NAMELESS SERIES OMNIBUS

NIKKI ROBB

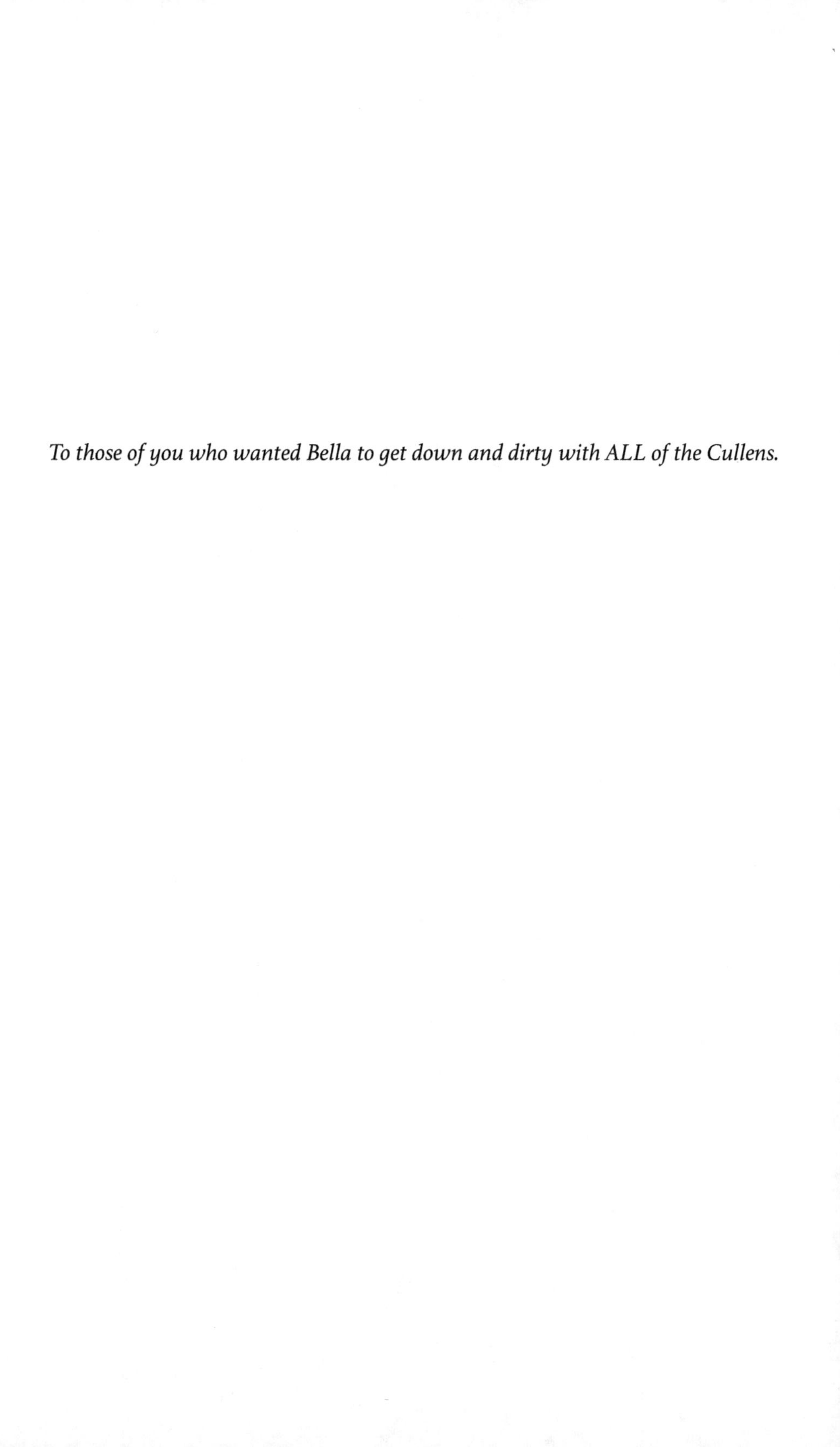

To those of you who wanted Bella to get down and dirty with ALL of the Cullens.

TRIGGER WARNINGS

This novel includes and alludes to things that may be concerning such as murder, vampires, blood drinking, graphic sex, sexual assault, rape, cancer, death of a parent and family member, non-consensual sexual encounters, victim-blaming, panic attacks, PTSD, discrimination, hate crimes, a brief reference to the LA Times Bombing, parental neglect, and harassment. Please consider these before continuing.

PART I

THE WANDERERS

ATHENA

You've read the stories and heard the tales about the things that go bump in the night, the monsters under your bed and in your closet. It's all pretty terrifying stuff to hear as you're growing up, never really feeling safe. You probably spent most of your childhood constantly checking every nook and cranny in your house, looking around every corner for what vicious and violent creature might be lurking there, poised to attack.

Growing up, and especially growing up as a woman, you learn two unsettling things pretty quickly in life.

One, the monsters from those stories aren't real.

Two, the monsters in the real world are even more terrifying.

Men don't need claws to claim a woman's unwilling flesh. Men don't need inhuman strength to pin a woman down. Men don't need fangs to drain a woman's life. Men don't have to be invisible, they don't have to hide in order to lure us to their traps.

No, sometimes, men are vile monsters all on their own.

That's the unfortunate truth though, isn't it? The lesson we were taught by Scooby Doo every week on TV. The unsettling fact that we all had to come to terms with as we grew and saw the truth of the world for the first time.

The real monsters are human.

1

ATHENA

iving in the middle of Nowhere, Maine sucks. For three months of the year, our little town of Shockgrove becomes a tourist playground, with crab shacks on every corner, and live music every night. For those few months, all the ridiculously expensive beach houses that stand empty every other month of the year are packed with housewives who are joined by their husbands on the weekends, college kids with big bank accounts and reckless attitudes, and those families who are rich enough to afford three months away from their jobs, duties, and lives to spend an entire summer drinking, swimming, and sunbathing.

During those three months, business is great, the economy booms, and my family's bookstore cafe becomes a hotspot that tourists just can't get enough of. We're right there on the pier, a perfect sanctuary on rainy days, or days when the sun's warmth is just too powerful for some of the newer visitors. They'd stop inside for tea, an iced coffee, and a good book. My family has owned this little shop for three generations. My Grandma and her husband started it back in the 50s when they would sell a cup of coffee for 75 cents. Then my mother took it on after Grandpa passed and Grandma just couldn't do it alone anymore, although she still spent most of her time in the shop. Citing that 'nobody can do it the right way anymore.'

It was only Mom and me for as long as I could remember. She never told me much about my dad, as far as I'm concerned he was a sperm donor who didn't deserve another moment of my time. Mom remarried once, but I tried not to think about that anymore. My stepfather was now in prison, where he belonged. Despite the many changes that occurred throughout our lives, this coffee shop-slash-bookstore was the one constant. The Maine Plotline was a Landry family business, and for three months of the year, business was good. Great even.

For the other nine months of the year, however, it was a ghost town, with a measly population of just over five-thousand people, and business frankly suffered. Not many people call little coastal towns like this home. It's always the stop along the way, the blip in the timeline of family memories, not the destination. But to me, Shockgrove was my beginning, middle, and likely my end.

It's like a vacuum, this town, and its people. I've tried to leave, trust me. Dozens of times. During sophomore year, my world turned on its axis. Sending me into a spiral I've fought tooth and nail every day since to climb out of. Trying to get out of this town at any and every opportunity. I applied to some stupid all-girls boarding school. Not that I would have minded being without men. I wanted nothing to do with men and their depraved desires for a long time. An all-girls school seemed like a dream I would never be allowed to have. Plus, it was obvious that I was bisexual at age fourteen when I first saw The Mummy and I wasn't sure if I wanted Brendan, Rachel or to be between them. I would have been fine with all women. Great, even. However, I didn't take into account the price of a boarding school education so that was promptly shut down. That, and Mom needed me at the shop. We couldn't afford staff, so for the longest time, it was just me and her, with Grandma when she could.

Senior year, I planned on heading away for college like so many of my classmates were going to do, but life had other plans. That's when Mom got sick. The best thing about Pancreatic cancer is that it's quick. She didn't suffer for long, and considering how much pain she was in for the short and fast end of her life, I could see that as a pro. But suddenly, The Maine Plotline was my responsibility. Grandma helped as much as she could, but she was getting older and she couldn't do as much as she wanted to. It was up to me to keep the business alive. It took me nearly two years longer than normal, but I got my business degree online while working full-time. And all of a sudden, I was twenty-six years old living in a small coastal town with a store that was practically bleeding money, and no way to escape.

I allot twenty minutes a day to feel sorry for myself about my lack of direction and passion in my life. From the moment I lock the doors at the end of the day, to the moment I finish cleaning and counting the day's drawers and leave out the back. That was it. During those few lonely minutes, I let myself lament about how I got stuck in this reality. I allow myself to dream about a life beyond this store, to dream about having more.

But the moment I walk out into the Maine evening air, the salty-sweet smell of the ocean prickling my lips, I lock away those thoughts until their cage would open again the next day.

That was how I lived my life.

I had just finished my daily mental sob fest and began the trek to my bike that was parked behind our building when my phone rang. I smiled at the name and answered, pinching the phone between my ear and my shoulder as I unlocked my bike.

"I had the literal best sex of my life last night with that guy I met at the Craving Crab. You know, the one whose address I sent you in case I went missing and you had to avenge my death. Well, I'm happy to report that the only thing I was dying of was too many orgasms. Yes, you heard me, this man had me quaking. I think I saw God. Anyway, he's going out again tonight but his friend's in town now, so he's bringing him along..." I flinched, knowing what was coming next. "So, you're going with me to keep his friend company so I can once again delve into the wondrous world of this man's cock without his stupid friend vagina-blocking." I'm pretty sure that was all in one breath. I chuckled. That was par for the course for my best friend. She's another victim of the Shockgrove vacuum. Her parents run the amusement park down on the edge of the pier and she's been doing most of the social media and event planning for them since she could hold a phone in her hand. She was good at it and even had a few TikTok videos go viral last year. Under her suggestion, they held a winter wonderland event that brought a few tourists in for the weekend. I knew the jump to social media was what The Maine Plotline was missing, but I didn't understand a single thing about marketing in that sense. Numbers and invoices, I got. Ring lights and trends, I did not. Davia offered to start a few pages for me, to even run them, but I knew I wouldn't be able to pay her what she was worth, so I never took her up on it.

"Hello to you too, Davia." I slipped the lock into my bag and straddled the seat of my bike, riding off along the dock. It was early May so the sun had only just set, basking my ride in a pink-orange hue. The tourists would be coming back in a few weeks, and not a second too soon if the store's financials were any indication.

"Yes, sorry. Hello, Athena. How are you?" She didn't wait for me to respond. "So be ready in an hour, ok?"

"I don't know, girl. I'm pretty beat." It was the truth, but more so than that, I wasn't really into the whole clubbing scene anymore. Especially not the Craving Crab, one of the only bars that stayed open through the off-season. It was always packed with locals during this time of year and you couldn't let loose with your neighbors breathing down your neck.

"You are not," she said matter of factly.

"Yes, I am," I teased back.

"I'm pulling the Vagina card." I nearly dropped the phone from between my shoulder and ear. Gripping the handles with one hand, I freed the other to rescue the falling device and pressed it firmly back to my ear.

"I'm sorry, the what?" I exclaimed.

"The Vagina card, I'm pulling it."

"And what the fuck is a Vagina card?" I said through a bout of laughter.

"You know, when you are the only thing standing in the way of my vagina and night full of mind-blowing orgasms, I can pull this so you have to help me," she spoke confidently like this was something that made perfect sense and she wasn't making it up entirely on the spot.

"You're ridiculous," I laughed, as I reached the edge of the pier and headed down the sidewalk toward my home. I smiled weakly as I rode past the light-house that sat tucked on the rocky shoreline. The faded white and blue tower was massive, standing out brightly against the dark black of the rocky cliff on which it made its home. It had been long since out of service after the last keeper of the lighthouse passed nearly a decade ago. It's supposed to be closed to the public, and it is, but Mom and I used to sneak up to the gallery and watch the stars at night, listening to the waves crash against the cliff below. It was our place. Right up to the very end.

Passing this lighthouse was the best and worst part of my everyday routine. On the plus side, I could feel her here. Her memory, our adventures.

On the downside, I could feel her here. Her pain, her death.

"Come on, you know I'd do the same for you!" She cried out, desperation lacing every word. That must have been some damn good dick.

I rolled my eyes, pulling them from the lighthouse and its ghosts, knowing that she wouldn't have to do anything of the sort for me anytime soon. I wasn't a virgin, unfortunately, but I certainly didn't have what you'd call an active sex life either unless you count my several vibrators at home that I used by myself.

It took me a while to feel comfortable sharing my body with anyone. And then after Mom died, I found the process of hooking up with random tourists whom I'd never see again quite pointless. Everything is temporary. Even pleasure.

"Please, Athena...Please!" I could practically picture her large brown puppy dog eyes and her thick lips pouting. She was a master of manipulation.

"Fine," I sighed as I turned the handles of my bike into my driveway. It was a long gravel road, you couldn't see my house from the main road and I liked it that way. My small cottage was nestled in a small grove of lush trees, whose newly formed leaves were a promise of a warm summer to come. The dark blue paint on the siding of my house came into view and I smiled. The one-floor cottage had two bedrooms, a kitchen, a living room, a laundry room, and one full bathroom. It wasn't much, in fact, it was the only thing I could afford after Mom passed and I sold the family home to cover expenses from having The Maine Plotline closed for two months. But it was home.

"You're amazing! Ugh, maybe we'll both get some seriously life-changing sex tonight." Not likely. Besides, I'd had 'life-changing' sex before, and I didn't want anything like that again. Ever. "I'll be there to pick you up in forty-five minutes," Davia cheered before hanging up.

I parked my bike in the small shed off the side of the cottage and made my way inside. Tossing a frozen meal into the microwave, I stopped by the baby blue record player that sat on a shelf in my living room. I threw on one of Mom's old records and felt the melancholic fog claim my heart.

The dulcet tones of Cyndi Lauper echoed through the house when I arrived home from a long day at school. Dropping my bookbag onto the bench in the foyer, a smile spread across my lips. When I came around the corner I saw my Mom dancing in front of her baby blue record player, her bare feet moving back and forth across the tile floor as she danced along to her favorite album of all time, "She's So Unusual." She sang along loudly, and badly. I did not get my slightly better-than-mediocre vocal talents from her, that's for sure. I wasn't phenomenal, but I could at least carry a tune. Her long red hair was naturally wavy, her beauty was effortless, something I appreciated, and hated about her. I had to spend a half-hour every morning trying to look as naturally radiant as she always did. She wore a loose-fitting, flowy floral shirt under jean overalls, not unlike Donna from the movie Mamma Mia, but she swore up and down that she 'wore it first'. A glass of white wine was pinched between her fingers and she swayed to the music. I leaned against the wall and watched her. For one song, then another. She noticed me somewhere between "When You Were Mine" and "Time After Time." Her off-key lyrics grew louder as she urged me to join in. I rolled my eyes, trying to shake my head, but her hand was gripping my arm and pulling me from the wall. Then we were dancing. Our voices blended in a glorious symphony of love and happiness, our bodies swaying joyfully to the music. Cares and worries slipped away when we were together.

You always hear people say that they wished they had enjoyed the people they lost a little more before they were gone. Wished that they'd loved them harder, appreciated them deeper, or made the most of the time that they had. Not me. I don't have a single regret about how I loved her. She was my everything, and I made every single second with her count. So no, I don't wish I had loved her harder, I wished I could have loved her longer.

With the music soaring through the halls, I made my way to my bedroom. A king-size bed took up the majority of the space, but I did have a very small walk-in closet where I had a vanity space. I actually loved playing around with makeup, I always had the best Halloween looks. In another life, I might have been a makeup artist. The life where I got lucky enough to get out of this town.

I spent the 10 minutes my food needed to heat up painting my features. I settled for a black and gold smokey eye with winged liner. Letting the smudged shadow frame under the eye as well. That sort of look always made me feel so confident. Like armor.

I skipped the foundation but went in with a little contour and concealer to give myself some semblance of bone structure. I ran my fingers over the small plastic case of my favorite red lipstick. I'd put it on after I ate. I didn't have much time left to do anything special with the mop of red hair on my head, so I pulled it back into a sleek ponytail and called it a day.

Forty minutes and a frozen personal pizza later, I was finished getting ready. I stood awkwardly in front of the full-length mirror on my closet door examining my outfit.

I'd pulled out something comfortable and safe. A pair of dark leggings and a Shockwave Community College crewneck sweater with the sleeves rolled up. My outfit was a large contrast to the dark and sultry makeup look I was sporting, but I liked makeup...and I normally hate dressing up. So this seemed like a good compromise. At least I put on a thong.

Not that I was expecting anything to happen tonight.

The knock on my door told me Davia had arrived, so I padded across my living room in my white Vans and opened the door.

My best friend was a knockout. Her long blonde balayage hair had been curled and effortlessly fell down her back and over her shoulders to just below her breasts. Speaking of those, she was wearing a full-blown corset. The dark red bustier barely held her C cups in. Her legs were hugged by tight leather leggings and she finished off the look with red heels. She looked like she was either about to do a strip tease, or go on stage in Vegas. Or do a strip tease in Vegas. There was a brief time in high school when I had a crush on my best friend. It was an annoying two months of not knowing how to act around her, and not knowing if she was bi. I eventually told her, and her exact words here, 'I'd be literally so offended if you weren't turned on by me, and girl you know I'd rock your world if I was into vagina.' I got over my crush and knew she'd be my best friend forever.

"You cannot wear that," she said, taking in my comfortable appearance. She brushed past me, her heels clicking against the wooden floor of my cottage.

"And why not?" I asked. "It's not like the Craving Crab is a nightclub. It's a local bar. There's pool playing, not pole dancing." I smirked, and she waved her hand as if to say I was being ridiculous.

"You need to look enticing enough to keep Greg's friend interested," she called over her shoulder on her way to my bedroom.

"I did my makeup," I retorted.

"And you look great, babe, which is why-" she mumbled from the room, "you need to be wearing this." She re-emerged from my bedroom with one of the few dresses I own. Of course. It was a dark purple body con, it barely covered my ass and the criss-cross design on the front was a far cry from modest. Davia bought it for me, and I tried it on exactly once and then buried it in the back of my closet never to be seen again. How the hell did she find it so fast?

"No way," I exclaimed, tossing my hands up as she approached.

"Yes way," she said, quickly grabbing the hem of my sweatshirt and pulling it over my head. Not exactly the best way to have my clothes ripped off of me. Although, not the worst either. I shivered, convincing myself it was from the cool air against my exposed skin and not the memory that echoed inside my head.

Once I was standing in front of my friend in nothing but my plain black bra, and she clicked her tongue.

"You don't have any better bra than that?" Her eyes scanned my body and I felt exposed in a not-fun way.

"Just give me back my sweatshirt," I cried, crossing my arms in front of me. She shook her head and pulled the purpled fabric down over my head and onto my torso. I groaned but ultimately shimmied into the dress. I pulled my leggings down, feeling the phantom wind nipping at my exposed legs.

"It's cold," I whined. Davia was already walking to my front closet and pulling out my favorite black leather jacket. I shrugged it on, and sighed, attempting to pull the skirt of the dress lower, only to show off more of my cleavage in the process. Looks like I needed to make a choice between showing off my ass or tits tonight. I saw her reach for a pair of black bootie heels and I nearly yelled after her, "No. If I'm gonna wear this outfit, I'm at least going to have comfortable shoes on." She looked down at my feet, studying the white vans.

"Fine, good enough." Then she made her way out the front door, her blonde hair bouncing as she swayed her hips in that sensual way. She never walked like that, unless she was on the prowl for a good dicking. I chuckled under my breath, thanking my past self for shaving my legs, as I followed her out.

***

An hour later, I was two Blue Hawaiians deep and already feeling the buzz when the door to the Craving Crab opened.

Davia gripped my arm in her hand, "That's Greg," she whispered, excitement practically oozing out of her pores. I followed the line of her gaze to the handsome man who had just entered the bar. His dark skin was on display under his completely unbuttoned short-sleeve button-down. He had a nice body, I guess, but it was early May and still cold...and he was wearing nearly nothing.

I turned to Davia, expecting to make a joke about his outfit, but she was practically drooling over him. I stifled a laugh.

I turned my attention back to the new arrival, he had spotted us and was making his way over in our direction, with a man trailing behind him. It wasn't until they were only a few feet from our table that I really got a good look at Greg's friend. Pale skin, sandy blonde hair, and blue eyes. He wore a dark blue polo and tan shorts. He looked like a frat boy on vacation. Which he probably was. He was decidedly, not even remotely, actually the farthest thing from my type. I tried to catch Davia's eyes to silently tell her I was going to kill her, but she was already out of her chair and flinging her arms around Greg's neck in a sensual hello.

I turned my murderous gaze from her and smiled at my date for the evening. His eyes were trailing my body appreciatively, something most girls loved, except I hated the way it made me feel to have his gaze on me. A vicious memory threatened to poke its way into the forefront of my mind, but I pushed it away.

"Hi, I'm Athena," I asserted over the music that filled the bar, extending my hand to him. The blonde boy took it in his own, and I felt his thumb rub a small circle on my skin, sending a shock through my body, and not the fun sexy kind, but the kind that had alarm bells going off.

I pulled my hand back, with some resistance. "I'm Louis, and you are hot as hell." Ugh, even his voice was a red flag. I fought against every fiber in my body that told me to grab my purse and run.

"Um, thanks," I replied, shifting awkwardly in my seat, casting a glance in Davia's direction. Davia and Greg had already locked faces in an incredibly graphic display of affection.

I was going to kill her.

"So, Athena, you look like you work out," Louis beamed, sitting down on the stool closest to me. I fought against the urge to kick it out from under him. Who the fuck says that to someone when you first meet them?

"I ride my bike everywhere," I answered bluntly, not wanting to give this kid anything.

"Yeah, you definitely have the rider's legs." I nearly choked on my drink as I turned back to him. He was not-so-subtly checking out my legs, the legs that stupid Davia forced me to have on display tonight.

"Ok," I gripped my glass and took a long drink, begging the pineapple rum to wash over my tongue and cover the bad taste of this date. It wasn't working.

Davia and Greg were all over each other for the next twenty minutes, she didn't even stop to introduce me. That man better have the best sex game in the world cause I'm never letting this bitch pull another 'vagina card' in her life.

I listened to Louis go on and on about his rugby team and their national title. Which would have been impressive had he not been trying to show me clips of his highlight film all night. I swear if I hear him say the word 'skirmish' one more time, I might ask them to hold everything other than rum in this next drink.

I was leaning my head on my palm, nodding with feigned excitement as Louis regaled the final three minutes of the 'most epic game ever' in excruciating detail when the door to the bar opened.

Framed in the dim orange light from the street lamps outside were four individuals. The moment my eyes caught a glimpse of their silhouettes I felt my breath catch in my throat. Tall and slender they slipped inside, the entire bar seemed to recognize their presence, like a cold chill of air traveling your spine. My hair stood on edge and goosebumps erupted over my entire body dancing along my skin like a sensual touch. The first individual in front had pale skin, nearly white, dark hollowed cheeks and a strong chiseled jawline. His honey-golden eyes were framed by dark circles, but he didn't look frightening. He looked strong. A kind of strength I found myself drawn to. His broad chest was covered in a black t-shirt, and he had an unbuttoned white jean jacket hugging his body. Dark black hair was pulled back and fastened in a bun at the nape of his neck. The ink from some tattoos threatened to poke out of the collar of his t-shirt and his ears and face were decorated with piercings. Dark jeans were tucked into tall black boots as he stepped inside.

Flanking him on his left was quite possibly the most stunning woman I had ever laid eyes on. Her silky black skin was blemish-free and nearly glowing. I watched her strong frame move across the floor with such grace that I wouldn't be surprised if she was royalty. Her long brown hair was braided into thick tresses, some were gathered at the top of her head in a thick cornet, while single strands fell down her back and onto her shoulders. Her lips were painted a bright candy apple red, the sinful color drew my eyes directly to her, and I felt myself licking my own lips in response.

On the other side of the man in the white jacket was a shorter individual wearing a grey button-down shirt, rolled up to the elbows. Their blonde hair was cropped short, just above their ears, hanging loosely across their tanned forehead. Their skin was a stunning tanned shade that looked like they received a healthy dose of sunshine, but could only really be achieved by lucky genetics. They, unlike the first two to enter the room, smiled warmly at those that they passed on their way to the table in the back corner. While the other two seemed to scream mystery, this one screamed comfort, but they were no less beautiful.

Bringing up the rear of the group was an imposing man, with marble-like skin that was pale and smooth. He had short black hair, slightly longer on the top than the sides, combed and slicked back. He wore an honest-to-god three-piece suit. The pants and jacket were a stunning blood-red color, and the vest had a golden design over a black button-down shirt unbuttoned to reveal the slim base of his throat.

I nearly lost the ability to breathe.

Who the hell are they? And why are they so fucking hot?

"Um, hottie alert," Davia whispered into my ear, the first thing she's said to me since her boy toy arrived, her mouth hanging open.

"Do you know them?" I asked back, vaguely aware of Louis still droning on about his game.

"If I did, do you think I'd be over here with you?" She joked. I couldn't pull my eyes from them as they took their seats in the corner booth. There was one singular red light above that booth and it cast an ominous glow over the drop-dead gorgeous newcomers. I was studying them, my heart beating quickly until the man in the suit turned his knowing gaze to me. His dark eyes looked nearly black from here and I felt a deep thrumming of my heartbeat in my chest and down below at my core, his eyes held mine and I felt the warmth pool between my legs. I don't know how long we sat there, staring at each other, but suddenly Louis moved his head until he was directly in my eye line. I ripped my eyes from the strangers for the first time since their arrival, my senses coming back to me in waves when I realized that Louis had asked me a question.

"I'm sorry, what?" He smiled, despite the annoyed look that flashed across his face.

"Do you need another drink?" Louis asked. On one hand, I really did want another drink, especially if I'm going to have to sit through another hour of Louis' company, on the other, I did not want this guy to think I owed him anything in return. He'd be lucky if he got a goodbye high-five from me tonight.

"I can get it, no worries," I started, beginning to slide off the stool. He put a hand on my thigh and I fought the impulse to slap it away.

"Allow me." He leaned in, his breath felt sticky and warm and smelled vaguely of Bud Light.

"No, it's ok. I can buy my own drinks." I pushed past him, trying not to be too obvious when I ripped my thigh from his grasp and made my way to the bar.

For the first time since Louis arrived, I felt like I could breathe. What was it about frat guys that made my skin crawl? Actually, I knew exactly what it was about that kind of guy that made me sick. These were the kind of guys who got everything they wanted, no matter what. Even if they had to take it. Davia knew my aversion to that type, and I better get like, unlimited favors from her for putting up with this tonight.

"Another?" Mike, the bartender asked. I nodded. Mike was a good friend of my mother's, but truth be told we hadn't spent much time together since her funeral. I appreciated how kind he was during that period of my life, but I had too much on my plate to try and maintain anything other than the business and my own sanity. A lot of relationships fell by the wayside.

"And you?" Mike asked, looking over my shoulder. I didn't have to turn to feel them there. The presence was thick, like honey. And just as tempting. I turned my head slightly to catch a glimpse of the sexy patron.

It was the pierced one. The one with the tattoos, and the hair, and the eyes... and the broad chest... and the strong hands...the one who... What was I saying?

"Four shots of bourbon," the man asserted, his voice a deep timber that nearly vibrated through my whole body. Oh god, yep, I'm definitely gonna need to use my toys tonight, I thought as I pressed my thighs together searching for some kind of relief.

"You got it," Mike replied, getting to work on our orders, leaving me alone with Mr. Tall, Dark, and Sinful. I suddenly forgot what to do with my arms. I first stuffed my hands into the pockets of my leather jacket but felt like my elbows were sticking out too far making me look like a chicken flapping its wings. Then, I leaned my forearms onto the bar in front of me, misjudging the distance and falling forward much further than I expected, which sent my ass jutting straight back as if in an open invitation. I stood up quickly with a groan under my breath. Did he see that? Did he like it?

I shook my head.

Get it together girl.

I risked one glance over my shoulder at the man, and found him staring directly at me, his honey eyes meeting my gaze with such an intensity that I wasn't sure I could look away if I wanted to.

We stood there, trapped in each other's gazes for what felt like far too long, and yet not quite long enough.

Fucking say something, don't just stare at him.

"Sup?"

The moment the meek word slipped through my lips, I stifled a whimper. Did I seriously just say, 'sup'?

If I could tear my gaze from his right now, I would facepalm.

He didn't respond, he didn't even flinch at my juvenile greeting. He just...watched me.

"Your drinks." Mike's voice drew the man's attention away, finally releasing me from his gaze. He slipped a twenty down on the counter, leaning in just enough so I could smell his woodsy scent, before gripping the shots and slinking away. I dropped a five on the counter and smiled at Mike before making my way back to my table with my drink. Avoiding looking at the table in the corner of the room.

I didn't want to look at Louis, and I definitely didn't want to look at that table, so I found myself staring at a poster of a shark holding a beer in its fin on the wall. Davia and Greg had vanished, probably to give each other those mind-blowing orgasms again.

I felt the faint buzz of my phone with a message from her.

> DAVIA: Same address as yesterday, but if you hear screams, don't come knocking ;) Have fun!

> ATHENA: I'm going to kill you.

> DAVIA: love you! <3

I shook my head, seriously contemplating revoking her best friend card, I turned back to Louis and found him sitting even closer than he was before, his eyes studying my drink.

"So, it looks like it's just you and me now." His attempt at a sensual seductive tone came across as creepy, and I seriously wanted to leave, but I had just gotten a new drink and I wasn't going to let this creep keep me from enjoying it.

I grabbed the glass and took a few long sips.

"Yep, looks like it." I didn't allow myself another glance at the table in the corner, but I knew they were still there, their presence was fucking magnetic.

My third drink was hitting me harder than normal, either that or the sheer sexual prowess of these strangers had me in absolute shambles.

"You wanna get out of here?" Louis asked, his hand finding my thigh again.

I went to brush his palm off of my skin but missed. My vision was blurring slightly. Shit, maybe I should have had more dinner.

"Actually, I am going to go home," I murmured, slowly standing, rocking off-balance on my feet.

Thank god I wore my Vans.

"Aww, come on, our friends are gonna be occupied for hours. You don't want to leave me with nowhere to go do you?" His lips brushed my cheek, and I felt bile rise in my throat, and my head swam. I couldn't focus on anything in my surroundings. I needed to get out of here.

"I'm going home. Alone." I heard the words slur despite my best attempt to keep them coherent. Something was wrong, and an eerie familiarity washed over me. I felt my entire body tighten in fear.

"I'll walk you," Louis offered, flinging an arm around my shoulders and leading me out the front door. I don't remember the walk from the table to the street outside, but as soon as I felt the cool night air hit my clammy skin, I knew I needed to vomit. I rushed to the alley where the dumpster was, and puked up the contents of my stomach. My lips were chapped, my mouth was dry, and my chest felt heavy.

Tears pooled in my eyes as my mind struggled to remain clear.

"Come on baby, let me take care of you." I felt Louis' hands gripping my hips from behind as I was bent over, his erection pressed against my ass.

No. No. No. NO. Please. Not again.

"Leave me alone," I cried, but the words weren't there. "Please, go away." My pleas were nothing more than grunts.

"Don't worry, it'll feel really good." The cold air hit my ass cheeks as my dress was pushed up around my hips exposing my thong. I tried to break free from his grasp but his strength felt insurmountable in my current state. I felt the hot tears spill down my cheeks. Memories slammed into my chest. Rough hands. The static of the radio. Whiskey. The senses of my nightmares.

"Stop. Hel-" They weren't fully formed, but I mustered every ounce of energy I had left to scream, but my shout was cut short by a slap across my face. The sting felt like it traveled down my spine as my head snapped back. I tasted blood.

I heard the tell-tale sound of a zipper and I tried to pull myself from him one more time. I had been a victim before, and I barely survived. I don't think I would be so 'lucky' if it were to happen again.

"Don't fucking move, you teasing bitch," he hissed through gritted teeth. "You wear this tight ass dress, showing off your fucking cleavage all night, and you don't give me the time of fucking day?" I whimpered, trying to pull from his grip as he pulled my thong to the side. I felt his bare cock notch against my entrance.

There was nothing I could do.

I screamed and pounded against the brick wall in front of me with every ounce of dwindling energy I had left. Hitting the bricks as if they were *him*. The monster from my nightmares.

Then I felt his vicious presence dissipate as he was pulled away from me. I didn't have the energy to stand on my own without his selfish hands holding me up, a sickening dilemma, but before I fell to the ground, a pair of hands caught me.

"Let me go, you fuckers!" I heard Louis exclaim. I couldn't see a thing, the world was tilting on its axis as whatever drug he fed me took over my senses.

I faintly heard the sounds of flesh hitting flesh, grunts of fighting, and groans of pain.

"You're going to wish you never fucking touched her," I heard a voice whisper. It was threatening, dominant, and calm, like a viper poised to attack.

"Fuck you!" Louis cried, but his tone was laced with fear. "Wait, what the hell are you?!"

Good.

I want him to be afraid.

I want him to suffer.

"Get her out of here," the dominant voice said. The arms that were holding me in place reached around so they could gather and lift me until I was settled in against their arms. Instinctively I laid my head against their chest, cold and hard, like tile flooring. I knew I should be afraid, worried that I traded one threat for another. But something about the grip on my body, the caring way they wiped my hair from my forehead, I knew I could trust this savior.

"Fuck, she's bleeding," an accented voice said. I felt the arms around me tense, as their face leaned closer to mine. I felt their cold breath against my lips. I willed my eyes to open, but the lids were too heavy.

"Control yourself, Laz." A feminine command.

I felt blackness slowly closing in on my consciousness when I felt the figure's face lean close to mine until our lips were mere inches apart. I wasn't afraid of being claimed unwillingly again though, something about this presence felt safe. Secure.

"Oh, shit..." The figure exclaimed, fear, wonder, and something else entirely laced their tone.

And then it all went dark.

2

ORPHEUS

"**A**re you sure we can't stay here longer than tonight?" Silas asked, sliding into our booth with four shots of bourbon in his hands. I didn't justify his stupid question with an answer, instead, I reached across the table and gripped my shot glass in hand.

"You got your eye on someone?" Samara teased, her red lips pursed to plant an air kiss. Silas elbowed her and she coughed, devolving into laughter.

"The redhead with the short-as-sin dress on." He nodded his head in her direction. Both Samara and Laz turned to look, but I refrained because I already knew what I would see. I'd gotten a nice look when we first arrived. As my companions ogled over the busty redhead, I fixed the lapel of my suit jacket.

"I could smell her arousal the moment we walked into the room," Laz whispered in a soft southern accent, licking their lips.

"I wonder what her blood smells like," Samara added. The three of them looked like a pack of ravenous monsters ready to devour their prey. Which, I guess they were.

"You know we cannot hunt in this area," I said, drawing their attention back to me. My Romanian accent was not as thick as it used to be, it's been nearly a century since I've returned, and time will dilute a lot of things.

"Who said anything about hunting her?" Silas tossed toward me, leaning back into the booth and letting his tongue run over his lip piercing. "I just want a taste." I saw the gleam in his eyes and barely stopped myself from groaning.

"You cannot feed on anyone in this town, Silas." It wasn't often that I went full coven leader on my companions. Oh who am I kidding...it's daily that I need to go full coven leader on them. The hungry, horny bastards are always getting into trouble. "Need I remind you that your hunger and libido are the reason we are on the run in the first place?"

That got his attention, finally drawing his gaze from the nameless redhead.

"You had your fair share if I remember correctly." Silas tossed back, an edge of anger in their voice. My mind flooded back to that night. The gilded mansion, the sensual offerings, the trap.

"Stop, both of you," Samara scolded, casually leaning back in the booth. "We all made mistakes, which is why we all made the choice to go on the move." It wasn't exactly a choice, but she was right, we all contributed to our current predicament. A mistake I will not be letting us make again.

"I do not like the way that guy is looking at her though," Laz responded under their breath. I'd noticed the blonde boy sitting entirely too close to her when we first arrived. He seemed so caught up in himself that he didn't notice his date was practically drooling as we entered.

She wasn't the only one.

"Yeah, that guy gives me the creeps. Do you see the way he's got his hand on her thigh?" Silas was back to looking at the mystery woman. I rolled my eyes.

"Can we stop talking about the girl and take our shots?" I exclaimed, exasperated.

Samara gripped her glass and raised it above her head. "To fresh starts." To her credit, she was a hopelessly optimistic soul. She saw our life on the run as a new beginning, and every time we picked up what little roots we managed to plant in one place and rushed to a new chapter, she saw it as an opportunity. I wondered how long that unbridled optimism might last. Or if she was truly just masking the pain we all knew she'd been feeling since we were held captive.

"To finally feeding soon," Silas teased, but I knew he wasn't joking, we had been very careful not to feed for the last three stops, and it wasn't going to be easy to resist much longer. But we had a plan and feeding in this small town where everyone knows everyone was not a part of it.

"To The Wanderers," Laz contributed, lifting their shot glass over their head. We'd been known as The Wanderers Coven long before our nomadic new life, but now it fits even more than it had then.

"To surviving," I added, then the four of us tossed our drinks back letting the warm amber liquid warm our cold, dead insides.

"Hey, what the fuck?" Silas exclaimed. I followed his gaze, although I didn't need to. He was clearly looking at the redhead. She was stumbling out of her stool, and the bumbling idiot beside her was gripping her exposed skin possessively. A growl rumbled in my chest.

"Leave it be," I bristled, matter-of-factly.

"She doesn't look good," Samara mused, sitting a bit straighter in her seat. Her fangs elongated slightly as she watched the couple.

"She's been drinking, she's fine. Leave it be," I repeated, adding an edge of authority to my voice. Her fangs retracted.

I heard the door open and close and knew that the pair had made their way outside. Hopefully, now my coven could focus on something else.

Silas was out of his seat immediately, crossing the bar to her vacated table. I rolled my eyes, and let my forehead fall into my hand.

Silas returned with her half-drank drink in his hands, slipping back into the booth he put the blue liquid down in front of him.

"Laz?" He said, sliding it across the table to them. Laz had the unique ability to discern the contents of any mixture. It kept us from drinking poisoned blood on more than one occasion. You can never be too careful with Hunters on your tail.

Laz gripped the drink and pulled it to their nose, inhaling deeply. Their eyes fell closed as they analyzed the drink in front of them. I eagerly awaited the moment that they put everyone's fears to rest and we could get on with our evening. I was looking forward to at least two more shots before we found our way to the inn.

No such luck.

Laz's eyes sprang open revealing the telltale sign of a near shift, bloodshot eyes, and red rims. Their fangs elongated and I quickly leaned forward to block their frame from anyone in the bar.

"It's drugged," Laz hissed in an almost violent manner, and suddenly all hell was breaking loose. Samara's sharpened fingernails dug into the table top and Silas sprung up out of his seat.

"Stop, now. All of you. Calm yourselves." I whispered with as much authority as I could. They turned to look at me, of course, they did. I was their leader. My heart remained calm. One beat every hour, that's all we got now. The result of our suspended animation. A reminder of the half-life we now led.

"She needs our help," Silas spoke through clenched teeth, his features had not shifted yet, but I knew he was nearly on the verge.

"Ground rules. She doesn't see you shifted, and he doesn't die." It was clear they wouldn't put this behind them without doing something, but at least we could stick to the plan. They nodded, tense. I stood calmly and led them out of the bar, keeping Laz close behind me. They had the good sense to keep their eyes tilted downward and their mouth shut as we walked past the remaining patrons.

I felt her fear the moment we were outside. It gripped my senses with a violent hold. Nearly inescapable. Her muffled cries of pain sent us all into action. Quick on our feet, we rounded the corner to the alley beside the bar. The sight in front of me was one I would never forget. Even if I tried.

The redheaded woman was braced against the brick wall next to the dumpster, her dress bunched around her waist, her underwear ripped to the side as this man stood behind her, ready to take from her what did not belong to him.

I saw red. I knew I had shifted, feeling the tell-tale prick of my fangs against my bottom lip as I wrapped my fingers across this bastard's neck and pulled him back. I felt my elongated and pointed nails dig into his flesh, and it took every ounce of self-restraint to keep from ripping his spine out through his neck and feeding it to him.

I was vaguely aware of Laz catching the small-framed woman before she fell to the ground, their eyes scanning her for injuries before carefully pulling her dress down to cover her. Her fear was consuming me, flooding my senses to the point where I could barely feel anything else. Not the cool night air, not the trembling of the man in my clutches. It was her and her terror. I'd never felt fear so poignant. If my blood wasn't perpetually chilled, it'd be boiling.

Silas joined me in restraining the asshole. Before I could stop him, his fist connected with the man's jaw. I held him in place as Silas landed another hit to his gut.

"Let me go, you fuckers!" The vile creature hissed. I caught a glimpse of the bruise that was already darkening on the redhead's face. I leaned my lips close to this asshole's ear, and calmly uttered, "You're going to wish you never fucking touched her." It was a miracle that I could restrain myself from screaming at this man, truthfully. But I wanted my privacy in order to punish him the way he deserved. To make him suffer.

"Fuck you!" He spat. Silas landed another punch on his ribs, I heard one crack. Silas' control slipped and I saw his eyes go red, his fangs sharpening as he stalked toward his prey. Shit. "Wait, what the hell are you?!" Fuck. He had seen us. We had been careless. There was only one way out of this now. I had to make another plan, and quickly.

"Get her out of here," I ordered Laz. They nodded, bending down to gather the woman in their arms. Then I saw it, deep crimson blood marring her stunning face.

"Fuck, she's bleeding." Laz's mouth fell open and their fangs begged for the chance to sink into this woman's life force. Hell, I was all the way over here and I still wanted a taste. This was not good. Her scent wasn't strong though. It smelled wrong, almost toxic. A blessing in disguise, because I'm not sure any of us would have been able to control ourselves with the already unsteady hold on our monsters had she smelled as good as I thought she would.

"Control yourself, Laz," Samara voiced calmly. She was the only one of the three of us who had yet to shift, sometimes her restraint truly surprised me.

Silas took hold of the writhing wannabe rapist in my hands and held a tight grip around his throat, keeping him from crying out. I felt my features return to normal, the red tint that the world had a moment ago slipped away as the cloud of anger cleared. But her fear was still there. Still gnawing at me. Everyone else? They were angry. I felt their anger burning violently, spurring me on.

"Oh, shit..." I turned to see Laz taking a deep inhale of the woman's scent, and I readied myself to jump in, to keep them from creating a second body we'd have to worry about tonight because there was no way this douche was surviving the next ten minutes. But instead, their features reverted, their eyes cleared and their fangs retracted. Shock colored their expression and filled the air around me. I didn't have time to analyze it or ask.

"Follow her scent, get her to her home, safely." Laz nodded, acknowledging that they had heard me, but didn't take their eyes from the woman in their arms.

"Samara, go with them. Nothing happens to her, do you understand?" Samara nodded, and I watched the two of them take off into the night, the woman's crimson hair swaying with every step Laz took.

When I turned back to the blonde whimpering mess, I was pleased to see that he hadn't passed out yet. If I was going to kill him, I wanted him to experience every ounce of pain I was going to put him through.

"There's a camera in front of the bar. You know what to do, Silas." He loosened his hold on the asshole's neck, and I watched in awe as my companion transformed. As often as I'd seen Silas' gift in action, it still amazed me. A moment later I was looking at two identical figures. Silas' form was now a completely accurate mirror for the fucker in my hands.

"What the hell?!" The man whimpered weakly, his voice strained from the crushing hold I had on his neck.

"You deserve to rot in hell," Silas spat in his face before taking off toward the front of the bar to lead the trail in the complete opposite direction. He was good at what he did. He would make sure at least a dozen cameras saw him walking home alone. Doorbell cameras, businesses, he might even step inside a gas station for a quick look around.

Having Silas and his ability was one of the main assets that have helped us hide the way we had for so long.

Knowing that we were taken care of as far as an alibi, I turned my attention back to the worthless creature in front of me.

"I normally don't drink spoiled blood," I taunted, stalking forward, letting my vision redden, and opening my mouth to display my growing fangs. "But for you, I'll make an exception."

He wanted to scream, but I didn't give him the chance.

3

LAZ

y entire body was on fire, like the very venom in my veins was eating me alive. My skin felt electrified where her body met mine. She was so petite. So vulnerable. The mere thought of what that man was about to do to her nearly sent me tumbling down a hole of lost control.

It was the scent of her blood that calmed me though, ironically. Her face was caked with it, and I saw the bruise beginning on her skin. I hope Orpheus and Silas made his death hurt. Her blood was so tainted by the drug that he had slipped her that I couldn't even get a smell of the *real* her beneath it all. Anger was the only thing I could feel.

There are many out there in the world that would call me the monster, but how am *I* the one they fear when men like him exist? It sickens me to my very core.

"Her scent leads this way." Samara ran beside me, her face stoic and calm. She always was the best in a crisis. I followed the direction she led us, holding this beautiful woman tight to my chest. Beneath the blood that was drying on her ivory skin, I could see her features. She had dark-painted lips, and her eyelids were darkened with eyeshadow and glitter. She looked positively stunning when we first arrived at the bar. Of course, I noticed. Her long red ponytail was silky, and smooth and smelled like wintergreen as her head lulled against my chest.

She was breathing steadily, but I was worried about the effect of the drug on her system.

"Can you do something for her?" I asked as Samara turned down a gravel driveway. We ran quietly, our footsteps barely registering on the rocky ground.

"Once we get her inside, I'll do what I can." I nodded, although Samara wasn't looking at me. We quickly arrived at a quaint blue cottage. I don't know anything about this woman, but somehow this home made perfect sense. It felt like her.

Which I understand was entirely ridiculous to say, but it's true. I hugged her tighter to my body as Samara gripped a set of keys from the purse in her hand.

I hadn't even noticed that she picked up the girl's purse. That's why I loved having Samara in our coven, she was detail-oriented. Orpheus saw the big picture, Silas and I were good at executing plans, but Samara never let things fall through the cracks. She unlocked the door and pushed it open, but then stopped just in front of the threshold.

"Shit," she exclaimed. Damn, this was going to prove to be an issue.

"Hey. You need to invite us inside." I caressed the side of her bruising face. Her brows furrowed as she stirred in my arms. "That's it, wake up." She groaned, her arms moving slightly. "Can we go inside your house?" I asked, calmly, and quietly. Then she nodded. My heart thumped in my chest.

"She's gotta say the words, Laz."

"I know that," I snapped. "Hey there, Darlin'. I need you to say something for me." She groaned again and I gently shook her in my arms.

"Darlin'?" Samara asked, teasingly.

Ignoring her, I gripped the woman's small frame and whispered in her ear.

"Tell me I can come in," I cooed in my silky southern accent. The slightest whimper escaped her mouth and I felt my length strain against my pants immediately. "Please."

"Come in," she mumbled against my chest. The words were no more than a jumbled gargled mess, but they were enough.

Samara cautiously stepped one foot through the door, and a sigh of relief flooded me. "Thank you," I whispered to my sleeping beauty as I stepped inside. The inside of her home was even more perfect than the outside. With cozy colorful furniture and bright abstract art decorating the walls this home felt lived-in, in the most comfortable sense of the word. A table with a baby blue record player sat against one of the walls. Several records were filed neatly on the shelves underneath it. I followed Samara into a room, the girl's bedroom clearly, based on the saturation of her minty scent. A king-sized bed took up much of the space, but the walls again were decorated with bright lively images. My eye, however, was immediately drawn to the bookshelf. Hundreds of titles, ranging from fiction to non-fiction, fantasy to drama. I snickered at the copy of Twilight that sat on her bottom shelf before moving to place her down on the center of the mattress. It wasn't lost on me the immediate sense of emptiness I felt the moment she was out of my arms.

"Should we change her?" I asked, glancing down at her dress, a few drops of blood had landed on the front of the purple fabric, and I wanted nothing more than to burn it so that she never had to relive what happened to her tonight.

"No, she needs to think she got drunk and came home to pass out," I growled at her words.

"She needs to know what happened to her tonight," I argued. She needs to know that he didn't violate her.

"Orpheus won't want us to get involved." She waved me off.

Get involved? The thought made me laugh. Somehow I was already so deeply involved that I was furious with the prospect of her not knowing the truth.

I opened my mouth to respond but Samara had already taken her place on her knees near the woman's face. She leaned in, letting her eyes drift closed as she sent her ability out.

I watched carefully as she worked, her palms gracing the skin of the woman's perfect face. Samara was one of the best healers our kind has ever seen. If there was anything physically wrong with the sleeping angel, she would be able to fix it. It's the mental scars from tonight that she would have to find a way to live with.

I felt my fists tighten at my side as the memory of that man behind her as she cried out for help returned to me.

I had half a mind to go find Orpheus and Silas right now to make sure that they made him pay. To ensure that they are dragging out his torture in the most deviant and violent way possible. But I knew they would.

I trusted them to avenge her.

"She'll be fine," Samara said, rising from her knees. Her index finger trailed along the woman's face and I watched as the bruise that was darkening on the woman's face slowly dissolved.

We had almost picked a different bar. There's another town about thirty minutes away with another joint. Had we made our way there instead we wouldn't have been here. We wouldn't have been able to stop him. She would have - "I'm glad we were here," I lamented, not liking the train of thought that my mind was taking. Samara simply nodded, her eyes remaining on the girl before us.

"I don't want to leave her just yet," I claimed, truthfully. A little ashamed at how attached I had grown to this human already.

"Me neither," Samara responded and I found myself breathing steadily again. Nodding, I took a seat on the far end of the mattress. I was careful not to let it dip too much under my weight.

Samara sank to the floor at the foot of the bed, her back up against the wall.

"Her blood feels wrong," Samara whispered after a while, her brow furrowing. I sighed deeply. "I helped as much as I could."

"It's got a lot of that drug in it." I thought back to the drink we left on our table. The blue drink she had been sipping on. If she only drank half of it and reacted like this, I shuddered to think of how the whole glass might have affected her.

"She could have died." Samara was only stating what I already knew. The question was, why did we care so much? It is not that we don't care about humans...ok well, we really don't. We only care enough to find the vilest of humans, the ones who deserve to die. But we all jumped to her rescue tonight. Each of us.

"I know."

We sat in comfortable silence for an hour, watching over our little human, listening to her steady breathing and watching her chest rise and fall until our phones buzzed.

ORPHEUS: It's done. Meet me at the inn.

A weight lifted from my chest. The world would be a better place without that scum in it. But then a different weight landed squarely on my shoulders. "I don't want to leave her all alone here," I explained as Samara and I stood from our seats.

"We can't watch her forever."

I knew she was right, so why did a part of me want to believe that we could?

4

SILAS

"Tell me again," I hissed at Orpheus as we sat in our motel room. The dingy floors and ugly wallpaper were a constant, annoying reminder that we were on the run and that the comfort and luxury that we had grown so accustomed to over our centuries of life was not only a thing of the past, but also the one thing that could get us killed. For real this time. I caught a glimpse of my reflection in a large square mirror that was mounted on the wall. Taking in my large frame, dark hair, ink, and piercings, I was thankful that I was myself again. I hadn't felt as skeevy in someone else's form as I did tonight in a while. That tool had it coming. And I for one, was glad I'll never have to wear his face again.

"I ripped out his throat, drained him completely and once I knew he was long dead, I relieved his body of his head and tossed the pieces of him out to sea," Orpheus explained nonchalantly, as if he wasn't describing the brutal way in which he murdered a man tonight. He leaned back in the armchair, resting his ankle on his knee. His red suit was still pristine. How he managed to feed and keep his suit clear was beyond me.

"Did you save any?" I wasn't starving right now, but I knew that soon we would be and if we already hunted in this city we might as well make the most of it.

"Of course, I did." Orpheus nodded to the mini fridge that sat in the corner of the room. I sauntered over and pushed open the door. The rush of air felt warm against my already cold skin as I looked inside. Six plastic water bottles

35

sat side by side, filled to the brim with dark crimson blood. I licked my lips at the sight. It had been too long since our last hunt.

I gripped one in my hand and smiled at the feeling of it in my hand, still warm.

"Drink up, Silas." Orpheus didn't smile, but he had a damn good smirk that really only showed itself when things went according to plan, or he just completed a particularly great hunt.

And considering all of our plans went completely to hell tonight, I'd assume he enjoyed tearing that asshole to pieces. I'd take the smirk over his bitching any day.

The first sip of the still warm blood had me groaning, an intoxicating heat and rush of pleasure bloomed in my chest. Drinking blood was an almost euphoric activity. It's why so many vampires feed during sex. But blood from the bottle, even fresh blood like this, didn't have the same effect that drinking directly from the vein did.

I swallowed down the whole bottle in seconds, and then when it was empty, I licked my lips and the tips of my elongated fangs to savor the flavor. I always forgot how dimmer and duller the world looked and felt when I was hungry. When I had fresh blood in my system it was like the entire world lit up like a damn Christmas tree.

All my senses were sharper, including my hearing, which is why I could tell that Laz and Samara were going to walk through the door in 5...4...3...2....

"I smell blood," Laz crowed the moment they crossed the threshold. I laughed, my large frame shaking as I leaned down and opened the fridge door again.

Laz moved quickly, grabbing a bottle and downing it in seconds. Samara was slightly more reserved than that. She always was. But she indulged all the same.

"I trust you had no issue getting the human back to her home?" Orpheus asked, business as always. He was seriously killing my blood buzz. Although I would be lying if I didn't admit I was also interested in how the human was doing.

"She's safe and sound," Laz replied. I found myself feeling strangely relieved at that notion. I still didn't quite understand my reaction to the thought of her in danger. Sure, I hated men like that, and we've hunted men for doing less, but the fact that it was her that was threatened. The sexy redhead who got all flustered around me. The one whose arousal I could smell the moment she realized it was me who was standing behind her at the bar. I nearly dropped to my knees to have a taste right there.

Then to see what that asshole was going to do to her? Trying to steal her arousal, the wetness that was entirely for my sake, and rape her? Anger began bubbling under the surface again and I bit down on my lip, struggling against the impulse to go find his rotting corpse and set it on fire so he suffers, even in hell.

Why do I care that much?

"We need to leave first thing tomorrow." All of our heads turned to look at Orpheus, who was standing slowly and removing his suit jacket. "Get a few hours of rest and we will leave before the sun comes up."

"You want us to travel during the day?" Samara asked, incredulous. It was a fair question. Although we had completed the necessary rituals to survive being in sunlight, it still wasn't a pleasant feeling. Like a bad sunburn. Compared to a fiery combustible death though, it was a walk in the park.

"The sooner we leave this town the better."

I felt the attitude in the room shift. Almost imperceptible, but it was there.

"I can't leave until I know she's ok," Laz spoke first.

"I agree," Samara added. Orpheus ran a hand down his face.

"You said she was safe and sound, what more do you want?" He was holding on to the last thread of his control. If there was one thing Orpheus hated, it was feeling out of control, and right now nothing was going according to his plan.

"I don't want to leave yet, either," I found myself agreeing aloud and Orpheus tossed his hands in the air above his head.

"You're all ridiculous, why are you all suddenly so obsessed with this damn human?" I didn't know the answer to that, but I was interested in finding out.

When none of us answered, he growled, low and threatening. He could be a terrifying creature when he wanted to be.

"Fucking fine," he said, giving in. I smiled at the prospect of seeing my sexy little redhead again. "One day. That's all."

I only hoped that would be enough time to satisfy this strange desire.

5

 ATHENA

The sunlight peeking through the blinds of my bedroom warmly embraced my face and I instinctively moved to shield myself from its brightness. Cool leather touched my forehead as I brought my arm to my eyes. Then I bolted out of bed, the rush of last night coming back to me in silent dreadful waves.

The bar. The outfit. Davia. Greg. Louis.

My stomach churned at the thought of his name.

Other than the fact that I was wearing the same dress from last night, with no idea how I made it back home, I feel fine. There's no blinding headache, dry mouth, or nausea that usually accompanies a morning after an evening spent at the Craving Crab, taunting me.

Ok, what the hell happened last night?

How did I get here?

What happened with Louis?

I slid off of my bed and padded carefully to the bathroom, my hair was ratted, falling from the ponytail it was confined to, and my dress was rumbled, but that wasn't what had my jaw dropping. It was the cracked red blood that was caked around my nose, and a spot on my lip. I couldn't see an injury beneath the blood for the life of me, so how did it get there?

I felt my foundation shift uneasily, as I stared at my reflection in the harsh white light of my bathroom. Memories swam around my mind like out-of-order puzzle pieces.

Louis and I were talking. Davia and Greg had left. I got another drink. Those sexy-as-sin strangers arrived. And then...

I struggled to wade through the muddled memories of last night, attempting to reform the picture from the hazy clues. My drink. There was something wrong with my drink. Did I leave? Did I come home alone? That thought had me sprinting from my bathroom to search my tiny cottage for any signs of visitors last night.

Please, god, don't let Louis be here.

Much to my relief, I found no signs that anyone was currently or had recently been in my home. With that fear settled, I lumbered to the kitchen to make myself a cup of coffee.

As the glorious sounds of brewing coffee filled my ears, I rushed to find wherever I had discarded my phone last night. Maybe Davia would have some answers.

It was only nine in the morning. The bright picture of my Grandma and I sitting in one of the booths at The Maine Plotline flashed up at me from my lock screen. I had three unread messages. One from last night and two from early this morning.

> DAVIA: Hey you minx, heard you left the bar with Louis. (Mike told me) Hope you have fun ;) I am three orgasms in, and we're recharging before the next round. Love you!

> DAVIA: Good morning! Louis never came back to the rental last night so you must have had a great night. Can't wait to hear all the sweaty details. 8=====D ;)

A vicious throb began in my head as I read her first two texts. Did we leave the bar together? He never went home? None of the puzzle pieces were matching up.

> DAVIA: Hey girl, Greg is trying to get ahold of Louis, can you have him call? They were supposed to meet up at 8.

My mind was moving a mile a minute. Bits and pieces of things were fighting their way back into my conscious mind. Nothing was clear, but I do remember one thing. One overwhelming emotion. Fear.

As I poured my coffee, I called Davia.

"Good morning sex kitten! Did you get my texts?" She answered, cheerfully. I shook my head.

"Davia, I didn't have sex last night." I was still trying to figure out what happened, but it had been so long since I had had sex, that I feel like if I did, I would be feeling it. Although I also should be feeling the alcohol and I felt perfectly fine.

"So what, you just talked all night? Jeez Athena, what a waste of good dick." She had a kind of subtle sexy morning voice that sounded almost sing-songy. It was a pleasant sound, except when it wasn't making any sense.

"No, I came home alone," I explained, hoping that the more I said it, the more it would feel like the truth.

"But Mike said you left together..." she started, but a deep call from the other side of the line cut her off.

"Is that Louis?" The owner of the voice was clearly annoyed, and it didn't escape me that this was the first time that I had actually heard him speak. Considering he never introduced himself last night, and he spent what little time he and Davia remained at the bar whispering naughty words into her willing and eager ears.

"No, just Athena. She says Louis never went home with her," I listened intently to what Greg would say to that.

"I thought you said they were together?" An edge of worry seeped into his tone.

"I thought they were." I could practically hear her shrug with indifference.

"Davia, can you meet me for breakfast?" I asked, hurriedly. If anyone could help me make sense of last night, it was her. As hard as I tried to keep the uncertainty and worry from my voice, I don't think I was successful. Somewhere deep in my mind, I felt the past threatening to resurface. Panic started to seize my heart, a lump forming in my throat.

"Sure, Dale's in twenty work for you?" My best friend was many things, impulsive, yes, sensual, definitely. Infuriating, most times. But supportive when she knew I needed her, always.

"See you there."

After hanging up, I took deep breaths and quickly cleaned last night's makeup and the mystery blood from my face. There were answers as to what happened last night somewhere. I needed to find them before I fell over the edge and the lock on my worst memories was broken. Maybe I needed to talk to Louis. As unfortunate as that thought was. It did seem like it was the best of my options. There were two people who left that bar last night, and one of them had no idea what the hell happened.

I tossed on my Shockgrove Community College sweater that Davia so rudely, and not at all sexily, ripped from my body last night. Pulling on a pair of soft black leggings and sliding my feet back into my Vans, I was ready to go.

Dale's was only a three-minute bike ride from my cottage. In fact, most of the town was within a ten-minute bike ride. That's why I never bothered learning to drive or getting a car. If I needed to leave the town, which I rarely did, Davia would take me, or I'd hop on the bus line.

As much as I hated it, as much as I loathed the idea of being trapped here, this town was my home. My entire existence. And I guess knowing every square inch of your hometown has its benefits. For example, I knew the secret path to a private beach area that I would take when I needed a few uninterrupted hours of thinking or reading. I knew the soft spot in the fence surrounding the lighthouse that would bend just enough for someone to slip through. I knew about the place just beneath the main pier that if you sat there at sunset you'd have a perfect view of the golden rays peeking out over the blue ocean. I knew this town back and forth, and while at times it felt stifling, it was a comforting pressure.

Dale's was packed, as it usually was this early on a Sunday morning. I locked my bike up and hurried inside to find Davia already seated. She waved me over, and I smiled, noticing that she was wearing the same outfit from last night, but had adorned Greg's button-down shirt over top.

"I ordered you a coffee." She pointed to the steaming ceramic cup sitting in front of the open chair. Thankfully, she let me take a full sip before she bombarded me with the questions I knew she was dying to ask.

"So, what the hell happened last night?" I sighed, trying to gather my still-jumbled thoughts.

"Truthfully, I don't know." It wasn't the best answer, but it was the one I had.

"What do you mean?" She wrapped her hands around her own cup and took a deep sip, patiently waiting for me to make sense. I wish I could.

"I went to the bar to get a drink-"

"And that hot tattooed guy was right behind you," she added.

"Oh, so you were paying attention to something other than Greg's mouth." She shrugged, unashamed. "Yes, he was there and I was being awkward as I am oft to do, then he left because he couldn't seem to get away fast enough." Damn, just the image of that broad-chested, long-haired masterpiece had me feeling tightness in my core. I wonder what that piercing on his lip would feel like as he licked my-

"Ok, but what about Louis, what happened with him?" Davia's question snapped me out of my panty-wetting daydream.

"Right, so I got my drink and went back to the table. That's when I saw you were gone. By the way, thanks for saying goodbye, bitch." She leaned back in her chair with a satisfied grin.

"I mean, we could have stayed but then you would have been getting a

show." I laughed with my friend, but it felt hollow. The question of what happened still loomed over me.

"So, Louis was talking and I was trying to figure out how to leave politely 'cause frankly, I've talked to brick walls that were more interesting than he was." Davia choked on her coffee, her hand came up to catch some drips as they sputtered from her mouth. "But that's where things start to get fuzzy."

"Fuzzy?" She asked as she wiped her face with a napkin.

"I don't know, I remember saying I wanted to go home. Louis told me he'd walk me. I said no. Then... nothing."

She stared at me for a long moment, her brows furrowing.

"Nothing?"

"Nothing until I woke up, alone in bed. Still dressed in last night's outfit. And-" I hesitated. I had theories about what happened in my lost time last night. It wasn't the first time, I'd lost time. Wasn't the first time I'd woken up with blood caked on my body. The feeling of fear. But did I want to worry her if it didn't even happen?

"And..." she prompted.

Taking a deep breath to steady myself, I continued. "And I had blood on my face. It looked like I may have had a bloody lip and nose last night." I saw her eyes dart to my features, quickly scanning to see if there were any obvious signs of injury.

"You're kidding me?" I knew she didn't think I was actually kidding her, but I could see the same theories I had beginning to form in her mind. Her face dropped.

"I don't know what happened, Davia. But I - nobody was in my house. It was locked and I didn't feel like I had... like I was... I don't think anyone touched me last night." I was rambling, it felt awful putting my fears into words rather than fleeting thoughts.

"Mike said he saw you two leave together. Oh my god, Athena. I'm so sorry. If that asshole drugged you, I'm going to fucking castrate him." Her eyes were burning, so honestly, I believed her.

"I just wish I knew what happened, it doesn't make any sense. These blank spots in my memory certainly feel like I was drugged, again. But I would be feeling the effects today if I were. I honestly feel fine." Fine is probably not the right word for it, but it was the one I was choosing to use at this moment.

A slight chill brushed against my neck as the door to the diner opened, a small chime sounding from the bell above the entry. I didn't turn to see the newcomers, but I felt a familiar presence that sent goosebumps erupting across my skin.

"Oh damn," Davia exclaimed, looking over my shoulder.

"It's them, isn't it? The group from the bar?" I knew the answer already, something about the air when they were around felt electric, like every molecule in the room chilled.

"Yeah, and fuck they look even hotter today if you can believe it." I couldn't. There was hardly anything they could improve upon their appearance from last night. "Wait, they were there last night!" She nearly jumped up out of her seat as the thought solidified to her. "They might have seen something. Or at least they can confirm if you actually left with Louis." It wasn't a bad idea. In fact, it was probably the best shot I had of figuring out what happened. But the thought of approaching them, trying to speak coherently in their presence, yeah I might have better luck just trying to remember on my own.

"Go ask them," Davia encouraged, using her hands to shoo me. I shook my head.

"I can't. That's so weird." I suddenly hated my choice of outfit, and the very bare makeup look I had done. My hair was pulled back in a claw clip, and if I had to face those insanely attractive people looking like this, I may die of embarrassment. "What do I say, like 'Hi, I know you were at the bar last night, did you happen to see if that dude I was with drugged me?'" Davia winced at my blunt words. I knew she probably felt a twinge of guilt at the whole thing, being the reason I was even out last night. But it was not her fault or her responsibility if that man was a monster. She also knew my history. She understood why this question was so painful to have unanswered.

"Do you wanna know what happened or not?" She pursed her lips and I knew she was right. They were there, there are four of them so chances are they might have seen something. Even the smallest bit of info might help me fill in these gaps that feel so volatile. To keep my mind from filling in the blanks with snapshots of my past, of *his* hands on my skin as he held me down. Of the feel of him inside of me as I cried out for help. I shook my head, forcing the image of his eyes back into the box I crafted for him a long time ago. If he was always going to be a part of me, the least he could do was remain locked away inside.

"I look horrible," I whined, gesturing to the 'everything' about me.

Davia reached across the table, pulling the claw clip from my head and allowing my red tresses to fall down across my shoulders. She ran her fingers through it a few times, trying to achieve the sexy bedhead vibe. She pinched my cheeks, bringing a faux blush to them. She leaned back in her chair and admired her work.

"So?" She smiled.

"You look hot, now go over there and see if they saw anything." I nodded awkwardly a few times before moving. By the time I was out of my chair, I felt my heart racing to an unhealthy degree. Only then did I turn to face their table.

It took only a second for me to realize that Davia was right. They *were* hotter today. The tattooed man who I accosted with the word 'sup' last night was wearing a tight white t-shirt over ripped black jeans. A jean jacket slung over the back of his booth. His arms were on display and his delicious-looking pale skin was decorated entirely in stunning black designs. From his fingers up until they disappeared under the sleeve of his shirt.

His hair that was pulled back at the nape of his neck last night was half up, half down, and a few wayward pieces hung haphazardly around his face, framing him like the work of art he was.

The shorter individual had their shaggy blonde hair slicked back, thick waves sitting against their neck. They had a black button-down tucked into jeans, and their soft eyes looked tired.

The woman was wearing a red sundress, and a black jean jacket, her hair flowing freely in braids down her back and a wide-brimmed black hat sat atop her head.

And the final member of their little group, the one whose eyes were nearly impossible to look away from last night, was wearing another three-piece suit, of course, but this one was a charcoal grey, with a black undershirt, unbuttoned slightly, just enough to show off the top of his sculpted chest. A dark grey tie was loosely tightened around the column of his throat.

And here I was in my ratty old crew neck making my way over to them. What a joke.

"Get their number!" Davia whispered-yelled after me. I rolled my eyes, my face flushing in fear that they might have heard her but as I neared their table none of them reacted at all.

After what seemed like the longest walk in my life, and also entirely no time at all, I was at their table. Four pairs of eyes turned to me, and heat pooled in my core under their intense gazes.

"Um..." Speak, Athena. Come on, say words. You know what words are right? Say them! "Hi."

Death itself could come for me right now and I would welcome it.

Their eyes watched me for a moment before three of their faces split into wide grins. Not the man in the suit, of course not. It didn't look like he knew how to smile, but the others did. And god, if that didn't make me feel like a million bucks.

"Sup?" The tattooed man said in his sinfully chasmic voice, a twinkle in his honey eyes. I couldn't stop the laugh that fell from my lips.

"Oh god, I'm probably just the most articulate girl you've ever met, huh?" Words, nice. I silently thanked my subconscious and my mouth for cooperating. The tattooed man's smile deepened and he let out a small chuckle. The sound was so fathomless that I felt it directly in my core. I watched his throat move with his laugh. A dark tattoo of a snake circled his neck, traveling up the side of his throat. "I, um, sorry. I'm Athena." I waved. Fucking waved. Like a dork. Ok, ground, swallow me up anytime now, please.

"Athena..." The woman replied, her voice was a rich rasp, almost melodic. She said the word as if it was the most delicious thing she's ever had on her tongue. My name had never sounded so delectable.

"I saw you all at the Crabby Crave last night." Fuck, no. "Wait, the Crave Crabbing. Shit. I mean the Craving Crab." Ugh, I need them to stop looking at me like that.

"Yeah, we saw you too." The shorter blonde said with a delectable southern accent that made me feel like I was in an episode of Yellowstone, their eyes meeting mine and holding me there in a comfortable embrace of gazes.

They saw me too. They noticed me.

Good thing you can't hear someone's internal screaming, because AHHHH-HHHHHHH!

My head turned to look at the man in the suit. He hadn't said a word since I arrived, his arms cautiously crossed in front of him as if he were bored with the entire encounter. I cleared my throat, ok enough being turned on. Time to get answers.

"I'm sorry if this is awkward, but um-" Ok, time to be honest, no matter how embarrassed I felt. "I was wondering if you saw anything last night because I think the guy I was with drugged me and I wanted to see if you saw where we went. Or what happened..." The words tumbled out of my mouth. It sounded pathetic. But also, anger coursed through my veins at the fucking thought that I needed to be worried about this at all. Stupid Louis. If he knew what was good for him, he would leave this town and never show his face again. I hated that I was in this position again. But most of all I hated that one single night was threatening to topple the years and years of hard work I put in learning to heal after the last time. Funny how trauma works like that.

The tattooed man nearly growled, an animalistic, threatening sound.

"Sorry, that was incredibly personal. I shouldn't have said anything... I'm sorry." I began to back away, shame blooming in my chest.

"Wait." The tattooed man reached out, his cold hand wrapping delicately around my wrist. A shockwave zipped through me at the contact and I swear to god, I think I whimpered. It seemed I wasn't the only one affected, because he quickly dropped his hand, turned his gaze from me, and cleared his throat.

"Um, please have a seat," the blonde said in that delightful soft southern drawl as they looked at their companion questioningly. Every fiber of my being told me to turn on my heel and walk the other way, that the answers they had for me weren't going to be worth the trouble, but something deeper begged me to stay. I had to know. I slipped into an open chair.

"My name is Laz," the blonde said, smiling warmly at me. Their features were soft and welcoming, but there was an inherent danger to them. Like they might be too perfect, like a porcelain doll. But I wasn't naive enough to think that they could be easily broken. "This is Silas," they continued, pointing across the table to the tattooed man who was still avoiding my eyes.

I nodded my acknowledgment and turned back to Laz.

"I'm Samara," the woman spoke, leaning forward until her head rested on her palms. She was so alluring, so stunning that even her voice felt like it was a siren calling for me, beckoning me out to sea. Her ocean was one I would gladly drown in.

"And the chatty one over there," she pointed with a nod of her head at the man in the suit, "is Orpheus."

It was oddly fitting. In Greek mythology, Orpheus is one of the very few individuals to have traveled to the Underworld and survived, exhibiting power over even Hades himself. Looking at this pale, dark haired man, I could see him taking on the God of the Underworld, and winning.

Orpheus was also incredibly naive and had very little trust in those around him. I guess I'd have to wait and see if he lived up to his name.

"Hello," I said, waving again. What is with me and the waving today? What am I, on Sesame Street?

"So your question," Laz said, slowly bringing my attention from the myth himself. "Yes, we saw something last night." Their eyes darted around the table as if checking in with the others. Oh shit. All awkward tension dissolved from my body and I felt the cold wash of fear blanket me again. No, please. My chest tightened and my breath came in shallow bursts.

"Ok, what did you see? What happened?" I was gripping the edge of my metal seat with such a tight hold that I was worried my fingers might rip through. If it happened again, if I lost another part of myself last night. I don't know if I'm going to be strong enough to hold whatever is left of me together anymore.

Laz took a deep breath, preparing to say something unpleasant. "We saw you two leave together, but you looked...off." Oh no. "We were concerned so we checked your drink." They didn't need to finish their sentence, I knew it was already true, but I guess hearing that my fears were accurate from someone else was validating, and horrifying.

"Ok, so he drugged me and then led me out of the bar..." I needed as much information as these strangers could give me. Even if it broke me.

Laz looked at me as if they thought I might break, which was a fair assessment. I didn't know what my threshold was, but I could tell I was nearing it.

"We followed you out, to make sure that fucker didn't do anything." Silas, the man with the piercings continued. Unlike Laz, his voice was not comforting, or nurturing. No, he was seething. I could feel the anger from here. I felt it too. "When we found you in the alley, he had your dress up around your waist, his pants were down..."

"Fuck," I cried, feeling the hot tears stream down my face. My breathing was ragged and erratic. Flashes played in my mind, replacing Louis' face with his, the monster. I leaned forward, hot tears staining my cheeks, as I felt myself crack. My breathing came in rough spurts. Panic gripping my heart as it did so often.

"No, Athena, don't worry, love." Samara jumped in, reaching a hand across the table toward me, but not quite making contact. "We stopped him before he had the chance."

Relief flooded through me like a tidal wave. The tension dissipated, but not completely. There was still the fear there, of how close I'd gotten to shattering again. God, how could I be so stupid? I looked away from my drink for a minute to read Davia's text, maybe not even that long. I should have known. I shouldn't have gone. I shouldn't have let Davia choose my outfit. I should have learned from the last time. I should have -

"Stop," Orpheus demanded. There was a faint Eastern European lilt to his words.

All eyes at the table turned to him, mine included. I watched him, trying to settle my breathing.

"You don't get to feel one ounce of guilt about what that asshole tried to do to you." It wasn't comforting, it was a command. One I was tempted to follow.

I wiped the tears from my eyes. How had he known I had begun a stupid descent down a victim-blaming spiral?

"Did you take me home?" Laz and Samara exchanged a glance, and Samara nodded.

"Yeah, you were coherent enough to give us your address, and your keys were in your purse. We got you home, and safe. And we stayed only long enough to ensure that you were ok." I nodded mindlessly as I took in this information. These four strangers were my fucking saviors last night. They saved me from a horrific fate, and while the scars from my past were well and truly still in place, they could have been flayed open all over again had it not been for them. Had they not seen me acting differently in the bar, had they not followed me out? If this wasn't a fucking shining example of how being a decent person can save lives, I don't know what was.

"What did you do to him?" I saw the pure rage rolling off of Silas and Laz and Samara certainly didn't look too pleased either. I simultaneously hoped that they didn't hurt him and that they ruined him.

"Sent his sorry ass on his way," Orpheus answered, ever the picture of calm and collected. I was glad that they didn't hurt him, and risked getting in trouble themselves, but a small part of me felt like Louis got off far too easily. "After getting a good hit in." Orpheus didn't smile, but a sort of dangerous smirk graced his thick lips. I watched them closely. Wondering how they tasted.

I couldn't help the nagging thought that Louis didn't go home last night. In a strange area, with no one he knew other than Greg, I don't know where else he might have gone. But I can't say I was too worried about it. He could sleep in the ocean with the sharks for all I care.

Orpheus brought his drink to his lips, covering another smirk as if he knew what I was thinking, and agreed.

"Thank you, all of you, for stopping him." That's all I could say. Words would never be enough. "I wish I could make it up to you somehow."

"You can give us a tour," Silas replied eagerly, his dangerous-looking face turning into a wide goofy smile.

"A tour?" I replied at the same time as Laz. Silas nodded.

"Yeah, we're just passing through, but we'd love to get to know..." he hesitated. "The surroundings," he finished. Orpheus was giving Silas what can only be described as a death glare, and Laz and Samara looked on the fence about the whole ordeal as well. Part of me knew they were probably just taking pity on me, the poor girl who got drugged last night. But another part of me could not pass up the chance to spend a few more hours in their intoxicating presence.

"Of course." Silas' eyes lit up at that. "It's the least I could do." Suddenly, I was making plans to meet these four beautiful strangers at the pier in one hour, and exchanging phone numbers with Silas to 'keep in touch'. I didn't miss the way Laz's eyes flashed, or Samara grumbled when Silas insisted that I only needed his number and he could act as a liaison.

I must have looked like a damn zombie when I arrived back at Davia's table after the four of them had left the diner because she was out of her seat pulling me into her arms.

"What did they say, I saw you crying. Oh god, what did they see?" Davia was a good friend. The best friend. But a huge part of me didn't want to burden her with this. Plus, she was so happy with Greg, and I know that if she knew about what his friend did, she would dump his ass flat. She knew what happened to me back then, in fact, she was one of the few who took my side without question. She was intimately aware of why something like this would break me. I didn't want to weigh her down with my issues. Again.

"They just said that Louis walked me out, and they saw us go our separate ways." Davia's relief was palpable. I hated that I had lied to her, but like it or not, there is a stigma in this world for victims of this kind of crime. Something I learned the hard way. This is my home, I don't want rumors and accusations to start flying in my direction again, not when The Maine Plotline is in such a delicate spot financially already.

I knew the truth, and that's really all that mattered to me. Nobody else needs to know.

After finishing breakfast, I excused myself to go change for my tour, a thrilling shiver of anticipation traveling up my spine the whole way home.

6

SAMARA

"You're a fucking idiot, Silas." Orpheus was once again berating him for suggesting this impromptu 'tour' with Athena. Hmm. Athena. Such a sensual name for such an appetizing woman. Her long red hair was tousled this morning, loose from the confines of its ponytail last night, and my fingers truly itched to be tangled up in it, pulling her closer to me as her mouth feasted on me. That only lasted a moment before I felt ashamed for thinking such a thing.

"You said we have the day, so I want to take the day." Silas' response was logical of course, except for the fact that it was daylight out, and without layers and an umbrella we'd be seriously uncomfortable on this stupid walking tour of Shockgrove, Maine. Silas held a bouquet of pink roses in his grip. I had rolled my eyes when he insisted that we stop at the market to grab them. But I did have to agree that the flower reminded me of Athena. Pink, like the blush on her face last night at the bar when we walked in, but prickly and strong when in the face of danger. She would like them.

"You wanted to see that she was fine, she was fine." Orpheus ran his hands down his face in annoyance again, as he often did when dealing with Silas.

"You saw her, Orpheus. She is anything but fine." He was right. She looked like she might fall apart at the seams at any given moment, it was a true challenge to keep my hands to myself, and not reach for her.

"I agree with Silas," Laz spoke from their spot under the awning. We had sprinted over to the pier where we were to meet Athena and sought shelter

53

from the blistering sun under a blue and white striped awning to a closed ring toss game. Too bad, I would have been so good at this game.

"Of course you do, you were head over heels last night." Orpheus threw his hands up in defeat, turning to lean against one of the metal support beams.

Last night, Athena had been in bad shape. Her blood was fucking toxic, it didn't even smell good, so you know that means it had some serious shit in it. Her heart was beating over time to try and keep her alive, keep her safe. Louis almost killed her, just to get laid. If Orpheus hadn't already ripped his head off and tossed him in the ocean, I might have torn off his dick and gagged him with it. There was nothing I hated more than a man who took advantage of women. Even with my tight grip on my control, it was fucking difficult to maintain my relatively calm demeanor after seeing the position she was in.

"Is her blood clean today?" Silas turned to ask Laz. They shook their head.

"Samara got as much as she could out, and it's definitely lessened, but the scent is still there." Laz was angry, their forehead creased with worry.

"I couldn't smell her, not really." Silas slumped down onto the ground, with his back against the booth.

"And why the hell are you trying to smell her?" Orpheus threatened.

Silas turned his eyes to the ground and shook his head as if he was trying to find the words. We all watched him expectantly.

"Oh fuck no," Orpheus exclaimed, having discerned something from Silas' silence and his emotion that I had not yet garnered.

"What?" Laz asked, eagerly.

"You've got to be fucking kidding me." I'd never seen Orpheus so annoyed, and insistent. And that is saying something.

"What the hell is going on?" I chimed in, their head turned to where I stood and I offered a glance that told them not to test me.

"Silas here thinks Athena is his mate," Orpheus fumed as if he was uttering the most outlandish phrase in the entire universe. As if there was a zero in a million chance of it being true.

I was obliged to agree with him.

Although

"How dare you?" Laz dropped to their knees before Silas, their hands finding the collar of his shirt.

"Hey, watch it! You'll stretch the fabric." Silas pushed Laz back, but they didn't drop their hands.

"Fuck your fabric!" They seethed.

"What is your fucking problem?" Silas stood, retreating from Laz's grasp, setting his roses down on the ground, safe from Laz's assault. I turned to Orpheus who was studying Laz intently.

"Abso-fucking-lutely not!" Orpheus looked like he was about to throw both Laz and Silas off the pier. "Not you too." His gaze burned into the side of Laz's face. I turned to them. They were fiery, and growling, all the things they normally are not.

Thinking back to last night, I could sense Laz's reluctance to leave her alone, but that couldn't have been because of any mate bond. They were just worried about her. Like I was. And she certainly isn't my mate.

Silas understood what Orpheus was getting at and when his gaze retrained on Laz, I saw the whites of his eyes darken with a red hue. Fuck. "She's mine," he hissed.

I looked over at Orpheus for a sign of what we should do, and I saw that he was already on his way to restrain Silas. I stepped up behind Laz and placed my hands on their shoulders, firm, but not to the point of pain.

"We are in public, during the day. Both of you cool the fuck off." Orpheus was our leader for two reasons, he was at one point the only person any of us could trust in the entire world, and he had this uncanny ability to put all of us in our place without even really trying.

But right now, it wasn't working.

"You do not get to claim her." Silas was screaming, if there was anyone else on this pier they would hear him no problem. This was dangerous.

"Neither do you," Laz replied, their tone a much more sinister drawl. Quieter, but in no capacity was it any less threatening.

"Hey, look at me," I called out, loud and firm. Laz turned their head slightly to put me in their periphery, never taking their eyes off their current opponent. Silas' eyes darted from me to Laz and back rapidly.

"Athena is not your mate." They both simultaneously hissed at the mention of her name. "She was bleeding last night, and neither of you felt the bond snap in place. Did you?" I know it hadn't because if it had, they would not have been able to control their frenzy until their cocks were in her and her blood was in them. The mating bond was not a subtle thing. It was powerful, raw, and animalistic. They would know if she was their mate. Plain and simple. None of this, 'I think' crap.

"No." Laz was the first to answer, their shoulders relaxing slightly under my palms. I trained my gaze on Silas, prompting him to answer. His calm took a few more seconds to wash over him, the whites of his eyes returning as the red retreated.

"No," he responded eventually, his breathing settled back to its normal rhythm.

"Then there's your answer. She's not your mate. So calm the hell down and stop acting like fresh turns." It was a bit of a vampiric slur for a newly turned creature. Usually synonymous with those who could not control themselves or their impulses. Exactly what these two fools were doing now.

They settled down, the tension dissipating. I sighed. I loved my coven. They were like a family to me. No, not just *like* a family, they were my family. The only one that mattered at least. One hundred and seventy-three years ago I had a mother and a father, but they did not have a child. They had a bargaining chip. They had a toy whose company they would sell to the highest bidder. My family saw an opportunity in my sharp features and thick curves. They saw the chance to get out of their current predicament, to escape. My flesh was their key to a new life.

And theirs was the key to mine.

Orpheus found me one night, hiding outside the brothel where my family had sent me to entertain for the evening. His harsh words and dominant personality scared me at first. He asked what I was doing, and I don't know why, but I told him everything, every little detail about my pathetic existence. It felt almost euphoric to tell someone else. To let them in on my secrets.

When I was finished, Orpheus got very quiet, his face stoic in an unreadable expression. Then he reached into his purse and grabbed a few coins. Exactly the price I had just finished telling him that my parents often charged for my company. My heart sank, and the euphoria I felt, feeling not so alone even just for a moment, drifted away as I nodded, wiping away the tears. Then I sank to my knees before him. He only wanted what everyone else wanted.

Or so I thought.

He pulled me up to my feet and growled. Yes, actually growled at me. And then he said the words that I have never forgotten no matter how many moons I've lived to see on this Earth. "You will never have to give any more of yourself than you are willing to give, ever again."

For one month, my parents would set "appointments" for me at the brothel. When I would go, I'd find Orpheus had already convinced the gentlemen to leave, and he would pay the price and ask for not a single thing in return. So for one month, I would visit the brothel, have a short conversation with Orpheus, take his money, and leave. I later learned that Orpheus 'convincing' those men consisted of him drinking their blood and hiding their bodies. I didn't know that at the time, he wasn't the bad guy, the men who were paying for a piece of my unwilling flesh were. I can't say I would have been too upset had I known their fate even then.

A large part of me feared that this man's generosity would eventually wear out, that one day he would see how little he gained from our interactions and he would demand payment in kind for the things he's done for me. But even after one month, that day never came.

I'd come to trust him, in a way that I barely even trusted myself. When he offered me the chance at a new life, it was the fastest yes I've ever said. And when he told me the price of my new existence, it was the fastest price I've ever paid.

Silas, Alora, and Laz joined our little coven not long after, each with their own stories of why an eternity as a creature of the night seemed like a better fate than the one they had been sentenced to. I shook off the sharp pain in my chest at the thought of her name.

We were a family, and nothing pained me more than seeing my family at odds with each other. Not in the sense of Silas pushing Orpheus' buttons and riling him up, but something like that... a mating bond...that could ruin the foundation of my little family. And that was something I simply couldn't have.

"There she is," Silas exclaimed, grabbing his roses from the ground, his eyes fixing on a point at the far end of the pier. He was smiling like a love-sick fool. Maybe he should seduce the poor girl, and fuck her to get her out of his system.

But one look at Laz and their smitten expression as they watched her approach, told me that simply couldn't work. No, if we were going to remain a family, nobody could have Athena.

"Behave," I heard Orpheus whisper as the bike approached. She had changed. Her form was now draped in a casual grey t-shirt dress, with a light jacket slung over her shoulders. Her hair had been tamed and loosely curled too. And her face was made up to have that natural 'no-makeup' look. You know the one that all the guys truly believed took no time and effort, but in reality, probably took a good twenty minutes of intense work to get the shading just right. The others won't see the effort she put into this little tour, but I do. And fuck, I like what I see. Her breasts were perky and thick, they bounced slightly as she dismounted her bike. I caught a glimpse of black lace panties as her dress rode up, and suddenly my clit was throbbing. Begging for the chance to rub against those panties and what lies beneath them.

I turned to look at the others, and of course, Laz and Silas were nearly drooling, their eyes were one second from falling out of their sockets. Orpheus was the picture of unfazed, but I noticed the way his jaw tensed and his fists balled. He liked what he saw too.

Damn, this girl has some serious magic or something. Why the hell were we all reacting this way for some human?

The word echoed around my head. 'Mate'. That wasn't possible, was it? Not for them, and certainly not for me.

She approached cautiously, timidly. I found myself stepping forward to greet her so that Silas and Laz could get a metaphorical grip on their cocks and calm the fuck down.

"Hi," she spoke, her stunning green eyes bearing into mine.

"Hi, Athena," I responded, once again loving the way her name felt on my tongue. I bet more about her would feel great on my tongue too.

"So, what brings you to Shockgrove?" She steered the bike to a post and locked it up before smiling back at me, her eyes giving me her full attention. I loved it.

"Just passing through on the way to our destination," Orpheus answered before anyone else could. A strange expression crossed her face as she absorbed that.

"Yep, just a couple of Wanderers," Silas teased, knowingly. I thought Orpheus was going to strangle him.

"Well, unfortunately, this isn't Shockgrove's most...exciting time of year." She sighed. Silas held out the bouquet of roses and her sweet eyes landed on them, widening in shock.

"Oh, wow these are gorgeous. Thank you." She smiled, bringing the roses to her nose and inhaling.

"They're from all of us," Laz interjected, and I shot Silas a look that told him not to fight back right now.

"Well, then thank you all." She made sure to make eye contact with each of us as she said those words. Then she turned and headed down the pier. I sent a glance to the others who made quick work of donning their long sleeve jackets, sunglasses, and hats. It wasn't a particularly sunny day, with the clouds blanketing the sky in a soft embrace, but I knew as well as the others did that the rays could still do their damage. I pushed open my black, Victorian-era parasol and followed after Athena, struggling to keep my eyes from her round ass as she walked.

Maybe we could all have a little fun together before we left? Hell, why was I thinking of that? We'd never done something like that together. I had never been attracted to my companions, partly because they are too important to me and sex can ruin even the strongest of relationships, and two, because I wasn't the least turned on by the idea of dick. The feel, the look of them, and the people they were generally attached to. I was very happy finding my pleasure in the sweet folds of women.

So why is it that this gorgeous woman with blood-red hair and pale skin has me thinking of sharing her with my friends?

It would be simple, I would bury my face in her sweet heat, tasting every inch of her release with my tongue while Laz took her nipples into their mouth and Silas fed her his tattooed cock. She would squirm under our hold, straining to get away from the sheer blinding pleasure I was wringing from her body, only to spear herself on Silas' dick. The act of sucking cock never appealed to me, but right now I couldn't stop picturing what her thick lips would look like stretched to accommodate my well-endowed friend.

"I can smell your arousal from here," I heard Orpheus whisper in my ear. He was a few steps behind me, but my hearing was impeccable. "Please don't tell me that you are going feral over this human too?" His voice was strained. Worried. He knew as well as I did that a mating bond would ruin the delicate family dynamic we've created and protected over the years.

"She's attractive. That's all." I believed the words, but my heart seemed to throb at the idea of her being nothing to me.

Strange.

"We cannot get distracted." Orpheus had taken a few strides to fall into step with me. Silas and Laz had flanked Athena and were asking her questions fitting for a tourist. 'How long does the season last?' 'What events does the city hold?' 'What is the best seafood place?' 'Does this town have a sex shop?'

My head snapped toward Silas whose honey eyes had darkened with sexual promise as he asked her that last question. Her face flushed a deep crimson. The blood beneath her skin burned hot with embarrassment.

Orpheus groaned and rolled his eyes.

But Laz, Silas, and I awaited her response eagerly.

"Yes, we do have one. I can show you...if you'd like." She looked up at Silas through the dark frame of her eyelashes, batting them twice before shyly looking away, her fingers toying with the pink roses in her arms. Ohh, she was good.

"Fuck yeah." Silas nearly jumped up and down at the idea of visiting a sex shop with Athena. The idea did sound kind of appealing.

"What was that you said about getting distracted?" I teased Orpheus, who had crossed his arms and was staring daggers at the back of Silas' head.

"Don't act like you aren't aware of what is coming after us, Samara. You understand more than any of us the danger we're in."

Nameless.

The violent, horrific group of hunters called themselves Nameless because they knew that if our kind ever were to find their identities behind their stupid masks, we would devour them like the weak, pathetic cowards they are.

The faceless legion had been around for centuries, passing their wicked legacy from generation to generation.

These Hunters were cruel, vicious monsters who not only aimed to eradicate all vampires from existence but to make us suffer violent deaths. Deaths that lasted for weeks, months even, draining us of our energy, and powers.

Methodically torturing us within an inch of expiration until we had no choice but to beg for a swift death that Nameless would lord over us until the moment that all fight had left and we were nothing but an empty husk that once was full of life.

I was one of the few who escaped their clutches. But my wife was not so lucky.

I shuddered at the memory of the lost fifth member of our coven.

"I know, Orpheus." He was right. We had escaped - albeit not all of us - but Nameless has our essence, they have our scent and they do not take lightly to their captives escaping. In fact, in all the years they've operated as a threatening shadow chasing our kind at every turn, no one else has ever escaped their clutches the way our coven had.

All except for Alora.

But she was the reason we survived, she was the reason we escaped. Her flesh was the key to our new life...

"We can't stay here, they'll find us." They would always find us. My unspoken response hung in the air between us. We knew it was true.

"We can't run forever, what good is a life unlived?" The others sometimes said my optimism was useless and unfounded, but my wife gave up her life so I could be here today. I wasn't going to waste a second of it.

"I don't like the way they look at her," I turned to see his face, his dark brows furrowed, a slight crease forming on his forehead.

"What are you getting from them?" I asked, knowing that Orpheus had been using his ability on the two of them by his concentrated stare.

He inhaled deeply, his eyes fluttering closed for only a second before he sighed. "They're smitten like a bunch of teenagers." I didn't need Oprheus' ability to read emotions to gather that. Laz was laughing at every word Athena was saying as if she was the most humorous person alive, and Silas was taking every chance he could to lean in and whisper in her ear, which always earned him a deep red blush.

"And you aren't much better," Orpheus remarked, turning his annoyed glare to me. I rolled my eyes.

"I'm not smitten," I scoffed. "I simply think she'd be a great lay." Orpheus ran his hands through his perfectly combed hair, messing it up to the point that he looked less put together, and more rugged. He was a handsome man if you liked that sort of thing, but he was truly his most breathtaking when he was about to fly off the handle.

"You're supposed to be the sane one," he nearly growled.

"Do you think there's any merit to their claim?" I asked him, letting my eyes drift back to the display of juvenile courtship happening in front of us.

Athena was telling a story about the origin of the amusement park at the end of the pier. The Ferris wheel and single roller coaster stood tall against the backdrop of the cloudy sky. Hundreds of booths and carts littered the space at their base. But here it was, a warm nearly summer day, and the gates were locked tight.

How these businesses survived this town during the off-season was perplexing.

"About her being their mate?" I nodded. "Absolutely not." Vampires mating with humans was not uncommon. In fact, it was pretty frequent. But the improbable part was the two vampire mates. Multiple mates were rare, accounts of them only really occurred in royal families or for the most powerful of our kind.

"You sound incredibly sure," I mused. I mean, I was sure too. I think.

"You said yourself, she was bleeding last night and the bond didn't snap into place. They would have known the second they scented her blood." I nodded, that was my reasoning too, but a nagging thought kept prickling at the edge of my mind.

Her blood felt strange last night. It was full of that toxic shit the blonde man had slipped her, it wasn't even appetizing, and that is definitely saying something considering before last night I hadn't fed in almost two weeks. So maybe the bond didn't snap because her blood wasn't her own last night? There was something strange about the way we all reacted to her being threatened. Even Orpheus had lost his cool, breaking his own rule to not kill the boy.

"Right." We came to a stop in front of a plain brick building off the beaten path. The outside was unassuming, specifically designed to camouflage the debauchery within.

There was a single neon sign in the window that told us they were open. Athena looked bashful, looking down at her feet.

"Here you go," she said to Silas, who was smiling at her like she was his next meal. He walked toward the door but turned back to look at her.

"You coming in?" She blushed, and I felt my core tighten at the look of her blood rushing beneath her perfect skin. I glanced at Orpheus, ready to take his verbal abuse at my reaction, but he was too busy staring at her face. His expression was empty, but there was a sort of heat behind his gaze.

Athena followed Silas into the shop, and Laz was close behind. Orpheus finally looked at me once she was out of view.

"So, this is getting complicated." He groaned and found a spot against the outside wall to lean. It was clear he wasn't going to go inside. And I almost didn't either, but there was a strange draw, like an invisible string begging me to follow after her. I obliged.

The store was like many others of its kind I've seen in my years. Dark red and purple walls and lushly decorated shelves. Phallic and damn near painful-looking contraptions lined the walls. A back wall was covered entirely in various lingerie, I tried not to picture Athena in the red nightie that would match her flaming hair perfectly.

Silas and Laz were arguing off in the corner, my advanced hearing picked up only parts of their frustrating pissing match. 'She's mine,' 'She looked at me first..' and on and on. I tuned them out and walked over to where Athena was quietly pursuing the aisles.

"I'm sorry that Silas convinced you to bring us here, he can be...childish sometimes," I said as I approached her. She smiled sweetly, a slight dimple deepening on her cheek. I watched it with rapt fascination.

"It's ok, I don't mind. I actually come here often." Her eyes widened as she realized what she just admitted to me. "Um, not like 'often' but sometimes. I've been here. Once, or twice. At least once. Oh god, I should shut up now," she spoke quickly with an anxious burst. I smiled and watched her face deepen with another blush.

"You don't need to feel embarrassed for taking your sexual pleasure seriously," I whispered. Her gaze locked on mine and I eyed the spot on her neck where her vein was pulsing loudly, tauntingly. "Do you have a favorite?" I asked boldly, waving a hand toward the various toys on display. She coughed to hide her shocked gasp.

"Um, I'm sorry?" She nearly spat out.

"Don't be sorry, give me a good recommendation," I flirted, which felt wrong, but also entirely right.

"Oh, um well that depends on what kind of.." she lowered her voice, I glanced over her shoulder at Laz and Silas who were still engrossed in their own conversation. "Stimulation you prefer?"

I smirked at her, my tongue darting out to wet my bottom lip, she tracked the movement.

"Well, I'm very gay, if that's what you're asking." She gulped, awkwardly and I chuckled. "But I enjoy a good penetration when it's the right person performing it."

She nodded, the scent of her arousal making my mouth water.

"You might like one of these then," she offered, avoiding eye contact now, studying the roses in her hand.

"What about you, Athena? What kind of stimulation are you a fan of?" It was pretty clear based on her reaction to Silas that she liked men, and if the way her breath was coming in shallowly, I could venture a guess that she was just as attracted to me as I was to her at this moment. Call me selfish, but I wanted to hear her say it.

"I'm bisexual," she whispered and a sweet smile spread across her lips. I wanted to taste it.

"Lucky me," I said the words before I could even stop myself, her chest was heaving and I felt like I was going to implode any moment.

"I don't normally talk about it so openly," she admitted shyly, but her eyes never left mine.

"Why not?" I asked.

She swallowed deeply, her eyes flicking to my lips and back.

"I've had.. I've got some stuff I've been working through. It's taken a long time to be comfortable with it again." I noticed how her heart rate picked up, coupled with the far-off look in her eyes.

"Hardships make us stronger. I know I am who I am today because of all the shit I had to go through. I'd wager you are too" Athena's eyes held a deep empathy that I remembered seeing in Orpheus' eyes that first day we met. I reached a hand to her, unable to resist, and ran my fingers delicately against her cheek.

The moment I touched her skin, I felt a shock wrack through my body, like a lightning bolt. I pulled back instantly, picturing Alora's disappointed face in my mind.

"Sorry, I shouldn't have done that," I rushed out before turning on my heel and hightailing it out of the shop. It took most of my focus to not run at full speed, but the cool Maine air hitting my face was a calming sensation. I took a few steadying breaths.

"You shouldn't have gone in," Orpheus spoke from his casual position against the wall. I turned around, finding his eyeing me carefully.

"I know." I walked over, found a space on the wall next to him, and got comfortable.

"Your emotions are all over the place," he confirmed what I already knew. "What's wrong? Don't tell me you think she's your mate too?" He begged. I chuckled half-heartedly, although it didn't really seem all that humorous.

"No, I don't think she's my mate." I let my head hit the wall behind me, taking a deep breath. "I already had one." Alora wasn't my mate in that mystical, fate-filled way, but she was my everything. She was my lifeline. My heartbeat. It had been years since she was taken from me, but even the vivid rush of desire I was feeling in my core had me feeling sick to my stomach with guilt.

I wouldn't want someone else. I promised Alora she'd be my one and only. I swore it to her before our friends and the stars of fate. Just because she's gone, doesn't mean that vow is any less iron-clad now than it was that day.

"Samara," Orpheus started. I let my head fall so I could look in his direction. "Alora would want you to feel love again, she would never want to keep you from experiencing the happiness that she used to bring you again." I smiled lightly at the memory of her bright blue eyes. "Just don't go trying to find it with this human, ok? Please?" He was exasperated, an emotion I didn't often see in him.

I laughed, fully and leaned my head on his broad shoulder. "I promise." I meant it, but I hoped I could keep it.

A few minutes later, Athena exited the shop followed by Laz and Silas, who was now holding a shopping bag. He had a mischievous glint in his eyes and I suppressed the urge to roll mine.

Athena resumed her tour, leading us down to the pier again, spending quite a bit of time on each of the shops along the way. She spoke so highly of the businesses on the boardwalk and their owners, it was admirable how much she respected them.

After a while, we came to a stop outside a small storefront just down the pier from the amusement park. Its worn red awning was weathered and tattered but in a cute vintage way. The windows were filled with shelves of books and cute wooden tables and cozy padded chairs. Gold Painted lettering graced the window, 'The Maine Plotline'. Cute.

"This is my store." My head snapped to Athena, she looked shy, as if she was embarrassed about her accomplishment of owning a store.

"You own this place?" I asked, realizing it was the first I'd said to her since we left the sex shop. She smiled and nodded.

"I do." She tossed a forlorn glance over her shoulder at the quaint storefront.

"Can we go inside?" I don't know why I felt the need, but I wanted to see if her business had the same kind of quaint charm that her home had. To see if her essence was plastered on every wall as it had been in her cottage. I smiled as I thought of her charming abode, and how perfectly it reflected this shy, bubbly woman in front of us.

"Oh, yeah sure." She fumbled through the pocket of her jacket for her keys and made quick work of the lock before stepping aside to allow us inside. "Please come in. I'm going to put these in water."

As we followed her into the shop, I noticed once again how intoxicating her scent was. I still couldn't smell her blood, but she had this almost wintergreen scent to her and it reminded me of a cozy winter day.

The first thing I noticed as we arrived in the shop was the colors. She had painted the walls with an almost ivy green, deep, thought-provoking, sensual. The light brown shelves sat against the walls, filled from floor to ceiling with books. Old titles, with worn and tattered covers, all the way to new arrivals, the scent of the printed words still prevalent. There was a small counter where there was a coffee machine and some pastries behind a glass case.

Sections of the store had been blocked off for small group and individual reading areas. Lush green velvet couches and plush black armchairs created an almost private feel.

It was gorgeous. Personal. Intimate. Everything I'm learning to expect from Athena.

"This place is incredible," Laz said, their fingers trailing over the spines of some books.

"Thank you," Athena responded, returning with a glass vase and placing the roses on the counter, a bright smile spreading across her face. Her features were soft and kind. Almost innocent. But her eyes held a sort of darkness that I found entirely too familiar.

"Have you had it long?" Silas asked, moving closer to her. He hadn't touched her again since this morning at breakfast, but that wasn't stopping him from getting as close as possible. A rush of jealousy spiked in my chest.

What the hell? Jealous?

A harsh sadness crashed over me at the thought of my late wife again. It's been years since we escaped Nameless, years since Alora sacrificed herself for our freedom. I've found myself attracted to other women since then, I've even indulged in some heavy petting, but I had not yet crossed the line and slept with one. I always stopped myself before it got that far. I couldn't stand the thought of her not being the last woman I was with. Alora wasn't my mate, but that didn't make our love any less powerful and genuine. The loss of her was potent and painful. Less and less each day, but still raw enough to sometimes take my breath away. I hated that I was feeling this way over someone new, having these dark thoughts, these dirty fantasies of Athena when it should be my wife that I'm thinking of.

How does one ever move on from a grief so potent? How can someone ever breathe again? How can you not hate yourself for developing feelings for someone else?

I took a deep breath and crossed the space until I was far enough from Athena to take a breath without inhaling her wintergreen scent.

The sooner we left Shockgrove, the better.

7

SILAS

*H*er body was a magnet. A powerful force drawing me into her orbit, holding me in place, and keeping me hostage in her universe. The moment my hand touched her skin at that dingy diner, the world around me ceased to exist. I had never felt so completely and totally absorbed by a person the way her energy consumed me.

She has to be my mate.

I feel it.

Orpheus and Samara were right, logically I knew that. She was bleeding last night, and although I had gone a little feral when beating that sorry excuse for a man, no bond had snapped into place.

I've been protective my whole life, hell, I'd kill for any one of The Wanderers and I have. But to feel so defensive of this human so quickly, to know that without a doubt I'd lay down my life at her feet if it meant her safety...that had to mean more.

I listened to her, excitedly telling the tale of the amusement park on the pier, and I hung on to every word as if it was the most interesting thing I'd ever heard. And from her lips, it was. I wanted to taste her, to sink to my knees and run my tongue over her center, send her into a shattering orgasm where she could do nothing but scream my name. I wanted to wear her thighs around my head like a crown. I wanted her. Plain and simple.

Laz was walking on thin ice, I don't know who they thought they were, laying a claim on her, when it was so evident that she was mine. I shook my head, allowing the murderous thoughts toward my companion to drift away.

67

Athena seemed to enjoy their company, they made her laugh. And fuck, that laugh was one of the most glorious sounds in the world, so if Laz was the reason for it, I'd allow them to be near her. For now.

Athena led us through her bookstore and I found myself mapping out all the surfaces I'd like to claim her on. The counter, the velvet couches, up against the bookshelves, having her pant and moan as pages fell from the sky from the impact of my cock in her soft folds.

Orpheus and Samara had taken to looking at one of the shelves near the front of the store; she'd been wearing a strange expression ever since she ran out of the sex shop. Laz followed Athena as she led them deeper into the store's depths. I watched as Athena smiled, describing the changes she's made to the decor in the last few years. I didn't care much about decor, or feng sway, or whatever she called it. All I knew is that this store was important to her, and therefore it was important to me.

"So, you're a bit of a bookworm then are you?" I teased, wetting my lower lip with my tongue and loving the way her green eyes traced the movement.

"I've been reading since before I can remember," she responded, her skin flushing again. I fucking loved making her blush.

"What kind of books do you read?" I took a step toward her, boxing out Laz who seethed behind me. They can suck my dick, it was my turn to have her attention.

I towered over her by at least a foot, and I loved that difference. She had to look up at me as I came closer, her neck straining under the movement. I watched the vein beneath her skin throb and I felt my fangs elongate slightly in anticipation. "I'm a fan of fantasy." She managed to say, but the breathless way her words came out told me she was as affected by our proximity as much I was.

I circled her, coming to stop behind her. I brought my lips close to her ear and whispered. "I'm a fan of romance. But none of that PG shit. No, I like the down-and-dirty stuff." I saw her swallow, the movement making her pulse quicken. I wanted to taste her blood so desperately. I was thankful I was behind her, so she couldn't see the way my fangs begged for her. I saw Laz staring at us, a sort of hungry jealousy in their eyes.

"Yeah, smut is pretty good," she responded in a near whisper. I watched her chest heave and the scent of her arousal nearly had me shifting right then and there.

I kept my face near her neck, letting my breath paint her skin with beautiful bumps, as my hands trailed the books on the shelf next to me. I didn't know these titles, but I was willing to bet something called "Devour Me" was going to be exactly what I needed. Careful not to touch her again, I reached around her until I was holding the book open in front of her face, my lips so close to her ear I could feel the pulsing of her blood in my fangs. I flipped the pages as her breathing became labored.

"Hmmm, let's see here." I stopped on a delicious-looking page and began to read. "'Her skin was slick with sweat as Drake hovered over her. His tongue traced a roadmap across her exposed skin, teasing her sweet flesh before taking one of the mounted peaks of her breasts into his mouth.'" I felt her tense beneath me, not in fear, but in pure anticipation. Laz was watching her with ravenous intentions. As long as they keep their hands to themselves, they can watch. I liked putting on a show. "'She felt his hands travel down her sides until his fingers dug into her thighs as he spread them apart, revealing her hot center, slick with desire for him.' Oh, this is getting good, don't you agree, Athena?" She nodded, wordlessly, her eyes glued to the pages I held open in front of her. I inhaled, prepared to continue, but the sound of her sweet voice stopped me.

"'His fingers trailed the sensitive skin near her core and she moaned. One brush of his touch against her clit was all it took for her to detonate. Her body raged with a flash of blinding heat as Drake slid a finger inside her folds. Stretching her. Pleasing her.'" Her words were breathy and sultry, and I felt my cock spring to life. It took every ounce of willpower I wasn't already diverting to controlling my shift to keep myself from pressing it up against her ass. I flicked my eyes to Laz, the outline of their arousal evident as well.

"Keep going, baby girl," I whispered into her ear and her lips parted to let a moan escape. It was the most captivating sound I'd ever heard. I would give anything to hear it again.

"'His cock was hard against his jeans and she reached for him, begging him to let it spring free and give her the pleasure she was aching for.'" Her scent grew stronger, more intoxicating. I was so transfixed on her, I barely noticed Samara and Orpheus looming in the stacks behind Laz, their eyes just as full of hunger as mine, I'm sure. Laz took a step forward, nearly touching her, but I didn't mind because their closeness simply made Athena's breath catch and a tiny moan escaped her lips.

"'She clawed at his fabric prison until she reached the prize she was after. His thick length stood erect as he looked down at her naked form, writhing and begging for him.'" Laz leaned forward, their lips dangerously close to her extended neck, she almost leaned into them. I saw the words on the page and before I could stop myself I spoke the line aloud.

"'Beg me to fuck you,' Drake demanded.'" Athena's head lulled back as she exhaled, my words finding their target in the center of her core. Laz and I had her caged in, her body was flush against both of ours and I could tell how much she wanted it. I looked at the next line and felt like I was ready to explode just with the anticipation of hearing her sultry voice read it.

"I believe the next line is yours," I barely recognized my voice, it was primal, hungry. All hers.

I turned my head just enough that I could see her lips, and my companions. Their faces were equally as eager to hear her performance as I was.

"'Fuck me,'" She paused. The room was filled with so much tension I was surprised we all hadn't shifted already. I exhaled, long and deep, my breath landing on her skin as she read the last word. "Please."

I closed the book, slowly, my fingers feeling numb with the ache to touch her again, and placed it back on the shelf. Laz was staring at her, their eyes held a slightly reddish tint, nothing she would notice, but I knew they were close to a shift. Hell, we all were. Even Orpheus, who stood with arms crossed, looked like he might try to devour her any second. And Samara, whose self-control could rival even the most ancient vampires, was teetering on the edge of a shift. All for this human.

My human.

We waited in tension-filled silence for a few moments, her body trapped between mine and Laz's. I'd fuck her right here, if she asked me to. And I'd let my friends watch. Just say the words, bookworm, and I'm yours. I wanted to believe that her arousal was for me alone. But from the way her body reacted to Laz's, I knew it wasn't.

"Yeah, those books are great." She said, matter-of-factly, the heat and desire that was so present in her voice previously was gone. Then she stepped out from my orbit, and moved toward the front of the shop.

If I couldn't smell her arousal still, I might have thought it was all an act.

So my girl likes to play games then? Good.

Let's play.

8

ORPHEUS

Fuck, this human was going to be the death of all of us. And I mean that quite literally. Her little performance in the bookstore was fucking intoxicating. Samara and I could smell her from the front of the shop, and it was as if our feet moved on their own accord. Drifting across the space until our eyes landed on her. Her face flushed, her chest heaving, her nipples peaked and pressing against the grey fabric of her dress.

The four of us watched her like she was our prey and our most prized possession at the same time. If she didn't break the spell she had on us by walking away, we might have all taken her right then and there. Hell, maybe we should have. Then we could have had a taste of this human that perplexes us so that we could get the hell out of this town. Nameless was after us, and they're never far behind. We cannot stay here, we shouldn't even be here now, but this devil of a woman had to go get into trouble.

As she continued to lead us all across this wretched little town, I began formulating a plan.

We had to leave, and soon. Fuck, we should have left last night after our shots. That was the plan. Silas nearly begged for a reprieve from our travels. We had been running non-stop for nearly four hours at that point. At our speed, we made it through the entire state of New Hampshire and most of Vermont.

Vermont was where we had hunkered down for a few weeks. It was safe enough, the town we found had enough people in it that we felt concealed, but not too many that we felt surrounded. But then we saw the symbol.

Two offset triangles, and a wooden stake. That symbol - painted, printed, projected. It has plagued our kind, like a shadow. No, not a shadow. This was far more sinister. More revealing. Like daylight. When we saw the symbol, it meant that we had been discovered, that Nameless was close. We couldn't hide anymore, just like daylight. They were gifted in manipulation, and scare tactics. It worked. Whenever we noticed the symbol, on a flier in the coffee shops we frequented, or painted on a billboard like some kind of taunting graffiti, we packed up and ran. Nameless had either the best or worst trackers in the world. On one hand, they gave us the chance to run, to get away. On the other, they instilled a sort of fear, a dark panic in us that followed us everywhere. So that even when we found respite, we were never truly free from their influence.

And we never would be.

Not until every last Hunter was killed. And I would not rest until this Earth was rid of their vile corruption.

Although they might say the same about me.

Perspective is funny like that. Hearing this tale, the tale of our kind being chased across the world, tortured within an inch of our lives, and hunted from our side might make a person sympathetic to our cause. However, hearing the same tale from the dirty mouth of a Hunter might change someone's mind about us. Might make them fear us. We were something to fear, of course we were. We kill, we drain, we hunt.

But that's where their tale ends. The Hunters. That's all they need to know in order to justify their attempt to eradicate my kind from the planet. The rest of the story doesn't matter to them. It doesn't matter that my coven only hunts monsters. People like that asshole at the bar last night.

In a sense, we are both Hunters. Nameless and us. Life and death isn't so black and white.

I watched my coven, Silas and Laz mostly, fawn over this red headed human. I also saw cracks in the wall Samara had expertly built around her dead heart. Her kind smile melting the cold exterior we had all so carefully crafted over the dark years since we've been running.

I don't trust her. No, I don't think that she intentionally got drugged and nearly raped as some sort of ploy to keep us in town. I don't think she's working with Nameless. That's not the distrust I feel when I look at her.

When I look at her, when my eyes involuntarily scan her body, appreciating her curves, and catch a glimpse of her twinkling green eyes, I don't think she will betray us. I think she will make us weak.

I feel it happening already, as I watch Silas and Laz. Their emotions tickling my senses like a soft embrace, their sickly sweet feelings toward this human. I felt them at the bar and I feel it more here.

A long time ago, I told my coven about my ability to feel emotions, and they saw it as an invasion of privacy. They didn't tell me that of course, but I felt it. They didn't need to tell me a lot of things that I was able to discern. Every member of The Wanderers is gifted, that's why we've been able to stay hidden from Nameless for so long. That's why we've been able to remain safe - if that's what you want to call it- from many threats over the years. But my particular gift, the way I knew when someone was plotting, when someone was anxious, or when someone was hiding something. It's what made me a good leader then and it makes me a good leader now. It's kept us alive.

They know that as well as I do. I try to refrain from reading them if I can. Sometimes I don't have a choice. Like with this human.

Athena's emotions this morning at breakfast nearly consumed me. Her guilt. As if she had any reason to feel guilt over what that fucker attempted last night. But what was worse, what truly gripped my soul was her fear. Unrelenting, deep, and broken beyond repair. I wasn't planning on speaking to her. Hell, I don't even want to look at her, but fuck, I was practically choking on her dread and I needed her to stop. For my sake if nothing else.

Now though, those feelings were still there, but dormant, a sort of constant cloud covering her. But the emotion that danced around her was happiness and lust. Both are equally as potent, and distracting.

I knew it was a bad idea to do this tour. Silas' little performance in the bookstore was exhibit fucking A. Her lust, her passion, her fucking aching need entered every single one of my senses at once. Drowning me in her desire. If I hadn't already felt that, the scent of her arousal would have alerted me anyway. Before I could stop myself I was watching. Watching the flushed look on her face, the way she pressed her thighs together to chase some relief, the way her eyes scanned the pages of the book and then landed on me as she said those words.

'Fuck me, please.'

No, I didn't trust her one bit.

"Well other than the lighthouse that's about all." I sighed, thankful that our waste of time has come to an end. It was a relatively warmer May day, and the sun was shining, which justified our hats and sunglasses, but made the long sleeve shirts and suit jackets we wore a bit uncomfortable. But I'd rather experience discomfort than the vicious sting of daylight.

I'm about to demand we make our way out of town when Silas opened his stupid fucking mouth.

"Show us the lighthouse?" I groan, I don't mean to, but it slips out and I see my companions eyes turn to me, Laz and Silas with an edge of fury. But it's her eyes that hold me. She watches me, her eyebrows furrowing. Disappointment dancing around her.

"It's ok, I've monopolized so much of your time already," she whispered, tossing her hands in a 'it's not a big deal' kind of way.

I felt their gazes, their anger, it pressed against the edge of my subconscious. I looked to Silas, then to Laz, then to Samara. They were waiting for me. Of course.

"Show us the lighthouse," I demand. It's not kind, not sweet. But that's not who I am, and if my companions thought they might get a different version of me, then they were fucking naive.

"Right this way," Athena says to me. Her green eyes held mine in an almost challenge until the moment she turned.

So we followed, I barely registered the elbow that Silas threw into my abdomen, he knew that it wouldn't hurt me. That wasn't his intention.

"Could you be less of a dick, please?" He asked.

"Could you be less of a love sick puppy?" I toss back, keeping my eyes trained ahead. Watching. Always watching.

"I saw you looking at her." It wasn't an accusation, or a threat.

"And?" I prompted.

"And... I think you know there's something here." He's referring to the 'mate bond' that he feels so strongly is there. I rolled my eyes.

"If you want to get your dick wet, be my guest, but don't be ridiculous with all this mate crap. You know as well as I do, that she's not your mate." I whisper. Luckily for us, Laz is talking Athena's ear off, asking questions about the lighthouse and its histories. Which she answers truthfully, but with a sort of fond sadness circling her. Interesting.

Silas growled, low, threatening, and I felt his hand come up and grip my arm. I turned my head to look at him for the first time. His eyes were dark, and bloodshot, to anyone he just looks like he needs sleep, but I know what that look is. Intimately.

"How can you be hungry? You fed last night." Our kind could survive on what he had last night for weeks, maybe longer if the vampire was strong enough.

"Because of her, I need her." His voice was laced with desperation. Fuck. So much for leaving after this tour.

"We can't stay here," I toss back, but I know from the look in his eyes that there is no fighting this. If he was already hungry, already craving, there wasn't much I could do to stop this.

"And I can't leave. Not until I know." I may be the leader of this coven, I may make choices that the others follow, but when it comes to this - to primal needs

- there is nothing more sacred to our kind than a mate bond, and if Silas was reacting to this human like this, I knew that we were not leaving until he was able to confirm or deny the bond.

"Fuck." I said, running my hands down my face. My mind was already shifting the plans I've made.

When we left Vermont, we knew Nameless would expect us to head West, toward the wide expanse of the United States. We covered our tracks as well as we could, left some breadcrumbs heading that direction, then turned to head East.

It was a stupid idea, heading to the dead end that was Maine. Which is why we made it. Nameless thinks that we are smarter than that. With any luck they won't catch on that we didn't go West for a few weeks.

We can stay for a brief time. It would have to be enough.

"I'll text you an address, meet me there after your fucking tour." Silas nodded, and I felt it. He was sorry, guilty. He didn't want to be the reason we didn't stick to the plan, but there was another emotion that floated through my senses, drifting off of him. Happiness. He wanted to stay with her.

I turned on a heel, not bothering to say anything to my coven or the human who seemed to have them wrapped around her little finger.

I had preparations to make, and not a lot of time to make them.

Looks like Shockgrove's population just grew by four.

9

ATHENA

I was still reeling from the...reading... in the bookstore. I don't know what came over me, why I, after being caged between Silas' powerful arms and Laz's strong body with the dirty book in front of us, felt the desire to read aloud. To say those words to them. To all of them. I'd read that book before, and I knew what I was going to read, but I did it anyway. Why? Because of the way Silas smirked at me, because of the way Laz's body gravitated toward me, the way Samara's eyes were on me the moment I stepped off the bike, and because of the way Orpheus, who had done whatever he could to avoid me, had come around the corner and stood among the stacks of books and watched me with ravenous eyes. Or maybe because I felt autonomy over my own desire for the first time in a long time. I felt like I deserved to feel what I was feeling without the guilt or the memories haunting me.

That's why I said those words. And, I think I meant them.

Which might be the most surprising of all, considering my close call last night. After the first time that my monster took what he wanted from me, I didn't feel attached to my body for months. And then when I finally felt like I belonged to myself again, I hated it. Hated the way it felt like I was wearing someone else's body around, trying to force it to fit. I would shy away from anyone who looked at me. Hated the way that no matter how sweet someone was, their faces eventually molded into his. I couldn't be attracted to someone without remembering his words in my ear.

"You've wanted this for so long, haven't you? I can tell."

It took years of therapy and hard work to let myself be aroused without

79

seeing him. And longer to let another person touch me the way he did. But I did it. I found strength and courage, and I moved past what he did to me.

And then it almost happened again. That is why I'm so surprised that even after all that, with the fear and the memories that Louis brought back, I'm attracted to these strangers. No strings or ancient memories attached.

My body feels this intense sort of pull toward them. Not to mention they might have saved my life last night. If not my life, at least my sanity. Hot as sin and respectful? Sign me the fuck up.

Ok, I need to calm down. I nearly dropped to my knees in front of all four of them. Even went out and bought a damn dress to wear for them. Who the hell am I? This doesn't happen to me.

They're not attracted to me, they simply feel sorry for me. They saw me go through something traumatic last night and they're throwing me a proverbial bone. A sexy, dirty-talking, kind, did I mention sexy, bone.

Ok, Athena, stop thinking of bones.

"So, do you come to the lighthouse often?" Laz asked, their gaze was trained on me and their face was the picture of interest. I'm not sure I've ever had such genuine, undivided attention before.

I led the group toward the hole in the gate and smiled at Laz. The waves were crashing against the rocky cliff below the lighthouse, and I could feel the wet sting of the ocean and taste the salted air on my tongue as I breathed. It was more potent here than it was on the pier, with no buildings or roller coasters to block the wind rolling in from the horizon.

"I used to." They didn't push, only nodding gently with a quiet understanding. Laz had this sort of pure and innocent nature to them, but the look in their eyes as they pressed their whole body to mine told me they were anything but. I came to a stop in front of the gate and turned to my companions, only to realize that Orpheus had left. I scanned the direction from which we came for him. Did he just fall behind? Silas came into my line of sight.

"He had an appointment," Silas offered. I nodded, wondering why I suddenly felt sad about his absence. He's barely said a word to me. I shouldn't care that he ditched my tour. But I do, and that feels weird.

"Well, welcome to Shockgrove lighthouse." I smiled and pushed the weakest part of the fence, my mind flooding with memories of my mother doing the very same. Her long auburn hair, her freckled face. She was gorgeous, and I loved every moment I had with her.

Sighing, I moved through the fence, only slightly aware of the others following closely behind.

The last time I was here, life looked quite a bit different.

I swallowed the lump in my throat and forced the tears that threatened to fall back. Her hand was frail, her skin pale. Her hair had lost its illustrious shine and had muted to a dull color. Her head was covered in a small knit hat, concealing the small patches of balding spots that she had developed from her brief stint in chemo. It was obvious pretty quickly that she wasn't going to survive her fight against this illness, and she made the decision not to spend what little time she had in a hospital bed, connected to tubes.

She wanted to die as she lived. Free.

I lead the group of strangers toward the entrance to the lighthouse, fighting off the vivid pictures that begged to be replayed. I hadn't thought of that day for a long time, but now I couldn't seem to keep the memories from flowing.

Me, smiling weakly as I pushed her wheelchair toward the edge of the cliff, close enough that we could feel the mist and see the waves dance along the shoreline below. I always wondered what it would feel like to be the waves. To build and grow until you're so full of emotion, or passion that you finally crash, exploding, sending a small piece of yourself in every direction. To have so much power that you make that big of an impact.

"Ok, let's go up," she said, meekly. She was getting weaker with every passing moment. It's a horrible thing. Watching someone you love wither away, seeing the light that used to shine so brightly behind their eyes dim each day until you know that at any moment the light may go out for good, and you'll be cast into darkness. I'd never been afraid of the dark until the moment I knew what her darkness would mean.

"There's no elevator, mom." She scoffed, tossing a hand toward me. The sleeve of her sweater rode up revealing her arm. Has it always been so skinny?

"Get me to the stairs and I'll climb them." She was so determined, her voice so sure that I almost forgot.

"Mom, you can't." I hated saying it, but it was true. She wasn't strong enough. She hadn't been for days. She's only been able to stand for brief periods of time. There was no way she would be able to climb the tower.

"I can, and you're going to help me." She started wheeling herself toward the base of the lighthouse, and I couldn't shake the terror that pulled at my heart.

When she reached the base of the stairs, the spiral staircase that we had climbed together over a dozen times throughout my life. A climbing staircase that led to a whole slew of adventures that we had with each other.

"I don't remember the last time we climbed these," she mused, her head falling back as she took in the sight of the steps.

"Me either," I responded, quietly. I promised myself the moment I heard she was sick that I wouldn't cry in front of her. She needed me to be strong and that's what I would do.

"You know how everyone always says, 'I wish I knew the last time, was the last

time?"' I nodded. "Well, now we do. This time, right now. This will be the last time we climb these stairs together and we're going to make it count." A sob lodged itself in my throat, as she tossed off her blanket. Her legs had lost significant muscle mass, and she also had lost weight so her already small frame looked impossibly tiny. She was so weak, I saw it in the heaving of her chest, the unwanted hitches in her breathing. She was slipping away, and all I could do was watch her go.

I moved forward, helping her stand, securing my arm around her waist, and navigating her arm to rest on my shoulders.

Together we stood at the base of the stairs, her fragile weight resting carefully on mine, and began to climb.

As I pushed open the door to the lighthouse, I found myself inhaling a sharp breath. It looked the same. I don't know why I expected it to change. Maybe because everything else had changed so drastically since that day.

"Wow, this place is pretty cool," Silas said as he entered the space. I felt heat then, burning me, licking my skin. I shouldn't be here.

"Athena," I heard my name, but I couldn't place it. The room began to spin and my breathing came in punishing spurts. "Hey, hey, look at me." I felt a presence in front of me, blocking my view of the stairs that were haunting me, but their face was unfocused and blurry.

The moment the stairs were out of my sight, I dashed out of the lighthouse and into the open air. I bounded across the field and stopped at the cliff's edge, letting the cold ocean air caress my skin as I breathed. Flashes. Always flashes. Bits and pieces of this memory with my mom, tainted with the residue of his touch on my skin. One trauma into the other. Like a sliding slope, when I was overwhelmed with one, the other wasn't far behind. I pressed my palm to my chest and forced my breath to come. Forced my eyes to remain open, trained on the horizon, and not focused on the glimpses of pictures that were escaping from the deep recesses of my mind.

"Athena, what's wrong?" I could focus again, the world slowly settling around me. Silas was in front of me, and I felt Laz and Samara flanking either side. Silas' honey eyes were full of concern and worry. He held his ground before me and commanded my gaze. His shoulders were moving up and down in clear and deep breaths. Before I knew it, I was mirroring his movements, my own breathing leveling out.

The panic subsided. The images of my frail mother and the monster who dared to impede on my memories of her locked away tightly, for now. I stood a little taller and nodded to Silas. "I'm sorry," I managed.

"Don't be sorry," Laz said, moving closer, but still maintaining some distance between us. I smiled at them. "I take it this place means something to ya?" I nodded again and was thankful that Laz didn't push. I don't know if I would be able to explain what had just happened to me.

A phone rang and I saw Samara pull it from her bag. She grimaced at the name, and her eyes darted back to me as if she wasn't sure she should leave me.

"I'm ok, it was just a panic attack. I promise I'm ok now." Something in her gaze told me she didn't really believe me. "I promise. It happens sometimes. I'm fine." She fought an internal battle for a moment more before striding off to answer the call.

I turned to Silas. "That's one way to end a tour," I joked and I saw his eyes soften. "I think I dropped my bag in there." I curse under my breath. That's the last thing I need, to go back inside after finally regaining my composure.

Laz took a step forward and I felt a sort of cold radiating off of their body. They watched me carefully, like I may break at any moment.

The two of them exchanged a silent look, one that was too quick for me to decipher. "I'll go get your bag," Laz said eventually, taking cautious steps away like they didn't want to leave me alone with Silas.

With a sigh, they turned on their heel and jogged off toward the structure.

When I turned my head back to the man before me, he was watching me, his entire body closer to mine than he had been before. I shivered from the cold rolling off of him, and from his proximity. He was so close to me now, I could see his dark hair falling out from beneath his hat, and a tattoo peeking out from his collar. The scaled design was intricate and dark against his unusually pale skin. I bit my bottom lip between my teeth.

"Do you want to get out of here?" Those words have gotten a bad rep. Usually spoken with a slurred speech by drunken frat boys to their catch of the night. But right now, coming from the lips of this handsome tattooed, sinful man in front of me as he watched me with caring eyes, they might just be the best words I've ever heard.

"Please." His eyes glistened with something dark and mischievous at the word, a hungry smirk claiming his lips and I felt the blush heat my face.

"Say that again." His dark timber vibrated deep, his tone gravelly and inviting. A challenge. I took a step forward, involuntarily, as if my feet were being pulled to him. He licked his lips, leaving a sheen across their surface, I watched them hungrily. I knew what he would do if I followed through on his request. And I was shocked to realize that I wasn't afraid. I didn't want to shy away from the affection. I didn't feel phantom hands on my arms as Silas held me. All I felt was him, and I wanted him. All I had to say was one little word.

"Please."

His lips crashed into mine, and suddenly I knew what it felt like to be the waves. It took me all of a moment to kiss him back. His hands snaked around my waist and pulled me flush against his rock-solid form and his lips devoured me.

My hands found the back of his head and my fingers tangled with his hair, pressing his face to mine. His tongue pressed against my lips, begging for entry and I opened, willingly, eagerly. Our tongues collided and I whimpered against his mouth as heat pulsated in my core.

I felt his teeth graze my bottom lip and he let out the most delicious moan I've ever heard. I pressed my mouth to his, trying to taste it. To consume the sounds he made.

One of his hands trailed along my side, up to my throat where he gripped. I gasped at the sensation of lost airflow. It wasn't enough to worry me, just enough to enhance everything I was feeling. My entire body was on fire and beneath his palm, I swear my skin sizzled. Heat and cold. Fire and ice. A passionate, blind, inferno.

Driven wild by this strangely vulnerable yet powerful position he held me in, I took his lip into my mouth, ran my tongue against the piercing there, and bit down.

"Fuck," Silas murmured against my mouth, his hand closing in tighter on my throat until small white dots began forming on the edges of my consciousness. I waited for the panic to rise, but it never did. It was delicious, deviant, and everything I never knew I would enjoy. The difference here was that I knew that Silas would stop if I asked. And that felt powerful. Like I had permission to enjoy this.

His fingers loosened their hold on my windpipe, but his palm remained steadfast against my skin. My breath rushed back to me in a gasp that he swallowed down, hungrily.

I lifted onto my tiptoes, to press into his body as much as I could manage. I clawed at his shoulders, needing more. My clit throbbed with the need to be ravaged by this man. He growled against my mouth, a strained, sinful sort of sound, as his lips pressed against mine.

I was lost in glorious desire, he could have asked for anything in that moment and I would have gladly given it to him. Freely and with my complete consent. I nearly forgot we were on the cliff's edge overlooking the ocean until the crashing of a wave against the cliffs below mirrored the intense beating of my heart.

Our lips separated, but his forehead rested on mine as we both swallowed gasps of air, greedily. My lips felt puffy, satisfied, and frozen, a feeling quite like the moments after finishing an ice cream cone. My lips curled up in a sated smile, and I felt Silas' body shake with incredulous laughter. Finally, we stepped away, he unwrapped his chilled arms from my body and the slightly chilled May air warmed me instantly.

His honeyed eyes were glistening as he smiled brightly at me. He was looking at me as if he had just won a prize, or like he was in awe. He was positively gorgeous and my heart pounded at the thought of him looking at me like that forever.

"You taste incredible, Athena," he remarked, a devious glint in his gaze as he ran his tongue along his bottom lip. I burned. My eyes were locked on his lips, wondering how soon I'd be able to feel them again, wondering how good they'd feel on other parts of my body.

Silas' gaze heated and he took a step forward, I readied myself for another passionate onslaught, but unluckily, or luckily, a voice pulled me from his spell.

"Here's your bag." Laz held my bag up for me, their voice holding a dejected tone, and their gaze avoiding mine. I grabbed it quickly, ignoring the strange feeling of guilt that was bubbling under the surface.

"Thank you, Laz." I tried to meet their eyes, but they kept them trained away from me, their lips pressed in a tight line. They had seen the kiss, of course, they did. We weren't exactly hiding it. Maybe their flirtatious banter wasn't just banter, maybe it wasn't just out of pity.

Maybe they actually liked me? The memory of their hard body against mine at the store came to mind. Would I have kissed Laz if it had been Silas who went for my bag? Yeah, I think I would have. Hell, I would have kissed Samara if she was in their place too.

The thought sent warm tendrils of excitement to my core and a flutter to my heart. How is it that I went from being the town's social pariah with a traumatic past to the town's social pariah with a traumatic past and three incredibly sexy individuals interested in me? Well, maybe not three. Samara ran out of that sex shop pretty quickly and hadn't said more than a few words to me since, but there was a heat in her eyes that I craved to see again.

Someone pinch me.

"We should head out, Silas. Orpheus called." I heard Silas sigh deeply before walking toward them. "Thanks for the tour, Athena." Laz tossed, stopping Silas in his tracks and moving away rapidly. Silas paused, watching after his friend, and I suddenly felt like a horrible person. All euphoria that had invaded my senses from our kiss was evaporating with each languid step Laz took away from us.

"I'm sorry, I didn't mean to hurt anyone's feelings." I didn't turn to see Silas' face, instead, I watched after Laz, following them until they met up with Samara on the other side of the fence.

Silas ran his hand through his hair and turned to face me slowly. "You did nothing wrong, Athena. I, however, knew about Laz's feelings for you and acted on my own anyway." I saw the guilt etched on his face.

"I should probably go, I'm sorry for getting in the middle." Silas' eyes darkened and a devious smile spread across his lips. "You ok?" I asked, not sure I wanted to know the reason for his shifted mood.

"Just thinking about you in the middle." My face flushed and a positively juvenile giggle escaped my lips. I was definitely picturing that now too.

"I've gotta go, but thank you." Silas stepped forward, his scent invading my nostrils again, sending a shockwave directly to my center. His whispered voice aimed directly at my ear, and the skin touched by his breath erupted in goosebumps. "For showing us around." His lips landed on my neck, a brief kiss, but it was enough to draw a moan from my mouth. "And for the kiss." He planted another light kiss on my jaw. I felt my mouth fall open, and my eyes closed. "And for this." His lips found mine and his tongue quickly entered my open mouth. By the time I kissed him back, he was already pulling away. A nearly ravenous look on his face.

"You have my number," his eyes darkened. "Use it." He took a few steps away before I found my voice again.

"Are you all leaving town?" I called after him, attempting unsuccessfully to hide the desperation in my tone.

He kept walking but turned over his shoulder to send me a wink. "Not without you." And then he jogged, meeting up with the others on the other side of the fence in moments. Leaving me, completely stunned and positively turned on.

I watched them leave, my heart thumping in my chest.

What the hell just happened?

Ok, time to remember the facts. These four sexy strangers saved me from being raped last night. Then, they took care of me afterward. This morning after comforting me, they asked me to give them a tour of the town where two - kind of three? - of them flirted with me relentlessly. Then, like a girl with a schoolyard crush, I read a dirty book with them, out loud. I made out with the handsome tattooed one, like sucking each other's face off kind of makeout, and then the other one whose cock was against my leg earlier got extremely jealous.

I need to go home immediately. If only to relieve this burning ache between my legs with one of my many many toys. Something about them all makes me feel so sensual, so free. Like I have the right to take hold of those sinful desires I've only recently let myself feel again. I needed to get home and douse this flame immediately, but the thought of his lips on mine made it increasingly difficult to put one foot in front of the other. I glanced over my shoulder at the keep of the lighthouse and sighed warmly.

Panting breaths and grunts of exertion echoed in the keep when we reached the top. I helped Mom sit on the ground, her back up against the sturdy railing near the lantern's enclosure, then found myself a seat next to her. From our spot, we could look out over the water, watching the sun dance along the surface of the crystal ocean.

"You're out of shape," Mom teased breathlessly as I struggled to rein in my breathing. She had a smile on her lips, but I could see the energy dwindling with each passing second.

"This is a very tall lighthouse!" I complained gaspingly, wiping the sweat from my brow with the back of my palm. We sat in silence for several minutes watching the world in front of us carry on.

That's what it was going to do after all. Carry on. After she was gone, the sun would still rise, the waves would still crash against the rocks, the wind would still blow. No matter how her loss would rock my world, no matter how bleak and lonely I would feel. No matter how much I wish I could stop the moon from retreating every dawn and beg it to stop time. To stay in this moment forever. It wouldn't.

"Promise me something," my Mom said, her voice was tired, but she had a sort of authority about her that I respected. Even now, in her state, she could command a room.

"Anything," I assured her. She let her head tilt slightly until she was glancing at me, her eyes missing the glistening twinkle that I'd come to love from her stare.

"Promise me that you'll still try to live." A tear slipped from her eye and slid down her smooth skin. Smooth and fragile. Young. She was too young. I couldn't respond without breaking my own promise not to cry in front of her, so I just nodded. Her chest heaved with the exertion. "I'm sorry I couldn't protect you from everything." Her voice was sad, filled with guilt that I desperately wanted to erase from her soul. This guilt was mine to bear, not hers.

"Stop, you did everything you could." She shook her head, tears falling more readily. "You did."

"There are scars on your soul that I could have prevented, scars you will have for the rest of your life, and I hate that I can't kiss them better." I had to focus all of my energy on not letting the tears that were building in my eyes fall. She was exerting too much energy. Each word seemed to take too much and give too little.

I gently threw my arms around her and hugged her. She leaned her head into the crook of my neck, but her arms didn't reciprocate. She was too weak. I could hear her labored breathing from my close position to her chest.

"My soul would have had a lot more scars had you not been there to shield me, Mom," I whispered into her ear, speaking through clenched teeth, emotion cresting in my chest.

"You'll have to shield yourself now, love." It was barely a whisper, she struggled to force the words through her tired lips. When I pulled back from her face she had gotten

even paler than before. Pain constricted in my heart. There wasn't much time left. I could see the sands of time running out in the dimness of her eyes.

"We should get you home," I said, jumping into action. "Grandma will want to talk to you." Tears were streaming now, I was completely unprepared to face this reality.

"Sit down, Athena," she demanded. I shook my head, preparing to pick her up and carry her back down the steps.

"We have to get you home, you should rest." I was rambling, I knew it. So did she. "I need to call Grandma and the doctor. We shouldn't have come up here." I was panicking.

"Athena." I paused, turning to look at my mother's face. It was an expression of acceptance, of submission. My breathing wouldn't slow.

"We have to go." She shook her head.

"Athena, please." A sob wrenched itself from my lips, a painful sound.

I crawled into the space next to her. "You knew when we came up here, didn't you?" I asked, choking on my sobs.

She nodded. I burrowed into her arms, laying my head on her chest. Pressing my ear against her skin so I could hear that heartbeat.

Thump. Thump.

"What about Grandma?" I cried.

"We said... our goodbyes already...now it's our turn," she said slowly. Using every ounce of energy she had left.

"I can't do this without you, Mom," I told her truthfully. Her breathing slowed.

"Yes you can, love." I could only hear her because I was so close to her. I gripped her in my arms, as tight as I could without hurting her.

Thump... Thump.

"I love you. I love you. I love you." I murmured into her chest.

Thump.

"I love you."

Thump.

"I love you."

...

"I love you."

With a dazed look over my shoulder at the lighthouse, I silently thank Silas for giving me another happy memory here, one that could soften the blow of my final minutes here with her.

"I love you, Mom," I whispered, feeling the weight of grief on my soul lighten with each step away.

10

ORPHEUS

"I understand that you are booked for the season, but I'd urge you to find me a listing." I was a businessman at heart. Negotiations, acquisitions, and analyzing risks. I think I was similar as a human, but I'm not entirely sure anymore. One of the curses - or I guess in some cases like Samara - blessings, of our second life, is that after a while the details get fuzzy, and you start to forget the mortal life you led, the people in it, the kind of person you were. The birth of your second life becomes the only one that matters. It takes a long time to dissipate, longer if it was particularly impactful, so unfortunately for Samara, her wicked past will still loom over her for a while longer. But I remember being quite detail oriented, and skilled in the art of negotiating from the very beginning of my second life, so I can assume that was a skill I picked up from my previous existence.

"I'm sorry, sir." The realtor's shrill voice grated against my subconscious. My fists clenched at my sides at her words. She had her platinum hair pulled back in a tight ponytail that pulled her skin taut, and her shapeless form was draped in a tight burgundy skirt and jacket set. Her feet were stuffed into ridiculously uncomfortable-looking heels. "We have no homes available for the season." I forced myself not to roll my eyes before reaching into my suit jacket and pulling out a large stack of cash. I've spent long enough in this world to know that when money talks, people listen.

"I will buy out another renter's contract, and give them a sizable donation so they can find new accommodations." The blonde's eyebrows shot up and she pursed her painted-red lips.

"Paying in cash?" Her gaze scanned me. "I think it is my duty to remind you that we do not stand for any sort of illicit activity in any of our rental properties." I couldn't control my eye roll then.

"Ma'am." I didn't miss her wince at the word. Or the feeling of embarrassment flooding her emotions. So she was one of those women who loathed the idea of growing older. Noted. Time to shift tactics. "Miss," I started, leaning forward on the counter until I could feel her heat. A sudden rush of lustful energy began radiating off of her, but to her credit, her face remained emotionless. "I'm sorry, I can see I've wasted your time." I darted my tongue out to wet my bottom lip and saw her eyes follow the movement. Her chest moved with deeper heaving breaths as she watched me, and struggled against the very potent and very real feelings of desire that were building in her.

I couldn't stop the part of me that unconsciously differentiated how this woman's rush of arousal felt in comparison to Athena's. From a completely objective standpoint, there was no contest. Where this blonde's emotion felt abrupt and harsh, like grabbing the handle of a hot pan without a glove, Athena's felt like a warm fire slowly building to a climax.

I did not just think of Athena and the word climax in the same sentence. I need to stop letting Laz, Samara, and Silas' emotions around her influence me.

"We have a home near the pier, right on the beach, it's booked for the season but the tenants usually only spend their weekends there." I leaned forward again until I was well and truly in her space, I studied her carefully, masking my face to seem like the most interested person she's ever spoken to.

"Do you think they would mind?" I asked innocently. She smiled, her face flushing at the undivided attention I was giving her.

"I think I can make it work," she giggled, wrapping a small strand of blonde around her index finger.

"You're a saint," I nearly hissed the word, but she fell for it, despite my clear indignation at the ridiculous claim.

"I'll work on getting the paperwork, you just wait right here." She winked and took off, dragging her potent and not-at-all-alluring scent of arousal with her.

I stood up straight as she disappeared behind the office door. I hated resorting to my charms to get what I needed, but with so much on the line and so little time to formulate this plan, I didn't have time to follow through on anything quite as... intricate as I would have liked.

I turned to face the front of the office, a full wall of windows, and a single glass door. A Shockgrove Vacation Rentals decal was plastered on the surface and blocked some of the sun rays that spilled through the glass.

I waited impatiently for a few moments for the blonde to return with my rental information. The sound of her heels clicking against the tile surface had me turning back to the desk, fixing my smile in place.

"Ok, we just need some of your information and we can get this all set up." She slid some documents across the desk to me. She held out a pen, waiting for me to grab it. As I did she purposefully brushed her hand against mine. I had to fight against pulling my skin from hers as she touched me. She smiled meekly.

I got to work on the paperwork, utilizing one of the many pseudonyms I've adopted to avoid any paper trails. David Green was a business executive from New York, he had been purchasing and distributing underage pornography. We decided the world was better off without him. His blood kept us fed for a few weeks, and his ID kept us hidden for longer.

"So," she started, glancing down at the paperwork in front of me. "David." She smiled at the name. "Are you here with a wife or a girlfriend?" I didn't respond at first. On one hand, I didn't want her to feel like I had played her, although I most definitely had. On the other hand, I had no intention of following through on any silent promises our eyes made to each other as I charmed her into getting me what I needed. I had to play this delicately.

"Actually, I..." My words were cut off by the most intense wave of emotions I had ever felt in my entire existence. My eyes widened as I looked at the realtor, the only other person in my vicinity. But this feeling wasn't coming from her. I doubled over as another wave of sheer panic hit me.

"Are you ok?" I vaguely heard the woman asking. I waved her off.

"I just need some air, I apologize," I gritted through clenched teeth. "I'll be right back." I stumbled out of the office and into the midday air, as my breathing became difficult.

Panic.

A lot of it.

I bent at the waist, a hand to my heart, I felt phantom beats from a heart that wasn't mine, rapid and violent as I fought against the wave of crashing anxiety. The sting of the sun's light as it touched my face was a mild inconvenience compared to the brutal weight of this emotional barrage. I looked around, thrashing painfully looking for the culprit. The person whose emotions were so vivid and so close that I felt them this deeply.

I was alone. There was nobody else roaming the empty streets.

My back hit the brick wall behind me, settling under the shade of an awning giving my tender skin a moment to recover from the burn, as I struggled to regain a semblance of composure. There was no explanation for this feeling, no reason that I was experiencing something this painful when nobody was around. Instantly, the thought came to me. What if something happened to my coven? I've never felt their emotions this strongly, and certainly never from this far away, but that doesn't mean it couldn't. Fumbling for my phone, I rang Samara.

She picked up after four rings.

"Orpheus," her voice was strained, I couldn't read her emotions from here, but if I had to guess I'd say she was worried about something.

"What's wrong?" I asked, masking the current vicious emotion that continued to swim around my head.

"It's fine. I think." I waited for her to explain. Had Laz or Silas been hurt? The tight feeling in my chest was slowly receding, but the cool embrace of the panic's hold on my heart was present, and I'm sure it would remain that way for quite some time.

"What happened?" My breathing had returned to a relatively normal cadence and despite the sweat gleaming on my forehead, I was feeling as if I was collected.

"We're at the lighthouse, I think Athena may have had a panic attack." My breathing ceased again, my entire body going frigidly still.

"How long ago?" I asked through clenched teeth.

"Just now, although she seems to be settling down," I heard the concern in Samara's voice for Athena, but I didn't have time to analyze it.

I glanced toward the lighthouse, it was barely visible from my position this far inland. It must be a coincidence. It has to be. There's no reason why I would feel her panic, not from that distance, and certainly not that strongly.

Back at the diner this morning I had felt her guilt and her fear, but had it been any stronger than normal? I don't know. My head was spinning, my skin was tender from the sunlight and my chest was tight as I cleared my throat.

"I found us a place since Silas insists we stay put."

"Text me the address and we'll meet you there." After issuing my agreement, I shot off a text with the address of our new rental, then sauntered back into the office to complete the paperwork.

I needed to focus on our safety, our plans, and our survival. I didn't have time to worry about if it was her panic that I felt, and if so...why?

I didn't have time to think about why the idea of Athena in a panic was sending murderous thoughts through my head.

11

SILAS

Her scent was still strong, each time the wind caressed me, a cloud of her minty aroma wafted up to my nostrils and I hardened instantly. Her kiss was fucking wicked. I'd never felt so out of control before. Never felt so overcome by mindless attraction.

And yet, still no mate bond.

Although, she didn't bleed today.

To our kind, you must scent someone's blood for the mate bond to snap into place. So logically, last night, when she was bleeding after her encounter with that piece of shit, it should have happened. It didn't.

So why, even with this impossible-to-refute proof staring back at me, was I so fucking positive that this woman was mine? How was it that my entire body, every fucking nerve ending sang when I was around her if she wasn't my mate? How am I already missing her after leaving her only five minutes ago, if I don't belong to her?

Mate or not, I am Athena's. And she is mine.

My eyes drift to my side, Laz had been quietly walking alongside me. Their anger was pretty potent, I didn't need Orpheus and his ability to confirm that. I shouldn't have kissed her, not without talking to Laz first, but they knew the moment that they walked away to retrieve her bag that they were giving me permission. Whether they knew it or not. Still, I couldn't help the guilt that was tugging at my subconscious. Samara walked ahead of us, her eyes scanning the street names, leading us to the address that Orpheus sent over.

"Laz..." I started, but they put up a hand.

"Not out here, ok? I am barely keeping myself together as it is, I don't need to shift and go all Dracula on your ass in broad daylight in front of our new neighbors." I smirked at that. I've been with The Wanderers for a long time. I have seen Laz when they are angry, like irredeemably angry, and that usually manifests itself in a sort of quiet simmering rage. Silence before the storm and all that. So the fact that they were speaking to me at all at that moment told me that I had not broken us beyond repair.

I watched my friend as Samara turned down a driveway. Trying to place myself in their shoes. If I had walked away to get her bag, would she have kissed them? Did she feel the same pull toward Laz as she did for me? If she had, and I'd walked back to see them locked in a passionate embrace would I have been able to stop myself from tearing them off of her? I'm not sure. The pent-up rage in their closed fist at their side told me that I was one wrong word away from having to spar with my friend. I pushed that thought away and followed Samara. There was a rental car in the driveway. Smart, wouldn't want the neighbors to think we run everywhere. Orpheus thinks of everything.

The moment we stepped through the front door and it closed behind us, Laz was on me. I fell to the ground and they caged me down with their body. Their hands gripped my throat with as much ill intent as they could manage. It was child's play truly in comparison to other fights I've been in, but I let them take and keep the upper hand.

"You son of a bitch!" Laz pushed down on my windpipe, not enough to do any real damage, which is how I knew that we were ok and they just needed to air their frustrations. I let them.

"What the fuck is going on?" Orpheus called from the stairwell.

"Silas kissed Athena, and Laz is gonna kill him," Samara rattled off, unimpressed, but I noticed a slight edge to her jawline. Like she wasn't too happy about my alleged indiscretion either.

"For fuck's sake."

Laz slammed their fist into my face, and it hurt, don't get me wrong, but it felt like any actual hatred was long gone and this was coming from a place of pain. "Get up you two, now." Laz graced me with one more hit across the jaw before dismounting and standing. They stalked off through the back door, the one that led to a pretty solid-looking patio, and down onto the beach. We watched after them for a moment before Orpheus sighed.

"Nice place," I said with a low whistle, massaging my throbbing jaw. The interior was bright, with that beachy nautical vibe that New Englanders love so much. Blue walls and starfish decor, hardwood floors, and a huge living room. The space was furnished with burlap and oak furniture that looked the appropriate amount of rich and rustic, no doubt so the bastards who rent this place in the summer feel like they're doing something special with their lives.

There was a spiral staircase that led up to a second floor, a balcony overlooking the living space here with vaulted ceilings. I only had a briefest thought of fucking Athena against that railing before Orpheus gripped my shoulder.

"So...you kissed her," he spoke with a slightly accusatory tone. "Anything?"

I shook my head, and he rolled his eyes, groaning as he walked away.

"She didn't bleed, Orpheus." He tossed his hands up before sinking onto the couch next to Samara.

"You could have bit her lip or something," He offered and I couldn't stop the smile that played on my lips. My tongue ran across my bottom lip and the piercing there, remembering how it felt to have her tongue do the same. Relishing in the memory of her teeth closing around my lip, claiming it as hers.

"She beat me to it." I fell back into the armchair that sat across from the couch and smiled at Orpheus. Samara's eyes flicked to my lips and I knew she wasn't thinking of kissing me, but rather imagining the person who had.

"You need to figure this shit out sooner rather than later. We have a place to stay, but I don't intend to make this an extended pitstop." I nodded. I knew the risks and I understood intimately why the Hunters could never be able to find us again.

Alora was my best friend. Samara of course fell head over heels for the girl, but she was my friend from when we were humans. Losing her was hard on us all, but it nearly killed Samara and I. Those Hunters will never get the chance to do that to another one of us, ever again.

"I know. I will. I'm not unaware of the risks here." He nodded, satisfied with my answer. He was right. I was going to have to get a whiff of Athena's blood soon. But I needed to wait until I was sure that toxic shit that that fuckwad from last night gave her was completely out of her system. I needed to be sure, to be absolutely positive. If I was going to leave this place without her, I needed a damn good reason.

"For what it's worth," Orpheus started, leaning forward to rest his elbows on his knees and clasp his hands together in front of him. "I can sense it - how you feel about her." My breath caught in my throat. He knew we hated when he read our emotions. "And before you go getting your panties in a twist, I'm not reading you intentionally, it's just that strong." I smiled then. I knew how I felt about her, but it was nice to have someone validate that it feels just as earth-shattering from the outside. "I can understand why, with emotions that strong, you are so focused on discovering if there's a bond here. I've never seen you feel this way for someone before." He paused before standing and walking toward the back door. He turned slightly then, a wistful smile on his lips, glancing over at the door that Laz left through, but not before tossing a slight look toward Samara on the couch. "If it changes anything...they feel it too."

I ran a hand through my hair, combing it out of its bind at the back of my head and letting it fall freely around my face while releasing a deep sigh. Of course, Laz felt this way. Did Orpheus intend to look at Samara? Could she be feeling similarly? She's always been so reserved with her feelings. It took decades for her to make a move with Alora. Shit, we were both going to need the time to determine if she was our mate. Athena was going to change everything. I just hoped we'd be able to handle it. As a coven. As The Wanderers.

A slight buzz from my pocket had my entire demeanor shifting. A total of five people had this number. Seeing as two of them were currently in my periphery and one of them wanted nothing to do with me right now. My options were down to two. My body relaxed when I saw a local number. Her number.

> ATHENA: So what do I get?

I shook my head, scrolling up to see if I'd missed another message. Something that makes more sense.

> SILAS: What do you get?

I typed back my response, quickly.

> ATHENA: Yeah...What do I get?

My eyebrows furrowed as I typed back.

> SILAS: For what, bookworm?

I smiled at her nickname, and the memory it elicited. God, what I'd give to go back to her shop alone and read each dirty scene in that entire place and reenact every single one with her.

> ATHENA: You told me to use your phone number.

I tilted my head in confusion, watching as the dots appeared again as she typed.

My cock twitched in my pants, and I bit down on my lip to avoid the moan that wanted to escape. I stood and raced up the steps toward the bedrooms, I found an empty one with pale green walls and a king-sized bed facing double balcony doors by the time she responded again.

I threw the door closed behind me and nearly sprawled out on the bed typing back. I had half a mind to say 'whatever the fuck you want,' which was technically true, but that's not the game she wanted to play right now. And I was more than willing to give her what she wanted.

A giddy excitement was budding in my chest, and my cock was hard, tenting my pants. I unbuttoned them and slid them off, leaving my boxers for the time being. If only just to avoid touching myself and exploding before I wanted to.

That fucking word. I was going to make her scream it the next time I saw her.

When she didn't immediately respond, I worried that I may have taken the game too far too fast, we only met last night for Christ's sake and didn't even speak till this morning after all. When my phone buzzed again I sat up against the headboard with a jolt.

And down go the boxers. With one hand, I type my message back, letting my other finally touch my aching cock, stroking it to offer some relief.

I was panting, breathing raggedly as I stroked myself to the thought of following through on my promises. Her next text came quickly.

I smiled as the bubble returned.

And again.

I nearly came from seeing the text bubble appear once more.

I struggled for only a moment to text back, while holding my cock in one hand before I gave up and called her. She didn't answer for a few agonizing rings, but on the fifth ring, her sultry voice echoed in my ear.

"Hi, Silas." I knew right then that I'd give nearly everything to have her say my name again. I was in trouble. I wanted to tell her how I felt, tell her how I never wanted to be without her. But I was playing a role in a game that we both wanted to play.

"Put me on speaker," I barely recognized my lust-filled voice as I gave the rushed command.

"Ok." She replied and I heard a slight rustling, then the sound amplified telling me that she had once again followed my orders.

"Good. Now undress for me. Completely," I ordered. I heard a slight moan escape from her lips on the other line and I thanked whatever devil gave me my new and improved hearing because I heard every glorious fucking note of it. "Tell me what you're doing. Explain it to me." I stroked my cock, slowly just enough to satisfy the primal need burning within me, but holding back enough to prolong this moment.

"I'm removing my dress." I closed my eyes and pictured the grey t-shirt dress she wore earlier. It fit her frame well, showing off her tits and ass like the taunting delicious features they were. "Now I'm removing my bra." I smiled but noticed the slight timidness in her tone.

"Describe it to me." There was an ounce of hesitation on her end of the line and my fingers stilled. "Athena, I love this game and I want to play it with you. But if you need me to stop I will." I heard a sigh, relief perhaps, coming from her side. "Just say 'blood' and we stop, ok?"

"Ok." She replied, the sensual tone returning to her voice.

"Let me hear you say it baby girl so I know you can." I felt like I was alight, burning from the inside out.

"I will say blood if I need you to stop."

"That's my fucking girl," I growled, and my hand resumed its torturous stroking of my cock.

"My bra is black, it matches my underwear." I moaned, loudly. I hope Orpheus and Samara had the good sense to leave the house, or at least throw some headphones on. Or hell, maybe they want to listen. Hear how I make her feel.

"Take them both off. I need you naked for me." I heard her movement confirming she was listening to my demands.

"I'm naked." She was shy, but there was something so sexy about that. She wanted this as badly as I did, but she wasn't sure she should let herself have it. Well, I was about to show her that she deserved every second of this and so much more.

"Show me," I strained, pressing the video chat button on the phone. I knew I should resist. To let the first time I see her like this be in front of me when I can touch her, feel her. But I couldn't. I needed her. I needed to see her, now.

She answered the video call and my heart would have stopped had it not already. Her hair was loose hanging around her face, framing her blushed cheeks perfectly. Her green eyes were filled with the same desire I saw at the lighthouse and her body... her fucking perfect body. Her breasts were thick and perfectly rounded and the hardened peaks were begging for my mouth. From this angle, I couldn't see past the soft planes of her stomach. I smiled at her with a devious smirk.

"You're being very good for me, Athena." I watched as her bottom lip was sucked between her teeth at that. I didn't miss the way her breath caught or the way she pressed her thighs together. "Set your phone down so I can see you. Lay back on the bed and spread your legs for me. Do it now, Athena." She nodded, a stunning picture, and did as I said. As she laid back and spread her legs, offering me the first glimpse of her perfect little cunt. I stroked my cock faster, pretending it was her I was thrusting into and not my hand.

"Fuck, baby girl. I can see how wet you are from here. Have you touched your little cunt yet, or were you wanting for me?" It was hard to keep this composed image of a dominant man when all I wanted was to sink to my knees below her where I belonged and taste her.

"I was waiting," she confessed.

"Touch yourself for me, Athena." I watched with rapt attention as her hands trailed along her breasts, slowly and carefully. Her fingertips brushed against her nipples just enough to send a jolt of pleasure through her. I grasped at my balls, matching her burst of euphoria with my own. Her hands traveled lower until they were nearly where I needed them. "That's it, baby. Touch your clit." She did and I nearly detonated on the spot at the sound she made as her fingers found her most sensitive spot. "Fuck baby, that sound is going to kill me one day." Her head lolled back and she continued her exploration of that bundle of nerves. I licked my lips to keep from begging her to come sit on them.

"Do you use any toys, Athena?" Her eyes snapped back toward the screen, her flushed skin looked delicious next to her mused red hair. She nodded. "Yes, sir." I fucking choked.

"Hell, baby. Say that again." I rasped through clenched teeth, holding on to my composure with a fucking thread.

"Yes. Sir." She separated each word letting her tongue really taste them. I was going to get that tattooed on my fucking skin. Right over the place where my fucking heart used to beat because if it was still alive I had no doubt it would be hers.

"Grab your favorite one." She blushed deeper but didn't argue. She rolled out of view for a moment and I was devastated at the loss until she returned and spread herself wide for me once more. She held up the purple wand. It had a bud on the inside, clearly built for insertion and clit stimulation all at once. "Put it in your mouth, Athena, get it nice and wet for me." Something flashed across her expression briefly and panic threatened to seize my heart, but she didn't say the word, and the look was gone almost as quickly as it had come. She raised the toy to her mouth and pressed it inside, not without giving me a show with her tongue. I groaned and stroked faster. I was going to fuck her so hard the next time I see her, nothing in the world could stop me. Not even Laz. She sucked on the toy as if it were a cock, her eyes closing as she groaned around it, the wet sounds making me feel fucking powerless against her.

"Fuck yourself, Athena. Fuck yourself the way you want me to fuck you." She gasped, and slowly removed the toy from her mouth. She dragged the tip of it down her torso, torturously close to her wet hot heat. When she slid the toy into her cunt, I sucked in a breath so deep I felt it in my core. She moaned loudly and I wondered if her house was secluded or if people would hear how well she took that toy for me. I didn't know which answer I wanted.

She held the device deep within her and smiled sinfully at me and then pressed a button. The vibrations might as well have been on my own cock, because I came with a roar as I watched her squirm beneath the movement of the toy. Her head fell back as she pressed the toy deeper and cried out as it stimulated her. "Fuck, that's it, baby." It didn't even matter that I had just come, my cock was already twitching back to life for her.

Then there was a knock on her door. She stopped, pulling the toy from her quickly and sliding off the bed embarrassed. I groaned in frustration that someone had interrupted my little game. Then an idea occurred to me and I felt the devious smile on my lips deepen.

"Do you have a robe, baby girl?" She looked at the screen, a deep blush of embarrassment on her face.

"Yes." She answered, timidly.

"Yes, what?" I goaded her. She bit her bottom lip.

"Yes, sir." I nearly came again.

"Put it on." She did, still following orders, I see. She deserves a reward. "Now slide that toy back into your wet little pussy." Her eyes widened in shock.

"What?"

"Put that toy back in your cunt, then go answer the door. Take me with you." She watched the screen like she was contemplating saying our safe word, and I would have let her. I know I was still playing the game, but if she wanted out, then we were out. She licked her lips and then nodded, slowly opening her robe just enough to give me a view of her sliding the purple toy back into her slick folds. She moaned and then closed the robe, hiding the evidence. She picked me up and took me with her to the door. I heard her frustrated grunts with each step as the toy stimulated her clit. I stayed quiet as she opened the door.

"Laz!" I jolted upright, leaning forward to try and see. She had slipped me into the pocket of the robe, so all I saw was faint light coming through a grey fabric. She was embarrassed, I felt it in her tone. She was in nothing but a light robe, because of my stupid game. I hated myself.

"Oh, I'm sorry. I didn't mean to...I um.." I could hear Laz's trepidation. On one hand, a very underdressed beautiful woman was in front of them, on the other, she hadn't been that way for their sake. I wondered if they would be upset to learn of the little game we had been playing. Once again the guilt I had felt earlier began to gnaw at me. If Orpheus was right, and Laz was feeling the same way I was, then I know I would raise hell. Laz would be the type to simmer in their anger, to hold it in until there was an explosion unlike any we've seen before. "I can come back... I'm so sorry." They were scrambling, anxious. Pulled between their desire for her and their desire to be courteous. To hell with being courteous. That's where the two of us differ. I can't say with any ounce of certainty that I wouldn't have already sealed her lips in a kiss had I been the one at the door.

"No, it's ok. I um... was just." She was nervous. I could hear that clear as day. There was a slight excitement to her tone too. When you've spent as long as I have learning to decipher tones, to replicate their mannerisms, you learn what people are saying when they aren't saying anything at all. And right now, Athena was saying that she was turned on, and I think the person in front of her had just as much to do with it as I had.

Jealousy flashed for a moment, but only a moment. Then a different kind of resolve flooded me. Laz was one of the best people I've ever known. One of the most genuine souls I'd met in the eternity I've been alive. Athena would never know a better person or a more attentive partner.

Could I share? Could I willingly give a piece of what I believe to be my mate to someone else?

The answer should have been no. The answer would have been no if I'd been asked it even an hour ago. But Orpheus had been sure to tell me how strongly he knew I felt for her and he needed me to know that Laz felt the same. Maybe even Samara as well. The same burning passion, the same clear and honest pull to her, they feel it too. Laz needs to know if she is their mate, just as badly as I do.

But if I'm going to share, I'm going to watch.

12

LAZ

After leaving Silas with a parting gift of my fist in his face, I stormed out of the beach house and down onto the shore. I didn't stop when I hit the water, I simply turned and let my feet walk while my mind struggled to get ahold of my heart. Sure, throughout the many many years that we have been a coven we've gotten into arguments, and even punched each other a few times, but this was different. I wanted to hurt Silas, even though I knew I couldn't. The entire walk home, every word he said only reminded me of the way his lips claimed hers. The way his hands explored her body and pulled her to him. I had never felt jealousy as potent or raw as I did then. I wanted to rush to them, pull Silas off of her body, and take his place. To finish what we dangerously began at the bookstore.

Sometimes I think I'm too cautious for my own good. I am the type of person who sees something I want, then I spend the next several days, months even, researching and understanding it. Laying out a list of pros and cons, and analyzing if this is something that I can afford to pursue. Then and only then do I go for it. Spontaneous, I am not.

But Athena makes me want to be. She makes me want to throw caution to the wind and dive headfirst into the unknown, as long as she's by my side. I think that if someone forces you to change who you are to be with them then that is toxic and dangerous...but if you find someone who makes you want to change, makes you *want* to grow and learn and be a better person then that's fate. I'm that fool who watches Grease and says that both of those people wanted to be something different and were looking for the excuse to go for it.

Sandy wanted a wild side, and Danny wanted a soft side. They brought that out in each other. Will they last? Who knows. But what changed between them, how they grew because of each other? That was fate.

That has to mean something. She has to mean something to me.

Before I realized what was happening, my feet had turned down her driveway. Orpheus unknowingly nabbed us a place only a few streets away from her. At least I think it was unknowingly.

I stopped at the end of the drive, watching the blue house with fascination. Now that I've met her, now that I've talked to her, it was even clearer why this house seemed like her. She was sweet and timid. But colorful and vibrant. Cozy. Like home.

I knew I should turn away and return home. There was no reason why I should be here right now. It was an invasion of privacy.

Then I heard it.

Soft, sweet moans wafted through the air. Not loud enough for any human ear to catch, but I heard it. I heard it all. Her breathy whimpers sent a shockwave directly to my core.

Near mindless, I took a step forward before I was able to regain composure and shake off the hooks she unknowingly had in me. I should leave. I should turn around.

I couldn't.

Caution to the wind. I walked forward, savoring each delicious moan that came from her home. But while I was focusing on her sweet voice, I heard another, and a chill ran down my spine. Silas. His dark and commanding tone was coming through a speaker. I was half tempted to call him and interrupt his little call with our girl. I shook my head. *Our girl?* I brushed my hands down my face, contemplating leaving again for the third time. Then I knocked.

I heard her stumble about the room, and I tried not to listen to Silas' words, afraid they'd only make me angry and waited for her to arrive at the door.

Her flushed skin was the most beautiful thing I'd ever seen. Her red hair was loose around her shoulders, tousled just enough to tell me she had been in an intimate position.

"Oh, I'm sorry. I didn't mean to... I um...I can come back. I'm so sorry." I averted my gaze despite every fiber of my being that begged me to stare, to soak up every moment of the time when she stood before me.

She drew her robe closed tighter and blushed deeply. I took a slow step back. Tell me to stay, Athena. Tell me to stay, please.

"No, it's ok. I um... was just." I smiled, turning my head back to look at her.

"I fear I may have caught you in an intimate moment," I said, smirking. I wasn't the best flirt, but I'd seen Silas and Samara engage in the act enough to replicate a bit.

She giggled, actually giggled, and I found myself grinning like an idiot at the musical sound. "This is embarrassing," she confessed.

"Do you want Laz to join our game, baby girl?" Silas' voice echoed from the pocket of her robe. So he was listening?

Game?

I watched her carefully as she fumbled with the phone in her pocket, her pale skin a deep crimson color.

"Uh, what?" She held the phone up to look at the screen. So it was a video call, then. What had he gotten to see from my delicious-looking Athena?

"Do you want Laz to play too?" Silas asked, his voice nearly unrestrained. I didn't have to look at the screen to see that he was nearing a shift. His eyes would be bloodshot. Hell, just seeing her in this robe had me nearly following suit. I can only guess what he's had the pleasure of experiencing and how much willpower it's taken him to last this long.

Athena glanced up at me, her green eyes shining with lust as she looked up at me through dark eyelashes. It's been a while since I had a heart, but if I still did, I knew it would be racing as I waited for her answer.

Silas was offering me a chance with her. Sharing. I'd never thought about something like that before, especially not with my coven, who are basically my family. But at this moment, I let the possibility swirl around my mind and it made my erection stand at attention.

"Yes," she answered, timidly, yet with a sort of barely restrained desire.

"Yes, what baby?" Silas asked and my eyes burned into hers.

"Yes, sir." She spoke to him, but her eyes were on mine. The words were for him, but the gaze, the desire. That was mine.

She was like a present I wanted to unwrap. I didn't need another invitation, I pushed through the door, thankful that she had already invited me in last night because right now I didn't care to wait for another second to claim her lips with mine. I pressed my mouth to hers and swallowed the gasp that she released before sinking into my hold. Her lips drank at me hungrily but slowly building like a fire, and I smiled against her mouth as my hands held her face to mine. I had plenty of time to explore her body, but right now I wanted her lips.

Her hands clasped around my neck, holding me firmly in place as her tongue begged for entry to my mouth. It was a passionate kiss, tender. We didn't feast on each other's mouths like animals, we didn't tear at each other's clothes - although my hands twitched to do just that. Instead, we kissed like lovers who were embracing the moment, living in it. Existing in this perfect instance with each other.

"Ah ah ah." I heard Silas from the phone that was now clasped in her hand behind my head. Athena pulled back, smiling shyly at me, and pulled her phone off to the side so that we both could see Silas on the screen, and he could see us.

"If we're going to play this game we need to set some ground rules. Take Laz to your room, baby girl." If I had heard him say those words at any other time I might have rolled my eyes, but here in the thick cloud of lust with Athena's body pressed against mine, I eagerly awaited his next command.

She pulled her body from mine, and I desperately missed her warmth. Grabbing my hand she led me through the living room toward her room. I smiled to myself when I saw the spot on her mattress where I sat last night, watching over her. How quickly I cared for this girl should have worried me, the way Orpheus was worried, but I couldn't care less how hard I fell for this human. Her red hair bounced with each delicious swing of her hips and I was about to lose my restraint. She moved to prop her phone on a shelf. From where it sat, you could see the entire bed. I found myself thinking about what she and Silas were up to when I arrived, and instead of jealousy coursing through me at that thought, it was curiosity, pure and unbridled passionate curiosity.

"Tell Laz our safeword, baby girl," Silas ordered. I flicked my eyes to Athena who was standing at the foot of the bed, an almost shy look on her face. She glanced down at the floor as she spoke.

"Blood." I groaned at the word on her lips, tossing Silas a look I'm sure he could decipher.

"Good girl." It didn't take my vampiric senses to tell how those two little words affected her. It was fascinating to see how Silas had fit so clearly into the role of a dominant personality with her. I was eager to see what my role would be with her. I'd be just about anything for this woman, do just about anything to see her blush at me the way she blushed at his words.

"Take off your robe." Silas sounded calm, collected, and dominant, but I knew all his tells, I knew how close he was to detonation. I wasn't far behind him.

She turned her eyes from the screen to me, smiling shyly before moving her hands to the collar of the grey robe. I moved to grip her wrist, stopping her momentarily. She looked up at me with confusion.

"Let me go first," I offered, and a dark desire crossed her face. "Is that ok, Sir?" I asked Silas. I don't know what possessed me to do so, but something told me that if I wanted this to continue I needed to play the game. Honestly, I wanted to. I noticed the surprise on both of their faces but didn't let it deter me.

"Yes. Undress for her, Laz. Put on a fucking show." And so I did. I took my time removing my shirt, buttoning each button as her eyes trailed my fingers. I even let my fingertips trail across my bare abdomen on my way down to my pants. Removing them and my briefs in one sweep. My length stood tall for her. All for her. Well, maybe a little for the game too. Not that I was attracted to Silas or anything, but I think I liked taking orders from him. Athena's eyes swept my body appreciatively, a coy smirk claiming her lips as she took in my endowment. I was girthier than most, I bet she was picturing how it would feel inside of her. So was I.

"Your turn, baby girl." Athena sensually dropped the shoulders of her robe one at a time, offering me just a quick glimpse of the skin beneath before dropping it all to the ground. As the robe pooled around her feet, I took an involuntary step closer. My shift right under the surface.

"Close your eyes, Athena," Silas ordered quickly and she followed quicker. I tossed a look at the screen and he shared a look with me, a silent check-in. I needed to be sure I was under control. I took a deep breath, feeling my fangs settle and the cloud dissipate, then nodded to him, the hesitancy from his face was replaced with his mask of dominance. "Show Laz our little toy." My eyes turned to her again, watching as she sat down on the bed and slowly, one leg at a time, spread her legs for me offering me the perfect view of her perfect sex, currently stretched by a purple toy.

"Athena. You are stunning." I whispered to her and I heard her soft moan tell me she was listening despite her eyes remaining shut.

"Do you want a taste, Laz?" I swallowed deeply, Silas knew as well as I did what else I desperately wanted to taste right now, but damn, her sweet arousal would be enough.

"Yes," I said, but it was barely more than a whisper, my breath was shallow in her narcotic presence.

"Yes, what, Laz?" Silas was lost to his own senses. I was too. And I loved it.

"Yes, Sir," I tossed back over my shoulder, my eyes stayed trained on the gorgeous woman spread before me like my own personal feast.

"Then do it."

13

ATHENA

Who the hell was I right now? Not the timid, scared, shattered girl I'd been for the last decade of my life. For so long I let that one horrific night cast its shadow on every day of my existence. But not here, not with these two. When I got home after the tour and the kiss, I grabbed my favorite vibrator - the one currently stretching me - like I had every other time I was turned on in the slightest. They were safer than being with a partner. Especially men. I didn't take the risk, I didn't give in to their advances. The few times I did manage to open myself and my legs for someone new, the memory was so vicious and deep that I wasn't in the moment. Not really. But right now? With Silas' words guiding me, with Laz's eyes on my naked body? I felt powerful. Like a woman who deserved passion. And no matter how many times I looked into either of their eyes, I didn't see *his*.

So when I went to grab that vibrator, instead I grabbed my phone and took the first step to take back my life. Now here I was, Silas' thick voice giving me commands, ordering me to do dirty things for him. A familiar thing, but this time...I knew I had a way out. That was the clear and honest difference. There was trust here. Something that was missing the last time. Something *he* never cared to build with me. Something I had with these strangers the moment I heard what they all did for me last night.

Laz's body was close to mine, I felt the cold air radiating off of them. How were they so cool when I was burning up, an absolute inferno burning within me?

With my eyes closed, my other senses were on high alert. Paying attention to every little movement. Noticing the way Laz's breath hitched as they sank to their knees in front of me. The way Silas groaned his approval. The slick sound of Laz pulling my vibrator from its place inside of me. I leaned back on my elbows and let my head fall back as I relished the feel of the toy rubbing against my walls. Once it was gone, I immediately missed the feeling of being stretched, but the loss was replaced with anticipation quickly when I felt their breath on my clit. I'm not sure I could ever be more turned on than I was at this very moment.

"Tell me how she tastes, Laz."

I lied. Definitely more turned on right now.

Before I could whine, begging for their tongue to ravish me, they closed their mouth over my clit and sucked. I screamed in pleasure as a jolt made my entire body tighten. They let their tongue take the lead then, dragging it through my folds, absolutely drenched with my arousal. They drank my taste like it was the greatest thing they'd ever had on their tongue. Their appreciative moans against my sex had me bucking off the bed. Their strong hands came to my waist and pressed me back down, holding me in place to endure this pleasurable torture.

"You taste like fine wine," they growled against my clit before swirling their tongue around it again. I gasped, my mouth hanging open. "Like the finest wine that's ever graced my tongue," They speared me, entering me as far as they could and I gripped at their hair, pulling their face closer. I needed more. I needed them deeper. Harder. I just needed.

I'd never experienced such blind euphoria. They slipped a finger into my folds, stretching me as they feasted on my clit like they were ravenous.

"Make her come," Silas demanded through breathless pants. I dared to open my eyes and catch a glimpse of the scene before me. Laz was buried between my legs, their eyes closed as they savored me. My eyes flicked to the screen to see Silas' dark eyes watching hungrily. His breathing was uneven, and I saw his shoulder moving in slow steady movements. He was touching himself. He was enjoying the show.

So was I.

"Yes, Sir," Laz whispered against my sex before they slipped a second finger inside of me, curling them slightly to reach that perfect spot that had my whole body shaking. I was on the edge.

I felt Laz's teeth grace my clit with a wicked promise and I toppled off the ledge. My thighs tightened around their head, holding them to me until the last wracks of my orgasm had had their way with me.

When I came back to earth, I looked over at them. Laz had sat back on their heels, a wicked glint in their eyes as they licked my arousal off of their lips.

"You are beautiful when you fall apart, Athena," Laz whispered to me, causing my heart to race.

"Are you satisfied, baby girl?" Silas asked, slightly less breathy than he had been just moments before. I wonder if he found his release. I wished I could have watched it.

"Yes, Sir." I smiled, closing my thighs slowly, not missing how Laz watched my every move with hungry intent. I almost leaned forward, ready to give everything and more to this person on their knees before me. Laz stood, grabbing my legs and throwing them open. I bit down on my lip again when they pulled me to the edge of the bed. I felt their hard cock notch at my entrance. Their eyes watched mine eagerly as they pressed forward slowly.

"Blood." My whole body froze as Silas said the word. I pulled back from Laz, and my arms crossed my body, covering what I could as I turned my head to look at the screen. Laz did as well, a look of equal confusion on their face. I saw Silas' face, and it was shock that colored his expression. As if he couldn't believe he said the word either.

"Sorry.. I uh." He was floundering. Laz turned to the camera so I couldn't see their face. Silas ran his hands down his face. "Fuck. Sorry. I just..." He leaned forward, closer to the screen so I could see the flecks of color in his irises. "The first time I see you speared on a cock baby girl, it's gonna be mine." My breath caught in my throat and Laz turned back to look at me briefly.

I slid off the bed and threw my robe back over my body as Laz gathered their clothes too, dragging their pants back up and fastening them. I took the moment to study them, now that my head wasn't clouded with lust. They had that kind of strength that wasn't obvious. Without a shirt, I could see the definition of muscles. They were one of those sneaky buff people. Their abs were there but had softer edges, much like the person to whom they belonged. Everything about Laz told me they were a chivalrous person, the one who will be kind to you, and care for you. The epitome of southern hospitality. But everything I just experienced told me that they held the capacity to destroy everything in their path. Myself included if I let them. And I just might.

"You were perfect, Athena. I'm sorry. I'm not used to sharing...yet." Silas said, tossing the last word to Laz who looked at the screen. The edge of dominance was gone from his tone,

"You did a great job of it." I smiled at him, feeling on cloud nine. Not only had I just had the first orgasm that didn't come from my toy in years, but I let someone else watch. I'd never even been eaten out before, let alone let someone else watch me as I come undone on someone's tongue. But in this perfect, sated afterglow I couldn't bring myself to feel embarrassed.

"Thank you, both of you," I said, tossing looks at both of them. Laz crossed the floor to me, pulling me into a hug. Gentle, soft, sweet. I sunk into it.

"I was the one who had the utter privilege of tasting you today, it's I who should be thanking you." I blushed into their chest. "I should probably head back, we just got ourselves a rental." My heart flipped.

"You're staying for the season?" I asked a little too eagerly, but I just had a taste of desire with them and I didn't want to stop. Well, they were the ones who had the taste but you get it.

"Looks like you're stuck with us," Silas added from the phone. I smiled like an idiot then, because I was happy. Because for the first time in a long time, I felt like I had autonomy again. I felt like I was allowed to want something and I wanted them.

I grabbed my phone and walked Laz to the front door. They gave me a sweet kiss, not long enough to send me into another frenzy, but long enough for me to taste myself on their lips and moan into their mouth.

When I finally let myself close the door and say goodbye, I leaned back against the doorframe and smiled, looking down at the handsome man on my screen.

"Well that was something," I said, an incredulous giggle escaping my mouth. He laughed with me, much more carefree now that we were out of the game. I liked that I got to experience both sides of him.

"You were something I never expected, Athena." I noticed that my nickname 'baby girl' was no longer in his vocabulary. Maybe that was just for the game, just like 'Sir'. I smiled. I liked our game. I wanted to play again. Soon.

"I can confidently say the same." He sighed.

"Can I see you tomorrow?" He asked as if I would say no.

"I work until eight, but then I'm free," I replied, twisting a strand of hair between my fingers like a girl in love. Fuck, I needed to get a grip. They were only here for the season. I couldn't fall for them.

"I'll see you soon," he promised, and I believed him.

After hanging up, I took a long shower, letting myself reflect on the last hour of my life and how utterly unbelievable it all was. Davia would never believe me, but I needed someone to talk to about it or I was gonna lose it.

> ATHENA: Davia, are you sitting down? Buckled in? Strapped down? Don't answer that. But boy, do I have a story for you.

DAVIA: Not strapped down. And probably won't be for a while. Greg's been at the police station all day. Louis hasn't come back yet.

I furrowed my brow, reading the text again. Where would Louis go after attempting to rape someone and getting caught?

ATHENA: Maybe he went home?

DAVIA: That's what I said, but Greg hasn't heard from him. Police aren't being much help though. Something about not being gone long enough yet.

ATHENA: That's weird.

DAVIA: You didn't see him go anywhere? Didn't hear him talk about going to see someone or anything?

I swallowed the lump in my throat. A sort of fear prickling at the edges of my senses. The story I told Davia was not the real one. She didn't know the sexy strangers had pulled him off of me and 'sent him on his way.' Was that all they did?

ATHENA: No. I have no idea where he would have gone.

DAVIA: Oh well, ok. Anyway… Your story.

She responded again quickly, before I had a chance to.

DAVIA: You fucked them didn't you?

My jaw nearly fell to the ground.

ATHENA: What?! How did you… No, not exactly. But it's better.

DAVIA: How can it be better than that?

DAVIA: Which one was it?

I answered honestly. Because it was the damn truth. Each and every one of them was a gorgeous fucking specimen. They each appealed to a different part of me. Laz made me feel safe. Silas made me feel desired. Samara made me feel powerful. And Orpheus... he made me feel seen.

I waited for a moment for her to respond.

I spilled the whole encounter over the next several texts, each scandalous deed had my body igniting with the memory.

I laughed, I could practically hear her saying this in my head.

ATHENA: It was the hottest thing I've ever done.

DAVIA: And you didn't even have sex?!

ATHENA: I didn't need to.

That was kind of a lie. I definitely needed it, like primally. But I understood why crossing that line in that scenario wasn't the best idea. I wanted each of them, but I think I wanted them alone first.

DAVIA: I'm so jelly it's not even funny.

ATHENA: Says the woman who is used to having wild sex nearly every night of the season with handsome strangers.

DAVIA: You're right. I'm so lucky.

I rolled my eyes, laughing as I typed my response.

ATHENA: You have to promise not to let me get attached.

I crawled onto my bed, wrapped in my towel, and pulled my knees to my chest.

DAVIA: Babe, the fact that you think you even have the potential to get attached is why I won't promise you a damn thing. You have no idea how hard it was seeing you close yourself off from everything, and everyone for so long.

Davia saw me at my worst. She and my mother were the only ones who truly believed me when I told them what happened to me. She saw every gritty detail, each horrid scar, physical and otherwise. When I was trudging through hell trying to find my way back to the light, she was right beside me, holding my hand.

ATHENA: What if I fall apart when they leave?

> DAVIA: Then that means you were healed enough to break.

> DAVIA: There was a time we weren't sure that would ever happen.

Tears began to fall down my cheek as I read the words. Was it possible that I had healed from that night? The road seemed so dark, so treacherous that at times I truly never thought I'd be able to see the light of day again. But that's the thing about healing from trauma, it isn't fast, it isn't even gradual, it's torturous, slow, and grueling. It takes years of enduring darkness until you see the light. But when the sun finally shines on you again? It's fucking worth it.

> ATHENA: I love you.

> DAVIA: I love you more.

> DAVIA: Have a great wet dream! <3 talk tomorrow.

I chuckled and tossed my phone on the bedspread and swapped my towel for a baggy t-shirt. My whole body felt electrified like tonight was some sort of dream. I was giddy, and excited. Already planning my outfit for tomorrow. I hope he wasn't too attached to me in dresses because I was out of them and I didn't have the money to go out and buy a new one every time I saw them.

I slid under the covers and curled up with my phone in my hand, smiling as I scrolled back through my messages with Silas.

Before I thought better, I composed a message.

> ATHENA: Goodnight, Silas. Thank you.

I was about to lock the phone and set it aside for the night when his response came in.

> SILAS: Goodnight, Athena. If I could dream, I'd dream of you.

It was a strange thing to say, but it still had my heart in absolute flutters. I was in a lot of trouble.

It was with new memories of my body being worshiped that I fell asleep, and for the first night in a while, I didn't dream of *him*.

14

ARCHER

My fingers were stained with blue paint, already drying and cracking with each movement as I packed up my truck. I tossed a glance at the wall in front of me that was cast in the warm light from my headlights.

The symbol was easy enough to draw, even without any artistic abilities. I was a musician, not a painter. Well no, I guess I wasn't a musician either anymore. I'm a Hunter.

Right.

Keep forgetting that part.

We received intel the day before that a vampire was spotted in this town. I say we, but it's the head office that gets the calls and distributes the jobs. In the last three months since my father's not-so-gentle reminder that it was time for me to join the ranks, I've been sent to just about every state, and about a hundred towns to plaster this symbol on every surface. I'm a fucking messenger at best. But I guess, if I had to be dragged into my dad's business, this was a good way to do it. Not like I particularly want to go around staking vampires. So yeah, I guess being the resident artist wasn't too bad of a deal.

Although I had only recently joined the team, I'd grown up knowing the truth about the world we live in. It's so much scarier hearing stories of the monster under the bed and knowing that they're real. My dad made sure of it. *"You need to understand that you are only ever safe in this world if you fight for your safety."* He would tell me that, daily. Pretty sure it was cross-stitched on a pillow in our house somewhere. I didn't resent my father. In fact, I was thankful that he devoted his life to protecting me and other humans from the monsters that lurk in the shadows. I guess, I just never thought I'd have to do that too.

My phone buzzed, and I instantly felt my shoulders tense. Where were they sending me next? Somewhere warm I hoped, although that wasn't common. I'm learning quickly that these creatures like to stay away from heat and sun. Probably because their disgusting flesh would rot off if they were in the sun for too long.

I relaxed when I realized it was my personal phone, not the work one, that was ringing. But it didn't last long when I saw the name of who was calling. I answered on the fourth ring. "Bennett." Don't let me fool you, I'm not the cool guy that answers the phone by saying his last name for any other reason than I saw it on Criminal Minds once and thought it was awesome.

"You finished with New Hampshire?" I offered a glance over my shoulder at the wall with the fresh blue paint.

"Yeah, just packing up." I slid into the front seat of the truck and turned the key in the ignition.

"Good." I waited for a moment for him to continue.

"So what am I vandalizing next? A billboard in Montana? A bakery wall in New York?" I heard him sigh on the other end of the line.

"It's time for you to start pulling your weight, kid." My brows furrowed as I pulled away from my latest art project.

"Those paint cans are pretty heavy," I retorted, knowing that wasn't what he meant.

"You've put off your initiation for too long." I gripped the steering wheel tighter, my foot pressing into the gas pedal a little too hard. "I can't keep covering for you."

"I know, dad." He'd been as understanding as he could be, I got that. If I was going to be a part of this business, part of the Hunters - even if I didn't want to - I was going to have to prove myself.

"Listen, there's been talk around the office. They don't like the way you've been dragging your feet." His voice quieted. "People who drag their feet can be pulled in the wrong direction. They think you might be a loose end." I swallowed hard, letting up on the gas, watching the speedometer return to a legal limit. "Do you know why Nameless doesn't have any traitors?" I nodded although I knew he couldn't see me. But he knew that I did. I'd heard him say that a million times. "Because they don't let people live long enough to betray them." Fuck. My father whispered one last thing, his voice was threateningly low. "Your resistance is going to get one of us killed. Maybe both."

My father was a good man, as far as I knew. He fought to protect the human race, how much more of a hero can he be? If my lack of motivation for the family business was going to be a threat to his life, I needed to get my shit together.

"Ok, what do I do?" I begged.

"They're not making a move on you yet, but they're watching. You need to do something big, and soon." I turned into the parking lot for my motel, parked, and flipped off the car, but I didn't move, just sat there staring at the brick wall ahead of me and listening to my father speak. "You need to find The Wanderers." I ran my hand through my box-dyed black hair with blue tips.

The Wanderers were our white fucking whale. The only vampires to ever escape our clutches after being brought to our headquarters. I was a teenager when it happened, but I remember hearing about it. It's all anyone could talk about. And when I finally started my service at Nameless, it was the cautionary tale we were all told. They escaped after taking down fifteen of our best recruits. It took years for them to rebuild, to get their strength back. From what I've heard, they've been chasing them since that very day, with no luck. The Wanderers consisted of five of the world's strongest vampires, well four now. Luckily, Nameless managed to pick off one while the others got away, weakening their numbers and probably effectively pissing them off. My father has told me the stories of how he was the one to land the killing blow on the former fifth member. Driving the wooden stake directly into her dead, cold heart. He earned himself a pretty big promotion that day. The Wanderers were each gifted with a supernatural ability, something we'd only just begun to test when they escaped so to this day, we don't understand it entirely. But we knew enough to know that they were damn near untouchable.

"How the hell am I supposed to do that?" I pleaded with him. He had to know that I wasn't cut out for this job. I could barely make it through training, let alone catch the most elusive and powerful coven out there.

"I have intel on where they might be. A source of mine from outside the network." My father never told me he had a contact on the outside who knew about Nameless and the existence of the things that go bump in the night.

"Who is it?" I asked eagerly, knowing that he would never tell me but deciding to ask anyway.

"No one you need to concern yourself with." A cryptic answer. Typical. And pretty par for the course with my old man.

"So this outside source was able to track The Wanderers before Nameless?" How was that possible?

"Don't worry about it."

"You're not giving me many answers here," I sighed.

"Stop asking questions you know damn well I can't answer." My father was a strong man, built like a fucking brick house. His entire torso was covered in battle scars, gunshot wounds, knife wounds, and bite marks. I traced a featherlight touch across the skin on my wrist, the raised scar, the reminder of who I should trust, and who I shouldn't.

Vampires cannot turn a human with a simple bite. Thank god for that, otherwise, most of the Hunters would be part of the legion of the undead by now. No, it was a lot more complicated than that. Had something to do with a shared transfusion or something? I don't know, I wasn't really paying attention to the training that day, I was mostly trying not to pass out. Blood made me a little queasy. I paid attention just enough to know I shouldn't drink a vampire's blood. Done. Got it. Say no more.

"Where are they?" I asked timidly, knowing very well that my father was about to send me into the lion's den and I was just a little gazelle. No, you know what. I wish I were the gazelle, but I'm that stupid kid that fell into the enclosure. At least the gazelle was part of the natural food chain. Not me, I'm just the idiot who got too close.

"My contact spotted them near some town called Shockgrove. Maine." I leaned back in my seat, stretching my legs. I glanced longingly up at the motel room I had booked for the night, knowing full well that I wasn't going to be sleeping there any time soon. Maine wasn't that far, I could be there by morning.

"Got it."

"I do not need to remind you how important this is. For both of us." He didn't. I knew. I fiddled with the rearview mirror, sliding it so that I could see the backseat and the duffel bags of supplies. The paint cans and the paint brushes were in the bed of the truck, where it didn't matter if people saw them. But these bags, full of the standard issue weapons any Hunter has the good sense to never leave the house without, those stay hidden. As much as I didn't feel like I belonged in Nameless, I was pretty handy with a wooden stake, not that I've actually staked a live vampire yet. Just the dummies we use in training. But still. I could hold my own. I've been sculpting my body to be a perfect weapon for most of my life, just like my father wanted me to. Guess it was time to finally use it.

"I won't let you down, dad." I wasn't sure if it was the truth, but as I put the car in reverse and headed back down the highway toward Maine, I knew I would do anything in my power to make sure it was.

15

SAMARA

Coffee didn't have the same effect on vampires that it did on humans. It took effect quickly but burned out quicker. I took slow languid sips, willing the magic concoction to take away this vicious headache I woke up with.

"You looked stupid happy last night," I offered to Laz as they sauntered into the kitchen of our rental. They had gotten home pretty late, and when they did, gone was their hostile attitude and reckless anger toward Silas. Replaced with something cheerier. And it didn't take a vampire to smell the lust on him. And not just any lust. Hers.

I hated how I already knew the intimate scent of Athena's arousal, but I did. I knew it and it made me feel wild.

"Or just stupid," Orpheus called from the back patio. He had the doors thrown open and was staring down the beach, watching. I knew what he was watching for. And I prayed we never saw it again, but I understood that was too big a wish to come true. Not while the Hunters were alive. Not while Nameless still existed.

Soon enough I would stop running and eradicate their stupid existence. I would not leave this life without dragging every single one of those fuckers with me to the grave. I'm undead, I belong in hell. So do they.

Laz ran a hand down their face, groaning. And I shook off my bloody revenge-filled goals to truly look at their face.

Their eyes were red-rimmed and bloodshot. Their skin was paler than it had been last night and their fangs were slightly elongated.

"Are you hungry?" I exclaimed and Orpheus was to us in a moment, his eyes scanning Laz's face.

"Fuck. You've got to be kidding me." Orpheus slammed his fist down on the granite countertop, it groaned under the pressure but didn't break. Thank god, because it's literally day one and I don't want to lose our security deposit already.

"What's going on?" I asked, looking between Laz and Orpheus.

"Those two, love-sick puppies, are hungry already." I furrowed my brows.

"What does that mean?" I hadn't heard of this before. A vampire getting hungry so soon after feeding? We'd just fed two nights ago. But even as I considered the improbability, a pang groaned in the pit of my stomach. Hunger.

Orpheus bounded up the stairs with reckless abandon, I quickly followed behind taking the steps two at a time. Laz didn't follow. I wondered just how weak they might be feeling. Orpheus threw open the door to Silas' room, and as I approached from behind, I gasped as I looked past him.

Silas sat on the ground, his back up against the bed but he had a hand on his stomach as if holding himself together. His cheeks were slightly sunken and his eyes were vacant of his normal cocky glow.

"Fuck, Silas. You ok?" Orpheus was down on his knees beside him in a moment while I stood in the doorway in shock.

"I'm just fucking hungry," Silas groaned. I sighed, thankful that he was alive, and seemingly still just as much of a jerk as always.

"How is this possible?" I asked anxiously, glancing between Silas and Orpheus as they exchanged a silent conversation.

"I don't know," Orpheus offered.

Once the shock wore off, I slid in on Silas' other side placing a hand on his cheek, and then I felt him. Sending my vibration of power through his body, my mind settling into his skin and dancing amongst his poisonous blood searching within him for the source of this ailment.

In life, I was an empathetic person. I think that's why I developed this gift when I was ushered into my second life. Despite the lot in life I was handed, and the terrible existence I had, I still tried to understand. Tried to see every-thing from their point of view, and put myself in their shoes. It was second nature. That's what got me through it all. The evenings at that disgusting building with horrid men claiming my flesh as if it was something they had been owed. I convinced myself that they did it because they needed to and that they wouldn't do it if they had another choice. Although, eventually I stopped trying to understand why my parents did what they did or why men were paying for my unwilling company. Stopped making excuses for them. At some point, you have to realize that bad people are just bad people no matter whose shoes you're in.

Silas' blood felt normal, I couldn't find any physical issues with his body. In fact, infuriatingly, he was in tip-top physical shape. But there it was. A void, hunger. It was palpable, I felt it in my own stomach as I discovered it in him. My fangs elongated slightly to accommodate the new hunger growing.

I pulled my hands back, severing the contact, and I felt the hunger subside slightly. I was feeling some mild version of the pain he was in. "What did you feel?" Orpheus asked. He was good at masking his emotions, probably from years of feeling others so strongly, but at that moment I didn't need his gift to see the worry painted on his face.

"There's nothing physically wrong with him," I started. "He's just...hungry." Silas lifted his hands in an exasperated motion.

"See, I told you so!"

"What does this mean, Orpheus?" A thought solidified for me. What if that man we killed was toxic? Laz was a little preoccupied that night, so they didn't check the quality of that asshole before we kinda dug in. Panic started to set in, if we had drunk soiled blood would this happen to all of us? Was it already starting for me?

"It means we have to leave," Orpheus spoke clearly. Confidently.

"No," Silas and Laz, who had finally made their way up the stairs, spoke at the same time.

Orpheus groaned and stood, pacing about the room.

"You need to feed, and we can't do that here!" Orpheus was right. It was a small enough town that any disappearances right now would be suspicious. We were lucky that the douche from the bar hadn't hit the news yet. But it would. They always did in towns like these.

"We will be careful." Silas tried to stand, finding his arms weak and eventually leaning back against the bed frame defeated.

"You can't even stand up, Silas!" Orpheus was losing it. Frankly, I understood that. This was unprecedented, and none of us knew how to proceed.

We hadn't even reached this level of hunger when the Nameless held us, not until the second month without blood, at least. But here they were now. Starving.

Why?

"I'm not leaving her!" Silas growled, his eyes bearing as much intensity as he could muster.

"I agree," Laz added from the doorway, where they had found a solid spot to lean against.

"Don't you two think this is some kind of fucking omen or something? You need to forget about this human and let us get out of here." Orpheus was nearly begging. I'd never seen him so out of sorts before.

"Don't you think it's rather interesting timing? We meet her, and all of a sudden we're hungry like we are starving for her! If you're looking for evidence that she's our mate, then there it is," Laz spat out. Tension filled the air. Orpheus' eyes burned into Laz and they stood their ground as tall as they could.

Wait, did they say "our" mate?

"You already scented her." Orpheus was grasping at straws, desperate to protect our family. He always has been. And I could see where he was coming from here. I was just as afraid of Nameless catching up to us again as he was. I knew the things they could do to us just as well as he did.

But if she truly is their mate, they deserve the chance to find out.

He knew that too, or else he would have bought this house for us. He was giving them the chance they needed, but he was worried too. Hell, the two of them just fed two days ago and were acting like they may desiccate within the hour. I'm worried for my family too.

If she belonged to both of them, maybe there was a chance she belonged to someone else too. I shook off the budding hope blossoming in my chest, forcing myself to picture Alora's gorgeous features instead of the sweet redhead down the road.

"You need to scent her blood soon," I spoke up. Three pairs of eyes found me. I stood and walked toward the window, shrouded in a dark grey curtain that kept the sun's rays from reaching my skin.

"What if it's not clear yet?" Silas asked, quietly. A simmering anger boiled within me as I thought about what he was referring to. Her blood that night had felt impossibly inhuman, toxic to nearly the point of no return. There wasn't a doubt in my mind that she would have died had she drank even a sip or two more. I don't understand how someone could do that. I also don't understand why it made me so angry, made my dead heart feel like it was constricting inside my chest.

It might be hypocritical of me to condemn a human for being a monster when that is exactly what I am. The difference is, I am the monster that people know to watch out for, not to invite in, the one from the stories meant to scare little children into submission. I'm a monster because I'm meant to be. Humans are monsters because they choose to be. Humans are subtle. You don't suspect them. You don't distrust them. But I've lived a long time, and there are humans who are more monstrous than I could ever be. They just blend in better.

"What if when she bleeds our hunger takes over?" Laz asked, quietly in a whisper.

"We won't let you hurt her," I said, immediately. It was the truth. I wouldn't let Athena be in harm's way. Not again. Even if I had to stand up against my family to make it so. Which was a strange thought that sent an even stranger emotion coursing through me.

Orpheus glanced my way, and I tried to shake the feeling he had surely felt within me.

"But just to be safe, you should feed before you see her." If for no other reason than to return their features to a more... normal look. Athena might not know what a hungry vampire looks like, but anyone with eyes could see that these two weren't at their best with their dark red-rimmed eyes and hollowed cheeks.

"We cannot hunt here," Orpheus reminded us.

"Then you and I double back," I said to our leader. "We head back the way we came a few hours, lead the trail in the wrong direction, and bring back a snack." I tried to calm the excitement I felt at the prospect of feeding. My hunger was growing every second. Orpheus looked like he didn't want to consider it, but to his credit, he didn't dismiss the notion immediately.

"It's a good idea, Orpheus." I leveled my stare at him, watching as he took his bottom lip between his teeth, holding in the retort he had prepared. Releasing a sigh and lowering his head, he nodded.

"Fine. Samara, let's go." Silas and Laz looked hopeful, a smile spreading across their faces. "You two, stay here and don't do anything stupid until we get back."

"Ah, but we can do something stupid when you return?" Silas joked and Orpheus leveled him with an annoyed glare before stalking out of the room. "Be back by seven, I have a date!" Silas sighed, relaxing again. Laz stepped aside to allow Orpheus to leave past them and then slowly moved into the room, sitting on the bed above Silas.

The two of them shared a knowing glance that held a deeper meaning than I had the ability to understand. Something like respect or acceptance passed between them. How had they gone from nearly ripping each other's arms off, to this? I wondered briefly if Silas could scent Athena's arousal on Laz as clearly as I could, and if so, why was he so calm about it?

"Do you think it's true?" I asked them both. "That she's yours?"

They exchanged another glance and Silas faced me once again, looking so feeble from his position on the floor. "I know it with every fiber of my being, with every phantom beat of my dead heart. She is mine." He looked at Laz. "She is ours."

My breath caught in my throat. "Ours," I repeated. So they intended to share the human? Why?

And why was I suddenly very envious of that notion?

"Then we will make sure you are well enough to see her tonight. To know for sure." I left the room and went to the room I had claimed for myself down the hall. It had pale blue walls and sandy shag carpet. The white lines on the bed were only slightly ruffled from my body weight on top of it the night before. I switched my sundress out for some comfortable dark black leggings and a black, off-the-shoulder sweatshirt that was perfect for going hunting. Blood didn't show up on black.

When I met Orpheus on the ground floor, he had swapped his suit for dark black pants and a tight black t-shirt. He looked disheveled, a far cry from the leader of The Wanderers Coven that I had come to know. This human was throwing everything off balance.

Love often did.

He led me to the rental car he had somehow gotten a hold of and we climbed inside. He must not have wanted to run, this time. The interior was a dark leather that felt hot against my cold skin as I settled down into the seat. Orpheus was quiet as he pulled down the driveway.

Silent questions hung in the air. But I knew he wasn't ready to ask or answer them so we sat in the quiet for an hour as he drove us back the way we came.

Shockgrove was a town that was so small, so insignificant, and yet it was changing everything.

Athena was changing everything. I just hoped we could survive it.

16

ORPHEUS

I'd never been the type of person to fall apart.

In fact, in my life, those that fell apart were often ripped to pieces. In order to survive this world we were in, you needed a cool head. I had that. I prided myself on being the calm one - the lighthouse in a storm. You do not survive as long as I have, with Hunters around every goddamn corner, without critical thinking, without planning. You don't survive as a coven in this world without understanding what it takes to survive, and doing it.

Something is happening to me here in this fucking town. For the second time in my long second life, I'm feeling shaken, and unstable. The first time that happened was at the hands of Nameless. I can't help the eerie feeling in the pit of my stomach telling me that I am so close to falling victim like I did last time.

I made the mistake of getting comfortable once, and we lost Alora because of it. I refused to make the same mistake again.

Yet, here we are, our coven in disarray, breaking every rule we've ever made. Rules that have kept us alive, kept us safe. All for a fucking human.

She's got a pretty face, sure. But no one is worth ruining my family for. No one.

"What are you going to do if it's true?" Samara asked, quietly from the passenger side. We would drive most of the way, just back to where we last stopped before making the unfortunate mistake of walking into a bar at Shockgrove, then getting out to run. Leaving our scent, and leading whoever is watching in the wrong direction.

Then we'd hunt.

I pondered her words for only a moment. "It's not," I answered her. She clicked her tongue, I saw her shake her head in the corner of my eye. "It's not," I said again, although it did sound less convincing the second time.

"Ok." She didn't sound too convinced herself. Her hands were folded in her lap as she watched me. "But what if it is?"

What if?

A mate was sacred to our kind. And rare. Not rare in the fact that they don't exist, but rare because of how our kind was Hunted so brutally, we seldom lived long enough to find the one to whom our soul belongs.

If Silas and Laz found their mate in this fragile human, I could only see three ways this story could play out.

First, Nameless would find out, because somehow they always did, and kidnap her. They'd use her to lure The Wanderers to their headquarters and when they had us in their grasp, they'd torture and kill her while we watched. Then they'd kill us, the way they tried to all those years ago.

Or she will die, either from an accident or illness or in old age, as humans are inclined to do and her death would cause catastrophic, irreparable damage to our coven.

Or lastly, and arguably the most improbable of the options, they would mate, she would agree to be turned and we'd add another vampire to our coven.

Even if that were to happen, we'd still be hunted. We'd still be vulnerable. More people in the coven meant more people that Nameless could use against us.

No, there was no happy ending here. There couldn't be.

"What we've always done," I said as I pulled off the highway into a rest stop. We'd run from here. Samara got out of the car, watching me with careful eyes. "Try to survive it."

The next hour was nothing but quiet breaths and the rustling of the ground and twigs beneath our feet. It was spring, so that meant that life was starting to begin again. It was an interesting concept. Rebirth. How something could die, and stay dead for a long while only to be born again. Find a way back to life.

An interesting concept, but ultimately impossible for someone like me.

Not that I'd ever wanted to be human again. I've been what I am for centuries at this point. The tiny shack I once called home in Romania is a distant memory at this point. Blurred by time and the way human memories seemed to dissipate the further we were removed from them. I don't recall the majority of my human life anymore. Nor do I care to. I like the person I am today. The monster I've become.

I love the family I've built, and I would do anything for them. Including this stupid, reckless hunt.

Samara and I made it to the city by midday, being sure to stay in the shadows of buildings and beneath awnings as much as we could as we stalked silently through the alleyways. We never hunted during the day. We weren't interested in having witnesses. But also, the type of person we hunted normally came out at night. For some reason, evil felt more comfortable in the moonlight.

We'd made the decision long ago, that if we were going to kill, it would be those who deserved it. Like that asshole from the bar. I felt my jaw tighten with anger every time I pictured his body pressed up against hers. Like he owned it - like he deserved her. I relished ripping his throat out, but now I wished I had made it last. I should have taken my time. Made him suffer.

He was a monster, I was his karma.

Samara and I wordlessly made our way through the metropolitan streets. Being not as careful as normal to cover our tracks. We wanted Nameless to track us here after all. We had drifted to the seedier part of town, where the bars didn't have windows and the cars had busted windows. In our experience, in the many years of hunting, we've found that those who live in areas like this aren't the monsters, but those that often found places like this comfortable, so they took advantage of it.

I couldn't stand people who took advantage of anything or anyone.

Samara nodded to a small white brick building, sounds of general debauchery and mirth flowed from the door. We entered together, making our way across the sticky wooden floor to the bar. Neon signs illuminated the space. Five or six patrons sat in chairs scattered about the bar, and a few scantily dressed women walked around with trays in their hands, as some danced atop the tables while the men ogled them.

Samara and I took two barstools and glanced around. Listening. We'd find our next target here, I was sure of it. The stench told me as much.

The bartender was this buff guy with tattoos that rivaled Silas'. He wore a jean button-down shirt, with the sleeves ripped off, exposing his tanned skin and the myriad of black and white pictures painting him. He had a deep scar that ran from above his eyebrow to his cheek and it gave him that sort of 'don't fuck with me' vibe that I could appreciate. He approached and set down a napkin in front of the two of us.

"Girlie, you're in the wrong place. The male dancers ain't here till Thursday." I rolled my eyes, contemplating if bigotry was enough of a reason to choose this guy for our hunt.

"I ain't here for the boys, buddy," Samara responded leaning onto the bar.

The bartender looked at her all perplexed for a moment before his face scrunched up in confusion.

"You don't look like one of those girls who likes pussy," he scoffed, flinging the towel in his hand over one shoulder. I gripped the wooden bar top to keep from reaching across the space and bashing his head in.

"And you don't look like an asshole so... wait, actually I guess you do." I managed to hold in my chuckle, but barely. The bartender looked angry, his gruff face turning slightly red.

"You gonna tell me you're a faggot too?" He said as he looked my way. "Get on out of here. We don't want your kind in here." And that does it. I glanced at Samara who looked back as if to confirm what I already knew. We had found our mark.

The bar was crowded, so we needed to isolate him. This is where Samara came in handy. I just hope that he'd fall for it, as everyone else had. By the time she turned back to face the bartender, her mask was firmly in place and she was the sensual bait she knew how to be so well. She leaned on the bar, pressing her arms together to push her breasts out just enough to be enticing for him. I'd never found Samara attractive in that way, despite it being obvious she is a beautiful woman. I guess, when I first saw her, I couldn't see anything but the broken girl, the girl whose parents had taken every ounce of light from her and snuffed it out. She was beautiful, sure. But it was her heart and her soul that called to me that night and every night for the following month. Not her body.

The bartender, like a typical 'alpha' male, looked down to appreciate the view she was offering down the neck of her loose-fitting sweatshirt.

"I said I wasn't here for boys," she whispered, seductively. "I'm here for the men." I had to force myself not to roll my eyes. I was disappointed, but not surprised when the bartender leaned forward into her space with a cocky smile on his face as he fell for her charms. Hook, line, and sinker.

For being such 'strong' and 'powerful' men, they always were the easiest to kill. It's almost like the whole 'alpha male' bullshit was exactly that...bullshit.

"Well, little lady, why didn't you just say that." He licked his lips and I nearly gagged. How Samara was able to keep a straight face as these men acted like fools in front of her was beyond me.

"I gotta take a leak," I said nonchalantly, slipping off the stool and heading back to the bathrooms. I knew Samara was watching, so she knew where to lead him when it was time. I watched the patrons as I walked, too engrossed in the show in front of them to realize we had even come in.

I hid inside the girl's restroom, in one of the two stalls. With any luck, the dancers had their own dressing room, and wouldn't be coming in here any time soon. We just needed enough to fill the flasks we each had stashed away in our pockets. It was going to be too risky to take more than that in daylight. But this should be enough.

Although, what we drank two nights ago should have been enough too.

While I waited for Samara to convince the asshole to join her in one of these disgusting stalls, I let my mind wander. Athena couldn't be their mate. She was bleeding that night, and the bond should have solidified had it been there. But I guess if I'm looking at the facts a little closer when we saw her in that position and saw what he was prepared to do to her, Silas and Laz definitely went off the rails a bit. So did I, for that matter. Which I didn't really understand. Why did we care so much, why were we blinded by our anger at that moment? I'd never lost control before. I'd never broken my own rules before. But there I was, changing everything. For her.

Infuriating, stupid human.

She was going to get us all killed. There were rules for a reason, they were supposed to keep us safe, and keep us from making mistakes and falling into Nameless's grasp again. It took so much from us the first time. Our security, our friend. I don't think we'd survive it if we had to do it again.

A few minutes later two bodies came spilling into the bathroom. I heard Samara's fake laughter as she pulled him into the room. Her hands went to his collar turning him so that he was facing away from the stalls.

"Damn girl, you just made my day," he said in a pathetic attempt to sound sexy. I rolled my neck back, stretching out. Letting the monster that hides beneath the surface of my nearly impenetrable skin come out to play. I felt the shift happen, like an old friend returning after a long trip away. Samara giggled unconvincingly, but he wouldn't care. He was the type who'd never care.

I quietly pressed the door open, the slight squeak of the door drowned out by Samara's fake moans of anticipation. His large body was leaning over her as she sat on the sink. His mouth was on her neck, sucking away. How ironic. Her eyes met mine and I nodded, moving closer. Always stalking my prey.

I was inches from him when I caught my reflection in the mirror behind Samara. My dark hair which was usually slicked back into place, was wild, hanging haphazardly across my forehead. My pale skin looked almost grey, with the tint of death. But the most captivating part of me was the full set of pointed teeth. The canine teeth on both the top and bottom rows were the longest, begging for this man's blood. My irises were bright red, and crimson veins nearly blocked out the whites, making it look as if a pool of blood was looking back at me. My ears had a slight point to them now, a feature we got from our bat ancestors. At my side, I flexed my hand feeling my nails elongate to a dangerous point. I was horrifying. The type of monster you'd see in your nightmares. The kind of monster that you could never be safe from. The type of monster you'd only see once. The face of evil itself.

The bartender's unsuspecting eyes flick up to Samara, glancing only briefly at the mirror before the horror settles on his face. He looked back to Samara only to find that she had shifted too. He was sandwiched between two demons. With nowhere to go.

Do you think he knew he was looking at his death?

Before he could scream, my fangs sunk into the skin of his neck. Silencing him. His call was drowned out by the rush of blood that was filling his mouth.

Blood.

It tasted like life. Like a promise. I swallowed greedily until I knew the man in our arms was dead.

"The flasks, Orpheus," Samara reminded me, her eyes fixed on the dripping red liquid as it traveled down his throat. I barely pulled myself back. There was a hunger within me that I hadn't realized was there before. Had I begun to fall prey to whatever hunger was plaguing the others? And if so, why?

Samara and I held the waste of space up and drained the remaining blood from his pathetic body into the flasks. Filling five of them before we ran out of space.

"There's still some left, Samara," I said, wiping the corner of my mouth. "Drink up."

She did. Sinking her fangs into his neck and drinking what little blood we left in his veins. Once she was done, she licked the wound, and the violent-looking punctures closed up, leaving smooth skin where our fangs had pierced him. I watched my reflection in the mirror waiting for my features to revert. My fangs receded, giving way to the white set of teeth beneath. My eyes returned to their dark shade, the red fading into nothingness. The tips of my ears rounded and I felt the elongated fingernails return to their normal length. Soon enough, the Orpheus that I presented to the world was the one looking back at me. The one who women often fawned over. The one who seemed trustworthy, handsome, and alive.

But I was the same monster I always was, no matter which face I wore.

17

ATHENA

I sighed deeply as I watched the clock on the wall. It was nearly closing time and we had three customers all day. The Maine Plotline was holding on by a thread. And so was I.

I started counting the drawer early, luckily I had my date with Silas to look forward to. I still couldn't believe what had happened last night. That kind of thing doesn't happen to girls like me. That happens to Davia, but never to me.

Except, it did happen to me. My body still tingled with the effects of a phantom orgasm. While I still had a lot of questions about what happened, why and what I should do next...one thing was abundantly clear. I wanted to do it again. I smiled at the vase of roses that sat on the counter. In a way, they were perfect to represent my strangers. They were soft and sweet like Laz, their pink shade was subtle and beautiful like Samara, but their scent was strong and intoxicating like Silas' presence. And then there were the thorns. Orpheus. They will leave eventually, just like these flowers will die. But with any luck, their presence here will bring me as much joy as these flowers have before it's all over.

The bell above the door rang, clueing me into the arrival of a customer. I eagerly made my way around the counter to greet them. Greg rushed in, looking around with a sort of frantic wide-eyed gaze. My heart rate picked up, half expecting to see his predator friend trailing him. I sighed deeply when I realized that he was alone.

He rushed forward, his dark skin looked ashen and his features were haggard. That clued me into the reason for his visit. Louis still hadn't turned up.

"Hi, Greg, right?" I asked as he reached me. His eyes scanned me furiously.

"Where is he?" He asked, a little unhinged and breathless. I took a step back, carefully placing the counter between the two of us.

"If you're talking about Louis, I haven't seen him since he left the bar." Greg ran his hands along his scalp.

"He never came back," he whined.

"Maybe he went -" I started.

"He did not go home!" Greg slammed a fist on the counter. I took another step back, a bit of fear gripping my heart.

"Ok, I'm sorry. I don't know where he went. We left the bar, went our separate ways and I haven't seen him since." I spouted the tale that I told Davia, knowing she would have relayed that to him.

He shook his head, looking down at the counter, his fists balling on the surface. I watched them with caution. I ran down a list of my escape routes, something you learned to do after going through what I did. I could head out the back, but he would be able to catch me. I could run for the office where my Grandma was currently doing intake inventory. But then she's in danger too. My eyes are scanning the area for anything that might be useful if it were to come to that.

"What did he say to you?" He was desperate, the bags under his eyes told me that he hadn't been sleeping since his friend left.

Disappeared?

I thought back to the anger pouring off Silas, Laz, Samara, and Orpheus when they told me what happened to me. They wouldn't do anything to him, would they?

"He asked to buy me a drink, I said no," I told him, truthfully. "Then I wasn't feeling well so I left." That again was true. But here's where the truth became fuzzy. "He walked me out, but I said goodnight and left, alone," I spoke slowly, carefully. Without the ire, I wanted to invoke. Just thinking about the fucking waste of space made my blood boil, but I wasn't going to do anyone any good if I told the truth now.

He pushed off the counter, spinning away from me with a strangled grunt. He was angry. Worried. I get it. If it was Davia, I'd be out of my mind with worry.

"I'm sorry, have you tried calling him?" I asked, but immediately wished I hadn't because he turned his eyes to me with such hatred that I felt it in my chest.

"Of course, I've tried fucking calling him." I took one more step back.

"I'm sorry," I whispered, trying to placate him. He groaned and put his hands into the pocket of his navy blue pullover hoodie.

"If you can think of anything else, please just call me. Davia has my number." And with that, he was gone and I felt able to breathe again.

I could have told Greg that the strangers from the bar were witnesses. But they didn't know the lie that I told Davia. I started to panic when I thought about the inconsistencies I was already creating. If - heaven-forbid- there really was something going on, and the police got involved, I was not going to look good. I needed to tell Silas and the others not to tell anyone. But then I felt guilty immediately about asking them to lie for me, even though I knew they would. Which was strange, because I don't even know them, but I feel like I know their souls. As corny as that sounds.

If Louis was missing, maybe my strangers knew something about it. Maybe they could help find him. Although, the idea of finding him was not appealing in any way, shape, or form.

I mulled over that thought for the next half hour as I cleaned up the front of the shop. The bell sounded again and I felt fear grasp at me for only a second before I turned and confirmed that Greg had not returned. Or worse, Louis. The man standing in the doorway was tall and slender, with more subtle muscle definition. He was facing away from me but I noticed his paint-covered pants and hands. An artist then? I smiled as I took in his dark black hair with electric blue tips poking out from beneath his baseball cap. He turned to look my way and his hazel eyes searched the area before landing on me.

"Hello! Welcome to The Maine Plotline," I cheerily offered, giving him a bright smile. He wore a white t-shirt, which wasn't much lighter than his pale skin. Dark freckles dotted the canvas of his body. "Can I help you find anything?" I didn't add the 'please', but it was there in my tone.

"Just looking around," he said, stiffly, although his eyes were warm and welcoming.

Feeling his gaze on me had me wishing there were other sets of eyes watching me right now. Laz, Silas... Samara...Orpheus.

I shook my head, simultaneously ashamed at how I let my mind wander to such dirty depths, and shocked because I met someone out in public, and instead of immediately being wary and nervous, with my mind reverting to its protective hole, I was thinking about the future, the possibilities. Maybe Davia was right, I was healing.

"Actually, do you have any records here?" I nodded, smiling. Bringing music to the store was one of the things I implemented when I officially took over. Grandma fought back against it, saying that we had our niche already and shouldn't mess with it. But since the success of the first shipment, she's been pretty quiet about it. In this day and age, you have to keep up in order to stay in business. Our little town didn't have a music store, so I filled that hole as best I could. Niche or not, we needed to adapt to survive. Next step...social media. Groan.

I led the man down the aisles, through the stacks toward the back wall. I'd decorated it with posters of some of my favorite bands growing up and I had a little corner nook set up with a cheap record player for someone to sit and enjoy.

"Here you go!" I fanned my arm out, showing off my contribution to The Maine Plotline's character. "There's not a huge collection, but we've got some good stuff in there. A few rare finds." He stepped forward, flipping through the selection.

"Are you looking for anything in particular? We've got a pretty nice amount of recent records, but I've got to admit I'm a bigger fan of the 70s and 80s."

"They certainly don't make music like that anymore, do they?" He spoke under his breath, pulling out a copy of Led Zeppelin's Self Titled album and scanning its condition.

"I agree!" I added eagerly. He tossed a smile my way before returning his attention to the record in his hands. "Led Zeppelin, good choice."

"You know, my favorite story about this band is how they got their name," he said, pointing to the album in his hand. "Entwistle was recording with Page, Paul Jones, and Beck when they were tossing around the idea of starting a band so he said-"

"That their band was going to go over like a lead balloon," I finished for him. His eyes met mine and a friendly smile spread across his face sending warmth to my chest. It was a safe smile, a promising smile. I liked it. I wanted to see it again.

"Yeah, that's right." He slid the album back into its place, his fingers quickly flipping through the rest. He took a breath, turning toward me with an excited look in his eye. "Ok, you can go to a concert for any singer alive or dead, who are you picking?"

I leaned on the wall, crossing my arms across my chest and thinking for a moment. Pondering his question, and enjoying being able to talk about this kind of stuff with someone.

"Freddie Mercury," I answered finally, earning an appreciative 'oooh' from the stranger. "Videos aren't enough, that's a performance you need to see live."

"You're completely right about that," he smiled.

"What about you?" He flipped through the bin, stopping when he came across a vinyl of Born in the U.S.A. "Springsteen, hands down."

"That surprises me." I mused.

"He's one of the best performers in the world," he argued, playfully.

"I'm not disagreeing with you!" I said, throwing my hands up in mock surrender, laughing with him. "You just don't seem like the Springsteen type."

"Oh yeah? What type do I seem like?" I took a step forward until I was on the other side of the bin of records, flipping through until I found London Calling by The Clash. I pulled it out and handed it to him.

"This seems like you."

"In what way?" He asked, scanning the album in his hands.

"Purely going off vibes." He chuckled at that.

"Well, I'm glad my vibes have good taste." He held my eye contact for a few long seconds before looking down again to continue his search through the records.

"In town for the season?" I asked, for some reason not wanting the conversation with the new customer to end. His hands ran along the front of a Chicago album.

"What?" He asked, turning his head toward me again as if he didn't hear what I said.

"The season, are you here for the tourist season?" Why was I so nervous? Why did I suddenly wish I could be friends with him? Why did I suddenly feel like I was yelling?

"Ah, no. Just passing through," I nodded, feeling a twinge of disappointment. I liked talking about music with people. Davia didn't understand it all that well, and Grandma hadn't listened to any new music since 1979.

"Well then, thank you for choosing to spend some of your short time here with me." I felt my face get hot. "With the store, I mean. Not me. Like you're not with me. You're here for the books and records. And maybe some coffee too? I have that. We have that." I chuckled awkwardly, wishing the ground would open up and swallow me whole. I desperately didn't want him to think I was flirting with him. I have enough hot people to warm my bed. The stranger's eyes softened and he smiled at me, his boyish, stubble-covered face lighting up.

"What's your name?" He leaned forward over the collection of records, resting his elbows on the wooden frame of the display.

"Athena."

"Nice to meet you, Athena." He shook my hand quickly, without a hint of lust or attraction, just a friendly encounter. I didn't feel leering looks being tossed my way or unwanted advances. I appreciated that almost as much as I appreciated the music discussion. He stood straighter, returning his gaze to the music.

"Well, I'll leave you alone, let me know if you need me," I paused, my eyes widening. "Anything. If you need anything." He smiled, a laugh bubbling in his chest and I turned away fighting the urge to facepalm.

When I arrived back at the front desk, I felt a giddy excitement fill me. Despite the many terrible things I've been through in my existence, I was still living. I was letting new relationships come to me, being open to embracing them. This stranger isn't sticking around, but instead of cowering away from him, I made conversation. I made a friend, for however brief a time it was. That's something I never knew I'd be able to do again.

A few minutes later, the stranger made his way up to the front, an album in his hand. The Clash, London Calling. I smiled at it as he slid it on the counter over to me.

"Great choice," I mused, ringing him up, trying to contain the bubbly satisfaction building in my chest.

"Yeah, I dunno, it just feels like the right vibe," he joked, fishing his wallet out of his jean pockets. I once again noticed the cracked paint on his skin.

"It's The Clash, of course, they have good vibes." He grinned, sliding his money across the counter.

I went to grab it, the tips of my fingers brushing his hand briefly, our eyes met quickly before I glanced away, clearing my throat and finishing the transaction.

"Are you an artist?" I asked him in an attempt to dissuade his burning gaze.

"I'm sorry?" He reached for the bag as I handed it over the counter to him.

"You have paint on your hands, are you a painter?" He looked down at his hands, his bag hanging from one finger. A strange expression crossed his face as he surveyed the blue paint that was dotting his skin.

"Ah, no, just helping someone paint something." He said, closed off, stuffing his hands into his pockets. The playful banter between us was gone. I nodded, quietly, suddenly confused about the entire interaction. The stranger didn't say anything else as he headed for the door.

"Wait, um, you never told me your name." He stopped with a hand on the door handle and looked over at me. His hazel eyes were filled with secrets I'd never know.

He looked as if he was waging a war within himself, but ultimately he smiled softly and said, "Archer."

He was gone before I could respond, and I filed away the interaction under people I'd never see again but would think about from time to time. How could I not with his kind face, his knowing eyes, and then there was the mystery.

"You go ahead and take off girlie, let me close up tonight." The sweet voice of my Grandma shook me from my fantasies. I turned to see her, standing behind me. She was older, and her body had begun the slow rebellion that everyone had to deal with as they grew up, but she still had a lot of life in her. She was the type of Grandma who fell in love with the 70s. Her hairstyle and clothing still reflected that. Her lower half was covered in bell bottoms and her yellow, white, and red vertical-striped shirt had bell sleeves that dangled off her wrists as she walked. Her kind green eyes were just like mine, and mom's, but her red hair had long since turned white.

"I can do it, Grandma, don't worry! You should head home and rest. Do you need me to walk you home?" She waved her hand as if to say I was being ridiculous.

"I'm an old woman, not an invalid. I can close up the shop tonight." She hip-checked me out of the way and took my spot at the counter. I chuckled.

"Are you sure?" I asked eagerly. The excitement for my date was quickly overshadowing my worry about the store. Which sent a burst of guilt directly to my heart.

"I've been closing this shop since long before you were even a little swimmer in your dad." I made a gagging sound.

"Stop, I beg you." She laughed and took a seat on the stool, separating the cash for counting. She hardly ever mentioned my dad. I knew they knew each other from the brief time that he and mom were dating, but he up and left 'the minute responsibility started weighing on him'. Grandma's words. I didn't ask her anything about him, all I know are the tidbits that the two of them used to slip into conversation. I don't care to know him. I watched her work for a moment. Her hands were wrinkled, her body frail and skinny and she paused to remember her place more than a few times. Something like fear coursed through me. I didn't want to lose her. I couldn't lose her.

But I would. And probably sooner than I would like to.

"Get out of here will ya? You're making me lose my spot." She waved me off and with a lackluster chuckle, I left.

It was bittersweet, having her here. On one hand, this bookstore was her baby. She built it from the ground up with my Grandpa, and it was her dedication that kept it alive. On the other hand, now when she was here, she was here alone.

When she lost her husband, my Grandpa, her world was shattered. She still had us, sure, but there's something so heartbreaking about losing your soulmate. She was a strong woman, and she's been moving on as best she could, but I could tell that there was a certain light in her eyes that wasn't as vibrant anymore.

"You've created something really special here, Grandma. I don't think I tell you that enough." She turned to me, leaving the cash on the counter in piles. Something like happiness swam in her expression.

"We all did. Every single person who's stood behind that counter has brought something important into this store." She was walking toward the bookshelves now, counting cash long forgotten.

Her hands came up and ran along the wooden shelves. "Your grandfather built these with his own two hands. After we spent our life's savings on this building, we didn't have two nickels to rub together." I had heard the story a million times, but I never tired of it. "He took a job at the lumber yard down the road just so he could get some of the discarded lumber for free." She traced her fingers along one of the very 'imperfections' she was referring to. A knotted piece of wood, which at one time had made that log unusable, but now it was what made the character. It was history. "That was his contribution. He built this place." She smiled, sadly. She loved talking about him, but it hurt her too. It always would.

"I was in charge of getting all the books you know, for the grand opening. Now, ask me how I got those books without a penny to spend on them. Go on, ask me." Her eyes shined with a bit of pride.

"How'd you do it?" I asked, sliding my backside onto the counter to sit.

"I drove to just about every library and bookstore on the East coast and convinced them to give me their overstock. They normally donated it or sent it back, but yours truly got them to give it to us. We opened the store with the strangest mod-podge of books you ever did see, but it worked." She laughed, and it was a melodic sound, it reminded me of my mom.

"You brought the music." I didn't miss the almost indignation in her voice at that. "And your mother brought the heart." She said softly.

"Yeah, she was good at that," I added. Grandma wiped a tear from her face and made her way back to the counter.

"Now, you need to go out there and make a baby so we have someone to take over when you kick the bucket." I choked on air and struggled to catch my breath, laughing along with her. It was a hollow sound though, seeing as I wasn't sure we'd survive the next year, let alone another generation.

"Gee, thanks, Grandma." She shooed me off the counter and started sorting through the piles again.

"Get out of here so I can count this dang cash, alright?" I leaned in, planting a kiss on her cheek, and then headed back to the office to pick up my purse. Walking through the stacks at The Maine Plotline felt like taking a trip down memory lane. No matter how much time has passed since the ones we love left us, their memory was as strong as the scent of freshly brewed coffee in the morning. Always here with us, embracing us. If I was ever missing mom or grandpa too much, I'd take a walk through the aisles to feel them again.

Leaving the shop, and stepping out into the cool Maine air, I found myself smiling. The pier was gorgeous when it was empty. Despite the financial and economical issues that came with a quiet town, I loved seeing it in this state. Quiet. Serene. Peaceful. The sky was a soft orange-pink as the sun neared the horizon, casting a brilliant light on the shimmering surface of the water. Seagulls dotted the sky, filling the air with their call. It was peaceful. Calm. It was home.

I felt the hairs on the back of my neck stand on end, not in fear, but in anticipation. There were eyes on me. I could feel them. It was a possessive glance. Eyes that felt like they knew me. And I wanted them to watch me forever.

I turned my head, seeing the culprit leaning against one of the light posts, his arms folded across his broad chest. He wore a tight black shirt with a white jean jacket. His muscular thighs nearly burst through the black skinny jeans he wore and a bouquet of pink roses was clutched in his hands. I found myself sauntering over to him before I had the good sense to stop myself. I worried only briefly about reacting this way to someone I only just met. What if I scare him away? Before I could worry, Silas stood up to greet me, rushing forward and throwing his arms around my waist. I clasped my hands around his neck and suddenly my feet were lifted from the ground as he held me. I laughed into his neck, the sound was carefree, hopeful. I'd missed feeling this free.

"Hello to you, bookworm," he chuckled against my hair, tightening his hold on me. Suddenly a thought occurred to me, Silas had been calling me bookworm, but when we were...well doing what we were doing last night, I was 'baby girl'. Like he had a different nickname for the 'me' in the bedroom.

I liked it. I felt like I had some kind of sexual secret identity, like a sexy Batman.

Silas set me down on the ground, my feet feeling secure but as he loosened his hold on my body, I somehow felt more off balance. Strange. I smiled up at him, his eyes searing into mine with an intensity that I'd come to expect from this man before me. I couldn't help the blush that spread across my face as I thought about our phone call last night, my skin felt blazing hot.

His fingers came up to trace featherlight touches across my cheek. He looked at me with such reverence, like he was in awe of what he was seeing, the way someone might look at a work of art or a wonder of the world. I'd never been given such attention before. It felt unearned but warm and welcoming.

"I love the way you blush." If I was flushed before, now I was a tomato. He chuckled, as his ice-cold knuckles graced my skin. He offered me the roses, and I smiled brightly and gripped them. "For you."

"You spoil me," I offered as I took a deep inhale of the delicious scent.

"We're just getting started." He winked and I had to press my thighs together to stave off the aching need building.

"Let me drop these off inside," I said, turning to head back to the shop. When I entered through the front door, the bell rang making my Grandma look up from her counting.

"Welcome to the - Oh, Athena! What are you doing back already? Was he a two-pump chump?" I choked on air and devolved into a coughing fit.

"Grandma, Jesus..." She laughed and I stepped forward, carefully adding the new bouquet to the vase with the last one. I smiled like a fool at the very full vase.

"Your grandfather used to bring me roses too," she mused, quietly. Smiling weakly at the arrangement. "The good ones always bring roses." I smiled, my cheeks already burning from the amount of happiness Silas had brought me.

"I'll see you later, Grandma." She gave me a wink and I was back out the door and standing in front of Mr. Tall, Dark, and Sinful himself.

"Come with me," he said, weaving his icy hand with mine and leading me down the pier toward the parking lot.

"Where are we going?" He simply tossed a coy smile over his shoulder and continued to the lot. He led me to the passenger side of a dark pickup truck. I tossed a quizzical look his way.

"You don't seem like the pickup truck kind." He laughed as he settled in the driver's seat and took off down the road.

"It's a rental." I nodded. We drove for a few moments in comfortable silence and I let my head drift to face him. He was relaxed in his seat, controlling the wheel with only his left index finger and thumb, his elbow resting easily on the door. His right hand, however, was in my lap, gripping my hand. I found myself trying to memorize the feeling of his hand in mine as if it was too good to be true. A dream that I really wanted to remember when I finally woke up and returned to the life that I deserved to have. The boring one, devoid of the type of passion that the man sitting next to me elicited. Holding his hand in mine felt like grabbing a handful of snow in the middle of winter, his frosty skin biting into mine. How was he always so cold? I might have written it off as a medical condition, had Laz not felt the very same. I tried not to dwell on that peculiar fact, but I couldn't help it. I studied him. The planes of his face were sculpted as if from marble, he was nearly perfect. His handsome, chiseled face was smooth, unblemished, and taunting.

"Like what you see, bookworm?" Silas joked, peeking over at me coyly from the corner of his eyes.

"I'm staring, sorry." I turned my head, diverting my eyes to look at his hand. My fingers danced along his skin, exploring him.

"I don't mind," he whispered with a seductive lilt to his voice. I smiled to myself but didn't meet his eyes again.

"Your hands are always so cold," I spoke, almost to myself, but I knew he heard me because his hand tensed slightly in my lap. I silently prayed I hadn't hit a nerve.

"Yeah, sorry about that," he said, nonchalantly, but I could sense his hesitation. He made no move to pull his hand from mine, but his grip loosened and I didn't care for how that created a pit in my stomach.

"It feels nice," I said, truthfully. Every time I was around him, and Laz too for that matter... and who was kidding Samara and Orpheus too... I felt like I was burning from the inside out. Like any moment my entire body might burst into flames that consume me in heated passion. So having their cool touch to balance me out felt...perfect.

"Good to know." He chuckled, using his thumb to rub circles on the soft spot of my hand near my thumb. I smiled like an idiot while I watched the movement. So simple, and yet it said so much.

A thought occurred to me then, the image of Greg's disheveled appearance, his threatening aura. I shivered.

"What's on your mind?" Silas asked.

"Oh, um, Greg visited me at work today. Louis's friend. The uh-" I paused, taking a deep breath. "The guy from the bar." Silas' hand tensed and I swear I heard a growl rumbling in his chest.

"Did he do something to you?" He asked through clenched teeth.

"No. He's just, well Louis hasn't been seen since that night and he's getting really worried. He was asking me questions," I said meekly.

"Do you want me to get him off your back? You don't need to talk to that douchebag's friend." I squeezed his hand appreciatively.

"It's ok. I um, ok this is going to sound bad, but I didn't tell Davia about what happened with Louis." Silas was quiet, waiting for me to continue. "She was happy with Greg, and she's already had to help me through too much in my life, I didn't want to burden her with yet another traumatic Athena story." We came to a stop at a stoplight, it cast a strange dark hue in the car. Silas looked threatening in the red light, but I wasn't afraid, if anything I felt safe. Like he would protect me from anything.

"First of all, you are not a burden, nor are the things you've survived." His eyes bore into mine. "Second, you don't owe your truth to anyone, not even your best friend if you don't want to give it to her." I sighed, not realizing how much guilt I'd been harboring over the whole thing.

"If he's actually missing, the police might get involved, and if that's so, Davia and Greg are going to tell them my story. The one I've been telling them. That we left the bar and went our separate ways." I didn't want to ask him to lie for me, especially if the authorities got involved. I felt sick to my stomach.

"As far as I'm concerned, that's exactly what happened," he said clearly, watching me with his honey eyes. The light turned green and he continued down the road. I felt a weight lift off of my chest and I held his hand tighter.

"Thank you," I whispered, looking ahead at the road. We drove in silence for a few minutes, but my curiosity, or fear maybe, got the better of me.

"Did you see where he went, after... After you got him off of me?" I asked, timidly. I wasn't sure I wanted the answer.

Silas looked like he was thinking, a soft smirk on his lips. "I think he headed West, saw him walking toward the gas station down the road from the bar." He looked like he had said something humorous, and I couldn't help but furrow my brow.

"Ok, I'll text that to Davia to tell him. He'll like to have a lead." I sent the message quickly, then returned my phone to my bag. Deciding to put the whole situation away. I was on a date and I was going to enjoy it without the ghost of Louis screwing it up.

I glanced up as I felt Silas turn off the road. It was starting to get darker, the sun creeping toward the horizon. His headlights lit up the sign for the Field of Films drive-in-theatre. I'd been here what felt like a million times growing up, my heart leaped in my chest. For a brief second, it wasn't Silas next to me in the car, but my mom as we drove in for yet another night of stuffing our faces with junk food and making fun of the characters on screen.

"Wait, Silas. This place isn't open for the season yet." I tried not to sound disappointed as we drove down the annex road toward the very empty field. Normally, this road is packed, bumper to bumper with cars of families coming to spend the evening under the stars.

"The owner needed to do a test run of the screens and projectors before the big season opener, and he was more than willing to let the owner of The Maine Plotline be the guinea pig." I smiled, Charles Greene owned the drive-in and he and I would often find ourselves in light-hearted arguments about films versus their book sources. He was yet another friendship I let fall to the wayside after everything happened. I should fix that. The pergola that sat at the end of the road at the entrance to the field was lit by soft white fairy lights and the string of Edison bulbed lights hung across the whole field strung from post to post, dotting the sky above the field with a soft starry glow. It was gorgeous, one of my favorite places in the world. I hadn't been back since before Mom passed. It never really felt the same. But driving toward the screen now, with Silas, I wasn't dreading it. I was thrilled. Despite my final memories here.

Silas slowed down by the pergola, where Charles was standing with a large smile painted on his face. "Charles, thanks again for hooking us up!" Silas spoke to him as if they were old friends, not strangers. And by the laugh that Charles gave him, he felt the same camaraderie.

"Thank you for agreeing to be my practice. I always hated doing the test run." Charles leaned toward the car window and his eyes landed on me. "If it isn't Miss Landry. It's nice to see you." He didn't say it with any modicum of judgment for my absence which felt nicer than I thought it would.

I leaned toward the window, trying hard not to focus on how being closer to Silas made me literally erupt in goosebumps, and smiled. "Hi, Charles! It's really nice to see you too." He nodded, his eyes holding a small ounce of pity. He knew my mother and probably missed her as I did.

"So what are we watching?" I asked, leaning back and removing myself from Silas' immediate aura because he was entirely too alluring and Charles was the one who was supposed to be putting on the show, not the other way around.

"Double feature tonight consists of Jumanji and Zathura," Charles said with a false presentation as if he was practicing for his future customers to return. "Pull forward, no matter where you park, you've got the best seat in the house." He laughed at his own joke and I couldn't help but smile at him.

Charles turned to the table behind him and grabbed a tub of popcorn, a large drink, and a box of Twizzlers, handing them through the window to Silas who took them and sat them on his lap. "There's the snacks you ordered! The station is 97.4. Well, enjoy the show. I'll be back to switch the film!" Charles disappeared into the projector building and Silas drove forward.

"You've been here for two days and you're already getting special favors from the locals?" I joked while taking a sip of the drink he had bought us. His eyes lit up with mischief as he turned to me.

"You offering a special favor, bookworm?" I choked on the drink and very unflatteringly had to cough to regain composure. He chuckled and parked, facing us the wrong way.

"Uh, I hate to be that guy...but the screen's that way." I pointed over my shoulder, but Silas was already getting out of the truck and walking around to the bed. I turned in the seat, looking through the back window of the cab.

Silas fiddled with a chest that had been strapped down in the back, opening it and removing items. When I finally got out of the truck and made my way to where he was working. I saw the several blankets and pillows he was pulling from the chest. Once he'd gotten his materials out, he placed the chest on the ground and got to work laying out the plush blankets into the truck bed. In a few minutes, the back of the truck looked like a cozy little hideaway.

"You came prepared." Silas slipped off his shoes, letting them sit on the ground before climbing up onto the bed and offering a hand to me. I did the same, letting him pull me into the back.

"You don't think I'd just drive a truck for fun do you?" We smiled at each other for a moment, a sort of romantic tension washing over us as we stood in the back of his rental truck with the soft twinkling lights shining above our heads from the string lights and the stars.

His eyes burned into mine, our breath mingling with each other. I didn't want to move, to break this spell because it felt unreal, like something out of a fantasy. He must have felt the same because he didn't move for a while, he just stood there, holding me in his arms, looking for forever in my eyes.

His lips brushed against mine and I sunk into them. Letting him taste me the way I so desperately wanted to taste him.

It was a fairly chaste kiss, probably because we both realized at the same time that the projection of the screen had started up, and Charles could no doubt see us standing up in the back of this truck. Silas pulled back with a grin on his face and slid down onto the blankets. He reached through the small window of the truck to the radio and set it on the right channel before settling down onto the pillows and blankets. He looked up at me, patting his chest and inviting me to snuggle into him.

I did.

That's how we sat for quite some time, while the previews played and I heard Charles' car drive off, leaving us alone. The movie began, and I watched with distracted attention. I couldn't focus on Alan Parrish and the shoe factory with the solid wall of muscle beneath me. My hand rested on his chest and I would get brave enough every so often to trace the planes of his stomach through his shirt. I heard his breathing catch, but he didn't react any other way.

"This is a perfect date," I whispered, instantly embarrassed. "I love this place." I tried to cover.

"Did you come here often growing up?" Silas asked, his lips resting against the top of my head.

"Mom would bring me all the time," I admitted, quietly.

"And now?"

I sighed, taking a breath. "She's not around anymore, so I haven't been in a few years." It was easier to admit this to him since I couldn't feel his eyes on me.

"Loss fucking sucks. I'm sorry you have to deal with it." I nodded, gripping his shirt and fighting back tears. It would be just my luck to cry on my first date with one of the hottest guys in the entire world.

"Thank you." I held back the waterworks, despite the stinging eyes. "Have you lost many people?" I asked because his tone had a sort of melancholic pain to it.

"Nearly everyone," he admitted quietly. My heart shattered. This strong-willed person next to me was harboring so much pain behind his playful eyes and it sent a vicious sting directly to my chest.

"Silas, I'm so sorry." I felt him shaking his head.

"I got used to it. Doesn't mean it sucked any less, but I'm not surprised when it happens anymore." His fingers ran through my hair softly as he spoke. "I'm numb to it now. The pain."

"Being numb doesn't mean you don't feel pain, it means you've experienced too much." He sighed.

"I guess you're right."

"Although, maybe it would be nice to feel numb about it. It's been a few years and I'm still feeling so raw, exposed." I traced my fingers along his abdomen mindlessly.

"Is it hard having so many places in town that hold memories of her?" He spoke softly, comfortingly. His hand was stroking my back.

"It was. But now I think I'm lucky that I feel her all over this town. That way I won't forget her." I hadn't said that out loud. That I was worried about forgetting her. When you lose someone... you lose them twice. Once when they first leave you, and again when you start to forget. When you can't recall the exact smell of their presence, when you drive past a place you used to go together without thinking about them, when you hear a song and can't hear their voice singing along. The second loss isn't talked about enough, but it's just as painful.

"Tell me about it?" He asked, quietly.

"About what?" I asked.

"About when she would bring you here." He wasn't pushing, but it felt like an honest invitation to share some of my favorite memories.

"We had this old hatchback, so we'd sit in the front seat together with all the widows up. We were so squished." I chuckled, the image of the two of us cramped inside the car, with blankets and pillows like we had created ourselves a little fort. "She would save up all month so we could splurge on all the drinks and popcorn we could eat." I smiled into his chest, a warm feeling spreading within me despite the coldness of his body against mine. "Sometimes, we would turn off the radio and we'd play a game and try to guess what the actors were saying on the screen."

It was a chilly summer night with the misty air rolling in off the ocean. Mom and I were packed into the hatchback with all our snacks. The flickering screen ahead of us was some romantic comedy. We had been laughing all night, my stomach hurt and probably partly from the excessive amounts of candy I had consumed.

"Ok, let's play," Mom said, turning the volume all the way down in the car and thrusting us into silence. "I'll take the older woman."

I smiled, situating myself in the car so I could fully see the screen, ready to play our game. The younger character came storming through the front door and the parent tried to stop her. My Mom spoke up, a thick southern accent coming from her mouth. "Now you listen here young lady, where have you been?" I giggled, chewing on a milk dud as I responded in an equally over-the-top accent, I think it was supposed to be Australian but ended up vaguely Eastern European.

"I'm a teenager now, Mom, I don't need to tell you where I am all the time. Jeez."

The Mom on-screen chased after the daughter and grabbed her arm. "You can't run away from me, girl. I told you I had something I needed to tell you tonight." Mom continued.

The teenage character went to slam the door, "Leave me alone! I'm brooding!" Mom and I both laughed, watching the action on the screen.

"It's important, and you're not gonna like it," Mom said as the character on screen pushed into the teenagers' room and paced along the floor.

"Unless you're here to tell me that we can get pizza tonight for dinner, then I don't care!" I said, playing the part.

"I have cancer," Mom said, I chuckled a little watching the character on screen scream something at her kid, Mom's character confession didn't fit the scene.

"That was pretty bleak mom, jeez," I said in my own voice before picking up with the character, trying to match the indifferent look on her face. "You're totally killing my vibe." I retorted in the accent, waiting for Mom to respond. The parent character began to speak, but Mom didn't. After a few seconds, I turned to glance at her. She wasn't watching the screen anymore. Instead, she was watching me. Her eyes glistened with unshed tears.

"Mom?"

"I'm sorry, baby. I didn't know how to tell you." A tear slid down her cheek and she wiped it away quickly. Breathing became difficult and my entire chest felt tight like I might fall to pieces at any moment.

"No," I said simply. Shaking my head. "No, that can't be. You can't be..." She reached out, grabbing my hand and pulling it into her lap.

"I'm so sorry." She watched me as if I was going to break, which I very nearly did. Shattering into pieces in the front seat of her hatchback.

"We'll fight it, we'll get your treatment. We'll fix this..." I couldn't fathom losing her. She was everything I had.

"It's not that simple, sweetie." She went on to describe to me her diagnosis, and the very bleak prognosis.

I learned two things that night.

One, my mother had cancer.

And two, that cancer was going to take her and there was nothing we could do about it.

I didn't realize I had tears streaming down my cheek until I tasted the slightly salty liquid on my lips.

"She sounds wonderful. I wish I could have met her," Silas' voice rumbled in his chest. It was saddened, comforting.

Then he moved from beneath me, sliding me off so he could reach into the truck through the window. I sat up, trying to wipe the remaining tears from my cheeks before he saw.

A few moments later, Robin Williams's voice was silenced and Silas was sitting back down. He looked at me, then spoke in an atrocious Russian accent. "I am going to play this game and there's nothing you can do to stop me." A laugh escaped my lips, nearly causing me to snort embarrassingly.

"What are you doing?" I whispered, despite us being entirely alone in this field.

"I believe it's your line." He gestured to the screen where Bonnie Hunt was mouthing something. I nodded, exhaling a quick laugh of disbelief.

"Who said anything about trying to stop you, I just want you to keep me out of it." Silas devolved into a fit of laughter at my positively horrendous English accent.

"At least let me borrow your dice, you know yours work better than mine," He continued, his accent even thicker and more incorrect.

"You can't blame the dice when you're the one who's bad at the game." I had tears pricking my eyes again, but this time from joy.

"What accent was that supposed to be?" He asked through breathless laughter.

"It was better than yours!" I retorted quickly, finding myself smiling deeply, freely. Silas watched me for a moment, his laughter slowly receding but leaving his smile firmly in place. Then his lips were on mine, claiming me as his own. I tangled my fingers in his long dark hair, pulling it from its tie at the back of his head until it fell loosely around his face. I drew him closer to me, rising onto my knees to get closer to him. He held my body flush against his. His hands firmly pressed against my back and ran along my spine in a taunting dance. My tongue pressed against his and he greedily kissed me.

My hands gripped the collar of his jean jacket, sliding it down his arms until his biceps were exposed and my fingers gripped at them, loving the way they strained as he fought to get closer to me.

His wicked fingers grabbed at the hem of my dress and tugged it up, but not removing it. I silently thanked him. We were still outside, and despite the very dirty things I planned on doing with him right now, I didn't want to be that exposed.

His hand teased the skin of my thighs and I felt my core tighten in anticipation.

With a hand firmly on the small of my back and one nearly touching where
I needed him to most, he leaned me back onto the bed of the truck. The blankets cushioned me. His mouth went to my neck then, his lips hungrily kissing
me there, I heard his groan with frustration as if he couldn't get enough of me. I
knew the feeling. I lifted my hips to meet his. I felt his erection just beneath his
jeans and right then, right there, I wanted nothing more than for him to
devour me.

18

SILAS

The scent of her arousal was driving me into a near frenzy. I had to force myself to refrain from sinking my fangs into the perfect flesh of her neck and discovering once and for all if she was my mate. Although, at this point, I didn't care. There was no way I was leaving this girl, not now, not ever. Mate or not.

My hands danced closer to her core and she moaned into my mouth, pressing her hips up. Seeking me. I ripped through her panties, literally ripping them apart like some sort of feral beast. She gasped into my mouth and I swallowed it.

I kissed down her neck again, ignoring the temptation to take her throat between my teeth and drink, and traveled down her body until my head sat nestled between her thighs. She moaned, arching off the bed of the truck and I smiled as I took her in. The camera phone didn't do her any justice. I didn't waste a second before dipping my tongue into her heat. The taste of her exploded in my mouth, flavors that I never knew were possible. It was a breathtaking, habit-forming kind of taste. A type of straining desire that I'd only ever dreamed of. She cried out as I feasted on her. Taking her clit between my lips and sucking, following her body's cues. When she pulled my head toward her center, I slid my tongue into her core, as far as I could reach, letting her control me like she controlled that toy last night. She'd never need it again. Not while I was around. Her breathing became shallow and I felt her thighs shake with promised euphoria. I thrust two fingers into her and she exploded around

167

them. I lapped up her release like I was starving for her. I'd never need anything else again. Not after having her.

"Baby girl, I need to feel you," I spoke with a strained jaw, crawling up her body and using one hand to free myself from the confines of my jeans. If I didn't get inside of her soon, I wasn't going to be able to refrain from tasting her the way I needed to.

"Do you have a..." She paused, her eyes landing on my cock. I gently pressed it against her clit, letting it slide in her arousal along the surface of her cunt. Never pushing in.

"I.." I paused, sliding along her opening. I didn't want to drop this bomb at this moment, but it was important for her to know. Especially because I never intended to have a barrier between me and her. "I can't have children, and I haven't been with anybody in a long time." Her eyes flicked up to meet mine, and her flushed skin looked radiant. Gorgeous, like the goddess she was. But a sort of sadness was in her gaze.

"I'm sorry to hear that," she breathed quietly.

"Don't feel sorry for me, I'm about to fuck the most beautful woman in the world. I'm the luckiest guy alive or dead." She smiled at that, but her face contorted in passion as I slid myself along her slit again, pressing down to give her just enough pressure.

She rocked her hips, begging me with her body to slam into her. But I needed to hear her say the words. I needed them since the moment she uttered them in her store, among the books. I needed her to whisper those words so achingly that I might cry out if I had to wait another moment.

"Beg me, baby girl. Beg me to fuck you," I whispered into her ear, her moan was delicious and she turned her head to meet mine. Her lips stole mine in a kiss. She wrapped her arms around my neck and held me there as if she was afraid I'd leave. As if she was trying to meld our bodies together as one. "Don't make me ask again, baby girl."

"I need you, Silas. Fuck me..." She pulled back, her green eyes burning into mine. "Please."

I slammed into her, my cock disappearing into her heat. She cried out and threw her head back, pressing her breasts against my chest. I groaned at the overwhelming feeling of it all. She clamped down on me, her wet heat welcoming me like it knew she belonged to me and I to her. I stayed still, letting her adjust to my size, and forcing myself to breathe, to calm down from this euphoric high that threatened to cloud my senses. The feeling of being inside her was more potent and addictive than any blood I'd ever tasted. My mind was cleared of everything I'd ever known except this moment. It was only her. And it would only ever be her. Always. I'd never felt anything more perfect, and looking down at her splayed out beneath me with her legs wrapped around my hips and her mouth slightly parted, I'd never seen anything as perfect either.

Then I moved. Slowly at first, savoring the way she seemed to squeeze me with every slight movement. She met me, thrust for thrust, sending her hips up, begging me for friction. I let my fingers trail down her torso, pushing her dress to the side and finding her clit with my index finger. She gasped as I pinched it between my fingers. I watched the space where my cock was disappearing inside of her in awe. There wasn't a doubt in my mind that she was made for me.

"Open your eyes, baby girl. Eyes on me." She did and I felt that space where my heart used to reside jerk back to life as if she was a lifeline I never knew I could have. Looking at her, seeing her face as I claimed her in every way I could, I knew this woman was my salvation.

So I did what any sane man would do when realizing that he was looking at his future. I started to fuck her as hard as I could. My fingers dug into her skin, and I worried only briefly about hurting her with my strength, but she matched my thrusts with her own, taking me the way she was made to. I couldn't believe how hard it was to ration my strength when all I needed to do was rut into her and mark her as mine. My hands gripped her hips hard, guiding her down onto my cock at a speed that probably wasn't quite human, but the way she cried out and moaned in pleasure, I knew she didn't mind. See, perfect for me.

My fingers continued their torture of her clit until she was detonating around my cock, her orgasm sending her over the edge and her walls pulsed around me. I pushed through it, prolonging her blinding passion. Her fingernails dug into my back, and if I wasn't nearly indestructible, she might have drawn blood. The thought spurred me on and I drove into her, chasing my climax and once it arrived, I felt my entire world shift on its axis. I came with a type of ferocity I'd never experienced before, my entire body wracking with pleasurable jolts. I came to a resting position, my weight on her chest, listening to her heart beating wildly. Neither of us spoke for a few long quiet minutes, we just savored the sound of our breath and felt our sated skin burn against each other. I was still inside of her, and I wasn't sure I'd be able to remove myself.

I lifted myself in my arms, looking down at her. She smiled up at me, her expression one of happiness and satisfaction. I wanted to bottle it. My eyes flicked to her neck, my tongue coming out to wet my lips slightly. I felt the briefest warning that my fangs had started to elongate and I hid my face from hers by burying it in the crook of her neck. She smelled like a forest after heavy rainfall, peaceful, and calming. Her blood ran hot through her veins and I wanted to taste it. At the very least I needed to scent it so that I could confirm once and for all that Athena Landry was meant to be mine.

My mind flashed back to the promise I made before I left for this date.

"Just promise me that you will wait until we're together. To scent her." Laz had finished drinking the blood that Orpheus and Samara brought back for us and was sitting with their legs crossed looking at me.

"Why?" I asked although I understood.

"If she's ours, I want us to find that out, together," they pleaded with me.

"I want her alone first." Laz nodded, but I noticed the strain in their jaw.

"Me too."

"So we each get her alone, first. Fuck her as long and as hard as she'll let us...then we'll scent her later?" I offered.

"Please." I didn't have time to think about why I liked hearing that word from Laz now all of a sudden. Maybe last night broke some sort of wall we had built between us, but I didn't necessarily hate the idea of Athena writhing in pleasure in the middle of the two of us anymore. Not the first time though. No, I need her all alone first so I can show her exactly how wild she makes me feel.

I sighed and slowly removed myself from her, immediately feeling the loss of her around me. She grumbled something about needing to go commando now that I destroyed her panties, but I only shrugged. I didn't see the problem.

We laid back down on the blankets, her head resting on my chest and her arms holding onto me, and for the first time in a very long time. I felt my heart race.

19

LAZ

I paced the front room, anxiously waiting for Silas to return. I tried not to picture what he was doing with Athena right now. Was he making love to her? Was he tasting her the way I had? Was he feeding on her?

No.

Silas and I may not always agree, but we're family, we're a coven and we made a promise, one I knew full well that he would not break. I trusted him. Maybe that's why I was starting to come around to the idea of sharing Athena with him.

He was an attractive guy, sure, but it was the way he looked at Athena that had me aching. The way he adoringly spoke to her, as if she was his everything. The way he commanded her pleasure. I could never give demands like that. That wasn't who I was. And it certainly seemed like Athena enjoyed that. So maybe it was a good thing she had someone else to satisfy her in an area I wasn't necessarily comfortable with. Now, I was desperate to find a place where I could satisfy her. I wanted nothing more than to be hers.

Samara was sitting on the couch in the living room, flipping through the channels aimlessly. "Sit down, will you? You're making me dizzy," she called from her seat, not looking over at me.

I sauntered over and plopped down into the cushions.

"He said he'd be back after the movies. Do you think they're..." I trailed off, not wanting to picture it.

'If I had to guess, I'd say, yes. They are." I groaned and ran my hands over my face. When I opened my eyes I saw a slight twitch of annoyance in Samara's jaw.

Samara was the first one to join Orpheus' coven. The two of them were together for a few decades before they found Silas and Alora, and then a while later...they found me.

Growing up in the south as a queer trans individual in the early 1900s before there was even a word for what I knew I was, I had never truly belonged. Uncomfortable in my own skin. Mistreated, and discriminated against for what I couldn't change. For what I didn't want to change. They didn't like that.

Samara found me one night after a particularly brutal reminder that I didn't belong because she had smelled the blood that pooled on the street beneath me. They'd left me there, intending for my mangled and beaten body to be a message to anyone else in our town who dared to be different.

Samara saved me that night. Found me on the brink of death and pulled me over, falling with me into a second life. A stronger life. Those men wanted me to be a message, a cautionary tale. Instead, I was their karma.

Once a human is turned, they have a brief window of time to cement the transformation, to make it permanent. The cost is death. The death of someone by your own hands. I knew immediately whose flesh would be my ticket to a new life.

Everything I'd ever known told me that vampires were evil, monstrous, death incarnate, and humans were their weak fragile prey. But how is that true if humans were the ones who damned me and a vampire was my salvation?

She introduced me to Orpheus, Alora, and Silas, and the three of them welcomed me with mostly open arms. I'm not sure Orpheus has ever been described as "welcoming" but he was thankful for the unique gift that I'd developed and suddenly I went from being forced to be something I wasn't to finally becoming *everything* I was. In every sense of the word.

Headlights shined through the window and I was out of my seat and at the door in an instant. I expected Samara to poke fun at me, to comment on my eagerness, but she was right there beside me, waiting for Silas' report of the evening.

Silas had barely set foot through the threshold by the time I bombarded him with questions.

To his credit, he answered them honestly, telling me each sweet detail of his date with Athena, without fuss. Samara even asked a few things as well.

"Did you..." I start and both Samara and I watch him expectantly. I can scent her arousal on him. He licks his lips and I wonder if he was blessed with a reminder of her on his mouth. I almost kissed him just to get a taste for myself.

"We did." He smiled to himself, a look of pure and undiluted passion and happiness on his face. I'd never seen him so content.

"Tell me," I asked, timidly. Silas and Samara shot shocked glances in my direction, but ultimately Silas found a seat and began regaling each salacious detail of the way he claimed her body. Samara perched on the arm of the couch and listened intently. I was riveted. Seeing her through his eyes. Imagining the way she writhed beneath him.

By the time he finished, I was as hot as I could be with my ice-cold skin, and I saw Samara breathing heavily at the description of Athena's soft moans. I saw a glimpse of someone sitting on the stairs.

Orpheus was propped on the top stair, his elbows leaning on his knees and he watched Silas speak with a dark heat in his red-rimmed eyes. We were all ravenous for her.

Damn.

When Silas finished his recounting of what he described as the 'single best experience he's had in either of his lives', I was out of my chair and heading out the front door.

"Where are you going?" Silas asked.

Without stopping, I tossed over my shoulder, "Where I belong."

I ran through town quickly. Taking the path that was now quite familiar to me, until I ended up at her house. The sweet blue cottage sat calmly at the end of the long drive. A single light was on the inside. I was knocking before I could stop myself. Not that I would either way.

I heard her shuffling along the floor inside the house, and I tensed in anticipation. It'd only been a day since I saw her face, but those hours felt longer than the entirety of my second life. Her mere presence was a drug to me.

The door opened and when I saw her face, I could have fallen to my knees. She was beautiful, perfect and she was smiling at me. I wanted her. I wanted all of her. I wanted everything with her.

"Laz," she said, breathlessly, but I was past the threshold and crashing my lips onto hers before she could say another word. She sank into my hold immediately, her arms resting gently on my shoulders. I kissed her with a quiet intensity, not the kind of blazing red hot passion that Silas had just finished telling me about, but the kind that started small and built and built until before you noticed it, you were at the center of a blazing inferno.

Our mouths melded perfectly, giving and taking in equal measure. My hands cradled her face, keeping her there. In this moment, with me.

I was only slightly aware of our feet moving together toward her bedroom. Nothing about our pace was rushed, or eager. It was as if time slowed and there was nothing in the outside world to worry about. There was only us, and this bond.

I pulled back from her kiss, my breathing ragged. Her room was lit by a single lamp on the end table, it emitted a soft warm glow, basking Athena's face in a soft glow that only accentuated her ethereal beauty. Framing her like the goddess she was. I exhaled sharply, absolute wonder filling me.

"You belong in the stars, Athena." She looked at me in question. "Your beauty is too captivating to view so closely. I fear you may have ruined me for everything. Museums, flowers, art. You are the most stunning thing I've ever witnessed, Darlin'. Nothing will ever compare again." Her eyes welled with tears, and her face softened with a look of adoration. I'd give my soul to have her look at me like that forever.

She reached behind her, letting her dress fall to the floor around her feet. She wore a black bra, but her lower half was entirely bare. I took my bottom lip into my mouth and bit to restrain myself from sinking down to taste her again. Not yet.

I followed suit, removing my clothes one item at a time as I felt her eyes on me. Watching me with an appreciation I never knew I had desired.

She slipped her bra off, one strap at a time, and then we were bare before each other. I felt her eyes scan me, the tension between us like a rubber band poised and ready to snap until I gave into the pull and embraced her in my arms.

So I did.

Holding her in my arms, her bare chest against mine, I finally understood what it meant to feel whole. I had been spending my entire life feeling incomplete and I didn't even realize the empty space was present until she was there to fill it. Her mouth trailed soft kisses along my throat and down my chest. Her tongue flicked against the hardened pebbles of my nipples as she explored me.

Then it was my turn. I led her gently to the bed, helping her lay back softly against the bedding. Her chest heaved with anticipation. I was taking this moment slowly. I would savor every second that I was granted the opportunity to worship her for the rest of my immortal life.

I took my time, letting my lips make contact with damn near every inch of her until she was writhing beneath me.

"Please, Laz," she begged.

"I will spend the rest of my life worshiping you, Athena. If you let me." She didn't respond other than the softest moan of approval as my tongue danced along her wet opening.

Her legs trembled around my shoulders and I pushed them apart with my hands, sinking my tongue deeper into her. She cried out.

"I need you," she whispered with seductive trepidation. I climbed up the bed until I was laying next to her. She turned her body so that she was looking at me. Her flushed face looked ever more delectable now than it had when I arrived, painted with the sweetest of blushes.

She pressed her hand on my chest, pushing me until I was on my back. She swung a leg over my hips and straddled me. I felt the heat of her center taunting my achingly hard length.

I saw a flash of something cross her face as she looked down at me. "I will use protection if you want me to, Athena. But you do not need to worry about getting pregnant with me." Her brows furrowed.

"What do you mean?"

"I can't have kids," I responded. Not exactly the sexiest conversation.

"You either?" She asked, nearly incredulous. I heard a hint of disbelief and I quickly thought of a response.

"All of us, actually. It's something the four of us have in common. We found each other because of our similar situations." Her eyes softened and I hated the half-lie I had to give her to explain why all four of us would be barren.

"I'm so sorry, that's..." She sat up, letting me follow suit beneath her, her hand gently brushing the hair from my forehead. Her green eyes held mine captive, the emotion in them was so pure I briefly worried that my touch would corrupt her, but quickly my selfishness overshadowed that. "I hate that you don't have the freedom of choice."

I had never really wanted a child, I grew up in a home that was so vile and toxic, I knew I wouldn't have the ability to be as impartial as a child deserved to be. Not with the trauma I still hadn't worked through, even after all these years. And I'd always just been thankful I didn't have to worry about it anymore, but hearing those words from her, understanding her, the reminder that the choice was taken from me burned in my chest. Just because I don't want the experience of parenthood, does not mean that I didn't deserve to make that decision alone.

"Thank you, Darlin'. I'm ok. It's never something I wanted for myself. So I've had time to process." She nodded, absorbing that information carefully. I leaned my head forward, kissing her neck. I wrapped my arms around her waist and gently guided her to move. Her slick heat was not touching my erection, but I felt her warmth and suddenly I was desperate for her to slam down onto me.

Her head fell back as my lips claimed her throat, I forced myself to focus on the soft sound she made as she let her inhibitions go so I couldn't think about biting into her perfect flesh.

Her breasts were arched forward and I couldn't resist taking one of the swollen peaks into my mouth, dancing my tongue around the sensitive area. She gasped and pressed into me further. Her center was flush against me, and she moved back and forth, gliding her slick opening along me and I felt her body tightened with anticipation. My arms tightened around her, urging her to move quicker.

Her breathy moans grew feverishly, then she was lifting up, removing her slickness from me and I nearly protested, but her hand came down to grip me, lining me up so that she could sink down. As she did, our eyes met. Inch by inch she possessed me and the feeling was unrivaled.

How is it that it took me a century to feel comfortable in my body, but only a second to feel so at home in hers?

It was a slow, torturous, delicious descent as she claimed every inch of me with her body. And when she was fully seated, I held her in place. My eyes burned into hers, watching as her lips parted, and her skin flushed.

"You are so beautiful, Athena." I don't know how long we sat there, with me so deep inside of her, unmoving, just gazing into each other's eyes. But I could have continued for a lifetime.

Slowly, she started moving again, and the sensation was divine. It was slow at first, not tentative, but savoring. But as her hips rolled, and her body adjusted to my length, I felt her inner walls tighten around me and I groaned, falling back onto the bed. I looked up at the goddess who was riding me, her red hair falling down her back as her head lulled and she turned her face to the ceiling. I'd never seen something so stunning. If I were a painter, I'd attempt to recreate the look on her face, the way her body fit onto mine so gloriously, but even the most talented artists on this Earth would be unable to capture her. She had the type of beauty that was impossible to recreate. A beauty that many would try and fail to emulate.

"You're staring at me," she mused through a light chuckle and deep moans. Her hips continued their adventurous exploration of me.

"Just trying to memorize this moment," I responded, truthfully. She leaned down until her chest was flush against mine, her warm skin felt like a fire against mine, but I welcomed the burn.

"Then let's make it memorable." Her lips caught mine and she began to move quicker, with reckless abandon. Her smooth movements were replaced by quick, sharp thrusts, and I pushed my hips up to meet hers. Our skin hit against each other as she rode me. My hands drifted from her hips, finding the swollen bud at her apex, her appreciative gasp urged me forward and I moved my fingers in time with her body sliding up and down on me.

I felt her begin to tremble, her release mere inches away. I wanted to give it to her. All of it. My life. My passion. My past. My future. She was the one. The one I'd need for the rest of my life. Nothing had felt right before, and nothing will feel right again, not without her.

The words wouldn't tumble from my lips, so I showed her with my body. Thrusting deeper and harder until she was exploding around me, taking me off the cliff with her. I'd follow her over any edge.

We were a quiet mess of heavy breathing and sweaty bodies, our souls holding onto each other.

I held her closely, the space behind my ribs feeling more alive than it has in decades, and I felt the overwhelming desire to breathe her in, to memorize her scent and her movements. To recall this very moment no matter where life takes me, to know I can think back to this incomparable experience. With her.

She lifted off of me, and I missed the connection instantly. But as she laid down beside me, and snuggled her naked form into my side, nestling her head on my chest, I realized that I craved everything with her. Not just the physical moments that her body belonged to me, and mine to her, but the soft, quiet moments like this. I wanted to wake up next to her, I wanted to make coffee in our kitchen, I wanted to watch tv late into the evening, I wanted long car rides, I wanted grocery runs, I wanted normal. I wanted a life.

I craved the mundane with her.

20

ATHENA

esterday was a dream.

I had the world's most romantic date with Silas, then spent the better part of the night indulging in the quiet ferocity that is Laz. They left just before 3 am, telling me that they needed to leave or they'd monopolize my entire night and I wouldn't get any sleep. I had argued last night, saying that I didn't mind, but sitting here now at work, trying to keep my eyes open. I understand why they had left.

My entire body tingled with the memory of both of their hands, mouths, and bodies claiming me. It was a type of sensual awakening that made me realize how dull my life had been before. Colors were more vibrant, songs were more exciting, and things were different. I was different.

I found myself staring at the pink roses in the vase on the counter. Seeing my newly realized passion in their colors. Smelling my euphoria in their scent. Feeling my freedom in their thorns. I would never look at pink roses the same way again.

The bell above the door rang and I looked up from my daydream to find the lethally handsome and equally dangerous Orpheus walking into my business. Shock was my first reaction. Then confusion. I stood from my stool behind the counter and crossed the floor to him. He wore a dark charcoal suit, his black hair slicked back and his eyes found mine. Burning into me the way they had the day of the tour. I hadn't seen him since that moment. Haven't said a word to him since he heard me reading that book out loud. Since he watched me, writing between Laz and Silas. Since I looked directly at him and said those words. My face flushed at the memory of his eyes on me from the dark.

"Orpheus, hi," I said timidly, instantly embarrassed by how flustered I sounded. His eyes raked across my body quickly, nearly imperceptible, but I felt the heat of his gaze on my form. My tight jeans and dark emerald green blouse hugged my curves deliciously. I'd dressed this morning with the knowledge and hope that I could very well see one of the wandering newcomers. Thankful that I felt confident and attractive because, under his stare, I was melting.

"Athena," he said quickly, attempting to be devoid of emotion, but I recognized that sort of breathless sound. He was good at hiding it, however, I was just as good at noticing it. That was a strange thought to me, considering I'd only met the guy a few days ago, and spoken to him truly only once.

"How can I help you?" I didn't miss the way his shoulders rose and fell quickly with forced even breaths.

"I'm hoping you can help me find a book." My eyebrows rose. I wondered if Orpheus was a reader. I could see it, but part of me thought that if he read, it wasn't smut and romance that he was spending his time with. He seemed like a non-fiction kind of guy. Some people read to escape the world they live in. I have a sneaking suspicion that Orpheus has trouble letting go of his control, even in his own mind. But I could be wrong.

"That's what I'm here for. Do you know what book you're looking for?" His eyes darkened and he stood incredibly still, I wasn't even sure he was breathing anymore.

"I'm looking for a book about a group of friends who've been together for most of their lives. Have been all each other had for years." I start flipping through the endless catalog of plots in my mind, there were several books like that, with that found family trope. "But then they meet this girl who starts sleeping with several of the friends. She's got them fawning over her." My eyes flick up and lock on his. Understanding washed over me at his words. It was clear what he was doing now. "You see, this girl has the potential to ruin everything this group has worked for. And one of them really doesn't want that to happen. In fact, he'll do whatever he has to ensure that it doesn't." He took a single step forward, but he might as well have been breathing down my neck. His presence was overwhelming.

"How does it end?" I asked, swallowing deeply. Another step.

"That's the thing, I haven't finished it yet." He was close to me now, too close - or not close enough- my mind and body couldn't agree.

"What do you hope will happen?" My tongue darted out to wet my suddenly too-dry lips. His eyes tracked the movement hungrily. His hooded eyes watching me the way he did that day among the stacks.

"That's the problem, there's a part of me that thinks this girl could be good for their group." His eyes scanned my face, darting between my eyes and my mouth.

"But the other part?" I breathed, quietly. I felt the frigid air rolling off of his body and I couldn't help but shiver.

"The other part of me wants the group to have their fill of her and move on, back to their lives." It stung, I couldn't deny that, but I couldn't act on that hurt now. Not when I was so deep under his spell.

"The whole group?" His eyes narrowed at that, heat in his gaze. I bit my lip and a soft growl rumbled in his chest. I felt the vibration of it in my bones. "You want them all to have their fill?" I was too enchanted by this moment to be embarrassed about asking if he wanted me the way the others had.

"I can't decide," he answered quietly. I believed him. His breath was cool on my lips. I took this moment to study his face. It was chiseled and hard. I could see the edge of his jawbone with perfect clarity. His dark eyes had no more color up close than they had from a distance. I was enthralled by him. My body's reaction was eager and needy.

He stood there in silent tension for a few more moments, his eyes watching my mouth with indecision.

"Why were you so afraid?" He asked, his voice still quiet, reserved. He must have seen the confusion on my face because he continued. "At the diner. You were afraid, I'd never felt fear like that before." His tone was almost sympathetic. "Why?"

That broke the spell, slightly. I pushed off of him, my hands meeting the hard planes of his chest with as much force as I could muster.

"That's none of your damn business, Orpheus." He didn't move, it was as if I was pushing against a brick wall. Instead, he gripped one of my wrists and kept my hand against his body. His eyes widened as his skin brushed mine and a shock spread from the point of contact.

"I know that, but you can tell me anyway." I was angry, I was turned on, and I was afraid.

"Let go of me," I screamed, feeling the tell-tale signs of the darkness creeping into my mind. I couldn't breathe.

His hold loosened, but he didn't let me go. The darkness on his face was replaced with worry. "What's wrong?" He sounded concerned but I couldn't focus on that. For a brief moment, the hand on my wrist wasn't Orpheus', it was *his*.

For a moment, I was lost.

It was a cold night, in the middle of winter. I remember the house felt empty because Mom was away at a conference for the weekend. It was the first time I was going to spend some 'quality time' with my stepfather. They'd only started dating a few years ago when I was in middle school and they tied the knot and he moved in just a few months ago. It was a hard adjustment. Adding a new person to our routine. It had just been Mom and me for so long, I resented his presence for a while, but I was happy that she was happy. She'd spent most of her life living for me, I didn't feel right about holding her love hostage. She deserved to feel loved by more than just me. Even if he gave me the creeps.

He was nice enough, but there was just something about the way he looked at me. The way he commented on my clothing like he simultaneously liked what he saw, and hated that I planned on going in public dressed like that.

He'd been harmless.

Until that weekend.

I felt sick after dinner. Like the world was spinning and I couldn't keep up. I went to bed early, trying to combat the dizziness and nausea, but just as I began drifting in and out of consciousness, the door to my room opened. I was stuck somewhere between sleep and reality when I realized he had me pinned beneath his body. His selfish mouth was stealing kisses. Whiskey. I tasted whiskey on his mouth. It was bitter, wrong. I didn't understand it. I couldn't believe it.

I didn't fight back. I couldn't. I was frozen. In fear, in shock, in pain.

He told me that I was his precious little girl. That he loved me. That I had told him I wanted him. With my outfits, and my back talk. He said I was asking to be punished.

He violated me that night in a way no one ever had, and while I wished the drugs had taken the memory of his vile hands and his vicious kisses, nothing could erase the fragmented pictures that would forever be imprinted on my soul.

Panic seized my heart and my breath didn't come. I struggled against Orpheus' hold. Bending at the waist, I pulled my hand from his grip. There was a tightness to my chest like rocks were being piled on top of me and I couldn't escape no matter how hard I fought.

"Athena," a voice sounded, but I couldn't focus on that. The edges of my vision blurred, and images flashed in my mind.

"Athena, please," the voice was strained as if the owner was in as much pain as I was. I felt a pair of cold hands grip my face, but I didn't pull away. Instead, I saw a pair of eyes that didn't haunt me. They were dark black. A comforting sight. "You're safe, I swear it," he cooed, softly, a look of worry on his face. I tried to focus on his words but found the breath was still not coming to my eager lungs.

"Name four things you can see," he demanded. When I didn't respond he held me still, moving his head so that he could hold my eyes. "Four things you can see, Athena. Name them now."

I nodded, drawing in shallow breaths. "Books," I started, feeling the light-headedness begin. My eyes darted around the space, willing the spinning room to slow so I could focus. "The lamps." I gasped, turning my head aimlessly. Needing to see more. Begging to see more. "The window." My anxious eyes landed on him. "You."

"Three things you can smell." I swallowed deeply, forcing air into my lungs. This time it came. Not easily, but it came.

"My perfume, the pink roses... you." He nodded.

"Good, you're doing well. Now tell me two things you can feel." His hands were soft against the skin of my face. I felt him holding me upright as my mind began to settle. Breath came easier. Everything slowly returned to focus. My eyes adjusted to the space.

"The ground under my feet," I whispered, he nodded urging me on. "You." The room stopped spinning. I felt grounded, firmly planted in reality. The memory locked tightly back in the box I created for him all those years ago.

"And one thing you can taste," Orpheus hadn't let go of my face, his eyes scanned my face furiously. Worry and fear. It had been a very long time since I had a panic attack so vivid, and so painful. Since he had been the star of my memories. Orpheus was a lifeline, holding out a hand for me as I waded through my tumultuous sea of traumatic experiences. My breath evened out, and there was nothing but Orpheus and me.

"You," I whispered before crashing my lips to his. He pushed me off, quickly, still holding my face between his hands. He looked at me with a sort of shocked expression for a moment. I worried that I had crossed a line. Worried that I had taken advantage of his kindness, blurring the lines of his consent. He watched me, a war of emotions crossing his expression. I felt shame and guilt seeping into my chest, but it only lasted for a brief time before a fire lit in his eyes, and throwing caution to the wind he closed the gap between us again, taking my lips with his.

He pulled my face to his, urging me to fully emerge myself in this moment with him. So, I did. My tongue sought out his, tasting him the way I longed to. His hands never left my face, and his body never pressed against mine, but that didn't make the kiss any less passionate. I longed for his comfort.

He tasted like bourbon and ice. A cold shock to my system that only brought me further from the horrors of my past. It was addictive and over-whelming.

He captured my bottom lip between his teeth and bit slightly, not to the point of pain, but it was enough to draw an eager moan from my lips.

I was so oblivious to the world, that I hadn't noticed the door open and the three patrons making their way inside The Maine Plotline, but I felt their gazes burning into my skin.

I forced my eyes to open and saw Laz, Silas, and Samara standing by the front door, their eyes full of seduction and lust.

A brief flash of embarrassment crawled up my spine and I went to push back off of Orpheus. Silas, Laz, and Samara were watching us with hooded expressions, not a trace of anger. Instead, they each looked as if they wanted a taste as well. I blushed deeply.

"Sorry to interrupt," Silas said, cheekily, stepping forward to hand me a single pink rose. Orpheus hadn't turned to face his companions, instead, his gaze was trained on my face as he breathed deeply. I tried to ignore it and grabbed the rose from Silas' outstretched hand.

"Hi, Silas. Thank you." I blushed as his eyes scanned my outfit appreciatively. His tongue traced his bottom lip, across that delicious piercing there.

"I told you that I wanted a few minutes with her," Orpheus addressed his friends without turning to them.

"We couldn't wait," Laz admitted sheepishly.

"I wasn't expecting you all," I said, the double meaning was obviously clear. I didn't expect them to be here tonight, but it was more than that. I didn't expect them in my life, in my bed, in my mind. My soul. These four people had laid a claim to a piece of me and I didn't know why, or how, but they did. And I never wanted them to let go.

"I told them about what you spoke to me about yesterday," Silas started. "About the asshole's friend from the bar." I sighed, still feeling so raw from the panic attack that even the thought of Louis was threatening to send me back over the edge. The slightest hitch in my breath drew their attention.

Orpheus' fingers found my chin, drawing my gaze to his face.

"Stay with me," he commanded. It was a soft request, but it was what I needed. I nodded, feeling the call of the void slip away.

"Thanks," I whispered to him as he dropped his fingers from my face. I looked over at the others who were waiting with patient expressions on their faces.

"Greg, um, Louis's friend, came to see me. He says Louis is missing. My friend Davia told me that he even went to the police. It was too early to report him missing then, but if he still isn't home, then it's only a matter of time before he goes back and police start asking around." I swallowed deeply, hating the idea of being at the center of yet another investigation. The cops in this town didn't prove to be sympathetic to a victim back then, so I can't imagine they would now.

"So, you're worried about being questioned?" Samara asked, taking a few steps forward. I shook my head.

"I didn't tell Davia the truth about what happened that night." I held the long stem of the rose in my hand and twirled it mindlessly as I continued. "I didn't want her to feel guilty for leaving me alone with him."

A few deep rumbling growls sounded in the room. It was a possessive sound, an angry sound. "Shouldn't she?" Orpheus said, his eyes were dark and unrelenting.

"No, she shouldn't," I said, an edge of annoyance in my tone.

"She left you with a rapist," he added as if I didn't know what had happened to me. As if I hadn't been replaying it every night since. "Sounds like a shitty friend." I was seeing red. Seething. "He got his chance because she left you alone and vulnerable." Orpheus was pissed, his fists clenching at his sides. I felt something snap, pain, and anger that had been building for a decade rushed to the surface.

"She was one of the only people who believed me when it happened the first time!" I yelled, tears pricking my eyes. That shut him up. Shut them all up. Their eyes were locked on me, the silence so potent I felt like it could detonate at any moment. "When the whole town turned on me, choosing to take *his* word over mine, turning me into a social pariah, she stood by me. She kept me grounded, kept me sane. When the cops and the town turned it all back on me when they tried to tell me that it was my fault when they tried to tell me that I was lying, seeking attention, she stood by me. She told me they were wrong!" I was a blubbering mess, falling apart before their eyes, but I didn't care. "When their voices were so loud, she was right there drowning them out. She was there for me, feeling every ounce of my pain right alongside me. So no, she doesn't deserve to feel guilt over this when it's not her fucking fault that that asshole was a rapist. And I don't want to hear you blame a woman for a man's actions ever again." Orpheus' eyes softened as he listened. "Do you understand me?" It was so silent, you could have heard a tear hit the ground. Nobody moved for a moment and I let the tears fall down my face, unrestrained. I'd spent too long hiding my emotions, and I was tired of it.

Samara was the first to move, her arms encircled me and pulled me into her body for an embrace. I dissolved into the hold, letting her stroke my hair. My hands balled into her clothes as I nestled my face into the crook of her neck.

After a minute or two, I was composed again, my tears had dried up and I felt a little lighter than I had before. I pulled back, looking up into Samara's brown eyes, expecting to see pity. But it wasn't pity I saw in her expression, it was a softer emotion, a deeper one. Her cold hand came up to cup my cheek and she leaned forward planting the softest kiss on my lips. It was brief, barely a kiss, but it meant everything to me at that moment. When she pulled back she smiled sadly at me, an unreadable expression on her face.

Samara stepped away, and I looked over at Orpheus for the first time since my outburst, he wore an expression of shame, and I hated it.

"I'm sorry," I whispered, and Orpheus was standing in front of me in an instant. Faster than he should have been able to.

"Don't apologize to me or anyone else for making your boundaries known, Athena. Ever." His dark eyes bore into mine and I nodded.

"I'm sorry for what happened to you, Darlin'," Laz offered from their spot near the door. I smiled sweetly at them and turned to see Silas who was seething.

"Who the fuck was it?" He asked through gritted teeth, his eyes an almost unnatural shade of red.

"He's in prison. It's ok." That seemed to placate him, a little.

"He was convicted?" Samara asked, gently. I shook my head.

"Not for what he did to me," I admitted, sheepishly. "Turns out, he was embezzling money from The Maine Plotline." I shook my head, that was such a horrific time of our lives. We nearly had to close the doors. We had no idea where the money was going, no idea why we couldn't seem to keep our heads above water. I remember the day they took him away in the police car. It felt like a hollow victory. On one hand, he was going away, being punished for his crimes. On the other, it didn't escape me that if he hadn't committed that entirely different crime, he would never have been held accountable for what he did to me. "I'm ok, I promise," I said, hoping it was convincing.

"So, what would you like us to say, should the authorities come to speak to us?" Laz asked, changing the subject. I mouthed 'thank you' to them and they nodded.

"I told Davia that you all saw Louis and I leave the bar and once outside we went our separate ways." Laz nodded, but the others looked furious. "Listen, I know I should have told the truth, but honestly, I can't be a victim again. I barely survived it last time in this town. The rumors, the judging." I felt my hand tighten around the stem of the rose. "I can't do that again, ok?" A sharp pain stung my palm. I winced, pulling my hand away from the rose, seeing the spot where a thorn had dug into my palm. I turned to the counter, feeling the blood pooling, and began to spill down my arm, dripping onto the pink petals of the rose, marring it with the red hue of my blood. I placed the rose on the counter, and reached for a tissue, using it to apply pressure to the wound. The pain was there, but dull. It was deep, but not deep enough that I would need stitches.

When I returned my gaze to my visitors, my heart skipped a beat and fear seized my heart.

I didn't see the handsome and beautiful strangers from the bar, or the soft and comforting faces of the people I've kissed, and made love to.

What was staring back at me were four ravenous creatures. Their eyes were blood red, dark veins running along their faces. Their ears were pointed, sticking out from their messy hair. Long, vicious fangs protruded from their gums, glistening violently in the warm glow of the lamps. Long claws stood ready for attack at their sides.

A scream caught in my throat, my heart pumping quicker than it had any right to.

"What.. what are you?" I gasped, my fight or flight instinct utterly broke, settling on the third option...freeze.

The four of them stalked forward, moving toward me in some kind of slow methodical hunt. I was their prey.

A raspy, violent sound ripped from their throats. A single word, spoken in terrifying unison, had my entire body clenching in fear and uncertainty.

"Mate."

PART II

THE FALLOUT

PROLOGUE

SAMARA

There is nothing quite as beautiful as a vampire joining ceremony. Although, I may be a little biased. Moonlight flooded the small clearing, casting a soft glow across the faces of the people I loved most in this world. Standing off to my side was Laz, their face was lit with the brightest smile I'd ever seen grace their features. To my left was Orpheus, his usually cold exterior softened in this moment of love and light. He wore a suit, as always, but he had swapped his usual dark tie for a bright red one to mark the occasion. Across the way, Silas stood with his hands clasped in front of him, an eager excitement coursing noticeably through him. He wore what he wore every day, dark jeans and a tight t-shirt, but he had the good sense to swap his jean jacket for a grey sport coat at least.

And then, standing before me, hands in mine, was the most beautiful creature to ever exist. My love. My chosen. My Alora.

Her golden hair was pulled up into a delicate tangle of curls and braids at the top of her head with stray pieces falling to frame her stunning face. She had that perfect olive complexion, a testament to her human parents' Sicilian ancestry. Her eyes were the color of the ocean, and their gaze felt just as deep. Her delicate frame was draped in a blood-red gown, as mine was. Her dress had a corset bodice that hugged her soft curves perfectly. Mine hung off my shoulders, showing off my dark brown skin that was illuminated by the light from the midnight moon, and flowed loosely down to the grass beneath our bare feet.

There was a soft ethereal nature to her as if she were some sort of mythic beauty. My own personal Helen of Troy. Her plump lips called to me the same way they had every day since I met her. Ever since the day she and Silas joined our coven, her intoxicating scent and mesmerizing gaze had laid claim to me.

She wasn't my mate, but what I felt for her was so powerful that I truly couldn't fathom any bond being stronger than the one I shared with her. That is why I asked her to commit to me, mate bond be damned. I didn't need some cosmic intervention to tell me that I belonged to this woman, and she to me.

The stars in the sky served as a million little reminders of the days I'd already spent worshiping this beauty before me, and a promise of the days I was swearing to devote to her from here on out.

"Alora," Orpheus began, but neither of our gazes traveled to him. We were too enraptured with each other. She had that effect. "Do you swear your commitment to choose Samara, tonight, and every night beyond?"

"I swear." Her voice was steadfast despite the happy sobs that were slipping past her delicious lips.

"You may now offer your promise."

Alora cleared her throat, pushing the flooding emotions down, and squeezed my hands in hers. "Samara, my love." She inhaled sharply, holding back the wave of cresting emotions. " I have spent so much of my life, both this one and the one that came before, feeling like a nomad. Wondering if I'd ever find a place to settle, a place to belong. And I did." She glanced at our friends, our family. " Here with The Wanderers, I found a home. But I didn't know the true meaning of the word until you offered me your love." Tears streamed down her face, painting her gorgeous features with crystalline streaks. "I make this promise to you before the stars and before our coven. A promise I will spend the rest of my unending existence upholding. You will be happy. You will be content. You will be loved." She was staring directly into my eyes, into my soul. "This is my vow to you."

I reached up to wipe my own tears away, smiling so wide that my cheeks were beginning to burn. I welcomed the pain though. It was a good pain.

"Samara," Orpheus continued. "Do you swear your commitment to choose Alora, tonight, and eve-"

"I swear," I interjected, eliciting laughter from all in attendance, but the melodic shimmering laugh of Alora was the only one that mattered to me.

"You may now offer your promise," Orpheus offered with a chuckle. He didn't often smile, but I saw the hints of one gracing his lips.

"Alora, I have known you were my chosen from the moment I laid eyes on you. There is nothing I wouldn't do to protect you, to honor you, to adore you. Our connection is something only a few are lucky enough to experience and I am bewildered and honored that you would ever consider allowing me to share this love with you."

She was crying now, tears of pure happiness, her face blurred in my vision as my own tears spilled.

"I will never love another the way I love you."

Orpheus held up a goblet between the two of us, the silver design was delicate and intricate, climbing vines and steadfast trees. "Fortify your bond. Make your choice."

Alora and I raised our wrists to each other's mouths, letting our fangs sink into the flesh there and drawing the venomous blood to the surface. Once the flow was steady enough, we allowed the essence of our individual lives to drip from our veins into the goblet, mixing together in a swirling whirlpool of life and promise.

She drank first, taking the cup eagerly in her hands, and sipped the proof of our commitment hungrily. When she pulled the cup from her lips, they were stained with a red tint, I couldn't wait to taste them. But first, I reached for the cup in her outstretched hand and took a sip of my own. It was a burst of sweet flavor, assaulting my senses with a slight jolt of euphoria. I smiled, handing the now empty vessel back to Orpheus.

Then I claimed her lips with mine, sealing the promise between us.

I meant what I said. I would never love another the way I loved her. Not as long as I lived.

1

ATHENA

You never know how you're going to respond to life-threatening situations until you're in one. Are you a fighter? Someone who pushes back against the threat and refuses to be a victim? Do you default to flight? Run away at the sign of trouble and never slow until your feet have carried you to safety.

In the past, I've been known to freeze. To completely shut down and while my body remained and endured the trauma, I was somewhere else. Deep inside the recesses of my brain where nobody could touch me.

"Mate".

Their long claws were thick and vicious-looking, sharpened to a point in a matter of seconds. Their eyes were red, the whites disappearing entirely, giving way to the veiny crimson hue, and their once rounded ears had tapered off to a fine point. But that wasn't the most terrifying part. Nor was the way their mouth hung open in a snarl to reveal razor-sharp teeth and two elongated fangs. No, what scared me the most was how they were watching me. Like I was their prey, their meal.

If I froze here, I would die.

So, realizing I had found myself in this life-and-death situation, staring into the ravenous faces of four vicious-looking creatures, I didn't freeze.

I ran.

Leaving behind the blood-covered rose, I sprinted to the back entrance of the store, a scream stuck in my throat. I didn't waste any time, throwing the door open and delving into the eerie night. The setting sun cast an orange-red glow on the town, and a soft layer of fog was rolling in from the ocean. Everything looked warmer like I was looking at my hometown through a sepia filter. It wasn't lost on me how quiet it was on the pier. Not a soul in sight. Normally, I enjoyed the peaceful calm that came from the small-town atmosphere. But at this moment, as I sprinted down the boardwalk, with my heart racing beyond what I thought it was capable of, I was begging for a savior.

I didn't dare look behind me to see if they had followed.

I wasn't naive enough to think I could outrun them - whatever it is they are, but I could make it to civilization. I could make it to safety. To anyone.

The sound of my feet pounding the wooden pier below echoed in my skull. Despite the quiet Shockgrove evening, the sounds in my head were loud, violent, and terrifying.

I felt them then, their presence. It was all-consuming, intoxicating, and dangerous. I had once craved that feeling from them, but now it felt like a chain around my heart. Goosebumps erupted across my skin and the hairs on the back of my neck stood at attention. A mangled cry escaped my lips. I felt so hopeless, but still I pressed on.

They were going to catch me. I was going to die. But I was never going to stop running.

Leaving the pier, I hung a right and sprinted toward the lighthouse subconsciously, letting my feet take me through the fence and toward the tall white and blue structure. Slowly, I realized I had no plan. I was headed toward the cliff, a dead end. Just as I was deciding if I'd rather take my chances with the rocky coastline below or the creatures in pursuit, I saw a figure standing near the base of the lighthouse.

Hope blossomed in my chest.

"Help!" I screamed out, making a beeline for the figure. Whoever they were. They turned to face me and I got a quick glimpse of their dark hair under a baseball cap.

Relief flooded me, the man from the store. He stepped forward to meet me and I didn't bother stopping my trajectory, I slammed into his firm body and held on for dear life, violent cries falling from my lips.

"Whoa, um, are you ok?" The man, Archer, I think he said, put his strong hands on my shoulders and gently peeled me from his torso. Then and only then did I look back.

Their presence wasn't as strong anymore, maybe they had given up the chase. But either way, I scanned the area behind me with fervor. My chest rose and fell as I struggled to regulate my breathing, still ragged from the fear and the fastest mile of my life.

"Chased... they're..." I stopped. My words fell silent. They're what? What were they? I'd never seen anything like it before. Were they monsters? Yes, they had to be. That much was clear. But somewhere beneath the fear, beneath the obvious, I remembered the way Silas made me laugh, the way Samara comforted me, how Laz worshiped me, and Orpheus grounded me. How could I reconcile those creatures I saw, with pointed teeth and bloodthirsty gazes with my wanderers? The ones I was starting to... truly care for?

"Breathe, ok?" Archer spoke, drawing my eyes back to him and away from the empty town behind me. I followed his command and let my breathing return to a relatively normal pace, but my heart still sped within my chest. "Tell me what's wrong," he pleaded, his eyes also scanned the area as if he was looking for the threat. There was a slight tick to his jaw, and one of his hands came to rest on something on his hip. I didn't bother looking at what it was.

For a brief moment, panic seized my heart as a horrific thought came to me. What if I led the threat to him, what if Archer gets killed because of me?

"I..." What the hell was I supposed to say? 'I think the people I was sleeping with are inhuman monsters and then they started chasing me?' Not the most believable claim. While I took a few more calming breaths, and my sanity returned with each passing second, I thought carefully of my next move. "I saw something, like a big creature of some kind." That much was true. "I ran. It chased me."

Archer's eyebrows furrowed, but not in disbelief, more like he was trying to decipher my words.

"What kind of creature," he asked, the muscles in his arm tensing as his hand closed tighter around whatever it was he was holding at his side.

I panted, taking a steady step away from Archer and the intensity of his questioning glare. He seemed genuinely worried for me, which was a sweet notion, but he was a stranger and I was a raving lunatic who nearly tackled him.

"They were..." I stopped, his eyebrow rose in question. "I'm sorry, I wish I could describe it. I just... I didn't stop to take mental pictures, you know. I just ran." That was a lie of course. I'm not sure I could ever close my eyes again without seeing the image of their warped and terrifying forms burned on my eyelids. He nodded, seeming to accept that answer, then lifted the hem of his shirt to cover whatever he had hiding in the waistband of his pants. A gun maybe?

Why did that thought make me even more uncomfortable? I took a step back, assessing this new potentially threatening situation for the first time.

"You're safe, there's nothing here now," Archer confirmed in an authoritative voice. He seemed calm and collected, but on edge like he was preparing for the creature I spoke of to show its face.

"I'm sorry, you must think I'm crazy," I offered, pathetically. Archer looked down at me, his eyes harboring a hint of fear.

"I don't think you're crazy at all." He held my gaze and all I could think of was how nice it was to have someone believe me. That was not always the case. In fact, in this town, it was quite the opposite all those years ago when I told them what my stepfather had done to me. Instead of comforting words of encouragement, instead of support, I received accusatory looks and disbelief. But Archer wasn't giving me one of those looks I knew so well, the kind that had a sort of pity to them. No, this look was genuine and I knew, without a doubt, that he believed me. "It's Athena, right?"

I nodded, pressing a hand to my chest and feeling the beating there as it gradually slowed to a more appropriate resting rate.

"How many did you see? Was it just the one?" He asked, and I looked up at him again, hoping my wide-eyed reaction didn't give me away.

This man believed me, he believed I saw what I saw. He seemed actually interested in helping me. I could tell him the whole truth. Tell him what I saw, and what they looked like. I could give him names.

I could do that.

But I didn't.

I shook my head. "Just one," I lied. He nodded again, mentally filing away my answer.

"You're hurt," he said, pointing to my palm. Glancing down at the wound, I noticed it had stopped bleeding, but my run had splattered the red substance all across my arm and onto my shirt.

"Did you hurt yourself before or after you saw the creature?" he asked, eagerly. I glared at him in question. This stranger is asking the type of questions someone might ask if they knew something. Could he?

"Before," I claimed, gauging his reaction. His breath hitched in his throat and he nodded to himself continuously for a few seconds. He slid his backpack off his shoulders and placed it on the ground. Kneeling, he grabbed a small box from the pack. I tried not to glance inside as he unzipped, but curiosity got the better of me. I caught a glimpse of several paint-covered rags and the blue cap of what looked like a can of spray paint.

Maybe he was a graffiti painter who tagged buildings illegally, and that was why he was so cagey when I asked if he was an artist. He closed the bag quickly before I saw anything else and produced a small first-aid kit.

He handed me a wet wipe and I thanked him, getting to work on cleaning my skin of the blood. Then he handed me some antibacterial ointment and I carefully smoothed the cooling substance into my palm, ignoring the sting and focusing on forcing the memory of the roses from my mind.

How had the sweet, kind, protective individuals who brought me those roses become the stuff of nightmares? There was this blanket of fear cloaking me from seeing past those red orbs to the eyes I'd become so fascinated with within the last week. Their hands had claimed my flesh, their mouths had been on my center. They kissed my neck. A shiver wracked through me at that thought. Those fangs, they've been so close to me. They could have killed me.

But they didn't.

That doesn't matter. They're still monsters.

Right?

After cleaning the wound, he offered me a bandage and helped me wrap it around my hand and secure it on my palm.

Archer and I stood facing each other, and a strange energy was coursing between us, something like camaraderie. I liked it. After a few moments of silence, I realized I had no idea what to do next. They know where I live and where I work. I left the store unlocked. I can't go home. I can't be alone.

My breathing was shallow again all of a sudden and Archer caught the shift in my demeanor.

"Hey, it's ok," he cooed.

"I just realized I have to go back to the store and that's where... Um, that's where I saw it."

"I'll go with you," he offered, earnestly. I sighed, a weight lifting off my chest.

"Are you sure?" He nodded before I'd even finished the sentence.

"I won't let anything happen to you, I promise." It was a sweet gesture, one that made me feel safe and protected. And I think the fact that I could tell he was hiding his own fear made him seem even more trustworthy.

I nodded a few times, taking long languid breaths before turning to face the direction of the pier.

"You're ok, Athena. I promise." He knelt down, returning the kit to his backpack. He dug for a brief moment into the pack to grab what looked like a canister of pepper spray and then he stood, slinging the bag over his shoulder.

He caught me looking at it and shrugged. "Can't be too careful, right?" I found myself wondering if pepper spray would work on those creatures. Probably not, but it was better than nothing, right?

Together, we left the clearing at the base of the lighthouse and I tried not to let the memory of Silas' lips on mine the last time I was here distract me from the very real danger he posed to me.

Because he is dangerous. They all are.

I can't forget that.

Archer and I slipped through the fence and out onto the quiet Shockgrove streets. The sun was setting rapidly, and I couldn't ignore the dread that was enveloping me at the thought of being outside at night, with whatever they were on the loose.

The walk to the store was slow. My paranoia caused me to constantly look over each shoulder. On the plus side, Archer seemed to be reacting similarly to the threat, his eyes scanned the space methodically, almost militant. I then noticed the toned arms and the broad shoulders that held his tactical back-pack. Not to mention whatever weapon he had in his waistband.

I wanted to ask him if he was a soldier, but I couldn't bring myself to make a sound. I felt so exposed out here in the open, walking amongst the quiet store-fronts, venturing onto the pier. Toward the monsters.

The closer we got, the harder it was to breathe. Archer placed a comforting and encouraging hand on my shoulder and led me to the front door of my store. The fairy lights were on, the open sign hung in the window, and the stacks of books inside stood steadfast and unchanged. It looked as if nothing was different, but that wasn't true, was it?

There was nobody inside. At least not that I could see. I paused with my hand on the cool metal handle before pressing inside. The chiming of the bell frightened me and I jumped slightly as it rang out. Archer was close behind me, and again he squeezed my shoulder, encouraging me forward into the store.

The memory of what I saw here only minutes ago felt so visceral, and yet so blurry at the same time. Like a dream.

A nightmare.

Everything was unchanged, except for me. I was changed.

The single pink rose I had left behind on my way out was gone, but the bouquet atop the counter remained in its vase. I hated the way my confused heart leaped at the sight of them.

Was it fear that made my heart beat faster, or something else entirely?

"Lock this door," he said pointing to the front door. I did. flipping the sign and securing the metal gate in its place. "I'm going to sweep the place, don't go far." Archer moved forward, disappearing into the stacks of books. Just as he rounded the corner I swear I saw him reach for whatever he had tucked in his waistband. I moved to the cash drawer quickly. Thankful for the first time all off-season for the slow day that made the final count incredibly simple. I secured the cash into the safe in the office and by the time I returned to the cash register, Archer was back. Whatever weapon he had grabbed was hidden again, but he still had that canister of spray in his hand. A faint smell of garlic pervaded the air.

"There's nothing here. We're safe, but it's getting dark and we should head out. Do you have someplace safe to stay tonight?"

I nodded. Davia would let me stay over without a doubt.

"Good, I'll walk you there."

I pulled my phone from my pocket and shot off a text.

ATHENA: Can I sleep at yours tonight?

DAVIA: You never have to ask that. But why?

ATHENA: I just don't wanna be alone.

DAVIA: None of your new fuck buddies wanna volunteer to keep you company?

ATHENA: I think I need my best friend tonight.

DAVIA: Then get your ass over here. I'll cue up Love Island.

I smiled for the first time since before seeing the real faces of the people I was falling for. It felt foreign on my face, but I enjoyed the hopeful bloom in my chest nonetheless.

After shutting the lights off and locking the back door behind us, the two of us headed back down the pier toward town. The red-orange light was fading with each step giving way to the soft glow of the stars and moonlight. With each inch that the sun sunk, my fear ramped up just as much. There was an almost inhuman quality to the stillness in town. Like the ghost town from all those horror films. I tried to keep my overactive mind from filling in the blanks of the story that was unfolding with images of death, blood and fear.

Was I the unsuspecting human who was seduced by the creatures only to be their victim? I shivered at the way that thought made me feel. I'd told them about my own issues with being a victim. They know I've had my own run-in with monsters in my past. Why now, were they here doing this to me, again?

I never wanted to be a victim again. I never wanted to feel helpless, like I had that night.

I led Archer through the streets toward Davia's house. Archer remained vigilant and I couldn't express how much it meant to me to have someone so clearly devoted to keeping me safe.

I just hoped this one didn't turn out to be a monster too.

Even I have to admit my track record isn't the most promising.

When we turned down Davia's driveway, the sun had completely disappeared behind the horizon and I felt a chill crawl down my spine.

"Thank you, Archer. You have no idea what you've done for me tonight." He nodded, a soft smile gracing his lips.

"I'm just glad you're safe." He sounded like he meant it. "Listen, if you see anything else I want you to text me, ok?" He was reaching into his backpack, grabbing a pen and a scrap of paint-stained paper. He scribbled a number and handed it to me. He must have seen the apprehension in my gaze as I looked at his outstretched hand because he quickly added, "I'm not hitting on you in a moment of vulnerability if that's what you're worried about. I just want to make sure you're ok." There wasn't a hint of manipulation in his gaze or tone, so I was inclined to believe him. I grabbed the number and nodded.

"It, um, well it means a lot that you believed me," I whispered the confession into the quiet night air. Archer sighed, not in pity, but something else colored his expression.

"I've seen my fair share of monsters," he said with a small melancholic chuckle. I watched his dark eyebrows scrunch together as he took a contemplative moment to gather his thoughts.

"Me too," I admitted, but it wasn't the transformed, blood-thirsty faces of the wanderers that I thought of, it was *his*.

His charming smile, the deep dimple, the perfectly coiffed blonde hair. He was one of those all-American homegrown hero types. The kind that had such a perfectly crafted and iron-clad public persona that nobody could even imagine their perfect golden boy was a villain behind closed doors. Mom fell for his charms, hell, we all did.

"Have a goodnight, Athena." Archer began back down the driveway, his eyes returned to their scan of the surrounding area.

"Be careful, Archer." He looked over his shoulder briefly and smiled.

"Always am." As he continued down the street, I watched him go, and found myself increasingly nervous for his safety. Maybe I should have told him the full truth so he could be prepared. Walking alone at night with *them* on the loose could potentially be life-threatening for him. But something about him told me he could handle his own.

Once my most recent savior was out of eyesight, I felt the eerie chill return, as if there were eyes watching me. I quickly slipped into Davia's home and locked the deadbolt. Leaning my forehead against the wooden frame, I sighed, releasing tension I didn't even realize had been gathering in my tight shoulders. An almost suspicious feeling gripped my heart. Why have I been so willing to place my trust in strangers who save me? Maybe I should have been more careful with Archer. I certainly should have been with the others.

A sinking feeling erupted in my chest at the thought of sharing my body with them...whatever they are. Although, beneath the fear and disgust there was another, heated emotion. Something that felt wrong, and dangerous, but exciting.

"Athena, that you babe?" Davia's voice called from the living room. Composing myself, I turned on a heel and walked in to greet my best friend.

A night with Davia was exactly what I needed. Despite the growing fear in the pit of my stomach and my jumpiness at every little sound, she had me laughing and relaxing within an hour. She didn't ask questions or comment on my obvious nervousness, which continued to be one of my favorite things about her. Eventually, I started to feel a little more back to normal, except for that soft nagging voice in my mind.

Just as I was beginning to feel like I was back on solid ground, my phone buzzed with an incoming call. Before even looking at the name on the screen, I knew who it was. Dread filled my heart and my palms were sweating as I lifted the phone to check the source of the call.

SILAS

I watched the name on the phone flash as the vibrations numbed my hand. I was still lost somewhere between fear and anger. They had lied to me. Had deceived me. Had hidden who they were.

I let the call go to voicemail, but I only had a moment of reprieve before the phone was ringing again.

I watched the call continue again, Davia's voice as she explained what was happening on the screen was a distant echo. Another minute passed and he called again. This time, instead of letting the phone ring, I pressed the power button, sending him to voicemail after a single ring, hoping that sent him the message.

A moment later, a text arrived.

> SILAS: Athena, please let us explain.

I swallowed the lump in my throat and took a few steadying breaths as another number joined the barrage.

> LAZ: Darlin', where are you? We should talk.

> SILAS: Bookworm, please. It's me.

My heart tightened, I drew my knees up to my chest and hugged them, reading and rereading their words. A tear slid down my cheek.

SILAS: I need to talk to you.

LAZ: It isn't what it looked like.

The anger that was already pooling in my chest was burning brighter with each text.

SILAS: Baby girl, text me back.

Trying to command me? Fury grabbed the wheel and I found myself excusing myself to go to the restroom. By the time I was leaning over the sink with my hands on the vanity, I had several more text messages.

SILAS: We would never hurt you.

SILAS: I'm sorry we scared you.

LAZ: I swear you're safe with us.

SILAS: We need you.

I saw the bubble, informing me they were texting again, but before he got the chance to send it, I blocked their numbers. There was a quiet relief in that silence.

It was a hollow victory.

On one hand, I needed this space. On the other, something told me that whatever they are, they're not going to be deterred by a simple block button. But tonight? Tonight, it was enough for me.

I returned to the living room and when Davia talked about the hot couple on the tv screen and their dramatic relationship troubles, I listened.

2

SILAS

he world was black and white before. I only thought I had experienced the joy of color, but the moment the scent of her blood reached my nose everything exploded into vibrant rich hues and I quickly realized I had never experienced what it meant to 'live' in my long life. The light felt brighter, and the smells were stronger. Hell, even the air on my skin felt softer, like a careful embrace. It was more. Everything felt...more. But it wasn't *everything* I was feeling, seeing, smelling... It was her. Her scent was thick, it invaded every single one of my senses, holding me in a vice grip. Wintergreen. Fresh, vibrant, and cozy. Sensual. Her blood called to me like a siren song, I'd welcome the depths of the ocean if it meant I could have a taste of the blood that ran in her veins, and the woman who owns my soul.

My vision zeroed in on her. There was no past, no future. There was only this moment. Heedlessly, I watched her. Her flushed skin, her perfect red hair. I needed her. My cock strained against my pants and my fangs ached with the need to sink into her perfect skin and drink the sinful elixir.

I knew then for a fact, a confirmation of what my soul already knew, this human was my mate. The one for whom I was created. The other half of my existence. I was incomplete without her, a shell of who I was destined to be. I belonged to her, mind, body, and soul. I would go to the ends of the Earth to protect her, to find her. To worship her. There was nothing in the world that could keep me from her.

So why the fuck was she running away from me?

She darted from the bookstore and I was so caught off guard that I couldn't move for a moment, a frustrated groan escaping my lips. My logic was locked in a cage of mindlessness. There was no rhyme, no reason, only her. My fingers gripped the stem of the now blood-covered rose. Her scent was addictive, beckoning me to have a taste. But no, the first taste I have of her will be directly from the source, not lapping drops from the thorn in my hand. I sprinted in the direction she retreated, only vaguely aware of my companions who were quick to follow along. Her long red hair bounced with each stride as she ran down the pier, away from me.

That simply wouldn't do.

I could catch her in a few seconds. I could have her blood on my tongue in a moment, driving my cock into her heat. She could be mine.

Just as I prepared to dart forward and catch up to her, I felt a powerful palm against my chest.

A growl wretched itself from my throat at whoever it was who dared to keep me from my Athena. My eyes settled on the figure before me.

"All of you, stop! Right now!" Her voice was strong, familiar enough to give me pause, but in the fog of the mate bond, I wasn't able to place it entirely. My eyes glanced after my mate again.

"Fucking stop! You're terrifying her!"

I cocked my head, how could my mate be afraid of me? I was her mate. I was made for her. It didn't make sense.

"Snap the fuck out of it, right now!"

I felt the hand on my chest push back harder and the sensation was almost grounding. The red vignette of my vision slowly receded with every step she took away from me.

I pressed forward against the hold on my chest because suddenly my mate was too far from me and I couldn't understand why.

"Silas, please!" The voice, Samara, I think, pleaded. "Laz, shake it off. Fuck. Orpheus. Help me."

I knew those names. They meant a lot to me, I think. Not as much as Athena. Hers was the only name that truly meant anything and ever would again. I needed her blood. Immediately. With every fiber of my existence. If I didn't, I would cease to be.

"Damnit," Orpheus exclaimed. I didn't turn to look at him though. My eyes were still trained on my mate as she ran. "God Damnit!" He yelled again.

"Shake it off, Orpheus, and fucking help me. If they go after her like this, they'll kill her."

At merely the thought of Athena in pain, I felt the world snap back into focus, the red film the world had taken on dissipated, and the fog of mindless want and need started to recede. My fangs retracted, and my fingernails returned to their normal length and suddenly, I had regained a hold on my actions. And the reality of what I had been prepared to do hit me.

"Shit," I exhaled a long breath, feeling the effects of the forced shift.

Samara sighed with relief, letting her hand drop from my chest. I glanced around at my companions, each of them breathless and tired. Their eye color had reverted to normal, but they were sunken, hollow. I'd never seen Orpheus look so...out of place.

"Thank you, Samara," Laz said, placing a hand on her shoulder. She nodded, focusing on her breathing. Again, I found myself utterly amazed by her willpower.

I glanced down the pier, noticing Athena had disappeared around the corner.

Fuck.

We shifted in front of her.

And we all...

Double fuck.

I was hit with an intense wave of hunger as the aroma of her blood called to me from the pink rose in my hand. I felt my already delicate will being tested. The barrier between myself and my monster was so thin it was nearly nonexistent.

Before I could fall even further back into the mindset of lost control, the rose was ripped from my hands. I growled as Orpheus tossed it over the ledge into the ocean below.

"You were losing it," Orpheus claimed, although, from his ragged breathing and strained voice, I knew I wasn't the only one.

"We need to get home now. We all need blood," Samara winced as if merely speaking the words was painful. A deep grumble sounded in my chest at the idea of drinking blood that wasn't Athena's, but I knew she was right. If we had followed through, the four of us? We would have killed her.

Samara kept us from doing that.

It was tense, and we had to hold our breath as we sprinted away so as not to scent her as we made our way back to our rental. Every step in the direction opposite of Athena was painful, it was like there was this hook in my soul begging to drag me back to her, but I knew I needed to get this hunger under control before we spoke to her again. After what she saw, we had a lot of explaining to do. We needed a clear and collected head to do that. Who knows how strong her pull will be the next time we see her? We need to be prepared.

There were only a few flasks left from Orpheus and Samara's trip to the city. We each grabbed one and gulped down every unsatisfactory drop, but it tasted wrong somehow. It filled my stomach and satisfied my hunger, for now, but my nearly-dead heart was begging for something else. Something I couldn't offer.

We had denied the nature of the mate bond, and somewhere in my mind, I knew we would face serious repercussions for that. The fact that I had just drank an entire flask of blood and could already feel the slight pang of hunger in my stomach was one issue.

The way I was so desperate for my mate that I felt the shift constantly dancing just beneath my skin was another.

"Fuck, this cannot be happening," Orpheus mumbled, his hands running through his hair as he paced the living room. Laz was rubbing their face in their palms anxiously.

"Except it is," Samara interjected, sinking onto the couch, her composure returning. I made my way across the room to her, sliding down onto my knees in front of where she sat.

"Thank you for stopping us," I whispered. Orpheus and Laz both paused, turning their gazes to watch our exchange.

Samara sighed, a tired smile playing on her lips. "You're welcome."

"How did you regain control?" Orpheus asked, coming to a stop near the edge of the couch. Laz leaned against the wall across the room, listening intently.

"It was blinding. The want," she started. I nodded, understanding completely. "We chased after her, but when we got outside, in the fresh air, I felt like I could breathe a little. Then reality hit me. Breaking through the frenzy."

My breath hitched at the memory of how mindless I had become, how willing I was to chase Athena and sink my teeth into her without any regard. I shuttered.

"There was a voice screaming at me, telling me that if we went through with it, we would kill her."

Laz, Orpheus, and I all growled at that sentiment.

"I think I was able to break free because I was reminded of how it felt to lose the love of my life. The memory of the pain and the desperate need to avoid ever feeling it again was what brought me back."

Silence filled the room as the four of us exchanged knowing glances. This new development not only changed our present but our future. There was no plan anymore. There was no more running away. We all knew it.

I allowed a moment of reflection before I spoke again. "Multiple mates," I barely murmured, but they all heard me.

It wasn't impossible, but unlikely. Especially for who we were. We weren't from any royal line, and while we were powerful individuals we weren't the most powerful of our kind by any stretch of the definition. Not when there are some vamps who have the ability to literally alter time and space. There was no logical explanation for why Athena Landry, a human from the middle of nowhere, was now at the center of our coven. The keystone to our delicate structure.

"I need to do some research," Orpheus exclaimed, angrily. I could see the delicate hold he had on his control and how close he was to losing himself again.

"I'll help you," I offered, standing up and making my way to him.

"I don't know much, but I know we can't deny the bond for long without experiencing ramifications." He grabbed the knot of his tie and pulled it down, removing it over his head. His collar was crumpled, and I took in the sight of him. Orpheus had never been this off-kilter before. I'd say we were dealing with the ramifications already.

"We can accept the bond tomorrow. After we feed again just to be safe," Laz piped in eagerly.

I nodded.

"You're all forgetting something."

Our heads turned toward Samara who had stood from the couch. She placed a hand on her chest and breathed slowly.

"She saw us shift, she's afraid of us. She won't let us anywhere near her."

A whimper escaped my mouth at the thought of Athena being afraid of me. Doesn't she understand I am her protector?

I reached for my phone then, seeing Laz do the same out of the corner of my eye. I called her. It rang for what felt like hours until it went to voicemail.

"Hi! You've reached Athena."

I felt my heartbeat in a single powerful thump at the sound of her voice. How had I ever not had that voice in my life?

"I'm sorry I couldn't answer the phone, but go ahead and leave a message!"

I hung up before the tone. When I said what I needed to say to her, I needed to know she was listening. I called again. Each ring felt like she was slipping away from me.

And again. When the third call was sent to voicemail directly, I felt a desperate fear grip my soul. I texted her, ignoring the questions slinging my way from Orpheus and Samara.

SILAS: Athena, please let us explain.

She had to give us that. She knew us. She knew who we were. She had rested her head on my chest, she had cried with me, she had screamed my name. She knew. She had to.

SILAS: Bookworm, please. It's me.

I was slipping into a frenzy, different from the one from before. This one was the flailing dance of a man who felt his whole heart being ripped away from him. I was only slightly aware Laz was also glued to their phone. Were they getting an answer?

SILAS: I need to talk to you.

Orpheus grunted in anger, and I heard the crashing of something against a wall and pieces of glass clattering to the floor. I was only vaguely aware of Samara comforting him.

SILAS: Baby girl, text me back.

I was running out of excuses to not run to her house right now and beg her to listen to me, but even through the fear of losing her, I knew she needed time to process what she saw and come to us on her own terms.

SILAS: We would never hurt you.

I hated that I had to even remind her of that. She should already know I'd never do anything that brought harm to her. She was everything to me. She will always be everything to me.

SILAS: I'm sorry we scared you.

Please answer me.

SILAS: We need you.

Each unanswered text was a scar on my heart. I glanced up at Samara who was doing her best to calm a raging Orpheus. Laz looked nearly as dejected as I felt, so I could imagine they had the same amount of luck getting through to her as I did.

I let my thumbs fly across the keyboard and typed another response.

When my phone buzzed with a message I gasped, my entire body flooded with endorphins. Everyone was to me in a flash, gathering around trying to peek a look at the screen.

"What did she say?" Laz.

"Is she ok?" Samara.

"Where is she?" Orpheus.

I flipped to the message and felt the venomous blood drain from my face, the pit in my stomach deepening.

Just like that, my already dead heart broke into a million pieces.

3

ATHENA

I didn't go home for two days.

I stayed with Davia, who only asked a few questions to ensure I was safe. I wasn't sure how to answer her, but I assured her I was ok. Whatever that meant. Grandma worked The Maine Plotline on her own, which made me feel horrible, but the idea of returning there nearly had me spiraling into a panic. I wasn't ready to face them again.

Not the monsters from that night, or the saviors from the bar. I couldn't face either version of them.

I tried to do research, but I had no idea what to search for. I didn't exactly understand what I saw, so I had no idea what words to even use to describe it. Turns out though there was a whole message board site dedicated to the sightings of monsters these people described as something eerily similar to what I had seen.

I read a lot. And no, not just smutty romance books. I read non-fiction, and contemporary, even books for knowledge, not pleasure. I feel like I have a rather wide range of understanding with which I use to view the world. That is why it is so disconcerting to be forced to rework the way I looked at my existence, to shift how I saw everything. If monsters exist, then what else is out there?

On the morning of the third day, I was exhausted from the night before when I spent countless hours scrolling through the message board. Scrolling past pictures of missing people whom others were convinced were taken by the creatures of the night. Some swore they saw werewolves out in the woods at night, complete with blurry pictures to 'prove' it. Others were adamant they had experienced alien interference. Ghosts, Gollums, Witches... reading the erratic wordy claims of these individuals a week ago would have made me laugh, but now all I could think of is how I would sound if I were to describe what I had seen. I typed it once. Fully prepared to anonymously post it to the board in hopes someone could give me answers, but it was so unbelievable I ended up deleting the entire thing and tossing my phone across the room for a solid hour before the potential answers the message board housed called to me again.

There was a knock on the front door and I heard Davia venturing to answer it. I tidied up her guest room, bracing myself to leave the house today when she called for me.

"Athena, someone's here to see you, babe."

Everything stilled. The blood in my veins, the beating of my heart. I felt each individual pump as if it were the drum pounding, beckoning me to my execution. Had they finally gotten tired of me hiding? Were they going to kill me for what I saw?

Fear froze me in my spot for a few moments until an unsettling thought entered my mind. What if they hurt Davia? Suddenly, I was jogging out of the guest room and making my way to the front door, expecting to confront the very demons that had entered my heart and my bed before revealing their true face.

But it wasn't them that was waiting for me just beyond the threshold. My relief lasted only a second before the two individuals standing on the porch flashed their badges to me. A sinking feeling rushed through me and suddenly I felt my very foundation shift.

"Athena Landry?" The woman closest to me said, her light brown hair pulled back in a bun, accentuating her angular features. I nodded, unable to use my mouth. "My name is Detective Barnes, and this is my partner Detective Argent." She nodded to the stout man to her left. He had dusty blonde hair that was combed back. They both wore dark black slacks and dress shirts. I swallowed the lump in my throat and nodded my acknowledgment.

"We have some questions we'd like to ask you, mind if we come in?"

I glanced over to Davia, who looked calm and collected despite the law enforcement officers standing a few feet from her. She nodded, ushering them inside. I stepped to the side, letting the two brush past me. Claustrophobia blanketed me the moment they were in my space like their mere presence was suffocating.

Davia sent a reassuring glance in my direction before shutting the door and following the detectives into the living area. The two of them took seats on the large beige couch.

"Can I get you anything to drink?" Davia asked, ever the gracious host. The two politely declined and Davia took a seat on the loveseat and gestured for me to join her. I hadn't realized my feet were cemented to their spot near the door. I took a settling breath then made my way to the loveseat, sinking onto the cushion next to my best friend. Her steadying presence was comforting despite the pairs of accusatory eyes that were now analyzing my every move.

"Miss Landry, do you know this man?" Detective Barnes asked, drawing a picture out of a folder at her side and sliding it across the coffee table toward me. Louis' smug smiling face looked up at me from the portrait and I hated the way even a picture of him made me feel weak.

"I've met him once, yes," I answered. I felt Davia's hand squeeze my thigh and I let her reassurance calm me.

"He was reported missing by his friend Mr. Greg Holden. When was the last time you saw Mr. Dells?"

Dells. Louis Dells. A weird sense of comfort floats over me, knowing the name of my villain. There's power in names. Rumplestiltskin could tell you that.

"Last Friday night, at the Craving Crab."

The stout man took some notes on a small flip notebook as Detective Barnes kept eye contact with me.

"Did you two leave the bar together?"

I tried not to let the memory of stumbling out the front door and into the dark alley enter my mind. I could tell them the truth right now. Tell them what really happened to me. Maybe they'd be sympathetic. Maybe they'd believe me.

But they didn't the last time.

My hands were sweating, and the skin around my fingers had been nearly completely peeled off, a nervous habit that had only been exacerbated by this entire ordeal. Mom sat outside the interrogation room, her simmering anger was a constant presence today, never directed at me, but I couldn't help but feel like I had played a crucial part in the events that led to her current state of mind. The older gentleman sat across the metallic table from me, his grey mustache was long and hanging over his upper lip as he took a sip of his coffee.

"That's how it happened," I finished, timidly. It was the first time I was taking my experience to the authorities. It took nearly a month to gather the courage to tell Davia, and a few weeks after that for her to convince me to tell Mom. It was a night he had to work late. I remember standing on the edge of the kitchen, watching her as she danced freely to the music playing from the baby blue record player while she

cooked. I loathed the idea of ruining her lightheartedness. Ruining her relationship. Her life. But I had to do it. I had to tell her. It wasn't my job to protect her from the truth, it was my job to protect her from the monster living and lying in our house.

After a long night of tears, reassurances, and promises. We got a room at the motel, and she asked me to write it all down. Every word, every moment. I hated it. Of course, I hated reliving the worst night of my life, but it was watching her face as she read the words that hurt me the most. Seeing her face fall, no matter how hard she tried to stay neutral for me when she read the things he said, the things he did. The way he stole my innocence out from underneath her nose. No matter how many times I told her it was not her fault, I could tell she believed it less and less each time I uttered the words.

She woke me up the next morning with breakfast from the continental buffet in the lobby and then told me she wanted to take me to the police station. I argued, of course, fear coursing through me, but she convinced me it was the right thing to do. She told me he should not be allowed to get away with what he did to me. She spoke with such fire and such passion that I believed her. I believed her when she said that others would want to protect me too.

It wasn't her fault she was wrong.

"Your father is a good man," the detective replied. My skin crawled.

"Stepfather," I corrected, meekly, with only a fraction of the ire I felt.

"I know how some kids get jealous when their parents remarry." He leaned back in his chair, nonchalantly and relaxed, like I hadn't just rehashed the entirety of my horrific assault for him moments ago.

"I'm not...I wasn't jealous." I stuttered through the words. Why was I defending my story? Why was he questioning me?

"Listen, I know him and there's no way he did what you're claiming. You teenagers need to learn not to make these false accusations just cause you're upset. You could ruin his life with talk like this." He took another languid sip of his coffee and my jaw fell open.

"You think I'm lying?" I asked although I didn't need to. It was all over his face.

"I think you're acting out because your Mom hasn't been paying you enough attention. See it all the time. Most try underage drinking and smoking before they go flinging baseless accusations around."

I felt my whole body tense, anger, fear, fury.

"I'm not lying. He did this. He actually... He drugged me."

The detective leaned forward on the table.

"And conveniently you waited over a month to come and report it? When we couldn't do a blood test to confirm your story." The way he said 'story' made it sound like I had told him a bedtime tale. Something insignificant. Not the biggest, most traumatic event I've ever had to endure.

"You're not going to do anything?" I asked, tears falling steadily down my face.

"Of course, I'm gonna do something." Relief. "I'm going to tell your daddy what you're lying about so he can discipline you." Fear. Unrelenting, uncontrollable, fear. Sobs ripped from my throat. "The police are here to help you when there are real problems, girl. You need to learn not to waste our time with lies."

The next hour was a blur. Mom was screaming at the detective, being restrained and then he came. At first, he looked terrified, like maybe he'd been caught and this was his end. I relished that look on his face. The guilt painted on every expression he made. But quickly enough he discovered just how wrong he was to be afraid. His perfect mask was firmly in place and he had the audacity to apologize to the detective that his wife and daughter took up his time with this. The graying detective shook his hand, muttering something about going golfing when he gets a handle on the two of us. I felt sick to my stomach and bile rose in my throat.

Mom refused to go home with him there. He rolled his eyes, denying every single thing I had admitted. But she did not back down. She believed me with every breath in her body and not once did doubt creep its way in.

Every once in a while, I felt him cast a disapproving glare in my direction as if I was the one in the wrong. As if I had broken some sort of silent twisted promise by revealing his true nature.

Fucking lot of good that did.

Mom and I moved in with Grandma when the divorce process began. It got messy, only in the sense that the entire town knew about it. The rumors ranged all over the board, but always painted Mom and me as ungrateful liars, the promiscuous whores. In every version, he was the one who was wronged. In every version, he was the victim.

The stares and whispers continued for years, every time I went to school I'd feel their stares on the side of my face, and hear their words in the hall. People would come into The Maine Plotline, only to get a good look at us, like the circus freaks we were. It didn't help that he still retained his portion of the business from the divorce. For years, I'd see him, work with him, and feel his eyes on me as I grew up. He finally moved out once the divorce was final and let us move back into my childhood home, but it felt tainted somehow. Mom did her best to keep us separated, but without the support of the law, there was little she could do besides get into screaming matches with him when he showed his face. Do you know how horrible it is to see your tormentor every single day and know that nobody who could do a damn thing about it cared enough to try?

When Grandma found a discrepancy in the books it felt like the universe was finally throwing us a proverbial bone. The trial was quick, painless even. The amount of clear evidence we had found in the financials of the store was enough to put him away for a long time.

The worst part?

Even when the town found out about his illegal activities, he was still the golden boy. The town still came to his defense. No one admitted he may have been the one who lied all those years ago.

The villain was the victim until the very end, and the victim was forgotten.

"We walked outside together, but we went our separate ways in the parking lot," I said finally. I knew the truth, and while I hated the idea of another monster like him roaming the streets, I couldn't be 'the girl who cried rapist' in this town again.

"Did you see where he went?"

What was it Silas had said? I wracked my brain.

"I think he was headed to the gas station down on the corner of 5th and Lake."

More notes.

"Why are you not staying at your own home, Miss Landry?" We've been trying to find you for two days now," the stout one piped up.

"I had a fight with someone I was seeing and needed some time to recoup," I admitted, willing the images of the four wanderers to stay locked away.

"It's rather convenient," he started, "that you go into hiding after Mr. Holden visited you to tell you about Louis' disappearance."

"I did not go into hiding," I asserted.

"You didn't return home for two days, Miss Landry. The timing of that is-"

"I am here at my best friend's house. A friend that I publicly and frequently am seen with. There isn't a person in this town who couldn't make an educated guess as to my whereabouts. If I were trying to hide, I chose a pretty shitty spot." I was seething. I was tired of the police accusing the wrong fucking people.

"Please don't get hostile, Miss Landry," he offered, casually, making my blood boil again. His stupid face reminded me of that aloof bastard sitting across the metallic table from me in that fucking interrogation room.

"Louis and I said maybe twenty words to each other the entire night. I bought my own drinks because I knew the second he walked through the doors that I wanted nothing to do with him. When I left, we went our separate ways and I've never seen him again." I stood up, feeling years' worth of pent-up distrust and anger fueling me.

Detective Barnes stood to make eye contact with me. She smiled softly. "You are not a suspect, Miss Landry. We are not even sure he didn't run away of his own volition. We are simply trying to get all the information we can."

I nodded to her. She seemed to be the most level-headed of the two. I wondered what might have changed if I had taken my report all those years ago to a female. Would I have been heard? Would she have believed me? Would we both be buried by a man with more power?

"Do you have anyone who can corroborate your story?"

I swallowed, turning my head to Davia. She nodded, urging me on. Her face was stoic, but I could tell she was fuming beneath the surface.

"There were four people in the bar who were just passing through town. They saw us go our separate ways." She nodded, indicating to Detective Argent to take down that note. He stood and leveled his stare at me.

"Do you know how we might be able to contact them?" He asked.

I thought for a moment about lying, and protecting their identities, which was utterly confusing, but then a sickening thought occurred to me. What if they were lying? What if they didn't let Louis go?

Pulling my phone from my pocket, I offered up Silas' phone number without offering their names.

"Thought they were strangers just passing through?" Argent mused in an accusatory tone.

"They were until I started sleeping with them." I saw Detective Barnes' eyebrows shoot up at my confession. Davia stifled a laugh to my side. "You'll understand when you see them." I tacked on.

As Davia ushered the two detectives out the front door I found myself truly struggling to rectify that the people who saved me from Louis were the monsters I saw. But they were. I had seen it. I felt them chase me.

But if they were truly monsters, they could have caught me.

If they wanted me dead. They could have found me.

"We'll be in touch," Detective Barnes promised as she crossed the threshold. "Please give me a call if you think of anything else." She handed me a card.

"Don't leave town," Detective Argent added, unhelpfully. The two of them sauntered down the driveway to their black sedan parked on the curb and Davia and I watched them pull away before slowly retreating into the safety of the house.

"Are you ok?" Davia asked. She had intimate knowledge of my personal experience with law enforcement.

"I just hope they find him soon so I never have to hear his fucking name again." I offered with a little too much anger. I sighed, remembering I hadn't told Davia everything that happened that night.

"You know, just cause I'm headed out of town for this stupid summit, doesn't mean you can't stay." She meant it. And that made me feel safe.

"Thanks for letting me stay here, Davia, but I think it's time for me to rejoin society."

She smiled softly. "You're welcome to *hide* here anytime you need to." She laughed as she emphasized the word. I threw my arms around her shoulders and drew her into a tight embrace.

I made my way back to the guest room to pack up and get ready for a day at The Maine Plotline. My first day back since... Since them.

Was I ready to see them?

No.

Was I missing them?

Maybe.

I'd never felt this confused in my life.

I pulled my phone from my pocket and made my way to my jacket which was slung over the arm of the accent chair in the corner. I dug through the pockets until I found what I was looking for. A moment later, I was typing in the number that was scrawled across the slip of paper into my phone.

> ATHENA: Archer. Hi. It's Athena.

It was a few moments before I saw his response come in.

> ARCHER: I was wondering if I'd hear from you. How are you?

How was I?

Confused, angry, afraid, utterly lost. But he didn't need to know that.

> ATHENA: Still trying to understand.

> ARCHER: I get it.

> ATHENA: I figured you might.

Which was a strange thought because I barely knew this guy.

> ARCHER: You ever heard Float On?

> ATHENA: Modest Mouse? I'm offended you think there's a chance I haven't.

> ARCHER: Didn't wanna assume and embarrass you in case you had shitty musical taste.

I laughed. A full, belly-shaking kind of laugh. It felt good, albeit misplaced.

ATHENA: Of course, I've heard the song.

ARCHER: Listen to it again.

I don't know why, but I did. Pressing play, I tossed my phone onto the bedspread and fell backward onto the mattress, closed my eyes, and let the song envelop me.

Three minutes and thirty seconds later, I released the breath I had been holding. A cleansing one. I felt like I had been given the world's most mellow pep talk. Smiling, I reached for my phone.

ATHENA: Thank you.

ARCHER: Have you seen anything since that night?

ATHENA: I haven't left the house, truthfully.

ARCHER: Understandably.

ATHENA: You really don't think I'm crazy?

I waited with bated breath. Worry rushed over me. He had seemed truly understanding the night he walked me here. Never once making me feel like I wasn't worthy of being believed. Which was a really nice feeling.

ARCHER: Not in the slightest.

I didn't take the time to think about it that night, and how quickly he trusted me because at the time it meant the world to me. But I would be lying if I didn't admit that here in the light of a new day, it was a little strange he didn't question it once. He heard me speak of a monster and instead of questioning it, he gripped his weapon and walked me home.

Did he know more than he was letting on? Was he a paranoid nut-job, or did he have a deeper understanding of the world that I could only ever dream of?

ATHENA: I'm rejoining the land of the living today though.

ARCHER: Definitely a better place to be.

I chuckled lightly, but there was that slightly nagging feeling in my chest that told me there was a chance he wasn't joking.

ARCHER: Are you nervous?

ATHENA: Yes.

I sighed, finishing packing the final items from around the room into the bag that Davia let me borrow. I'd take the clothes she lent me home and wash them before returning them. Although, I loved the soft off-the-shoulder blue and white floral shirt she gave me to wear today. It reminded me of something Mom would have worn. Maybe Davia would let me keep this one.

ARCHER: Want me to walk you to work?

Did I? On one hand. I needed to go back to my real life and stop being so afraid. On the other hand, if I was going to be confronted by...*them*... it was entirely possible it would occur at the store where I last saw them.

ATHENA: I don't want to inconvenience you.

Which was the truth, but also I was silently hoping he'd do it anyway.

ARCHER: You still at the place I left you at?

ATHENA: Yeah.

ARCHER: Be there in 10.

I smiled at the phone, and slowly relief began to replace the cloud of fear that had been present for who knows how long. I took the next few minutes mentally preparing myself to exit the safety of this oasis for the first time in two sheltered days.

Venturing out to the living room, I saw Davia had dressed for work and was gathering her things into her large grey messenger bag. Her small black suitcase sat by the door. She had her blonde hair curled slightly, the top layer twisted up in a claw clip at the back of her hair. She wore a light pink dress with a grey overcoat which traveled down to her knees.

I used to think Davia was the most attractive person I'd ever seen in real life. And while she was undoubtedly, and annoyingly, stunning...I couldn't help but feel my mind flash to the faces - well the normal faces - of my wanderers.

No. Not mine.

I thought of Samara's flawless skin, and the way her eyes managed to make me feel like she actually *saw* me. All of me. I thought of Silas' powerful tattooed hands, the way they possessed my body in a way I'd never thought I'd want to feel again. But it was a worshiping connection, the type of domination that reminded me with each punishing touch that it was *I* who held the power. I thought of Laz's loving gaze, the way their soft hair fell so delicately across their forehead when they looked at me with what felt like an emotion I was not, and would never be, worthy of. I thought of Orpheus. Of his dark black eyes. Of his overwhelming scent. The way he so clearly understood how to calm me. As if he knew my soul more intimately than I could ever hope to.

I thought of them all. Their bodies, their souls. I had been drawn to them from the moment I saw them. Was that because of *who* they were? Or *what* they were?

Did it matter?

Maybe.

No.

I don't know.

"Are you ready?" Davia asked from over by the couch. I was shaken from my internal dilemma, the mental pictures of my wanderers slipping away.

"I have to be."

She nodded. She had been so wonderful these past few days, but I knew her nosy-by-nature personality was on the verge of exploding. "I got into a fight with them," I stated. Davia stopped to look at me. "I was falling too hard, too fast and I realized I didn't even know them. I needed to take a step back. To find myself again. Clear-headed."

She pursed her lips, seemingly absorbing this new development.

"Need me to kick their ass?"

I chuckled, before crossing to her and pulling her into a hug. She held onto me. "I could take most of them, I bet."

The humor dissipated and I pulled back, suddenly worried for her safety. Davia was one hundred percent the type of friend to confront them if she ever saw them about town, and while they hadn't come to hurt me, yet, that didn't mean anything when it came to her.

"Promise me you won't, ok?" I urged, infusing as much seriousness as I could into the warning. "Promise me."

Her face fell. "Are you scared of them, babe? Did they do something?" I saw the fire building in her eyes. Was I afraid? I was. Yes. But am I still? Working on it.

"No, nothing like that. I swear."

She sighed.

"I just...I don't think I'm ready to burn any bridges with them and that would be hard if you go over there pouring kerosene all over the place."

She smirked. "You say the word and the whole town goes up in flames. You know that."

I hugged her again. Letting my lips press a gentle kiss on her cheek. "I know. I won the best friend lottery."

She pulled back, gripping her bag and slinging the strap over her shoulder. "Don't you forget it."

Knock. Knock.

I jumped. How could I not? Now that I was aware, as vaguely as it was, of a world beyond what I could comprehend, I was jumping at everything.

Davia answered and I sighed as the door swung far enough to reveal Archer.

"Who the hell are you?" Davia asserted, and I jumped forward.

"Davia, this is Archer. He's..." I stopped. What the hell was he to me?

"I'm a new employee of The Maine Plotline. I'm training today and Athena is going to show me the ropes." The lie fell so expertly off his tongue.

"I didn't know you were hiring," Davia accused, an eyebrow cocked in my direction.

I hated the thought of lying to my best friend. Literally hated it.

"Grandma needs to take a step down." Truth. "Archer here is helping me out." Also true. Semantics didn't matter much, but it placated me slightly to know I didn't outright lie to her.

"Ok, so why are you here?" Davia popped a hip and rested her hand on her waist. She was without a doubt one of the most intimidating women in the world. She could make people eat out of the palm of her hand and then thank her for the pleasure.

Archer was composed, but I noticed his eyes scan her, a coy smile playing on his lips. "Walking her to work. Wanna join?" When Archer smiled a small dimple appeared on his right cheek.

Davia's eyes narrowed and her tongue ran along her teeth as she surveyed him. "No," she replied plainly.

"Then, it was a pleasure." He tilted his head. "I'll wait outside, Athena." He took a few steps back, tossing another cheeky grin in Davia's direction before retreating hallways down the driveway. Davia watched him walk for a moment before closing the door and turning her attention to me.

"You have ANOTHER boyfriend? You're five for five with the hot strangers and while I'm incredibly happy for you, seriously so thankful that you're feeling healed enough to move on and take back your sensuality. Love you so much. I'm also so pissed because how dare you? Seriously. Leave some for the rest of us, Jesus." She pointed an accusatory finger in my direction.

"I am not dating this one, he really is just a friend who's helping me out," I replied with a laugh. She tossed her hands up and went to leave.

"Have fun living my dream!" She sauntered out the front door with her suitcase in tow, I was close on her heels, and she grimaced at Archer who was leaning against her car.

"Do you mind?" She bit. Archer shifted his weight off the car and smiled brightly at her.

"Not at all," he teased. She maintained her glare the entire time she slipped into the driver's seat, started the car, and backed down the drive. "I'll only be a few hours away babe, so call me if you need me to come back and castrate anyone." She called out the window, her eyes landing maliciously on Archer.

He laughed as we both watched her car disappear down the street. "Your friend hates me," Archer offered a few moments later, chuckling.

"She's just protective of me," I said, warmly. My best friend was the fiercest defender of my emotional safety. I loved her for that.

"You ready for this?" Archer asked, his gaze free of judgment. I appreciated that. Nodding, we began the trek to the pier. We made idle chatter, it felt comfortable between the two of us.

Arriving at the store felt like a dream and a nightmare rolled into one. I sighed deeply, resting my hand on the door before disengaging the lock and lifting the gate.

So many memories were made in this place in the last week. Reading that book out loud with Silas, feeling their heated gazes on me. The pink roses. Orpheus calmed me expertly, then pressed his lips to mine.

Their red eyes, pointed claws and sharpened fangs.

Too many memories.

"Give me a second, ok?" Archer offered before leaving me standing near the front of the store to go for another sweep of the space. Once again, like a militant soldier. I flipped the open sign in the window, switched on the fairy lights that danced along the display window, and decorated the ceiling. It felt good to be back at work, despite the fear that had me constantly checking the front door.

When I turned back to the counter, the dying pink roses stopped me in my tracks. Their petals had lost their vibrant color and instead were lightening to a soft brown. Their leaves, once rich green, were decaying. Their scent wasn't as strong. I found myself wishing I could simultaneously smell their strong aroma again, and never smell it again.

"Hello there, young man," a familiar kind voice called out. Archer's head poked into the office, his body going rigid. My grandma popped out of the room and smiled up at him. His eyes flicked to mine as if asking for confirmation of who this person was.

"Hi, Grandma," I offered, moving across the floor to embrace her. She held me back, planting a kiss on my hair. I looked over at Archer who relaxed slightly, and continued into the store.

"You're a sight for sore eyes," Grandma whispered into my ear as she held onto me.

"I'm sorry I've been M.I.A," I said as I pulled back.

She waved me off. "Don't worry about that one bit, you know I love working at the store."

I smiled, noticing how strong she seemed. She might not be able to do it every day like she used to, but she really did live and breathe for this place. "I know, but I've got it today. You go rest."

Her phone rang in her hand, she glanced at it briefly and I couldn't help myself but look at the screen.

My heart skipped a beat. "Is that who I think it is?" I challenged, as she sent his call to voicemail.

"Depends on who you think it is," she responded aloofly.

"Why the hell is my dad calling you?" I asked, probably a little too angrily, but I couldn't help it when it came to him.

"I know he's done wrong by you, Athena. And trust me, he's heard an earful from me about it. But he and your mom were together for a while before he took off. I knew him well once," she sounded pained by that.

"So he'll call you, but not me?" I didn't mean to sound so jealous.

"Now, I'm all for bashing the guy for his choices as much as he deserves, but he never called you because that was your mom's wish, not his."

I shook my head. "There's no way that's true."

"Listen, girl, I don't know what happened between them all those years ago, but what I do know is that he calls to check in on you every once in a while, so I tell him and then we leave the conversation at that." She waved me off. "I don't forgive him for his cowardice and for leaving, but I also know how hard it is to be separated from your daughter." A tear slid down her cheek, and my heart was constructed at the thought of my mother.

"Why didn't he call me after she died?" If my father cared so much about how I was doing, he should have the guts to ask me himself.

"He doesn't know," she replied, sheepishly.

"What?"

"He doesn't ask about her. He knows she didn't want anything to do with him, and he respects that. And I just... I guess it's nice to talk to someone who doesn't know. To talk to someone who thinks she's still living life to the fullest."

I sighed, grabbed ahold of her hand, and squeezed.

"How often do you talk?" I asked, not entirely sure I wanted the answer.

"Not very, I swear to you." She crossed her heart and held up a Girl Scout Salute. I smiled lightly, still feeling the twinge of anger budding behind the action.

"Who's your guest?" She teased and I rolled my eyes. "He's a cutie."

"Just a friend."

She smiled, crossing behind the counter and looking at the bouquet of decaying roses. "You never did tell me how that date went," she teased.

"It was perfect," I replied, honestly, with a hint of shame and sadness.

"You don't sound too happy about that," she accused. I moved to the counter and rested my elbows on the surface.

"I just think it was too good to be true, ya know?"

She squinted, a pensive look crossing her face. "Or was it too good for you to believe?"

"I've got the store today," I said, ignoring the way her gaze made me feel exposed. "Go home, and relax!"

She contemplated for a moment, and I thought briefly that she might continue to push the subject, but thankfully she finally agreed and headed toward the door.

"Just to be clear, I'm leaving because you have a handsome visitor and I don't wanna be a third-wheeler, not because I need a break." She winked and left before I had a chance to reiterate to her Archer was just a friend.

"Place is clear." Archer had come back from the back of the store and settled in near the counter. "If it makes you feel more comfortable, I can stick around. I was just going to be doing some research today and this is as good a place as any."

I smiled at him, without fully giving him my attention. My eyes were still drawn to the expiring roses.

"That would be great, Archer. Thank you," I offered, mindlessly walking toward the vase on the counter.

I felt the tiniest, most imperceptible draw to them grow with each step. Like a rope was wrapped around their stems and the other end secured onto my heart. The closer I got to those roses, the less fear harbored in my mind. With each step, the image of their monstrous faces was replaced with their soft eyes, gentle hands, and tormenting tongues. These roses and their withered existence ironically gave me a fresh perspective. A long time ago, people painted me the villain without letting me explain, without truly hearing me. Nobody cared what the truth was. I wasn't offered the option, but maybe my wanderers should be. If nothing else, they at least owed me their truth. And I owed them a listening ear.

So with newfound determination and resolution, I pulled my phone from my pocket and unblocked two very important numbers.

"So how long have you been working here?" Archer asked, finding a comfortable spot on one of the couches near the front. I slid my phone back into my pocket, suddenly feeling lighter, and made my way to the coffee machine. I made quick work of brewing us each a cup.

"My entire life basically," I answered, as the milk steamed. "This store has been in my family for a long time."

"It's a really cool place, when I'm in here I feel like I'm scrolling through a 'dark academia and woodland fae' Pinterest board."

When I turned, giving him an arched eyebrow he threw his hands up. "What? Can't a guy enjoy a little interior design?"

I fell into an easy laughter I hadn't experienced in a few days and instantly was once again thankful for his presence. "Sure you can," I assured him, pouring the hot liquid into blue ceramic mugs.

"All I'm saying is, you should be proud of this place." I turned to face him, mug in hand, and smiled.

"I am." I sat the coffee down in front of him, and then it hit me. "Oh, shit. I didn't even ask you what kind of coffee you like." I shook my head. "I'm sorry! I can make you something else!"

"Hey, no worries," he comforted. "What kind did ya make me?"

I glanced down at the cup on the table. "It's a white chocolate mocha."

"That's my favorite," Archer replied, earnestly. I tilted my head and eyed him incredulously. "No, I'm serious! I swear. It really is my favorite." He made a crossing his heart motion that looked so playful and easy. I couldn't help but notice that this was how it was starting to feel being around him. Playful and easy.

"It's my favorite too," I agreed and Archer took a slow sip of the coffee, releasing a satisfied groan of approval as the taste reached his tongue. I chuckled and sat down on the opposite side of the table from him, enjoying my coffee as well. We drank in comfortable silence for a few minutes.

"So, still not sticking around for the season?" I inquired, replaying his answer from the first night we met in my mind. He shook his head, swallowing his current sip of coffee.

"No, I'm not staying long," I couldn't help but feel a little saddened by that. Archer had quickly cemented himself as someone I enjoyed spending time with. Well, that and he willingly protected me the other night. That kind of chivalry makes an impression.

"That's a bummer. Who am I going to go to the summer series concerts on the pier with?" I teased.

Archer smiled, but then a small blush darkened on his face.

"I assume you could ask your friend... What was her name again? Danielle? Delilah?" Something in his coy phrasing and shy smile told me he knew exactly what her name was. I smirked and leaned back in my chair.

"Davia?" I said, amused. He nodded, over the top.

"Oh, that's right."

I watched him as he avoided eye contact, fiddling with the cup in front of him.

"You could always go to those shows with her unless she has someone else she normally goes with. Parents, boyfriend... You know. That kind of person."

"Are you fishing to find out if Davia is single?"

He had the gall to act appalled. "What? Jeez, no I'm just... you're... Ok. yeah, Yeah I was," he admitted, defeatedly. We devolved into laughter together, the melodic sound filling the space with a type of liveliness I had desperately been craving.

"She's single, and she's also a serial one-night-stander," I said, and Archer nodded his head, absorbing the new info. "Can't go to those concerts with her anyway," I resolved, downing the last of my coffee.

"Why not?" He asked.

"Davia doesn't know the difference between Kid Rock and Kidz Bop."

Archer visibly flinched. "Yikes."

I nodded solemnly. "So, where are you from? And why did you choose Shockgrove as your latest pit stop?" I asked, leaning my elbows on the table and resting my chin on my hands.

He looked like he was contemplating the answer, his brow furrowed.

"I grew up in the Midwest. I'm talking corn fields, cow-tipping, and 'drive your tractor to school' kind of rural." He seemed nearly ashamed of that fact. "Knew I wanted to get out of there, but it was kind of impossible."

"Why?" I asked.

"Because of the family business," he replied, sincerely.

"You didn't want to join?"

He shook his head. "No, but there wasn't much of a choice." He seemed upset, and I nodded. I understood the pressure of joining a family business, but the difference here was clear. I loved the work I did, and this was a passion I developed myself. It was a perfect fit. But if I hadn't loved this job, I still would have done it, out of obligation. And I would have been miserable.

"I'm sorry," I whispered.

He thanked me under his breath.

"Is it a painting business?" I asked, he looked up at me sharply, a confused expression on his face. I gestured to the blue paint stains on his hands that were receding, but still there. He anxiously clasped his hands together in front of him.

"Yeah, something like that." He seemed cagey and I decided it was best not to press the matter.

"What would you do if you got the benefit of a choice?"

He sighed deeply, a soft smile playing on his lips. "I've always wanted to be a musician."

"Do you play? Write? Sing?"

He nodded. "All of the above. I can play five instruments, but my favorite is guitar." The passion in his eyes was undeniable. I couldn't help but feel a prick of pain at the thought of him suppressing his dreams.

"That's really impressive," I gushed. "You'll have to play something for me sometime!" I eagerly offered. He leaned back in his chair.

"Maybe," he promised, with a slight smirk.

We spent the next few hours getting to know each other. A few customers came and went, buying mostly coffee and pastries, and one hardcover of Moby Dick. Throughout it all, the exchange between Archer and me was easy and freeing.

But the ease of this conversation and the vase of roses on the counter served as a reminder of the conversation I needed to have soon. And it was going to be anything but easy.

4

ARCHER

I really couldn't believe my luck. When I arrived in this little town, I thought it was going to take me days to figure out where The Wanderers were hiding out, then days after that to plan my attack, and then probably a few days to gather the nerve to carry it out.

It was fate really that I had ventured out to the lighthouse that evening. I've been sent to enough coastal towns during my tagging assignments, but I never had time to just sort of soak it in. When I drove into town the decommissioned lighthouse felt like a beacon to me, despite its state. I was drawn to it, in a weird sort of quiet way. Like a whisper. When I got there, in the orange hue of the evening, with the fading light dancing against the waves as they crashed, I felt like a normal guy. Someone on vacation, just relaxing and taking in the view. Appreciating the natural beauty of what this world has to offer.

But I am not normal.

That truth slammed into me almost as hard as Athena had as she barreled toward me. The look of terror and incredulity on her face was so familiar. I'd seen that look before. The way she was struggling to describe what she had seen, the fear hiding behind her mask.

A monster. She had seen a monster.

Now, unless Shockgrove had another monstrous visitor in town, I was positive that I found my trail.

Jackpot.

Walking her to her store was not entirely selfless of me. Not that I wanted her to walk alone with the creatures of the night still out and about, but if The

Wanderers left a witness? Maybe having her near me was the bait I needed to capture them once and for all.

That was as good a plan as any. Stick close to their loose end in hopes they come back to tie it up. Then I'll be ready.

Fuck. When did I start thinking of human beings as bait and loose ends?

I always said I wasn't going to lose myself to this business, but here I was, not even a single kill in and already I'm hoping the vampires will come to terrorize this girl so I can capture them.

Who's the monster in this scenario again?

Them. Of course, it's them. Vampires. They prey on the innocent. They drain blood and leave their lifeless forms in a trail of death and destruction behind them. They kill without reason, take what they want, and damn the consequences.

They are the real villains.

The entire walk back to her store, I felt my heart in my throat, beating quickly and violently. My fingers were tense, holding tightly to the acidic spray. It would be enough to incapacitate them for a few hours. I just had to get close enough to do it.

The wooden stake that rested on my side felt like it was burning me alive as it brushed against my bare skin. I'd never used it on a living creature.

No, stop that, Archer. They're not living. Not anymore.

When we got to her store, I could feel it instantly. Hunters are trained to understand and recognize the smallest details about vampires. I could analyze anything in this room and decipher if they were here, but I didn't have to. The hair on the back of my neck stood at attention, goosebumps erupted across my entire body. The air was thick, like blood. They were here.

I found them.

"Lock this door," I offered to her, as I headed down the aisle to the back entrance I clocked the last time I was in the store. "I'm going to sweep the place, don't go far."

I knew she was doing as I asked, but I didn't bother to look back. I let my hand rest on my stake, and once I knew I was far enough from Athena, I pulled it from its place. Holding it in front of me. Ready.

The stake was a dark brown wood, meticulously filed to a sharp point. A metallic band encircled the girthiest part of the stake that read 'nisi nox'. The creed of Nameless. A promise our organization has made to the world of mortals, even though they'll never know.

Save the night.

That's what we're trained to do. To protect mortals from the vicious creatures who hide and hunt in the dark.

I let the air fill my lungs, willing my heart to slow as I take cautious steps forward. Stake in one hand, spray bottle in the other. Quickly, without stopping my motion, I spritz the mixture on either side of my neck. It was a little trick taught to us at the facility. If a vampire gets close enough to take a bite out of your neck, you're already dead...but this way you take them with you.

As I ventured through the stacks of books, the musty smell of paper in the air, I wondered briefly if I was hoping to find them, or hoping not to. I knew what my father had said. That I needed to make a statement. To prove my loyalty and allegiance to Nameless before they see me as a liability and erase me from existence. And a part of me really wanted to do that. Make my father proud. Make Nameless proud. Help rid the world of monsters. But another part of me, the part that has never done more in the field than paint a symbol on some walls, was panicking. I'm not cut out for this. I'm not a fighter. A Hunter.

But I have to be.

When I arrived at the ajar back door, I could sense them. I may not have trained against actual vampires, but I've seen them. I know what their presence feels like.

The first time I ever saw a vampire, I was nine years old.

"You're gonna be brave in there, right, son?"

I remember the way my father had bent down, his knee resting on the ground. His fingers came up to fiddle with the collar of my shirt. My palms felt clammy.

I swallowed the lump in my throat and nodded once.

"Good." His hands came to rest on my shoulders and his eyes searched my face. He only looked at me like this when he was serious. Which was a lot of the time, but I knew why today was special. He told me to be ready. To be brave. It was the day I was going to see my first vampire.

"I know you're probably scared," he started, but I shook my head. I was scared. Really scared, actually, but I knew better than to let him know that. "If you're going to be a Hunter when you're older, you need to learn how not to show fear. Vampires sense that and they will not hesitate to kill you."

I felt my heart beat faster and my chest heave with anxious breaths. I glanced at the large iron door that led to the vampires. Dad told me once that nightmares live behind this door. I used to lie awake at night, worrying about what was in there. Making up fantastical stories, and images in my mind. Today, I'd see if they were true.

"I won't be scared, Dad."

He shook his head, lifting a hand to stop me. "Don't call me that here, kid."

I shut my mouth, hanging my head in shame. "I'm sorry, sir."

He gave me a pat on the back and stood, his frame towering over me. He reached into his back pocket for something, producing it in front of me.

"Stay behind the red line, don't let them get into your head, kid."

I nodded to hide the way my body shook.

"I'll be watching." Then he slid the black mask onto my head, securing it over my face. I'd seen my father wear a mask much like this before. I remembered always wanting to wear it, wondering when it would be my chance. Now that it was here, I wasn't so sure I wanted it.

When he was satisfied with my preparations, he offered a quick nod and moved to the iron door. He slipped a key into the massive lock, the sound echoed in the empty hall... When he pushed it open, I felt the cold air brush against my warmed skin. There was so much fear. I felt like I was drowning in it... My blood pulsed with fervor as if it wanted to taunt the creatures beyond the door.

With one last swallow, I puffed my chest and stepped across the threshold into the long, dank hallway. My eyes slowly adjusted to the low light. There were only a few dull bulbs lining the space, casting an eerie shadow across the floor. The air escaped my lungs as the door was shut behind me, locking me inside. I forced long settling breaths, despite the growing panic. Knowing my father was watching my every move. Studying me. Judging me.

Large iron gates lined the walls and as I took tentative steps forward, I couldn't see into the darkness of the cages. I'd passed three sets of cells without seeing anything, but I wasn't relieved. It was only a matter of time. Only a matter of when.

I think I walked past seemingly empty cages for a whole minute before I heard the softest groan. My entire body froze, fear coursing through my veins like ice.

"Hello?" I called out meekly, toward the cell where the sound permeated from. In the darkness of the hallway, I couldn't see more than a foot or two into the depth of the cage. If there was a back wall I couldn't tell. My eyes glanced down at the red line on the ground, crudely painted. I planted my feet firmly behind it.

"Hello?" I asked again. I had almost given up, writing it off as my mind playing tricks on me when a soft, feminine voice spoke from the depths of the cell.

"Hi there." The voice was weak, but other than that, it sounded positively... human. My eyebrows rose in shock as a beautiful woman slowly appeared from within in the shadows. Her clothes were torn, and her face was dirty and sunken, but she was pretty. Long blonde hair curled around her face, hanging down her back and over her shoulders. Her blue eyes were bright enough to reflect even the dim light. "What's your name?" She asked, tilting her head slightly, her blue eyes scanned my form. I swallowed the fear and confusion that were beginning to intermingle and cleared my throat.

"My.. um... I'm," I paused. I felt the cool fabric of the mask brush against my face, a reminder of my supposed anonymity. "I'm a Hunter," I replied with as much false bravado as I could muster, which earned me a soft chuckle from the woman behind bars.

"Do you want to know my name?" She asked, smiling down at me with a mischie-

vous glint in her eyes. I nodded my head. "Evangeline. My name is Evangeline." It was a pretty name, fitting. She looked like an Evangeline. "How old are you?" She took a step closer to the iron gate, and I found myself glancing down at the line to ensure I hadn't crossed it.

"I'm not afraid of you," I offered. She smiled again, leaning her head against the bars.

"I don't want you to be." It was so matter-of-fact, so concise. I almost believed her. "I'm two hundred and seventeen years old," she whispered, a contemplative look on her face.

"You're a vampire," I echo her volume. Her eyes flicked to me.

"Yeah," she starts. "I am."

I studied her, she looked calm, sweet even. If I saw her on the street I might even feel comfortable saying hello.

"I'm not going to hurt you, Hunter," she expressed, sinking down onto the ground. She sat with her shoulder leaning against the bar, her profile turned to me.

"Do you know why they have me in here, little one?" She queried. I shook my head. "They think I'm a monster." She glanced up at me, her eyes met mine directly. She looked at me as if she could see right through the mask to the scared little kid beneath.

"You are," I asserted, shakily. She sighed, letting her head fall back and her eyes travel to the ceiling.

"You don't even know me," she scoffed. "Tell me, kid, what about me makes me a monster?"

I scanned her face, her weak form, and her soft eyes. She was right, she didn't look the part of a monster, but she was one. I knew that much. She was here for a reason, my dad wouldn't do this if he didn't have to. We were saving the world. We were protecting humans.

"You are in disguise," I trembled.

"Aren't we all?"

"How many people have you killed?" I inquired, she looked back to me as if the question didn't surprise her.

"Have you ever asked your daddy that question?" She bit. I bristled, and my heart rate quickened. She noticed my reaction, smirking softly. "Thought you weren't afraid of me."

I swallowed the lump in my throat.

"I'm not," I lied.

"I'm going to tell you a secret, little Hunter, and I need you to promise that you'll never forget it, ok?" She moved until she was sitting up on her knees with her hands gripping the bars in front of her, she looked hopeless, afraid, and weak.

"Ok," I agreed. She smiled.

"This world is full of monsters, and not all of them look like me. They're not always so obvious, with large claws and fangs. No, some monsters are hiding in plain sight, pretending to be the heroes," she seethed. "You're better off not trusting a single person besides yourself."

I listened intently to her anger as it poured out of her.

"After all, you're the only one you can trust."

"I can trust my dad," I argued, although a small tremble in my voice gave away my hesitation.

She leaned toward me, a look of pure concern on her features. I felt drawn in. Before I could stop myself I had taken a step. Her eyes scanned my masked face with reverence. It was so disorienting, so unlike anything I expected from a creature like this, that I didn't even flinch when her gentle fingers came up to brush against my mask. When she slowly gripped the edge of the mask, I didn't shy away. When she began to remove it, I didn't stop her. Cool air brushed against my skin as Evangeline studied my bare face. The way she looked at me was so motherly, so caring. I didn't realize how much I craved that until it was dangling in front of me. "Little Hunter, you can't trust anyone."

She moved faster than I'd ever seen a creature move. Suddenly my body was pressed up against the bars and my arm was pulled into the darkness. My eyes had barely adjusted to her speed when the pain radiated from my wrist. A scream erupted from my lips as I looked down my arm to the woman who had sunk her fangs into my skin. Her kind blue eyes were gone, replaced with a violent bright red. Her hands wrapped around my wrist and held me in place as she drew my blood into her mouth. It stung, like a thousand hornets attacking the exact same part of my body. I tried to pull away from her, to retreat behind the safety of the red line I had foolishly crossed, but her hold was steadfast and impossible to break free from. I pushed against the cage which she was holding me to, swinging aimlessly into the darkness within. My vision slowly started blackening along the edges, as she drained the very life from my veins.

I had almost given up, my escape attempts becoming weaker and weaker the more blood was stolen from me, when a metallic clang sounded through the hallway. A rush of air brushed against my face as the ax swung, barely missing me. Something cold and wet splattered across my skin. The force against my wrist receded, but the pressure of the fangs on my skin did not. When I looked down at my injured wrist, I saw the severed head of Evangeline. I didn't register the rag that was thrust in my face until it had wiped the substance from my skin.

"Don't fucking taste any of that shit, clean your face."

I barely recognized my Dad's voice, I was still frozen in fear, unable to tear my eyes from the head attached to my wrist.

"Archer, snap the fuck out of it."

I wasn't breathing.

"Jesus Christ," he said under his breath before a bucket of water was tossed onto my face, drenching me and washing away the remnants of whatever it was that had gotten on me. The cold shock of the water finally brought air back to my lungs. The world was technicolor again. Tears fell down my cheeks as I tried to pull my arm back through the bars, but the head attached was too wide and when it hit the bars, the fangs ripped at my tender skin. I screamed in pain again. My panic was so vivid, I knew I would never be able to wash this memory from my mind.

My dad's hand clasped around my arm, above where the head was attached, quickly, he helped relieve my wrist of its new accessory, sending a few jolts of pain up my arm. Finally, I was able to pull it back from the darkness of the cage, cradling the bleeding appendage against my chest. As I stumbled back to behind the red line, I watched as my father slammed a wooden stake into the chest of the headless form on the floor of the cell. He stood a few moments later, pulling the stake from its place, and turned to face me, I saw the dark black mask covering his features. He looked calm if a little out of breath, but I knew my father well enough to know that this was him when he was angry.

He gripped my shoulder and led me quietly out of the hallway, away from Evangeline's corpse. He didn't speak to me until we were safely locked behind his office door. He pulled his mask off with a grunt and turned back to me with disappointment oozing from his pores.

"I'm sorry," I whispered, knowing it wasn't enough.

"What the hell were you thinking?" He asked, his voice eerily even and restrained. He moved to his desk and took a seat on the ledge.

"I wasn't," I replied, timidly. My father nodded to himself.

"Clearly."

He ran a hand through his soft strawberry-blonde hair and sighed.

"Show me your arm," he demanded, holding a hand out for me. I winced as I extended my tender wrist toward him. He studied it in silence for a few moments before grabbing a small white box from his desk drawer. The liquid he poured on the wound burned, but it was like a pinch compared to the fire of Evangeline's fangs. Once it was wrapped and the gaping red wound was no longer in my eyesight, I started to feel the shock wear off. Tears stung my eyes.

"Don't cry," my father scolded, but I couldn't help it. "That's part of being a Hunter. Look." He slid off his suit jacket and began rolling up his shirt sleeve to reveal several white raised scars in the shape of vampire bites littering his skin.

"Why did you cross the line?" He inquired, as I memorized the way the scars looked against his pale skin.

"She felt safe," I answered, quietly. I was ashamed of how I acted.

Reaching behind him, my father grabbed the bloody stake from the place where he discarded it. Taking a rag from his pocket, he wiped it down, although I don't think the nearly black blood of the vampire would ever truly be gone. It would stain this wood, the way this scar would stain my skin, and this memory would stain my soul. "You need to understand that you are only ever safe in this world if you fight for your safety." He held out the stake for me, and I grabbed it with shaky hands.

That was my first day as a Hunter.

The Wanderers had been here, but they were long gone. I slid the forever-stained wooden stake back into my waistband and locked the door.

I walked Athena to her friend's house and watched the door from a distance for a few hours waiting for their arrival. Eventually, I determined The Wanderers either didn't care enough to kill her...or maybe they cared too much. Watching the front door, I thought about the fiery redhead inside. The night I walked into her store I was simply following a feeling. I felt their presence, it led me there. I half expected to see the vamps inside, that's how strongly I felt their influence, but instead, I ran into an innocent human. The ease of our chat was a breath of fresh air for my morally corrupted lungs. It'd been so long since I just talked to someone, in fact, I got so caught up in the feeling of normalcy I hadn't even thought to interrogate her on if she'd seen them. It wasn't until she mentioned the paint on my hands that I remembered just why I shouldn't be making easy conversation with her.

It was another stroke of fate that she found me at the lighthouse. There was something so familiar about the hollow look in her eyes. A kindred spirit. Just as terrified of what she'd seen as I was. As I still am. She's brave though, I have to give her that. And I can't say I hate the companionship of our conversation. She and I could have been friends in a different universe I think. If there weren't monsters out there if I wasn't hunting them. But as I staked out the house she was staying in, attempting to protect her from the creatures of the night, I knew there was no chance of us having a normal friendship. Nothing about any of this was normal, so despite the briefest glimmer of a blossoming friendship, I had to keep my distance. I'd be gone soon anyway. With four vampires in tow, hopefully.

The next morning, I watched the house for the majority of the daylight hours, and a good portion of the evening. At night, I went back to the store and tried tracking them, but whatever trail they might have left was long since cold at that point.

The next day, I checked in periodically between canvassing the entire town.

The third morning, when I was sure no one was going to venture to the house where Athena was staying, I made my way back to the pale blue and white lighthouse and climbed the solitary staircase to the top. This town looked even smaller from this vantage point. Those monsters were out there somewhere. As I leaned my arms along the railing, looking out over the crashing waves, my fingers absent-mindedly traced the scar on my wrist. The bite mark was a constant reminder of what I had to lose if I ever let my guard down again.

Ring. Ring.

I pulled my phone from my pocket and glanced at the name. With a groan, I answered.

"Bennett."

"Progress report?"

I rolled my eyes, leaning further onto the railing of the lighthouse.

"Hello to you too," I joked.

"There's no time for jokes, son. You need to make a move and you need to make it soon. They're going to discover The Wanderers are settled in that town any day now and Galvin will send the Hunters. Your chance will be gone." He sounded desperate. A far cry from the usually put-together calm leader he was.

"I know," I sighed. "I have a lead. I'm following it." There was silence on the line for a moment. "

"Good. See to it that you get this done, kid." I nodded, although I knew he couldn't see me.

"I will. Hey, you ever gonna tell me who your contact was that knew they'd be here?" I couldn't help but feel curious. I'd walked around the town quietly studying each face wondering if they were the ones who had told my father. Wondering who knew about the monsters under their noses?

"It's just an old friend from another life," he said, solemnly.

"Are they a Hunter?" I asked.

"Don't worry about that," he dismissed me. "Just get the job done." The line went dead. I held the phone to my ear for a few moments longer, not sure what I was expecting to hear.

Just as I was devising a plan to draw them out of hiding, my phone buzzed with a text from Athena, and suddenly the plan created itself.

An hour later, after greeting Athena, and engaging in a verbal sparring match with her firecracker of a friend, we were at her bookstore.

She was starting to trust me, and truth be told, I was starting to enjoy her company too. She was smart, had great taste in music, and her bravery was inspiring. I've seen some Hunters take longer to recover from an encounter with vampires. She was growing on me. And I can't deny that it felt good to have someone to talk to again.

If she was going to be the bait for this plan, I was going to protect her. No harm will come to Athena Landry. Not while I'm alive.

5

ORPHEUS

I've had the unfortunate pleasure of enduring torture three times in my life.

The first time was rather early in my second existence. I was still quite young and without a guide or mentor to show me the ropes of how to survive in this new reality that was thrust upon me. I was struggling to maintain control over my bloodlust. Three elder vampires caught up to me somewhere near Moldova and chained me up in a bunker, claiming I was 'soiling' the vampire name, and drawing unwanted attention. They were right, of course, but as a young fresh-turn with little to no regard for anyone's safety, including my own, I didn't take that new development lightly. They took on a sort of 'educator' role, promising to let me go once I learned to control my instincts. Their methods were brutal, savage even. Before I had gone through the proper ritual to survive in the daylight, they'd set me up in a chair just in front of a window and slowly pull back the curtains, inch by inch. They did this every day. For two years. The light scarred my flesh, permanently in some places, and their lessons were drilled into my mind. They let me go once they were sure I was 'trained'.

I have always appreciated what they did for me, teaching me how to control my emotions. It certainly made it that much more satisfying when I found them again years later and spent three months prolonging their violent and painful deaths.

The second time was just a few years back when Nameless got their fucking hands on us. We had been evasive up to that point. Careful, of course, but we weren't implementing anywhere near the level of countermeasures I put in place in recent years. It was a trap, of course, it was. I should have fucking seen it. It isn't often that our coven runs into other vampires. We'd avoided meeting in large numbers after the Hunters grew to be a more serious threat, but that night we had been invited to a night of vampiric debauchery, mirth, and above all...blood.

Silas had met a woman while out in the town early in the evening, just as the sun set. She was a gorgeous temptress. She promised him a night of sex, blood, and mindless passion.

Silas fell for it. Hook, line, and sinker.

But then again, so did I.

The mansion was dark when we arrived, we weren't tipped off to that though. Of course, they would try to hide their party from prying eyes. Nameless could be anywhere, right?

Right.

That sensual female vampire sold us out to the Hunters, making a deal with them that they would let her go if she delivered the elusive Wanderers to their doorstep.

She fulfilled her part of the bargain.

And they staked her through the heart.

They held us for months. I don't understand why they didn't just kill us and get it over with at first, but after a few of their 'interrogations,' I realized quickly that they were running out of leads. They were so desperate to find more blood-sucking vamps that they were reckless enough to leave us alive.

Although 'alive' is definitely not what I wanted to be. I had endured everything they threw at us before. It wasn't any more painful than my time with my 'teachers' in Moldova, but my companions hadn't. The torture wasn't unbearable because of what they were doing to me, it was unbearable because of what they did to *them*. My family. I felt every second of their fear, their agony, and their desire to die. Their emotions were so potent, I was choking on them. Each day, their screams were knives in my chest. Their burnt skin was acid on my body. I was the reason they were all vampires, after all. It was my doing that they were forced to withstand this. It was my fault.

The torture of knowing their pain was my doing was worse than anything Nameless could do to me.

The third time I suffered through torture was in the days following the shocking revelation that Athena Landry, a human from Maine, was my mate. The two days when my body, and the bodies of my coven, burned through blood faster than they had in our entire second existence. The two days when we had to hunt more frequently in order to fucking survive. When we were moving around the house like zombies, with sunken eyes and hollow cheeks, our dead hearts aching with each phantom beat. Our bodies desiccated from the inside out the longer we fought against the mate bond.

The torture of watching my family start to fall apart and knowing there was nothing I could do. The torture of realizing my soul belonged to someone and discovering she wanted nothing to do with me.

I've never felt this helpless, this lost. This torture was agonizing.

Just yesterday, I walked past Silas' room and saw her frame peeking out through the crack in the door. Her long red hair and her soft innocent face looking back at me from the floor length mirror. I nearly sprinted in and wrapped her in my arms. It took me a few moments to recognize it was Silas using his gift in order to see her again. He stood there in front of the reflection and studied her face, her eyes. Wanting to feel her near him. I understood the urge.

Luckily, or unluckily, I could feel her. Even from this distance. Her fear was so fucking potent. It ebbed and flowed, though, as if she would suddenly remember our encounter again after a moment of reprieve. But the emotion I felt that sent me into a spiral of agony was her pain. She had lost connections she started to cherish. She felt their loss nearly as strongly as I felt hers.

I'd lived a long life. I've endured things that would test even the strongest of constitutions. But this. This torture had the potential to kill me.

"We can't keep this up for long," Laz said, plopping down into a chair in the office I'd commandeered for research. I glanced at them over the top of the laptop screen. Their usually tanned skin had lost some of its luster. Despite feeding this morning, they looked hungry, but that was becoming a constant state for all of us. A flask of human blood, which used to sustain us for weeks, was now barely getting us through the next few hours.

Silas and Samara had left the day before to hunt. They had tracked down a trafficking ring in a city a few hours from here. After setting the women free, they had their pick of the predator buffet. They brought back an entire cooler full of blood. If my current calculations were right, the blood they brought would only sustain us for three more days. We had to find a solution by then, because even though there was no shortage of evil people in this world to feed our bloodlust, Nameless would be looking for that exact sort of hunting pattern. And since we were going to be here for as long as it took to convince Athena that we were hers, we needed to be careful. We couldn't be careful if we were hungry.

"I know."

"We need to go to her," they said, quietly. I leaned back from the screen, letting my hands rest behind my head.

"I know."

They groaned and ran their hands through their sandy blonde hair. Their emotions were overwhelming. I felt every ounce of want and desire they did, which only increased my own tenfold. But I also felt their despair, their fear. It was potent. Sickening. "I've never felt like this before, Orpheus."

I nodded my agreement. They were right. I'd never experienced this either.

"I feel so incomplete. I need her," they whispered.

I've never needed anyone. Truly never. I'd been taking care of myself for as long as my mind can recall. And yes, I love my coven, and I'd die for them, but their companionship was purely a selfish thing to combat my growing loneliness. I didn't *need* them. But, Athena? I now understand why Silas and Laz were so desperate to stay. They had recognized the connection first.

I should have.

The way her eyes met mine as we walked into the bar that night. The way she held me captive in her gaze and I had to force myself to look away. The way I so eagerly jumped at the chance to destroy the man who dared to put his hands on her. The way I was so drawn to her in her bookstore.

Fuck.

I spent so long trying to keep my coven safe that I didn't dare indulge in the sinfulness that was Athena Landry. I ignored all the signs because I couldn't accept the truth. While Silas and Laz were basking in her attention, I was always watching. And now, I may never get the chance.

"What did you find out?" Laz asked, indicating to the computer.

"Not much, you can imagine how many hoops I had to jump through to get to any real information." It was essentially a nightmare trying to wade through hundreds of unsubstantiated claims from thousands of 'believers' to even find some truth among the tales.

"What I do know is the longer we wait, the harder our thirst will be to control."

They nodded at that, and already I saw their fangs slightly elongated.

"We either need to accept and complete the bond, and soon... or..." I paused, afraid to continue. As if by speaking the words, I'd be speaking the possibility into existence.

"Or?" Laz prompted.

"Or we can reject it."

Laz growled, their eyes reddening. Long fingernails dug into the arm of the chair.

"Never," they snarled. Their fury hit me in the chest like a brick wall. I put a hand up to calm them, and steady myself against the onslaught of anger radiating off of them.

"I know, I can't stand the thought either…But-"

"There is no 'but.' She won't reject us." Their voice was full of fury, but I recognized the fear that trembled behind the facade.

"If she doesn't accept us…" I started, hating the way the words felt on my tongue.

"She will!" They stood, their voice booming. I heard Samara and Silas making their way upstairs.

"But if she doesn't," I repeated, standing to meet their gaze. "We need to know how to reject it so we can survive."

"I won't survive without her," they spoke with such conviction, and their emotions flooded with a deeper sadness than I could even comprehend, that it made me pause. A small part of me, the logical part which used to be the most dominant, wanted to argue. Tell them we've made it this long without her, we could do it again. But the rest of me, the part that belonged to Athena, the part that was hand-crafted by whatever fates there were to be hers, wanted nothing more than to agree.

"I don't know why you're even bothering with this argument, Orpheus," Silas interjected from the door frame. "She is ours. She'll realize it soon."

"Maybe not soon enough," I sighed exasperatedly. "We are running out of time, I won't lose a single one of you because of her fear." I didn't care how much my heart yearned for her, or how much my body craved her touch. I refused to lose my family. If she doesn't want to be a part of it, she doesn't have to be.

But fuck. I need her to.

"You're acting like you don't fucking care if she accepts the bond. What kind of mate are you?" Silas challenged and I saw Samara place a warning hand on his chest, slightly angling her body to fit between the two of us.

"I'm trying to think realistically here, Silas! There is a strong chance she will reject us. All of us."

He growled and stepped forward, but Samara's hand kept him from crossing the threshold into the room.

"You're weak, Orpheus," Laz spat.

"Somebody has to protect this family!" I screamed, feeling my hands balled into fists at my side.

"Athena *is* a part of our family!" Laz glowered. I heard Silas grunt in agreement, and I glanced slightly over to Samara who had been quiet this entire time. Come to think of it, she had been pretty subdued for most of these past few days. Her emotions had been a mix of desire and guilt. Overwhelming, agonizing guilt.

"Not if she doesn't want to be," I replied, calmly, fighting against the devastating flood of feelings that were pouring out of my coven. Laz stormed off toward the door, to join the others. They paused just before venturing out into the hall and turned over their shoulder to glare at me.

"I'd sooner die than reject her. And if you can't say the same then you don't deserve her." With that, Laz pushed past the others and disappeared down the hall. Silas shook his head, and a cloud of his emotions surrounded me.

His disappointment was suffocating. "By the way, the cops called me about the douche from the bar. We're expected at the station in an hour."

Shock colored my expression, but Silas was gone before I could respond.

When Samara and I were alone, I placed a hand on my chest and forced a few steadying breaths, mentally begging my gift to give me a moment of reprieve.

"Overwhelmed?" She asked from her spot across the room. I nodded, afraid my voice would come out breathless should I attempt to speak. I sunk into the office chair and let my head fall back and drew a few shallow, anxious breaths. I heard Samara crossing the floor to me, but I didn't look up to meet her gaze.

"I was getting a little stifled myself, I can only imagine how it felt to *feel* it all," she offered, meekly.

A few moments passed before I regained enough control to turn my face to hers. Samara's guilt was still potent enough to invade my senses but felt like a calming balm compared to the volatile nature of Silas and Laz's anger.

"I'm just trying to keep my family together," I admitted, quietly. My strength was not a front, I wasn't some hard-shelled monster with a secret soft interior. I was strong. I was tough. The way I show my love and dedication to someone wasn't through soft embraces and meaningless words of affirmation. It was through action.

It was ok with me if they couldn't see that now - if they weren't hearing what they wanted from me, because I would do whatever I had to in order to protect them, whether they liked it or not.

"Yeah," she mused, timidly. Her eyebrows furrowed as she took a deep breath.

"Are you ok?" I asked, scanning her face.

"Huh? Oh, yeah. Just hungry." It wasn't a lie, per se, I could see the tell-tale signs on her face, in the redness that was slowly permeating her eyes, but there was more to it. I felt it. She looked up at my face and must have seen the look on my face because she sighed. "I don't know why I ever try to lie to you." She chuckled softly, without any real humor behind it.

I remained silent, allowing her the space she needed to formulate her response. She toyed with her fingers in her lap, mindlessly picking at the skin around her nails. "I don't think I can do it," she admitted, finally.

"Do what, Samara?"

"I can't move on from her." A tear slid down her dark skin, painting the surface of her cheek with a single path of pain. "Alora was my chosen, Orpheus. She was my wife. My everything. My life. I stood beneath the stars and the moon and I promised my heart to her and her alone. If I accept this mate bond, I am breaking my promise to her." Tears flowed more freely now although her face remained stoic.

With my particular gift, it's easy to comfort others by saying 'I know how you feel' because it's true. I do. I feel it all, I understand intimately how they feel. But I've learned an important caveat to my gift in my many years of existence.

I may know how they feel, and be able to experience it for myself, but never in my lifetime have I or will I be able to truly understand the depths of their emotions as intimately as they can. No matter how much I wish I could, I cannot save them from the cages they forge for themselves.

Samara's affection for Alora grew over time, building each day. I could see it, but it didn't take my gift to acknowledge the budding love between them.

"What brought this on? Just a few days ago you were smitten, following her into sex shops and kissing her at her store?" I asked.

She groaned. "A few days ago she was just an attractive stranger whom I would have enjoyed spending an evening in bed with."

I looked at her, questioningly.

"Now she's... it's just, it's too much," she whispered, before taking a shaky breath. "We talked about it once," she continued, "what would happen if we found our mates."

I leaned forward, watching her face as she spoke.

"We swore to each other that we would reject it," she choked on the word like it felt painful even to utter it. "We promised each other. It was us, and only us. Till the end." She maintained control of her outward display of emotions despite the wave of guilt I felt coming from her.

"It was," I said, calmly. She glanced up at me through moistened eyelashes, inquisitively. "It was you and her till the end, Samara."

A sob wrenched from her chest, but she was quick to regain composure.

"Just because her end and yours are not the same doesn't mean you didn't keep your promise to her."

She nodded, but I could tell she wasn't buying into it.

"I feel like I'm being ripped apart from the inside. Athena's kiss felt like coming home, but Alora *was* my home." She wiped the backs of her hands across her face to catch the stray tears.

"Those can both be true."

She scoffed, letting me see the slightest bit of hidden emotion behind her walls. "How do you reject a mate bond?" She asked, straining against the question.

"Samara I-"

"How do I do it, Orpheus?" She asserted again. I sighed, running my hands down my face.

"Ok, so let's say you reject it. You sever this fate-given tie and cast your feelings for Athena aside."

She whimpered at the thought of it.

"Let's say you do all that, but Laz and Silas manage to complete the bond. What then? Would you stick around, seeing your coven reap the benefits of a mate bond with the one you let get away?"

Her facade broke for a moment and a cry nearly escaped her lips. She shook her head. "I'd have to go."

"Go where?" I demanded, quietly.

"Anywhere!" Her careful grip on her emotions was slipping with each passing second.

"And leave your family?" I argued, my voice raising slightly.

"Alora was my family!" she screamed as she stood, once she recognized her outburst, her hands clenched at her side and she took a few slow breaths to calm herself.

It wasn't working.

"How do I do it, Orpheus?" She begged, her wet eyes pleading with me.

"You have to transfuse with someone else," I whispered. The act of sharing blood was how someone of our kind was created. I've turned a few vampires in my life. It's a slightly intimate process, depending on where you decide to take the blood from, but the pain overshadows any romantic undertones rather abruptly. A human must drink from a vampire at the same moment a vampire drinks from the human. It activates the venom in our blood, sending it catapulting through their veins to their heart, suspending it in lifeless animation. "In order to reject a mate bond, you have to create a new vampire." Samara's eyes were wide, and I felt the disgust filter into her emotions.

Vampires didn't have an organized 'government' body, just the royal family, who are more for show than anything else, but there were some unspoken rules that the monarchy liked to agree on.

Don't expose our kind to humans.

Don't sell out our kind to Nameless.

Close the wounds after feeding. Regardless of if the victim is alive or dead.

Don't create new vampires, unless necessary.

If our population were to grow too exponentially, we'd have a harder time avoiding breaking rules one and two. So for the most part, turning a new vampire was reserved for life or death, or mate purposes.

"Damnit," she exhaled. "So if she doesn't accept us, in order to survive we'd have to double our numbers?"

I nodded curtly. We'd each have to find a human and condemn them to a half-life.

She absorbed that for a moment, her eyes glazed over as thoughts I could never hope to understand flitted through her mind. Then she stood, the only indication of her discomfort was the hard line of her jaw, and the way her fingers wrestled with themselves. She nodded once, before moving to exit.

"Samara," I interjected, as she paused by the door frame with her back to me. "Talk to her first." She didn't respond. "Just promise me, before you go making irreversible choices that you will talk to Athena first." Her shoulders rose and fell with quick breaths. "Please."

She glanced over her shoulder at me, and I saw her raw unfiltered expression for a brief moment. "I don't make promises I can't keep." And she was gone.

I fell back into the chair with an exasperated sigh.

That was a problem, an issue I'd need to address soon... but first, we had to go make a statement at the station. We needed to feed and get our story straight.

Shockgrove was proving to be a significant problem, and for the first time in my entire existence, I had no idea what to do.

6

SAMARA

Walking into the police station was like finding a source of fresh water after days of traversing the dry desert. We had each swallowed down a bottle of blood from our reserves before leaving the house ten minutes ago and while the hunger wasn't ravenous, it was there. Like a pit in my stomach that was noticeable and slightly painful. Orpheus was right to be worried. If we run out of blood before they accept the bond there could be an accidental bloodbath on its way to Shockgrove, Maine.

It didn't matter to me. though. I had already made up my mind.

I had to reject the bond. I made a promise and I wasn't going to go back on my word.

The station smelled like stale coffee and body odor, but that stench wasn't enough to mask the scent of mouth-watering fresh, warm, blood. Even so, I tried to focus on the displeasing aroma to avoid focusing on the other, more tasty smelling one. Several people milled about the bullpen with various levels of urgency. When we approached the front desk, the secretary smiled at Silas and Orpheus with stars in her eyes. So I rolled mine.

"How can I help you today?" She gushed, twirling a strand of light brown hair around her index finger.

"I was called by a Detective Barnes," Silas offered, tight-lipped, without an ounce of flirtation or cheekiness. It was an odd thing to see from my normally very sensually forward friend. She didn't get the message, because she giggled flirtatiously and reached for a phone to call the Detective.

A few moments later, we were ushered into an office at the corner of the bullpen. The room was bright, sunlight poured in from the several windows that lined the walls, my skin felt tender under its warmth. The burn was manageable, but I found myself tilting my body away from the window nevertheless. Awards and certifications decorated the free space between each window and a large mahogany desk sat near the back wall.

The four of us each grabbed a seat in the open black leather armchairs and waited for the Detective to arrive.

It was silent and tense. I've never felt such a distance between my family. Even when Alora died, we came together in the wake of the tragedy, supporting each other through the loss. But this, this was tearing us apart.

Something I never thought could be possible. We'd been through so much together, and came out the other side stronger that I had truly thought our bond was impenetrable. I glanced over my shoulder at the bullpen behind us. Along one of the walls there was a small holding cell, and I felt my body tense as unwanted memories overtook my senses.

I'd lost count of the days. From our cells, we could not see the sky. We had no indication of time passing down here. The torture seemed to come at various times and lasted for varying lengths, but I could be mistaken. Things tend to blend together when you're a prisoner.

"Don't fall asleep, Samara." Alora. After weeks of being separated, with only their voices drifting from adjoining cells to keep me company, I was beginning to forget the nuances of her face. All of their faces. The exact shade of their eye color. The shape of their noses. The memory of my wife and my coven was starting to fade at the edges. A taunting vignette with the ability to eclipse the pieces of me that made me whole. It was reminiscent of the way my human memories had slowly begun to slip from me, not nearly fast enough, but similar nonetheless. Orpheus said it was a side effect of the hunger. Without blood, our hearts forgot to beat at all and slowly our minds started to think we were dead. Well, really dead. It had been weeks since we last even scented blood and that was only when Nameless used it to torment us. We hadn't tasted the life-giving elixir for so long that I couldn't remember the way it tasted, or the way it slid over my tongue and warmed my entire body, setting it alight.

"I'm not asleep," I whispered with what little energy I had.

"You have to stay strong, baby." Her lilting voice had a hard edge to it. Fear, maybe? Orpheus would know better than I would. He was fortunate, or perhaps unfortunate in this case, enough to have a gift that traversed distances. Me? I had to lay my hands on the wounded person to help them. For the first few months when I would hear my wife and my coven scream in agony - sustaining injuries that were vicious and painful - I knew I could heal them if only I were granted a moment, a single moment to touch them, I could alleviate their suffering. But I couldn't help them.

"Why?"

I'd been fighting for months. Spending each and every day grasping onto my sanity with every ounce of strength I had left. Holding out hope that if only Nameless let their guard down for a moment, we could all escape and return to the life we deserved, the life we fought for. As each day passed, that hope waned like the very memories in my heart.

"Because, I'm going to get us out of here," she whispered. I didn't have the energy to be shocked or surprised. And it wasn't like I hadn't heard it before from Silas, Orpheus, and Laz as well. Hell, I'd even uttered the same words myself a few times over our tenure in these cages.

"Heard that before," I heard Laz whisper from their cell a little way down the dank hallways. Their southern lilt seemed to deepen and become thicker the hungrier they got.

"Alora..." I started, but I heard her shush me softly.

"Samara, I mean it." She was whispering so quietly that I knew the guard down the hall couldn't hear her. Our advanced hearing certainly made it easy to hold private conversations, although that particular gift had started to fade as well with our faltering strength. Eventually, I wouldn't be able to hear anything at all. "I drank blood." I sat up as quickly as my frail body would allow me to. I heard the others perk up as well.

"What do you mean?" I asked, trying to reign in my curiosity.

"When?" Silas asked, eagerly.

"Who was it?" Orpheus interjected.

"The last torture session in The Room." I shuttered at the label we had given the site of our 'interrogations'. It was a small metallic room with walls of pure aluminum, silver chains were reinforced into the cement floor. That's where they put us. The room was rigged with a sprinkler system. A toxic mixture of what Orpheus theorized as holy water and garlic concentrate would spray down from the ceiling dousing us in acidic torture. Horrors beyond what I could comprehend had been given out to us in that room as if they were earned. "They were cleaning up after their most recent scenting taunt. They must have thought I was passed out, which I nearly was." I cringed, my whole body tensing. I hated the thought of Alora in pain. "They spilled the blood." I pulled my knees to my chest and held them close. Just the thought of the red liquid crawling across the floor toward me made my mouth water.

"How'd you manage to drink it?" Orpheus asked, eagerly. He was starving, we all were.

"It wasn't much, barely a mouthful, before they dragged my body out of there." I growled at the image.

"Did they see you?" Silas inquired.

"No, and it wasn't enough to quench the hunger, but I have some of my strength *back. I can take the guard. I know I can,"* she promised, *and for the first time in a long while I felt the glimmer of hope.*

I should have known not to trust it.

The door to the office swung open and two individuals waltzed in. A taller slender woman and a shorter man with graying hair. They both looked rather haggard, and tired.

"Hello," the woman began as she crossed to the desk. "My name is Detective Barnes, this is Detective Argent. Thank you for stopping by." Orpheus, ever the frontman, reached a hand forward for the both of them to shake. I avoided breathing in their scent, although not entirely appealing, blood was blood and I was hungry.

"My name is David Green," Orpheus offered, and Laz and I exchanged a quick, imperceptible glance.

We had used aliases for a century. It helped us hide from Nameless, but we had never been questioned by the police, so we never had to use an alias for something so formal and so prone to an investigation. If the police chose to look into that name, they would find the very fragile cover we implemented, but it wouldn't take much to look deeper and find the falsified records. It was enough for a rental company...but the police? That was an avenue we'd never tested before. Before I could even begin to think of the name I would offer, Orpheus continued.

"This is Cal Freeman, Haven Jones, and Marcie Phillips." I schooled my reaction, smiling and tipping my head slightly toward the detectives whose eyes were scanning us.

"Heard you're just passing through town. Not staying for the season?" I watched Orpheus handle their questions expertly, like the leader he was born to be. He offered clear and concise information that sounded invested enough to give a reason for our continued presence in town, but nothing in-depth enough to raise any questions. He was a masterful protector.

"So, where did you say you saw him go?" Orpheus looked toward Silas to allow him to offer the answer.

"He went down the street, sorry, I don't really know the names- " Silas began. The Detective nodded before urging him on. "He went toward that gas station though, down the street from the bar. Didn't watch long enough to see if he went inside though." Silas was the one who wore Louis' image into that gas station. He would have been seen on cameras all over town on his way out. That was his job, and he was good at it.

Detective Barnes seemed to accept the information, but I noticed the suspicious look brewing on the man's face.

"Why'd you follow them out?" Argent asked, his eyes narrowing on all of us.

I felt Silas and Laz tense next to me, the memory of why we followed them outside fresh in their heads. I waited a moment for Orpheus to answer, but when I glanced at him he was still, taking a deep breath to calm himself.

I spoke up, quickly demanding the attention of the Detectives. "It was my suggestion actually." Barnes and Argent turned to look at me, patiently waiting for me to explain. "I guess it's a force of habit. If I see a woman who may be drunk being led out of a bar by a man, I tend to keep a particular eye on that just in case she needs any help." I saw the respect flash across Detective Barnes' face while Argent nearly scoffed and was just short of rolling his eyes. Bet he was the kind of guy who said 'not all men'.

"Do you think he's ok?" I asked, feigning platonic worry.

"We have no reason to suspect anything to the contrary at the moment," Detective Barnes answered diplomatically. "Well, thank you for taking the time to come down and talk with us." Orpheus shook their hands, and soon enough we were back out on the sidewalk in the open air.

Silas and Laz both exhaled, deeply. Their eyes were tinted slightly, but I could tell they still had a grip on their hunger.

"Let's head home," Orpheus offered, beginning the trek toward our rental. We had to pass the pier to get there, and on the way here, the four of us were silently walking past with our eyes fixed on the slightly aged red awning of The Maine Plotline. We stared at it like lovesick fools. I mean, they were the lovesick ones. Not me.

I couldn't be lovesick. There was no love here.

The walk there was painful, a sort of invisible string was drawing us to that small bookstore cafe. The walk home was worse.

The first flash of red hair in the wind had each of us coming to a stop. Our feet were glued to their spots. My heart was racing at the sight of her. She was wearing a blue shirt, showing off her creamy shoulders, and tight blue jeans hugging her curves. She sat on the park bench that was outside her store, a book in her lap. Her hair swirled around her face as she read.

She was stunning, and breathtaking, like a wonder of the world. For a brief moment, I forgot.

I forgot I planned to reject this fated bond between us. Forgot I made a promise that I will not break. Forgot I couldn't have her.

"Athena," the soft, pained and longing voice was Silas'.

"She's perfect," Laz added.

I hated that my heart wanted to agree.

Laz and Silas took a step forward, but Orpheus was quick to put his hands out, blocking their trajectory.

"We can't go over there, you'll scare her." Orpheus, ever the realist.

Silas grabbed his phone from his pocket, without ever removing his eyes from her form. I shook my head. He had been trying to call her several times a day since the night she blocked his number with no success. But that didn't stop him from attempting.

He dialed her number and held the phone to his ear.

"Holy shit, it's ringing," Silas exclaimed, barely containing his excitement. Laz and Orpheus were turning to him quickly.

"Speaker, now," Orpheus demanded, and Silas obliged, holding the phone out for us all to hear. The ringing felt like a lifeline. We'd been adrift in the open water for two days with no sight of land, but here she was, giving us a reason to keep swimming.

Our gazes traveled down the pier to where Athena was resting. She closed her book, sliding it onto the bench next to her as she shimmied enough to grip her phone from her pocket. Her free hand came to rest on her chest when she looked at the screen. I could see her shoulders rising and falling slightly faster, but the same fear we saw in her that night wasn't present.

A glimmer of familiar torturing hope bloomed in my chest.

It rang again, and again. She didn't leave her spot. She didn't answer. She didn't even move. It was like she was stuck.

"Come on, bookworm, answer the phone," Silas whispered. His voice was full of a type of pleading I'd never witnessed from him.

Another ring.

Then another.

With each ring, I felt my confidence waiver. She was fighting a battle inside her own mind, I could see it from here. Could feel her turmoil, her struggle. I wanted to tell her it was ok. Tell her we would never hurt her. That we would protect her.

Another ring.

She pulled the phone to her chest, and sighed, her shoulders slumping as she exhaled. Her chin lifted and she looked to the sky as if she could find the answer in the clouds.

She pulled the phone from her chest, staring once more at the screen.

Then she answered.

The dial tone ended, making way for the sort of buzzing silence that told us she was there.

My heart beat once, hard and strong. Renewed energy filled me and even the constant hunger waned for a moment.

"Athena," Silas said, his voice low and sultry, his eyes never left her form. "Thank you for answering."

She sighed, and even her soft breathing felt like a soothing balm on my burning chest.

"I want to explain everything, we all do." Laz and Orpheus were nodding along. Orpheus was wearing his usual charcoal suit, but the collar was slightly crumpled, not the pristine sharp edge he was used to sporting. His grip on himself was slipping. He needed her to hold onto.

"You are safe with us, I swear that to you, darlin'," Laz interjected softly. Their eyes shining with unshed tears as they watched her sitting on the bench.

"We know we scared you, and I'm so fucking sorry about that," Silas exclaimed, running a hand through his hair, pulling a few strands free from the tie at the back of his head.

She breathed, softly, calmly, still not responding, but still not hanging up. That was enough.

"Athena," Orpheus started, his usually calm, collected voice wavered slightly. "We owe you answers. And we're going to give them to you." I watched as she wiped a tear away with the back of her hand. "What we're going to say will not make any sense to you, and it will sound like we're lying, but I need you to promise that you'll keep an open mind."

I glanced over at him, breaking my concentrated gaze on Athena for the first time. His face was contorted with a strained emotion. Orpheus has only ever told four people about what we were. And three of us were here with him now.

It wasn't a secret he offered up freely. It wasn't something we go around advertising. Especially not over the phone. But we may not ever get the chance again if we didn't take it now. I knew it, so did he.

I looked over at the gorgeous woman who was intently listening to the call. Her chest heaved with labored breaths, her eyes watered with tears of confusion, her red hair gently swayed in the wind. She hadn't seen us yet, so we were seeing her in all her natural beauty. She was stunning, but it was more than that. She was powerful. She was strong. She was a woman who had been beaten down by the world, by the people who were supposed to protect her and when she came out the other side, she crawled her way through the impossible to put herself back together as well as she could. I understood that. Watching her, I felt my chest burn with want. My hands begged to touch her. My lips yearned to brush against hers. I wanted Athena. I needed her.

But I couldn't have her. It was going to kill me, but I was going to reject this bond. This connection that was making me feel alive, that had me nearly thinking I would be able to move on. I had to turn away from it. I tore my eyes from the object of all my joy and turmoil and looked at my friend, Orpheus. His frame was now blurry, from the tears that had started to gather in my eyes.

Despite the protest in his mind, Orpheus spoke the next words carefully... like a promise.

"There is more to this world than anyone realizes, things that may be considered myth to one person, could be another's very existence." He swallowed the lump in his throat. "It is imperative that even if you feel like what I tell you is false, you keep this truth close to your chest."

Silas and Laz were locked on Athena, their gazes somewhere between forlorn, and hopeful.

"We are not human, although I can assume you've already put that together." She inhaled sharply on the other side of the line. I didn't dare look back at her to see how her body reacted to that revelation. "We have been called many things throughout history, Night Walkers, The Undead, Damphir..." He took a long breath. "But most commonly we are called Vampires."

I couldn't resist. My eyes involuntarily searched for her again and I watched as she let the phone fall from her hand onto the bench. Her hands cradled her head and she shook it back and forth. We stood there, at the edge of the pier, watching her compose herself after hearing what we had to admit. But still, no matter how much we yearned to comfort her, our feet remained steadfast. Silas was holding the phone in his hand so tightly he was close to breaking the device. Laz was as still as death, their eyes glued to her, their hands rigid at their sides. And Orpheus was watching her like he was seeing his future. He could hide his affection, mask it behind his protective nature, and it might even work for Laz and Silas. But I saw it. Every painful ounce of it. He was drowning in his desire for her. It was changing everything for him. It was changing everything for me too. I wish I could embrace the change. Embrace this new chapter. Move on. Athena might be the future I was promised by whatever fates there are, but if I dive headfirst into a new future, I'm betraying the one I promised to Alora.

Athena was a worthy partner. Anyone would be lucky to share in her wisdom and kind heart. It just couldn't be me.

She rocked back and forth for a moment longer on the bench, while we watched. Then she gripped the phone in her hand, her sweet sighs sounded so desperate.

She prepared herself, taking several long breaths. Finally, with the phone pressed firmly against her cheek she spoke, in a voice that sent a shockwave directly to my heart, a second beat. I was shocked, feeling how lively my heart had become. The second in just a few minutes. More than the one beat an hour I was so accustomed to. She was doing that to me.

"Tell me everything."

ATHENA

I felt their eyes watching me, my skin burned under their gaze, but I refused to acknowledge them. I wasn't ready to invite them back into my personal space, but I would hear them out. I wasn't sure what I was expecting to hear, but nothing could have prepared me to hear those words. "...we are called Vampires."

I was stunned. Speechless. I waited for the punchline that deep down I knew was never going to come.

It was impossible.

It was a lie.

It was make-believe.

Although, even as my objections rattled inside my brain, the truth behind the confession rang true above it all. Their bright red eyes, the long fangs, the claws, how they reacted to my blood. The most insane of explanations was the sanest thing I had heard in days.

My first instinct was to react in fear. It's a conditioned response to 'monsters'. After a long deep breath, I let my body sway back and forth as if bouncing the information around my brain would help me absorb it.

They could have killed me.

They didn't.

There was a lot I didn't know, and I wasn't naive enough to believe I didn't need to know it, but I was ready to let them control the conversation.

"Tell me everything," I demanded.

Several shocked inhales sounded over the call. I knew if I looked toward the end of the pier and saw them standing there, they would take it as an invitation to come to me, and I wasn't ready for that. Not until I heard it all.

I also wasn't sure I was ready to see their faces, the ones I had come to care for, and longed to see.

"I was turned first," Orpheus began, his voice even. "I lived in Romania, well it wasn't called that back then, but that is what you call it now." I nodded, knowing he could see me. Could they see everything? I knew they were far away, but how good is their vision? If I breathe can they see my chest rise and fall? If I sweat will they see the bead run down my forehead? Maybe that's why it felt like they truly saw me. "I was ill, with no cure in sight. The healers had considered me a lost cause. They'd given up trying." My heart tensed almost painfully at the thought of Orpheus being abandoned to die alone. "I don't know who turned me, I don't remember it. But I spent the first several decades of my new existence learning how to control my thirst." I swallowed the lump in my throat. "Many, many years later, I found Samara."

I heard a whispered conversation beyond the phone that I couldn't quite make out, there was a slight shuffle and then I heard Samara's melodic voice. "Orpheus saved my life." I could hear the reverence in her tone. Her pride at knowing Orpheus, at being a part of his group. "He gave me a chance at a life where I could make choices for myself." Her voice cut out to make way for a muffled sob, I nearly turned to look at her.

"The others all joined our coven when they needed to escape most," Orpheus continued. "For one reason or another, we all had been dealt pretty shitty cards in our first life. This existence, this transformation. This was the escape. The second chance." I nodded my head. I could understand the urge to escape. Honestly, I can't even say what I would have done had I been given the same choice in those few months after going to the police about my stepfather. When the entire department and the town turned me into a liar and a whore.

Desperate people do desperate things, like begging to become a vampire.

"We've been a coven for a very long time," Silas interjected. "The closest thing to a family most of us ever had." I smiled softly at the fondness with which Silas spoke about them. I felt similarly about Davia. I had a wonderful mother who worked tirelessly to make sure I never felt like I was missing anything without having a father figure in my life. However, without any siblings, sometimes I did feel that tiny twinge of loneliness, at least I did until Davia filled that space with all her loud-mouthed glory.

"We take care of each other, we fight for each other...we would die for each other." The conviction with which Silas uttered those words nearly took the breath from my lungs.

"You would *kill* for each other," I whispered, shivering from the cool wind as it blew my hair around my face.

They were silent on the other side of the line for a few moments and I tried not to read into it. I told them I wanted to know everything, and I did. Even this. Especially this. I needed to understand, in order to decide what I would do next.

"Yes," Orpheus spoke the single word as if it shamed him. Which loosened the fear that was attempting to grip at my heart.

"You have to understand something very important about us, darlin'," Laz's sweet accented voice was breathy, they sounded desperate. "In order for us to survive we must consume human blood-"

I inhaled sharply at the admission of what I already had believed was true, and they continued quickly, "but we will only hunt those who deserve it," they continued. I couldn't help but scoff.

"Who decided you had the right to choose if someone deserves to die?" I bit, with more malice than I was anticipating. I've seen the news stories and read the papers. Every day people are being killed because someone 'decided' they deserved it. Women all over the world are being killed because men believe they "deserved" it. I couldn't help but feel disgusted at the notion.

"Louis deserved it," Orpheus seethed.

I stopped breathing.

Somewhere, deep down, I had considered that unbelievable and terrifying possibility after seeing their true faces, but even then, I didn't know if I wanted to hear the truth. To know Louis was dead, because of me.

"Don't you dare, Athena," Orpheus growled. It was such a demanding tone that I couldn't stop myself from turning my head in his direction. There they were, the four of them, the vampires. Standing steadfast at the end of the pier, huddled around a phone. All eyes trained on me.

I was locked in their gaze, unable and unwilling to pull my eyes from them.

They looked how I remembered them, their beautiful features prominently on display masking the inhuman creatures within.

Despite all the fear, and the logic telling me to cut ties, to run, to find Archer...there was this undeniable connection sizzling between us like a piece of paper over an open flame. Beautiful, powerful, deadly. I didn't stand a chance of staying away from them.

"You will never feel guilt over that scumbag's death, do you understand me?"

I heaved, breathing erratically as I watched Orpheus take a step forward. Just a single step, but it lit my core with electric energy. The others followed behind as he took slow deliberate steps toward me. "Never again will you blame yourself for the actions of another. Never again will you let their wrong-doings cause you pain. I can feel your guilt, Athena, and he does not deserve it."

I found myself nodding at him as he approached, the others hot on his heels with equally ravenous looks on their faces. I wanted to tell them to stop. Wanted to keep my distance, but their pull was just too strong.

"We kill monsters, Athena. Evil people who hurt others, who take what doesn't belong to them as if it is something they are owed."

My shaky breath comes quickly.

"We are not heroes-" he stated, as they breached the halfway point. Now that they were closer, I could make out more of their features. Their eyes, their lips. Things that have simultaneously haunted and comforted me. "We are not villains."

I inhale sharply at the hungry look in their eyes, and not a hunger that scares me, but one that excites me and has my core tightening in anticipation. They're close now. Twenty feet or so, I can nearly feel the cold radiating off of their bodies. Orpheus hung up the phone and spoke directly to me.

His voice was clear and intoxicating. "We are yours."

I put my hand up.

They stopped their approach, watching me for signs of distress, no doubt. Worried expressions cross their faces. Their stunning, handsome faces.

They paused to look at me as if they adored me. Their eyes scanned my form and I felt so secure under their watchful gaze. And even as my body longed to bridge the gap between us, to welcome my strangers from the bar back into my life, I knew I could not confuse those people with the ones standing before me now. I had to be careful, and smart. Logical. And logic was telling me to keep my distance until I knew everything.

"You turned into vampires in my store. Your eyes, your claws... You looked like-" I started, feeling like I was rambling and unable to contain it.

"Monsters." Laz finished for me.

I nodded.

"You chased me, I felt it. I thought you were going to..." I swallowed, putting a hand on my chest as I stood to face them fully. "I thought you were going to kill me."

They all simultaneously growled, in anger, but I wasn't afraid.

"We would never hurt you, Athena." Samara was the first one to speak, her eyes full of care, adoration, and sadness.

"But-" I began.

"No." Silas bristled. "No buts, bookworm."

My heart leapt.

"We would all rather die than to see any harm come to you, by our hand or another's." Silas looked like he wanted to reach for me. I almost let him.

"When you were in the store, you all said something," I started slowly, trying to make sense of my thoughts. "You said 'mate.' What does that mean?" I saw Orpheus and Samara exchange a quick glance and more emotions than I could ever perceive past through that one look.

"It means you are our fated mate, Athena. We were crafted by the stars to belong, mind, body, and soul to you." Laz wiped a tear from their eye as they explained it to me. "And you were forged to be ours."

I'd read a thousand books featuring the concept of a 'fated mate', and it was a beautiful story device used to give readers hope. To mimic the silly belief of soulmates. Had I grown up wishing there was someone out there who was perfectly tailor-made to love me? Of course, it was nothing but a childish dream.

"That's not real," I stuttered, taking a single step backward.

"Neither are vampires," Orpheus claimed. "And yet, here we are."

My heart began beating faster, as if it may just up and jump out of my chest onto the pier at my feet.

"I don't understand," I stumbled. Silas took a tentative step forward and I raised my hand again to stop his approach. His honeyed eyes softened with a mixture of pain and want.

"Mates are a powerful thing to our kind," Samara began, her face twisted as if it physically pained her to be in my presence. She wouldn't make eye contact. "It's like this intense draw, this string connecting your soul to theirs." She tilted her head toward the others. I noticed Orpheus toss her a forlorn look, but didn't have time to analyze it further.

"When someone is mated, their connection only grows stronger," Silas added. "They're stronger, faster, some say that any power they have before is enhanced after they complete the bond."

"What do you mean, complete the bond?" I asked, and watched as the four of them shared timid glances. "Whatever it is that you're thinking about hiding from me, don't." I smoothed the hem of my shirt idly, letting my hands fall to my side. "I said I wanted to know everything, and I do."

Orpheus stepped forward, but this time I did not retreat.

"In order to complete the bond," he began, his eyes darkening as he watched me. Inside I felt like cowering under his intense stare, but outwardly I stood my ground. "We need to taste you, Athena." A blush crept across my face, heat spread through my lower belly.

Orpheus smirked darkly, as if he could tell exactly what I was feeling.

"What?" I stammered.

"Your blood," he clarified, in a low husky timber. "We must taste your blood to complete the bond."

That admission did strange things to me. At first, I felt disgusted, but quickly that small tug at my heart tightened in anticipation. My heart soared. As if that was exactly what it wanted, exactly what it deserved. What it was made for.

"Would that kill me?" I whispered, afraid.

"Of course not," Laz growled between clenched teeth.

"You will always be safe with us, bookworm," Silas pleaded.

"What happens to me if you drink my," I lowered my voice, "blood...do I become.." I trailed off, timidly. A wave of uncertainty blanketing the rush of desire that had previously been there.

"That's not how it works," Samara explained sadly, a tenseness to her tone.

"How does it work, then?"

I watched as they exchanged yet another hesitant glance.

"Don't lie to me, please," I begged.

"In order to transform, you would have to drink from us as well," Silas whispered, just loud enough for me to hear. I glanced around the pier for any listeners, but there was no one close enough to overhear. Over my shoulder I tossed a glance back at The Maine Plotline and saw Archer sitting at the front counter, he was holding a book, but I could have sworn his eyes were watching us.

"What happens if you don't complete it? The bond," I asked, quietly. I heard a few soft whimpers from them.

"If you don't accept the mate bond, we will need to either reject it...or we'll die," Orpheus explained, his calm demeanor was undercut by a barely restrained anger.

The thought of any one of these people standing before me dead was making me feel physically ill, like I might lose my balance and pass out. The blood rushed from my face and I felt dizzy.

"Are you feeling ok?" Laz asked, anxiously.

"Yes, I'm..I'm fine. Just...processing," I rambled. They watched me cautiously for a few moments, ready to intercept me should I fall. I could make heads or tails of what I was feeling. What I was considering. I needed to understand the whole process and the pros and cons in order to make a logical decision here. I'm not talking about going on a date, I'm talking about solidifying some strange supernatural bond with four literal vampires. A decision like this requires time. And information. "How do you reject a bond?" I asked, quietly.

Silas and Laz let out a soft moan of agony. Laz's eyes welled with unshed tears. Orpheus watched Samara closely, something unspoken passed between them.

"We would have to create a new vampire," Samara breathed, nearly imperceptibly. She still hadn't met my eyes, and I couldn't deny the twinge of disappointment and rejection I felt at that realization. Laz and Silas looked shocked by that admission, had they not known?

Did she want to reject me? Is that why she can't look at me? Is that why Orpheus keeps watching her? Does she not want me?

Why does that thought bother me so deeply?

"Athena, please... don't," Silas begged, a hopeless look on his face. "Don't ask me to reject you, because I couldn't. I wouldn't be able to." Laz nodded their agreement. I couldn't stop myself from glancing at Samara to gauge her reaction.

She quickly wiped a tear from her cheek as she looked out over the railing toward the ocean. What I wouldn't give to understand what she was thinking right now.

"How long.. How long do I have to decide?" Orpheus couldn't hide his wince at my inquiry, but he schooled his expression quickly. The mask of professionalism was firmly in place again.

"The timeline is moving quickly, we will need to complete or reject the bond within the next few days. Three at most, I'd say." I nodded, shocked by how soon I'd have to decide the course of my future. Of all our futures.

"Ok," I started. "Thank you for telling me all this, for trusting me." It was earnest. I may not be able to sympathize with having a secret of supernatural origin, but I do understand a little bit about having a secret so big it could disrupt your entire existence. "I need some time to think. To absorb."

Orpheus, Laz and Silas nodded.

"Take the time you need, darlin'. We're not going anywhere," Laz assured me. I didn't even know how much I had needed to hear those words until something hollow inside my chest felt whole again.

I begin to take a step back, but pause and scan each of them again. They really are impossibly stunning, crafted from marble kind of beautiful. Now when I look at them, I still see the creatures from the store, but there's more to it now. There's more to them. I had just started getting to know them, just started learning about them, and indulging in the sinful pleasures they promised me.

Maybe I needed more to make this choice. Maybe I needed them to help me decide.

"I'd like to go on a date, with each of you, to talk, to spend time together. I want to make sure I make the right choice."

Silas's smile was blinding as he beamed. Laz exhaled in relief and Orpheus smirked again, darkly, in that way that feels so promising. Samara still hadn't looked at me, but I knew she heard me because her chest began to heave with labored breaths. If she didn't want me, I needed to hear that straight from her lush, red-painted lips.

"Name the time and place, bookworm," Silas agreed eagerly.

I nodded, promising to text them, then I turned to retreat into my store. The moment I turned my back to them, I felt a weight settle on my chest, and with each step away from them that weight got heavier and heavier. By the time I was back inside the store, my mind was swimming.

On one hand, the fear that had been looming over me since that night had dissipated. But on the other hand, what they had confessed to me was shifting everything I had ever known about the world, and everything I ever thought I'd want for myself.

Sure, I saw myself growing up and eventually settling down with a partner. Although, I knew I wasn't likely to leave Shockgrove, and the pickings were rather slim in town. But I had never considered multiple partners. Multiple people devoted to giving me care, and pleasure. I blushed, as I leaned against the cool door.

"Who were they?" Archer's voice broke me from the spell I was under. I quickly composed myself and smoothed my hair.

"Oh, just some friends who are in town for the season," I replied, hoping I wasn't appearing as flustered as I truly was.

Archer studied my face casually, then looked over my shoulder out the window toward the pier. His face was tense, his paint-stained hands were clenched at his sides. I narrowed my eyes at him, his body language was guarded, like he was angry at my interaction with them.

"Hey, I'm going to go out and grab some lunch, do you want anything?" He said, nonchalantly, quickly sliding out from behind the counter and walking past me toward the door.

"Uh, no. I'm ok. Thanks." He grunted his acknowledgment before slipping through the door and disappearing onto the pier.

I watched after him as he briskly walked back toward town. Shaking off the strange interaction, I took a seat behind the counter.

I had a lot of information to process, and some decisions to make.

One thing was clear though. I needed to confirm I cared enough about these strangers to agree to being bonded to them for my entire life.

Oh shit. How long would that be?

Were they going to want to turn me? Is that something I even wanted?

Panic was creeping into my consciousness, but I pushed it away, forcing myself to take deep breaths.

Tackle one problem at a time, Athena.

One breath at a time.

One step at a time.

One date at a time.

8

LAZ

Her wintergreen scent was even stronger than I recalled. In the days since I had seen her face, or heard her voice, I spent a lot of my time building up this image in my head, trying to remember every small detail about her, on the off chance I'd never see her again. The way she smelled, moved, the way she tasted. The memory of her I crafted was so vivid, so incredibly perfect that a small part of me worried I was putting too much pressure on the real Athena to live up to this indescribable version of her in my mind. But all it took was one glance to know nothing I could ever create would hold a candle to the perfection that was Athena Landry. My mate.

She stood her ground, keeping us at a comfortable distance, but the distance to me was anything but comfortable. I yearned to touch her, to feel her body pressed against mine. I needed her. But despite the pain I was in from restraining myself, the interaction went about as well as I could have dreamed. Well, maybe not dreamed. In the dream version of that conversation, she would have accepted us, and allowed us to drink from her right then and there so I didn't have to waste another useless second of my life on living without her by my side.

All things considered, it was a success. She wanted to try. She wanted to think it over. She wanted to spend time with us. With me.

I'd do whatever it took to show her the life she deserves to have with me.

We walked home in a daze, nobody said a word, but I'm pretty sure Silas' smile never faltered. He was on cloud 9, or whatever the supernatural equivalent might be.

We walked in a daze, distracted by the realization of our current situation. We had a chance to convince her. She was allowing us that, and I knew I was going to take it seriously.

When we arrived home, we let out a collective sigh of relief.

"Well, that went better than expected," Silas finally said, breaking the tension. The two of us erupted into soft laughter. Days of worry and fear escaping with every exhale. Things had gotten dark, and while we weren't entirely on the other side of the tunnel yet, there was hope. And hope is something worth holding on to.

"I'm not gonna tell you assholes what to do, but don't fuck up your dates, ok?" Silas teased, but I knew he wasn't kidding.

Orpheus watched Samara with a piqued interest that seemed... odd. There was something they weren't telling us. They were acting strange earlier, and now they were sharing silent loaded glances as if they were having full conversations with their eyes.

"I wonder who'll be lucky number one," Silas mused, resting his head back on the headrest of the chair. His exhaustion was evident. We hadn't been sleeping very well, how could we when our hunger was keeping us up half the night, and our desire for her occupied the other half?

We didn't have to wait long for an answer.

Ten minutes after we arrived home, we were scattered throughout the living room, in a collective state of exhaustion. I don't think any of us had realized just how impactful the threat of losing Athena had been to our well-being.

Silas sat with his head lulled back and his eyes closed, a soft snore sounded from him. Orpheus and Samara sat side by side on the couch, idly watching whatever mindless show was on, they were struggling to keep their eyes open too. I felt the sting of exhaustion, of course, but there was something else pumping, the adrenaline that comes from planning a perfect date.

I was scrolling through my phone, making notes, preparing a menu and finding the perfectly paired wine. Before too long, I had crafted the single best evening. One fit for someone like Athena.

I was swiping through the wine list of a local market when the notification banner appeared at the top of my screen with her name.

My heart thumped loudly once and I felt the toxic blood in my veins rush to my cheeks. If I were alive, I'd be blushing.

ATHENA: Hi, Laz.

A smile spread across my lips at the memory of her sweet voice speaking my name. I was eager to hear it again.

And because I couldn't contain myself.

I hoped it wasn't too much for her to hear, but it was the honest truth. Even before the bond revealed itself, I felt this draw, this connection to her. I couldn't leave her then, and I sure as hell couldn't leave her now. Not after knowing her.

What on Earth did she need to apologize for? This whole thing was our mess. Our fuck-up. We should have told her exactly what we were the moment we could. We waited too long.

I would say my heart skipped a beat, but it only beats once an hour so that's not a very good analogy. My fingers brushed across the screen hurriedly.

That was a lie.

I'd love her more.

I was never one for taking charge. Not in my former life, and certainly not in the coven. We had enough natural leaders with Orpheus and Silas constantly butting heads. I was content being the follower. It wasn't mindless though, my following. I was analytical, I put a significant amount of thought into what I chose to do with my life, and who I chose to spend it with.

When I was first turned, I did feel like I owed Samara a significant debt for saving my life, so I remained with her coven for years in order to learn how to control and adapt to my new reality. When I felt like I had a firm enough grasp on the person I had become, I spent a lot of time trying to determine if being a member of the self-proclaimed Wanderers Coven was what I wanted for myself.

I had to decide if Orpheus' hot headed attitude and strict rules were the

kind I could see myself following. I had to decide if I could cope with Silas'
recklessness. Hardest of all, selfishly, I had to decide if I could stand to see
Samara and Alora living so authentically when a similar expression of queer-
ness was what landed me face down in the streets in a puddle of my blood in
the first place.

Before there was even a description for how I felt about who I was, I knew I
never quite fit the binary boxes that society labeled for me. I've had intense
feelings for men and women alike, faced with so much persecution that I
sometimes didn't even know which way was up. There was a certain freeness to
Alora and Samara that I couldn't help but resent.

For a while, I wanted to leave. Wanted to get out of there and wallow in my
solitude as a person who had enough courage to know exactly who they were,
but not enough to become them.

Alora and Samara helped shape me. In their own way. Once I was able to
move past the anger and jealousy, it was like looking at a snapshot of what
could be.

As time moved, so did the standards, and the terminology.

I will never take for granted how lucky I have been to live through the
emergence of this sort of tentative acceptance. I am who I was meant to be, and
in every way, I owe that to Samara and Alora.

I may be a follower, but I know what I want, and I will protect my right to
have that for as long as I live.

LAZ: Meet me at the pier at 8?

I anxiously waited for her response, watching the bubbles appear and
disappear with her thoughts.

ATHENA: I'll see you there.

The next few hours were a blur of nerves and phone calls. I was given an
opportunity to prove to Athena that she has nothing to be afraid of with us, and
I was not going to mess it up.

After changing approximately five times, and downing a bottle of blood to
quench my hunger, I finally descended the stairs to the living room, where
Silas was laying on the couch.

"I take it, you're up first?" He asked, eyeing my wardrobe. A soft linen
button up, and tight khaki pants with rolled cuffs.

"Yeah," I answered absentmindedly. My mind was racing.

He stood, making his way over to me. His presence had always been thick and intoxicating, he had that kind of effect on everybody, but I couldn't help but wonder if recent activities were affecting the way his presence sent shocks of excitement through me. Or the way my entire body tensed in anticipation as he towered over me.

We hadn't discussed what happened between us with Athena that night. Not really. I wasn't sure anything really did happen. For all I know, Silas could have been swept up in the energy that night, the palatable lust that was rolling off of Athena's body and echoing through her moans. It was Athena he was turned on by, not me.

"You ok?" He asked, tilting his head to study me. My fingers were intertwined in front of me and I fidgeted with them nervously.

"I don't know," I replied honestly. He nodded, agreeing. My breath caught in my throat and I felt my eyes beginning to sting with hot tears that began to fall, freely. Through heaving sobs, broken and breathless, I admitted a truth I had been trying so hard to hide. "I'm scared, Silas."

He watched me carefully as I spoke.

"I'm so scared," I finished.

His honey eyes glanced down at me though his soft black lashes. "She's going to accept us, Laz. I know she will." He spoke with such conviction that I nearly believed him.

"She has to. Or I won't survive this."

Silas' hand clasped around the back of my neck and pulled my forehead to his. We stood there locked in a comfortable embrace for a moment. His breath mingled with mine as we drew comfort from each other.

"Just go out there, show Athena how amazing you are. She'll see it." He put a little more pressure on my neck, pressing me into him. "I know she will."

I let my hands drift up to rest on his hips, gently, not commanding. It felt comfortable, this embrace, like it was something we'd always been doing, although we were not the affectionate type before Athena showed us we could be.

Embracing the affection I had for Silas would not diminish the blinding passion I had for her.

After a few moments, Silas pulled back. His eyes were glossy and sincere. "Bring her back to us, Laz. If anyone can do it, it's you," he pleaded in a whisper. He looked so vulnerable, a way I had never seen before. Not from him. Before I could stop myself, I raised my hand to his face and let my thumb brush against the skin of his cheek.

We've considered each other found family for nearly as long as I'd been undead, but right here, in this moment of vulnerability, this was the most intimate we had ever been.

"I will," I promise. A new determination in my soul.

Silas nodded, leaning into my palm ever so slightly. Just enough to let butterflies loose in my stomach.

When he pulled back, stepping out of my personal space, I felt his absence. Which was a strange, but not an unwelcome, feeling.

With a nod, and newfound determination, I left to prepare for my date.

An hour later, after I was sure everything was as perfect as it was going to get, I made my way to the end of the pier. Despite the chilly Maine evening, the setting sun managed to burn my exposed skin, slightly. Not to the point of pain, but enough to remind me I was alive. Or my version of it.

My elbows rested on the wooden railing as I looked out over the restless sea. Waves crashed against the wooden posts below, lightly spraying my face with a mist. There was something familiar about the ocean. Not in the sense that I spent much time around it, because I hadn't, but this vast open body of water held so many secrets that even those who devoted their lives to studying it couldn't confidently say they really knew it. In some sort of weird way, being a vampire felt like that.

The sun was creeping toward the horizon of the water, sending golden rays scattering across the surface. Fractaling against the blue canvas with glittering reflections. It was not often that The Wanderers stayed in one place long enough to enjoy it, to come to know it. To relish in its beauty. Being on the run has destroyed these sort of calm contemplative moments. This was just another thing Athena was giving back to us.

I wasn't foolish enough to think we would never have to run again, but I was beyond thankful for Athena's gift of a reprieve.

In the time since we arrived in Shockgrove, Maine, we had begun to live again. To stop and smell the proverbial roses. She has inadvertently reminded us of something we had come to forget.

There was more to life than simply surviving it.

Sometimes it's ok to sit and watch the sunset over the ocean. Sometimes it's ok to spend an entire afternoon reading a good book. Sometimes it's ok to let responsibilities and fear fall away.

Sometimes it's ok to live.

I heard her footsteps approaching, but I forced myself to remain calm. Taking slow breaths to counteract the urge to taste her blood. She might not be aware of my sensitive hearing, and I want her to acknowledge me when she's ready. Her scent invaded my nostrils as she neared me, I inhaled shakily, fighting back my fangs. All I wanted to do was sink my teeth into her skin and claim her. I wanted her to be mine. Finally, and formally. I wanted her to wear my bite on her body like a promise.

"Hi Laz," she said with a fair amount of false confidence. When I turned to face her, I couldn't breathe. She had substituted her blue blouse from earlier for a deep hunter green shirt with soft patterns. The sleeves were held together at the wrist by ties and her legs were hugged by dark wash jeans. She was stunning. The kind of beauty that wasn't forced or pressured. Her face was painted in a dark makeup look, very reminiscent of that first night we saw her at the bar and just as she had that night, she was captivating me. Her red hair was bound at the base of her head in a loose bun, tendrils hung in every which direction and danced in the wind.

"Hello, there." I smiled warmly. She was close to me, closer than she had been since the night she ran from us, and my body was reacting in a nearly feral way.

"Thank you for meeting me," she added nervously, her eyes dancing around to the nearly empty pier. There were a few stray people walking around, which probably made her feel safer. The thought sent a jolt of pain to my chest.

"Thank you for giving me the chance."

She smiled, and briefly I saw the warm-hearted Athena who laid in bed beside me that night. It felt like forever ago. "Walk with me?" I asked, offering my extended hand. She eyed it for a few moments, studying the fingertips as if she thought the claws might return at any given moment. Which, I guess they could. I sighed, quietly, careful not to let my disappointment show on my face.

Slowly I pulled my hand back, letting it settle at my side. "Everything is at your pace tonight, ok?" She nodded, relief flooding her face. Stuffing my hands into my front pockets, I smiled and began heading toward the back half of the pier. She fell in step beside me, maintaining a few feet buffer.

"You look gorgeous tonight, Athena." I glanced over at her out of the corner of my eye to find a soft blush creeping onto her cheeks. The rush of blood beneath her skin had my body reacting. Heat coursed through me, warming me in a way only she could.

"Thank you." A soft laugh escaped her lips, and I wanted to capture it with my own. We walked in comfortable silence for a few minutes until we reached the steps that led down to the beach below. The moment we set foot on the sandy shore, I leaned down, slipping my shoes off and gripping them in my hand. She did the same and as she sunk her toes into the soft chilled sand, her body relaxed. I saw the exact moment when her comfort overtook her fear and I could have jumped for joy, but I had a date to impress.

She walked beside me, her smile infectious as I led her to the large blanket and basket I had set here a little while ago.

"What.." she asked, pausing and a small gasp sounded from her.

"Do you like it?" I asked, watching her as she surveyed the scene in front of her. She nodded, smiling timidly.

"It's beautiful," she choked out, holding back a flood of emotions. I moved to sit down. Placing the basket beside me, as a buffer. She settled in, her shoulders were tense and I saw her glancing around to ensure we could be seen from where we sat. I knew she would be worried about that, so I scoured the beach to find the spot that could be seen from the main road behind us, and anybody walking on the pier. She seemed to realize that and with a released breath she relaxed.

"My mom used to take me for beach picnics all the time," she recounted, smiling out at the water. "She would pack us some lunchables and juice, well I would get juice she would get wine," she chuckled softly. "And we'd sit there for hours just sort of talking about anything and everything." The sadness in her eyes wasn't desolate, instead it looked hopeful, like the remembering wasn't as hard as it used to be.

"You speak so fondly of her," I said with a hint of admiration. She hung her head slightly.

"She was my best friend." She sighed.

I reached into the basket and produced a bottle of moscato. She giggled as I popped the cork and poured her a glass. "We are definitely not allowed to drink this out in the open," she warned playfully as she gripped the stem of the glass in her hand. I poured my own glass and felt my entire body shake with laughter.

"If anyone asks, it's juice." I offered her a wink and her genuine smile felt so rewarding. A prize I was entirely unworthy of, but would cherish nonetheless.

"I wish I could have met her. Your mom," I whispered, truthfully. Athena nodded, sipping from her glass.

"I think she would have liked you," she laughed, half-heartedly. "You know, if she could get over the whole vampire thing." I studied her face as she spoke, trying to gauge her reaction.

"Can you?" I asked, she turned her head to face me, and I was struck breathless by the way the receding light painted her face in a warm amber glow.

"Get over the whole vampire thing?" She clarified, and I nodded. With a deep sigh, she looked back over the water, and I had to force myself not to stare at her bare inviting neck. "I'm trying to." It was the answer I expected, but it still gripped at my heart and sent a sharp pain through me.

"And if you can't?" I asked, turning my eyes away from her. Instead, I focus on the blanket beneath me, tracing the checkered pattern with my fingertips anxiously.

"I don't know," she replied. I took a drink of the wine, willing the sweetness to overpower the sour taste in my mouth as my hunger flared. "How did you.." she started.

"Become a vampire?" I finished for her, still averting my eyes.

"Yeah ."

I downed the rest of the wine and set the glass down, digging the base into the sand. I hugged my knees to my chest and sighed. "It's not a fun story," I warned.

"You don't have to tell me," she offered, but I shook my head.

"No, it's ok. I don't mind telling it, but it's hard to hear. It helps to know the story had a happy ending. It just took some time to get there." I heard her shift slightly, turning her body to face me, offering me her undivided attention.

"I was born in 1898." I heard Athena inhale sharply. "If you think that's a long time ago, wait till you talk to Orpheus," I offered, playfully. "I grew up in the south. Texas to be specific. A place where even to this day, it's not safe to be who you are. Especially when what you are is something they've never seen before. Something they don't understand." I saw her head nodding out of the corner of my eye. "I knew I was different. I found passion with men, with women, but that wasn't the crux of it. I never felt like me. Back then there wasn't a word for it, but I knew I had never, and would never, fit their mold. But despite that, I found love. His name was Charles." I paused, breathing deeply, letting the salt tainted air fill my lungs. "We hid our relationship from the town and the world. He wanted to remain hidden forever, he would have been content to live his life in the shadows, but that wasn't what I wanted. I would never tell his secret, but I wanted to tell my own." I wet my dry cracking lips with my tongue. "That angered a lot of people. It started innocently enough, with death threats." I chuckled, it was a humorless and hollow sound. "When it became clear I wouldn't change, couldn't change, they graduated to more violent displays of discontent." I swallowed the lump in my throat, carefully navigating this treacherous part of my history. I rolled my sleeves up, ignoring the sting of the setting sun's rays on the pale skin, to show her the scars that danced along the surface of my arms. So faint that you'd have to know what you were looking for to see them. But the visibility of a scar has no bearing on the severity of the trauma.

Sometimes the deepest scars are the hardest to see.

"Jagged, vicious little slices, given to me by men who decided it was their right to mutilate my body," I seethed through clenched teeth. A tear slipped from my eye, and flowed down my cheek. Suddenly, a soft, warm hand pressed against my skin. Her touch was a salve on a burn, an embrace after an injury. I turned my head to face her, leaning my cheek into her hold, eagerly. More tears slipped through the confines of my eyes as I scanned her face. There was so much empathy, so much care flooding her expression. I had never felt more visible than in that moment.

"One night, those men decided they had had enough of my existence. They decided I would be better off dead." Athena was crying, her hand pressed into my skin as her thumb wiped away the tears as they fell. "For hours, I endured their torture. Hit after hit, slice after slice. I wanted death. I begged for it. Those men hated me because they didn't understand me. They were afraid because I was unknown, but at least I understood it.Their hatred wasn't the worst part.. No, the unbearable part was that it was Charles who struck the final blow." She tilted her head to the ground, her hand fell from my face, a sob wrenched from her throat. "He hated me because he understood me intimately. He hated me because I was an extension of his own guilt and shame. He hated me because he loved me."

Her hands clenched into fists on her lap. I reached a hand out to her face to return the calming gesture. She allowed my hand to grip her chin and tilt her head up, her eyes met mine. Glossy and red, they still looked beautiful. Her skin was a soft canvas, I'd almost forgotten how it felt to touch her, if she'd let me, I'd never forget again.

"Samara found me in the street, she offered me a new life, with a new family, and I took it."

She closed her eyes, and leaned into my hand.

"Because of that, I've lived long enough to put a name to my identity. I lived long enough to see people like me living freer than we ever had before. There is still a long way to go, but the distance we've traveled so far is no small feat. And I got to witness it." They smiled softly. " It was like I had been spending so much of my life walking around in the wrong size shoes. They protected my feet, they got me from one place to another, but they were clunky and I would trip up. I couldn't walk unhindered." I held their hands together in front of them. "Because of this life, this second life...I got to try on new shoes."

A single tear fell down her face. "You found your size," she whispered, and I turned to face her, a rush of euphoria blooming in my chest. I smiled, choked up, holding back a sob. I nodded, letting the truth of those words hit me.

"Yeah... I found my size," I answered. "See? Happy ending." She let out a sound that was somewhere between a sob and a laugh and I smiled sweetly at her.

"How do you do that?" She asked.

"Do what?" I brushed my finger against her chin.

"Find the bright side in something like that." I sighed, letting my hand fall into my lap. "How do you look at those scars everyday and survive?" She trailed a light touch across the scattered white lines on my forearms. "You carry these, but it doesn't seem to weigh you down. My scars are invisible, but they still feel unbearable."

I furrowed my brows and exhaled slowly. "Come with me," I said, standing up and once again extending my hand to her. This time she accepted it. I pulled her with me toward the shoreline, the rush of cold water brushing against my bare feet.

"Where are we going?" She asked, playfully, giggling when the cold water startled her.

I scanned the water quickly, my eyes searching the crystalline water. "What are you doing?" She asked, as I bent over at the waist, reaching my hand into the ocean and finding what I needed.

I turned to face her, holding out the oyster in my palm.

"I don't get it," she said with a slight smile.

I cracked the oyster, opening the shell enough to see the soft-white round pearl inside. Athena inhaled excitedly and watched as I removed the pearl and placed it in her palm.

She studied it. "Did you know only oysters that are wounded in some way can produce pearls?" I said softly.

She glanced up at me with disbelief in her features.

"It's true," I continued. "Essentially, if an unwelcome or outside substance enters the oyster, like a parasite or a grain of sand, the oyster gets to work creating layers upon layers of protective cells to defend itself from the intrusion. Those layers build up and eventually become a pearl. The more wounds the oyster endures, the more pearls are created."

She looked back at the pearl in her hand with an expression of wonder, a tear slid down her face.

"Each scar becomes something valuable. Something beautiful," I closed my hand over hers. Her eyes met mine. "Your pain will always be with you, Athena. But that doesn't mean it can't be a beautiful part of you. That doesn't mean it's not worth carrying."

My hand was resting gently on hers while her chest heaved with labored breaths. I looked down at her lips as they parted slightly. I wet my lips again and her eyes traced the movement intently. A soft inhale was the only sound between us.

Suddenly, her lips crashed to mine and everything around me exploded into vibrant sounds and colors. The world had been a dull excuse of existence, but with her kiss she introduced me to what life can be. Her hands snaked around my neck and held me to her, and I stole kiss after kiss from her willing lips. Euphoria like I'd never experienced before flooded my veins as her soft moans were muffled by our kiss.

My hands tangled in her hair, holding her against me with restrained desire. Her scent was driving me to the edge of my restraint. Hunger pulsed through me. I needed her blood nearly as much as I needed oxygen.

I felt my fangs begin their slow descent, and I pulled back, turning my face from her and rushing back up the beach toward the blanket.

"What's wrong?" She asked breathlessly, chasing after me.

"I just need a second," I answered, through tight lips as I sank down onto the blanket, my body facing away from her. I felt the mindless creature beneath my skin threatening to break free, but with each breath I placed another brick up in the wall between us. I knew my eyes had darkened, and my claws had elongated, and I hid my face from her so she couldn't see me. I wouldn't survive it if she ran again.

Her hand gripped my face and she applied pressure, forcing me to turn to her. I fought it for a moment. "Please, I don't want to scare you," I begged, but she persisted, turning my face to her. The moment her eyes landed on me, I expected her to drop her hand and leave me there, but she didn't. She sat there, her hand exploring the skin of my face. Her eyes scanned my sharpened features as if she was looking for something specific.

"This is still you," she whispered, and I nodded. Entranced by her bravery, her kindness. The mindless need to complete the bond mixed with the mindless desire to please her, and I felt my fangs retract, my eyes returned to their normal shade and she watched with fascination.

"It's me. It's always been me, Athena." Something in her expression shifted then, like a barrier had been breached.

"I know," she whispered before claiming my lips with hers again. Her kiss was soft, but demanding. It felt like a promise, and my heart burst to life.

My hands held her to me, cradling her like the prize she was. I could live a million lifetimes and never earn her affection, but I would spend the rest of my existence trying.

Her fingers danced along my exposed forearms, brushing against the scars as if she was acknowledging each and every one. Her tongue pressed against my lips begging for entry and I opened willingly, letting her in. I would always let her in.

In a flash, her leg swung over my hip and she was straddling me. I was only vaguely aware of the public nature of our reunion, but I couldn't care less. Her heated center pressed against my length, and I felt it harden to a nearly painful point. She slid across me, chasing her own desire through our clothes-covered bodies.

"I've missed you," she admitted against my lips, and I groaned as her center created friction against my eager need.

"You'll never have to miss me again," I promised. She rode me eagerly, her breathing coming in ragged spurts. I met her trust for thrust, despite the confines of our clothing, I felt her burning heat and knew any intimacy with Athena had the ability to claim me mind, body and soul. She sped up, her hips moving in disjointed quick movements, as she chased her release. I slipped a hand down the front of her jeans, and the first brush of my fingers against her swollen bud was met with an encouraging moan. I slid through the slickness there eagerly, and impatiently. Pursuing her orgasm as actively as she was. She rocked onto my fingers, guiding me lower to her core. I slipped a finger inside of her heat and she cried out, tossing her head back. Her heart beat matched the pace of my breathing. Slow, steady, needy.

"Oh, Laz," she exhaled, and I nearly came from the sound of her voice. My fingers pressed against her center, in and out, sliding easily though her slick desire. Her breathing ramped up as she climbed to the heights of passion. Our bodies were communicating through a language I would only ever be able to speak with her.

"I'll never get tired of watching you fall apart, darlin'," I whispered through my own ecstasy.

When she reached her peak, she let out a scream, I pressed my mouth to hers to muffle the sound. Those sounds were mine and I'll be damned if I let anyone reap the benefits of hearing her scream for me.

She bucked against me, riding the last of her release, and I knew nothing would ever compare to basking in the beauty of her desire. I restrained myself, focused only on her. A feat I would have considered impossible, but most of my energy was diverted to keeping my fangs from sinking into her throat.

When she slowed her movement, and looked down at me, her flushed cheeks darkened with embarrassment. She started to dismount, but I held her in place with a wicked smile, letting my fingers press deeper into her. She moaned at the renewed sensation.

"Don't go," I pleaded. She smiled, softly, laughing.

"I've never done that before. Publicly, I mean," she admitted, shyly. I gripped her hips tightly with my free hand and pressed her down onto me again. She moaned. I let my fingers dance against her clit once more before removing them from the front of her jeans. She sighed at the loss.

"Me either," I agreed, my eyes landing on her neck, I watched intently as the vein pulsed just beneath the surface. Taunting me. Instead of tasting what I so desperately needed to, I slid my finger into my mouth and sucked the sweet taste of her arousal off. The delectable taste satisfied my hunger, for a moment.

Her eyes darkened as she watched me, but I couldn't focus on anything but that spot on the column of her throat.

"You are trying not to bite me right now, aren't you?" She deduced. I swallowed, turning my eyes to her and nodded. She bit her bottom lip with a contemplative look on her face. "What happens if I let you?"

I couldn't breathe for a moment as the anticipation of doing just that seized me. "If we accept the bond, then we belong to each other. Forever."

She absorbed that answer for a few seconds before she dismounted, swinging her leg back over mine and sliding down onto her spot on the blanket. She leaned back, laying down so that her gaze was trained to the sky, a sort of wistful look was painted on her face. She raised the pearl I gave her above her eyes and studied it.

I slid down until I too was laying on the sand. Her ragged breathing was beginning to slow, and I hoped regret would not find its way into her mind.

"Your forever, or mine?" She asked, quietly. Turning the pearl in her fingers. I let that question ruminate in my brain for a second before answering the only way I could.

"My forever is yours, Athena. However long you want that to be."

"So you wouldn't want me to become a...like you?" She held her hands tightly against her stomach as she watched the night sky overtake the orange and pink reflections.

"I only want what you want for yourself. This life was the right choice for me. That isn't the case for everyone. I would never take that decision from you." She sighed.

Her phone vibrated and as she checked it, I saw the coy smile form on her lips. "Tell Silas that I said he can wait his turn." She giggled, tossing her phone down onto the blanket.

"He wants to have our date tonight." I rolled my eyes playfully.

"Of course he does," I lamented. She laughed and rolled over until she was resting on her elbows the pearl pinched between her thumb and forefinger.

"Does it not bother you?" She asked, suddenly serious. "Sharing my time, attention ...body?" She added, meekly.

"At first, the thought of sharing you with him made me want to rip Silas' head clean off, I nearly did, in fact," I recalled, a slight chuckle ringing in my voice. "But, the more I have gotten to know you, the more I am intimately aware of how much you have to offer. You are everything, Athena. It would be selfish of me to keep that to myself when you deserve every ounce of love you can get."

Her soft smile deepened, a strand of red hair blew into her face. I brushed it back behind her ear and tried to memorize the look she was giving me.

"Go meet Silas," I said. Her eyebrows shot up.

"But I'm with you," she argued.

"And you always will be, even when you're not." She turned her face to the sand and furrowed her brows.

"This is not a selfless act, darlin'. The sooner you have your meetings with the others, the sooner you make your choice and the sooner I get to claim your pleasure and make you mine." It was a bold claim, but one I was positive in making. After the way she looked at me, the way her body sought her ecstasy from mine, I knew it was only a matter of time. Athena was mine. She knew it too.

Her face darkened with a blush, and she leaned forward to brush her lips against mine.

It was a vow.

As she got up, dusting off the sand from her clothes and slipping the pearl into her pocket, I stood to meet her. "You have no idea how much today has meant to me," I stated, earnestly. She smiled, unhindered and freely, a stark contrast from the looks of fear she was harboring at the beginning of the evening.

"I think I might," she offered before pressing her lips to mine once more then turning to head back to the pier.

I watched her walk away, but this time I was confident she would come back.

9

ARCHER

If you would have told me a week ago I'd be tailing a coven of extremely powerful and dangerous vampires through a small New England town, I would have called you a fucking liar. But here I was, following two of the four creatures across town. When I saw them earlier, it was like a time machine had captured me and forced me into my worst memories. The several months where The Wanderers were prisoners of Nameless were infamous in our line of work. I had never seen them, but I knew who they were the instant my eyes landed on their forms on the pier.

Once the shock of seeing them, right there, out in the open, during daylight no less, had worn off, I focused on Athena's reaction. She was frightened and hesitant, that much was clear from her body language, but there was a familiarity there I had not expected. She knew them. Intimately, I'd wager based on the way they respected her boundaries. She put her hand up, and they paused. Keeping their distance from her. That wasn't a quality I expected from these blood-thirsty monsters.

I studied the interaction through the lens of a Hunter. Or at least I tried to. I couldn't help the way my palm itched to grab my stake and move to protect Athena from their vicious nature. But I knew I had a job to do and I was not going to be able to do it without the benefit of my anonymity.

That's why I haven't used the paint yet, haven't made the mark, and haven't let them know I was here. They would figure it out eventually, I'm sure, but with any luck, I'd be dragging their asses to Nameless by the time they pieced it together. And then it'll be too late for them.

I sprinted after them initially, but I lost their trail. I spent the better part of the afternoon trying to pick it back up. I cursed myself for getting so close, and being unable to follow through. I could practically hear my father's voice calling me a disappointment. A few hours later, as luck would have it, I saw two of them emerge again in town. This time I was determined not to lose the trail.

I haven't spent much time in the field, but I know how to tail someone. The tall one with the suit looked around him, and checked his surroundings a few times, a habit I can guess he picked up after his encounters with the Hunters. The woman with him, the only female left in the coven after my dad killed the other, walked dazedly, staring forward. A few times, Suit Guy glanced in my direction, but I schooled my reaction and willed myself to remain calm. I couldn't let my own fear get in the way of completing this mission. From protecting Athena, and all humankind, from these monsters.

I followed them through the streets, silently begging them to lead me to their den. Wherever it is they're calling home base for now. If I can find that, I'll be able to get the jump on them. Just as I started to feel the bloom of hope in my chest, I saw Suit Guy's eyes catch on something off to his left. He whispered something to the woman who carefully gazed over her shoulder in that direction.

My eyes followed theirs to see the most obvious undercover cop car I'd ever seen. Through the darkened windows, two individuals sat stoically. I couldn't make out their features, but their forms were obvious enough. Without slowing their walk, the vamps turned and headed in a new direction.

Damnit.

The car remained still. Turns out, I wasn't the only one hoping to get a peek into the secret life of these creatures. As they turned down a new street, heading back toward town, I silently cursed the cops for their incredibly pathetic attempt at remaining inconspicuous. Now, who knows how long it'll be until they lead me to their den? They certainly won't go there while they're being followed.

I remained a few hundred yards behind them all the way to the diner at the corner of town. They slipped inside, Suit Guy ushered the woman inside first and offered a quick scan of his surroundings before following her in. The neon sign read 'Dale's,' and the moment I stepped inside I felt like I had been transported to the 50s. The diner had charm, the kind you don't really find in big towns. I can see why a quaint town like this attracts so many people during its season. It's got quirks. I could probably be happy here if I was allowed to.

The vamps took up a booth in the corner of the diner, and I thanked my lucky stars it was crowded enough in there to justify my sliding into the booth right behind them. The hair at the back of my neck stood at attention, everything in my entire body told me not to put my back to them, but if I wanted to hear anything in this loud place, I needed to be close. Sliding on a pair of headphones to give me an outward reason for ignoring the world in favor of listening, I strained to hear them.

"Of course, they're tailing us," Suit Guy exclaimed, quietly seething.

"They're hoping we make a mistake," the woman replied. Funny, I'm hoping for the same thing.

"We won't." Suit Guy was very resolute, it was almost admirable. Almost.

"What are we supposed to do, Orpheus?" The woman asked. Orpheus, a fitting name for a creature of the underworld. I made a mental note of that as he replied.

"I wish I knew." He sounded defeated. An attribute I hadn't expected from the fearsome and ruthless leader of The Wanderers.

"We can't stay here long," she stated.

"What can I get ya to drink?" I jumped slightly at the voice. Glancing over at the petite older woman wearing the baby blue dress with a pad and pencil in her hands.

"Coffee? Decaf." I say, and she smiled, jotting it down. I try to focus on the continued conversation behind me but some things were lost to me in the loudness of the encounter.

"Sure thing, sweetheart. Be right back." I expected her to head away, but she slid down to the booth behind me.

"Anything to drink today?" I awaited their answer eagerly. I had no idea if vampires could even consume human sustenance.

"Any chance you have a mimosa?" The waitress giggled, no doubt finding herself enamored by the lead vamps charms.

"No such luck, honey. But I can get ya orange juice, what you do with it once it's at your table is your business." Orpheus offered a soft chuckle.

"Just a water then, Maureen." My eyebrows rose. The big bad evil vampire took the time to learn the waitress' name and address her as such."And you, sweetie?" The waitress, Maureen, asked.

"I'll have chocolate milk." After the waitress assured them she'd be right back, I heard Orpheus let out a low choked laugh.

"Shut up," the woman exclaimed playfully. "Chocolate milk is delicious and you know it." I couldn't quite wrap my head around the fact that I was listening to the so-called 'most dangerous coven of vampires' joking about chocolate milk.

"Do you think she'll accept?" the woman asked, quietly, nearly too quiet for me to hear. I heard Orpheus sigh. Accept what?

"I couldn't possibly fathom a guess. She was so afraid of us, Samara. You don't just forget that kind of fear." The woman, Samara, took a deep breath.

"You know why I can't do it, don't you?" Do what? Fuck, I wish they'd stop speaking so vaguely.

"I know that's what you're telling yourself."

"I'm going to do it... reject the bond." Bond? I leaned back, trying to ensure I didn't miss a single second of their hushed conversation.

"You know what that means, right?"

"Of course, I do. I'm not making this choice lightly, Orpheus." Samara raised her voice briefly before calming herself again.

"So what is your plan then? Run away with your fresh turn? Start a new coven? You would leave your family?" My head was spinning. None of this made any sense to me, but I made mental notes on each and every moment, each word.

"I can't stay and watch you be happy."

"Then stay and be happy yourself!" There was a silence then that was only broken when Maureen came back to drop off our drinks. She started at their table this time. Asking for their order. Orpheus coldly asked for a few more moments to decide. When she came to my table, I ordered the very first thing my eyes landed on from the menu. She sauntered off to place the order and I retrained my focus.

"I can't."

"No, you can. But you're deciding you aren't allowed to. You're placing this arbitrary restriction on yourself. Nobody else is forcing this on you. Not me. Not Silas or Laz. Especially not Alora."

Samara sucked in a sharp breath.

"Don't be an asshole, Orpheus." She exhaled on a long slow breath.

"Do you truly believe you cannot accept this bond?" He asked and I heard the tension in his voice.

"I know I can't."

Maureen dropped my food, a Belgium waffle apparently, onto my table and then made her way to the vampires again. "Just the drinks for us today, Maureen." I started scarfing the waffle. I'd need to be done before they left if I wanted to continue following them.

"Ok," Orpheus finally said after a few moments.

"Ok?" She asked.

"Ok, I promised you once that you'd never have to give any more of yourself than you were willing. And I meant that. If you can't accept the bond. I won't either." He sounded confident in his statement, but something about the way his breath hitched told me he was anything but.

"I would never ask you to do that," Samara offered exasperatedly.

"I know, you don't have to ask me. I'm offering." Orpheus continued. "You are my family, Samara. I spent centuries suffering in agonizing loneliness. Until I found you. Nothing, not even a mate bond could make me forsake the bond I've created with you." I heard a soft sniffle. Samara must have been crying.

"But she's your mate." My heart rate quickened. Were they talking about Athena? Was Athena this vampire's mate? Holy shit.

"And you're my sister."

"What about Laz and Silas?" The other two, I noted.

"They will have each other...and her." He sounded strained as if the very thought of it was painful.

"I can't let you..."

"I'm not asking you, Samara. If you decide you cannot accept the bond with Athena, then neither will I. This is not some sort of trick, this is not my way of pressuring you. I mean every word I say. No matter how much it will hurt. No matter how much of my soul I'll be leaving behind with her, I choose you."

A strange emotion stirs within me - something vaguely resembling empathy, but I quickly stamp that out, finishing the last bite of my waffle.

"But if you're going to reject her, she needs to hear it from you." Orpheus challenges, and I heard Samara wipe away a few tears.

"And you? Will you still meet with her?"

"I will," he answered.

"Thank you, Orpheus," she whispered, so vulnerable, so full of love. I had no idea how these people were considered villains.

"No need to thank me. Especially not until we do what we have to. We can't do it in this town, there's already so much heat surrounding the missing guy." My ears perk up.

"I know. I don't suppose you think we have enough time to find someone willing?" Fuck, are they talking about...

"We have maybe two days tops. It took weeks for me to explain the nuances to you, for you to fully understand what you were in for. We won't have the luxury of that kind of time."

They're going to make another vampire.

They're going to kill someone. Someone who's not willing.

Fucking monsters.

They slid out of the booth, and after dropping a twenty on the table, I followed suit. Far enough behind that I could just barely see them in the distance, but it was enough. With this newfound determination, I felt brewing within my chest, I tracked them all the way to a white beach house just off the beaten path. They filed inside and I crouched in some brush outside a house across the way.

These creatures nearly made me feel sorry for them. Showing me a type of humanity I didn't think they were capable of.

Every new thing I learn about them makes them more confusing. Maybe this is how they've brainwashed Athena, by charming her. She doesn't know the real monsters behind their skin. I would show her the truth, I would protect her from falling into their trap. I would save her.

10

ATHENA

Walking away from Laz, with the slick evidence of my arousal between my legs, I struggled to make sense of just how quickly desire for Laz overcame my fear. It felt like my soul was seeking something it could only find in their arms. Was it mindless lust, or was it this mate bond? I wasn't sure. But one thing was clear. I wasn't afraid anymore. I don't know when it happened, but it did. There wasn't a doubt in my mind that these people were not going to hurt me.

But even with that obstacle out of the way, I still had a decision to make. A life-altering decision. Just because I'm not afraid, doesn't mean I want to bind myself to them for the rest of my life.

Does it?

The thought of waking up early and spending a lazy Sunday morning filling out the crossword with Laz certainly does sound like a dream come true. But all dreams end, and I need to be sure I'm willing to survive the nightmares before I get lost in the dream.

SILAS: Follow the roses.

Before I had a chance to text back, asking what he had meant, I arrived at the top of the stairs to the pier and instantly understood. Scattered across the wooden walkway were hundreds of pink rose petals. Tears tickled my eyes, but I held them back. The wind was relatively still, but the slightest breeze had their delicate forms dancing along the ground. There was a clear direction,

301

leading directly to The Maine Plotline. I swallowed the lump in my throat and followed the path.

Guilt seeped its way into my mind. Was it wrong of me to accept the pleasure they were offering me without giving them an answer about the bond? Should I refrain from getting physical with any of them in order to keep my mind clear enough to make an educated choice?

Probably.

But the moment I entered the open store and felt Silas' presence envelop me like a lust-filled cloud, I knew I wouldn't be able to resist.

"Silas?" I called out, my voice heady. "How'd you get in here?"

Then, venturing around one of the stacks was Mr. Tall-Dark-and-Sinful himself. His torso was covered by a tight white t-shirt that accentuated his biceps and showed off the intricate black serpent tattoos on his alabaster skin. Dark black jeans hugged his thighs, and a silver chain hung from one of the pockets and dangled against his leg. Black hair hung loosely in his face and down to his shoulders, and that delectable lip ring glistened in the light. Fuck, he was sex on legs.

"Bookworm, if you don't stop looking at me like that, we're going to have to skip all the important stuff I had planned and skip right to the after-party." My core tightened at that idea, remembering the way he dominated my body at the drive-in. What could he do to me when we were in the privacy of my store?

"Hi, Silas," I whispered, carefully avoiding scanning my eyes across his chest again.

"Hi," he replied, the sweetest little smirk spreading on his lips. I was dazzled, utterly and completely. He was stunning. "I'm sure you have questions, and I know Laz probably answered several of them, but I want there to be no secrets between us. No walls. I want you to ask me anything, and I'll answer it."

I nodded, thinking about the wealth of information Laz had offered me. There were plenty of questions I still needed answers to, and I know it's important for me to understand everything there is to know, but looking at him and seeing the inherent sadness between his eyes - the sadness I put there with my fear and indecision - I had only one thing I wanted to say.

"I'm sorry," I spoke into the emptiness between us. The air felt charged.

"I'd be a liar if I didn't admit that these last few days were some of the most painful I'd ever experienced."

I winced, and he must have seen me because he stood from his relaxed state and took a tentative step forward.

"But you don't have to apologize to me."

I shook my head. "Laz said the same."

"Laz was right," Silas stated, confidently. He stood his ground, keeping several feet between us. A buffer that was simultaneously clouding my mind with lustful thoughts and allowing me to breathe.

"But I am sorry," I offered, eagerly.

"Stop apologizing." He commanded.

"Yes, sir." The word slipped out as if it was the most natural response in the world. Silas' eyes darkened sinfully, and his tongue ran along his bottom lip. A delicious-sounding groan rumbled from his chest and seemed to hit me directly in my core.

"Fuck, bookworm," he sighed, running his hands along his face in agony. "You are trying to kill me aren't you?" I smiled innocently, and his hands clenched at his side. I took a step forward. "I'm trying to be a gentleman here," he groaned.

"Uh-huh," I replied, continuing my trek toward him.

"I wanted to answer your questions, give you context and information... conversation.." He was stumbling over his words, clearly battling against his desire for me and his desire to respect my boundaries.

Fuck my boundaries.

When I came to a stop just a foot from him, I felt the cold roll off of him in waves. It felt like the brisk morning air. Comforting, welcoming. I looked up at him through my dark eyelashes and was once again awe-struck by his beauty.

"I do have questions. A lot of them." I brought a hand up to his chest, letting it settle against the material of his shirt there. He inhaled sharply and nodded while his eyes tracked my movement. "But I think we have some lost time to make up for first." He looked shocked for the briefest of moments until I added. "Sir."

Then it was all over for me.

His demeanor switched from the relaxed and sassy Silas I had come to enjoy, to the dark and dominant lover, I'd come to burn for.

"So, my baby girl wants to play, huh?" I nodded arousal flooding between my legs. "Words, baby girl, use your words."

"Yes, sir." He hummed darkly, taking a slow step back.

"I'm going to give you everything you want, but first..." he smirked wickedly. "I want to read with you." A thrill shot through me at the idea of what he has planned for us. If our 'reading' last time is any indication, I know it's going to be sinful and delicious.

"Stay here, do not move until you are told. Do you understand?" I swallowed the lump in my throat, pushing away the smallest threat of memory from that night so long ago, when I was told a very similar thing. "Answer me," he snapped.

"Yes, Sir," I squeaked out.

Silas let his eyes travel over my form once more before stepping away and disappearing into the stacks of books. I stood silently for a long while, listening eagerly for any sign of his plans. Finally, he spoke.

"'She stood cautiously at the edge of the room,'" I heard his voice echo sexily from somewhere deep in the belly of the store. "'Desire flooded her lower core. She knew if she went to him, she would be lost to the lust he was promising.'" I smiled. "Hmm, this book sounds interesting. Time to lock the door, baby girl. Do it now." I turned and locked the door behind me, smiling at the irony that just a few days ago I was locking this door to keep him out, but here I was locking myself inside with him. "Good, now come and find me, come read with me." I followed his instructions eagerly.

"'With each step, her core fluttered with anticipation. One thing was abundantly clear.'" His voice was getting louder as I ventured through the stacks. The fairy lights cast a soft glow over the aisles. The dark-painted walls and cozy velvet furniture scattered throughout only added to the torturous temptation that surrounded me and set my skin alight. I tensed as I peeked around every corner, trying to follow his beckoning call.

"'She wanted him to find her, wanted him to claim her in every way a man can claim a woman.'" Excitement danced across my skin. Was it wrong? Maybe. Did I care right now? Not one bit.

I turned a corner to see Silas lounging on a dark green velvet loveseat, his body lazily sprawled across the furniture.

He held a book in front of him, but his coy smirk told me he knew I was there.

"'She wanted him, nearly as much as he wanted her.'" He looked up from the pages, and his honey eyes met mine directly. My heart skipped a beat. He laid the book down on the cushion next to him and stood slowly.

I remained glued to my spot, watching him with careful eyes.

"He needed her forgiveness," he continued, the dialogue from the book long forgotten as he spoke from his own heart. "He needed her to know she was safe with him."

"She wasn't afraid anymore," I added, and I watched as the worry drained from his face, replaced with dark eagerness.

"He would go to the ends of the world to satisfy her." He took another step forward, his presence overwhelmed me in the way only he could.

"She was working on letting him," I whispered, venturing into his space. His lips were inches away, and the taste of his breath on my mouth was sweet and intoxicating.

"He wanted to kiss her." He whispered, and I felt the brush of his lips against mine.

"She wanted him to fuck her," I pleaded against his lips.

Silas' shocked laugh was the kind of dark sound that sent a flood of desire to my core. I groaned. "Ask politely," he taunted darkly.

"Please, sir."

His mouth was on me in an instant. Our kiss was a violent display of passion and need. My hands gripped the base of his shirt and pulled it up, breaking our kiss for only a moment, but his lips claimed a place on my bare neck and he ran his tongue over the vein there. His fingers made quick work of the buttons on my jeans.

I was suddenly lost to my base urges. My hands moved where they wanted, searching for some sort of relief. His lips brushed against my chin, and then the space just below my ear, and finally finding the column of my throat. My pulse quickened. His mouth found mine just as his hands pushed my pants down my legs.

"I can sense your arousal, baby girl. You want this cock don't you?" I nodded, whimpering against his mouth. "Say it," he growled.

"I want your cock, sir."

My hands gripped his waistband and he helped me relieve his perfect body of his clothing. His thick length sprung free and pressed against my bare skin. The chill his body gave me at our point of contact had me shivering in anticipation.

Then his palm came to my throat, closing around the column eagerly. A move he'd done before, but this time, ever so briefly it wasn't Silas there. A flash of perfect hair and an unassuming all-American smile had my body seizing. "Blood," I whispered.

Silas' hand was gone from my throat in an instant. "Athena, hey. Are you ok?" I nodded, softly, but ashamedly. "Where'd you go, just now?" I wiped a tear away from my cheek.

"I'm sorry, It's not you. I just.. Fuck. I hate that he still has this much power over me." Realization crossed Silas' face.

"The one who hurt you" He stated, and I nodded.

"My stepfather." His eyes burned with heat and anger I'd never seen in him before. The corners of his eyes darkened to a deep red. But still, I couldn't find the good sense to be afraid. "He... He held me like that. He told me to stay still. Not to move. He commanded me." He instantly understood.

"Bookworm, you should have told me. I never would have..."

I stopped him by pressing a quick kiss to his lips. "I wanted you to do it, Silas. I wanted you to make me forget him. I wanted the memory of your hands to replace the feeling of his." Was it fucked up that I wanted Silas to dominate me when that was the crux of my very trauma? I don't see it that way. I see it as allowing myself to heal by regaining the agency he stole from me. "I want the last person to do those things to me to be you, not him." There it was. The broken truth. Silas leaned his forehead against mine and our breath mingled.

"I will erase every kiss he ever stole from you. I will wipe away every memory of his selfish hands on your body. I will eclipse his hold on your soul, Athena. Because you are mine. Mine to worship. Mine to command. Mine to protect." He growled the words, like some sort of primal beast, and I felt my arousal return with full force.

"Erase him, Silas. Please." He kissed me again, with more passion than he'd ever displayed before. There was a deeper meaning to this kiss, the way his hands encircled my waist, and dug into my bare skin. His length hardened against my stomach, and I rubbed my body against him with reckless abandon, seeking the cathartic passion he was offering me.

His hands snaked up my back, and slowly made their way to my throat. His eyes settled on mine, a silent question. I nodded.

"That's my fucking brave girl." His praise had me nearly buckling my knees. "Does my hand on your throat make you wet? Are you eager for me?" His fingers dipped into my folds, running through the slickness there, eliciting a moan from my lips that he eagerly swallowed with his mouth on mine. "Fuck, you are soaked for me, aren't you? Because you know how safe you are with me, don't you, baby girl?" I nodded, whining against his mouth as his fingers circled my clit. "You love following my commands, because you know you have all the power, isn't that right, baby girl?" His fingers slipped inside, and my hands went to his shoulders in earnest. "Answer me."

"Fuck!" I exclaimed as his thumb pressed down on my clit and his fingers curled to hit that spot so deep inside. "Yes! Yes Sir!" He smiled against my lips. My hips moved, riding him excitedly as he expertly worked my body to orgasm. I detonated around his fingers, feeling my walls pulse around him.

"I need you," I exhaled, riding the last of my release, my hands snaking down his chest searching for his thick cock.

"Ah ah ah," he teased, pulling his fingers from me and pressing them against my lips. I opened them wide and willingly and he slipped them inside. I let the taste of my arousal flood my tongue and I moaned around his fingers. He groaned as if in pain before withdrawing his hand from my lips. "Good girls ask nicely to be fucked. Say that magic word, baby girl."

I smiled at him, his lust-filled eyes revealing just how hard it was for him to hold himself back. I had that effect on him. Then I whispered our little phrase, the one that was so deeply ingrained in the facet of who we were. Words I once spoke in this very spot. I hadn't meant them nearly as viscerally then, but now it was a vow, a promise. A declaration. "Fuck me, please."

He moved quickly, gripping my thighs and hoisting me, my legs circled his waist and I felt his length hard and ready pressing against my opening. I gasped, clutching his shoulders. With one hand, he held me there with ease, and the other slid between us, brushing ever so slightly against my sensitive clit.

His cock was notched at my opening and I couldn't contain my eager breaths. The mask of this dominant Silas was slipping, giving way to the breathless, handsome man who utterly adored me. His eyes held mine as he lowered me down onto his length. I felt each glorious inch as he stretched me. When I was fully seated, we both let out a long delicious sigh.

"Holy shit. You were made for me, Athena." His breathless admission felt so personal, so full of passion that I felt my heart tighten with a new emotion. "You were made for *us*," he added, with a grunt as he withdrew entirely only to thrust himself inside of me again.

The truth hit me like a ton of bricks. I *was* their mate. I *was* made for them. Despite whatever I planned to do with that truth, the fact remained the same. And I think I was starting to like it. The idea that I was crafted to fit someone so perfectly. Four someones.

"Does my girl like that?" His hands were on my hips and he lifted me with ease, bringing me slamming back down onto his cock. I cried out with each thrust. "You like the idea of belonging to all of us, don't you? You want to know what it feels like to take us all at once don't you?" I whimpered. "You'd take my cock in your cunt, and Orpheus would take your ass. We'd stretch you so full, but you wouldn't be able to scream because your mouth would be buried in Samara's pussy or choking on Laz's length." I cried out as his hips slammed against my thighs.

"Yes, please!" I begged, but I wasn't sure what I was begging for. Was it him, or this fantasy he painted for me? Either way, my body was tightening with anticipation as I climbed closer and closer to my release. Without breaking his pattern, Silas pressed my back up against a bookcase. The wood creaked under the force as it bounced against the wall. He released my hip and pressed his fingers against my clit again sending me tumbling blindly into a euphoric orgasm. A few books fell from the shelf behind us from the force of our bodies. "That's it, oh shit. You're so tight." He gasped as he chased his own release. His body stilled as he rode out the last of it and his head rested on my chest. Our heaving breath was the only sound for a long moment. Soon, too soon, he lifted me off of his length and helped me set my feet back onto the ground.

Despite the cold radiating off of his body, I felt like I was on fire. I leaned into his hold, my cheek pressing against his bare chest. My heart was beating quickly, violently, and as I focused on it a thought seeped into my mind.

Pulling back quickly, I looked up at Silas. "I can't hear your heart beating," I exclaimed worriedly.

Silas smiled, holding my chin gently in his cold grasp. "A vampire's heart beats so infrequently it's nearly dead." I gasped, but Silas turned my eyes to his. "Before you came into my life, my heart would only beat once every hour." I couldn't wrap my head around that. "But the first moment I kissed you, and every moment after that, it's been more alive than it's ever been." I pressed my ears against his chest and we stood silently, nakedly embracing, as I listened for his heart.

Thump.

I started counting. A minute passed. Then two. Then three.

Thump.

"Three minutes," I stated.

"For me, that's racing." He kissed the top of my head.

He took a step back from me and began sliding his jeans back onto his body. I followed suit until the two of us were fully clothed and resting on the velvet loveseat.

I leaned into his hold and we sat comfortably together as if it were the most natural thing in the world. As if we'd been doing it forever.

"Do you have anything else you need to know, bookworm?" He asked, a bit of trepidation in his tone. I traced the ink on his forearm.

"Why snakes?" Silas lifted one of his arms, showing off the swirling designs of scales that decorated his body.

"Snakes are misunderstood. They're not aggressive creatures and they won't strike out of malice, they don't go looking for trouble. But if they, or anything they care about, is threatened, they'll defend themselves till their last breath." He spoke so reverently. I smiled.

"That sounds just like you," I mused. He chuckled.

"I also have an affinity for wrapping my body around anyone who's brave enough to get close." As if to demonstrate, he tightened his hold on my waist. I sank into his hold eagerly. A few moments later, I shifted in his arms, slightly uncomfortable due to the question I wanted to ask.

"Why did you choose to become a vampire?" I asked, the word still feeling volatile on my lips.

"Has anyone told you about Alora?" I shook my head. "Alora was once a member of our coven before she died." His voice wavered with a thick agony. I sighed, and a brief flash of shock bloomed in my chest. Another member of the coven? Was she my mate too? Did I lose a piece of myself before I even knew it was missing? A sadness blanketed me, and I felt Silas' arms tighten around me. "She was my best friend growing up, back when we were humans. I had lost my parents pretty young, too young, so Alora and her family took me in. She was my family. My sister." I squeezed the arm that was encircling my waist, thankful my back was to him so he could not see the tear that slid down my cheek at the longing and pain which was evident in his tone. "We were freshly adults when Alora's parents died. But it still hit her pretty hard."

"I'm so sorry, Silas." He sniffed, and I felt his body move as he breathed.

"For what?"

"You lost them too." His arms tightened around me.

"Yeah. For the majority of my life, they were the only thing between me and the foster care system. Which was not exactly cozy and comfortable in the 1890s."

I took a slow breath, letting the new information about Silas sink in.

"After they died, Alora and I moved out to Los Angeles, trying to make a new life for ourselves, and we did. For a while." His voice shook, slightly. "In 1910, we were walking downtown together, enjoying the weather when we walked by the LA Times building."

I listened intently, a soft alarm going off in my head.

"When the bomb went off, we were on the street out front." His hold tightened on me.

I gasped, tears falling down my skin.

"The reports have fluctuated from a gas leak to a widespread union conspiracy. But it didn't matter. The two of us were fighting for our lives in a hospital bed for days, I could care less how we got there. It was a blur, really. I couldn't tell you what all they did to us to try and bring us back. But all I remember the whole time was begging them to let me see Alora, and they wouldn't. I spent those days in pain, not knowing if I'd lost the last member of my family."

I felt his pain as if it were my own then, my chest tightened.

"One night, I snuck out of my room. Ignoring my broken bones, and pushing past the pain from the injuries. When I got to her room, she was in a coma. I nearly lost it." His voice quivered. I gripped his arm in my hands and squeezed it reassuringly. "Orpheus slipped into her room to find me crying. I didn't find out until much later that he was robbing the hospital of blood bags, and it truly was just luck that he found me. I don't know if it was the meds or the pain, but I was so vulnerable that I just spilled my entire life story to this stranger. When I was done, he offered me a chance to live, a chance to save Alora."

I was suddenly so thankful for the chance encounter that Orpheus had all those years ago.

"Twenty-one people died in that bombing. Twenty-three if you count Alora and I joining the legion of the undead." He chuckled.

"You almost died," I choked out, and suddenly Silas rearranged himself so he was looking into my face.

"I didn't. I had to survive so I could make it to you."

I nodded and leaned forward pressing a kiss to his lips.

"Tell me you're mine, bookworm," he whispered against my lips in a soft plea.

I felt like his. All of theirs. I wanted nothing more than to be the mate they wanted me to be, but despite the outpouring of love I've received and felt, I couldn't make this choice yet.

"I want to be, I do."

He sighed, but I saw the understanding on his face.

"I need time," I whispered.

"I've waited a century for you, Athena. I'd do it again."

With Silas' arms around me, I let him tell me more about the first years of his second life, my decision getting closer and harder with each passing second.

11

ORPHEUS

Silas and Laz returned last night with content smiles on their faces, and despite the ever-present hunger in their gaze, they looked satisfied. A twinge of jealousy flashed within me when I looked at them. While they assured me Athena had not accepted the bond yet, that they hadn't had the distinct pleasure of sinking their teeth into her perfect skin and drinking the blood that coursed in her veins, I couldn't help but feel like these two had once again surpassed me. Their relationship with our girl was leagues beyond where I stood with her. And that was my fault and my fault alone. I had only indulged in her once, that kiss. The way her trembling body calmed when she looked at me made me feel like I was her anchor. The one thing keeping her grounded. Her lips met mine in a desperate comfort-seeking way and I was lost to her. I always would be.

Even if I had to leave her.

Samara was the first member of my family. The first person to combat my loneliness and win. If she had to leave, I couldn't let her go alone. No matter how fucking painful it was going to be to turn my back on my mate.

I slept like shit last night, tossing and turning, knowing most likely Athena was going to request a meeting with me today, and I'd have to look at her in those perfect emerald eyes and tell her the truth.

That I wanted her more than anything on this Earth, but I couldn't have her.

By four a.m. I knew trying to sleep was futile so I got up, threw on a pair of jeans, and made my way down the stairs. After downing a blood bag to curb the hunger, and pouring a coffee with entirely too much sugar in it, I pushed through the glass doors and found myself leaning on the railing overlooking the beach. The water was peaceful this morning as the moon began its slow descent to the horizon. Breathing a lungful of the crisp salty air felt like a calming embrace. Fuck, it felt good to have a place that felt familiar.

It had been so long since we'd felt 'settled' in a single place. Mostly because settling meant getting sloppy, and getting sloppy meant getting caught.

I was worried about that happening here.

What were Laz and Silas going to do if they saw the Nameless mark in this little town? Something tells me they're just reckless enough to ignore it. Without me there to bark orders at them, they would try to fight, and they would lose. And chances are Athena would be caught in the crossfire.

My chest tightened at that thought. My free hand, not holding the mug of coffee, gripped the railing with inhuman strength. The reason we survived for so long, and were able to avoid being captured by Nameless again is because we didn't make mistakes. And yet, since the moment we arrived in Shockgrove, mistakes are all we've made.

How long did we have until they found us?

The sun began its slow climb to its perch in the sky, casting a warm amber glow across the dazzling water.

My shoulders had just started to relax when my phone vibrated in the pocket of my jeans, effectively erasing all instances of calm I had been feeling.

The name on the caller ID made it worse.

"Detective Barnes," I answered coolly.

"Mr. Green." Her voice was relaxed. I tried not to let my frustration over finding them tailing us yesterday seep into my response. I had the eerie feeling that someone was watching us, and sure enough there they were.

"How can I help you?" I heard her clear her throat on the other end of the line, and I waited with bated breath for her to play her hand. Whatever that might be.

"I wanted to inform you that we have closed the missing person case for Mr. Dells."

I bit back the sigh of relief that nearly fell out of my mouth.

"Was he found?" I asked, with false eagerness.

"No, but camera footage confirms he left town on his own accord. We've reached out to neighboring towns to keep an eye out for him, but without any threat, the case is closed," she answered quickly. *Thank you, Silas.*

"I'm glad to hear that he seems to be safe," I replied, diplomatically.

"Yes, well." She paused, waiting for me to offer something else. I didn't. "I apologize for concerning you in this matter."

"Not at all, you were just doing your job." After a brief goodbye, I hung up and felt a small weight lift from my shoulders. Another potential threat dodged effortlessly thanks to Silas' gift. I couldn't help the silent dread that began to fill me at the thought of trying to survive on the run without his power.

We all worked so well together, it kept us sharp and prepared. Without our united front, were we just biding our time until it all comes crumbling down?

I heard the door creak open behind me and I tossed a quick glance over my shoulder. Silas sauntered out, his broad, bare chest on full display. Only dark jeans hung low on his hips.

"You're up early," I said, returning my gaze to the ocean. His satisfied, content, lust-filled emotions were vibrant and powerful.

"Had a sex dream, had to wake up and take care of business," he teased, leaning on the railing next to me.

"Please refrain from informing me of that ever again," I replied, nonchalantly, but jealousy was roiling within me. The cup in his hand smelled of blood.

"How is your hunger after engaging in intercourse with her?" I asked, attempting to make the act seem as clinical as I could in my mind so I couldn't picture the way her body stretched to take him, or how well she would take me.

"Intercourse?" Silas asked, raising an eyebrow. I nodded, and he chuckled softly before it died out. "Worse," he finally stated, taking a sip of the red liquid in his cup. "Definitely worse."

I groaned. If the timeline was accelerating this quickly we would be out of blood by tomorrow.

"And Laz? Same for them?"

Silas nodded, and I peeled my eyes from him again and watched the tide rush in, then out.

"You and Samara need to make a good impression, I think she'll accept us. I know she feels this bond too. She just needs to give herself permission to."

I didn't respond. How could I? Was it my place to tell Silas what Samara's plans were? What I was planning to do with her. Maybe not, but he deserved to know, nonetheless.

"Right," I said, absentmindedly.

"What is it, Orpheus?" He asked. I couldn't seem to look at him.

"Samara is intending to reject the bond," I whispered, but I knew he heard me because he nearly dropped the cup of precious blood from his hand.

"What the fuck," he exclaimed. "Why would she do that?"

"I think you know the answer to that, Silas."

That calmed him slightly, his frantic breaths returned to normal, and he leaned forward on the railing again, this time burying his head into his arms.

"Fuck, of course. I can't believe I didn't even think about that." He was in pain, I could feel it. "I can't imagine how she feels right now."

Alora had been Silas' best friend. They were attached at the hip for their first few years in The Wanderers and still were even after Alora found something special with Samara.

"She's going to reject her mate because of Alora," he whispered to himself, not as a question, but as an answer.

"Yeah, she is."

"So what, she'll just sit there and watch us fall in love with Athena every day? That'll hurt like hell. Even if she rejects it."

I didn't answer, I didn't turn to face him. His eyes burned into my profile, a quiet realization.

"She's not going to stay...is she?"

I shook my head.

"Did you try to talk her out of this?" Silas asked, his voice raising slightly.

"Of course, I did," I answered.

Silas groaned.

"I've told her she's allowed to move on, but she will never be able to until she believes it herself." I shook my head, ignoring the guilt building in my chest.

"If she goes out on her own, Nameless is going to find her." He downed the last of his blood and set the cup down on the railing. "She'll never survive alone."

Again, I stayed silent.

His questioning glare deepened.

"You already know that, though," he accused. I didn't give anything away despite the pit of despair forming in my stomach. "You're going with her." It wasn't a question. He knew.

"You said yourself, she'd never survive alone." I tried to hide the traitorous emotional crack in my voice, but of course he caught it.

"Orpheus," Silas whispered, the sound was full of the brotherly love we had created together. "Athena is your mate." He was angry. I ignored him. "She is your mate!"

"You think I don't know that?" I snapped, turning my molten gaze to him. "You think I'm not intimately aware of what I will be losing here? Because let me promise you, I am."

He just stared at me. "Then why?"

"Because Samara is my family," I whispered, feeling Silas' anger and sadness roll off of him, enveloping me in a blanket of his agony.

"What about me?" He screamed, a tear sliding down his face. "What about Laz? Aren't we your family?"

I choked down a sob. "Of course, you are," I assured him.

"Then why the fuck are you planning to abandon us?" He was yelling now, it was only a matter of time before Laz and Samara were aware of our conversation, if they weren't already.

"You'll have each other, and..Athena," I added with a pained whisper.

"You're a coward," he seethed, quietly. "You both are."

I turned to follow his gaze to see Samara had arrived and was standing at the threshold of the glass doors. Her eyes were glassy with unshed tears.

"Silas," she started, but Silas only stalked off onto the beach. My eyes darted to Laz who stood motionless behind Samara.

"Tell me that's not true," Laz begged. "Tell me, you aren't doing this."

Samara shook her head, unable to give them what they wanted. Laz nodded to themselves a few times, shock and betrayal coloring their emotions. Samara reached for them, but they pulled back violently.

"Don't." They pushed past Samara and followed after Silas.

"Fuck," she exclaimed under her breath and I felt her guilt rear its ugly head again. "Why did you do that?" She cried.

"They deserved to know," I reply, letting my mask of indifference slip away entirely.

"Our family is falling apart," she lamented, watching after Silas and Laz.

"They'll be ok," I lied.

"I thought Silas would understand. He loved Alora, shouldn't he be glad I'm taking my vow to her so seriously?" Her voice cracked with sadness.

"I was there that night," I stated. "When you and Alora made your promises to each other."

She wiped a tear from her cheek.

"Do you remember what she promised you?"

She nodded. "Every word."

"She promised you would be happy, content, and loved," I reminded her. Samara sniffled. "Look at you, Samara. You are anything but happy and content right now."

She sobbed.

"Have you considered that by keeping your promise to Alora, you're breaking her promise to you?" I whispered, I didn't want my words to hurt her.

Her sobs continued and I almost couldn't stand to be in the presence of that much pain

My phone vibrated with a text from an unknown number.

My heart beat once. That single text had injected a sort of hope in my veins I hadn't felt in so long, while also seizing my heart in a sort of dread.

She sent an address for a crab shack just down the pier from her store. After issuing my agreement, I pocketed my phone and turned to find Samara in her state of distress.

"I meant what I said, if you're out, then I'm out."

Samara looked up at me through wet eyelashes.

"Are you out?" I asked, attempting to mask the hope I had that she would change her mind. There was a slightly longer hesitation in her response, but then she nodded, effectively dashing what little hope I had.

"Ok, I'm going to go get ready. I'm meeting her in a few hours." I began walking away but then Samara's meek voice stopped me.

"What are you going to tell her?"

"The truth," I uttered as I retreated into the house.

Silas and Laz had not returned before it was time for me to leave, and Samara had not come out of her room since locking herself inside after the confrontation.

I wore the same burgundy suit I wore the night we arrived in this little town and our life was turned upside down. Call it a full circle moment, or maybe I just wanted to feel her eyes on me the way I did that night before I ruined everything that was growing between us.

I pulled open the cooler of blood and winced at how little remained. One flask each. We weren't going to survive without more soon. It had been a few hours since I drank my four a.m. fix, but the hunger wasn't unbearable. I could probably keep it under lock and key while I have this conversation. I can't imagine she'll want to drag it on for very long anyway. Not after hearing what I have to say. I closed the cooler without taking another flask.

I was at the pier a few minutes later, ignoring the sense of dread that was settling over me with each and every step toward my mate. Mostly because I knew that every step I took toward her was only a step I'd have to take away from her.

The crab shack was empty when I arrived except for a few employees who sat around making themselves look busy. Boredom rolled off of them.

I grabbed a table near the window, overlooking the water and I found myself once again entranced and watching the sun glistening on its calm surface.

I felt her the moment she entered the restaurant. Her nerves were screaming for me. I felt her emotions so fucking clearly, like I truly couldn't tell if it was her or me feeling them. I stood as she arrived at the table. She was wearing the same grey T-shirt dress she wore the day of our tour. The day I felt her panic so clearly I nearly was brought to my knees. I should have known right then what she was to me, but I couldn't see what I didn't want to.

"Hello, Athena," I said, coming around the table to hold her chair out for her. She blushed deeply and I had to suppress a groan at the look of her delicious blood blooming beneath her skin. She nodded her thanks and sat down.

Settling back into my chair, I found myself admiring her. Her strength, her bravery. There was a twinge of fear threading through her emotions, but her courage and determination were front and center. Driving her.

"I've already done this twice and it doesn't get less awkward." She giggled and I wanted to bottle the sound to keep with me when I left.

"Do you mind if I start?" I asked and she shook her head, gesturing for me to continue. "I wanted to first and foremost apologize to you, Athena."

She looked at me curiously.

"For everything that occurred at your store that night. From the moment I sent you tumbling into your worst memories, to everything that happened after."

She furrowed her brows at that, tucking a strand of her soft red hair behind her ear. "Everything?" She asked, timidly. A soft bloom of lust broke into her emotions. My fangs bit into my bottom lip as they tried to descend. A deep breath managed to force them back. Here it was. The moment of truth.

"Yes."

Shame, and rejection. Both emotions flooded my senses.

"Wait, allow me to clarify. I do not regret the moment we shared, Athena. In fact, your kiss was the single best moment of my entire long existence."

She smiled, blushing again. "Laz did mention that you have been...around for a while."

I nodded. Just then, a waiter came to the table and took our drink and appetizer order. All the while, I didn't remove my gaze from her.

"A 'while' is a bit of an understatement," I replied once the waiter had left. She waited for me to continue. "I was turned in the mid eleven hundreds."

"Holy shit," she exclaimed loudly, before clasping a hand across her lips. "Sorry, I just...wow. That's. Laz wasn't kidding."

I smiled, sadly at the wonder in her gaze. It was such a stunning sight. Her amusement. I could spend my entire life showing her new things if only to be blessed with that look again.

"And in all that time, you've never had anything better than our kiss?" She asked, tentatively, but I could feel the spark of jealousy. She thought I was lying. She was considering the other women I might have passed time with. If only she knew how little those women mattered, how insignificant and forgettable their touches were.

"No matter what pleasures I've experienced before, nothing compared to the moment you claimed my lips with yours."

She released the slightest moan, the sound hitting me directly in my core.

"However," I started, noticing her nerves return to the forefront. "I should not have indulged until you knew the truth about what we were."

She nodded. "I agree, but I can't fault you for guarding your secret. You had no idea who you could trust."

Here we go.

"I also should not have indulged until I knew what my decision would be." I tried to keep my tone even and steady.

She studied me.

"A mate bond is sacred, I'm sure the others have explained that fairly effectively."

She nodded.

"And I should have withheld my affection for you until I was positive I could accept the bond."

She tilted her head, watching me. Her emotions settled calmly, a quiet storm. "You don't want the mate bond," she stated.

"Fuck yes, I do, " I snarled before I could contain it. My nails dug into the table.

"I don't understand," she said, shaking her head. The coldness in her tone sent icy jolts through my heart.

"I want you more than anything I have ever wanted in this existence. I want to sink my fangs into your perfect skin and mark you as mine and mine alone. My body fucking burns for you, Athena."

She gasped, her lust enveloped me instantly, driving me absolutely fucking crazy.

"You've barely said ten sentences to me," she added, breathlessly.

"And yet, my eyes were the ones you could not look away from that first night," I replied, darkly.

Her tongue darted out to wet her bottom lip and my eye tracked the movement hungrily. "So you do want this bond?"

I shook my head. "I do, but I can't."

"So why are you meeting with me if you don't want-"

I raised my eyebrow.

"I mean, *can't* do this?" She asked, watching me with the same fervor I watched her. I tried to ignore the strands of disappointment that were threading through her desire.

"You deserved to hear it from me," I offered her, with my attempted mask of indifference in place. Her cold eyes were full of fearful rejection.

"Well thank you for your candor," she snapped, contritely. A bite behind her words was hidden behind a mountain of sadness. She pushed back from the table and tossed a twenty-dollar bill down before turning to leave.

"Athena, wait," I nearly begged. It couldn't be done yet. I wasn't done yet.

"You've made yourself very clear, Orpheus. I am not expecting anything from you. You are not obligated to fulfill this bond any more than I am. You're free."

I felt anything but free as she stalked away from me. Her pain danced around me, invading my senses like a nightmare would invade a dream.

The moment she exited the restaurant, I expected a reprieve from the torture of her agony, but it never came. If anything the burning pain grew more intense the further she got from me. I stood from the table, offering my apologies to the waitstaff through clenched teeth, and raced out of the building after her. Her red hair was blowing in the wind as she stalked down the pier toward her store.

So I ran. My feet pounded the wooden planks below me as I flew across them. My heartbeat caught me by surprise. It was violent, vicious, pounding against my ribcage as if it were actually alive. She made me feel that way.

My hand grasped her by the arm and pulled her into an open alleyway between two buildings. The brick structures offered a slight shield of privacy from the pier's walkway, but the ocean was still visible over the railing near the back of the buildings. I turned her so she was facing me, backing her up against the brick wall until she was caged between it and my form. Her gasp was so delicious I nearly bent down to taste it. Heat rolled off of her, and fear laced with want danced around her in a taunting cloud.

"What the fuck, Orpheus?" She exclaimed, but I couldn't answer her. My chest heaved as I stared down at this perfect creature. This fucking goddess. She was my Eurydice. The woman I was destined to love, but destined to lose due to my own selfish distrust. But even the tales of the beautiful nymph goddess of nature paled in comparison to this stunning creature before me.

"I..." How could I explain this? How could I prove to her how desperately I needed her, and how no matter that, I couldn't have her? Suddenly, my breathing came in ragged spurts, my heart beat again to my surprise, and utter torture. It was such an unfamiliar feeling, but so fucking wonderful all at the same time.

"Orpheus," her voice pierced through the cloud of despair. Her hand came to rest on my cheek, fire against the ice of my skin. "Talk to me."

"I made a promise to Samara." I had made the decision that it wasn't my place to divulge her secrets to Athena, but I needed her to understand. I needed Athena to know why I was doing this. I couldn't bear the thought that she might think I didn't want her. "If she goes, I go with her." Athena absorbed the new information.

"She's going to leave too?" It wasn't an accusation, and her emotions weren't full of rejection this time. Just pure worry.

"She had a chosen once, not a mate, but their connection could rival some of the more powerful bonds out there."

Athena inhaled deeply, feeling the weight of my confession. "It was Alora, wasn't it?"

I wasn't even shocked that she knew her name, not after having her conversation with Silas. I nodded.

"She doesn't think she can allow herself to commit to this bond. Not after losing Alora." To Athena's credit, she seemed to be taking all of this rather calmly.

"And you're going to leave with her," she continued.

"She's my family," I said again, although, after Silas' interjection this morning, I could admit it felt slightly less noble of an admission.

"That is the most selfless thing I've ever heard, Orpheus." Her emerald eyes watered slightly as she looked at me with adoration.

"Fuck. I want to be selfish with you, Athena," I added, stepping forward until her breasts were pressed against my chest. Her arousal invaded my nostrils and I groaned, burying my nose in the crook of her neck. I didn't allow my skin to touch hers, instead hovering just above making contact. The space between us was electric, charged with something I'd never had the fortune of experiencing.

"I'm not ready to give you up yet," I whispered, it was a soft, broken sound.

"So don't." I pulled back and looked at her questioningly. "You can't stay, but we can have today." I stared at her, feeling her words wash over me with a hope I didn't dare feel. "Be selfish, Orpheus."

That was all the permission I needed. My lips captured hers and I pressed her body into the brick wall behind her by driving mine into hers. She moaned at the friction. Her kiss was not gentle, and neither was mine. We were ravenous hungry creatures who were soaking up every ounce of pleasure they could before the moment ended. Her fingers threaded through my cropped hair and pulled my face to hers. My tongue danced with hers, an exchange of promises we weren't able to say aloud. I tore my lips from hers and began kissing my way down her perfect skin, stopping briefly at her throat. The smell of her blood was so powerful now that I had gotten a whiff. How had I missed the clear indication that she belonged to me? It was as obvious as the sun in the sky now. Hunger flooded me, and I paused a moment, resting my forehead against the skin of her neck, sucking in spurts of cool ocean air to stave off the monster that was threatening to rear its ugly head.

"How does it feel?" She asked, breathlessly, her chest heaved, and brushed her pebbled nipples against my chest. "Drinking blood," she clarified. I moaned, my length strained against my slacks.

"Fuck, Athena. You're trying to make me lose control," I exhaled a slight chuckle.

"You won't hurt me," she asserted. How far she's come in these few days. How brave my girl was.

"Never," I swore, despite the agonizing need to taste her.

"How does it feel?" She asked again.

"Blood from the vein tastes like the most delectable thing on the planet. It's euphoric and earth-shattering. It fills you with a sense of power and longing."

She shivered under my touch where my nose nestled against the column of her throat.

"Now, when someone drinks from you, it's an aphrodisiac. You'll feel heat and arousal flood your core. You'll be so close to a release that you might just beg for it."

She sighed sensually, letting her head fall back against the brick behind her.

I kissed her neck, the spot where I would have marked her had things turned out differently. My tongue slowly slid over the exposed skin and she released a guttural groan, her desire was so potent I was drowning in it.

"I wish I could have you," I whispered against her skin, feeling her shiver under my touch.

Her hands danced along my back, leaving trails of electrified paths in their wake. When her hands disappeared from my body, I growled my frustration, but it was quickly replaced with desperate whimpers when her hands gripped the hem of her grey t-shirt dress and lifted it slightly. Her eyes scanned the surroundings. Looking down toward the opening of the alleyway. From where we stood, nobody could possibly see us. I could do whatever I wanted with her in this alley and only she and I would know. I was on my knees before I could take my next breath.

"You want me to devour you, little nymph?" I looked up at her from my position and was struck by just how beautiful my Athena was. Her dress settled around her waist, giving me a perfect look at the soft white panties that covered her core. I pressed my lips against the fabric letting the first taste of her arousal brush against my willing and eager lips. She sighed, resting her hands on my head.

"Yes, Oh god, yes," she cried out, quietly.

"The gods aren't here right now. It's just you and me." She whimpered, pressing my head into her hot center.

I pressed a kiss to her core, feeling her slick wetness soak through the fabric barrier between my lips and her folds. "Taste me, Orpheus," she pleaded, and if I thought I was hard before, I was sorely mistaken. My cock was pressing painfully against my pants, but I didn't dare relieve my ache until her needs were well and truly met.

"Your wish is my command, little nymph." It took minimal strength to rip the fabric from her body and reveal her wet hot center. I wasted not a moment of time before burying my tongue inside of her, eliciting pained passionate moans from her delicious lips. Her taste flooded my mouth and I knew no matter how long I lived, I'd never taste another thing this sweet. Her hands worked my head, pressing me further into her, and I let her drive me. She rode my face with reckless abandon, seeking her every desire. I let her use me the way she so desperately needed to. I was her plaything, perfectly molded to make her every wish come true. Her satisfaction was mine.

I slid two fingers inside of her as I offered special attention to that exquisite bundle of nerves at the apex of her perfect cunt. She bit her bottom lip to avoid releasing the scream I knew she was teetering toward. Her breathing ramped up, and her amped-up heart rate only made the blood under her skin pump faster, sending me into a frenzy of epic proportions. My hunger was rivaled only by the desire for her.

As my mouth ravaged her, I felt my fangs elongate, but I couldn't stop them. When the sharp point brushed against her clit, I heard her gasp. I hadn't turned entirely, but I felt small qualities of the creature inside of me venture to the surface. When I looked up at her, I knew what she was seeing. Nearly blood-red eyes, and elongated fangs. A monster feasting on her center. I readied myself for her to push away and keep me from finishing my task, but instead, when I looked into her eyes I didn't see fear. I saw curiosity.

And all I felt was lust.

She rode my face harder, holding my head to her. I was careful not to let my fangs break the skin, but the soft gasp she released every time they brushed against her was too damn delicious for me to resist. Her walls tightened around my fingers and her hands held me to her center as she found her release. I hummed my appreciation and watched her come undone from my rightful place on my knees before her.

Her body settled with heaving breaths and satisfied sighs, all while I remained in my spot tracing lazy brushes of my tongue against her sensitive core.

"If we were mates, I would never leave my knees," I whispered, pressing my forehead against her stomach.

"We are mates," she returned, breathlessly.

I glanced up at her and saw a gaze filled with admiration and care. It was nearly too much for me to handle.

"I know," was all I could say.

She sank down to her knees in front of me and took my face in her hands. Her eyes searched mine, and I wondered if she found what she was looking for in their black depths. "If you're going to ask me to say goodbye to you, I want you to make me scream it." Her hands fumbled with my belt, and then the button on my slacks. When her delicate fingers managed to free my length from its confines, she marveled at my size. She hiked her dress up and strad-dled my legs. I felt her heat slide against my cock as she climbed into position, pulling a groan from both of us.

"Anything you need, little nymph."

She positioned her slick entrance over the head of my cock and didn't waste a single second before slamming down on top of me. Her perfect cunt swal-lowed my every inch expertly.

"Oh, fuck, Athena," I gasped out and she began swirling her hips teasing me, and forcing friction against her clit. I helped her, bringing my fingers to her center and sliding them along that bundle. Her head leaned back, exposing her throat to me.

I kissed the skin there again, reverently.

"Take it all, Athena. I'm yours. Use me." I had never been a selfish lover, it wasn't in my nature. I got pleasure from my partner enjoying themselves. If their body was brought to a beautiful, explosive climax, I never needed to even be touched to feel accomplished. Not that I didn't fucking love the feel of Athena's pussy strangling my cock, but I didn't need it. All I ever needed was her pleasure. I could never have sex again, and the memory of the way her face twisted in desire would sustain me for the rest of my existence.

I tried, unsuccessfully, to forget that this could be mine - if I didn't have to leave.

Athena bounced harder, using my shoulders for stability, her walls tightened as her climax neared. I let my other hand sneak around to her tight hole and I felt her curious surprise as I slowly circled it with my index finger. I watched her face, memorizing the way her lips fell open as she moaned, the exact color of her green irises, and the way her hair flowed down her back. My mate was perfect, and I would never forget it.

"Say it, Athena," I growled through clenched teeth.

"Goodbye!" She screamed as I pressed a finger through the ring of muscles. Filling her completely.

When she orgasmed, she cried out and buried her face in the crook of my neck to muffle the sound. Her teeth bit down on the skin of my neck and that was all I needed to topple over the cliff of passionate oblivion with her.

I held her there longer than I needed to, as I rode out the last of my climax, but I couldn't help but remember that once I removed myself from her, I'd never feel this kind of euphoria again.

Luckily for me, she didn't seem like she was in much of a hurry to leave.

"Will I ever see you again?" She asked, a tiny flash of hope blooming in her emotions.

"I don't think I could survive watching the others reap the benefits of a bond that should have been mine."

She nodded as if it made perfect sense.

"If I can't have you, Athena, I can't see you. I'll only be reminded of what we could have been."

She plastered a fake smile on her face but a tear slipped through her eye and I had to refrain from darting out and licking it. "Thank you for this. It was the perfect goodbye."

"It was," I agreed.

She hesitated to stand and withdraw from our joined position, but she knew, as I did, that our time was up. When she stood, I felt something inside my chest crack. My heartbeat pulsated loudly and more lively than I'd felt in my long second life, and I suddenly hated the feel of it in my chest. The wretched organ came back to life just in time to break.

We righted ourselves, smoothing our clothes and hair in silence, an attempt to prolong the farewell that was acidic on our tongues.

"Goodbye, Orpheus. I wish you every happiness."

I didn't have the heart to tell her I was leaving my every happiness behind with her.

"Goodbye, Athena."

She left first, something I was thankful for because I wasn't sure my feet would have allowed me to take one single step away from her. When she disappeared around the corner and back toward the main pier, I let the full force of her pain hit me. It held my soul and my nearly dead heart in such a grip I almost hoped it never let me go.

Would I still feel her emotions this powerfully after rejecting the bond? I didn't think so. So even though this pain was violent and agonizing, I wanted to feel every single second of its sting, because the moment it ceased would be the moment I lost her.

12

ATHENA

I was well and truly past being afraid. Now, the only thing I was worried about was keeping the fragments of my heart that belonged to my wanderers from shattering into a million little pieces. Samara and Orpheus were going to leave. They didn't want this bond with me.

A pain unlike anything I've ever felt struck me each time I thought about it. I felt like my chest had been flayed open and I was going to lose myself entirely. I'd been trying to figure out if the way I felt about them was the bond or simply a school girl crush, but nothing about the way I felt knowing two of the pieces of my soul weren't going to stay screamed 'crush'. Since the moment I left Orpheus in that alley, I felt a tidal wave of misery crash over me, and I haven't been able to come up for air since.

It was only going to get worse.

There's a special kind of torture in finding your soulmate only to lose them.

The afternoon shift at The Maine Plotline moved by in a blur. I hadn't yet texted Samara, and I debated if I even could bear it. I knew what she was going to tell me, and I didn't know if I had the strength to hear it.

Archer stopped by for a few hours, and thankfully he didn't inquire about my near zombie-like emotional state. He made me laugh, which was like a bandaid over a bullet wound, but it was nice nonetheless.

When he left, he promised he would call me later. I still wasn't sure what he was up to in town, but his companionship was too nice to question.

A few minutes until close, I sat by the counter with my phone opened to an empty message history with Samara. I had gotten her number, and Orpheus', from Silas the day before. He eagerly gave them to me, urging me to meet with them as soon as possible. I knew he wanted to complete the bond, although he didn't pressure me.

I was lost in a daydream, staring at my phone, when a loud crash jolted me from any semblance of peace. The glass of the front window shattered violently, flying in every direction. I turned my head to avoid the assault of the tiny sharp shards, but I felt them pelt against my skin leaving tiny cuts. I cried out as something heavy and pointed caught my shoulder. A sharp pain permeated through my entire body. I winced and stammered backward into the wall. Shock was all I could feel as I looked down to where the offending object sat. A dark red brick, sitting amongst the shattered glass, with white painted lettering.

'Lying Bitch'

Tears flowed from my eyes and blurred my vision, and I shivered from a combination of the pain in my arm, and the cool night air flooding in from the now open front window. My unhindered hand pressed against my shoulder, feeling the sticky warm blood there. I winced again at the tenderness I found. My blood slid down my arm and pooled on the floor near the brick.

White-hot, blinding pain seared through my arm, and I looked out through the window, but all I could see was the quiet Maine night sky.

I reached for my phone, and a sob escaped my lips at the exertion. I held it in my bloody grasp, my entire soul begging me to call them, but all it took was a glance at my blood that was spattered on the floor and crawling down my arm to remind me that they should not be anywhere near this mess.

The phone rang.

SILAS

I answered before I could think otherwise.

"Athena, are you ok?" Silas asked frantically. I heard rustling behind him. And it sounded like someone was wincing in pain in the background.

"What - how did you-" I started.

"Are you hurt?" He pleaded.

"I'm ok, just...I'm ok. Can I call you back?" I asked, trying to hide the pain from my voice.

"What's going on, Athena?" Laz's voice came through the phone.

"I'm going to call you soon, ok?" I assured them.

"We're on our way," Laz asserted.

"No!" I yelped.

"What do you -"

"Just give me a little bit of time, ok? Don't come here!" I begged. I heard them inhaling sharply on the other end of the line. I leaned my head back against the wall, feeling the blood pour out of my arm. I needed to call some-one, and soon.

"Athena-" they started.

"I am bleeding all over the fucking place and you being here will only make it worse, ok?" I exclaimed through the pain. "Just give me a little bit of time to fix this and then I will call you. Please." I waited for their response.

"I'm calling 911 now," I heard Laz say. There was some slight rustling and a hushed conversation. "They're en route, Athena."

"Thank you," I said, weakly. Feeling the effects of the blood loss.

"Call us the second you're safe," Silas commanded.

"I promise." I hung up, knowing they wouldn't be the ones to end the call, but I didn't want to worry them any more than they already were. I took shaky breaths and leaned into the wall for support. The world was getting foggy, I needed someone.

I sent a quick text to Archer asking him to come to the store and I felt calmer the moment he responded that he was on his way.

I'd come to trust him, and as far as I knew, my blood wasn't going to send him into some weird frenzy. Archer arrived first, he must have been close. His eyes were wide with worry as he hopped through the open window and beelined directly for me.

"Holy shit, Athena. What happened? Are you ok?" He didn't seem to care about getting his hands or clothes dirty, because he gently pulled me against him, careful to avoid aggravating my shoulder. I couldn't explain it, but the moment I was in his hold, I felt comfortable. Safe. Protected.

"Somebody threw a brick through the window," I stuttered, feeling my body shake as the shock began to wear off.

"Who did this?"

I shook my head, although now as my mind cleared from the initial jolt, I could think of someone who might consider me a 'lying bitch'. Especially with the timing of the phone call from Detective Barnes I got this morning, it wasn't that unreasonable of a guess.

"I didn't see anyone, but.. but.." The sound of a back door swinging open had both of our heads snapping in that direction. I whimpered, in fear and pain as Archer situated me behind him. His hand went to his waistband and I saw the top of a weapon hidden there. It wasn't metallic like a gun, but instead looked wooden, like a blunt end of a club or something.

We waited with bated breath for something to arrive through the door, but nothing came. Eventually, the calm night was disturbed by distant sirens and echoed shouts as the police and paramedics made their way down to my store on foot from where they parked their vehicles at the mouth of the pier. Archer didn't leave my side as the police took my statement, not exactly stating Greg's name outright, but alluding to my recent case involvement with Detective Barnes, and the paramedics checked my wounded shoulder.

They assured me I would only need some stitches, and the bleeding had already begun to stop.

They called me lucky.

Archer squeezed my good arm that was looped through his when they said that. As if he knew how unlucky I had felt at that moment.

There was a sort of wicked irony about the whole situation. My vampires had protected me from Louis, but in doing so they created a threat in his unstable friend. And now, if I didn't want to force them into a potentially painful situation, I couldn't even call them.

The paramedics were adamant I get taken to the hospital, and I told them I would once my grandma arrived. She got there about twenty minutes after my call and walked straight over to me, pushing past the hordes of people analyzing the scene.

"Oh my god, you beautiful thing. Are you ok?" I nodded, letting tears slip through my eyes. She hugged me close to her chest. "Shh, shh, it's ok." Her warm voice was like a cooling balm against the painful burn in my chest.

Only after she assured me, multiple times, that she would take care of the shop, did I allow the paramedics to take me.

Archer had a soft exchange with my grandma and although I couldn't focus on what was said, the two seemed chummy, comfortable with each other. After he said goodbye to my grandma, Archer accompanied me to the hospital and sat by my side as they patched up my arm.

Once whatever pain meds they had given me started to take effect, I started crying softly. Archer reached forward, gripping my hands in his.

"Hey, you're ok, Athena. You're safe now," he whispered. His eyes watched me carefully, without an ounce of pity, but with all the worry in the world. "Do you want to talk about it?" He asked, and I shrugged, wiping tears from my cheek. "You told the police it might have something to do with another case you were involved in?"

I nodded.

"Are you in danger?"

I motioned to the bandages on my arm that now covered the seven stitches I had to get. "Apparently," I teased, and he cowered at that.

"Fuck," he leaned back in the pale blue chair. It creaked under the shifted weight.

"Hey, um, thank you. For coming when I called."

He held my gaze as I continued.

"Davia's still out of town, and anyone else I could have called is well, a little squeamish with blood."

His eyebrows furrowed the slightest bit at that. "Hey, I know I haven't been here long, but I'm glad you felt like you could call me. I guess I am sort of getting used to your company, and I would have hated it if you had died," he said with all the delivery of a joke, but the solemnity of the truth. It felt nice.

"Last week, there was a guy at the bar who was kind of coming on too strong."

Archer listened intently.

"I didn't like the vibe I was getting, so I told him I was going home. He walked me outside." I paused. Wondering why I suddenly felt the urge to tell the truth, the *real* truth to him. After the momentary lapse, I continued. "We went our separate ways, but apparently he never went home." This statement felt more toxic now that I knew without a doubt what had happened to Louis. He was ripped away from me before he could violate my body any more than he already had, and he was killed. Probably drained of his blood by my vampire mates.

That thought didn't scare me as much as it did before.

"His friend thinks there's more to the story. He's getting a little aggressive," I added.

There was a tick in Archer's jaw that indicated his anger, but his face remained void of any clear indication of his feelings. "Has he tried anything like this before?" He inquired and I swallowed the lump in my throat, sitting up and wincing at the slight pain in my shoulder. Even dulled by the meds, it was one hell of an injury.

"He came to my store and confronted me. He was aggressive, but I didn't think he'd go to this length."

Archer was fuming. I could see the urge to go find Greg dancing behind his eyes. I needed to ensure my wanderers didn't go after him or else we'd have another body on our hands.

"The missing persons case was dismissed today, so that might have something to do with the snap."

I groaned as a thought occurred to me.

"What is it?" Archer asked.

"I just realized that I have to tell Davia about this. She was sleeping with the guy."

Archer reached for my phone at the same time as I did and held it in his hands. "Allow me," he offered. I raised one eyebrow. "I will gladly tell your incredibly attractive best friend that her previous, sub-par, lover is a psychopath and she needs to find someone else to spend her nights with."

I rolled my eyes, but ultimately let him find her number and input it into his own phone and step into the hall to make the call. She was gonna give me an earful for giving 'a stranger' her number. I would talk to her soon, but I was so tired, and I secretly was thankful I didn't have to answer her million questions right now.

I grabbed my phone which Archer had sat back down on the bedside table and sent a message to my grandma asking how the store was. She sent back an answer quickly telling me the money was secured, the insurance company already called to start a claim, and Mr. Harley from the hardware store brought a bunch of his buddies down to help board up the window until it could get replaced.

I felt a weight lift off of me. I don't know what I would have done if there was irreparable damage done to that place. It was my home. It meant everything to me.

Archer was still in the hall, and I faintly heard him verbally sparring with my best friend in a playful, yet annoyed manner. They'd be good for each other if he was planning on sticking around Shockgrove.

Suddenly, my phone buzzed with an incoming phone call.

I smiled and answered.

"Hi, Silas. I'm fine now. I promise."

I heard several exhales of relief on the other end of the call. My heart did a little flip wondering if Orpheus and Samara had also been worried about me.

"Holy fuck, bookworm. You worried the shit out of us," Silas exclaimed.

"Are you hurt?" Laz interjected.

"Who the fuck did it?" Orpheus. His demanding tone was so different from the sweet, and attentive lover he was, but it turned me on just the same.

"I think it was Greg." I heard a loud growl and a crash as if something was thrown against a wall.

"That douche's friend?" Samara asked, and a slight pain stabbed my chest at her voice. I hadn't talked to her yet. She might not know that I know she's planning to leave me. It colored this encounter with a somber tone.

"I can't have you going to avenge this," I whispered, keeping an eye on the door. "I mean it, you cannot retaliate." Silence. "I'm not kidding. If you hurt him, I can't accept the bond. I need to know I can trust you."

"He hurt you," Silas whined.

"Yes, he did." Another growl. "But if we retaliate, the cops will be all over you." There were a few hushed words exchanged on their end, and no matter how I strained to hear them, I couldn't. "Promise me," I demanded, when I heard nothing, I repeated myself with more fervor. "Promise me."

"Ok, we promise," Laz finally said. "Are you sure you're ok?"

"I'm a little banged up, but a few stitches and I'm good as new," I tried to interject a little bit of cheeriness into my tone to mask the pain that still radiated through me despite the drugs.

"We should have been there," Silas whispered, sheepishly, and my heart nearly shattered at how broken and betrayed he sounded.

"I was bleeding all over the place and I knew that was going to be an impossible situation to put you through," I admitted.

"We could have handled it," Silas claimed, but even I knew that wasn't true.

"How did you know I was hurt? Was it a mate bond thing?" Again there was a slight pause.

"We can explain it all soon, but you should rest," Orpheus finally answered, his voice tense.

"I'm sorry I never got to schedule my date with you, Samara," I said, nonchalantly, trying to hide the quiver in my voice.

"You were understandably preoccupied, Athena." Her smooth tone was simultaneously a comforting embrace and a sharp stab.

"Come over to my house tomorrow morning? I'll make us breakfast." I tried my best to sound calm. If she was going to tell me what I think she was and break my heart, I'd prefer to fall apart in private. "Wait, do you even eat breakfast?" I thought back to the last time I saw them at Dale's. They had food on their table and I think I recall them picking at it.

"We can eat human food, although its benefits are in taste alone," Samara responded. That was a small reminder that my vampire mates were hungry for more than scrambled eggs. "But, you were just injured, you shouldn't be cooking anything for me," she interjected.

"I'm injured, not dead." I attempted to make a lighthearted joke, but I should have known better. Several low growls sounded through the phone. "Tomorrow morning, ok?"

She sighed, and I could imagine the look she was exchanging with Orpheus at that very moment.

Finally, she replied. "Tomorrow morning," she agreed.

After the others made me promise to give them updates, I hung up, just moments before Archer returned, a smirk on his face.

"Not many people can go a round with Davia Adams and live to tell the tale," I joked. "How did it go?"

He sat down in his chair again and offered me a smile. "She's going to call you in five minutes."

"I thought you said you'd take care of it for me?" I laughed, but secretly I did want to hear her voice.

"I bought you five minutes, that was monumental," He removed his baseball cap and ran a hand through his dyed black hair. The flashes of blue looked dull in the fluorescent lighting.

"I guess you're right," I sighed. "How'd she take the news about Greg?"

"She mumbled something about 'good dick always being attached to assholes.'" He mimicked her tone, and I found myself belly-laughing, then wincing at the movement.

"She demanded that I put you on the phone."

"But you bought me five minutes," I added. He smiled, then a look of accomplishment on his face.

"Impressive, huh?"

I smiled at my new friend, a warmth blooming in my chest at the friendship and camaraderie I had found with him.

"Revolutionary."

Archer reached forward then, resting his hand on the exposed forearm of my good arm.

"I'm really glad you're ok, Athena." He looked at me the way a friend would. I nodded, willing the stinging tears to stay put.

"So when do I lose you?" I asked a soft pang in my chest at the thought of losing Orpheus, Samara, and Archer.

"I'm not sure," he said, weakly and I felt a cloud of sadness blanket us. "But hey, maybe when I'm finished with this current job I'm on, I can come back. I think I'd like Shockgrove during the tourist season."

I beamed brightly at him and gripped his hand in mine. "Shockgrove would be lucky to have you."

He smiled at me, unfiltered and unrestrained.

The moment was interrupted by the ringing of my phone on my lap. Archer leaned back, rolling his eyes. I laughed, gripping the phone in my hands.

"I'm pretty sure that was only three minutes," I teased. Archer stood, grabbing his backpack from the ground at his feet and slinging it over his shoulder.

"Well I'm not a miracle worker," he added before offering me a nod and exiting the room. I smiled after him, and mentally prepared myself for the coming onslaught of questions.

I answered the phone and answered all of Davia's questions, as thoroughly as I could, including the biggest question of why I gave her number to Archer. By the end of our conversation, I had a sneaking suspicion she wasn't as upset about that as she was pretending. I loved my best friend, and I felt how much she cared for me in every single word, every single threat to kill me for not calling her first. I had to remind her she was hours away at a summit, and she scoffed, saying, "As if that's enough to keep me from you."

She promised she would be home tomorrow, despite how I begged her to stay put, telling her I was fine.

When she finally let me hang up, and the doctors signed my discharge papers, I felt a weight lifted off of my soul. Greg was out there, and he was angry, but I had never felt more loved and protected in my life than I did at that moment.

Four vampires willing to kill for me, a new friend who sat by my bedside as I recovered, and my best friend in the world leaving her important work event early just to make sure I was ok.

I'd been through a lot of pretty horrible things in my life, but if it all led me here, to these people. I couldn't help but be thankful for the sunshine that peaked through the clouds.

Even if tomorrow morning it'll be eclipsed by the looming goodbye.

For now, I was going to soak up that sunshine because god dammit, I deserved to.

13

SAMARA

"Will you stop breaking shit?" Orpheus exclaimed again when Silas threw something at the wall of our rental and it shattered onto the floor in broken wooden splinters. "She's ok."

"That fucker deserves to rot for what he did," he seethed, his eyes reddening by the second.

"I agree, obviously, but you heard her," Laz interjected, putting their hands on Silas's chest. A strangely intimate look passed between them as Silas allowed Laz to invade his personal space. "She doesn't want us to retaliate. And we have to respect her wishes." Silas groaned but did not pull away from Laz's touch.

I understood the urge. I wanted nothing more than to rush to her side and heal her of this pain. To take it away from her so she doesn't have to suffer because of our hasty actions. It wasn't lost on me that we were the reason this Greg guy lost his friend, and therefore somehow blamed Athena for it.

But she had asked us not to.

And we needed to listen.

"Go get some sleep," Laz offered quietly to Silas, their eyes locked in an intimate expression of something. They'd never been that touchy-feely before. It kind of shocked me to see it. I glanced over at Orpheus to gauge if he was noticing the same thing I was, but he was too busy running his hands through his hair, his own control slipping rapidly.

"We all should get some sleep," I offered. They glanced in my direction. "Tomorrow, Athena will have talked to us all. She very well may decide to accept your bond tomorrow night." I said to Silas and Laz, who bristled at the mention of it.

"I can't believe you're still thinking of rejecting her," Silas said, his anger about Greg replaced with his ire toward me. It had been frosty at best around the house since Orpheus revealed my intention this morning.

When Orpheus arrived home from his lunch date with Athena, I hadn't expected to scent her on him so strongly. For the briefest of moments, I thought he had gone back on his word to me and decided to stay with her. Which he would have every right to, but it stung all the same.

But one look at his dejected, lost expression told me all I needed to know. Whatever moment he and Athena shared was not a celebration, but a goodbye.

"Please, just try to understand," I whispered so my voice could not betray me.

"I can't. I can't understand it at all," Silas roared.

"Silas," Laz warned, holding onto his arm.

"Tonight is the last night we will ever be a family," he started, a quiver in his lip. "Do you realize that? If she accepts the bond tomorrow, and you two idiots reject it. You'll run off with your new vampires and we will never be a family again. Never be The Wanderers again. Don't you get that?"

My chest tightened.

"Of course, I know that! It's all I can think about, Silas." I was crying, tears streamed down my cheek.

"Don't you care?" He asked, his eyes glassy.

"I care more than anything. This is breaking my fucking heart. I know that by rejecting this bond, I'm not just losing her," I choke out, unable to even say her name. "I'm losing Laz, and I'm losing you. The last living person who loved Alora as much as I did."

Silas glared at me, pain and suffering burning behind his gaze.

"You know what she believed in above everything else?" He asked, his voice an even, low tone, full of hurt. "Family." He finished before I could respond and I nodded, knowing that. My wife had valued her family more than anything on this Earth. "And here you are about to shatter her family."

I gasped, a painful stab in my heart.

"She would be so fucking ashamed of you."

The words found their purchase in my heart and I fell to my knees, tears pouring from my eyes. Laz had pulled on Silas, whispering "Silas...That was low," just as Orpheus ordered, "Get him out of here."

A few moments passed and I knew Silas had retreated from the room with Laz, leaving me alone with Orpheus. He knelt down in front of me, and my blurry gaze found him.

"He's just afraid of losing you," he offered, quietly. I nodded. "You should get some rest, tomorrow is going to be a hard day." He helped me to my feet and then slowly wrapped me in an embrace.

I excused myself to my room, and there in the still of the night, with the soft moonlight flooding through the cracks in my blinds, I mourned. I mourned for my wife, for my mate, for my family.

I mourned until I had no tears left to cry, and then and only then, did sleep finally take me.

***

The morning came sooner than I would have liked, something about the way the sun peered through the blinds and cast painful streaks of light across my skin felt appropriate. I found myself sitting there absorbing the pain for longer than I should have because deep down I felt like I deserved it. I rolled out of bed and donned a soft pink sundress with a keyhole neckline and long bell sleeves. The color was a bright contrast to my dark skin, and I spent a few silent minutes applying makeup to my face, doing my best to hide the red-rimmed eyes that were evidence of my despair last night.

I considered waking the others to discuss last night, but as I passed their doors, I couldn't bring myself to cross the threshold. Instead, I slipped out of the house quietly, after downing half of the last blood bag in the cooler, and headed to Athena's house around the corner.

The walk to her little cottage was brief, but each step felt like it dragged on. I found my feet making a detour before my head caught up. I slipped inside the market and smiled briefly at the cashier before purchasing a bouquet of pink roses. The flower that, at one point, meant nothing to me, but now would forever be a reminder of the love I could have had.

Their sweet aroma enveloped me as I returned to the streets, heading to her.

Turning down her driveway, I felt my heart in my throat, unbeating, but in pain nonetheless. I could barely stop the shake in my hands to knock on the door.

When she answered, the wave of her scent crashed into me, followed soon thereafter by the worry at her current state. She had done her makeup this morning, painting her perfect features with a soft bronzed glow and darkening her eyelids with a deep brown that made her green eyes pop. Her hair was left down to fall in gentle waves down her back. But it wasn't her beauty that gave me pause, nor did the slight white powder that seemed to be dusting her face and clothing. It was the dark bruise that marred her perfect skin, poking out from beneath the gauze bandage on her arm that I could see from underneath her t-shirt sleeve.

My eyes landed on that bruise and I couldn't see anything else. Her pain. Her injury. It was our fault. That was a fact I simply couldn't get over.

"Are you in pain?" I asked, and I saw her eyes follow mine to where her arm was covered. She shrugged.

"It's better than it was." I knew she was covering up the full scope of the injury in order to appease me, and that only made me angrier.

"Come in," she offered, stepping aside and welcoming me into her home for the second time. She must have had a similar thought because she followed up by asking, "Do you have to be invited in?"

I smiled, softly, passing her to enter her living room, trying to tear my eyes from her injury with little success.

"Yes, but you've already invited me in. The first night."

She nodded, processing that as she closed the door behind me.

"Well, um, thanks for coming. I've got a few things going." She brushed past me and headed to the kitchen, the minty scent of her skin mixing with the deliciously sweet aroma of her blood had my body tensing against the urge to indulge in her. A flash of hunger exploded in my throat.

Once I had composed myself, I turned to follow her. To say the kitchen was a mess would be putting it lightly, flour was dusting nearly every surface of the kitchen, and suddenly the powder on her clothing made sense. Cracked eggs sat on the counter, waffle batter sat in pools across the counter, and a slight sizzle came from the stovetop where pieces of bacon were being fried beyond recognition. She cursed under her breath and rushed to remove the pan from the offending burner. I watched her carefully as she favored her good arm, holding the other close to her frame. Fury seethed through me again. She struggled to set the pan down and turn the burner off with just one arm. I rushed forward, helping her.

"Here," I said, switching the burner off. Ignoring the way her breath hitched when I brushed against her skin. I stood still in that moment, soaking up her sweet heated gaze and the way her heat rolled off of her. Her eyes held mine captive, and I wasn't sure I'd be able to step away if the world ended.

It took nearly every ounce of my willpower to step back from her orbit. Clearing my throat, I safely put the kitchen island between the two of us. She composed herself and slowly turned to face me. Her soft breathing was strained.

"Sorry, I um, didn't realize how hard it would be to cook with only one good arm."

I nearly stepped forward to heal her right then and there, but I wasn't sure the intimate connection would be a very good idea at the moment, so instead I offered, "Let me, please?" I indicated toward the waffle iron, and she followed with her eyes.

"You don't mind?" She asked sheepishly, shame coloring her face.

"Not in the slightest," I said, moving around the island toward the cooking station. To my relief, Athena countered my movement and kept her distance. I felt like I could breathe and think when I had this space between us because when I was up close and personal with her I wanted to throw caution to the wind and lose myself in her. "How is your store?" I asked, keeping my gaze on the work ahead of me and stirring the eggs. The less I looked at her, the better. I was likely to throw myself at her if I stared at her too long.

"The insurance company is going to pay for a new window, thankfully. We should be getting it by the end of the week." She spoke with such pained worry. I knew she was mourning the destruction wrought upon her bookstore, and I knew she felt responsible.

"It's not your fault, you know," I murmured. I heard her sigh behind me.

"It's not yours either." I paused, pouring the batter into the waffle iron, and turned to face her. She was leaning against the island with her good arm, and staring directly at me. Her eyes seemed to delve all the way into my soul.

"Except that's not true," I tossed out, peeling my gaze from hers. It was safer not to look at her. When I looked at her, I saw things I shouldn't see, like a future. "He wouldn't be harassing you if his friend hadn't gone missing."

"And his friend wouldn't have gone missing had he not tried to rape me," she said bluntly. I felt my back tense under her gaze, but I focused on continuing to prepare our food.

"I do not regret his death, I only regret that it has caused you trouble," I stated, matter-of-factly, gathering two sage green ceramic plates from the cabinet above the sink.

"I know you're planning to reject the bond, Samara." If I didn't have incredibly quick reflexes the plate in my hand would have shattered across the kitchen floor. My name on her lips sounded like heaven, wrapped in the hell of her words.

"What?" I asked, turning toward her with wide-eyed shock. She simply watched me, curiously.

"I didn't mean to just blurt it out like that, but I couldn't avoid it anymore. You wouldn't even look at me. It was getting awkward." She chuckled softly and I joined her, suddenly relieved it wasn't a painful secret any longer.

"I'm sorry," I said, meeting her gaze and not shying away. There was no way those two words could accurately acknowledge all of the ways I feel I let her down.

"I know," she answered, with a shy smile. I turned away from her and plated the food, focusing on the task so I couldn't drown in the dread of what came next.

I set the two plates of food down on the island and quietly Athena took a bite. She moaned at the taste, and I groaned at how that moan made me feel. My core tightened and I wanted nothing more than to hear that sound again. And again. And again.

I avoided thinking of how I'd much rather spread her wide on this kitchen island and have her for breakfast and took quick bites of the waffle.

We ate in silence, save for a few of those delicious moans. Finally, she cleared her throat. "Tell me about Alora." I stopped mid-bite and nearly choked on the piece of waffle in my mouth. "Sorry," she offered quickly, handing me a napkin. As I reached for it, my fingers brushed against her skin and we both gasped. Her skin was electricity against mine, shocking me with a jolt of magnetic energy that made me feel fucking alive. I instinctively bit my bottom lip, forcing the pooling desire between my legs to calm.

I pulled my hand from her, leaning breathlessly against the island. Guilt flooded my senses. She had just asked me about my wife, and I was being turned on by her mere presence. I hated how weak that made me seem.

"Alora," she prompted again. "She was your partner right?" She asked without a single ounce of judgment. I nodded.

"My wife, my chosen." Athena licked her bottom lip softly, averting her eyes from mine. She took an idle bite of food. "She was the strongest person I've ever known." I felt the tell-tale sting in my eyes as the thoughts of her grew heavy and painful.

My memories of her were so hard to reconcile. How beautiful they were, how horrifically they ended. No matter how I tried to separate the love we shared from the torture we endured, I couldn't seem to.

"Was." Athena noted the verb tense, and although I'm positive Silas or maybe even Orpheus had already told her the unfortunate truth about my wife's demise, she wanted me to tell her.

"Yeah, was," I repeated.

"What happened?" Athena asked, quietly, her eyes scanning my features.

I hated reliving this moment, but if Athena was going to understand why I couldn't be with her, she needed to know why. I took a long, steadying breath, and began.

"She died saving our lives."

"Are you all ready?" Alora's voice whispered from her cell. I tensed, gripping the bars of my cage with a painful grasp. Despite my exhaustion and brutal hunger, I couldn't help but feel a bloom of hope in my chest, blanketed by overwhelming fear.

"Remind me why you think this is going to work?" Orpheus asked, quietly from the cell next to mine.

"Because it will." She asserted, and I couldn't help but smile at the pure optimism of my wife, however misplaced I feared it was.

"It's our only chance," Silas exclaimed quietly, and weakly. We hadn't fed in nearly two months. Our bodies were slowly deteriorating. But Alora had gotten lucky, or as lucky as a prisoner can get, and managed to get a single taste of human blood. It wasn't enough to quench the thirst, or even offer much strength, but it would have to be good enough.

"When we get out of the cage, we can feed each other," Orpheus offered, excitedly. He had been trying to find a way to get his blood to us since the very first week. Vampire blood, while still delicious and often euphoric, didn't give us quite the same amount of strength as human blood, but a weak vampire could still kill a strong human. We just needed something to stave off the overwhelming hunger. We needed to get out of the cages, and then we could do this.

"If all goes well, we can share a guard for dinner before we get out of here. Just be ready to move. Don't get caught in bloodlust. Ok?" Alora warned, and although I knew the dangers and logically understood a bloodlust trance could mean the difference between life and death, I wasn't sure I'd be able to control myself the moment I tasted blood again.

We waited patiently for an hour or more, I wasn't entirely sure. Time seemed to work differently in the darkness of these cages. Finally, the thick door at the end of the hall opened and a single guard wandered in. He walked down the center of the aisle, firmly keeping his feet on the safe side of the painted red line. His eyes scanned the other cages, although we hadn't had a fellow prisoner in a few weeks. There was an elder vampire trapped in one of those when we first arrived, He'd been there for weeks at that point. He wasn't very good at conversation, and every time Orpheus pushed him for recon or answers, the elder would usher a hopeless response. He seemed to have accepted his death long before we arrived. And a few weeks later, death came for him after all.

The guard scanned the cage next to me, his eyes filled with a sort of disgust and contempt, as if somehow in this scenario we were the monsters when he was starving and torturing us. I glared back at him, tracking his movements carefully. He met my gaze before slowly moving along, His eyes darted to the cage next to mine, Alora's, and his steps faltered.

"Fuck," he exclaimed under his breath. He gripped the walkie-talkie on his vest and pressed a button. "We've got a dead one."

My heart, which hadn't beat in almost three hours, constricted. I pressed my body against the bars straining for a look at her. She had to be ok, it was her trick, of course.

Right? I couldn't think straight, my shift was so close to the surface I could nearly feel it.

"Bring the cart," he called into the walkie-talkie, and I felt tears stream down my cheek. Please let this be part of the plan.

"Alora?" I couldn't help the cry on my lips. "Alora, please. Answer me!" I was risking the entire thing, but the pain in my chest mixed with the exhaustion won over any logic. "Alora!" I screamed.

"Shut up!" The guard called over to me. "The bitch is dead."

I screamed, a guttural painful sound. "Alora! No," I beat against the bars of the cage with all the strength I could muster, which wasn't much.

The guard got a sick little smirk on his face and leaned toward me just enough so I could see the evil in his eyes. "Be quiet, or you'll join your little girlfriend."

"I will fucking rip you to shreds," I growled at him, he attempted to remain composed, but his face drained of color and he faltered, stepping back from my cage. I didn't even notice then that he had crossed the red line, unaware of the horrors that awaited him on our side of the barrier.

A pair of hands reached out through the cage next to mine and in a blink of an eye, the guard's neck was snapped and his lifeless body fell to the ground in front of my cage. His lifeless eyes looked up at me from the floor.

"Samara, get the keys," Alora's heavenly voice called to me, and I sobbed with relief.

"Alora?" I cried out.

"Yes, my love, I'm ok. Please get the keys." My vision blurred with tears, but I pressed my hands through the bars to the lump of human flesh next to me.

"Good work, Alora," Orpheus praised, but I didn't miss the hitch in his composure. He was just as hungry as the rest of us, and here in front of me was a dead human body, filled with blood. Blood that, if we drank it now, would give us enough strength to fight our way out of here.

"Toss me the walkie Samara," Silas called. I reached for it, unclipping the device from the vest, and slid it down the wall toward his voice. A few moments later, I heard the voice of the guard call into the walkie-talkie, "False alarm, the bitch was trying to pull a fast one. All clear." I smiled, weakly as I searched the body for the keys. Silas' gift had come in handy more times than I could count. His facade might just be the thing that saves us today. My fingers found the keys at the guard's belt and I made quick work of the lock on my cage. When it clicked open, I felt a sort of freedom and hope I didn't know was still possible.

I stood over the limp body at my feet and my shift was so close I couldn't contain it for another second. My fangs elongated and I descended on the body at my feet. Sinking my teeth into his still-warm flesh. The first taste of blood was so impossibly *perfect, the world around me fell away until there was nothing but its taste. I drank, and drank, gulping the liquid down like the ravenous starving creature I was.*

"Samara! Stop!" The faint scream of my wife was the only thing that penetrated the bloodlust haze. Slowly, logic returned, and shame bloomed in my chest. I pulled my fangs from the body and turned to face my wife, seeing her face for the first time in two whole months. The taste of blood, still fresh on my tongue, was nothing compared to the power I felt from seeing her crystal eyes.

I unlocked her cage, and embraced her, my wife, my chosen, for the first time in too long. Her arms circled my waist and held me close to her frail body. I didn't realize how much her touch meant to me until I couldn't have it.

"Guys, I get it, I do. But get us out," Laz whispered. It took a nearly unbearable amount of willpower to peel my body from Alora's and unlock my coven's cages. When the last cage was opened, I turned to notice Silas, Laz, and Orpheus all latched onto a different part of the deceased guard, stealing what little bit of his blood I had left in his body. Silas, who was now disguised as the very guard he fed from, smiled and the picture was so inherently wicked. Alora set a hand on my shoulder and smiled, turning me to face her.

"You should feed," I whispered, relishing the way her hand felt on my body. She nodded, hungry eyes locking on my neck. She dove in and sunk her fangs into the soft part of the throat. She drank eagerly, and I held her there. Each slow draw of my blood to her mouth was another reminder of my love for her. She should have drank from the human instead, gathering more than just 'enough' strength. Maybe if she had she would have been stronger.

She retracted her fangs, kissing the spot, her tongue sealing the wounds at my throat.

"Are you ok?" I gasped, scanning her frame for injuries, of which there were plenty.

"I will be," she assured me with a kiss on my lips. I placed my hands on her cheeks and sent my healing power surging through her nonetheless. Finding each cracked rib, each tear of flesh, and fixing them. She let out a sigh of relief. "Why didn't you tell me what you were planning, I thought...I thought for a second there that I'd lost you."

"That's what I was counting on," she replied sheepishly. "I needed you to scare him."

I nodded, hating it had come to that, but thankful I had her here, in one piece in front of me. I brought my lips to hers again, sinking into a kiss that said every word that went unsaid these last few months.

"We need to get out of here, now," Orpheus exclaimed. He looked strong and focused. The little bit of human blood he got was doing wonders at returning our fearless leader to his former glory.

Silas stripped the dead guard at his feet and slipped into the tactical gear he wore.

I nearly growled at him, the facade of the guard a vicious reminder of the torture we'd endured.

We slipped through the hallway carefully, Silas leading the charge, the cells lined the space taunted me as we walked past. I would rather die than return to one of these. Alora's hand gripped mine, our fingers intertwined, and I felt grounded.

When we arrived at the thick iron door, the air was filled with unspoken tension.

"We are a coven," Orpheus whispered. "We are a family. And we will make it out of here together."

"But, if someone is lost, do not turn back." Alora squeezed my hand as she spoke.

"Alora," I whined. She shook her head.

"Promise me," she said to me. "Promise," she offered to the others. Silas, Orpheus, and Laz softly agreed, but I shook my head, tears staining my skin.

"It won't come to that," I cried.

"I hope you're right." She pushed a strand of my loose curly hair behind my ear.

"Are we ready?" Silas asked, and as his eyes - the wrong shade thanks to his facade - scanned each of us for our acknowledgment. Then he pressed on the door and crossed the threshold.

Nameless headquarters was a dark warehouse, industrial in its design and function. The few times we'd been allowed to see where they were dragging us, we'd seen conveyor belts, and what looked like a weapon manufacturing floor. Normally, it was loud and active in this place, with shouts and machinery. But now, either by a stroke of luck, or a sick cruel sense of hope, the space was quiet. We moved carefully against the wall of the open factory floor with our claws elongated, poised to attack, but nobody came.

We moved at a pace that was slow for our kind, but we didn't dare get caught up in the false sense of security.

We had nearly reached the other end of the factory and a large set of double doors that had to lead outside when a sound echoed across the expanse. We rushed forward, ducking behind the machinery. Alora pressed her head into my chest and I felt her breathing come raggedly. I kissed the top of her head, willing myself and her to calm down. Laz and Orpheus were at our back, their nerves were so palpable I could choke on them. Silas stood up, his guard-shaped form, gazing in the direction of the sound.

"Foster" a voice called from across the space. I glanced at the door, nearly a hundred yards away, but so close I could almost feel the fresh air on my skin. Silas waved his hand nonchalantly.

"Need something, Bennett?" He asked calmly. I cringed at the name of the guard who'd overseen some of our worst torture sessions. How Silas could say his name without seething was beyond me. They had been careless, letting us hear their names. So cocky and confident that we would never escape. But we knew their names now,

and have seen their faces. And if we get out of here, we won't let them forget what they've done to us here.

"What the hell are you doing over here?" Silas shrugged.

"I was gonna head outside and get some fresh air, those bloodsuckers smell like shit." I could hear the tenseness in his voice and I knew he was feeling the pressure bubble up. His eyes darted every so briefly to where we were hiding. His head made the slightest nod toward the door.

"You were supposed to check in," the voice accused, getting closer. I buried my face into Alora's hair, willing my breathing to slow.

"Jesus, can't a guy have five minutes to erase that stench from his nose?" Silas took a step back toward the door.

I glanced over at Orpheus and Laz, their eyes tracked Silas' movement carefully. He would open the door and we would make a break for it. They readied themselves, getting their feet beneath them and preparing for the race of a lifetime. Alora and I followed suit, my shaking hands pressed against the cement floor.

"Where are you going?" The guard asked an edge of disbelief in the tone. Alora and I shared a worried glance.

"Outside, I just told you," Silas teased again, taking another step toward the door. He was so close now. Come on, open it.

"Freeze," the guard, Bennett, called, and I stifled a gasp. Silas' eyes widened and he put his hands up, no doubt a weapon of some kind was now pointed at him. His eyes flashed briefly toward us.

"What the fuck, man?" Silas said, trying to maintain his cool, but even I could see it slipping by the second. He took a few more careful steps toward the door. "Just calm the hell down, and I'll be in for a check-in soon." He reached the door and as he put his hands on the metallic surface, the four of us in hiding sprinted. With new blood running through our veins, we were able to sprint with the speed we'd so dearly missed these last few months.

"Code Black!" Bennett screamed into his walkie and suddenly a vicious-sounding alarm blared through the air, a bright white and red light flashed, but we were at the door. So close, we just needed to get outside. They'd never be able to catch us out there.

We pressed against the door with all our force, but it didn't budge. Fear and panic seized my heart.

"Fuck, it won't open," Orpheus screamed, his fists banging against the door.

"The door won't open from over there," the voice seethed, angrily, threateningly. "And Foster would have known that you fucking filthy bloodsucker."

I swallowed the lump in my throat.

"You're trapped, so give up," the guard yelled.

My eyes scanned the area, sounds of running footfalls were echoing through the space, and we would be surrounded soon. We would be dead soon. So close to freedom, and it was all going to end.

"There," Alora whispered through clenched teeth. She nodded toward a panel on the wall near where the guard was standing, we'd passed it on our way here. "There is a key, I bet that opens the door."

"We're too fucking far from it now," Orpheus hissed, his eyes reddening and his claws sharpening.

"We could reach it!" She exclaimed.

"That's suicide, Alora! No," Orpheus snapped.

"What the hell are we going to do?" Silas asked, his form slowly returning to normal now the jig was up. His hands ran along the seam of the door searching for a weak spot.

"We were so close!" Laz cried, digging their claws into the metal of the door with no luck.

We were going to die. The horde of guards was almost there. The one guard held a weapon pointed at us, a dark mahogany stake in one hand, a gun in the other. The gun to slow us down, the stake to finish the job. It was the Hunter's method. That or their garlic and holy water mixture. The guard stared at us, his strawberry hair wild and disheveled as he glared at us with determination.

"Nowhere to run, Wanderers," Bennett taunted.

"We could fight our way out." Silas offered, anger pouring off of him.

"Impossible," Orpheus growled.

"Damnit," Laz lamented. They leaned their head against the door, the barrier keeping us from salvation.

Alora turned to face me, her eyes shining with tears. Her hand gripped my face and I reveled in her touch for a brief moment. Her lips crashed against mine and I soaked up her kiss as if I was starving for it. Her tongue pressed against mine and I let myself fall into her arms, kissing my wife with every ounce of promise and love in my body. Telling her everything I couldn't bear to say aloud. A century of thank you's and goodbyes.

If I had to die, at least I would die with her. At least she would know that I loved her. Whatever afterlife was allotted for my kind, I wanted to enter it with her at my side.

She broke our kiss, her cheeks stained with tears. She looked at me with every ounce of the love we shared.

"I love you, Samara," she sobbed.

"I love you too, Alora."

Then she ran.

For the briefest of moments, time slowed and I couldn't comprehend what had just *happened. One second, her soft curves were safe in my arms, the next she was sprinting toward the danger.*

"Alora! Damnit!" Orpheus called after her, and the world resumed. My wife was making her way across the factory floor toward the horde of guards, toward the panel on the wall. I took a step involuntarily, ready to follow her to the ends of the world.

Arms circled my waist and held me still. I fought against them. "Let me go!" I screamed, but the arms tightened. I watched in rapt horror as my wife dodged a shot fired from the barrel of the guard's gun. "Alora!" I yelled, scratching at the arms that now acted as yet another cage between my chosen and myself.

"Laz, stop him!" I was only vaguely aware of Laz grabbing a hold of Silas beside me who was nearly as feral as I was at the prospect of Alora heading into the fray alone.

"Fucking get your hands off of me. Alora!" Silas screamed, but Laz grunted, forcing their arms around his thrashing form.

"Samara, stop," Orpheus whispered against my ear, but his voice was nothing but noise. My heart felt like at any moment it would rip out of my chest and follow her itself.

Alora managed to make it past the first guard, but he got a shot off just in time to clip her shoulder. She faltered, crying out in pain.

"No!" I shouted.

"She's ok, she's ok," Orpheus chanted and he held steadfast against my attacks, but he didn't sound convinced.

Blood flowed down her arm, coating the floor beneath her as she made her way to the panel at the wall. The room flooded with Hunters, armed and angry. They converged on Alora. She winced as she pushed through them, but despite their persistence, she managed to knock a few down to the ground at her feet.

She threw herself into the wall, her hands gripping the key and twisting it.

"That's it, Alora," Silas whispered beside me, he had stopped fighting Laz, but his voice was full of fear. I understood it. I felt it too.

The door behind us creaked as the mechanisms whirred to life. Cool air brushed against the back of my neck as the door to our freedom slid open.

"Come on, baby, come on," I cried, watching as Alora began her fight back to me. She pushed past more guards, taking a few more hits. Bullets riddled her body, but still, she fought. Silas screamed just as Bennett plunged his stake directly through Alora's heart, her agonizing wail piercing the air. I stopped breathing. The light in her eyes went dim, she fell to her knees. Her hands came up to her chest to feel for the wound. Her eyes met mine and I watched the life drain from her gaze, before she fell to the floor, unmoving.

"Get up!" I shouted. "Get up, baby please!" My throat was raw from my screaming, but I couldn't hear myself, I couldn't hear anything. There was nothing but her

form, lying still amongst the Hunters. There was nothing but her. I pulled on the restraints around my waist. I needed to get to her. I needed to save her., I could heal her. I know I could.

"Samara, stop, she's gone." Orpheus cried, his voice broken.

"Silas, please, help us," Laz pleaded. I raged against the hold, managing barely to break free, but just as I began my sprint to my wife, another set of arms grabbed me.

"Please Samara, I can't lose you too." Silas cried into my ear.

'No! Put me down. Let me go! Let me save her," I demanded through my vicious sobs. "Please, I can save her! I can-" I thrashed, but the arms were already dragging me through the door. My view of Alora's body was obscured as the Hunters rushed forward toward us. Bullets rushed past us, I heard Silas curse as one hit his skin.

"We have to go, Samara, please," Silas begged, pain lacing every word, every breath. "If we die, her sacrifice will be for nothing." Only then did I rip my gaze from her. Silas' eyes were red, tears painted his face and I saw the pain I felt so vividly mirrored in his expression. I knew he was right, but dammit, I couldn't move. I don't remember the next several minutes, I might have run, I might have been carried. I don't know. All I could see each time I closed my eyes was her face, the shock, the blood, the goodbye. My wife was dead, and I couldn't save her.

I was crying, the image of her death was so vivid in my mind despite the years that have passed since. It had been so long since I'd let myself fully relive that moment, the moment I lost her.

"Samara." Athena's soft melodic voice gripped my hand and pulled me back from the depths of my darkest memory. I blinked away the tears and let my eyes land on her. She had been crying as well, her glassy green eyes looked even more stunning beneath the wet sheen of tears.

"Words will never be enough to make up for what you went through. What you've seen." She started to reach across the island toward me, but I saw her restrain herself and bring her hands back to rest in her lap. I nodded, wiping the tears away with the back of my hand.

"I've been living a half-life since that day," I explained. "I'm not whole, Athena. I haven't been since I lost her."

She nodded, understanding.

"That's why I can't be your mate. Not because I don't care for you, not because I don't want to, but because you don't deserve someone who's broken." I sobbed, the truth of my pain flowing so easily through my painted lips.

She rushed around the island, and pulled me into an embrace, carefully with her injured arm. Her arms held me together as I fell apart. I cried into the crook of her neck and she brushed my hair from my face. Her wintergreen scent enveloped me, soothing the pain in my chest. I clung to her like the life-line I wished she could be.

"Being broken does not mean you do not deserve love, Samara," she whispered into my hair.

I pulled back from her hold, putting some much-needed space between us. I shook my head and licked my bottom lip. The salty taste of my tears was acidic, a reminder of the death that followed me.

"Please don't try to convince me to change my mind," I begged. The words *'because for you, I would'* remained unsaid.

"I'm not going to force you to love me," she whispered. "I understand why you feel you need to do this, and I'm not going to stop you."

I furrowed my brows. "You're not?"

She shook her head. "No, I'm not." She moved around the island to the coffee maker and poured herself a cup. I watched her move carefully, favoring her good arm, and carefully maneuvering around with her injured one.

She turned and took a slow sip of her drink before moving back to her place on the other side of the island.

"When my mom died, I thought I was going to die right along with her," Athena said eventually, her voice was even and calm.

"I'm sorry for your loss, Athena," I apologized, softly, settling into a bar stool across from her.

"Thank you," she replied, a solemn smile on her lips. "Basically, I'm trying to tell you that you don't have to explain yourself to me. I know it's not the same thing, but if someone showed up out of the blue claiming to be my fated mother, I wouldn't take that very lightly." I inhaled sharply. I had expected the guilt to soften when Athena understood why I had to reject this bond between us, but instead, it grew. The pit in my stomach was painful. The loss of her was growing nearer and I couldn't find the silver lining amongst the growing clouds in my mind.

"All I'm trying to say is that you don't need to worry about me. You don't need to be upset or afraid that you're hurting me," she spoke calmly, but even I noticed the almost imperceptible twitch in her jaw. "I will be ok."

I sighed, not feeling the relief I had wished would come with those words.

"But will you?" Her eyes bore into mine.

"What do you mean?" I asked, a slight defensive edge to my tone.

"Don't mistake my question, I would never push someone to *get over* their grief. I know that's not how it works," she continued. "But you are immortal, Samara."

I couldn't help but notice how she said that with such ease. How far she's come in such a short time.

"You have, thankfully, a lot of life left to live. Resigning yourself to a loveless existence is torture, and I can't bear to think of you putting yourself through that."

"I can't-" was all that escaped my lips.

"You haven't rejected me yet," she started, her voice caught. She exhaled a shaky composing breath and started again. "You haven't rejected me yet, so I'm still your mate." Tears flowed freely down her face and she forced herself to press on. "And if you can't promise yourself to me, can you at least promise that one day - one day when it doesn't hurt as much when you wake up and you can finally breathe again." She struggled to compose herself. "One day when you can think of her without that stabbing pain, you'll be open to love again. Promise me that you'll let yourself love when the time is right. Even if it can't be now. Even if it can't be with me." Her voice cracked on that word, her careful hold on her sobs slipping.

My heart shattered as her words penetrated the shield I'd so carefully constructed around my soul. In her features I saw the hurt, the type I felt every time I thought about leaving her behind and severing this bond the fates have given us.

I closed the gap between us before my mind could catch up to my feet. I held her face in my hands and she leaned into my hold as her tears flowed. And there, staring into her green eyes, it finally hit me just how selfish I had been. It wasn't just me who would be affected by this rejection. It wasn't my pain to carry alone. This bond was hers as much as it was mine. While I prepared to carve a piece of my heart out and leave it behind, she was going to let me, despite the torture it would cause her. She would do it, without trying to stop me, not because she didn't want to stop me, but because she loved me enough to let me go. I watched her heart break in real time before my eyes, knowing she would never ask me to change my mind because she respected my decision. My heart hummed to life, a heat blooming in my chest. It beat against my ribcage in a solid thump with more promise and hope than I had felt since the night I lost Alora. A giggle escaped my lips at the shock. Athena studied my face inquisitively.

She watched me carefully, a timid expression on her face, but her eyes scanned my face with what could only be described as hope.

When I looked at Athena when I focused on this powerful bond tying her soul to mine a nearly golden thread of connection, I no longer felt the pain of loss and betrayal, but instead, something deeper thrummed inside of me. A soft glimmer of light and memory dancing through my soul in unrestrained tendrils of blood-red passion and love. I closed my eyes, focusing on the tug of that strand of memory that beckoned for me. Asking for my attention. I shut my eyes tight, willing that familiar warmth in my soul to crest to the surface. Begging it to envelop me in its comfort. A whisper in my ear, clear as day.

'*You're allowed to love again, my chosen. It's ok.*'

I don't believe in ghosts, which may be a tad naive considering I'm a vampire, but I don't believe in souls sticking around long after their bodies have decomposed, but fuck, at that moment in the cozy kitchen of Athena's cottage, I would swear on my very existence that Alora spoke to me. Tears flowed from my eyes and I felt my body shake with a laugh of disbelief. Years of pain and anger and guilt slipped from my body with each exhale. I felt lighter than I had in years.

'*Thank you, my chosen,*' I whispered back through the channels of my mind. The warmth of her soul flooded through me like a promise.

When my eyes slid open, I saw Athena with an unfiltered gaze for the first time. Her soft red hair, her caring green eyes. Her creamy skin, and lush lips. The bond thrummed between us with a new vigorous life. I could see that golden bond in my mind so clearly, so vividly. And as I exhaled my fear and my pain, I saw that strand of memory, the piece of me that was Alora's, but instead of dissipating into nothingness, it wrapped itself around the bond. A beautiful display of gold and red, a mix of past and future. A reminder that Alora would always be there. No matter who my heart belonged to, she would forever be a piece of it.

My cheeks hurt from the smile that spread across my face. She studied me with careful curiosity, her fingers brushing against my face.

"What happened just now," she asked, quietly. Without accusation or expectation. Just pure worry and care.

"You just brought my heart back to life," I whispered on an exhaled breath, running my thumb along her tear-soaked cheek.

She looked up at me with love and wonder, a soft smile playing on her lips and I couldn't wait a single moment longer. My lips met hers and I poured every ounce of the affection I had been withholding into the kiss. Words that had gone unsaid, moments that had been avoided. The walls were well and truly down now and I sank into her kiss.

She tentatively kissed back for a brief moment, fear coating her tongue. I pulled back and let my breath mingle with hers.

"Is this goodbye?" She asked, breathlessly with an edge of heartbreak in her tone. I wanted to wipe every ounce of trepidation from her face, I wanted to erase every fear from her soul. I wanted to apologize for the pain I put her through by losing myself in her embrace.

"Athena, I can't leave you. I can't believe I even thought for a second that I could," I whispered, planting a kiss on her throat just above her clavicle.

"What are you saying?" She pleaded, leaning her head back to give me more access to her bare skin.

"I'm saying that you are my mate, and I intend to be yours."

She moaned at that confession, the sound causing my core to clench. "What about Alora?" She pressed on my shoulder with her good arm, putting some space between us. Her eyes searched mine.

"She's always going to be with me, I'll always love her. She's here now, in here," I placed a hand over my heart. "She will always be my chosen."

Athena's eyes searched mine for hesitation, or worry, but she wasn't going to find it.

"But, for the first time, I'm ready to love again, Athena." The words were a liberation, the key to the cell that I never truly escaped that night. But here, with my mate in my arms and my chosen in my heart, I finally took a full breath of fresh air.

Her smile brightened as tears continued to flow from her eyes, but they were tears of joy, of adoration. She crushed her lips to mine and kissed me back, passion and promise exchanged through our careful touches and selfish lips. I once compared her kiss to the feeling of coming home, and I realize now, as our tongues press against each other that I could not have been more right. Her kiss is transcendent, comforting, and perfect and by indulging in her I feel like I belonged again.

She went to toss her arms around my neck and she groaned in pain. Her lips pulled from mine and she cursed cradling her injured arm.

"Forgot about that," she lamented, with a soft laugh. I reached for her hand, and with a soft smile on my lips, I helped her stand from the stool.

"Where are we going?" She asked, her lips shimmering and freshly kissed. She placed her hand in mine, and gently I led her through her living room, past the baby blue record player, and headed into her bedroom. Her eyes darkened with lust and I struggled to keep my hands to myself as I helped her lie down. Athena's eager breaths came in quick spurts and she leaned back on the comforter. Her chest rose and fell quickly with anticipation. Her eyes watched me with heat burning within her gaze.

"What are you going to do?" She asked, cautiously.

"I'm going to kiss it better," I promised before slowly unbuttoning her jeans. Her breath hitched as I slid them down her legs, leaving just the thin white fabric of her panties behind.

I hovered over her body, letting my breath trail a path along her skin as I climbed up to grab the hem of her shirt. She gasped as I ripped it in half, exposing her perfect breasts.

"Samara," she moaned, and I nearly lost control right there and forgot my current mission, but the bandage on her arm served as a reminder of the more pressing matter.

"Shhh, I'll take care of you," I urged before planting a healing kiss against Athena's chest. Through the point of contact with her skin, I can feel the injuries and their lasting thrums of pain. I plant another kiss on her shoulder, willing my healing touch to wash away the physical trauma. Athena moaned beneath me, writhing in pleasure as I planted another kiss above the bandage on her arm, then below. My fangs threatened to elongate as my lips grazed so close to the wound. The bandage and stitches did nothing to mask her scent, so close to her blood I struggled to keep myself focused and push the hunger down. But as my lips brushed her skin, I felt the full force of the abuse her body had been through and suddenly nothing mattered more than healing her.

My fingers trailed up and down her stomach, brushing delicately against the top of her underwear and the underwire of her bra. She groaned in frustration each time my fingers changed direction, ignoring the source of her desire.

Kiss. Erase the bruise. Kiss. Close the wound. Kiss. Ease the ache. Kiss.

She moved her arm, tentatively, testing the range of motion. Her eyes widened as she realized the pain was gone.

"How did you..." she began, but my lips brushed against her stomach and her words were lost.

"I think you'll be pleasantly surprised to discover what my lips can do, Athena." I chuckled, kissing a trail down her stomach to the seam of her underwear. She groaned a pleasurable sound that had my hands itching to spread her wide.

I placed a soft kiss on the fabric that separated her heat from my mouth and her thighs pressed against my head slightly as her back arched. I gripped her thighs and pressed against her legs forcefully, letting her fall open for me.

"Samara, I need you," she gasped and I let go of the fragile hold I had on my control. Using my slightly elongated fangs, I ripped through the fabric barrier and then delved into her core. She was soaking wet, her arousal pooling at her center, and it was all mine. I slid my tongue through her folds, eliciting the sweetest sounds. I hummed against her, the vibration had her shaking beneath my hold. She writhed beneath me, her eager body pressing into my mouth as she rode me. I focused my tongue on her clit and pushed two fingers into her heat. She let out a scream as her orgasm snuck up on her. I drank every ounce of her release and her breathing slowly returned to almost normal.

I kissed each thigh before sitting up and studying my stunning mate. She was gorgeous, but there was something so elusive and artistic about the way she looked when she was in the throes of passion. I needed to see more. I climbed up her body again, trailing wet kisses across her skin, pausing briefly to slide the fabric of her bra down enough for me to take a nipple in my mouth and roll it along my tongue. She sighed pleasantly, pushing her chest into my mouth.

"I want," she whispered, stopping to moan as my mouth continued its worship of her breasts.

"What do you want, Athena?" I spoke against her skin.

"I want to taste you."

I clenched, my core tightened and desire flooded between my thighs.

"Anything for my mate," I answer, teasing kisses against her exposed skin. She sat up, pressing on my shoulders until I was lying flat on my back on her bed. She eyed me hungrily like I was the prey. And I kind of liked that.

She let her warm breath dance along my skin as she pushed up my sundress, helping me throw it off. Only my pink satin panties remained, her lips brushed against my skin and she kissed up the length of my leg, stopping just at my apex before kissing up the other. I gripped the bedspread in my fist at my side as I fought against the urge to tangle my fingers in her hair and bury her face in my center.

The first drag of her tongue against my panties elicited a scream from my throat. She smiled up at me from her place between my spread legs and dove into my core again, this time sucking on my clit through the fabric.

Her fingers hooked on the top of my panties and finally slid them down my legs, the air brushed against my already sensitive clit and I shivered as Athena leaned toward my core and let her breath dance along my folds.

"Fuck, Athena, please," I begged, and she placed a gentle kiss on the space where my thigh met my hip.

"Does my mate need my mouth?" She whispered, sinfully. I threw my head back and voluntarily pressed my legs open further.

"Yes, I do. Please." Before I finished, her tongue pressed into my folds. Spearing me. I cried out, my fists twisting in the sheets.

She devoured me as if she was starving, and only my arousal could save her.

"Fuck," I exclaimed as she focused her attention on my clit. She dragged her tongue through my folds, lower, lower until it brushed over the tight ring of muscle. I gasped, but her mouth had already made its way back to my center.

With one finger, she pressed circles against my clit, while her tongue entered me and claimed every inch of my pussy. I was nearly lost to bliss, nothing could beat this feeling. But I was wrong. Just as I teetered over the edge of my own release, with her fingers on my clit and her tongue fucking me, she slid a finger to that tight hole. Circling it, spreading my slick arousal around it. I moaned as she pressed in. Devouring me, owning me so completely. When her finger was fully seated in my ass, I exploded around her. Lights and colors flashed in my eyes and I released a scream. Her tongue traced lazy strokes up and down my core as I rode her face, drawing out my orgasm as long as I could.

My hands released their hold on the sheets and I felt my chest heaving, my heart beat again, harder than before and I smiled at the feel of it existing inside of me as something lively and not a useless organ.

Athena crawled until she was resting over me, her lips glistened with evidence of my arousal, and an earth-shattering smile plastered on her face. I pressed my lips against hers and loved the way her taste mingled with mine.

"I want to lose myself in you," she whispered against my lips, and I felt every crack that had ever been in my soul fill with promise.

"I want that too, you have no idea," I started, pressing another kiss to her lips. She moaned and I captured the sound with my mouth, hoping I'd be lucky enough to hear it forever. "But first, if you're willing...." She sat up, her hair falling down her back in waves, as she watched me. "I think there's a bond that needs to be completed."

<h1 style="text-align:center">14</h1>

ARCHER

$\mathcal{I}$ was moments away from ambushing the house and enacting the plan when the female, Samara, left the house this morning. I cursed under my breath at the lost opportunity. I wasn't dumb enough to think I could have acted through the night, if I was going to survive this, I needed to do it in daylight when its harsh rays might act as another rope around the throat of The Wanderers.

I watched her leave and swore to myself I was going to do it the second she got back. I don't know how long I sat there in the bushes across the street watching the movement within the house, trying to psyche myself up to go through with this.

The stake on my hip burned against my bare skin, and the smoke bombs, specially engineered to release a mixture of garlic and holy water, felt heavy in my palms. Sweat gathered at the nape of my neck, and fear coursed through my veins just as easily as my blood. I was a Hunter, but I didn't want to be.

I wanted to make music and escape from this world where monsters exist and I'm in charge of killing them.

I wasn't cut out for this. No matter how much my father claimed it was in my blood.

The mid-morning sun was bright, I had to use my hand to shield the glare from my eyes. There was a small gathering of people in the clearing. Several trainees, like myself, stood in a row facing the altar. My eyes landed on my father, who stood at the back of the robed figures who faced us. His eyes were light, and he practically beamed with pride from behind his black mask as I stood there, weapon in hand, prepared to make a pledge to spend my life killing vampires.

The man at the front, Doctor Kline Galvin, stood tall. His face was masked, but his eyes scanned us, disapprovingly. He had a Ph.D. in occult studies and never let anyone forget how well-versed he was in the unnatural. The Galvin line had acted as the head of Nameless for as long as the organization had operated in the dark. He held a metal brand over an open flame, slowly rotating it for maximum heating. My father told me once about the brand. Even showed me his, it was this ugly, violent-looking scar that rested between his shoulder blades. Raised angry white lines to form a disfigured image of the Nameless calling card. The symbol of the Hunters. Two triangles, and a wooden stake. He said it had hurt, but the pride in doing what he was born to do far outweighed the pain. He said it would be the same for me.

One by one, my classmates made their way up to the altar, exchanging whispered words with Dr. Galvin. Then he would lower the heated metal to their skin. The sound was an almost evil-sounding sizzle, it made my stomach churn. But what was worse was the smell, an acrid scent of burning flesh. I forced myself to breathe only through my mouth. A few of my classmates screamed as the brand scarred their skin. Their cries of pain were met with disapproving looks from the council. Then it was my turn.

I begged my hands not to shake as I made my way across the clearing to come to a stop in front of Dr. Galvin. His dark blue eyes passed over me with interest as he leaned forward.

"Your father assures me you will be one of the greatest assets Nameless has ever seen." His voice was rough and textured, and I could almost feel its bass rumbling in my chest.

I couldn't find my voice so I simply nodded.

"Hmmm," he mused, leaning back and scanning me again. "I hope he was not lying." I swallowed carefully, hoping he could not see the fear in my eyes. Suddenly, I was thankful I had a mask on. It hid the way my teeth bit into my bottom lip to keep my whimper from escaping.

"Archer, son of Jacob Bennett, do you swear your oath today to Nameless, and pledge your life to protect this world from the creatures of the night?" He asked in a loud whisper.

I bowed my head, silently begging my voice to remain calm even as I responded, "Nisi nox."

He motioned for me to offer him the bare section of flesh for the brand as he lifted the metal rod from the fire. I swallowed, and slowly unbuttoned my shirt, sliding it off to offer him my shoulder. Right where my father's mark was.

I didn't get a warning before the searing brand made contact with my skin. The pain was so absolute and so overwhelming. I waited, begging for the pride to eclipse the pain the way my father swore it would.

But it never did.

And so I just burned.

Sometimes when I was especially stressed I would mindlessly rub the scar on my wrist, the bite mark I garnered from trusting Evangeline all those years ago. The ugly, raised white lines reminded me so vividly of the brand that sat on my shoulder blade. Yet one came from the villains and one came from the heroes.

How thin was the line between the two?

After an hour or so, I watched as the female vampire returned back to her den, but just as I began to prepare for the attack, I stopped dead in my tracks. Athena was standing next to her, hand in hand. Her face brightened with a smile. The vampire stopped just outside the house, twirling Athena in her arms, and embracing her, pressing her lips against her throat. I nearly jumped out from my hiding space to save her, but she did not scream, she did not cry out. Because the vampire did not bite her, no, she simply kissed her.

My mind swam with questions and confusion. Had Athena fallen so deep into their trap? Or was she seeing something I couldn't? The two of them laughed, and I could hear the melodic sound dance in the wind. It was a carefree, happy sound. Not the sound of someone who was at the mercy of monsters.

They disappeared into the house, and I strained to listen for the tell-tale sound of death and destruction. Waiting for her to scream for help. But it never came.

Minutes passed in silence. I was frozen in indecision. An hour had come and gone before I made a choice.

I tossed my weapons into my pack, and slung it over my shoulder, setting off down the road.

I couldn't very well do the job with a human inside anyway.

But as I walked away, leaving Athena in that house felt like a death sentence, no matter how smitten these creatures seemed. They were still monsters and Athena wasn't safe. She'd never be safe. She was a human amongst monsters.

I stood at the end of the street, the road out of Shockgrove taunting me. I could just leave, leave Nameless, leave Athena, leave this fool's quest to capture The Wanderers. I could start over somewhere far away. Without monsters, without death.

Even as I thought it, the reality of my situation slammed into me. Nameless could track a coven of elusive and powerful vampires, if I thought for even a moment that they couldn't find me if they chose to, I was an idiot. No, like it or not, this was my life, and according to my father, if I didn't act on this task soon, my life very well could reach a rather abrupt end.

My heart clenched and beat against my chest as I glanced back at the house. Athena was inside a vampire den. Her vulnerable human blood was there for the drinking. Something very similar to grief flashed across my emotions. It's only been a few days, but something about her makes me feel like a real person. Her companionship and conversation have brought me more hope and normalcy than I ever thought I'd be able to find. I cared about her, and I cared about her safety.

These vampires looked like they were in love with her. I heard them call her their mate. If that was true, were they going to claim her? Turn her? Kill her? I gripped the stake at my side just as my phone vibrated.

I didn't need to check the caller ID to know who it was.

"Bennett," I offered, calmly, not drawing my eyes from the house.

"What the fuck is taking you so long," he spat. I winced at the harshness of his words. And then sighed at the unfortunate familiarity of the tone.

"This coven escaped Nameless, slipped through the hands of dozens of highly trained Hunters, and you expect me - alone, I might add - to do the job the Hunters couldn't?" I bit back. My father's silence was evidence of how infrequently I challenged him.

A long moment passed before he sighed. "You're right." The phone nearly fell from my grasp at that admission. One I'd never heard from his lips, and doubted I'd ever hear again. "Galvin is getting restless. He sent a group to a nearby town. They are zeroing in on The Wanderers, and I want you to complete this before they interfere." He sounded so desolate, so worried this was the last chance either of us had to set things right. I slid my hand through my hair in frustration.

"I know, I'm trying. Things just..." I glared off toward the house, "got a little complicated."

"How so?" He asked.

"There's a woman here, human. They seem to have taken a liking to her." I hated talking about Athena like a pawn in this long-winded game.

"Are they drinking from her?" He inquired so nonchalantly like he was asking about the weather.

"No," I replied. I had tried not to be obvious or creepy about it, but I scanned all the places on her skin I could see in her hospital gown. There were no noticeable bite marks. "I think."

"Hmm," he mused. "Have you tried to use her to lure them to one place?"

I had to forcibly avoid growling at that concept. I hated that, at first, that had been my intention. Now that I know her, I couldn't imagine using her like that. Shame clouded my senses.

"She is a human, Dad. Or have you forgotten that we are supposed to be protecting them?" I seethed, quietly. Barely containing the anger that bubbled under the surface.

"And you know as well as I do that one human life in exchange for millions is worth it every time."

I let my arm fall to my side, my phone dangling by my thigh as I took a steadying breath. Once I had composed myself enough not to scream at my father, I brought the phone to my ear again.

"What have I taught you?" He prompted. "You -"

"You are only ever safe in this world if you fight for your safety," I finished, dejectedly.

"That's right, son. Don't forget it."

I hung my head.

"When do you think you can make your move?"

I glanced back up at the house. The place where, at that very moment, all four of the remaining Wanderers were inside, undoubtedly distracted by the human that seemed to capture their fancy.

"Today," I whispered, but the word felt like ash on my tongue.

"Then I'll see you tomorrow."

"What about the human?" I asked, careful not to give away how much I had come to care for this particular human.

"If she's dead, ensure you are not implicated."

I winced, the mental picture of Athena lying dead on the floor, her green eyes lifeless, pierced me.

"And if she isn't dead?" I should have talked to her. Should have told her everything. She doesn't understand. I could have helped her understand. Kept her far away from these creatures. She would be safe.

"Don't let her see you. Knock her out if you have to." I nearly protested, but I knew what he would say. He would see how attached I'd become to her, he'd see right through me.

"Ok," was all I could say.

"Do not mess this up, Archer," he concluded before hanging up. No words of advice, or encouragement.

My goodbye hung dead on my tongue. Pocketing the phone, I slid my pack off my shoulders and reached inside for the materials I would need to feasibly complete this job. My truck was parked just off the street. The tarps were prepared to cover any cargo in the bed. My throat seemed to close with the reality of what I was about to do.

I could only hope Athena would understand why I had to do this, that she would forgive me for disappearing on her without an explanation. If she was even still alive after being subjected to whatever sick torture those vamps had planned for her. I wish I could be here to protect her. To help her in the aftermath.

With one last composing breath and a mindless trace of my fingers across the bite mark on my wrist, I headed toward the house.

15

ATHENA

I didn't know what to expect when Samara came over this morning. Heartbreak, pain, tears. That's what I had my money on. That's the fear that starred in my dreams last night. Never in my wildest imagination did I think we would share such a cathartic moment and release our inhibitions. Never did I think she would accept me as her mate.

But she did. My heart was almost too full, I was afraid it might burst. I felt my pulse in every inch of my body as Samara and I got dressed. It wasn't lost on me that Samara choosing to stay, also meant the obstacle that stood between Orpheus and me was now gone. A shiver wracked through me.

The bond.

I was about to complete a bond with four vampires.

My four vampire mates.

And I couldn't feel anything except excitement.

There was still the question of how long this bond would last. I didn't know if I was particularly interested in giving up my mortality to become a vampire. But all I know was my soul yearned for theirs and I deserved to indulge in the pleasure of them for as long as I could.

Samara led me through the streets of Shockgrove, a town I'd known my whole life. A town where I have lived, lost, cried, healed, and learned to trust again. The lighthouse stood as a beacon against the purple midday sky. The slightly chilled air caressed my cheek, and I couldn't help but think it was my mother's warm comforting embrace, telling me she was proud of me.

Samara's hand in mine felt like an anchor, holding me steady. I followed

369

her down the sidewalk and came to the overwhelming realization that I would probably follow her anywhere she asked me to.

That thought should have terrified me, but no matter how hard the little voice in my head tried to pierce through the happiness I'd crafted for myself, there was nothing but bliss.

She twirled me, our melodic laughter mixing to create a sound so fucking pure I almost cried. Her lips grazed my throat, and I released a content sigh. There was something so right about her lips on my skin.

"Are you ready for this?" She asked, her breath dancing across my exposed throat. I let my hands trace a path along her back. "We don't have to do this if you're not sure." Her reassurance wasn't needed, but I enjoyed having it none-theless.

I smiled brightly. "I'm sure."

Her dark eyes glistened with something that looked like pride, then she gripped my hand and pulled me onto the porch of a beautiful white beach house. Each step closer had my heart beating quicker until I almost wasn't sure it was beating at all.

Stepping through the threshold, I instantly felt enveloped by their presence. Their scents were so strong here, so saturated with their essence. It was intoxicating, sensual. I took a long languid breath, inhaling every ounce of them I could.

The living room looked positively touristy, and I stifled a laugh thinking about Orpheus willingly sitting next to a decorative bowl of seashells.

My eyes trailed along the walls, taking in the paintings, and tapestries when the hair on the back of my neck stood at attention. Goosebumps erupted across my exposed flesh, and I knew without a doubt they were there. My mates. I felt their eyes on me as if it were a physical touch. I bit my bottom lip, closing my eyes to revel in the sensation as their gaze caressed me.

When my eyes opened, I saw them.

Silas was leaning suggestively against the doorframe across the room, his arms folded in front of his chest offering me a clear view of the climbing serpents starkly contrasting against his cream skin. His honey eyes watched me with a hint of hunger, in every sense of the word. Laz had come to a stop on the staircase and sat down on one of the steps. Their hands were clasped in front of them as if they were holding themselves back. Their face was painted with a tortured expression. My eyes trailed up, landing on Orpheus, who was watching me from a perch on the second floor. He wore dark dress pants and a black button-down, but the top two buttons were undone and his tie hung loosely around his neck. Disheveled was a delicious look on him.

But just as I was admiring them, and the way their gazes trailed delicate passes across my skin, I heard a growl.

"Samara, she shouldn't be here right now." Orpheus. My eyes snapped to him. Looking closer now, I noticed his hands were gripping the railing in front of him, nearly digging into the wooden banister. Flicking my eyes to Laz, they weren't much better, their nails pressing into their skin as they forced their hands to remain clasped in front of them.

Looking over to Silas, I saw the tenseness of his shoulders more clearly now, the way his face was twisted.

I was wrong, they weren't just hungry.

They were starving.

"How bad is it?" I asked, my voice a timid whisper.

Samara put a gentle but firm hand on my shoulder and moved to stand between the others and me. Her body was rigid and poised. Fear clenched my heart. Not fear that I would be hurt, but that I was too late.

"The scent of you feels like barbed wire in my fucking throat," Silas whispered, his voice was animalistic, devoid of his typical cocky attitude.

"What were you thinking, Samara?" Laz lamented, grunting through held breath. "She's not safe right now."

"There was blood left this morning," Samara rasped, her body tensed.

"Half a flask," Silas growled, his body straightening. Samara put an arm out in front of me.

"Calm down, you need to get a handle on yourselves before you do something you might regret," Samara insisted, with an edge of worry. I felt my breath coming in ragged pants.

"Why did you bring her here?" Orpheus asked, his hunger slightly more restrained than the others, but there was an obvious hunger there.

"Because she is ready to accept the bond," Samara relented. I heard sharp gasps from Silas and Laz. Orpheus sighed deeply, his head falling forward.

"Fuck," Silas exclaimed, but it was not flirtatious, or even loving. He took a step forward like a predator. I stood my ground.

"Silas, back up." Samara had put her hand up, commanding him to cease his trek forward.

When I glanced back at the stairs, Laz was standing, their eyes full of guilt as they watched me. They were so close to losing every ounce of control they had.

"They need to drink," I whispered to Samara.

"They can't, not like this," she replied over her shoulder, without tearing her gaze from the others.

"Why not?" I asked.

"Because we're too hungry to control ourselves, Athena," Orpheus declared from his place above us all. "If we tried to feed on you-" I didn't miss the way his throat bobbed as he swallowed roughly at the thought. "In this condition, we wouldn't be able to stop."

A shadow of fear settled over me.

"You won't hurt me," I claimed, but it was met with a scoff.

"You have no idea what you're talking about," Orpheus spat as Silas and Laz continued to take stalking steps forward. Samara took a step back, herding me toward the door.

"You won't hurt me," I repeated with fervor. Deep down, despite their hungry gazes, and sharpening teeth, I knew it was true beyond a shadow of a doubt.

"We could kill you!" Orpheus screamed, his raspy timber echoing throughout the house. Laz and Silas were closer now, their closeness sent a shiver of anticipation where there should have been an air of caution.

"Samara, drink from me," I ordered. Her eyes darted over her shoulder to me in a brief display of confusion.

"If they smell your blood they won't be able to stop themselves." She turned back to face Laz and Silas. "We.. we won't be able to stop."

"You will. I trust you."

Samara groaned, and I saw her willpower waver. She wanted it, as much as they did.

"Samara, don't," Orpheus commanded, anger pouring off of him.

"Samara, do it," I reiterated, my eyes meeting Orpheus'. He pleaded back at me in silent gazes. Was I making a mistake? No, I don't think I was. I was listening to my heart, and trusting this bond thrumming between us.

"You won't hurt me." I said again, and as my eyes locked on Orpheus, I felt Samara turn to face me. Her eyes were ravenous, her careful composure slipping with every passing second. Laz and Silas stood flanking her.

Tearing my eyes from Orpheus, I stared at the stunning woman before me. Her chest heaved as she took me in, her eyes reddening.

"Do it."

The first strike of her fangs against the skin of my wrist was unlike anything I'd ever experienced. The mixture of pain and pleasure was so overwhelming I whimpered at the intrusion. Samara was locked on my arm, her mouth closed over the wound. Her eyes were closed as she drank, and as I watched her, my heart exploded with emotion. Every moment with Samara passed through my mind.

I put a hand on her cheek and silently begged for her eyes to meet mine. She opened them, and finally, the red orbs met mine, a moment later, she pulled her fangs from my skin. Her tongue darted out to lap up the traces of my blood that remained on her lips.

I leaned in, kissing her and loving the unfamiliar taste of copper.

When I opened my eyes, Silas and Laz were transformed, their ears tapered off to points, their nails elongated. I reached for them, the overwhelming desire to connect with them overpowering any hesitance. Silas reached me first. His hand snaked up to grab my throat, a gasp escaped my lips at the shock of his touch and his burning stare. His nails didn't puncture the skin, but their pressure offered a sort of delicious danger to his hold. He tilted my neck back, forcing my breasts to push forward toward him. His fingers tightened around my windpipe, as he released a feral growl. Silas' fangs connected with the skin above the swell of my breast just as the edges of my vision began to blur. My hands came up to his head, tangling in his long dark tresses. My heart was beating out of control, pumping blood directly into his willing mouth. Just when the pressure on my throat reached critical mass, it disappeared. I gulped down greedy gasps of air, as he continued his indulgence. My breathing returned to normal and I glanced down at this perfect man, this stunning creature. His mouth had not relented. I kissed Silas on the forehead and whispered.

"You won't hurt me."

His eyes flashed up to me, as I watched the internal battle he fought against his own insatiable hunger, but soon enough his honey irises emerged victorious, and he took a step back. His mouth was painted dark red, and I watched it with my own hunger, my chest heaving in time with his.

I turned my head and reached for Laz. Laz jolted forward at the beckoning and dropped to their knees in front of me. Their clawed hands tore at the hem of my shirt, raising it just enough to clasp onto the flesh at my hip. A cry of euphoria escaped my lips as the point of contact sent jolts through my entire body, this sensual action so close to my core had my walls tightening with ecstasy. I was so fucking close to a release from the deliciously torturous connections with my mates. My toes curled as I held them to me, beckoning them to drink. They sucked my blood down eagerly, grunts of passion pervading the air. I leaned my head back, enjoying the way Laz's hands gripped my thighs and pulled me into their hold. Their tongue brushed across the bite as they drank which had me nearly begging for the release that was just teetering on the edge of my senses. My hands came to a rest on their shoulders, digging my own fingertips into the hardened flesh there.

Once my hand brushed against their skin, they pulled back, a look of fear and disgust on their face at the thought they could have hurt me as they reverted to their human form. I smiled down at them, hoping they could see just how happy I was, how perfectly and utterly content I felt. My body ached from the explosion of emotions, I felt this connection to each of them solidify and crystallize. I was seeing their features more clearly, feeling their breath as if it were my own. I was wound so tight, my desire built so precariously, I feared a subtle gust of wind might be enough to topple me into oblivion.

I felt my warm blood sliding across my skin from the stinging wounds on my body, but I couldn't focus on that as my eyes tracked Orpheus stalking down the steps toward me. Silas, Laz, and Samara were watching me with rapt attention, I could feel them so intimately, as I waited for my final mate to claim me.

He somehow managed to keep his transformation restrained, only the darkened corners of his eyes and the elongated fangs gave away just how fragile his control truly was. He was beautiful, they all were, in this almost half form. Lethal, and powerful. A mixture of human and vampire. Beautifully monstrous humanity. When I saw them now, I saw creatures worthy of the second chance at life they've been given. I saw creatures who deserve love, acceptance, and passion. And I was going to give it to them.

When he reached me, his head lowered to the wound on my breast, where Silas had claimed me, and his tongue darted over the bite, a long languid lick. I moaned wildly, ravenous for him. He gripped my arm in his hand and lifted my bleeding wrist to his mouth, repeating the process. His control was slipping with each and every second, I saw the monster begin to take hold as he sank to his knees and tasted Laz's mark on my skin.

All four of my mates released a guttural groan of pleasure and pain all in one as I gasped.

Orpheus was on his feet again in an instant, the creature well and truly taken over, and before I could comprehend it, his fangs were buried in the skin of my neck, at the hollowed space where my shoulder met my throat. I screamed out as my orgasm wracked through me. I was lost in the blinding pleasure, feeling the bond snap into place as if it were some tangible thing. My legs quivered, from passion or blood loss, I wasn't sure. But it was a type of pleasure I couldn't even begin to describe. There was only his mouth on my skin. Only the bonds from my mates. There was only us.

As I slowly recovered from the release, I felt the painful draw of my blood into his mouth, and the blend of pleasure and pain began to lean towards pain.

"Orpheus," I whispered, putting my hand on his cheek. He didn't respond, didn't remove his fangs from my skin. "Orpheus, listen to me." I glanced over his shoulder to Samara, Laz, and Silas who were frozen in their place, watching the blood pour from beneath Orpheus' mouth. "It's me," I whispered, feeling suddenly lightheaded.

The others didn't see my concern, instead, they simply watched with hunger as my last mate drank from me. "Orpheus," I commanded, my voice raised, I felt my strength wane, as my consciousness started slipping away. "It's me, Athena. Your mate. Please." I gasped as the pain increased. "Please!" It was a whimper, a cry, but he heard me. The pain subsided as he withdrew his fangs from my veins. He darted away, leaving me standing up against the wall alone. His back was turned to me, but I could see his turmoil. The guilt, the shame.

I struggled to maintain my balance, using the wall behind me as a steadying force. Silas, Laz, and Samara watched me, their eyes full of worry, but the careful grasp they had on their monsters kept them at a distance. I stepped forward, strength returning to me with each stride across the floor. As I passed, I felt Silas, Laz, and Samara fall in line behind me. Flanking me. Following me.

My hand came to a rest on his shoulder and he spun to face me, inhumanly fast, but I didn't blink. I stood my ground in front of him, his dark hair was wild and his face was locked in the visage of his creature. Red eyes, long fangs, pointed ears, vicious claws.

Most would shy away from him, many probably have.

I did once.

But not anymore.

I lifted my arm, bringing my palm to press against his cheek. His skin was smooth and cold to the touch. He groaned, it was an angry sound but he leaned into the touch.

"I almost drank too much," he seethed, in that vicious-sounding voice. I shook my head.

"But you didn't." He closed his eyes taking shallow breaths.

"I could have killed you," he sobbed, his clawed hands in fists at his side. I gripped his tie in my free hand and pulled him closer.

"But you didn't."

His red eyes were darting around the room, looking everywhere but at me. No matter how hard he tried, he couldn't regain control.

"Orpheus. Name four things you can see." He exhaled incredulously, nearly scoffing, but his breathing didn't slow. "Now."

He struggled to focus on something, anything, and I watched him closely as he forced his eyes to focus on his surroundings. "Samara," he began. I nodded, a soft smile playing on my lips at the name of my mate. "Silas, Laz," he continued and I brushed my thumb against his sharp cheekbones. His eyes landed on mine. Settling for the first time. "You."

"Three things you can smell," I prompted. He struggled to sniff in one smooth breath, his chest still heaving, but the fists at his side had come unclenched.

"The ocean," he said. I glanced over his shoulder at the waves that lazily crept up the beach toward the house. "Blood," he relented, his eyes locking on the wound at my neck, but just as I worried he was reverting back into his panic, his eyes found mine again, the red irises slipping away to reveal his dark black eyes. "You."

I rewarded him with a soft brush of my thumb against his lips, finding my blood there. He moaned.

"Two things you can feel," I whispered, watching in awe as the tips of his ears slowly rounded in front of my eyes.

"The ground under my feet." He smirked and I felt my eyes sting with unshed tears. "You."

"One thing you can -"

His lips were on mine before I could finish, his kiss was possessive and full of unspoken promises. His tongue begged for entrance and I moaned into his kiss at the metallic tangy taste of my blood on his lips. My fingers tangled in his hair and I pressed my body against him, feeling warmth bloom in my core.

He pulled back, breathlessly resting his forehead against mine. "I almost lost you," he sighed. I held him tighter.

"But you didn't."

He pressed another quick kiss on my lips before leaning his head down to my throat, and the exposed wound there. His tongue darted out to taste it and I threw my head back to give him better access. He was in control, I felt it in every ounce of my body. This was Orpheus.

When he lifted his head, he smiled over my shoulder at my other mates who had been watching closely.

"Are you still hungry?" I asked aloud for them all.

"I'll always be hungry for you," Orpheus offered, sending a blush to my face. "But I am in control now."

I looked over my shoulder at the others, waiting for their response.

"I feel better than I ever have," Silas whispered, and Laz nodded in agreement.

"You were everything I needed." Samara brushed her hand against my arm, and I shivered.

I turned to face them fully, leaving one hand resting on Orpheus' chest.

"But we took too much," Samara lamented, her eyes full of worry as they scanned me,

"That was reckless," Laz interjected, guilt painted on their expression.

"I'm so sorry," Silas added at the same time.

I put a hand up to stop them. "I don't want your apologies or worries."

They watched me as I met each of their gazes. Seeing passion and power in Orpheus, care and love in Samara, adoration and trust in Laz, and desire and certainty in Silas. My mates. Standing here now, between them, I realized I never knew what belonging felt like. Like Laz, I'd been wearing this town and my past like an ill-fitting pair of shoes, but now with them at my side, with this bond burning so strongly in my soul, and suddenly I'd finally found my size. An unfamiliar feeling pulsed between us, something I can only really describe as magic.

"What do you want then, little nymph?" Orpheus asked in a dark, sinfully sensual tone.

"I want my mates to claim me as theirs, now and forever."

Silas was the first to move, his lips crashing against mine in a clash of tongue and teeth. I felt Laz pressing up behind me, their lips placing eager kisses against my shoulder. A hand gripped my jaw, drawing me away from Silas. Samara leaned in, replacing his lips with hers, her tongue danced along the seam on my mouth begging for entry. I moaned into her lips as Silas lifted my shirt enough to capture one of my hardened nipples in his mouth.

I opened my eyes to find Orpheus watching us with ravenous attention. A dangerous smirk on his red-tinted lips.

He leaned back against the kitchen island and studied us. Seemingly perfectly content to enjoy this from the sidelines. I'd let him, for now.

"Do you want your mates to play our little game with you, baby girl?" Silas teased against my breast, his cool breath on the moistened skin sending shock-waves through my body. I nodded. His teeth clenched around the peak, and I winced. "What do you say?"

Samara broke our kiss to look at Silas, her gaze curious. I smiled at her before turning my taunting gaze to Silas. "Yes, sir." I heard every single one of my mates groan as those words crossed my lips and I was struck with how much power I had over them. They may be nearly indestructible immortal beings, but they were falling at my feet.

"Why don't you tell them what our safeword is," he commanded, darkly.

"Blood," I whispered. Orpheus ran a hand down his face to stifle a moan, the evidence of his arousal straining against his dress pants.

"Very good, baby girl. Now do us a favor and take off your clothes." Silas stood back, offering glances to Samara and Laz in a request for them to do the same. Laz obeyed quickly and eagerly, and despite the slight hesitation in Samara's movements, the heat in her gaze told me she wanted this moment with me, with all of us.

"Who knew you were such a bossy lover, Silas," Samara teased.

Silas winked at me. "Athena knew."

I felt my face flush as I reached for the hem of my shirt to pull it off over my head. I savored every hitch of breath and soft moan. As I stripped down, I was not ashamed or afraid of my nakedness, there was an empowering sort of magic to the way they watched me. Silas growled, a sort of darkness to his stare.

"Touch yourself, baby girl. Show us how ready you are for us," Silas commanded. I bit my bottom lip, humming with appreciation at how the words made me feel. My hands trailed down the planes of my stomach, inching lower, torturously. I ached to be touched, but I wanted to savor each second of their attention.

My fingers reached the apex of my thighs and I dipped them into the warmth of my folds. I groaned at the sensitivity I found at my clit. Drawing my fingers through my slick wetness there a few times and relishing the feeling, I tossed my head back and let the sounds tumble from my lips. I withdrew my fingers just long enough to hold them out for Silas. He stepped forward, capturing them in his mouth. Both of us groaned.

"Enough playing around, Silas," Orpheus called from his spot near the island. He was collected, his ever-present composure firmly in place, but I could see just how much this was affecting him.

"What do you say, baby girl? Are you ready to be fucked by your mates?"

All I could do was nod. I was blind with desire, there was nothing but them and their bodies. I needed them like I needed oxygen.

Silas smiled and lifted me by my thighs, urging me to wrap my legs around him. He stalked over to the couch and slowly lowered me onto the cushions, my head rested on the arm and I watched him with bated breath. I felt Laz and Samara follow after, but Orpheus stayed put, his eyes trailing me. Watching.

"I'm going to give you my cock while Samara sits on your face and you're going to use those perfect fingers of yours to get Laz ready," Silas rattled off with a sinful eagerness. I was so wound up I felt like my body was a livewire just waiting to detonate.

Silas and Laz stripped down, revealing their toned bodies. Laz looked like the picture of Southern comfort. Soft tones arms and a hard planed stomach, their golden skin on full display. Silas' tattoos never ceased to stun me. The dark trails of ink covered most of his torso, dancing down his arms and traveling lower on his body to his perfect length. I didn't want to think about how painful that might have been, but the design made him look so dangerous, so forbidden. It was enough to have me whimpering for him.

He settled between my open legs and gripped his cock in his fingers, pressing it lightly against my opening. His other hand gripped my thigh, holding me open for him.

He pushed in, inch after delicious inch, and I cried out at the welcome intrusion. He cursed under his breath as he seated himself fully inside of me. My walls stretched to accommodate him.

Laz came to a stop near my torso, dipping their head to take a nipple into their mouth. They worshiped the hardened peak with their cold tongue and I felt the shiver rush through my entire body. My fingers wrapped around their hardened length and they hummed appreciatively as I gave them languid strokes. I arched off the couch just as Silas withdrew nearly to the tip only to slam back into me again. Before I could cry out, Samara situated herself above me on the arm of the couch and lowered herself to my mouth. I drank up her arousal as eagerly as she drank my blood, and she rocked back and forth, riding me for her pleasure.

Every inch of my body was electrified by pleasure. I'd never felt this aware, this adored. As Silas pounded into me, Samara slid her sweet pussy along my willing lips. I quickened my strokes on Laz's length and they continued to taste my nipples.

The connection that thrummed between us, so completely obvious and strong now, was pulsing with lust, intensifying the emotions. Samara's breathing quickened and her fingers tangled in my hair as she neared her release. I sucked her clit into my mouth, and she cried out, her orgasm bursting within her.

Silas picked up his pace, his cock hitting the deepest parts of my body with each thrust. "You take me so well, baby girl," he grunted as he slammed into me. Samara stood from my face and I took gulps of fresh air, ragged and panting as Silas continued his delicious torture. I flicked my eyes to Laz who understood what I wanted and moved closer so I could take their length into my mouth. I let my tongue swirl around the head, and Laz moaned, the muscles in their abdomen twitching, eager to thrust into my hot willing mouth, but they restrained. I reached for their hips and pulled them into me, taking as much of them as I could into my throat.

"Oh, Athena," they whispered, a sound of passion, of adoration. I loved it so much. Their fingers caressed my face and I worked their length.

"You look stunning with their cock in your mouth and Samara's cum on your lips," Silas growled, their control slipping as they pressed in again and again. Their pace was relentless and eager. I cried out, the sound muffled by Laz's cock. Silas' fingers dug into my hips as he drove into me chasing that high, I felt him tense and pulse as he found his release. A string of expletives tumbled from his lips as he emptied himself inside of me.

I picked up my pace on Laz's length, their hands brushing loving touches across my forehead.

"You are the most perfect creature I'd ever seen," Silas whispered before withdrawing from me. The absence of him made me whimper, the vibration jolting through Laz. They moaned.

"Samara," Silas ordered, breathlessly. I couldn't see what they were doing, but a moment later, Samara had situated herself between my legs, straddling me. Her core was inches from mine. I mewled in anticipation.

She pressed her core to mine and the first brush of her clit against mine sent me tumbling into an orgasm that she rode out, the friction was so delicious, so intense that a third release came slamming into me before I'd even recovered from the second. Laz had lost control of the gentle lover and was thrusting into my mouth forcefully, and I swallowed each inch happily. With Samara dragging her slick folds against mine, she cried out, reaching another release quickly and a salty taste erupted against my tongue as Laz followed suit, spilling themselves into my throat. I swallowed every precious drop. When Laz stepped back, and Samara stood, I felt utterly used and satisfied, but still, a deep ache burned in my stomach. My eyes flicked over to where Orpheus stood. Somewhere during all that, he had lost his dress pants and unbuttoned his black shirt, it hung open to reveal his trim physique. Hard planes of muscle and a soft dusting of hair. My eyes trailed down to his erect and exposed cock as his hand trailed careful strokes down its length.

His eyes were locked on mine as he stalked forward. When he reached me, he knelt down, stealing a kiss from my lips. "That was the most beautiful thing I've ever seen," he whispered against my kiss-swollen lips. "Now it's my turn."

My thighs clenched at the promise.

"I will love watching you with them, little nymph. I could do that for the rest of my life. Seeing you take your pleasure from them. Cry out as they work your body." I smiled, and I heard the others release a soft sigh. "But when you are with me, I will not share." He moved to position himself behind me on the couch, spooning me. He lifted my leg and carefully adjusted our position. I could feel the press of his length against my slick opening and I gasped. "I will wait my turn, I will watch you ride all three of them for hours if that's what you want. But when it is my turn, you're mine and mine alone." Silas chuckled, lightly.

"Do you understand?" Orpheus asked, pressing slowly into me, the feel of him drove me wild.

"I do," I whispered.

"Leave it to him to be possessive." I heard Silas offer in a teasing tone.

I almost retorted, but then Orpheus was sliding home. This position made it so I could feel him so deep inside of me. His arm wrapped around my waist as he controlled our pace. A slow, torturous tempo. I tried to speed up, but his hands remained steadfast, forcing us to revel in this.

"God damn, baby girl," Silas vocalized, his eyes watching the place where Orpheus and I were joined with a look of wonder and lust.

Orpheus slid his fingers down to brush against my clit and I felt my release cresting again. He worked me slowly, savoring the feel of my walls tightening around him. His lips pressed against my throat, where his fangs had just claimed me. I released a heady sigh as his fingers continued their worship of my clit.

Each careful thrust of his cock into me was a promise. A reminder of who I belonged to.

My orgasm exploded claiming my body, and I was vaguely aware of him following me over the cliff of passionate oblivion.

When my breathing slowed and my heart rate returned to normal, I felt the weight of exhaustion for the first time as well as the light ache of exertion in my muscles. But above all of that, I felt the bond. This love, this connection. It gave me strength. I wondered how I'd ever gone without it. Orpheus stood from the couch, and I rolled back, resting my tired limbs.

Laz's hands were first to touch me, a gentle caress against my cheek. The four of them helped me dress and gave me a glass of water. I promised them I was fine, but they fawned over me nonetheless, and I felt like my heart might burst from the rush of love.

The others took seats near me around the living room, their hair perfectly mused, their chests rising and falling with content breaths. I looked around the room, studying them. My mates. How lucky was I to find people that not only knew my body as if it were their own, but made me feel so safe, and so protected?

"Your bites aren't bleeding anymore," I stated.

"Our saliva counteracts the bite," Samara said, a soft smile on her lips. "When we take the time to lick the wound it will disappear entirely, as if nothing happened. We always do. It's like an unspoken vampire rule to close the wounds before leaving." I felt my heart clench with fear and disappointment that my bites might not have left a permanent mark on anything other than my soul, but my eyes flicked down to my wrist, where Samara had made her claim. To my satisfaction, there was still a mark there, evidence of our connection, but it wasn't a bite mark as I anticipated. Instead, raised white lines formed an outline of hanging wisteria circled my wrist climbing up toward the elbow in a gorgeous fine-line design. Like a white ink tattoo on my skin, the floral pattern was stunning, and so perfectly Samara. She watched me as I brushed a finger across it. As I did. I felt her. Intimately, as if by touching this mark I could focus on the bond I had with her and her alone.

I lifted the hem of my shirt to see Laz's mark on my hip. Climbing up my upper thigh and just above my hip bone was a white design of the phases of the moon. Changes and exploration. Something new. Laz beamed at me with pride and honor as I stroked the design and felt that connection burn brighter.

I stood from the couch and moved to the mirror which was fastened on the wall between the two front windows. Immediately my eye flashed to the lightning strike that spanned the right side of my throat. Starting from the base of my ear to the top of my shoulder, white disjointed lines decorating the surface stared back at me. My fingertips brushed it and Orpheus pushed to the forefront of my mind.

Finally, I pulled at the neck of my shirt, revealing the loosely coiled serpent design that sat just below my left clavicle. Its detailed scales were so intricate. I ran a touch along the snake's body and suddenly my senses focused on Silas.

"They're gorgeous," I uttered, holding in sobs of pure happiness.

"How do you feel?" Laz asked carefully.

"Like I have a family again." They looked back at me with matching gazes of love. My heart was beating for them, and theirs for me. I could feel them through the bonds that decorated my body as if they were merely extensions of myself.

The sound of breaking glass echoed through the house as both windows shattered. I bent forward, covering my eyes as shards flew around me. My mates were with me in an instant, their bodies covered mine from the assault. I tried not to panic, letting the comfort of their presence soothe me, but then I noticed the smoke spilling from a small metallic device that had landed amongst the glass on the floor.

"Fuck," Silas cursed, weakly.

"They found us," Laz cried, falling to their knees, clutching their chest in pain.

'No, no, no, no," Samara cried, but each repeat of the words was weaker and weaker as she stumbled back against the wall, losing her balance.

I glanced around at my mates, their faces twisted in worry and fear as the smoke enveloped us. I waited for it to affect me, but I felt perfectly fine.

"What's happening?" I pleaded as Samara slipped to the ground. Silas crashed against the wall as he attempted to hold himself up.

"Athena...run..." Orpheus forced out before collapsing onto the floor.

I dropped to my knees, tears pooling in my eyes and obscuring my vision. "Wake up!" I cried, pressing my palms against their limp forms. "Oh my god, wake up!" They didn't budge, the smoke blanketed the area, covering their forms. I tried to wave my arms around across the floor, eager to be in contact with each of them. "Please, please," I sobbed.

I was too distraught, too focused on the pain in my chest to hear the figure slip through the open window and come to a stop behind me. All I saw was a brief glimpse of a shadow amongst the smoke before something hard crashed against my temple and everything went dark.

16

SILAS

The world was finally in focus. Suddenly there was nothing but her. Her blood on my tongue felt like electricity, oxygen, sunlight. It was powerful, and alive. Nothing in this world could ever compare to the feeling of my body inside of hers, her walls constricting around me, holding me there as if she couldn't bear to be separated.

These last few days have been agonizing. Knowing that she was so close but that there was this cavern of distance between us. My family was on the verge of falling apart, and I was so close to forgetting why I cared enough to continue existing.

And then...Athena.

Her kind heart, her pure soul...her.

She was exactly what we needed. All of us. Orpheus needed someone he got to relax with, someone he trusted enough to take the metaphorical 'tie' off around. Laz needed someone who they could tend to, someone they could worship. Samara needed someone to help her heal, someone who could fill the void left by Alora without erasing the memories she left behind. And I needed someone to love me.

I've had a family. I got lucky with Alora and the other Wanderers, but I have never been in what I would consider love. Not in the way Alora and Samara were, or Laz with that asshole from his hometown, before he took the cowards way out. I'd never experienced that. I'd only ever indulged in sex and physical pleasure. But now, it's her. I have her. And I love her. Without a doubt in my mind. I love Athena Landry, and she loves me. She hasn't said the words but she doesn't have to. I know what love is. I've seen it. And I see it in her eyes when she looks at me. I hear it in her voice when she says my name, I feel it in her touch when she places her palm on my face.

She is everything I never knew I could have. And now that I have her, I would do everything in my power to keep her safe.

I would burn down this entire world for her.

As my body began to betray me and I heard her frightened screams, I had one thought. One singular, overwhelming thought. That I was going to make whoever did this to us regret every breath they've ever taken.

My consciousness began to slip from my grasp as she cried for us. For me.

The mixture of holy water and garlic isn't lethal to a vampire, not in any capacity, but what it does is vicious. It sinks into the pores and freezes its victims from the inside out. Suspending them in time. My lips stilled, and my eyes dried out from the inability to blink. They tried unsuccessfully to focus on the white smoke that circled me.

I wasn't able to move, to speak, to call out for her, but I could hear everything. Every sob, every desperate call from her lips. The way my name, all our names, sounded like a broken scream. Hearing the woman you love fall to pieces and knowing you can do nothing to stop it is a fate worse than death.

A fate that I can't wait to force onto my captor.

I heard the sound of footsteps, heavy and crunching against the broken glass, and I wanted to scream to her, to tell her to get out. To get free. But I couldn't speak. I couldn't scream. I couldn't help her.

The sound of something heavy connecting against flesh threatened to topple my sanity. Suddenly, a loud thump vibrated across the floor, my eyes focused through the dissipating wisps of smoke to see her, unconscious and lying in a heap on the floor. I lost every ounce of control I had. Anger surged through me, but with nowhere to go, and no way to release it, it felt stifling, and overwhelming. Like I might explode at any moment.

I watched in rapt horror as she was dragged from my view, her red hair trailing behind. My heart, newly revived, felt cracked and split right down the center.

The footsteps disappeared, along with my mate, and I knew it was only a matter of time before our captor returned for us. I needed to do something. I needed to save my family. To save my mate.

But still, I couldn't move.

I wished I had been knocked out. I wish I couldn't hear a single thing. Wished I didn't know what had happened, because having the complete awareness of what was occurring, and none of the ability to act on it was a special kind of torture.

Focusing every ounce of energy I had left, I tried to move a finger, but it felt as if I knew there was an appendage there, but it did not belong to me anymore. So far removed from myself.

I screamed and trashed against the mental cages that have been forged around my consciousness to no avail.

Eventually, the footsteps returned. I could see more clearly now that the smoke had lifted, but my vision blurred from the dryness. Dark boots, dark wash jeans, dark clothes... and there. There it was.

A confirmation of what I already knew to be true. The mask that covered my captor's face. A Nameless mask. They found us. They caught us. Again.

I tried once more to move a finger, a hand, anything. There was a sort of tingling sensation radiating through my arm, and despite the pain, and all the anger bubbling beneath my surface, I felt it. My finger bent. Slightly, barely at all, but it was a movement. Unfortunately, it was not enough to save my family. Not enough to save my mate.

I wanted to cry. I couldn't.

Not when I saw the figure drag Samara out of the room. Not when they returned for Laz. Then Orpheus. Not when I felt their hands close around my shoulders and hoist me up, dragging me across the floor. Not when I felt the broken glass from the windows dig into my flesh as I was pulled through the living room and out onto the porch. Not as I was tossed into the bed of a truck in a heap with my family with their equally stiff bodies feeling like rocks beneath me. Not when a bright blue tarp was secured over the top of us. Not when our captor started driving away.

The driver stopped and I couldn't hear what he was doing, but there were voices. Someone was here. If only I could signal for them. If only I could let them know we were here.

I focused on my hand again. I had nothing left. I felt so weak, so helpless. But that wasn't good enough. Athena deserved better. She deserved my every-thing. I let thoughts of the people I love fuel me.

Orpheus and his quiet strength. His determination and ferocity in protecting those he loves.

Laz and their soft devotion. The way they love with every ounce of their heart, unreserved and unrestrained.

Samara and her will. Her control, the way she acts only when she must and only as she should.

Athena and her heart, her soul, and her mind. The way she trusts, the way she heals. People who've gone through half the trauma she has would turn it all off, and hide themselves from the world. But not her. She opened her wounded heart. She continues to do so, despite the pain, and the past. Her courage. I could do this for her.

With those thoughts and the images of my family flashing in front of my face, I channeled it all into my hand. It moved, slowly, inch by inch, but it moved. I felt the cool rush of air brush against my skin and suddenly, my hand was poking out from beneath the tarp. The voices continued. I just needed whoever it was to see me, then maybe they could help. My mind and body felt exhausted like I might pass out at any moment. It wasn't much, but maybe, just maybe, it was enough.

With that thought, and that sense of accomplishment rushing through me, I let the exhaustion take me away.

17

ATHENA

My head hurt.

That was the first thing I noticed as I came to. My body ached from blood loss, exhaustion, and exertion. My throat was dry, and each breath caused a sort of white-hot pain to radiate. My eyes blinked, struggling to focus on my surroundings. I groaned as I tried to sit up, my body felt heavy and worn out. As my eyes adjusted, I saw a familiar view. A normally comforting setting that at this moment was offering nothing except confusion and worry. The Maine Plotline was quiet and only soft rays from the evening sun were poking through the door. The rest of the light was blocked by the board that covered the front window. I glanced around trying to make sense of what had happened, to no avail. Pieces of the last few hours came back to me in flashes. Breakfast.The beach house. The bond. The smoke.

My head snapped around.

My mates.

I tried to call out for them, but my throat was searing. I glanced down at my wrist to see the floral wrapping design signifying one of my bonds and touched it quickly. Samara was there, I felt her, but she was weak. I repeated the motion on the other three bonds receiving the same alarming sense. One thing was abundantly clear. They were in trouble.

I grabbed my phone from my pocket and dialed their numbers. The line was dead. Each unavailable beep sent me closer and closer to spiraling. I slammed the phone down on the counter and paced, dragging my hands through my ratted hair.

My mind was spinning as I tried to piece together the muddled facts. The sound of the bell above the door had hope blooming in my chest. I turned eagerly, mentally begging to see my mates return to me, safely. But I was not so lucky.

A figure stood silhouetted in the door frame by the waning evening light. As he took a step inside I gasped with recognition.

His eyes burned with anger and hatred. I saw them so clearly. Felt his ire so intimately.

Greg.

He took a few menacing steps forward, and I stepped back.

"Greg, what are you doing here?" I asked nervously, my eyes glancing over at my phone on the counter. So far away.

"I came to give you one last chance to tell the truth," he replied, he sounded so unhinged. I couldn't get a hold of the shaky breath that came out in spurts.

"Please, just leave me alone," I begged, backing up against a bookshelf, the wood slammed into my shoulder blades and I winced at the soreness there.

He continued his slow deliberate steps forward. "See, I know for a fact something happened that night that you're not telling the police." His eyes scanned me with disgust. "So fucking fess up."

He was only a few feet from me now, and fear gripped me. I tried to make a break for it, heading for the phone, but his hands darted out, grabbing my biceps forcefully and holding me in place with a painful hold. I tried to scream, but he pushed me back into the bookcase, sending a jolt of pain down my spine as a few titles fell off the shelf to the ground below.

"Stop, please!" I cried.

"Tell me the truth," he demanded, his bloodshot eyes staring into mine.

"He tried to rape me," I shouted, trying unsuccessfully to pull from his grasp again.

"You're lying," he screamed before pushing me into the bookcase again, his fingers dug into my arms to the point of pain. I cried out at the pain. His breath reeked of alcohol and the scent stung my nostrils.

"I'm not! I'm not," I whimpered, tears flowing from my eyes. "He tried to rape me and those strangers saved me. They pulled him off of me and took me home. I swear." Now that I knew what my mates were capable of, I wasn't all that afraid of telling this one asshole about their interference. But my heart broke a little as the concern for my mates and their current situation returned in full force.

He watched me for a moment in silence, before a soft smile played on his lips. "He didn't try to rape you. You probably begged for it."

I shook off the sting of his accusation, not an unfamiliar phrase.

"I didn't," I yelled, but he dug his fingers into my arms harder, I felt the warm, sticky blood begin to trickle across my skin bubbling from beneath his fingernails.

"Don't fucking lie," he screamed into my face, and I turned my head from him, shutting my eyes. "You're a goddamn slut! You think I haven't seen you around town with your 'strangers'?" He spat the word. "I bet you're fucking them all too, aren't you?"

I sobbed, unable to manage words.

"Where is Louis?" He barked again.

"I don't know!" I cried out, I didn't even recognize my own voice. It was a broken, weak sound.

He pulled back, slamming me into the bookcase again with more force. My back exploded in pain at the impact and books flew off the shelf raining down on top of us. By some stroke of luck, a heavy tomb clipped Greg on the side of his face. He cursed and dropped his hands from my skin, cradling his head in his hands. I didn't dare wait another second. I sprinted past him, pushing through the door and out onto the pier. I called out for help. A familiar sense of deja vu hit me. There was no soul in sight.

I pressed against the bonds again as I ran, begging for them to feel me. To find me, but the connections laid dormant. Nobody was coming to save me.

I had to save myself.

Greg was behind me, I felt him begin to catch up. His presence was eerily similar to that ominous smoke back at the beach house. But this time, I was ready. I veered toward the railing of the pier, and his footfalls sounded behind me. I reached the railing and allowed myself only a moment to breathe, before turning to face my assailant. I stood my ground, gritted my teeth, and pushed every ounce of pain away from my mind. He barreled forward, a crazed obsessive look in his eyes.

I waited, watching his strides as he made his way to me, drawing strength from the connections that thrummed within my soul. My mates weren't there physically, but their influence was so visceral. I felt them in every step, in every breath. Their strength was mine. And I needed every ounce I could muster. Just as his arms rose to grab at me, I ducked. With his momentum he was hurled into the railing, but not quite over. The wind was knocked out of him and I knew I had to take advantage of the opportunity. I let loose a punch against his face and he groaned in pain. He tried to turn back to me, blood spilling from his mouth, but I landed another punch before he could react. I ignored the stabbing sting in my hand and let loose years of aggression on him. Punch after punch, I saw my step-father, I saw Louis, I saw the cops who never believed me, the townsfolk who judged me. I saw them all and I hated them. He whimpered under my assault, but I wasn't done. When he was weakened and his arms came up to protect his face, I gripped his arm and used every little bit of my remaining strength to push him over the railing. I heard his scream get cut off as he hit the water below and only then did the weight of his assault lift off of me.

Glancing down at myself I saw the bruises and blood decorating my arms like a gore-tainted work of art. I was so dangerously close to passing out. I had to get to somewhere safe. Soon.

I stumbled away from the railing, not even bothering to look for Greg in the crashing waves below the pier. He could disappear into nothingness and I wouldn't bat an eye. I limped toward the main street at the end of the pier feeling every injury throb violently, it was nearly enough to take my breath away, but I pressed on. My painful grunts echoed through the night air as I stepped onto the street. The sound of tires squealing startled me, but I wasn't strong enough to move out of the way. A pair of headlights illuminated me in the early evening light. The truck had stopped just short of me.

I vaguely heard the car door swing open.

"Holy shit, Athena. What the hell happened to you?" Archer's voice was strained, and worried. I forced myself to focus on him. The sight of him blanketed me in relief. I released a sob and fell into him. He held me up and I embraced him as best I could and cried. "Athena, talk to me. What happened?" He inquired angrily.

"Greg," I whispered and Archer cursed under his breath, his hands pressing gently against my back. My legs gave out slightly but Archer managed to catch me, righting me.

"Whoa, ok, ok. Here." He helped me over to his truck, leaning me against the passenger door. I pressed my body against the truck's frame and felt the extent of the injuries and exertion from the last twenty-four hours so vividly. I was lightheaded.

"I'm dizzy," I offered, meekly. Archer steadied me and looked over my shoulder into the bed of his truck.

"I have some water in my truck. I'll get it." He made sure I had a solid grasp on the side of the truck before he leaned into the cab. I gripped the metal and struggled to stop the world from spinning. I tried to focus on one thing, staring at the blue tarp inside the bed.

I calmed myself by studying it. Listing off what I could see as a way to focus on staying upright and conscious.

The bright blue color reminded me of a pool on a hot summer's day.

The silver rings had rope looped through them to tie it down.

The bumpy shape from whatever was beneath it.

The hand that poked out from beneath it.

Shock flooded my brain, I shook my head trying to make sense of what I was seeing. I stumbled a little but leaned onto the truck to ground myself and stared at the hand. Was it even real?

But as I continued to stare, I knew it was.

A gasp caught in my throat when I saw the swirling black ink painting the back of the hand and inching up the arm.

I knew those tattoos. I knew those fingers.

Silas.

Panic invaded my senses, and all I could feel was unrelenting, devastating fear.

"Here, drink this," Archer said, offering me a bottle of water. I was too weak to hide my fear. "What's wro-" his eyes followed mine and he saw it too. Silas' hand. Clear as day. He groaned with frustration. Something like guilt playing on his face.

"I can explain, I swear," he started anxiously, but I was done listening. I inhaled, readying a scream, but before it could escape my lips, Archer's hand clamps down over my mouth and nose, bringing a strip of wet fabric to brush against my skin. The scent of whatever he had doused the cloth with invaded my every sense, and the dark vignette around my vision blurred. I lost my balance, but Archer caught me, holding me tight to his chest as the world began to slip away into nothingness.

He looked down at me with traitorous green eyes, but they too were disappearing into the darkness of my own mind. Before I was lost to the void of my consciousness, I heard his whispered words.

"I'm sorry."

PART III

THE HUNTED

PROLOGUE

ARCHER

*Y*ou *need to understand that you are only ever safe in this world if you fight for your safety.*

Being a Hunter means protecting the night from the monsters operating in the dark, risking your life to save people, and doing anything necessary to bring those creatures down.

Even if it puts innocent people in danger.

Nisi Nox.

If given the choice between one human life and a hundred, the choice is obvious. Or at least, it should be.

It used to be.

No one warns you how much harder it is when the life at stake is someone you care about. Those superhero movies lie to you. They make it seem like you can save both the girl *and* the bus full of citizens. But that's a lie. You have to choose.

I had to choose.

In the heat of the moment, it felt right and impactful—what I was doing to these creatures. While they choked on the toxic mixture I subjected them to, struggling for breath and scrambling to escape, it felt like I'd done something right. I had protected innocent people. I made the night and the world a safer place.

Nisi Nox.

But when the adrenaline slipped away and the fog settled, suddenly, there were bodies at my feet and a lump in my throat. How do you know who's the hero and who's the villain? And what happens if you're neither?

Not good enough to be a hero and not bad enough to be a villain.

Just not enough.

I suppose the perspective you're meant to adopt is the one that's handed to you. The viewpoint you hear the most often usually becomes the one you identify with, doesn't it? The victors write history, and the hero is typically the protagonist.

But the same story told from both sides might change your mind. Or it might not, but at least you'd have all the information. Maybe Athena will understand once she hears my side. Maybe she won't. I am safe because I fought for my safety, and I fought for hers. I want to be the hero in her story, to protect her from the clutches of these creatures.

I just hope she hasn't already picked her side.

1

ATHENA

I don't know what death feels like, so I could be dead right now, and I wouldn't even know it. I've recently learned that being 'dead' doesn't necessarily mean that you're 'not alive,' so it's anyone's guess. My body certainly felt like it had gone through a ridiculous amount of trauma. There was a buzzing sound that continued its persistent, angry assault on my ears, growing stronger each moment that my consciousness came back to me.

Alive then, I decided. I don't know for sure, but I can't imagine I'd still be in this much pain had Lady Death come to sweep me away.

A faint smell permeated the air, no, not the air. It felt like the scent was attached to me, stuck on my skin. I wasn't able to break free from its acidic nature. Light began to seep through the darkness, through small cracks in my eyelids as they rose, heavy and labored. Blinking, I adjusted to the sight before me. I was in an office. A massive wooden desk sat steadfast in the center of the room, an oversized chair resting behind it, empty. Bookcases lined the walls. I could have been fooled into believing this was a regular office had it not been for the cases of weapons that taunted me. Sharpened knives, crossbows, guns and ammunition, and wooden stakes. Dozens of them. Pointed and stained with a dark red, nearly black, blood. The type of stain that told me this weapon had taken more than one life. I felt sick and leaned forward to pull my eyes from them.

My heart pounded in fear and worry. Where were my mates? Were they alive? Were they safe? Were they here?

That's when I felt my hands bound behind me. Rough rope dug into the flesh at my wrists. Panic began to crest as I pulled against my restraints. Cries escaped my mouth as I struggled, to no avail. I hated feeling so weak.

I couldn't even free my fingers to brush against the bond on my wrist. I couldn't focus on my mates because of the fear; it was too potent and overwhelming. My chest heaved as I felt the panic beginning to sink its claws into my heart.

Instantly, a thought took root in my mind.

If I was a vampire, I could have saved them. I could escape.

It was a shock as the thought crossed my mind. I mean, sure, I had considered that possibility. Whenever I thought about what a future could look like for me and my mates, there was only one way we all ended up happy, and that was if I was turned. I didn't really understand the process or the consequences, and I couldn't imagine being so hungry that I might rip into Davia's throat at the next movie night. So, I didn't say anything. I hadn't vocalized the truth that it was something I could have wanted. Something I still wanted.

But here in this dimly lit room, tied to a chair, afraid, in pain, and tired of being weak, the thought was clear, clarified in the crucible of our situation. If I was a vampire, I could have saved us. I could have saved myself. I could get out of here. I wouldn't be stuck. I wouldn't be trapped. I wouldn't be so goddamn weak.

My eyes scanned the room quickly. "Ok, Athena, four things you can see…" I struggled. "Weapons… desk, there's a…it's a chair, then there's a… window," I whispered. "Three things… Three things," I closed my eyes tight, holding them shut against the onslaught of fear that stole my breath. "Three things…" I gasped. My mind slipped to Archer. The friend I had gotten to know, the person who had protected me, cared for me and came to my rescue. How had I been so blind? How did I let my guard down again? How did I let myself trust the wrong person? Again.

Tears streamed down my face, and I thrashed against my restraints. "Help!" I screamed. Unable to contain the urge anymore.

My throat burned from whatever substance was used to knock me out. I didn't notice the door had opened until a blurred silhouette made its way into my tearful vision. I pushed back against the chair, trying to move away, but I could not get even an inch of distance between myself and the visitor.

"Please, please…" I cried out.

"Athena." The sound of his voice sent an icy jolt of warning down my spine. "I'm so sorry."

"Fuck you," I spat up at him. As my vision cleared, I took him in. His green eyes were tired, and his black-dyed hair looked shaggy and unkempt.

"I guess I deserve that," Archer responded, slowly moving further into the space. I cringed back.

"Stay away from me, you monster!" I screamed. His hands rose in front of him.

"Athena, please. I can explain everything, but you must listen to me."

I laughed, a wicked, exasperated sort of cackle. "Listen to you? You drugged me, you knocked me out, you tied me to a fucking chair!" A painful memory returned to me. "You had Silas in the back of your truck! Where the fuck are they?" I demanded.

"Do you know what they are?" He asked with an edge of anger. I felt an eerie chill pass through me as the thought solidified.

"Do you?" I seethed.

He sighed, running a hand down his face.

"I do," he answered, finally. Looking at Archer, I didn't see any trace of the music-loving, kind-hearted man I'd gotten to know. Here in front of me was a stranger. His strong arms were weapons, and his eyes were a trap. He wore dark jeans and a white t-shirt, but the weapon he so often had hidden in his waistband was on full display—a wooden stake.

Was that the only way to kill a vampire? There was so much I didn't know about my mates. So much time I lost because of my fear. There is so much I might never get the chance to learn.

I felt sick.

"Let them go," I begged with a quiet intensity.

"I can't do that." He took another step forward, but I snarled in his direction. "They are monsters, Athena. Vampires." He waited for my response. I didn't give him an inch.

"Maybe you haven't noticed, but you're the one who kidnapped five people," I growled at him. He winced, and I might have felt sorry if I cared about him.

"Not people, vampires," he corrected.

"Then what the fuck am I?" I screamed, and the air hung thick between us. "A casualty?" He stared me down, something resembling sadness in his gaze.

"I'm trying to keep you safe," he argued, a sort of pleading tone to his words. I scoffed at him.

"By tying me to a fucking chair and chloroforming me?"

He took a frustrated breath and threw his hands up. "I am a Hunter. I kill vampires, and I protect humans. It's what I do."

Kill.

That word sent a sharp pain through my chest. I would have fallen to my knees if I wasn't bound to the chair. They can't kill my mates. Oh my god. What if they had already? I wouldn't survive that.

"Where are they?" I asked in a whisper, afraid that anything louder would send me toppling into a spiral I wouldn't recover from.

"They're locked up," he responded, equally as quietly.

"Alive?"

It was his turn to scoff.

"They aren't alive, Athena. They're vampires."

I rolled my eyes.

"So what's your big plan here, Archer?" I spat his name as if it were a dirty word. "Kill them, and then finish me off because I've seen too much?"

He wore a shocked expression. "Of course not," he stammered. "I won't let them hurt you."

"You're the one hurting me!" I ushered back quickly.

"We can go back and forth on this all day," he groaned, running a hand through his hair. "The point is, I did what I did to protect you. I had hoped you'd be able to see that."

"Yeah well, I don't."

We stared at each other for a few silent moments. He started to turn.

"What are you going to do to me?" I asked, trying not to let my fear quiver in my voice.

He looked back at me over his shoulder, his green eyes gleaming with unshed tears. "I'm going to protect you. Even if that means protecting you from yourself." And then he was gone. And I was alone.

2

ORPHEUS

Vampires are some of the most indestructible creatures on this Earth. If not *the* most indestructible. Our skin can be pierced, but unless it's a wooden stake to the heart, it doesn't do any lasting damage. We can be shot, take literal bullets to our chest, arms, hell, even our throats, and still we'd heal. We'd have one hell of a scar, but at least we'd still be breathing. Our hearts would still beat once per hour. We can survive plane crashes, bombings, and diseases. We can live forever—century after century.

So why is it that our indestructible nature can be so easily thwarted by a mixture of aerosolized garlic and water that's been prayed over by a priest?

I should have known what they would try and that we weren't safe there. But I didn't, and now my coven was paying for that mistake.

Athena.

Fuck.

Just the thought of my stunning mate being left behind made me want to rip someone's throat out. As my vision blurred and my consciousness faded, it was her voice that I heard. Her scared cries, her anxious breathing. If they hurt her...

My eyes adjusted to the darkness of my cell. I could freak out, I could thrash against the bars, I could threaten death, I could do a lot of things. However, that tactic didn't work the first time, and I've spent a lot of energy these last few years preparing for this exact scenario. I knew that Nameless would catch up to us one day, and we would be right back here. The others focused their energy on staying out of their clutches while I'd been preparing for what to do when we returned. Some may consider that a pessimistic mind-set, but I knew the reality of what was chasing us. I knew that if nobody was going to be realistic, I had to be.

Despite the plans, I couldn't help the anger that it had come to it. Just because you prepare for a storm doesn't mean you want to be caught in the eye of it.

As I pressed my face against the bars and peered out, the long, narrow hallway stretched before me like a serpent's den. The air was damp and heavy with the musty scent of decay, and a pervasive silence enveloped the corridor, broken only by the faint echoes of distant water droplets dripping onto the cold floor. The stone walls were rough and uneven, covered in patches of moss and grime, with the occasional flicker of faintly glowing fluorescent, providing the only source of feeble illumination. As I stood there, taking in the sight of the familiar and foreboding dungeon, the familiarity was like an ashen taste in my mouth. I shivered as my eyes scanned the scratches along the cell's back wall. Like a rabid animal was once held within these bars. I guess I was in a bit of a mindless frenzy when I made those marks. How thoughtful of the Hunters to place me back in my old cell. Unfortunately, in this case, familiarity does not breed content.

I came to rather quickly. It was faster than the Hunters expected but not fast enough to avoid being tossed in here. Having Athena's fresh blood in my system was like a jump start. Her potent blood would keep us strong for at least a week. Longer than they expect. We can use that. That will help my plan. We just have to be smart about it.

"Fuck!" I heard Silas exclaim from the cell to my left. A metallic clanging sound permeated the air, and his growls of effort echoed down the stone hallway.

"Silas," I called out, pressing against the bars. Still, he raged on. "Silas," I commanded again.

"We've gotta get out of here," he growled, anger, pain, fear. His emotions slammed into me like a freight train, and I held onto the bars to stave off the onslaught.

"I know. Please save your energy for when it will count." That seemed to appease him a little bit.

Just then, two more sets of emotions slammed into me.

"Samara, Laz, are you hurt?" I asked. I heard soft groans as they came to. It was a few moments before Laz responded.

"Nothing I can't handle." Their southern drawl was thicker than usual, as it tended to be when they were under pressure.

"Samara?" I called.

I felt her grief so potently. Being here isn't easy for any of us, but there's a certain special kind of torture reserved just for her.

"They put me in her cell." Her voice was timid, soft, and weak. None of the rest of us spoke. There weren't any words. There would never be words. "She…" Samara started, but sobs wracked her chest.

We listened to her fall apart in silence.

But we would not be silent forever. Nameless was going to regret ever crossing The Wanderers.

As Samara's grief floated about, dancing in my senses, I felt a shock of fear and anger so thick and volatile that I knew it could only belong to her—my mate.

"I feel her," I spoke aloud.

"Athena?" Laz clarified.

"Yeah, I can feel her." I let out a sigh of relief. She was alive. But the relief was quickly replaced by worry. "She's afraid. She's angry."

"Do you think she's still in Maine?" Silas asked, hopeful. Although I had been able to feel Athena from a vast distance before, there wasn't a doubt that I was feeling her too strongly now for her to be several states away.

"No," I responded, but I wasn't sure if that was good news or not. On one hand, when we finally broke out of here again, we wouldn't have to wait long for her to be back in our arms. On the other hand, she was a prisoner of Nameless just as we were, and who knows what vitriolic lies they were feeding her now.

"How did they find us so quickly?" Laz asked, defeatedly. I leaned my forehead against the cool metal bars.

"Maybe it was Louis? The missing person's case?" Samara offered, seemingly fully recovered from her initial shock of grief.

"Or maybe the ring of traffickers was too close. We should have gone further," Laz added.

"Did anyone see the symbol?" Silas asked, anger still lacing every word. He was seething with barely restrained fury. His shift would be close behind.

"No, nothing." Samara.

"I thought we had time." Laz.

"We can't dwell on that now," I stated, feeling their emotions shift to sadness. "We're here, and we can assume they have Athena." Three collective growls. I understood the impulse. I was going to tear the head off of any fucker who dared to put a hand on her perfect skin but in due time. She needed me to have a level head right now, but I admit that was getting harder with how strongly my coven emotions were slamming into me.

"They're going to regret this," Silas growled, an inhuman sound that told me he had shifted. His fangs were out, his skin was paler, his claws had elongated, and his eyes were blood-red. I could picture it clearly despite being unable to see him.

"Yes, they are," I agreed.

Deep in my chest, safe behind the layers of protection I had crafted, laid my bond with her. As if it were some tangible physical thing. I felt it there, burning brightly and offering me energy and power that I could only ever dream of before. It felt almost...enhanced. There were stories about mate bonds enhancing the latent power of vampires after completion, but so little has been studied that it was mere gossip and tall tales. But I felt it here. The connection with her was like a fiery inferno in the pit of my chest that was forging me into something better, something more substantial. I didn't know what it would mean or how it would manifest, but it was yet another advantage I hadn't factored into my plan and another thing the Hunters would never see coming. We weren't the same Wanderers that they held captive last time.

No, we have something even more vital to fight for this time. And something that's going to fight for us right back.

"What are we going to do?" Samara asked with a slight quiver in her voice.

"What we always do," I replied. "Survive."

3

ARCHER

*M*y father never hugged me. It wasn't his thing. He's never been the touchy-feely kind of guy. Growing up, he would shake my hand when most parents would engage in some sort of physical connection with their children. So, it was incredibly jarring and strange to be in his embrace right now. His arms tightened around my shoulders, and he pulled me close to him—a slight chuckle in my ear. I patted him on the back once, twice. Entirely unsure how to react.

"I can't believe you did it, son," he said, pulling back from our embrace, his hands fixed on my shoulders painfully.

"Yep," I offered awkwardly.

"You have no idea what everyone's been saying. You're going to go down in history for this, Archer. Do you realize that?" His eyes glistened with the promise of fame that I never wanted.

"Sure." I shrugged.

His face fell. "What the hell is wrong with you?"

What was wrong with me? I didn't know. I wasn't exactly jazzed about becoming a Hunter, but I should be celebrating right now. I captured The Wanderers. Nameless' white whale. I did that. Alone. And yet… I didn't feel all that relieved.

"I just…"

He put a hand up. "Stop."

I watched him for a second. He pinched the bridge of his nose between his thumb and forefinger, and an exasperated sigh escaped his lips.

415

"You have been dragging your feet through life, son. You didn't start the academy until I forced you to." He groaned. "You wasted most of your life playing on that stupid guitar, and now that you've actually done something worthy with your life, you're acting like an ungrateful child."

I winced as his words found their mark. My father looked a lot like me. His eyes were a deep emerald, his hair a soft auburn color, the same as mine before I went and dyed over it. His toned muscles and his strong jawline were like mine, too. There was a time when I was his perfect mirror, and yet, there's a world of difference between the two of us.

"I did what you asked, Dad," I stated plainly. He nodded, letting loose a soft, incredulous chuckle.

"Yes, you did. Galvin is very impressed. He's going to expect big things from you from now on."

I simply watched him. I didn't know if I'd be able to respond in a way he'd deem acceptable. After a while, I broke the silence. "Where is Galvin?" I didn't want to run into him while roaming the halls randomly.

"He's been laying low for a while. A mission went south, and he had to hide until we could fix the situation." My father waved a hand in front of his face as if it wasn't a big deal to have the head of our underground vampire-hunting organization in hiding.

"And did you? Fix the situation?" I asked.

"Not yet, but Galvin assured me he is working on it."

I nodded, thankful that there wasn't a chance of an unexpected meeting with the frightening ruler of Nameless.

"What did you do with the human?" He asked.

The human.

Athena.

I hated how clinical it felt to talk about her. How little my father cared about what happened to her.

"She's in your office," I started. His eyes opened wide. "I didn't want to put blood that close to The Wanderers in the cells," I finished quickly, hoping that would placate him. It seemed to because he nodded.

"We'll have to interrogate her, figure out what she knows.' He began to pace in front of me. "She'll need to be analyzed. Figure out if she's an asset or a threat."

"And what if she's a threat?"

"You know we cannot operate without our anonymity, and if what you've told me is correct, she knows your face and real name." The thought stabbed me in the chest. Was Athena a threat because of how careless I had been?

"So what?" I prompted.

"Do you need me to say it?" He asked, an edge of disappointment in his tone.

"Yes, I want you to say it out loud. I want to hear you tell me what you would do to that innocent human being in there." I tried not to let my voice rise above a whisper, but the intensity was burning behind each word.

"She would need to die," he spoke so clearly, so confidently, like the words didn't make him sick. Like it wasn't a murder, he was suggesting.

"And if she's an asset?" There was only one way out of this for Athena, and I would do whatever it took to lead her down that path.

"She would join us."

I sucked in a sharp inhale. "You're kidding me. It's death or submission? Those are the options? Sounds an awful lot like this oppressive regime I've read about in my history books. You know, that guy was the villain, right," I spat sarcastically.

He almost responded when his phone buzzed in his pocket. As his eyes scanned the caller ID, he sighed and sent it to voicemail before retraining his eyes on me.

"We are in a war, Archer," he glowered. "People die in wars, and there is no happy ending for everybody."

"Right," I responded defeatedly. I knew I wouldn't win this battle with my father, and I couldn't focus on this anymore. I needed to figure out how to get Athena out of here with her life and freedom.

"Do I need to conduct this interrogation?" He asked.

"No," I replied. He nodded, scanning my form.

"You've made a great capture, kid. This wasn't a small feat, and people will not forget it. But even the tallest towers can be brought down by a single weak beam. So, don't make mistakes." He turned on his heel to head down the hallway, leaving me alone.

I sighed, glancing up at the door to his office and imagining the woman behind the door. She needed me to be innovative. She needed me to prove to her that those creatures were monsters. She needed to believe it.

And I knew just how to do it.

4

SAMARA

Being in this cell even a few days ago might have killed me. Sensing Alora here, her pain, and her last few moments. Noticing the ghosts of her dancing in the corner and lurking in the shadows. The memory of her was so thick I was nearly choking on it. And I used to think that would be my downfall.

But despite the distance between us, I felt my mate holding my hand. Her soft touch on my face caressing it, encouraging me to wade through these troubled waters. With her grounding me, I could face these memories without losing myself.

It hurt being here, but instead of feeling Alora's death, I just felt her. And that made it all ok. Athena gave me that peace.

"You really think it will work?" Silas asked, his voice gruff. He had been entirely shifted for nearly the last hour. His anger was potent enough for me to feel it. I could only imagine what Orpheus was getting from him.

"I do," Orpheus responded casually. He was good in a crisis. While the others often praised my willpower, Orpheus usually held it together the most efficiently. If I didn't know him so well, I'd think he was completely fine with being back in Nameless' clutches. But I did know him, and I could tell how much being separated from Athena was hurting him. The sooner we put his plan into motion, the sooner we would be reunited with our mate, and the sooner we could finally get revenge on Nameless for all they've done to us and all they've taken away.

"We won't get very far if you're in a constant shift," Laz offered quietly.

"I can't help it," Silas growled.

"Let Athena help," I said softly. Athena wasn't a vampire, so she never bit us when we completed the bond. Which meant that we did not have a physical manifestation of our bond with her on our skin like she does with us. But she's still there in my soul. If I focused hard enough, I could feel that bond, visualize it, and follow it to her. She's there. She's always there. "Lean on her," I advised, doing the same. I traced the bond in my mind, hoping she could feel my passion for her in that mental touch. The others were quiet, no doubt trying to focus on that connection.

She made me feel strong—a better version of myself.

"It's gotta be convincing, Silas," Laz urged. Orpheus had a good plan, but Laz was right. If we couldn't pull it off, there was nothing else to do.

"They likely aren't going to hold us for long. They're not going to risk losing us again. So we've gotta start now," Orpheus reiterated. "I mean it. No matter what they throw at us, we take it. Ok?" I nodded.

The door at the end of the hall opened with a loud metallic clanging sound —a familiar, eerie sound that sent goosebumps across my flesh. It was time to put this plan into motion.

"Shift back, Silas, now," Orpheus ordered. I didn't have time to ask if he had done it.

The weight of footsteps was heavy, steadfast, and confident. As the man came into view, I knew immediately who he was, despite the mask covering his face. I would know his frame anywhere. The last time I saw him, he was driving a stake through my wife's heart. Fury bubbled under the surface of my skin. It took every ounce of the willpower I had to remain calm.

He stopped several feet behind the red line and clasped his hands before him.

"Hello, Wanderers." The sound of his voice was grating, like nails on a chalkboard. It ground against my soul. "I see you've made yourselves right at home."

I could practically hear the smug smirk on his face behind the mask.

"Bennett, right?" Orpheus asserted. I gripped the bars and watched his body language carefully. He tensed at that. They never expected us to escape the last time, so they got careless and let some of their anonymity slip. Not enough. There are a million Bennetts in this state. I couldn't find him without a first name. And I tried. We all tried for a long time. It wasn't enough to find him outside these walls, but it was enough to throw him off balance here. And that's the advantage we needed.

"Hmm," he stood calmly as if he weren't facing off against four ferocious vampires. We've been preparing for your return to us." His shrouded eyes scanned each of us; it felt like a violation, his gaze on me.

"So have we," Orpheus retorted with a smirk—all part of the plan.

"You know, the Hunter who captured you mentioned that you've been out in the sunlight." He leaned back against the empty cells on the opposite side of the hall from us with a casual, taunting attitude. "That's a fun new little development."

There was a vampire living in New Orleans who was rumored to have the ability to make it so that vampires could exist in the daylight. It was a heavily guarded secret and an even more heavily guarded vampire. Her compound was acres upon acres of guards and traps. It took us a whole year to convince her to see us and a few months after that to persuade her to perform the ritual on us. It was only when we told her our story that she truly listened. As it turned out, she had lost someone to Nameless' clutches, too—her husband. Unfortunately, or fortunately, depending on how you look at it, the man she described was none other than the man who was two cages down from us when we arrived. The man who had all but given up. She asked about him. We told her the truth. She cried. We cried. Eventually, she performed the ritual. It was painful like she was burning our body from the inside out, but when it was done and we stepped out onto the lawn of her manor, feeling the rays of light for the first time in a century, or in Orpheus's case, even longer, I couldn't help the tears that fell.

She made us promise to use this new ability to our advantage. We swore we would.

"Are you waiting for me to tell you how we did it?" Orpheus asked, provoking him.

"Would you tell the truth?" Bennett asked with a slight chuckle.

"Unlike you, Bennett, I'm not hiding what I am."

Bennett's hands tensed at his side. "So what is it? Complete immunity? Or is there a threshold?"

We stayed quiet. He laughed. "Of course there is." He moved to a lever on the wall. I immediately noticed it was not there the last time we were here. I would know because I'd memorized every inch of these walls. "Are you going to tell me what that threshold is, or should we find it together?"

Before Orpheus had a chance to respond, Bennett flipped the lever. A loud mechanical whirring filled the air, and I cringed at how overwhelming the sound felt to my advanced hearing. I looked up to see that the ceiling of the cell was sliding back to reveal a clear pane of glass and a blistering sun. The light flooded into every corner of the cell, chasing every last shadow away. The rays hit my skin, searing. I stifled a cry.

I heard my companions cry out as the sun's rays assaulted them.

The sun burned it a way it hadn't since before the ritual. My flesh felt tender and raw under its heat. I tried to fold over myself, hiding my uncovered skin, but there was no reprieve from the blistering warmth.

"That glass above you? It's specially designed to enhance the sun's rays."

I winced as the heat burned through the clothes on my back. I pressed against the walls, trying to find the slightest shade, but there was no hiding from the burn. Every inch of the cell was basked in shining vicious light. And it charred my skin. Tears stung my eyes, but I endured the torture. I would not let this monster see me fall apart. He didn't deserve the satisfaction.

I felt like I was being flayed open, laid bare beneath the blazing inferno. My skin was so warm I felt like it might burst into flames any instant. There's something so vulnerable about being betrayed by your own skin. In the last few years, I'd come to appreciate the sun's warmth again. We weren't immune to its light, but the pain was minimal in comparison.

I heard Silas let out a string of curses, and Laz stifled a scream. Orpheus was stoic and silent as usual, but I could feel their injuries, the way the fiery sun was assaulting their skin and violently blistering their bodies. Shock filled me then when I realized just how intimately I could feel them, in fact. Fully and completely. I could see the burns and sense the edges of the blisters. I could feel them as strongly as I could if I were touching them. Despite the burning light that was still viciously licking at my sensitive skin, I felt hope.

My entire body was in pain, stinging, violent pain. It felt like a thousand needles were prickling at me, but I focused on this new development of my power—this latest extension of myself. Eventually, the pain was numbing, and the light receded as Bennett flipped the lever back.

Silas felt it most in his hands, which he had used to shield his face. The palms were raw and tender. His arms were faring not much better. Laz, like me, had attempted to shield from the rays by folding over themselves, so their back had gotten the worst of it. Orpheus' face was the part that burnt the most for him, as if he had stood his ground, refusing to shy away from this display of torture.

I let my mind analyze their injuries, study them, and embrace them. I'd never been able to do anything like this before. The excitement flooding me was nearly enough to overshadow the unbearable pain that was radiating through my body from the assault.

"You've got new tricks, but so do we," Bennett said before leaving the hall. I watched him go, and once we heard the tell-tale lock at the door, I listened to my companions truly let the weight of that settle on them.

"Fuck, I'd almost forgotten how bad that fucking hurts," Silas seethed. I let my mind focus on his hands. The palms. Red and angry.

"We're not going to have to pretend to let the torture weaken us if it's all like that," Laz whispered meekly. Their back was throbbing in my mind.

"We'll manage," Orpheus said through clenched teeth, no doubt trying to hold back the wave of emotion he had held so tightly to his chest. He tried to remain calm for us, tried to be strong. However, I knew he felt our pain. Each of us was forced to live our own pain while he lived all of ours as well as his own. The involuntary waves of our agony always found their way to him. He hid it well, how much that affected him, but I knew how hard that was for him. Feeling the injury deep in his skin, I let my gift sweep over his face.

If I could feel their injuries from this far... maybe... Just maybe.

I focused on the burns, one at a time, letting every ounce of my ability pour through the connections my mind had made to their worst wounds. It felt strange, an entirely new sensation, but no less powerful. It flowed through the channels of my mind, finding purchase on their burns, seeping into their skin, cooling them from within, calming the angry burns, urging the skin to reform. It was harder to navigate, but within seconds, I felt the burns disappear from their flesh, and their injuries fell away. Only then did I let my healing wash over myself.

"What the fuck?" Silas asked incredulously.

"How did-" Laz.

"Samara," Orpheus interjected. "Did you just-"

"A bond makes us stronger," I whispered, feeling the last remnants of the sting recede from my skin.

"Holy shit," Silas exclaimed. "No fucking way."

"Are you all ok?" I asked.

"Like it never fucking happened," Silas responded excitedly.

"I feel fine, perfectly fine," Laz said with a laugh.

"Are you drained?" Orpheus whispered eagerly.

"Not at all," I replied, taking stock of my current state. If anything, I felt stronger than before. More resolved.

"This changes everything," Laz added, and hope laced every word.

"Yes, it does," Orpheus said, and I could hear the smirk playing on his lips. I looked down at myself. My dress was tattered and torn, and the edges were seared from the fire that was nearly flaming on my body just moments ago.

"Can you feel her?" Silas asked. "Is she hurt?" I steadied my breathing and closed my eyes. Focusing my power on my mate. She was far enough away that it wasn't as easy of a task as it was for me to feel my coven, but after a few moments of intense focus, I found her. Her influence felt like a salve, a reward, every good thing I'd missed for many years. She was mine.

"There she is," I whispered.

"Is she ok?" Laz asked.

I let my power wash over her body, analyzing her pain and injuries. Her body had taken some hits, a contusion on her head, and her throat and shoulders were bruised. Long and thick bruises formed on her back as if she was slammed into something repeatedly. But the worst part was her hands. They were swollen, and tiny cuts danced along the knuckles. It was evident that she had to use them to defend herself. A growl escaped my lips.

"She's hurt," I seethed.

"Heal her," Silas urged angrily.

"Wait," Orpheus interjected before I let my power flow through the connection.

"What do you mean, wait?" Silas argued.

"We are vampires, so our skin healing won't make them suspicious," he started. "But Athena is human. If her injuries suddenly disappear, they're going to notice. We'd lose this advantage, or worse, they'd think she was one of us somehow."

I cursed under my breath. He was right.

"Can you relieve the pain but leave the outward facade of injuries?" He asked.

I'd never tried to do anything like that before. Why would I have?

"I'm not sure," I answered truthfully, trying to keep my focus on each of the vicious little injuries that littered her body.

"Try," Orpheus demanded in a soft, almost pleading sort of way. The thought of her in pain was agonizing, but the idea of putting her under unnecessary scrutiny in this place was worse.

I zeroed in on her internal pain, trying my hardest to ignore the outward bruises and wounds despite how my power itched to erase those from marring her perfect skin. Letting my ability wash over her felt like taking a long, languid breath of fresh air after being locked inside somewhere stifling. She felt like a relief, like the moment of calm at the end of a dangerous ride. I smiled and let my power get to work. I imagined kissing her skin and taking the pain away. If I couldn't press my lips to her skin, at least I could do this.

With each rush of my power, I felt her pain recede slowly but effectively. It pained me to leave those cuts untouched, to let the bruises on her back remain, but I took solace in the fact that she wasn't in pain anymore.

That's when I felt her. Stronger than before.

Thank you, Samara.

Her whispered words felt like they were spoken directly into my ear, so much so that my eyes sprung open, and I turned in hopes of catching a glimpse of her, but she wasn't there. I whispered back through the channels of my mind.

Athena?

I waited a moment, then another. Finally, her voice returned.

Samara? Can you hear me? Is this real, or am I hallucinating?

I giggled.

"What is it?" Orpheus asked. I pressed against the bars of my cell and smiled brightly for the first time since waking up in this hell.

"Have you ever heard of mates being able to speak telepathically?" I asked, focusing then on the bond.

It's real, sweetheart. It's me.

I heard her sigh.

"No," Orpheus responded.

Are you all ok? Athena asked.

She was in pain, and yet she asked about us, her mates. My heart thumped once, firmly against my chest.

We will be when we get you out of here. I offered back to her.

"She's talking to me now." I heard Silas and Laz gasp.

"So little is known about multiple mates. Perhaps it's got something to do with that?" Laz offered. I shrugged, although they couldn't see me.

What can I do to help?

I shook my head. *Stay safe and alive.*

"What is she saying?" Silas begged.

"She's asking how she can help," I said, pride lacing my tone.

You too. Thank you for kissing it better.

My chest warmed in that love-filled way, a vastly different heat than the sun that had just torn through my skin.

I wanted to respond, to tell her that I wasn't 'alive,' but ever since she came into my life, she had been making me experience life in a way I never thought I'd be able to again. I may not be alive, but Athena made me want to be, and that was enough.

"We're going to get out of here," Orpheus said, determined and clear. I had heard him say those exact words a dozen times the last time we were here.

But when he said them this time, I actually believed him.

5

It felt like warm honey spreading through my entire body. I could feel her healing powers take hold of the pain that was throbbing in my limbs and my chest and wipe it away.

I don't know how, but I could speak to her through that bond that thrummed so powerfully inside my chest. Over the next day, or maybe longer, I tried to establish the same line of communication with each of them with little success. I hadn't even been able to reestablish the link with Samara. Suddenly, I felt even more lonely than before. I didn't know how heavy the toll of their loss was on my soul until I heard Samara's voice. And I wouldn't be able to settle until I could speak to them all and hear directly from their lips that they were okay.

Well, as 'okay' as anyone could be when trapped.

The door creaked open, scratching the wooden floor below violently, and I cringed. Light flooded into the room, sending wicked shadows sprawling across the floor. As my eyes adjusted, a silhouette came into view.

My heart rate sped up as I saw them.

"I told you I didn't want to talk to you," I spat as Archer entered the room, closing the door behind him.

"I need you to understand why I did this, Athena," he pleaded. He looked tired as if he hadn't slept in days. Well good, I hope he never sleeps again.

"Understand why you've kidnapped me? And my mates?"

His eyes burned with shock. "They cannot be your mates, Athena."

"Fuck you," I growled, the words slipping out in an animalistic possessive

427

way. Archer ran a hand down his face and stopped a few feet from me. I noticed the bulky file folder in his hands for the first time.

"I'm not the monster here," he said, letting the file fall to the table to the side. He opened it, and papers spilled out across the surface of the desk. I tried to fight my curiosity and ignore his apparent attempt to goad me, but my eyes drifted toward the documents nevertheless.

What I saw was unimaginable.

Pictures, reports, and statements. Mangled bodies, blood-stained skin, and clothing puncture wounds deep into their throats. The pale, lifeless figures stared up at me from the pages, and I watched them in horror. Death. So much death on these pages.

I felt bile rise in my throat, and I forced myself to look away from the images. I heard rustling but refused to turn back to Archer.

"I'm sorry," Archer started quietly. "I didn't want to upset you, but you needed to understand what we're trying to prevent here."

I looked at him tentatively to see that he had filed away the photos.

"Who were those people?" I asked, meekly and unsure if I even wanted the answer.

"Victims," he replied. I shook my head. I was trying to piece together the jumbled mess of information flowing through my mind.

"My mates aren't like that," I asserted, confident but shaky in my conviction. He lifted the folder and turned it so I could see the labeled tab. Two words were printed along the top. Two words that stole my breath and clenched my heart. Two words and the world changed.

The Wanderers.

I gasped and felt tears sting my eyes. "No, no. They..." I struggled to find my breath. "They only kill monsters, people who hurt others." It was what they told me. And I believed them. I believed every word. Louis had been trying to hurt me. That's why he ended up the way he did.

A look crossed Archer's face, which looked a lot like pity, and he flipped open the folder. He took a deep breath and slid an image from the confines of the folder. With a deep breath, he turned it toward him. The woman in the photo was small young, maybe mid-twenties at most. Her soft brown hair was messy and sprawled on the concrete floor beneath her body. Her lifeless eyes stared into nothingness, and the blood that coated her shoulder was deep crimson. The two puncture wounds were vicious and angry-looking. I tried to avert my eyes, but I couldn't seem to look away from her.

"This is Lily Anders, a kindergarten teacher in Kentucky. She just turned twenty-four when she was murdered."

I swallowed the lump in my throat as Archer set the photo down and pulled another. The older man was dressed in a business suit. His wrinkled black skin was ashen, his eyes glazed and dead. The puncture wounds on his throat taunted me.

"Victor Brown, a civil rights activist from Montgomery, Alabama. He marched in The Selma Marches in the '60s and the women's liberation arches in the '70s. He survived all that only to die by the fangs of The Wanderers."

A soft sob fell from my lips as he discarded that photo and reached for another. The couple in the picture took my breath away. She wore a gorgeous white gown, painted and marred by the blood that ran from the puncture wounds on her neck. Her groom was discarded before her, his arms twisted unnaturally as he lay there. Their hands froze on the ground as if reaching for each other, even in death.

"Violet and Zander Freedman married just four hours before they were killed. They had a two-year-old at home."

Another photo.

Another story.

"Jennifer Kaufman, foster mother of 4." He slammed the photo down onto the desk. "George Haroldson, special education teacher. Bethany Terrison, Olympic hopeful." The photos fell from his grasp onto the desk, and I could no longer contain my sobs. "Francessca Dodson, ten years old." He held that photo in front of me for longer than the others. A look of pain on his face as he watched me take it all in.

'Stop," I cried, forcing my eyes to look away from the small frame in the photo before me. My head hung forward, and tears fell down my cheeks in steady streams. I heard Archer shuffle about, and then he was kneeling before me, his hands-free from the file.

"Did those people look like monsters to you?" He asked it so gently, as if the tone of his question could soften the pain in my chest.

It didn't.

I shook my head, sobbing. Archer reached for my shoulder, and I shied away from his touch. He pulled back, looking ashamed and guilty.

"I'm sorry," he stated. "That was... I just. I needed you to understand how dangerous they are, Athena. I can save a lot of lives by killing them."

I cried out, pain radiating through every nerve in my body at the thought of losing any of my mates and what they might be capable of.

"You're so lucky, Athena," he began, and I scoffed. "They could have bitten you. They could have killed you." I shook my head.

"They did," I whispered. His eyebrows furrowed.

"What do you mean?"

"They did bite me," I answered weakly, remembering the moment their fangs pierced my skin and laid claim to my heart, body, and soul. Tainted now by Archer's demonstration.

Archer's eyes scanned my throat and then my arms frantically.

"No..." he started.

"They wouldn't do those things," I whispered to him, knowing with every fiber of who I am that they were not responsible for the evil acts harbored within that file. "They wouldn't."

"But they did," he pleaded, his eyes begging with me. I shook my head.

"You said they bit you?" He asked, looking at my throat again. I nodded, hating the way he made it sound like a death sentence or something to be afraid of when it was the most beautiful experience of my life. "Where?"

"My throat, chest, hip, and wrist."

He sat back on his heels, looking at the image now painted on my skin.

"Those markings..." he whispered. I nodded again.

"The mate bond."

He shook his head, muttering under his breath. "There would be puncture wounds." A thought occurred to me then, a memory that seemed so distant now.

"The saliva in a vampire bite counteracts the wound," I whispered as the revelation came.

"What?" Archer asked from his position on his knees before me.

"A vampire's saliva counteracts the wound, closes it up." I felt a bloom of hope in my chest. "Those photos all had the bite, clear as day. That's not my Wanderers." I was ashamed that it took me this long to put it together.

"That's not possible," he stammered, but I saw the slightest edge of suspicion in his eyes.

"Archer," I said, trying to catch his eyes. He looked up at me, and for the first time since I realized what he had done, I saw the same Archer who was my friend with soft green eyes and tender gaze. "I am not lying to you. I was bitten. Their saliva closed my wounds. They do not leave punctures like that." I gestured to the file that sat on the floor by his knees. "I don't know who killed those people, Archer, but it wasn't them," I remembered back to the unspoken rule they told me about. "It probably wasn't a vampire at all."

He shook his head, disgust coloring his features. "You're brainwashed, do you even hear yourself?" he stood and paced around the room. "Saliva magically closing a bite? Are you kidding me?" He ran his hands through his hair.

"We can prove it."

He turned back to me, his eyes wild.

"Let them bite me. They'll show you."

He laughed a sort of crazed chuckle, disbelief pouring from him. "They would kill you, Athena! Don't you see that? They are trapped here and haven't fed for two days. They would drain you completely!"

I shook my head. "They won't."

He tossed his hands up in defeat. "You're unbelievable. How far have they gotten their hooks in you?" He dug into the file, sliding the pictures around till his hand found the one he wanted.

When he turned the picture to face me, I felt a sickening twist deep in my abdomen. Louis' smiling face looked up at me. The photo looked like it was a few months old. His hair was shorter than it was that night at the Craving Crab. I visibly shied away from the photo.

"They killed him, didn't they? The missing guy?"

I looked up at him, hating the way his figure blurred in my vision from the tears that were forming. I didn't respond.

"They did. They did it," he confirmed from my silence. "How can you defend them, Athena? They are murderers, monsters!"

"Louis tried to rape me!" I screamed. My throat was raw, and I hated the way the word felt on my tongue, like ash and death. Archer's eyes softened, and a sharp exhale spilled from his lips at my confession.

"What?" he asked, nearly under his breath.

"Louis drugged my drink and took me outside of the bar," I started, feeling the weight of the memory settling on my chest. "He had my underwear down, and he was about to... He was almost.." A sob fell from my lips as I tried to compose myself. "But then they found me, they saved me. They *saved* me, Archer. The only monster in that alleyway was Louis."

"No..." he whispered, and just one word was enough to shatter my composure. He didn't believe me. Of course, he didn't believe me. No one ever did.

"Please...They aren't the villains here."

He glared at me, a mixture of disbelief and anger on his face, before turning to leave the room.

"Wait, Archer, please!" I called after him. He paused but didn't turn back to face me. "You may not believe me, but I'm telling you the truth."

"Athena..." he started.

"One of us is going to be wrong about this. Please just... consider that it might be you."

His shoulders rose and fell as he took a deep breath before exiting the room and leaving me alone in the darkness again.

6

SILAS

Samara's healing powers helped relieve the pain of the burns but not the memory of their sting. It had been a while since I considered the sun a weapon. I hated how quickly I had forgotten. How easily I fell back into the mindset of humanity. The sun was the hardest goodbye I had to make when I was turned. I had no family besides Alora, and she turned with me. I didn't have many friends or prospects, so the one thing I honestly had to give up was sunlight.

At first, being thrust into darkness felt like a payment I was willing to make, but after months, then years, then decades of surviving only at night...it began to take its toll.

Being gifted the ability to survive in sunlight again was the only thing that helped hold me together after losing Alora. Knowing how much she would have loved to feel the rays on her face again hurt, so despite the slight burn, I would sit outside and feel her there with me.

To have it ripped away again so brutally, fucking sucked.

I couldn't wait for the day that I got to sink my fangs into Bennett's throat and drain his worthless life from his pathetic body. He didn't deserve to walk this Earth for another moment, but I would wait until the time was right.

"Two weeks is too long," I whined, leaning my head against the cold metal bars of my enclosure.

"If we act any sooner, they will expect us to be full strength," Orpheus added. I hated how cocky he sounded, although I knew he was right. "We need to give it enough time for them to think we're weak."

I nodded, sighing.

"That will be too long to be away from her," Samara whispered. I knew what she meant. My soul was also crying for Athena.

"She's strong, and we must be strong for her too." Orpheus' tone was laced with love. There was a time I'd never thought I'd hear him speak about another person like that. He was always so solitary. Even in our coven, he found his reasons to be alone, to isolate himself. Feeling everyone else's emotions constantly can't be easy, so I never blamed him. It was hard, though, to see how lonely he was. If you had told me a year ago that he'd be helplessly head over heels, for a human no less, I would have laughed. But Athena changed everything when she walked into our lives. I saw how she had started healing wounds in Laz, Samara, and Orpheus that were so old and deep that they'd all but given up on feeling whole again. She was mending us, she saw our scars, and instead of shying away or trying to hide them away, she kissed them and told us we deserved the happiness she promised. Samara, Laz, and Orpheus deserved that.

"So we have a timeline," Laz started. "And a plan."

I nodded along. It was a good plan. Orpheus clearly had put a lot of thought into our inevitable need to escape from here again, and the plan has only become more solid with the development of Samara's gift. Orpheus hinted that his gift might have progressed as well, although he wasn't sure exactly what the nature of it was now. Laz and I, however, felt entirely...the same. Not anymore powerful than we had before. Which was fine by me. I didn't join my soul with Athena's for some supernatural upgrade. However, Orpheus is convinced that new skills can still develop over time.

"Do we finally want to discuss theories as to why we're all mated to Athena?" Laz whispered, but we could hear them clearly.

"It doesn't matter," I said, probably a little too forcefully, instantly regretting how harsh I had sounded.

"I know, but it certainly is interesting. Considering it's so rare," they continued, ignoring my outburst. I was thankful for that. I knew they hadn't meant offense.

"Any chance one of you is vampire royalty and forgot to tell us?" I joked with a soft chuckle.

"The monarchy hasn't had an heir," Orpheus began. The royal family was more 'for show' than anything else. Our King has held the throne for nearly two centuries. His Queen was killed before I was even born as a human, and as far as any of us know, he hasn't created an heir.

"Could be illegitimate," I added unhelpfully. To create an 'heir,' a vampire must drink the human nearly dry before allowing them to feed on the vamp's blood. Then, after the transformation, the fresh-turn must drink first from the vamp who created them. It solidifies some sort of preternatural bond. No one is naive enough to think the King has never made another vampire, but there's never been a purposeful heir as far as anyone knows.

"So, short of being a bastard child of the royal line, the other multiple mate covens have been vamps with indescribable power," Orpheus added.

"We're all fairly powerful," Samara interjected.

"Yes, but not in comparison to these other covens. We're talking vampires with the ability to alter time and space," Orpheus continued. I had heard him talk about those gifts before. There was still so much I didn't know about my new existence. That's what happens when you're on the run.

"There's time-traveling vampires?" Laz whispered incredulously.

"There were," Orpheus replied solemnly. "Most of them have been hunted."

"How do you kill a time-traveling vamp? Couldn't they just keep rewinding until they escaped?" I asked.

"It's foolish to assume that the Hunters haven't considered countermeasures for most of our gifts."

I sighed, feeling anger course through my veins. Those Hunters have created such a horrific state of fear in our community. I couldn't wait for the day that we finally end them once and for all.

"Maybe we're not the powerful ones?" Samara whispered.

"You think Athena is?" Laz asked incredulously, but I could tell they were genuinely considering it.

"She's the common denominator here. She could have an extremely powerful latent vampire gift." Samara spoke so quietly as not to alert the guards or cameras of her theory.

"If that's true, we can't even allow the Hunters to consider it," Orpheus returned forcefully. "Who knows what lengths they'll go to to "study" our kind."

The thought of Athena being turned into a vampire sent a weird swirl of emotions through my chest. On the one hand, I wanted to spend eternity with her, and I wanted to live my life without worrying about her growing old, without worrying about her mortal form and how vulnerable she was. On the other, this life - although it was my salvation - is a curse, and it would be foolish of me to think of it any other way. I wouldn't wish this life on anyone who hasn't thoroughly prepared for what it meant.

"They're trying to eradicate us. They wouldn't make a new one," Laz started. "Would they?"

"We cannot trust their words, only their actions," Orpheus replied, his voice laced with fear. We've seen firsthand what sort of 'actions' these Hunters perform. "Think about it. They held us captive for over two months. We were weak, fucking inches from desiccating. If they wanted to kill us, they could have. So why didn't they?" He asked.

"Because they're looking for something else..." Samara finished.

"Exactly."

We were quiet for a moment. What could they be looking for? What could they learn by torturing us within an inch of existence? What would they do to Athena?

"I want to destroy them," I said, finally breaking the silence. Laz grunted in agreement.

"We need to focus on getting out of here," Orpheus said calmly.

"And then what?" I spat. "If we get out of here, where do we go? Do you want us to run forever?"

He didn't respond.

"Athena won't leave her grandma or Davia. She won't go on the run with us, Orpheus. She shouldn't have to."

"The Hunters will never stop," Orpheus pleaded.

"Then we stop them! Here and now. I'm tired of running, aren't you?" A tense quiet fell over us. My breathing slowed as I waited for him to respond.

"Of course I am." It was a whisper. Defeated. Ashamed. "But I can't risk it. I can't lose any more family."

I inhaled sharply at the confession.

"I don't know what to do." It was an admission that we had never heard from his lips. Orpheus, the leader of our coven, had always known what to do. He was the man with the plan. To hear him so defeated, so lost...well, it was a perfect example of how fucking dangerous this whole thing was. We fucking barely escaped last time. Even with Samara and Orpheus' new potential powers, getting out alive will be a challenge. Let alone take the Hunters down in the process.

I let my head rest on the metal bars of my cage, wishing I could replace their harsh touch with that of my mate. Two weeks was too long, but I knew without a doubt that I would make up for every second of lost time the moment she was in my arms again.

ARCHER

My head was spinning when I sat down at the bar. The dive was a staple for us Hunters, as it was the only establishment within twenty miles of our little operation. The Wooden Stake was owned and operated by Hunters, of course. Who else would be stupid enough to name a place, The Wooden Stake? The moment I stepped inside, I was enveloped in an atmosphere that immediately transported me to another time and place. The main area is a dimly lit, cozy chamber adorned with dark wood and heavy velvet curtains that hang in thick folds, muffling sounds and adding an air of secrecy. Antique weapons and hunting paraphernalia adorned the walls, from wooden stakes to silver-bladed weapons, each telling a story of battles against the undead and unnatural. I did not come here often, but I needed a drink and a clear head tonight. It had been nearly a week since I stopped in to speak with Athena. Someone else had been tasked with bringing her meals, although I've been informed she was not eating. I wanted to go in there and convince her to believe me, to trust me, but I just couldn't get her words out of my head.

I glanced around the dimly lit room. The patrons come from all walks of life. Some were seasoned hunters, bearing scars and grim determination etched into their faces, while others were newcomers seeking guidance. The bartender was a Hunter I didn't recognize, but I saw the raised white scar from the brand on his forearm. I didn't know how to make sense of the feeling I got when I looked at it. There was an almost sickening apprehension building in the pit of my stomach. The scent of burnt flesh was still so visceral in my memory.

"What can I get ya, kid?"

I narrowly resisted rolling my eyes at the belittling honorific. I may not have recognized the bartender, but there was an excellent chance he would have recognized me—Son of the great Jacob Bennett.

"Whiskey rocks, please."

With a nod, he turned to get my drink, and I stared at his back. He wore a tank top showcasing his ridiculous muscles, which was probably his desired effect. It also showcased the bite marks that decorated his skin. Several deep and angry white scars stood out against his olive skin. As he poured the drink, I studied those scars. Two deep puncture wounds, flanked on each side by several thin pinpricks from the vamps, additional sharpened teeth. His scars looked a lot like mine. Mindlessly, I ran my thumb across the marred flesh at my wrist.

Athena claimed that vampire bites could be closed. Then why do we all carry these scars? Why is my skin forever marked from that day? Why did my father, this bartender, and so many other Hunters have bites decorating their skin?

I shook my head. What was it that Athena had claimed? A vampire's saliva. How did she expect me to believe that? Well, it's not like the Hunters would give a vampire a chance to lick the wound.

Not that it would do anything if they did.

"Starting a tab?" He asked. I shook my head and tossed some bills down on the counter. He grabbed them and strolled away to help the other Hunters on the far end of the bar.

The first sip of the drink sent a warm rush through my entire body. A few sips later, I felt my phone vibrating violently in my pocket. With a sigh, I reached for the phone.

The name on the caller ID screen had my blood turning cold, erasing any ounce of warmth I had just felt.

DAVIA

"Fuck," I cursed, sitting up straighter and glancing around at the other patrons. Other than the bartender, there were four other people here. Two Hunters were seated at the far end of the bar, and two more were sitting at a table by the jukebox. Fleetwood Mac played through the bar, masking any conversations the others were having. If I couldn't hear them, they wouldn't be able to hear me. Right?

My hand gripped the phone tensely. A sheen of sweat formed on my brow bone. I considered sending it to voicemail. Strongly. But something told me Davia wouldn't be deterred so easily.

Had she realized Athena was gone? It had been over a week.

I cleared my throat and answered the call.

"Well, well, well, did you miss me?" I answer, trying to interject the same charm I usually had with her.

"Have you seen Athena?" She was all business; her voice had no edge of accusation, but I knew she was only calling because she thought I might know something. I took a deep breath and relied on every ounce of training I'd ever had.

"She didn't tell you?" I began. I had to skip town. I left about a week and a half ago. I hope to make it back for one of those summer concerts, though. She invited me." It took all my energy to keep my voice calm and steady.

"When did you last see her?" Davia demanded.

"Whoa, what's going on? Is she ok?" I asked, feeling a twinge of guilt grip my chest.

"She's missing," Davia answered, her voice wavering briefly, unable to contain her fear and worry. I hated how I was the cause of that pain. I swallowed the lump in my throat and refocused on the task at hand.

"What the fuck? Since when?" I laced my voice with as much worry as I could.

"Nine days now."

I didn't miss how her voice caught, full-on an emotion she was too afraid to share.

"Have you gone to the police?" I asked carefully.

"Yeah, they are concerned that.. um... " She held back a sob, composing herself. "They're concerned that Greg has something to do with it." There was so much guilt in her voice. "They've tried to find him, but he's missing too. He hasn't been back to his rental. They think he... They think he might have taken her." A full sob escaped her lips then, and I let my head fall forward into my free hand.

Moral dilemmas were becoming more and more frequent lately. Having the police consider Greg was perfect for many reasons. It kept them from looking at me and gave them a trail to follow. BI could tell that Davia already felt so much guilt from introducing Athena to that douche's friend for her to think he was behind her disappearance and that it was all her fault was almost too much for me to bear. Almost.

"I knew I shouldn't have left town until that asshole was behind bars for what he did to her." I heard Davia sniffle on the other end of the call. "Just, um, let me know if you hear anything, ok?" She pleaded so helplessly.

"Of course," I promised, but it tasted like ash on my tongue.

I tried to view the situation as if I were hearing it all for the first time. What would I say if I didn't know exactly where Athena was?

"Have you tried talking to those people she was seeing?" I asked as evenly as I could.

"They're not in town either. Their rental was tossed, and windows were broken in. Cops aren't sure what to make of it all," she finished with a defeated tone.

"Shit," I whispered, trying my best to ignore the treacherous guilt that was threatening to eat me alive. "Are you ok?" I asked, knowing the answer.

"Of course I'm not okay. My best friend is missing, and it's my fault," she bit.

"Don't say that," I interject.

"Why not?" She asked, sniffling again. "It's the truth. I asked her to come out that night, and if I didn't make her go, or if I didn't leave her to go hook up if I was a better person... literally none of this would have happened." She cried softly, anger laced her words.

"Davia, come on, that is not true," I offered quickly. "If Greg is behind this, then it's nobody's fault but his." The words felt vitriolic in my mouth.

It's nobody's fault but mine.

She was quiet for a few moments, and I could tell she didn't care for that logic right now.

"Just let me know if you hear anything," she said sharply before hanging up. The silence on the other end of the call was the loudest thing I'd ever heard.

Shoving the phone back into my pocket, I grabbed my glass and downed the rest of my drink in one gulp. I begged the warmth of the liquor to thaw the cold, eerie guilt that had blanketed me, but it didn't.

The stool next to mine was pulled back, and I saw a figure sitting down out of the corner of my eye. He slid his phone onto the bar and reached for his wallet.

"You don't normally come here," my father said as he waved over the bartender. I didn't turn to look at him and watched as the muscled man behind the bar brought him a gin and tonic. When my father had his drink, I felt his eyes burn into my cheek, but I didn't turn to meet his gaze.

"It's been over a week. Have you made any progress with the girl?" He asked casually, but I knew better. He probably had tracked me down to ask this specific question.

I didn't want to tell him how difficult she was being. I wasn't sure what he might do to her if he learned she wasn't budging. A few weeks ago, I'd say we would let her go. But now? I'm not sure my father would be willing to let her go, knowing all she does. That thought sent a confusing feeling to my heart.

"Slow but steady," I replied, opting for vagueness.

"Does she know the truth about vampires?" He asked, taking a swig of his drink.

There it was. Moment of truth. Was I going to lie to my father to save her life? Or was I going to betray her and sentence her to death? I felt my hand tremble as I motioned for the bartender to pour me another drink.

"You ever heard of a vampire bite closing up? With like saliva or something?" I tried to say it with as little interest as possible. He took another drink, and I turned my head just enough to gauge his reaction. My father was skilled at hiding things, his emotions mostly, so I didn't see much of a response on his face. But as good as he was at hiding, I was just as good at reading. I learned from him, after all.

"That's the type of question someone asks when they let delusions win," he answered finally.

"Not delusions, Dad. I'm just curious," I respond as the bartender slides another drink before me.

"Did that girl say something?" He asked, an almost imperceptible sliver of worry gracing his features.

"No, I was doing some research," I replied evenly. My father made a slight humming sound and took another drink.

"Why the hell would you be looking into something like that, kid?" He seethed. "You know as well as I do that vampire bites do not disappear." He gripped my wrist and held it up so that I could see the scar. I pulled my arm from his hand and bit my lip.

"I'm not a kid." My eyes met his. This time, I wasn't backing down. His eyes narrowed, and he clicked his tongue before turning and taking another drink. His phone vibrated on the bar. The caller ID read *Carmen*. He quickly sent the call to voicemail and slid the phone back into his pocket. His jaw was tense, and I felt his body go rigid next to mine.

Who the hell is Carmen?

"Right," he mused quietly, moving on without addressing the call. "So the girl. She gonna be a problem?"

I couldn't help but sigh, a soft, incredulous chuckle falling from my lips.

"What's so funny?" He asked.

"I just can't believe this is my life sometimes," I answered finally, looking over at him and taking a long sip from my drink.

"Protecting the human race from monsters?" He asked, an edge of arrogance lacing his tone.

"Treating an innocent human like she's a threat," I bit back softly. I was resisting the urge to bolt out of the bar.

"She is a threat," my dad said calmly. I had always seen this man as my hero. The man who was protecting humans from the creatures of the night. The man who would save us all. Now, as he sat before me and tipped the amber liquid to his lips, I saw a liar. How many innocent people have been caught in his crossfire in this unending desire to eradicate vampires? Does he care?

"Right."

I shook my head and took another drink, downing the rest of the liquid in one gulp. I let the burn calm my ever-growing suspicion. Questioning things can get you killed here.

"Do I need to remove you from this case, Archer?" He asked coldly.

For a brief moment, I entertained the thought of leaving Athena and this mind-fucking case behind me. Shoving it onto someone else's plate to worry about. The only reason I was so confused and conflicted was because I got to know Athena. I wouldn't care as much if she remained a stranger. It would have been easier if she was someone else's problem.

But the thought of my father, or one of the other vicious Hunters, back at Nameless getting their hands on her and sinking their brand into her skin made my blood begin to boil.

"No, I've got it. I've established a rapport. You'd have to start all over with someone new."

He seemed to like that answer.

"What are you doing with The Wanderers?" The question tumbled out of my mouth before I could stop it. His eyes scanned the bar for any listening ears.

"Testing their limits," he admitted with an almost sinister smile. My stomach churned at the admission. Torture. He was torturing them.

"Why don't you just kill them," I asked, trying not to let the disgust I was feeling seep into my tone.

"Doctors may be able to learn surgery on a cadaver, but they will never understand medicine until they practice on living flesh," he offered the metaphor so calmly.

"What are you trying to find out?" I asked, seeing a sort of glint in his eye.

"Everything." Finishing his drink, he pushed off the counter and stood from his stool. He left a couple of bills on the bar and turned to face me.

"Three days, Archer. By this weekend, she will either need to join our ranks, or we will be forced to eliminate the threat."

I swallowed the lump in my throat and nodded. My eyes followed my father's imposing figure as he exited the bar, but even when he was gone, I couldn't seem to fill my lungs with air.

I let my head fall into my hands and sighed, feeling the tightness in my chest overwhelm me. How did I get here? How did I become... this?

I don't remember when I left the bar or when I arrived back at HQ. Everything happened in a slow haze. Suddenly, I was turning the door handle on my dad's office and stepping into the darkened room to see Athena, visibly paler and weaker than the last time I saw her. Her head lifted meekly, and her eyes met mine with an almost hopeless expression before slowly letting her head fall forward again.

"Athena," I said, stepping forward into the space. "You haven't been eating."

She didn't respond, remaining quiet and staring at the floor before her. I knelt in front of her, hoping she would make eye contact with me again.

"You need your strength," I whispered. She ignored me still. I didn't know when I made the choice or even why I made it in the first place, but I found myself desperately searching for answers that, at this crossroads, only she could offer. That fact was why I whispered the following words. "If I'm going to allow them to bite you, I need you to be strong enough to survive it."

Her head snapped up, and her eyes widened in surprise. Clearly, as shocked to hear what I had to say as I was to hear myself say it.

"You're going to let me see them?" She asked eagerly. Life was returning to her features with every passing moment.

"I don't.." I paused, realizing how dangerous this road was to travel. "I don't believe you yet. But I think if anyone seems so certain of something, they deserve a chance to prove it."

She smiled so brightly, so reminiscent of those easy afternoons at her bookstore, that I thought she might actually forgive me for this after all was said and done.

If she was still alive, that is.

"When?" She pleaded.

"Most everyone is gone for the night. We'll go now."

You'd think I had promised her a million dollars the way her face lit with hope.

"You're sure about this? I can't save you if they want to kill you, Athena."

She nodded eagerly.

"They won't hurt me. They're mine." There was a sort of apparent certainty and confidence in her tone that made me believe her. At least believe her enough to let her try.

"Come on, we have to hurry." I loosened her bindings and helped her stand from the chair. Her legs nearly gave out beneath her from lack of use over the past few days. I cursed under my breath quietly, feeling overwhelming guilt over her treatment, or rather lack thereof.

"Stay close to me, ok?" I commanded, and she nodded eagerly.

Glancing out the door into the hallway, I quickly led Athena through the silent passageways of the Nameless Head Quarters. I felt her holding her breath behind me, in either eager anticipation at seeing her vampires again or fear of running into someone she shouldn't out here in the hall.

By either a stroke of luck or fate itself, we made it to the door to the holding cells without being spotted. When we arrived at the iron doors, I swallowed the lump in my throat, remembering the last time I stood there.

"Archer." Her whispered voice brought me back to reality. "Are you ok?"

I couldn't help the guilt that crested in my chest at the fact that she was worried about me even though I was her captor.

"The last time I walked through these doors, a vampire nearly killed me," I stated, holding up my wrist for her. Her green eyes scanned the scar that was present there.

"How long were they held captive?" She asked an edge of judgment in her tone. My eyebrows rose in response.

"I don't know…" I admitted, hating the way her question had me rethinking everything I had known to be true.

"Captivity can change a person," she whispered, adverting her eyes from mine, but the words found their mark in my gut.

"I have to ask one last time, Athena," I started. "Are you sure about this?"

"Positive," she replied quickly, without hesitation.

With a deep sigh, I inserted the thick key into the door and pushed it open. The dark hallway was just as I remembered—eerie and desolate. It seemed to stretch on endlessly, each cell identical in its quiet desolation. Every step we took reverberated through the corridor, echoing the sound of solitude.

As we pressed forward, the darkness ahead seemed to grow even more oppressive. The long path continued, and with each step, we descended further into the heart of this chilling dungeon, toward The Wanderers, toward the memory of my worst experience.

"Stay behind the line," I offered, closing the door behind us and effectively locking us in. My heart rate picked up violently as I moved closer to the cell that used to hold Evangeline.

"Athena?" I heard a whispered and strained voice from down the hall call out.

Next to me, Athena nearly squealed with excitement at the sound of the vampire's voice. She began to jog forward, and I rushed to keep up with her. The moment we arrived in front of The Wanderer's cages, I felt my stomach pit deepen.

"Oh my god," she gasped.

The vamps exploded into a chorus of exclamations.

"Baby, you're here!"

"Oh, bookworm. I missed you."

"Darlin', you're ok!"

And the one from the diner, Orpheus, sighed deeply, letting his head fall forward in relief. A look of pure love and adoration painted on each of their faces. Athena began to rush toward them, but I gripped her shoulder to keep her from crossing the line into their outstretched arms.

The Wanderers released a collective growl.

"What the fuck is he doing here?" The tattooed one asked, staring at me with a murderous gaze.

"Baby, are you ok? Are you hurt?" Samara asked, her eyes scanned the woman at my side. Either she was a skilled performer, or the worry was genuine.

"I'm ok, I promise," Athena whispered. I turned to see a tear sliding down her cheek. I couldn't comprehend what I was seeing. True and honest emotion. I knew that Athena had claimed to love these creatures, but truthfully, I believed she was simply under some sort of spell, lost in their intoxication. But watching the relief on these vampires' faces proved that not only did she love them, but the feeling was mutual. I also couldn't help but notice that they were still relatively lively. Typically, after this many days of not feeding, the vampires in captivity start to show signs of decomposition and aggravation, but not The Wanderers.

Curious.

"How did you get out?" The shorter blonde one asked. Athena turned over her shoulder to glance at me.

"He's giving me a chance to prove to him that you're being set up."

I observed their reactions. Shock and mild confusion flashed across their faces. Orpheus narrowed his eyes at me.

"What do you mean, little nymph?" he asked.

"They have a file on you here, of all the people.." she paused. "Of all the people they think you've killed.

"Let me guess," the tattooed man began. "All little kids and puppy dogs, right?" His eyes flicked over her shoulder to rest on me. "Typical, Nameless scum."

"You're monsters who survive on the blood of innocent human beings," I spat at him, although I'd be lying if I didn't admit that the phrase did not feel as definite as it once had.

"That rhetoric certainly would make it easier for your kind to commit genocide," Orpheus seethed, his dark eyes blazing.

"You'd have to be alive for it to be considered that," I barked back.

"Please, stop," Athena interjected, looking between us. I broke the heated eye contact with Orpheus and turned my eyes to her. "I'm here to prove to you that they didn't do that, right?" I nodded curtly. "So please, let me."

I scanned the vampires before me. Their features were primarily human despite their slightly darkened red eyes. I expected a frenzy. I expected their hunger to take over, erasing the humanity from their disguises.

Although Evangeline was once just as composed. Until I got closer.

"This is a bad idea," I whispered, drawing a hand through my hair. "They're going to kill you, Athena."

Each vamp let out a growl at my statement.

"If you think we'd hurt one hair on our mate's head, then you are more idiotic than I first suspected," the tattooed behemoth said through bared teeth.

"Archer, they won't hurt me," Athena assured me, her tone filled with a kind of trust I'd never experienced myself.

"What is he talking about, bookworm? What are you going to prove?"

She stepped forward, but my grip remained on her shoulder. "I'm going to let one of you drink from me. Then close the wound."

I instantly felt the collective hunger rise in the room. But it wasn't the kind of hunger that told me she was in danger, but rather the type of hunger that told me she was coveted and desired.

I scanned their lust-filled expressions, and my confusion only grew.

"Will you let them all feed from me?" Athena asked, eagerly turning her gaze to me. I looked over at her, seeing her pale face and remembering her aversion to eating anything we had provided over the last few days.

"Even if they won't drain you dry, having four vamps feed from you would kill you in your condition." The moment the words were out of my mouth, the vamps hissed.

"What have you done to her?" Orpheus seethed.

"What condition?" Samara begged.

"She hasn't eaten in days," I began. "On her own volition," I added when their gazes turned murderous.

"The Hunter is right, little nymph. You wouldn't be strong enough for each of us to feed on you. And well..." he paused, shame filling his expression. "We're all pretty hungry right now." It was the first time they had mentioned their hunger, and honestly, now that they did mention it, they didn't seem like the rabid animals my father always made them out to be. I didn't know if it was part of some game to get us to lower our guard or if they genuinely weren't feeling the effects of their hunger. Either way, Orpheus didn't seem to want to take any chances with Athena's health.

"If you can't control yourself, then we shouldn't do this," I stated matter-of-factly.

The tattooed one gripped the bars of his enclosure and glared at me. "We can control ourselves just fine."

Orpheus cleared his throat softly, and the others seemed to take a step back.

"Only one," I responded, scanning their faces.

"As much as it pains me to say it, I agree with the Hunter," Orpheus bit back. Athena nodded, accepting that condition, but then she let her gaze fall to the floor and idly played with her fingers.

"I... I can't choose. I won't choose," she replied after a moment.

"We won't ever make you choose, Athena. Never," the blonde responded in a soft southern lilt.

"It needs to be the one of us who's most in control at the moment, just to be safe," Orpheus replied diplomatically. Athena nodded, accepting that.

"So, which one of you is it, then? Who's more in control of themselves?" I watched their faces momentarily as they attempted to determine the answer.

I hated the thought of leaving it to chance and letting them decide something so huge and vital so arbitrarily. I had made the choice before I even realized it, and suddenly, the flesh on my arm split beneath where I had pressed the blade of my knife into my skin.

A test, I told myself as I watched their reactions to the fresh, warm blood that poured down my arm onto the ground below.

Their eyes tracked it almost immediately. Reddening. They pressed forward in their cells, their features sharpening into the monsters I knew them to be. But just when I was prepared to fight back, to reach for the stake in my waistband and protect myself and Athena from their vicious natures, they surprised me.

Taking deep breaths, The Wanderers did something I didn't know a vampire was even capable of.

They controlled themselves.

Their features softened as they shook their heads and took calming, steadying breaths.

The shock must have been on my face as I tried to make sense of the information swirling in my mind. It was Orpheus who spoke first. "There is a lot you don't understand about us, Hunter." His red eyes seared into mine, and for the first time, I thought I believed him.

I looked back between him and Athena, who was staring at him, all of them, with such love and admiration in her gaze.

"Go ahead," I whispered, hating how the words felt on my lips. I was effectively betraying everything I've ever known. Every lesson that had been force-fully drilled into my head. Every time my father told me a horrific story or every time I attended a Hunter's funeral after these violent and unstable crea-tures mutilated them.

My hand instinctively gripped the handle of the wooden stake in my waist-band as Athena rushed forward past the red line on the ground, and I braced myself for the tearing of flesh, the spilling of blood. Destruction. Death.

But it never came.

They didn't bite her. Instead, the moment she reached the first cage, she pushed her arms through the bars and embraced the creature within like they were her life source. The tattooed one held her back, breathing in her scent, but not once did his fangs penetrate her skin. Instead, he just soaked up the moment. When Athena repeated the process with each of the vamps, I watched in awe, unable to formulate any words. If it was all an act, it was one hell of a convincing one. She had tear-filled reunions with each of them, and with each passing second, years of hatred and fear began to slip away.

"Are you being treated well?" Orpheus asked tenderly as he flicked his eyes over to me briefly.

"Where they're holding me feels like a five-star hotel compared to these cells," she cried, tears slipping down her cheeks. "I've missed you all so much."

"We've missed you too, love," Samara added.

"I just found you. I can't lose you," Athena whispered, pain lacing every word. Her tears felt like barbed wire wrapping around my heart.

"We need to hurry," I choked out, hating how weak my voice sounded. I sounded broken. Like a man who just realized most of his beliefs have been wrong.

Athena wiped her wet eyes and nodded, turning back to her vamps. "I can't choose," she repeated.

I watched as Orpheus toiled over a decision in his mind. Eventually, he stepped forward, gripping Athena's hand through the bars and tenderly kissing the knuckles—an outpouring of emotion that I never expected from The Wanderers's vicious leader.

"Samara has the best self-control of all of us, and she'll be able to combat her hunger the easiest."

I waited to see if there would be some sort of argument or fight, but they all seemed to agree with Orpheus' assessment. They shared her love, affection, and blood so seamlessly, without a hint of reservation or jealousy. It was a strangely beautiful thing to witness.

Athena nodded, kissing Orpheus' hand where he held her before turning and stopping before Samara's cell. The vamp's eyes were full of intensity and heat. So much so that if I hadn't needed to witness the bite, I would have preferred to turn around and give them privacy.

Athena approached Samara slowly, their gazes locked together. When Samara reached out a hand through the cage and caressed Athena's cheek, pushing a strand of red hair behind her ear, I could feel the love bursting in the air.

"I will never hurt you," Samara whispered, bringing Athena's arm to her lips and planting a kiss on the inside of her wrist.

Athena let a small gasp out at the contact and nodded. "I know."

Then Samara sunk her fangs into the flesh of Athena's arm. My own scar burned with the phantom memory of the pain, and Evangeline's red, empty eyes flashed in my mind. I waited for Athena to call out in agony or to beg for my help. But instead, she let out the softest moan and caressed Samara's face as she drank. That alone would have been enough to shock me, but then Samara did something unbelievable.

She pulled away.

Her lips were painted red with Athena's blood, and her features had sharpened, but there was a humanity in her red eyes that there never was with Evangeline.

I found myself stepping forward, my eyes trained on the dark red wound on Athena's wrist that was obscured by flowing blood. Like a moth to the flame, I approached. Without letting Athena go, Samara let her tongue dance across the wound, a step that I was entirely unfamiliar with. We Hunters never stuck around long enough for a vamp to try something like that with us.

Samara pressed a kiss into Athena's palm, then placed her cheek there. Closing her eyes, she sighed, relishing in the physical contact.

When Athena pulled her hand back, she turned to find me hovering just behind her. She held out her arm for me, and I watched as the skin around the wound began healing. Slowly, nearly unnoticeable, but within a few minutes, Athena's pale skin was unblemished.

As if nothing happened.

I stumbled backward, my breath rushing out in ragged spurts.

"Archer, you see the truth now, don't you?"

I shook my head—not in disagreement, but in disbelief, in hurt. This truth could not exist simultaneously with all the truths I've ever known, and no matter how prepared I was to test the theory, I never considered this outcome.

"We need to get you back to the office," I muttered, unable to make eye contact with her.

"Archer, please," she pleaded.

"Athena, we're going to get out of here. I swear to you," Orpheus claimed, not even bothering to whisper in my presence. Maybe he saw just how broken I'd become and no longer saw me as a threat. Was I a threat? Could I be if I needed to be? I wasn't so sure anymore.

"We'll see you soon," the blonde promised lovingly.

"You're my soul, bookworm," the tattooed one pledged.

I needed to process new information, but until then, I had one last question to answer.

"Athena, please. We need to go now. I.. I need a minute to think about this," I begged.

She glanced at each of her vamps, placing a hand on her heart and nodding solemnly. "Ok. I'll go with you."

She stopped by my side and waited for me to lead her out. As we began our walk down the hall away from The Wanderers, I heard one of them call out.

"If she is harmed in any way, I will personally hold you responsible," Orpheus warned. I didn't turn to look at him. Instead, I quickly rushed Athena back through the iron doors at the end of the hall. She followed me silently, trusting me to guide her safely through the hallways back to the office.

She even allowed me to replace her bindings when we arrived. She was calm. Content.

"How are you so calm right now?" I asked incredulously. She sighed deeply before meeting my eyes.

"You let me see them," she claimed, a single tear sliding down her cheek. "I needed to see them."

My eyes trained on my father's desk— a sturdy wood behemoth, just as intimidating now as it was all those years ago. He never let me in here unaccompanied while I was growing up. He was rarely not occupying that leather chair, but now that his room had become a pseudo-holding cell, it meant that he had vacated the space for the time being. Leaving his things open and unguarded.

My feet carried me behind the desk before I could even stop them. I felt Athena's eyes on me, and I ignored the way they burned into my skin. The top drawer was relatively standard. Office supplies, post-its, pens, paperclips. It was strange thinking that a Vampire Hunter still had use for such mundane supplies. The next drawer was a little more detailed. Files on different vampire sightings and the personnel files on each of the cadets from this year's class. So many names of people being indoctrinated into this life the same way I was. The brand burned slightly as I scanned the files.

Three more drawers and I hadn't found anything that might explain this new development. All the while, Athena remained silent, just watching me. I almost gave up. I wasn't even sure what I thought I was going to find. Just something. Anything that could help me make sense of this jumbled mess in my mind.

Then I saw the latch.

Small, silver, hidden. Sucking in a deep breath of air, I pressed down. When a metallic release rang out, I could hear my blood running through my veins, echoing in the silent room.

The small compartment beneath the final drawer hung open, waiting for me to dive into the answers it held. I hesitated. I couldn't help it. Everything was changing, and something in my gut told me that the contents of this hidden compartment would ruin me. I sat crouched behind my father's desk, thankful that Athena's eyes couldn't reach me from where I was.

My hand slipped into the darkness and wrapped around the hilt of a metallic weapon. My heart pumped wildly, viciously, uncontrollably. Everything was leading up to this moment—my whole life, my training, meeting Athena, capturing The Wanderers, defying my father.

The weapon looked like a dagger, but instead of one long blade, there were two thin, pointed prongs in its place. It was like a thicker, more violent version of those skewers I used to roast marshmallows with, but something told me that this weapon was not used for such frivolity.

I rolled up my sleeve and slowly pressed the tips of the blades against my skin, where I had punctured it down in the cells. It stung, and I winced in pain. The hollow hilt warmed to the touch and whirred to life. Suddenly, the small blade emanated a soft glow, and as if it were being vacuumed, my blood was drawn by the device, drained from my vein, and pooled into the hilt. I cried out and pulled the blade from my skin, stopping the painful process before it could do anything else. As the blade was lifted from my skin, there they were. Two perfect puncture wounds. It was not unlike all the photos I had shown Athena, albeit it was much shallower. Every photo. Every single one.

My head was spinning, and my heart thumped in my chest as I stared at my blood that now sat in a thin layer within the hollow hilt.

Shock. Grief. Anger. Betrayal.

There was no chance of me sorting through my emotions at that moment, but one thing was sure. I needed to get out of this room as soon as possible. Without bothering to clean the blade, I threw it back into the compartment and closed it. Standing from my crouched position, I ambled toward Athena, who simply watched me.

There were a million things I wanted to say, but I couldn't find a single word worthy of the current state of my thoughts.

I glanced over at the day-old food that sat untouched on my father's desk.

"I'll get new food sent up for you." I began to leave, but I heard her call out my name. I paused, unwilling to turn to see her, tied to that chair by my hand.

"You know, don't you? You know that they didn't do this. Please, tell me you see it."

I swallowed the lump in my throat and fought the sting in my eyes.

"I have to go," I mumbled before rushing out of the office door and locking it behind me. I couldn't catch a full breath if I wanted to.

And I'm not so sure I wanted to.

8

LAZ

On the morning of our twelfth day in captivity, Bennett decided to see how Vampires reacted to being doused in holy water. He started with Silas. It was a clever tactic. Honestly, I had to hand it to him. Silas was the most physically strong of the four of us, so when his screams echoed through the cages, it was a clear indication that we were in for some pain. If even the strongest among us couldn't handle the torture, we stood no chance. He took Samara next, and in true Samara fashion, she managed to hold in her screams for a while, but even her iron will eventually stood no chance against the burning liquid. I wondered how much of her longer resistance had to do with the blood of our mate that flowed through her body. I knew Orpheus' plan was for us to convince Bennett that we were in much worse shape than we truly were, but something about her screams and the way Silas was still shivering in pain in his cage told me there wasn't a whole lot of pretending going on.

Because Bennett and Orpheus had some strange 'macho stand-off' energy between them, and his idea of torture for our leader is to make him wait for his turn and listen to the pained screams of his coven, I was next.

In another horrific display of their torturous renovation of these cells, three small sprinkler heads lowered from the ceiling, and a moment later, the evil little spouts were showering me with liquid death. It sliced against my back as I crumbled to my knees with a scream trapped in my throat. The physical pain had always been something that didn't affect me as hard as the emotional and mental anguish I had faced in my life, but damn, first the sun, then the holy water. It was enough to make me reconsider.

I pushed all thoughts from my head as I let the water wash over me, drenching my clothing and clinging to every inch of my skin. It burnt the way acid might affect a human. It was vicious and violent. A perfect cocktail. Three parts holy water and one part garlic. Nice touch, I thought as I analyzed the makeup of the liquid. It hurt. Unimaginably. I let my mind focus on her, my mate. Her soft red curls, her stunning green eyes, the way her lips part slightly when she's experiencing pleasure. Her image, so clearly burned into my mind, was the one thing that could soften the sting of the water against my skin. I focused on the chemical mixture. I felt its contents as it poured onto my skin. Despite the strength she gave me, I still felt the fierce sting pelt against me. Fuck, I'd give anything for this to be nice soothing water right about now.

The mixture continued its persistent assault on my skin, but with each passing second, the sting subsided until the liquid running down my skin felt almost...relieving?

I focused on it. I felt the chemical makeup of it in my mind. It couldn't be true. But it was.

It was water.

I glanced at Bennett out of the corner of my eye, expecting him to make some comment about it, but he didn't. Instead, he watched with evil intensity as his torture continued.

Had I done that? Had I changed the chemical makeup of his holy water acid? I'd never been able to do such a thing before. I covered the smile that played on my lips with my fingers and sent a warming embrace down the bond to my mate. The woman whose love made me powerful. The woman who made me a better version of myself.

Stay strong, Laz.

I heard her voice echo in my head.

Athena, darlin', is that you?

I called back through the channels of my mind.

It's me. I'm here! You can hear me!

I nearly smiled, but I knew that Bennett was watching closely, so I hid the movement of my lips with a snarl before calling back to her through the channels of my mind.

I can hear you.

I felt her joy push through the bond.

I feel your fear, Laz. It's ok. We will get through this. Together.

I felt my heart nearly burst from the adoration I held for her as I responded.

I know we will.

The mental connection faltered, then slipped away, but her strength remained.

With her in my heart, I could withstand any pain.

But Bennett couldn't know that.

So, I fell to my knees and screamed out in agony, maybe a little over the top, but hey, it wasn't often that I was given the opportunity to put on a little show. When the water stopped, relief flooded my body. I felt Samara's healing touch graze my back, working at undoing the damage the water had done before my gift worked its magic, but I didn't dare let that relief show. Instead, I held my knees to my chest and heaved long and labored breaths. I heard Samara and Silas doing the same. The Hunters would be letting their guard down any day now. They have been torturing us and withholding blood from us. They will be expecting us to be weak. The truth is, at this moment, I've never felt stronger.

Bennett whispered some overt taunt to Orpheus before turning on the spouts in his cell. I heard Orpheus let out a grunt of pain as the mixture landed on his skin. I closed my eyes tightly, focusing on the rushing water's sound, feeling how it hit the ground and spread across the concrete floor. I willed for the harmful chemicals within the water to dissipate, begging my mind and my power to remove anything that could hurt him.

I couldn't tell right away if it had worked. Sounds of agony echoed from Orpheus' cell, and it was so convincing that I couldn't tell if it was real or his attempt at convincing Bennett. But when I focused on the liquid again, it had run clear. The water was pure and harmless.

I heard Bennett take cautious steps toward Orpheus' cell when the rushing water subsided.

"Why are you doing this?" Orpheus pleaded, and I couldn't contain the smile on my face. I let my chin fall to the floor so nobody could see the joy on my face. There isn't a universe where Orpheus would beg like that. He was pretending. Which meant we were winning.

"Our world would be better off without your kind," Bennett spat back. I rolled my eyes. 'Blah blah blah, racist shit.' That's all he ever said, like a broken record of unyielding hatred. I couldn't wait to kill him. Bigots really got me riled up.

"Why won't you just kill us?" Orpheus cried out. Oh, he was good. Let the Hunter see weakness and get him to show his hand.

Bennett chuckled darkly, a great sign that an evil villain monologue was about to occur. "I'll kill you when I'm good and ready," he responded.

"You're a monster," Orpheus seethed.

"Oh, I'm the monster? That's rich, coming from you lot," he was becoming unhinged— exactly where we needed him. "Always hiding in the shadows. Preying on the helpless. You monsters aren't worthy of the gifts you receive."

Bingo.

"We didn't ask for these gifts," Orpheus whispered, playing directly into his hand.

"Well, soon enough, you won't have to worry about those anymore." Bennett stepped away, letting his murderous gaze wash over each of us before he headed down the long corridor and disappeared behind the metallic door.

Standing, I attempted to wipe the excess liquid from my clothing as Samara spoke.

"What happened, Orpheus?" She sounded almost frantic. "When I went to heal you, I didn't feel any injury." I smiled brightly.

"I'm not sure," he responded.

"You can thank me for that," I called out softly, making my way to the bars of my cage and leaning my arms on the cool metal.

"What do you mean?" Silas asked, grunting as he stood to his feet.

"I guess it's my fun little upgrade courtesy of our mate," I beamed, feeling so proud of my bond with my beautiful Athena.

"You could manipulate the contents of the water?" Orpheus whispered as a question, but his incredulous tone told me he already knew the answer.

"What the hell, why didn't you stop mine? Hurt like a fucking bitch," Silas griped.

"I didn't realize I could until it happened to me," I called back.

"So far, all of us, save for Silas, have received some sort of power upgrade," Orpheus began.

"You still haven't told us what your fancy new skill is, Orpheus," Silas teased. "And I already have the coolest power ever, no upgrade needed, thank you very much."

I chuckled at that, and the others joined in with soft, gleeful laughter. As our laughs settled, I sighed deeply.

"We have been here for over a week and were just tortured, and yet here we are...laughing," I whisper. The others release their own content sighs. We all knew the reason for our strengthened resolve this time around. It was her.

"When we make our move, we're going to need to kill them all." It was Silas who first broke the silence. "We all agree on that, right?"

I nodded but didn't voice the words. It was the only logical choice, but that didn't mean it was any less daunting. Even with our strength intact, they outnumbered us at least ten to one. They were intimately aware of our weaknesses and were trained on how to exploit them. It's the reason they were such a formidable opponent. The reason that so many of our kind have been eradicated. That is why we were among the few covens left, as far as we know.

"It's been almost two weeks. When are we doing this, Orpheus?" Samara asked, an eagerness to her tone.

I heard him take a deep breath and walk a few paces within his cell. I imagined him wringing out the water from his clothes and running a hand through his tangled mop of hair.

"They're after our gifts. Bennet and his useless big mouth just made that abundantly clear. As far as we know, they are only aware of yours, Silas. From the last escape."

I shuddered as the memory of that night came into focus.

"We can't let them discover what we can do, especially not now that our powers have grown. If they put it together if they find out why we're stronger now..." He didn't have to finish that thought. We knew. If the Hunters knew that Athena's bond to us was what made us stronger, they would either try to turn her to see what sort of amplification happened when we were all vampires. Or... they'd eliminate the bond and weaken us.

I refused to let either of those things happen.

Not like this.

"So tomorrow?" Silas prompted.

There was an anxious silence that filled the cells then. Despite the newfound upgrades and the game we had been playing, we still had to perform the Herculean task of escaping the Hunter's facility for a second time. And I knew I wasn't the only one thinking about how not all of us made it out last time around.

Five in, four out.

And that was when all of us were vampires, strong, fast, and powerful. This time, we had a human to protect. This time, there were five in... and we were going to do everything in our power to get five out. No matter the cost.

"Tomorrow," Orpheus responded. "We make our move tomorrow."

9

ATHENA

Two thousand, eight hundred and twenty-three.

After finishing my count of the ceiling and floor tiles in this room for the seventh time, I released a long and pain-filled sigh. It had been a few days since I saw my Wanderers, and I was getting restless. I felt their absence so profoundly, so viciously, but another sharp pain was snaking its way through my soul. Just the thought of what my absence was doing to my grandma was enough to wrench a sob from my chest. She's been through too much lost too many people. I wish I could tell her I was alive. That I was ok. That I was coming home.

After Mom passed, Grandma was the one who remained strong while I fell apart at the seams. Her gentle strength was steadfast and comforting. To anyone, it seemed she was handling the loss incredibly well. But I knew her better than that. She was broken. Her soul had splintered, and in the absence of two pieces of her heart, she was lost. She refused to show that to anyone, though. I pressed my eyes tight, trying to picture her face, latching onto her memory in search of that same comfort.

"Are you ready, Athena? Guests are arriving." My grandma called from the base of the stairs. I was jolted from my thoughts. My feet had brought me down the hall toward my mother's room. As I looked into the space from the safety of the threshold, the air felt heavy with grief and the remnants of happy and horrific memories. The sunlight filtered through the soft white and blue curtains, casting a muted glow on the familiar surroundings that had once been filled with the warmth of my mother's soul. Everything seemed frozen in time as if the world outside had moved on while this

room remained suspended in a bittersweet moment. This room hadn't been hers in a while, not since she stopped being able to make the trip up the stairs.

The bed was neatly made with the light purple comforter we'd picked out together. The floral pattern on the bedspread, once a comforting sight, now felt like a distant echo of happier days. A photograph on the bedside table of the time when Mom, Grandma, Grandpa, and I went to the Zoo. Those frozen smiles seemed to mock the somber reality of the world I found myself in now. Half of those smiles were gone now.

"Almost," I called back, trying to turn my head away from the site before me but finding myself unable to tear my eyes from the ghosts of the past. My feet moved on their own, taking step after cautious step into her space.

The silence was palpable, broken only by the occasional creak of the floorboards beneath my tentative feet. The room echoed with memories. Each piece of furniture held a story of its own. The dresser we painted together in the backyard. The purple plush loveseat we saw on the side of the road that she fell in love with and begged me to help carry the three blocks home in the rain. The books on the shelf she would read to me when I couldn't sleep, and the books she swore she would read one day but never got the chance to. The bed where I would crawl beneath the covers in the middle of the night when I couldn't sleep and I felt like the monsters under the bed would get me. She'd brush my hair out of my eyes and hold me tight, promising me that monsters didn't exist.

I heard a soft murmur of conversation drifting up from the stairs, reminding me of the world outside – a world that continued to move forward.

Summoning the strength to leave the room, I took a deep breath and steadied myself, breathing in the lingering scent of her perfume. How long until that scent dissipates? When you lose someone, you lose them a million little times. Over and over and over again. I will lose her the first time I watch a sunset without her. The first time I hear her favorite song. The first time I take a deep breath in this room and, her scent doesn't greet me. The first time I find the love of my life and she isn't there to walk me down the aisle. I have a harrowing feeling that I'd be losing my mom for the rest of my life—a little bit more each and every day.

The hallway felt endless as I made my way toward the staircase. As I descended, the murmur of voices grew louder. The somber atmosphere of the wake encircled me before I even reached the bottom landing.

As I entered the living room, the sting in my eyes intensified as I watched friends and family huddle together, sharing stories and offering condolences. Mom would have loved to have everyone she cared about in one room like this. All the business owners from the pier, Davia, her family, our neighbors, and the community members who knew and loved her. They were all here. There, at the heart of it all, stood my grandmother. She smiled a soft sort of grin that was a beacon of resilience.

Though clouded with the same grief that we all shared, her eyes bore a quiet *strength that perplexed me. She had weathered her own storms, lost her own battles, and emerged on the other side, and still managed to smile. I couldn't fathom the sort of strength required for that kind of feat. Grandma noticed me standing at the base of the stairs, and with a gentle nod, she beckoned me to her side. In that simple gesture, she conveyed a silent understanding that needed no words. As I approached, she enveloped me in a tender embrace, her arms a source of comfort in the midst of sorrow.*

With a soft squeeze, Grandma guided me to join the crowd of people gathered. She spoke of fond memories, shared anecdotes that celebrated my mother's life, and expertly navigated the delicate line between grief and remembrance.

Amid my mother's wake, surrounded by tearful eyes and heavy hearts, I couldn't help but marvel at her strength. In that moment, as we faced the collective ache of saying goodbye to my mother and all the memories we had shared, I found solace in the last remaining member of my family.

Tears fell down my cheeks and landed on my lap as I let myself wallow in the misery of knowing what my absence was doing to her. To them all. Another constricting sob spilled from my throat as I considered Davia. Would I ever see them again? Would I ever see the shop again? Even if I somehow escaped this, would I ever be able to return home? If I had to choose between my mates and my family... I couldn't do it. Even the thought of being forced to decide had my stomach turning over painfully.

The door handle turned, and I willed the tears to slow, composing myself as best I could. I didn't want Archer to see me at my weakest. My body tensed as I braced for the confrontation. My shoulders were screaming at the pain of being bound behind my back for so long. I was sure they would be permanently damaged if it weren't for Samara's gentle touch that came to me each night to ease the continuous ache. Footsteps inside were followed by the door closing once again. He hadn't said anything yet, so I kept my head down.

He waited by the door for a moment before turning to head for the desk. It wasn't until he had taken a few steps that a dangerous realization came to me. That wasn't how Archer walked. The gait was off, and the pattern was more assured. Archer walked around me as if he felt like I could break with one wrong move. No, these steps were confident, strong, and heavy. I lifted my head just enough to peer up at the figure through the curtain of my lashes and unkempt hair that had fallen into my face.

His broad shoulders were draped in a well-tailored black suit. His dark, auburn hair was neatly combed away from his face. He had a prominent brow bone and a sharp jaw that carried the slightest echo of a 5 o'clock shadow. I had never seen this man before, and yet something about him seemed familiar. He didn't turn to look at me but ruffled through some of the things on the desk.

What was he looking for? I diverted my eyes from him as his shoulders squared to face me.

"You must be wondering who I am."

I was, but I didn't let him know that.

"I don't think it's in our best interests to share personal details just yet." His voice was grave, like he had lost his voice recently, and his timbre was still a result of that. "So you can call me J."

I didn't respond, and I didn't raise my eyes to meet his. He slowly made his way around the desk toward me. Instinctually, I shied away from his advances. He stopped just a few feet short and leaned back on his desk, crossing his legs at the ankle and folding his arms across his chest. I couldn't tell without looking at him, but it seemed like my reaction amused him. Perhaps fear was a response he expected from his prisoners, and I was delivering.

"This is my office that you've been holed up in. Can't say I'm too happy about the stench."

I cringed. Truthfully, I'd gotten a little nose blind to myself. Archer and the other door guard brought me food. When Archer couldn't be bothered to show his face, both let me use the restroom when needed, but I still hadn't taken a shower.

They offered to let me take one a few days ago, but the idea of being naked in this place, being vulnerable with all these men around me, thinking I'm their prisoner? Not a chance. If my *stench* kept them from placing their hands on me, then I would wear it proudly.

"I'm sure Archer told you why you've been here for so long," he prompted, but again I stayed quiet. If you let someone talk long enough, they are bound to give away their secrets. "Chatty little girl, aren't you?" He grumbled frustratedly.

He unfolded his arms to grab the desk on either side of his hips that rested on the edge. His fingertips rapped against the wood for a few painfully quiet moments. Finally, he sighed and pushed off the desk to step forward. I forced my body not to react. I refused to give this man an ounce of the fear he so clearly craved.

"Maybe I can see why my son has been wasting all this time getting you to cooperate," he whispered under his breath. Son? I tried to picture Archer with a similar hair shade, and it was so clear. Of course. That's why he seemed so familiar. I'd seen those features in my captor.

"I do not cooperate with kidnappers," I stated with as steady a voice as I could muster. He seemed pleased that I had finally responded.

"Clearly." He then moved to another side of the room, opposite the big desk. He opened a cabinet I had found myself staring at on more than one occasion and grabbed a glass container with a dark amber liquid swirling inside. He poured a shot into an empty glass and replaced the carafe. All the while, I watched his back. He was strong and confident. He was playing a mind game with me, and I wouldn't let him.

"So, J, are you here to tell me I get to go home now?" I asked, trying to craft a facade of bravado for the intimidating figure in front of me. He turned again, and I kept my eyes hidden behind my hair but watched him with rapt attention. Each move he made was deliberate, like a well-choreographed dance—perfectly designed to intimidate and scare me.

"Give me a reason why I should," he asked casually as if he was considering accepting my business proposal and not deciding the fate of my freedom.

"I'm not a threat to you." It was the truth. I wanted no part of whatever was happening here. I wanted to leave this place with my mates and never return or think about this time of our lives again.

"It does not take physical strength to be a threat to me," he started, taking a long drink from his glass. "That is a guarded secret, something I work very hard to ensure my enemies never learn."

"I'm not your enemy."

"But you know who my enemy is. And my son tells me you've become very comfortable with them."

I swallowed deeply. How much did Archer tell him?

"Did your son also tell you that The Wanderers are being framed for everything you think they've done?"

This caught him off guard. For the first time since he walked through the door, there was a moment when the perfectly designed exterior cracked. It was gone before I could even register that it had happened, but I had thrown him off.

I could do it again.

"So, you do know what they are and what they've done," he mused once he had composed himself.

"Allegedly," I replied. He choked out a soft laugh.

"Were the graphic photos in this file still not enough to convince you?" He accused, his hands sliding through the discarded files on his desk.

"They didn't do that," I spat.

"You don't know what you're talking about, little girl."

"I'm not a fucking 'little girl' so stop calling me that!" I barked. He held his hands up in feigned surrender and chuckled.

"What's your name?" He asked.

"Thought we weren't sharing personal details," I tossed back, lacing my tone with as much indignation as possible.

"Let me tell you how this is going to go, little girl," he seethed, spitting those words with so much venom I almost felt my chest go numb as they found purchase. "You're either going to tell me what you know about The Wanderers, or you're going to die."

"I don't really like those options," I whispered, buying some time to think.

"Too fucking bad, you're forgetting who has all the power here."

"Hard to remember when I have no idea who you are. As far as I know, Archer is the one in charge here."

He rushed forward, another crack in the facade. I braced myself for his attack, but he stopped himself just before his hand made contact with my cheek.

"You're trying to rile me up," he said with pride like he had just deduced something impossible.

"It's working," I replied, lowering my chin to hide the smirk on my lips.

I could practically hear his teeth grinding from here.

"You want to defend those monsters down there, huh? What makes you think they didn't do what they're accused of?"

I could tell him the same thing I told Archer about the closing of the wounds, but something about the way his breathing was becoming ragged told me this man before me only had so much restraint left, and fuck, for some reason, I didn't want him to hurt Archer. I have no idea why I cared what happened to that traitor, but damnit. I did.

"Because I know them, they wouldn't do that."

His laugh had ice running through my veins.

"Oh, I see what's going on here. Did you whore yourself out to them? Is that it? Are you their fucking blood bag?"

My blood boiled.

"Do not call me that."

"Ah, I've hit a nerve then. You'll sleep with blood-sucking murderers, but you'll draw the line at being called a whore? How self-righteous of you."

"If anyone is a murderer here, it's you."

The composure he had held such a tight grip on had snapped, and he pressed forward, leaning down into my space. His hand grabbed at my chin and forcefully pulled it up so that I was forced to make unhindered eye contact with him for the first time. His emerald eyes burned with anger, and his lips were pulled back in a snarl. His hand on my skin sent a shockwave of panic through my body, and I couldn't control the fear then. What was he going to do to me? Could I stop him?

As I began spiraling, I saw his eyebrows furrow as he took in my face. His unfamiliar gaze held me captive as a shadow of an emotion passed across his hardened face.

"What is your name?" He asked again, his tone more inquisitive than angry this time.

When I didn't answer, choosing instead to suck in lungfuls of cool air to stave off the panic attack that threatened to claim me, he pulled back, dropping my chin and taking deliberate steps backward.

As he left, a strange look twisted his features, a mix of confusion and something more profound – a vulnerability that contradicted the menacing aura he exuded. His eyes once filled with a cold intensity, now held a hint of turmoil, as if an unexpected revelation had shaken him to the core. I strained against my restraints, watching with a mix of fear and curiosity as he cast one last glance back at me. There was a momentary hesitation in his step, a pause that betrayed an internal struggle. It was as if the walls he had meticulously built around himself were crumbling, revealing a vulnerability he hadn't anticipated.

When he left, closing the door behind him and leaving me alone in darkness once again, I didn't feel the similar sense of dread and fear close in around me. Whoever he was, he was affected by what I had said, by what he saw in here. For just a moment, I felt like maybe, just maybe, we could win.

10

ARCHER

The dull thud of my wrapped hands meeting the heavy bag echoed through the dimly lit gym. Beads of sweat trickled down my forehead as I unleashed a barrage of punches, each strike a desperate attempt to drown out the nagging doubts that had taken residence in my mind.

The rhythmic sound of flesh meeting fabric became my makeshift therapy. With its cold metallic scent and flickering fluorescent lights, the gym was a refuge where I could grapple with the guilt and confusion that clung to me like a heavy shadow. The pain against my knuckles was the last thing keeping me grounded. With each jab, I tried to silence the voices questioning my cause's validity. Was I fighting for the right side, or was I mindlessly following a path that had been hand-crafted by my father to promote death and destruction? The bag absorbed my uncertainty as I let the turmoil loose in each punch.

As I threw hooks and crosses, I couldn't shake the image of the kind-hearted redhead being held hostage in the office just a floor beneath my feet. Her words lingered in my mind like a haunting melody, a discordant reminder that taunted the possibility that she held a truth I was unwilling to acknowledge. The guilt gnawed at me, threatening to unravel the very fabric of my convictions.

The heavy bag swung in response to my blows, an unwitting partner in this internal battle. As I threw myself into the workout, I couldn't stop the onslaught of worry that maybe my father and this cause I was fighting for was, in fact, wrong.

My father's convictions were so strong, so steadfast, I had unquestioningly believed them. I considered them the indisputable truth, but Athena's convictions are just as strong. She was just as convinced that her Wanderers were the victims here as my father was convinced they were the monsters. How do you uncover the truth when both sides believe they're on the right side of history? Flashes of facts, memories, and conflicting truths that I had been force-fed flooded my mind with each punch of the bag.

Evangeline had bitten me. She was going to kill me.

She was being held captive and tortured.

The Wanderers killed that missing guy.

He tried to hurt Athena.

My father had some strange device that leaves behind vampire bites.

Vampire bites can close.

The Wanderers didn't kill Athena when they had the chance.

My father wouldn't do the same....

Breathing heavily, I finally relented, letting my battered hands fall to my side as I stepped away from the heavy bag. The gym's air felt thick with the residue of my internal struggle. With a sense of purpose, or perhaps desperation, I approached the gym's exit.

As I descended the stairs, the weight of all this uncertainty closed in on me, making me feel claustrophobic. I had made a choice, one that would have me walking a tightrope between loyalty and doubt. I would listen to her. She deserved to tell her side of this story, and I needed to hear it.

I'd listen to her and come to my own conclusions. Then, I would make the choice that had been looming over me for the last two weeks.

The corridor was empty, except for the owner of a muffled voice coming from around the corner near Athena's room. As I approached, I lightened my steps and listened as the familiar voice became clearer.

"Listen, I just wanted to check in." My father's voice sounded calm on the outside, and to anyone else, the demeanor would be believable, but I knew his tells and could hear the slight hitch and the way his voice pitched up. He was nervous. Shaken. I hugged the wall and carefully listened, straining to hear the voice on the other end of the conversation.

A muffled sound echoed from a phone speaker. It was too quiet to make out any words, but the feminine voice seemed frantic.

"Wait, slow down," he urged. Another few moments of quiet as he listened to the response. "Yes, we got them. I told you we would. But that's not why I'm calling. How is Athena?"

I furrowed my brow. Was this his mysterious contact? The one who told him we would find The Wanderers in Shockgrove. Why was he asking them about Athena?

"How long?" He followed up, a tenseness in his tone that I'm not sure I've heard since the day I crossed the red line. The voice responded, and I heard my father groan a pain-filled, angry sound.

"Why the fuck didn't you call me?" he hissed. The voice on the phone raised, and I knew my father was getting an earful for the tone he just used. "Right, no, I know... I was busy. Fuck." He groaned as the memory of Carmen's name appearing on his phone at the bar returned to me. "You should have tried harder to reach me," he accused. "Because I'm pissed off, Carmen. I'm her fucking father. I should have known she was missing."

My blood ran cold, and my lungs weren't capable of taking a breath. My father's cryptic conversation suddenly made chilling sense, and the weight of his words settled over me with a suffocating intensity. As the words reverberated in my mind, a nauseating realization dawned. Our hostage, the woman I'd kidnapped, the woman who I betrayed, was not merely a stranger caught in a dangerous battle with the monsters of the night....

She was my sister.

The world around me seemed to warp. The walls felt like they were closing in as I grappled with the enormity of this revelation.

"I'll fix this," my father spat before hanging up the phone. I slid down onto the floor, my legs unable to hold the weight of both me and this new secret. My father's breaths came in rapid spurts. I'd never witnessed him having a panic attack, but if he did, I'd assume it would sound something like this.

"Fuck!" He yelled, and a crashing sound came not long after. His phone exploded into pieces as the tech splintered against the wall and slid across the ground. He stormed off in the opposite direction, luckily for me, because I was not sure I could move from this spot if the building came crumbling down around me.

I don't know how long I sat there, flipping through my childhood memories, combing through each one, and looking for a clue, some indication that my father had this monumental secret. There was nothing—nothing I could think of that might have pointed to this entire other family that my father left behind.

Athena told me how old she was during one of our conversations, and I was less than a year younger. At the time, she teased me about it almost like a sibling would. What happened in that short time to force my father away from her and into his new family?

I felt sick to my stomach, and the walls around me were spinning. His lies had kept my sister from me. What else could he be lying about?

There wasn't guilt in my chest anymore. At least not the kind that worried me about questioning my father and everything he'd taught me. Our entire relationship was a lie. My whole life was a lie. When I stood from my seat on the floor and braced myself on the wall, I felt determination. Clarity.

The walk to her room was short, but it may as well have been miles. By the time I approached her door, I had made the choice that just an hour ago weighed so heavily on my chest and felt impossible.

When the door opened, she raised her eyes to meet mine, and something I can only describe as regret and love overtook my senses. How could I have possibly missed it? The more I looked at her, the more the intricate tapestry of our shared lineage unfolded. The red hair, the green eyes — they were markers of a hidden connection that now bound us together. She was my sister, undeniably.

She looked relieved to see me. Something I felt entirely too unworthy of. Her eyes searched mine with a mix of surprise and hope. The air between us crackled with unspoken words, the weight of our shared history hanging like an invisible thread.

"Are you okay?" I asked, my voice a low murmur.

She nodded, the confusion evident in her eyes. "I wasn't sure you were going to come back."

I stepped toward her, determined and resolute. She didn't shy away but instead watched me with rapt attention as I crossed behind her and cut through the bindings at her wrists, freeing her.

She said nothing, but I felt her questioning gaze burn into my skin.

I held out a hand, and she took it tentatively, rising from the confines of her captivity. The room seemed to expand as we stood there, siblings who were now united by a shared determination to unravel the truth. But she couldn't know that. I wouldn't be responsible for telling her who had done this to her. She had already lost so much in her life. I couldn't be the one to give her a father only for him to be a monster.

"What are you doing?" She whispered, fear lacing her tone. She didn't trust me. I deserved that, but damn if it didn't hurt to know that my actions had caused my sister harm. It was the fear in her gaze and the nerves in her voice that spurred me forward. There wasn't a doubt in my mind any longer. The choice had been made.

"I'm going to get you out of here, Athena. I'm setting you free."

11

ORPHEUS

It was well into the evening when her emotions slammed into me. Since we completed the mate bond, I have been able to feel her more intensely. Honestly, I'd been able to feel everything more intensely. But her emotions felt different this time than they had these last few days. It wasn't fear that she was feeling panic or anger; instead, I felt relief and hope flood her. It was a euphoric rush of positive emotions that I hadn't felt from her since we last saw her. Something had made her happy...hopeful. I hated not being able to form that mental connection with her that both Samara and Laz had, but that fact didn't make me jealous as it may have at one point in time. Instead, I was thankful that at least one of us had been able to connect with her so she didn't feel so alone.

Leaning forward against the cool bars of the cage, I focused on her and the hope radiating from her emotions. Despite being a dangerous energy to feel in a place like this, it warmed my chest. I couldn't help but wonder what had her risking disappointment to feel it now.

"Laz, Samara, have either of you spoken to Athena tonight?" I whispered, knowing my coven had heard me just fine. Despite being trapped for two weeks, our strength remained relatively intact. Thanks to our mate. We would need blood soon, but we weren't withering away like we had been at this point of our last capture.

"Not yet," Samara offered.

"No, I tried earlier but couldn't get through," Laz added. "Why?"

"I feel her, it's strong."

I heard Silas rush to the bars of his cage quickly before hissing in my direction, "Is she hurt? What are they doing?" His emotions slammed into me, forcing their way inside my mind and body.

"I'll heal her!" Samara growled.

"If they hurt one hair on her head, I swear..." Laz joined.

I nearly doubled over at the force of their worry. Fucking hell. I was highly susceptible to their emotions lately. It had been getting worse the last few days. The last torture session with Bennett nearly ripped the breath from my lungs. I hadn't noticed any fundamental shift in my power since that first day other than the potency of the emotions I felt. I knew that something happened, but so far, all that's changed is that it was getting stronger, and not in the way I'd necessarily prefer. I pressed a hand to my temple and rubbed. It was frustratingly agonizing, feeling everything so intensely all the time. My family's pain during the torture sessions was the one thing that genuinely threatened to topple every ounce of resolve I had.

"Please calm down," I bit back, harsher than I needed to, but I needed them to get a grip on themselves and soon. "You're killing me."

"Sorry," Laz whispered, and I noticed them settle into a calmer latent worry rather than the fierce stabbing concern I'd just felt.

"She's not in pain or afraid. In fact, she's feeling almost hopeful?" I whispered because even though we had been holding onto the clear confidence that we would survive this, hope was still a dangerous thing to harbor.

"Hopeful?" Silas clarified as his emotions returned to his standard tense resting rate.

"She's relieved about something," I added, focusing again on her damn near gleeful emotions now that my coven had settled their own.

"What would she feel relieved about in here?" Laz asked. I shook my head, unable to answer.

"Maybe that Hunter is bringing her back to see us," Samara offered hopefully. She had been the one to benefit the most from Athena's last visit, having fed on her. The moment when Samara fed on her, I felt every second of the euphoric rush. Every ounce of drained blood felt like it ran through my own veins. It was a blinding bloodlust. I had not felt the emotions of a feeding that intensely in my entire existence. It felt like I had been the one whose lips were pressed against her skin, and my fangs that were piercing her arm. But it didn't offer any reprieve from the desperate need I felt. It only made me more ravenous for her.

"Bennett's boy," Silas added. "When we get out of here and start ripping out throats, remind me to start with him."

"He brought Athena to us," Samara countered.

"He captured us," Silas responded.

I felt their blood boiling and their fury beginning to ramp up again. "Please, both of you, stop getting worked up for five goddamn minutes," I exclaimed, pressing my fingers to my temples.

"What's wrong with you?" Laz asked softly after a few moments.

"Nothing," I tossed out. But they weren't having that.

"Tell us the truth, Orpheus," Laz demanded calmly.

"The mate bond amplified my power," I began, rubbing calming little circles into the sides of my skull.

"That's a good thing, right?" Silas asked, but I could feel Samara's pity overpower anything else.

"You're getting overwhelmed by it all, aren't you?" Samara added quietly. I nodded, knowing she couldn't see me, but I didn't want to give voice to the concerns.

"I don't get it. What's going on with your power?" Silas asked with a twinge of worry flaring in his emotions.

"It's like... every radio station in the entire county is playing at full volume simultaneously," I tried to explain. It was a pitiful comparison, but there weren't really words that could accurately describe just how vicious the feelings were when they all flooded in.

At that moment alone, I could feel Athena's relief, my coven's worry and pity, Bennett's fury somewhere in the compound, and various pools of fear, anger, and happiness seeping from each guard within the building—all at once.

"Damn," Silas relented.

"Yes, well, it would help a lot if you could keep yourselves under control and don't go flying off the handle," I nearly begged. I hated how weak my voice sounded. I needed to get a handle on this and fast if I wanted to keep a level head.

"We'll try," Laz promised. "Won't we?" They prompted.

"Well, yeah, but I can't promise anything," Silas said. I sighed softly as I felt the guilt rush through him. He often felt things the strongest of the four of us. I didn't even need to use my ability to know how he was feeling most of the time, but I knew he would try. That was enough for now.

"So, Athena is feeling hopeful. Can you tell why?" Samara offered, bringing us back to the conversation.

"No, but it's strong." I tried to tune out everything else to focus on her. The energy radiating off of her was getting closer. "She's coming this way." Rustling sounds from the other cells echoed as my coven each stepped forward and tried to lean through the bars.

Another set of emotions began to overpower hers as she neared our hallway. This feeling was fueled by anxious nerves but held an undertone of guilt, regret, and determination. The emotions of someone who has done wrong but was fixated on making it right.

The door at the end of the hall slid open quietly. We may never have heard it if it weren't for our enhanced hearing. Someone was being covert. I braced myself for a fight, taking a steadying breath to stave off the torrent of emotions swirling around in my chest. I'm not even sure I knew which emotion was mine anymore.

I couldn't see the door from my position, but I felt her presence when she entered the hallway. Her emotions were so sweet and so vivid. Her hope called to me, sending warmth bubbling through my chest. I wanted her in my arms, in my bed. I wanted her safe.

The second set of emotions was suffocating: anxiety, uncertainty, betrayal, guilt. There was something almost desperate about the way this person's emotions swirled about the room. I gripped my chest, taking a steadying breath and forcing this new onslaught of feelings to subside, but it wouldn't settle. Whoever was accompanying Athena was overwhelmed. And so was I.

When Athena came into view, a sob lodged itself in my parched throat. She looked tired, but the smile plastered on her face outshone the very moon. Her eyes latched onto mine, and she broke into a sprint, tears streaming down her face. She crossed the painted line on the floor and snaked her arms through the bars to embrace me. The weight of her relief flooded me as her skin touched mine. Her heat warmed me soul-deep, and I basked in her comfort like a cat in the sunlight. In her arms, just for a moment, I didn't feel the assaulting emotions quite as strongly, as if her presence could quiet the torrent of swirling feelings prodding to enter my mind.

"I missed you," she whispered, pressing a soft kiss against the bare skin just below.

I couldn't respond. There weren't enough words. Instead, I pressed a kiss to her exposed neck, intimately aware of the way her blood ran just beneath the surface but not feeling hungry in the slightest.

She pulled back and offered me a soft glance of love before continuing down the line to greet her other mates. However brief, their reunions were filled with relief and warmth. I felt every second of them. It was all so potent I felt claustrophobic for the briefest of moments, surrounded on all sides by the wall of their feelings. Shaking my head, I pulled my eyes from the reunions and shut them tightly, hoping to find a reprieve from it all.

When I opened them again, I saw the little Hunter boy standing anxiously against the wall opposite us. His hands were nervously shoved in his pockets, and he frequently glanced over his shoulder at the entrance to our little torture cavern.

"What are you doing, Hunter?" I asked, drawing his nervous eyes to mine.

He sighed, pressing his back against the wall. "I'm fixing my mistake."

Silas scoffed. "A mistake? Typical Hunter logic, you kidnap and torture us and call it a simple mistake."

"I am going to get all of you out of here," the Hunter said, and I felt the wave of hope crash into me from all sides.

"Why?" Samara asked tentatively. I watched as Athena stepped toward the Hunter and felt an involuntary growl build in my chest.

"Because I'm not my father," he replied, casting a forlorn look at Athena. Twinges of guilt radiated from him in vicious strokes.

Interesting.

"How do we know it's not a trap?" Silas barked in anger.

"You outnumber me, and you're vampires. If this were a trap, it'd be a pretty stupid one," he claimed, and I felt his fear. He was worried, scared. He was telling the truth.

"Archer," Athena whispered, crossing the distance to him. "We need to go."

He nodded, swallowing the lump in his throat.

"I'm going to get you out of here, but I can't do that if you kill me," he pleaded.

"No promises," Silas seethed.

Athena moved back to Silas and pushed a hand through the bars, instantly calming him. "Just let him do this for us," she begged.

The Hunter, Archer, moved forward tentatively, his eyes glued to the painted line on the floor as he approached cautiously. He held his hand up, a key within his grasp, and I simultaneously saw the fear in his eyes. I heard the gasp escape his lips as he stepped across the line toward my cage.

I waited patiently, watching him with darkened eyes as he unlocked the lock and opened the bars.

Suddenly, there was nothing between me and the Hunter who captured us. There was no weapon, no holy water, no garlic, nobody to stop me. I heard his heart race as the blood pumped beneath his skin. I could have his blood in my system in an instant. I could bleed him dry and escape this place with my family in the time it took him to blink.

I could.

I flicked my eyes to Athena, who stood and watched with a nervousness swirling around her. She didn't want me to hurt this Hunter... Archer. And so, for her, I wouldn't. I stepped past the pale figure who had locked his eyes on me in fear and swept up my mate in my arms as Archer moved to Samara's cage.

Athena melted into my arms as if she belonged there, and her lips crashed into mine, and I drank her kiss as if it were the only thing standing between me and death. Because she did, and she was. My hands encircled her waist, ignoring the temptation to explore every inch of her and kiss away each painful reminder of our time apart. When she pulled back, her green eyes bore into mine.

"I missed you," she whispered.

Love.

That's what I was feeling. It was so potent, so clear.... so overwhelming. I doubled over, hands shooting to my temples as if my fingertips could keep my brain from exploding.

"Orpheus, what's wrong?" Athena's voice broke through the haze just as Samara's hands touched my shoulders.

"You're ok, you're ok," Samara whispered to me as she let her healing power travel through my bloodstream. I wasn't injured physically, but I'd be lying if I didn't admit that her healing balm dulled the raging headache to a low thrum of pain. I stood and met Samara's eyes. Nodding my thanks, she smiled before turning and hugging Athena and indulging in her own little reunion.

Archer released Laz, who gave him a less-than-friendly gaze before rushing to Athena. When Archer reached Silas' enclosure, I stepped forward, feeling my brother's anger and fury seeping through his pores.

"Silas,' I warned as Archer unlocked the last lock. Silas rushed through the bars and had Archer up against the opposite wall by his throat instantly. Archer's fear coiled around my throat as if it were me that Silas held captive in his grasp.

"Give me one good reason you deserve to breathe," Silas seethed.

Athena rushed forward, but Samara managed to hold her shoulder. Silas would never hurt her, but he was unpredictable when he was like this, and the fact that he was starving was only another reason she should stay back just until we could calm him down.

Archer's hands came up to hold onto Silas' arms, and as he struggled for air, I found myself unable to take a full breath either. "I..." he started. "I can't.." He finished defeat in his tone and his eyes. Guilt again filled my senses.

"Put him down, Silas," I ordered in a forceful whisper. My tone left no room for argument. I wasn't asking. I was demanding as the leader of this Coven. Silas knew that by the annoyance that flooded his emotions as he let Archer's feet hit the ground again.

The Hunter rubbed his throat and forced in gasps of air. "I want to help you. I know it doesn't make any sense, but.." He looked toward Athena with an air of familiarity. If I couldn't tell that he wasn't feeling an ounce of romantic feelings toward her, jealousy may have reared its ugly head. There was undoubtedly a type of care in his gaze that was perplexing, but I had no time to analyze that now. "Athena helped me see that my father has been feeding me lies, and you don't deserve to be punished for the lies of a Hunter," he spat. My eyebrows raised in surprise at his vitriolic tone.

"Please, let him help us," Athena begged, stepping forward to rest a hand on Silas' arm. He captured her lips in a brief but heated kiss before nodding.

"Sorry, bookworm," he whispered into her ear before pulling back and glaring at Archer. "Ok, Hunter. Get us out of here."

Archer nodded, gulping heavily. His fear was potent, and he refused to show us his back. Smart move. "The guards are going to be switching shifts soon. They don't leave any gaps by the door on the main floor anymore," he said, eyeing us. "But there are a few solid minutes when they don't watch the windows on the upper floor during the shift. You up to scaling the wall?" He asked with a bit of teasing as he looked at Athena. Her eyes went wide.

"We've got it," Laz interjected, throwing an arm around Athena's waist and pulling her to their side. "We've got you," they whispered to her. A wave of lust radiated from her, and I cleared my throat as heat coiled in my stomach, pushing away the feeling of her arousal because if I let myself feel it, I'd need to take her right here in this dungeon and we definitely did not have time for that.

"We need to work fast, and we don't have time for mistakes," Archer continued. "I know it's been a while since you were last here, but my father didn't spend that time just waiting for your return. He's been preparing for this. New weapons, new safeguards. If he catches us, he won't let you go."

"What do you need us to do?" Samara asked, always the calm one. I could feel Silas' resentment at being told to follow a Hunter's lead almost as clearly as I felt Athena's hope return. I took steadying breaths. I needed to get a handle on these fucking emotions before I lost my head.

Archer explained his plan, and I listened intently. It was simple enough but needed to be timed precisely, leaving no room for mistakes. We'd make our way to the complex's third floor, then sneak out through the windows in the exercise gym. Apparently, there weren't cameras in the gym, but that didn't account for the cameras in the halls.

"I've disabled the cameras in here and the hall leading to the gym, but they'll notice the looping soon. I'm not the most accomplished hacker. So, we need to move now." Archer stepped toward the door he came from but then quickly spun to face us, realizing he had accidentally turned his back to us.

His anxiety threatened to rage against my chest.

"We're not going to harm you, Hunter. Just get us out of here, and we will be even," I promised, ignoring the glare that Silas was now giving me.

Archer cast his eyes across each of us briefly, landing on Athena. That same strange familiarity washed over his face, but finally, he nodded and turned to lead us from our cages.

My Coven fell into line behind him. Wordlessly, we encircled Athena, protecting her on each side. It felt so right to have her near us again. Even now, I felt the mate bond within my chest thrum with glee at her proximity. I loved hearing her heartbeat despite its quickened rate from the danger surrounding our current task. I tried to focus on her, and only her, but the other emotions surrounding us were so charged and heightened that I was having a hard time focusing on my own breathing, let alone someone else. Instead, I focused on putting one foot in front of the other and keeping Athena safe. I would deal with this new facet of my power when we were safe.

I felt Athena's gaze on the side of my face, and I turned to look at her.

She knew not to speak as we neared the door she had just arrived through, but her eyes asked the unspoken question.

I nodded, trying my best to reassure my mate that I was okay. I didn't need her worrying about me when she needed to focus on keeping herself safe. She gripped my hand in hers and squeezed, and I let her touch ground me the best it could. We reached the door and Archer listened quietly at the iron frame. He pressed his hands against its surface, waiting for the right moment to open. Just as he moved to push through the door, I felt a new set of emotions. Two guards were just beyond the door. I felt them as they strolled through the hall. I sent my hand out, encircling Archer's wrist and holding him back. His heart rate quickened, and his breathing became labored as pure, unbridled fear coursed through him. His hand shook in my grasp. I saw the beginnings of a panic attack and quickly removed my hand from his wrist and whispered, "Two guards just outside." It took him a moment to calm his breathing, but when he did, he nodded first to me and then to himself. I'd seen that reaction before, in Athena when she had her panic attack back at her bookstore. He had PTSD, and by the way, he was cradling his wrist that held a raised white scar, I knew exactly what had caused it.

A wave of my own guilt ran through me at that thought.

I quickly pushed it down and tuned into the set of emotions beyond the door. I could feel their trajectory clearly, tracking them despite the barrier between us. I guess, in that respect, my newfound amplified powers would be helpful. I just hoped I could keep them from overwhelming me long enough to benefit.

"They've gone around the corner. We're clear," I whispered to the Hunter, and he swallowed the fear, schooling his expression, and moved forward again. We pressed through the door and spilled out into the hallway quietly. Even with my advanced hearing, I could barely hear our footfalls. We'd need to remain as quiet as possible to get out of here undetected. From here, I could feel almost fifty other people in this building. Moving about like ants in a maze. Their emotions called out like beacons. Helpful...and distracting. I focused on our path, trying to scope out who might be crossing us.

Archer led us toward the back staircase for a few painfully tense minutes, his eyes darting to me as we came to each corner for confirmation. I'd offer a tight nod to confirm we were clear, and we'd continue. Never in my life did I think I'd work *with* a Hunter, but Archer didn't seem like the Hunters I'd encountered before. He was different. I wasn't planning on grabbing a beer with him anytime soon, but I'd let him lead us out of here. I'd trust him to do that. I didn't sense an ounce of dishonesty in him, and there was something protective in his gaze when he looked at Athena, which made me want to believe him. It was apparent that Athena did.

When we reached the stairs, Archer glanced at me, and I tried to focus on the beacons of emotions. There were three guards on the next floor, but they weren't near the door to the stairway.

I nodded, and he began to climb.

Step after step, I did my best to remain focused on those three guards. If they took one step toward our direction, I wanted to know about it.

We made it another ten steps up the staircase before I felt it.

Blinding, violent, unrelenting rage.

It burned through my veins like acid, eating away at my very skin. My knees buckled under me, and I collapsed onto the steps. Silas grabbed my shoulders and held me steady before I could slip backward.

The beacons of emotions from the other guards grew, their anger and determination growing stronger with each passing moment. My chest tightened, and I struggled to remain quiet, resisting the urge to scream out and release the tension from the pain building in my body.

I recognized Athena's hushed voice as she spoke to someone, and they responded, but I couldn't drown out my emotions well enough to hear what they had said. There was nothing but rage. I was drowning in it.

Suddenly, her hands came to rest on my cheeks, and I tried to force my eyes open to meet hers, but the pain was too great. Her lips pressed into mine, and I tried to zero in on the place where her skin met mine.

She called out to me in the darkness like a beacon. Like a lighthouse. She was the only thing that could keep me from falling into the deep end. "Be here with me," she demanded against my lips. "Nothing but me and you, Orpheus. Do you hear me? There's nothing but you and me. Drown it all out," she begged. I forced my eyes open to meet hers, finding watery green eyes staring back at me. "Feel me, only me," she cried, bringing my hand to her chest so that I could feel her heartbeat. It was racing but strong and powerful, and I couldn't help but love the way it called to me. "Four things you can see, Orpheus." She commanded, and I felt the corners of my lips try to twitch into a smile before the rage burned another hole in my chest.

"I can't.." I strained.

"Drown it out," she begged.

I shook my head. "I can't." How could I shut out something that felt so over-whelming and all-encompassing?

"Yes, you can!" She whisper-screamed. I heard Archer's voice in the back-ground, but I couldn't feel anything past the fury and my mate's hands on me. "You're stronger than this. You always have been. Drown. Them. Out!"

Her words felt like a crashing window. Shattered pieces of the power in my soul came crashing down in fractals around me. Suddenly, there was only her before me. It was as if a switch had been flipped, instantly dampening the over-whelming surge of emotions that had been bombarding me from all directions. The chaos around me began to lose intensity— like a roaring storm gradually subsiding into a gentle rain.

With each passing moment, the weight of the emotional burden lifted, and I could feel a sense of clarity and lightness washing over me. It was as if a heavy curtain had been drawn, shielding me from the relentless onslaught of feelings that had previously threatened to engulf me. The world's noise faded into the background, replaced by a serene stillness that enveloped me completely.

In that newfound calm, I could finally hear the gentle whisper of my emotions rising to the surface. It was a revelation. For the first time in my second life, it was my emotions and mine alone that swirled within me.

My eyes locked with Athena's, and I pressed a kiss onto her lips, an incredu-lous laugh slipping through my lips.

"Are you ok?" she asked, a flash of something crossing her face. Worry probably...but I didn't know for sure. I didn't know because I couldn't feel her emotions.

There was peace.

"You helped me turn it off," I whispered, throwing my arms around her waist and pulling her to my chest.

She pressed a kiss to my throat, and I felt the burn of lust build in my lower stomach, making my cock twitch for her, but I pushed that unruly reaction away and stood with her in my arms.

"Sorry," I offered to my coven and Archer, who watched us with rapt atten-tion. I'm ready now. We need to hurry. Someone has realized we're gone."

I felt the power thrum within my chest. It wasn't gone, but I had control over it in ways I never had before. I tested it as we continued up the stairs, switching it on and off. By the time we reached the landing on the second floor, it was as easy as breathing. I smiled at Athena before telling Archer that the hall was clear and sliding the overwhelming power off, placing those painful emotions into a box and sliding it away until I needed to call on it again.

Athena had saved me in ways I'd never knew I could be saved. Her love set me free from the mental cage I had been forced to occupy for centuries. She had given me more than just a reprieve from the pain, but she's offered me a type of control I'd been craving. She was saving me over and over again, and when we got out of here safely, I was going to do everything I could to show her how thankful I was.

12

SILAS

I was going to kill Orpheus when we got out of here.

Who the hell did he think he was, promising the Hunter that we wouldn't kill him? I'd been planning and running through the very detailed and excruciating ways I had planned to make this fucker pay for what he put us through, for what he put Athena through. I was going to enjoy exacting my revenge slowly and violently. And this fucking suit and tie-wearing jackass stole that chance from me.

I was fuming as we made our way through the halls, and I was fuming as we climbed the stairs. Hell, I was fuming when Orpheus nearly slipped and fell. There was a split second when I considered not catching him. We were only halfway up the staircase. He wouldn't die. It would just hurt him—a lot. And if you asked me, he deserved it.

But he's my fucking brother, and I fucking love him for some stupid ass reason, so I caught him before he went headfirst down the stairwell. He had the audacity to be all in pain and make me worry for him...the fucking jackass.

My eyes watched the little Hunter like a hawk. He was jittery, and I was ready to take him out the second he showed even the slightest sign of betraying us. I couldn't look at his stupid ass face without remembering the way I was frozen in my body as he hauled me into the back of his truck.

Orpheus may look at the Hunter and see our ticket out, but I look at him as I see the reason we need the ticket in the first place. I was really looking forward to ripping out his intestines and hanging him from the rafters... dammit. Stupid Romanian bastard always ruins my fun.

Archer and Orpheus worked in tandem, like old fucking buddies or some shit, to navigate the halls toward the gym. We heard shouts echoing through the halls, but luckily for us, they seemed to be headed for the first floor. They wouldn't expect us to escape through the second-floor window. It was a good plan. Even though he was a stupid fucking Hunter. The alarms began blaring, and suddenly, the lights dimmed, and an eerie, almost green light flooded the hall. I pressed in closer to Athena and watched our backs as our eyes attempted to adjust to the color, but it hurt. The color was bright and invasive. It felt like I was staring directly into sunlight.

"What the fuck?" I cursed quietly, rubbing my eyes.

"It's designed specifically to affect a vampire's eyesight," Archer explained quickly. "I warned you, he's prepared for this. We need to hurry."

I wanted to punch him, but I couldn't fucking see him. Douchebag.

"We can't see," Laz exclaimed.

"Athena, can you lead them?" Archer asked, and I felt her hand come to rest on my arm, sending calming waves through me.

"Hold onto me," she whispered, and I felt my coven gather closer to her. We were rushing through the hall now, and I hated the way my blindness made me feel so helpless. The alarm was high-pitched to mess with my hearing, but I could still smell them. They weren't onto our trail... yet.

"In here, come on," Archer said, and I heard him push a door open. His footfalls echoed in the room, and I knew we had reached the gym. The smell of sweat invaded my nostrils. The light was diluted in this room, just enough that I could make out shapes around us. "The windows are on the other side. Hurry!" Archer took off across the floor, and Athena did her best to keep each of us close as she raced after him. I listened as Archer opened the window, and fresh air hit my skin for the first time since we were abducted. My heart raced, and I felt agonizing hope fill my chest. We would be free soon. I hadn't let myself believe in the possibility until this very moment. This close to the window, the green light was weak enough for my vision to return to me at mostly total capacity. It was nighttime outside, and the moon-light poured in, washing away the green. Good. That would help us disappear.

"Come on, climb out," Archer ordered, and I ignored the urge to tell him to shut the fuck up and stop telling me what to do because, as furious as I was, he was the reason I could taste the freedom beyond the window.

"Athena, go," I said, leading her toward the window.

"Um... Maybe you should go first so someone can catch me if- Well." Her eyes looked out and down toward the ground outside the window. It was a drop that would be a piece of cake for us but could kill a human being.

"Laz, Samara, go out on either side. You can help her down when we send her out," Orpheus demanded.

"I can't leave her..." Samara started, and tears had formed in her eyes. She was terrified of leaving Athena behind because the last time one of us was left behind... I gripped Athena's hand in mine.

"I will protect her, Samara. Get out there and be ready to jump. I have her." I promised her. Samara and I shared a brief moment before she nodded and slipped out of the window with Laz close on her heels. Losing Alora had nearly broken us both, and I would never let another one of us be lost in this fucking building.

"Silas, get her out of here," Orpheus looked to me, watching the door from which we came, basked in green light. His jaw tensed.

"They're coming, aren't they?" I whispered low enough that only he could hear me. He nodded.

"Go, get out there. I'll send her out. I can blend in if we're not out in time." I could see he wanted to argue, but we didn't have time for that, so he pressed a kiss to Athena's cheek and offered a quick nod to Archer before following Laz and Samara out onto the ledge. I was lifting Athena toward the window when the doors to the gym slammed open. My muscles tensed, and I conjured the only image I could, holding onto Athena tightly and pressing her to my back as I turned to face the incoming guards. I felt my skin tingle as my disguise formed, and I heard Archer inhale sharply beside me in shock.

"What the fuck are you doing here, Bennett?" One of the guards bellowed as he approached. His eyes landed on me, and he shook his head. "Sorry, sir. I didn't realize he was with you."

"Are you going to stand there and berate my son, or are you going to find those fucking vampires?" I called out, hating how Bennett's voice felt in my throat.

"You told us to check this floor," the guard questioned.

"I also told you to find the bloodsuckers. Do I need to ask you again?" I felt Athena press her face into my back, and I tried my best to hide her from view.

"Who is that?" One of the other guards asked, leaning to see around me. I took a step forward, prepared to rip each of their throats out, but then Archer stepped forward and pulled Athena with him. I was a fraction of a second away from turning my fury back on him, but then my eyes landed on Athena, or I guess I should say, the random person who stood in Athena's spot.

Confusion washed over me as I took in her appearance. Her long red hair was cropped short and had a dirty blonde tint. Her ordinarily soft features were angular and sharp. Brown eyes covered her green orbs, and her body was plump and thick. I shook my head, trying to make sense of what I was seeing.

"New recruit," Archer said, showing off the 'not-Athena," who looked equally perplexed. She didn't seem to notice that she looked nothing like herself. Good, if she did, she may not be able to hold in the shock that I was now fighting against.

"Now, are you going to stand there like fucking idiots, or are you going to follow orders?" I bellowed. The guards nodded, agreeing quickly and backing out toward the door. We watched them go, and I took a moment to breathe before letting the facade fall away. When I did, Athena's visage also melted away, revealing her.

"Neat trick," Archer whispered before ushering Athena, who was now looking much more Athena-like, toward the window.

She looked dazed but went to climb through. "Wait, Archer. What will happen if they find out you're behind this?" Her tone was full of worry.

"I'll be fine. I'm just glad I could do this for you," he whispered, and I saw him brush away a tear that slid down his cheek.

"Come on, bookworm, we gotta go." I helped her through the window, and she watched Archer.

"Thank you, Archer," she whispered before stepping out onto the ledge and into the waiting arms of her other mates. I turned back to the Hunter and scowled.

"This doesn't make up for what you did," I spat.

He nodded. "I know."

I nodded once, the most acknowledgment he would get out of me, and moved to slip out the window. I was halfway out when the door to the gym opened again.

"What the fuck have you done, Archer?" Bennett's voice echoed through the room, and I hurried to slide out the window. Samara and Laz were already helping Athena down the ledge, and Orpheus was ahead of them, watching our exit path. I turned my head back to the Hunter. He backed away as his father and the guard that accompanied him advanced.

"You've been lying to me, to all of us." Archer reached for the stake in his waistband. Shock flooded me. Would he actually use it against his father? Was he really so opposed to what his family did here that he'd fight him?

"You ruined everything," Bennett said, indicating with a nod to the guard at his side. The guard grunted, rushing forward and grabbing Archer in a less-than-friendly headlock. Archer cried out and tried to wrestle free from the hold.

"I should let this guard fucking kill you for your treason," Bennett seethed, eyes wide and hair wild. He was a madman, angered and unstable.

The guard let his fist fly, a punch landing on Archer's face. I smelled the blood as it poured from his now broken nose. I felt my shift just under the surface, and I barely held it together.

"Silas, come on," Orpheus called from the ground below. His voice came to me through a haze of hunger and fury.

I watched through red-tinted eyes as Archer attempted to stand up, but the guard was faster, sending another punch at him as his father watched on. This one landed with a sickening crunch, and more blood filled the air. I was damn-near ravenous. My hands gripped the windowsill, and I watched as the Hunter who captured us took blow after blow, ordered by the Hunter who tortured us.

"Silas, get your ass down here," Samara seethed. "We need to go." She was afraid, understandably.

"Bennett's got the kid," I whispered, knowing they could hear me.

"Fuck," Orpheus exclaimed.

"What's wrong? What is it?" Athena's worried tone broke through my near shift and cleared my head. The monster slipped back into the shadows of my mind as I watched Archer stand to face his father.

"You made it all up, Dad. All of it," he spat, blood pouring down his chin.

"You don't know what the hell you're talking about," Bennett yelled, watching as his guard dropped a kick in the kid's stomach, sending him toppling backward.

My fists clenched.

"What is happening up there? What's going on? Talk to me!" Athena begged her other mates.

"Archer's dad found him," Laz answered softly. Damn them and their big mouth.

"Is he ok?" She asked with worry in her tone.

"We have guards headed this way," Orpheus declared through gritted teeth.

"Is Archer ok?" Athena demanded.

"We need to go," Orpheus said, reaching for her, but she pulled back.

"Not until I know he's alright," she stated.

I focused again on the Hunter, who was on the ground in a heap, blood pooling on the floor below him.

"You're worthless, you know that?" Bennett exclaimed, stepping forward. I ducked further onto the ledge so he wouldn't see me. "You always have been. You and you're fucking naiveté. You have no idea what you just did. No fucking clue who you just released back into the world."

"Yes, I do," Archer said weakly, lifting his battered head to face his father. "I know exactly who I just released back into the world. I know exactly who she is. And so do you!"

My brows furrowed at that, confusion coursing through me, but Bennett understood the vague confession. The color drained from his face, and his steps faltered. What the fuck was that supposed to mean? Did he mean Samara or Athena? What the hell was going on? On the ground, Orpheus was trying desperately to get Athena to run while she struggled in his hold. We were running out of time.

"You will have to answer to Galvin, and I won't be able to protect you from that. Do you understand what I'm saying?" Bennett seethed, nodding again to the guard at his side, who landed another kick to Archer's chest. He curled around the hit and cried out in pain.

"Was that him?" Athena cried out. Her voice traveled to my ears, but luckily, Bennett didn't seem to hear it. She needed to be careful.

"You'd let Galvin kill me?"

My breath caught in my throat. Based on Archer's state, he wasn't too far from death already.

"I'd have no choice." With a frown, Bennett shook his head, dismissing the guard. Together, they turned on their heels and rushed out of the gym, leaving Archer, broken and bloody, on the floor. The Hunter's breathing became shallow as his body went slack.

In all my years of existence, I'd made a point of living my life to protect others from those who sought to hurt them. I'd stop monsters, far more evil than I, from taking what didn't belong to them, be it sex, skin, or blood. I'd fight for those who couldn't fight for themselves or had fought and lost. It was ingrained in who I was to be the silent protector, even when I felt like I couldn't. Even when it didn't make sense. Even when I fucking hated them.

That's why I found myself climbing back into the window, despite the protests from the ground, scooping the unconscious boy in my arms, and then taking the jump from the window in one leap.

Looks like we're taking the fucking Hunter with us.

Great.

13

ATHENA

The moment Silas landed on the ground near us with Archer in tow, the panic that had been building began to subside, only to ramp up again once I saw the state of the man I once considered a friend. He had saved us, he had set us free, and he'd almost died because of it. Guilt threatened to topple me over. I didn't realize I had been crying until the salted liquid painted my lips.

"We need to go, Athena. Please, we don't have time." Orpheus begged me harshly, and I knew he wouldn't use that tone unless necessary. I nodded, trying to pry my eyes from Archer's limp body, and climbed onto Orpheus's back. "Make sure he doesn't have anything that can be tracked." Silas and Samara tag teamed, rifling through his belongings, tossing Archer's phone on the ground, and smashing it. They nodded to us where we stood.

Then we were off.

Orpheus was fast. In the darkness of the night, I couldn't make out a single shape as the world around us blurred. I felt my mates running alongside us, but I couldn't see them in the kaleidoscope of air and darkness. With each stride away from the Hunters' compound, I felt relief replacing the fear and pain. I let the gentle sway of Orpheus' steps calm my racing heart. We survived —all of us. My heart constricted as I thought of Archer's poor, battered face. His father had done that? How could he do that to his own son?

Those who are meant to protect us can do the most harm.

The small voice in the back of my mind reminded me as a flash of perfect teeth and combed hair threatened to replace the forest's darkness with the memory of his face. I closed my eyes and pushed back against the thought of him. He had been a frequent visitor in my consciousness this past week. The feeling of being trapped, the helplessness...it all felt so familiar. I couldn't help but slip into those waking nightmares of when his calloused hands trailed my skin when his wicked lips took from me what I was unwilling to give.

I took a deep breath and focused on the feeling of my mate beneath me. His muscular body was chilled, and I let the cold comfort wash away his sweaty memory. Soon enough, I managed to force my stepfather back into the box reserved for him in the corner of my mind.

I don't know how long we ran, but I felt Orpheus's stride stagger. He was putting on a brave face, but I saw it in the way his shoulders tightened and the crease in his brow.

He was weak.

"Stop," I said into his ear.

"Not yet," he replied, the fatigue evident in his voice.

"Stop right now, Orpheus," I demanded, and he slowed his footfalls with a sigh. When we came to a stop, I slid off his back and let my feet hit the ground. I didn't miss how his body seemed relieved not to carry the extra weight.

"We can't stop, Athena. We're not out of danger yet. These woods are all theirs," he began, but I put a hand up to stop him. I heard Laz, Samara, and Silas come to a stop behind me as well.

When I turned to look at them, I saw it for the first time. The effect these last few days had had on them. They weren't ok. They weren't desiccating into nothingness, but they were weak and tired and hungry. I stepped forward, seeing Silas' near-red eyes as he held Archer's bleeding body in his arms.

"You need to feed," I whispered.

"We need to get out of here," Orpheus argued, strained though at the prospect of feeding.

"We'll be quick, but you need the strength," I said, stepping forward and offering my throat to him. His eyes darkened with hunger and lust, and his tongue came out to wet his lips before he tore his eyes from the pulse at my neck.

"We might lose control," he pleaded.

"You won't," I responded, grabbing Samara's hand and bringing it to my chest, letting her feel my heartbeat. "Samara has kept me strong. I can do this. Please let me do this for you."

Samara let out a whimper, a delicious sound that I couldn't wait to taste when we were safe, but now she needed something else from me, and I needed to give it.

"Darlin'," Laz warned as I reached for them, bringing them to my side and offering my wrist. Their eyes locked on my pulse, and they began to shift.

"Silas, please," I beckoned him forward. He was so close to losing his control that it didn't take much pushing for him to set the bloody Archer down on a nearby patch of soft ground and step toward me, pressing his front to my back and claiming my throat with his fangs. I bit my lip to stifle the moan as the pressure built. It was an otherworldly experience, having him drink from me. Samara pressed a gentle kiss against the inside of my forearm before sinking her teeth into the flesh and drinking. My head fell back as heat pooled in my core. Laz licked my wrist with their tongue, which made the cool night air tingle against my skin. I shivered in anticipation, but then they were biting down, taking languid sips of my blood.

I felt like I was on fire, a burning inferno of passion, as my eyes locked onto Orpheus, who was entirely shifted. His sharp ears and bright red eyes had once terrified me but now made me feel coveted, desired, and protected. He stalked forward and claimed the side of my throat opposite Silas and pressed his body to my front. Once his fangs were inserted into my skin, I couldn't stifle the sound anymore. I groaned as an orgasm ripped through me, sending shock-waves to every extremity. They pulled slow and steady gulps of my blood into their mouths, and I writhed in their hold, gasping with release.

Laz was the first to pull away, followed by Samara. Their vampire forms drifted away to reveal their heated gazes. Silas released his hold on my throat, licking the wound and sending a jolt of pleasure directly to my core. Orpheus took a moment longer to release his hold, but soon enough, he was drawing back, using the back of his hand to wipe the excess blood from his lips. The sight of my blood on his skin shouldn't be as tempting as it was. Unfortunately, I didn't have time to explore his mouth with mine as I desired.

"Are you ok?" Orpheus asked tentatively.

I nodded, smiling. "I'm perfect."

He released a sigh before offering me his back again. I climbed on and watched as Silas retrieved Archer.

"Samara, can you help him?" I asked. She pressed a soft kiss to my lips.

"I healed him as much as I could on the run here. He's alive and stable. I'll do more when we get where we're going." She smiled softly, and I instantly felt better.

"Speaking of, where are we going?" I asked as we began to run again.

"I've been preparing for this for a long time, little nymph. I knew someday they'd catch us again, and we'd need to escape," Orpheus replied in an even tone despite the incredible speed at which we traveled. Even the minuscule amount of blood he took was already making a huge difference in his strength.

I held him tighter, hating how much fear they had been living in for all these years.

"I have a safehouse about an hour's run from here. We'll be safe there until we figure out what to do." He squeezed my hand, and that was enough to calm my nerves as he continued his trek through the forest.

Sometime later - it may have been an hour, but I had no way of knowing for sure - Orpheus slowed to a light jog. "Are we here?" I asked.

"Nearly," he replied softly. "We could have been here earlier, but I wanted to double back and cover our trail."

I nodded.

Right. We needed to cover our trail because we were on the run... from Vampire Hunters. I felt my stomach flip as the reality of our situation settled on me. However, I didn't have time to dwell on that feeling because the dense canopy of trees suddenly gave way, revealing a small meadow nestled within the heart of the wilderness. Moonlight filtered through the gaps in the foliage, casting patterns of muted light and shadow across the vibrant carpet of wildflowers that blanketed the expanse. A narrow trail wound its way through the meadow, leading toward a seemingly abandoned two-story cabin standing at the edge of the clearing. Despite the wear and tear evident in its weathered exterior, there was an undeniable warmth to the rustic structure.

Above the cabin, the canopy of leaves stretched out like a protective shield, enveloping the area in a cocoon of privacy and seclusion. It was as though the forest itself conspired to keep us concealed from prying eyes, both on the ground and in the sky.

Approaching the cabin, I felt a sense of tranquility wash over me at the promise of safety within the cabin walls. Orpheus did not stop to let me admire the sight for any longer before sprinting up the steps with me firmly attached to his back. I heard the others follow closely, and within a few moments, we were all locked safely inside the cabin's living area. A faint scent of aged wood and must served as a reminder of the cabin's long solitude and lack of use. Yet, despite its apparent disuse, the cabin's interior seemed prepared and ready, as if it had been patiently awaiting our arrival. That thought sent a wave of sadness to my heart. How long had my mates been waiting for this moment? Had they ever considered there would be a time when they didn't need this safe house? Or did they always know they'd be here someday?

The main living area had sturdy, well-crafted wooden furniture draped with dust covers. A plush sofa and armchairs sat around a stone fireplace, their cushions invitingly plump, which only reminded me of my exhaustion. A thick rug lay beneath, its intricate patterns softened by time and wear.

Orpheus set me on my feet and helped me steady myself as feeling returned to the tired extremities before he returned to the door. Beneath his touch, I noticed a modern element that seemed out of place amidst the rustic charm of the cabin—a security system. A keypad lock adorned the door, its sleek design starkly contrasting the weathered wood around it. As Orpheus armed the alarm, I watched and heard the system whir to life. Motion sensors dotted the room's corners, their small lights flashing to confirm they were on and ready. Now that I was looking, I saw several cameras littering the space, and I knew that if I had paid enough attention, I would have seen them outside as well. I eyed the camera that was aimed at the front door. Its unblinking lens was a silent sentinel watching over us. I felt that wave of relief course through me.

Once Orpheus was satisfied with the arming of our safehouse, he turned to face us where we stood. My eyes drifted across the haggard faces of my mates, watching them as they let the weight of the last few hours, especially the previous weeks, settle over them. We stood together in a heavy silence, each fighting our internal struggles against the demons within. Every dreadful moment of the past two weeks seemed to seep into our very bones, leaving an indelible mark on our souls. There wasn't a doubt in my mind that we would remember what had occurred for as long as we drew breath. Some of us were fortunate enough to escape physically unscathed, but the scars ran deep, and they always would. I understand intimately that scars, whether seen or unseen, have a way of persisting.

"What is this place, Orpheus?" Laz asked calmly.

"A safe house," he replied.

"Obviously, but since when did you have this?" Silas interjected.

"Since about two months after we escaped the last time." The words hung in the air, and the others all inhaled a shaky breath.

"Why didn't you tell us?" Silas asked an edge of anger in his tone.

"Because you all wanted to believe that we were safe, but I knew we weren't." Orpheus ran a hand through his hair, and I took this moment to really look at him. He was still in his suit pants, but his button-down shirt was tattered, ripped, and singed. My chest tightened at the thought of what they had to endure there. Again.

"There is a state-of-the-art security system, with alarms for a mile perimeter. The kitchen is fully stocked with blood, but I do have some non-perishables as well," he added, tipping his head toward me. "Each bedroom has clothes in our sizes," he continued, trying not to make eye contact with any of us. Laz was slack-jawed. "You'll need to share with Samara." He shot me an apologetic look.

"Thank you," Samara said eventually, her voice hoarse and tired. "Thank you for this, Orpheus."

Then Samara began to cry. My chest ached as she sobbed. I rushed to her, pulling her gently into my arms, and she nestled her head into my neck and folded her arms around me. The return to the Hunter's cages was obviously hard on each of them, but I knew this memory held a special kind of torture for her. My heart broke for Alora, the love of my mate's life. Oh, how I wished I could have known her. Could have saved her. "I'm so sorry," I whispered against Samara's hair, pressing delicate kisses to the top of her head.

"Silas, get Archer set up in the basement. There's a couch down there... and some extra security measures," I heard Orpheus order, and I sighed. They would, of course, be wary of the man who captured them, but at least they were helping him.

That's how I knew, once and for all, beyond a shadow of the doubt, that the Hunters tried to plant in my mind that my Wanderers were not the monsters that Nameless believed they were.

Silas and Laz ventured toward a door that led to what I assumed was the basement Orpheus mentioned and disappeared with a still unconscious Archer. I heard Orpheus take some steps further into the house, leaving Samara and me to have this moment alone. We sunk down to our knees on the wooden floor, and still, she cried into my arms.

"I was so afraid," she whispered. I ran a hand along her spine, applying just enough comforting pressure.

"We're ok," I replied because it was true. We had made it out—all of us.

"I felt like I couldn't breathe, like at any moment they would take another member of my family from me." Samara sat back on her heels and placed a palm on my cheek. I was mesmerized by her dark eyes glistening with moisture. Despite the hardness of her features, she was stunning and seemed so soft and vulnerable in the gentle moonlight.

"I know." My heart constricted. I couldn't imagine the pain she had been in, feeling the memories flashing back, seeing the same scenarios play out, unable to stop them. "The memories are the hardest part," I added, swallowing hard.

She leaned forward and pressed the softest kiss to my forehead.

"You made it bearable," she promised, and I loved the way her eyes captured mine like she saw so deep within me that my soul was laid bare before her. "Thank you."

I ran my thumb along her bottom lip, loving how her cold breath sent shivers of anticipation down my spine. "No, thank you. You kept me healthy. You healed me."

"We healed each other," she admitted, and I ushered my agreement in the form of a soft kiss pressed against her parted lips. She moaned slightly as I drank her kiss. I pulled back, locking eyes with my mate again, and the mark on my wrist thrummed with energy.

"Why don't we clean up, and then I'll see what else I can do for Archer?" Samara offered, and the mention of Archer had a wave of guilt cresting.

"He's hurt because he helped us," I whispered, a tear sliding down my cheek. Samara caught it with her finger.

"He's alive because he helped us," she replied quietly. "I'm not sure Silas or Orpheus would have let him breathe if he hadn't."

I nodded. I figured as much. Hell, in those first few days, I may have killed him myself if it meant I could be free again.

"He'll be ok. We'll make sure of it. Like I said, he's stable." She pressed her promise in the form of a kiss on my lips, and I leaned into it hungrily. Feeling my core tighten at the feel of her lips against mine.

She pulled back, smirking. "Let's go take a shower, Athena."

I shook my head. "I need to call my grandma. She's probably so worried." My heart constricted. "I'm all she has left." A tear slid down my cheek, and Samara caught it with her thumb. "And Davia, too! And what about the cops that are looking into us? I mean, disappearing in the middle of an investigation is pretty suspicious." Another thought occurred to me, and my stomach sank. "What if they found Greg, and he told them what I did to him?" I was fully panicking now. Samara's hands came to my shoulders and squeezed.

"Breathe, sweetheart."

I tried, but inhaling felt impossible.

"Look at me, and breathe," she commanded, and I finally locked my eyes on hers and took a long, languid breath.

"There is a lot to figure out, there are a lot of questions, but they can wait for tomorrow."

I started to protest, but she shut me up with a kiss.

"It can all wait for tomorrow, my love. You've been through something horrible and need a moment to process that."

I nodded, not sure I fully believed her, but I felt the calm start to wash over me.

"So, my beautiful, perfect mate. Shower with me." Her words held a wicked edge that I instantly felt guilty about being excited about, but I quickly squashed that guilt.

We'd just been through the unthinkable and came out the other side. We're alive. We're safe. For now, at least. I deserve a moment of indulgence. She's right. These problems would still be here tomorrow.

Samara stood and took my hand, leading me through the rest of the unfamiliar space. Once we reached the top of the stairs, I let her lead me to the master bathroom. Although to call it 'master' anything felt disjointed, seeing as it was a short room housing a slightly larger than small clawfoot tub and a curtain that hung haphazardly from the ceiling. I didn't care, though. The promise of running water and my naked mate was too great a distraction. The door closed behind us, and Samara slowly reached for the hem of my shirt. I was instantly aware of just how long I'd been wearing this same shirt and cringed. I hope she could peel it off my skin without it sticking. She didn't seem to have the same reservations I did because as the shirt was lifted above my head, her eyes scanned my body hungrily.

"Do you know how beautiful you are, Athena?" She asked, trailing a finger along the waistband of my pants. I groaned at the pure need that raced through me at her touch. My head lulled back as she slid the pants down my legs, tugging my panties with them. I didn't have a moment to feel self-conscious about my current state of hygiene because she was up instantly, leading me to take a careful step into the claw foot tub.

"You're joining me, right?" I nearly begged as she stepped back. She smiled and reached for the hem of her ruined sundress, pulling it off her body in one move. I felt my jaw loosen as I took in the image of her perfect naked body. Her breasts were perky, and the nipples pebbled in desire. Her long legs were like roadmaps that led to my favorite destination. I might have moaned.

She stepped into the tub with me, pulling the curtain closed around us, offering us both an air of privacy. The moment the water hit our bodies, we both sighed in contentment. It was chilly, but honestly, I didn't mind the cold temperature anymore—not with my mate's ice-cold hands running along my body.

I let her hands explore the plane of my stomach as I let my hands get tangled in her dark, naturally curly hair. "Let me wash your hair," I asked, and Samara smiled. She handed me a bottle from the shelf, and I got to work, lathering my hands in the glorious-smelling soap. It smelled of lavender and sea. I ran my hands delicately through her hair, listening to her soft instructions on washing her hair properly. She groaned as I took my time with each curl. When I held her back so she could lean back and rinse the soap from her scalp, her hips pressed against my own, and I eagerly pressed back, my needy clit begging for friction.

She stepped back, earning her a frustrated groan, but she only smiled and got to work on my own ratted locks. Her magical hands made a miracle of my hair, easing out the tangles with gentle fingers. I pulled the body wash from the shelf and took a dollop in the palm of my hand. I offered her the same, and she smiled, putting her hand out, palm up for me.

Our hands quickly found each other's bodies and moved in gentle, soap-covered circles across our skin. I lathered her body up, staring at her shoulders, her chest, moving gently to her sides, then brushing ever so slightly against her hardened nipples. She inhaled sharply and paused her own exploration of my body to close her eyes and enjoy my touch. I circled her nipples with my fingers, working slowly and sensually despite the growing pit of need in my core. I pressed a kiss to her exposed throat, and she let her hands wrap around my waist.

My fingers drifted south, exploring every inch of her perfect body until I reached the apex of her thighs. I spent a few moments genuinely lathering the soap onto her body, but I didn't ignore the way her chest rose and fell with the friction I was providing. Once I was content and rinsed her body under the stream of water, I found her clit with my index finger and stroked it.

"Athena," she moaned, and I felt invincible. My name on her lips was something I could never get enough of. I slid two fingers into her pussy, loving the way her core tightened around me.

She gasped, and I took the moment to capture her mouth in a kiss. I drank her moans as I pumped my fingers into her over and over again. Her hands came to a rest on my breasts, and I sighed with pleasure as she caught my nipples between her thumb and forefingers and hardened them to a point.

"Fuck me with those fingers," she commanded in a soft tone, and I obliged instantly, picking up my pace and letting my thumb find her clit as I continued. Her breathing ramped up, and she bucked against my hand.

"You look so beautiful when you're coming," I whispered against her throat before taking a bite of the skin there, and she detonated around my fingers. I felt her walls clamp around me as I drew out the last bits of her release. Her fingers had climbed to my shoulders as she held on for dear life. When her breathing returned to normal, I slid my fingers from her pussy and couldn't resist the temptation to taste them. I slid my fingers into my mouth and groaned as her sweet taste invaded my tastebuds. I was so lost to the taste of her that I didn't notice she had dropped to her knees before me until I felt her cold breath on my sensitive clit. My eyes flashed open, but I left my fingers in my mouth as she positioned my legs where she needed them.

The first draw of her tongue through my folds was nothing short of pure euphoria. I gasped, gripping the top of her head to steady myself against the onslaught of passion. My legs were weak as she devoured my pussy. Her tongue danced in sinfully intricate movements along my soaking wet slit. I whispered her name softly, like a prayer, and she groaned as her tongue assaulted my clit with blinding need. The vibration was enough to make my heart race, my breathing came in rapid spurts, and I felt the orgasm cresting as my mate consumed me.

Her fingers slid into my aching pussy, and her tongue continued its devious attention on my clit, and I felt as if I were flying. Floating above my body, looking down at this sinful and stunning moment of passion.

The muscles in my stomach contracted, telling me I was close, and I whispered in a panted breath, "Don't stop."

She took that moment to slide one of her hands through my slick folds and back even further, teasing the entrance to my tight hole, and I inhaled sharply at the slight bite of anticipation. She slid the finger in, and I moaned at the fullness as she expertly worked me.

Her tongue was on my clit, her fingers were in my pussy, and another finger was pressing into my ass, and I fell apart. I saw stars as the climax crashed into me. Samara didn't pause to let me ride the wave, instead pushing up into me with a punishing pace as her tongue sucked my clit into her mouth. I screamed her name and tried to pull my body away from hers as the tightness built further in my core. She didn't let up, relentlessly pounding into me and torturing my clit. "Please," I begged, unsure if I was begging for her to stop and let me recover from the intense orgasm or if I was begging her to push me harder and see what was waiting for me on the other side of orgasm number two.

She chose for me and picked up her pace, pounding her fingers into my holes and lapping at my pussy eagerly. I felt the tension build and build, pushing beyond anything I'd ever felt, and suddenly, I exploded again. Warm liquid squirted out of me and ran down my legs. Samara drank every drop, and I had to grip her shoulders to avoid collapsing to the tub floor. Once the tremors in my body stilled, she gently removed her fingers, and the emptiness was unbearable.

When she stood, and I met her eyes again, I noticed the glistening liquid on her lips and face. I groaned in embarrassment, covering my eyes with my hands.

"I'd never done that before," I whispered. Samara gripped my wrists in her hands and removed my hands from their spot, forcing my eyes to meet hers. There was a kind of prideful heat there that warmed my entire body.

"That was the most beautiful thing I've ever seen, Athena. Never feel embarrassed for chasing your pleasure with me," she commanded, her eyes still full of lust. I nodded, still feeling the creeping blush warm my skin.

After that, we washed up for real, taking extra care to ensure that any of our cuts and bruises were healed, thanks to her power. When we were finished, we wrapped ourselves up in towels, and she led me from the room.

The moment the door to the bathroom opened, I saw my other three mates standing in the hallways with hooded, lust-filled expressions. I blushed, suddenly feeling very exposed. I met each of their eyes, matching their expressions with my own. My core tightened again, obviously prepared for a round three...four, and maybe seven.

"Shoo, you three. She's still mine until she's dressed again," Samara claimed, gripping my hand and leading me down the hall to a room.

I think I heard Silas scoffing and whispering something like "no fair" under his breath, but there was a light chuckle from the others, and I felt the tense worry that had been plaguing my heart since the day we were taken crack and started to drift away. They hadn't broken us. They hadn't ruined us. We were going to be okay. Eventually.

14

🍷LAZ

fter Samara shooed us away after making our mate scream in overwhelming pleasure, I felt equally amused and frustrated. Silas groaned and slipped into the bathroom, muttering about needing to take the edge off himself. I closed my eyes and tried not to picture the way his strong hand would look as it ran along his hardened shaft as he thought about our perfect mate. Something had shifted between Silas and me the moment we shared Athena over the video call, something that didn't make any sense but also wasn't all that scary.

I shook my head and hurried down the stairs to busy myself in the kitchen and avoid hearing Silas' grunts as he released. I was having a hard enough time after hearing Athena's explosive climax without adding Silas to the mix. Orpheus slipped into his room, and I needed this moment of peace to feel the last few days.

So much had changed. We had a mate. Our powers changed. We survived the Hunters again.

I opened the fridge and pulled out one of the several dozen blood bags, and held it in my hands. I let my power wash over it, analyzing the blood.

O Positive. It's not my favorite, but you can't be picky at times like this.

Wait. Maybe I can.

I focused on the blood in my hands, feeling its contents as intimately as I had the acidic rain, and willed it to shift. To change. There was no bright light or tingling sound, but when I checked the contents of the blood again, feeling its chemical makeup, I gasped with shock.

509

AB Positive.

I'd changed it.

A gleeful chuckle escaped my lips, and I took a slow, languid sip of the shifted blood, which was delicious. Nowhere near the taste of my mate's blood, but tasty nonetheless. The strength was returning to my body by the second, and after a moment, I felt back to normal. Physically, at least. The mental damage would take more than a bag of blood to recover. I took only a few sips before returning the bag to the fridge. I had no idea how long we'd be here, and we needed to conserve as much as possible.

I heard delicate footsteps come down the stairs, and I turned to greet her with a soft smile. Samara looked exhausted, but her eyes held a sort of sweet satisfaction to it, no doubt a byproduct of her shower with our mate.

"You need to rest," I noted, indicating to the bar stool at the kitchen counter. She sat and let her head rest in her hands, releasing a soft sigh.

"I need to check on the Hunter first," she replied.

"We should probably stop calling him that," I pointed out, and Samara nodded.

"I suppose you're right. He's probably just as hated by the Hunters as we are right now," she said sadly.

"Do you want me to come down there with you?" I asked as she glanced toward the door to the basement, a look of trepidation on her face.

"He can't hurt me," she stated, and I nodded.

"I know that." I waited as she looked back at me and then nodded gently. Pushing off the counter, I moved across the floor toward the basement door and opened it, removing the several locks that Orpheus had installed.

"Let's go," I said, gesturing for her to lead the way down the stairs. The basement was precisely what I would have expected from a log cabin. The smell of must was thick as we ventured down the creaking wooden stairs. If we both tried to stand on one step at the same time, I was sure that it would buckle under the weight. The air was thick with neglect, the scent of disuse assaulting my senses with every breath.

Dust particles danced in the dim moonlight that filtered through small, dirty windows and cast eerie shadows across the worn concrete floor. The silence was stifling, broken only by the occasional drip of water from a leaky pipe somewhere in the darkness and the soft snoring from the unconscious man who lay on the sheet-covered couch. I heard his heart beating strongly in his chest, which had me sighing in relief. The way his heart had stuttered and sounded so weak when Silas first carried him out of the window was concerning. Samara did what she could to heal the internal injuries on the run, keeping him alive, but he was in bad shape. He required far more than a short burst of healing energy from a tired vampire. Hopefully, Samara has recovered enough to help him now. I'm just glad Athena couldn't tell just how bad it was. For some reason, she is fond of the Hunter... or ex-Hunter.

Samara sank to her knees at the side of the couch and looked down at the man before her. His face was swollen and covered in angry red wounds. I could barely see his left eye behind the swelling at the socket. His chest rose and fell with labored breaths.

"How is he?" I asked.

"Alive," she answered with a groan. "His father did this to him?" She asked, with an edge of anger in her tone.

She lifted her hands and carefully placed them on his bare arms. Her new ability didn't require her to touch the target anymore, but I imagine that the concentration of healing magic was stronger through touch, and she needed as much as she could get at the moment.

She quietly got to work, and I could feel the thrum of energy in the room as she sent her healing magic barreling through Archer's body. I loved watching Samara as she worked. She was so confident in her ability, which she should be. Her healing had saved our coven more times than I can count.

I watched in fascination as the damaged skin on Archer's face slowly receded, giving way to unblemished pale skin. His breathing slowed to a standard rate, and I felt the fists at my side relax.

Sitting back on her heels, Samara sighed. "He's ok," she muttered quietly. I nodded and smiled.

"You always amaze me, Samara," I said into the basement's darkness. She smiled as she stood, touching my shoulder and squeezing once.

I looked down at the sleeping form and felt the slightest spike in my power. I shook my head, waving away the intruding feeling.

"What's wrong?" Samara asked, worry crossing her face.

"Nothing," I responded, checking in with my power silently. It wasn't angry or threatened, it wasn't trying to save me or fix anything, but it felt like it had something to show me. I ran a hand along my face and tried to pull the new power back to my body, but it was persistent and jumped toward Archer.

"What do you want?" I muttered under my breath.

"Who are you talking to?" Samara asked.

"My power is trying to latch onto Archer," I explained, feeling that distinct pull from my chest as my power slammed into Archer's bloodstream.

"Why?" Samara looked between the two of us.

My power slid into his blood, analyzing its contents and components. My power danced along the edges of his veins, and my mind was flooded with information as it studied it.

My power had never felt so sentient before, never like it had a mind of its own, but here it was, guiding me through Archer's body.

Wait.

"What is it?" Samara asked, scanning my face.

There it was, clear as day. Exactly what my power was trying to show me. I gasped and stuttered a few steps back.

"Laz, you're scaring me," she said as she gripped my shoulders, holding me in place.

"Sorry," I said, shaking my head, feeling my power return to my control now that it had shown me what it needed to.

"Are you alright?"

I nodded.

"Yes, I'm fine. But things just got a little...complicated."

Samara watched me carefully, but I couldn't elaborate, not yet. What I'd just discovered needed to be something that Athena knew first, and I wouldn't take that away from her.

"Let's get some rest," I urged, and she agreed after a moment of hesitation.

We climbed the stairs, replaced the locks on the door, and then moved into the kitchen.

"Where is Athena?" I asked, hoping she didn't press me on what my power had discovered down there.

"She went to one of the rooms to sleep."

I nodded.

"You should go be there with her," Samara offered with a smile.

"Are you sure? She's probably overwhelmed."

She waved a hand in front of her, dismissing my concerns. "She needs her mates. And you need her."

Samara's words drew my attention to the ache in my heart. It began the moment we were taken and separated from Athena and hasn't stopped since. Not even escaping with her had calmed the pain. Samara was right. I needed my mate. I needed her in my arms. I needed to know she was safe, to feel her breathing, to hear her heart beating. I needed to be reminded that we were alive— or at least, our version of 'alive.'

She tilted her head toward the staircase with a smirk. "Go."

I offered a gentle smile back to her and then sprinted up the stairs. Walking past the door to her room, I sighed when I could hear her soft breathing. I forced my feet to head toward the bathroom. I couldn't sleep in my current state.

After the briefest of showers, I wrapped a towel around my waist and headed into the room that Athena was currently occupying. As the door slid open, the light from the hallway illuminated her sleeping form. Her red hair was splayed casually across the pillow, and her soft, creamy skin seemed to glow. My chest tightened at the sight of her, safe. Breathing. Alive. I smiled at the pile of muscles at her back, pressing her back to his front. Silas's eyes found me, and heat curled in my stomach as I moved into the room.

"I'm not leaving," Silas warned, and I smiled, letting the towel fall to the ground at my feet before sliding into the sheets on Athena's other side.

"I didn't ask you to," I whispered before sliding my arms around my sleeping mate's body. My fingertips brushed against Silas' chilled torso at her back, and I stifled a groan but didn't remove my hand. He didn't make a move to pull back, either.

"She's out cold," Silas remarked, staring down at her face with adoration and love. I pressed a kiss to her forehead and breathed in her intoxicating scent.

"Good, she needs rest," I responded quietly, letting my hand trail along her side and the oversized T-shirt she wore. I tried not to react when my hand made contact with Silas' inked skin again.

"She's the only reason we're alive right now," Silas whispered.

"I know."

Silas let his arm, which was folded around Athena's midsection, lift to encompass me as well, and I sank into the feel of his protection. His fingers trailed lines along my ribcage, and my skin erupted in goosebumps. I met his gaze, and there was a sort of longing there.

"We never talked about this," he mused.

"About what?" I asked, knowing what he was referring to but needing to hear him say it. His fingers slid along my skin again, and I groaned, pressing my torso into Athena's form.

"Whatever this is, between us," he whispered, and I think I saw a hint of embarrassment in his expression. If he could have, he may have blushed. "*Is* there something between us?"

"Do you want there to be?" I asked quietly. My voice lowered with lust.

"I think I liked telling you what to do," Silas replied, pulling his bottom lip between his teeth. My tongue darted out and wet my lips. I loved the way his eyes tracked the movement.

"I think I liked that too," I admitted in the darkness, emboldened by his touch and heated gaze.

"But-" he began, and I tried not to let disappointment flash on my face. "I think it's because of her," he continued. I raised a brow.

"What do you mean?"

He lifted his arm to run a hand through his hair, and I tried not to show how I missed his touch when it was gone.

"I've thought about our moment on the video call a lot," he began.

I swallowed the lump in my throat. "Me too."

"I've thought about being there with both of you, being able to touch her, to touch you...to instruct you on the best way to pleasure our mate. To show you how to make her scream by making you scream first." I inhaled deeply at the image he was painting. "And I love it." He smiled softly. "But then I think about having that kind of moment with you alone, without Athena, and I just-" He stopped, frustrated at the lack of words. I paused momentarily and allowed myself to think of the same scenario. Silas and I alone. It was a pleasant enough thought, but he was right. The heat was different than when I picture the three of us together.

"I think I understand," I replied softly, feeling resolute. "And I agree."

Silas sighed, relief flooding his features. I smiled and let my hand grasp his arm gently.

"You and I are like gasoline and tinder. She's the match," I whispered. "We're only complete when she's there."

He looked so relieved I almost laughed.

"I was worried you wouldn't understand," he admitted in a rare moment of vulnerability. I smiled at my friend.

"So, you want to share?" I asked, and even saying the words made my length harden at the prospect.

His eyes darkened, and a devious smirk lifted his lips. "I would love to share." I shivered.

"Good," I whispered, licking my lips. "We should discuss what we're both ok with. You know, boundaries. Just in case," I urged because I do not doubt that I'd let Silas pump into me from behind while I feasted between Athena's open legs if that's something he'd like to do, and I needed to know how far to push him.

"You're right," he said, and suddenly, his devious smirk was replaced by a shy smile. "I never thought I'd have to have this conversation with you."

"Do you want to stop?" I asked. I'd been with men before, many, in fact. But to my knowledge, Silas had never experimented with his sexuality, and I don't think he's ever been with an AMAB non-binary person before.

"No," he replied quickly. "I just... You may need to lead the conversation." He shrugged, then let his arms wrap around Athena again.

"Ok," I began, finding the words. "So, let's start simple. We only engage in any sort of physical intimacy when Athena is present, agreed?"

"Agreed," he responded, nodding.

"So, kissing. Are you ok with kissing me?" I asked, watching his eyes dart to my lips and back up.

"Yes," he said, and I instinctively bit my lip as I watched the heat in his eyes burn brighter.

"Great." I took a deep breath. "What about hands? Can I touch you?" He groaned.

"Yes," he said quickly and eagerly. His eagerness had heat building in my core.

"You can touch me too," I replied, not recognizing the lust-filled voice that was spilling from my throat. "Mouths..." his eyes closed, and I felt his hand find my side again. "Can I put my mouth on you?"

"Gods, Laz," he whispered, almost like he was in pain. "Yes, you can put your mouth on me."

"You can, too, if that's something you'd like to do," I offered, suddenly feeling very exposed under his gaze. I waited in the dark for a few painful moments while he hesitated to answer.

"Can't promise I'd be any good, but I think I'd be interested in trying." My length twitched at that, and I groaned as my core tightened.

"Ok, so..." I paused, not knowing how Silas would respond to the next one. "Penetration," I whispered.

"Fuck," Silas said with a moan, closing his eyes.

"Giving?" I prompted.

"Hell, yes. I'd give." His eyes met mine, and a moan escaped my lips.

"Receiving?" I asked even quieter, barely making a sound. He took a deep breath and slowly smiled at me.

"I don't know about that one," he admitted shyly, and I smiled assuredly at him.

"That's ok, that's why we're having this talk," I reassured him. He nodded, pressing a kiss to Athena's hair.

"But none of this matters if she's not okay with it," he said, and I nodded profusely.

"Of course, if she's uncomfortable with this, we forget all about it," I replied.

"I'm ok with it," Athena's quiet voice startled me, and I nearly fell off the bed.

"Fuck, bookworm," Silas said, a hint of embarrassment in his voice. "How much of that did you hear?"

"Enough to know it's something you both want," she admitted, looking up at me with bright eyes and pressing her palm against my bare chest. "And..." she bit her lip, and I wanted to bend down to taste it. "I want it too." Shock flooded me. "I really want it."

Silas locked eyes with me, a mixture of shock and lust, and I felt myself harden even more as my mate pressed her body against mine. Silas pressed in behind her, trapping our perfect Athena between our bodies. She closed her eyes and let herself feel both of us.

"Tell us what you want, baby girl," Silas commanded, and I had to stifle my moan at the dominant tone he so quickly slipped into. It had its effect on more than just Athena.

"I want you to kiss Laz," she begged, and I watched as Silas lifted himself on his elbow and leaned across Athena to grip the back of my head. His eyes locked with mine, and I searched his for any sign of hesitation or regret, but all I saw was lust and pure need.

I let Silas control me, relinquishing all the power to him as he pulled my lips down to meet his. His kiss was demanding and needy. His tongue ran along the seam of my lips, and I opened to allow him in. He pressed his tongue into my mouth and explored me with his kiss. Athena was pressed in between us, and I heard her heart rate spike as we kissed above her, our hardened lengths pressing into her from both sides. I submitted to Silas' punishing kiss with a whimper that he drank up eagerly before pulling back. His eyes had a red tint as he looked at me again.

"What next, baby girl? Ask for what you want to see." Silas left his hand tangled in the shaggy and damp hair at the base of my neck, and I loved how I could simply let him control this moment and feel completely safe.

Athena opened her mouth but shut it quickly, a blush creeping onto her cheeks. Silas leaned down and captured her lips with his, and I watched as he devoured her kiss. The hand at the back of my head directed my head to their kiss in a silent command, and my lips pressed against theirs.

The three of us pressed delicious kisses against each other's mouths, and I honestly lost track of whose lips and tongue I was drinking up. I was drunk on passion. Silas pulled my head back, breaking the three-way kiss far too quickly. Both Athena and I let out pathetic sounds of disapproval at the loss.

"Don't be shy, baby girl. Tell me exactly what you want Laz to do to me," Silas whispered into her ear, and I watched as her nipples pebbled against the fabric of her t-shirt. I couldn't help myself. I closed my mouth around one of the hardened nipples through the shirt, and she arched into my mouth with a moan. "Words, baby girl, use your words," Silas demanded again.

"I want to watch Laz put their mouth on you, sir," she replied breathlessly, and I pulled back from her nipple with a tortured groan.

"Anything for you," Silas moved quickly, pushing Athena up against the headboard so she could watch. Then he crawled to the far end of the bed on his knees. His eyes were dark with desire as he beckoned me forward with a single finger.

I crawled toward him on all fours as if I were under some sort of spell, wholly lost to his command. My length pulsed with anticipation. I stopped just before Silas and turned my head to see our mate. Her eyes were hooded with lust, and her legs were pressed together, chasing some kind of relief. I couldn't wait to taste her arousal, but first, I needed something else. I turned back to Silas and looked up at him as he gripped my hair in his hands.

"Put me in your mouth, Laz," Silas said, jutting his hips toward me. I was suddenly very thankful that we both had crawled into Athena's bed naked, and there was nothing between Silas and my mouth right now. I leaned forward, letting my breath dust along his shaft and loving the way his body shook. My tongue darted out and connected with the thick head of his cock, and he threw his head back with a gasp. I ran my tongue along the underside of his shaft and relished the sounds I was drawing from his lips before repeating the process two more times.

"Stop playing with me, and suck me," Silas commanded angrily.

"Yes, sir," I smiled just before opening my mouth to take him as deep as I could.

He cursed, and I heard Athena gasp as I took Silas to the back of my throat. "Your fucking mouth, Laz." Silas praised, and I preened under it as he began pumping his dick into my throat. I hollowed my cheeks, giving him everything I could. Athena's gaze on me felt like a blazing inferno.

I let my gaze drift to my mate and nearly came on the spot as I saw her legs spread before me, her fingers circling her soaking wet core as she watched us.

"Do you like the way Laz sucks my cock, baby girl?" Silas asked, straining as he pressed into my mouth again and again.

"God, yes," she gasped, reaching up with her other hand and lifting the shirt to allow her access to her needy nipples. She pinched one between her thumb and finger as the assault on her clit continued.

"Yes, what?"

"Yes, sir," she replied breathlessly, and I found myself moaning around Silas's cock. Tasting the bead of precum on my tongue.

I lifted my hand to cup Silas' balls, and he cursed again, rutting into my mouth in one forceful thrust before pulling his hips back and sliding his dick from my mouth. I looked up at him in disappointment, but a thrill shot through me at the devious look on his face.

"Laz, make our mate orgasm with that talented tongue of yours, will you?" He said with all the guise of a question, but I knew it for what it was—another dirty demand. I crawled on my hands and knees over to where Athena was pressing her fingers into her core, and I wasted no time in pushing her hand out of the way so I could taste her for myself. The combination of Silas and Athena's arousal tasted like a beautiful rosé, a perfect combination of flavors. She pressed her core into my mouth as I explored her soft folds with my tongue. I pushed a finger into her wet heat, and she shattered. I lapped up her arousal eagerly, loving the way her orgasm vibrated her whole body.

"Come here, baby girl," Silas said as she settled from her last orgasm. He had laid beside us and gestured for her to climb up to sit on his face. I groaned as she did what he asked and landed on his eagerly awaiting tongue. I watched with rapt attention as he devoured our mate. My hand gripped the base of my length, and I ran my touch along it, chasing any sort of release.

Silas' hands came up to our mate's sides and pulled her down so that her ass was pressed up to the air, but he continued his exploration of her clit with his tongue. "Laz," he whispered against her sex.

"Yes, sir?"

He moaned like he liked it when I called him that. I did, too. "Get her ass ready for you."

Athena whimpered, and I matched the sound with my own but moved closer so that I was straddling Silas' hips. My length was dangerously close to his, and even the proximity was enough to send shivers down my spine as I leaned forward and circled my tongue around Athena's tight hole.

She jerked against my mouth, but Silas gripped her hips and held her in place against his mouth. I slowly pressed a finger past the ring of muscles and sighed when she rocked back against my touch.

"She's eager," I muttered, feeling Silas' cock twitch against my thigh and pressing a second finger into her.

"More," she gasped, and I obliged, pumping my fingers into her quicker and harder. Silas held her against his mouth, and she pressed her head into the bedding above him. I let my tongue slide around where my fingers were currently inside of her, and she cried out as I pressed a third finger inside of her —stretching her walls and preparing her to take me there.

She bucked back against my fingers with reckless abandon, and I smiled.

"She's ready," I whispered, and I watched as Silas pressed his tongue deep inside her core once more before lifting her from his mouth. I kept my fingers pressed into her as he slid her down his body and hovered her above his rock-hard length.

"Say 'blood' if you need to stop, baby girl," he reminded her before slamming her down onto his length. She cried out, and I had to stifle my cry as I felt his cock against the walls within her. She leaned forward, pressing her chest against Silas and giving me complete access. I moved with her as she rode him, chasing her satisfaction. I pumped my fingers gently to prepare her for the sensation of being possessed by both of us at once.

"Laz." With one word, Silas told me what to do, and I slid my fingers from Athena's ass, but instead of pressing against her hole with my length, I slid off the bed and came to a rest near Silas' head. He tilted his gaze toward me as Athena bounced on him.

"Get me wet for her, sir. Please." I begged, pressing my hips toward his mouth, and there was only a single moment of hesitation before his mouth dropped open, and he took my length into his throat.

Athena's eyes were locked on the action, and she slowed her hips to a more sensual pulsing as she watched Silas suck me.

I struggled to stay upright as he used his tongue to bring me to the brink, getting me drenched for what I needed to do. I was going to come soon, and I needed to come inside of my mate, so I pulled back, trying to memorize the almost lust-drunk look on Silas' face as I climbed back up onto the bed behind my mate. I pressed her chest down onto Silas so her tight hole was exposed for me, and I pressed the head of my length against it. She gasped as I jutted my hips forward slightly, just enough to slide an inch inside. Silas had stilled his hips, but I saw his fingers circling her clit.

"Relax for your mate, baby girl," Silas whispered, and she did. I pressed into her more, about halfway seated into her tight ass.

"Fuck, Laz, I can feel you," Silas exclaimed, closing his eyes and groaning as I pressed further until my hips met her cheeks and I was entirely inside of her.

She was stretched so deliciously around us both, and Silas was right. I could feel every inch of his hard length inside of her. We sat there, unmoving for a moment, breathing heavily as we each adjusted to the new sensation.

"Fuck me," Athena begged, and Silas and I locked eyes before giving our mate everything she needed.

Silas pressed up into Athena from below while I pounded into her from behind, and she cried out, curses and pleas falling from her lips as we thoroughly fucked our mate. Silas pressed his thumb against Athena's clit, making her shake and tremble as she neared her climax. Silas' eyebrows furrowed as he neared his own as well. I let one of my hands slide below where we were joined to our mate and gripped his balls tightly, offering just the right amount of pressure. He surged forward with a gasp, which sent Athena tumbling into her explosive orgasm, and Silas was close behind. The pulsating of his cock within her vibrated my length, and with another pump, I was coming undone as well.

I don't know how long we lay there, joined in a way so intimate and vulnerable yet completely safe simultaneously. I eventually slid out of her, and Silas lifted her off of himself and led her out of the room to use the restroom. When they returned, he handed me a washcloth, and I smiled as he helped me clean myself. I was thrilled to see this new side of Silas—the caretaker. Once Silas was satisfied with our care, he gripped Athena's hips and moved to lay her down in between the two of us. Hands comfortingly traced lines along skin, and I couldn't even tell where I ended and the others began. We just... were.

"I love you," Athena whispered into the darkness. "I love you both. More than I ever thought possible." My heart thumped loudly as it spurred to life as it always did in her presence.

I pressed a kiss to her cheek and then her lips and watched as Silas claimed a kiss for himself.

"I love you too, bookworm," Silas replied against her lips.

With a thumb beneath her chin, I tilted her head so she would look at me.

"Love isn't a strong enough word, but it's a good start," I said before kissing her again. I felt Silas' hand on my shoulder, offering a comforting squeeze, and I couldn't believe my luck. There was a point in my life where I never thought a moment like this would be possible, but here I was. Unapologetically myself, with people who loved me exactly how I was.

I was still smiling as the three of us drifted off to sleep.

15

ATHENA

When I woke, I was sated, sore, and happy, but even as I lay there in the embrace of two of my beautiful mates, I felt a hollowness and dread threaten to shadow the joy in my heart. I tried to slip out of bed without disturbing Silas and Laz, but the moment I moved, they both shot up at the waist with teeth bared and claws at the ready. I wasn't scared but rather startled as I sat up fully and captured their bodies in my arms.

"Sorry! It's just me. You're okay. You're safe," I whispered into Silas' neck before pressing a soft kiss there and doing the same for Laz. Their rigid bodies relaxed under my touch, and I sighed.

Would the memories of our trauma haunt us forever?

Silas was the first to lay back down, slinging an arm over his eyes with a groan.

"Fuck, I forgot what that felt like..." Silas said, pressing his other palm against his chest.

"What what felt like?"

"Fear," he replied. "My heart hasn't raced in.. well since.." I lean down, pressing my ear against his bare chest, and listen to the heart beneath the skin. I wouldn't classify it as 'racing' by any human standards, but it certainly seemed to come quicker than it had the last time I listened to his barely beating heart.

"I'm so sorry," I whispered against him. Laz leaned into me and pressed a kiss against my back, and the three of us simply held each other for a moment, finding comfort in our collective fear.

"I need to get up," I said, pulling my head off Silas and looking down at him. His eyes looked so tired, with sunken hollow circles beneath them. I turned to see a similar look of exhaustion on Laz's face. "You both should get more rest."

Silas shook his head, but I grabbed his chin between my fingers and kissed his gentle lips.

"Sleep, both of you." I saw the moment he succumbed to his exhaustion again and smiled softly before sliding off the bed. Laz kept their eyes on me as I reached for the door, but when I looked back for one last glance before sliding out into the hallway, I heard the soft rhythmic breathing that indicated sleep.

Once I was in the hall and the door was closed behind me, I hurried to the bathroom to freshen up. Last night, while perfect in every way I could imagine, had left me feeling sticky from the fresh sheen of sweat my mates had worked out in me.

The stream of water was colder than I would have liked, but I guess I shouldn't complain. This far out in the middle of nowhere, we're lucky to have running water at all. As I washed away the events of last night, without the comforting body of one of my mates to distract me, I couldn't stop the onslaught of terrible memories from flooding in time with the water.

As the water cascaded over me, steam enveloping the small shower stall, I closed my eyes, hoping to find solace in the sanctuary of the bathroom. But instead of the usual sense of relaxation, a flood of memories crashed over me, threatening to drown me in their intensity.

The events of the last nearly two weeks replayed in my mind like a vicious reminder on an endless loop. The sudden attack in my store, fleeing for my life from a crazed Greg, throwing him over the railing, the feeling of terror as I was drugged and helpless in Archer's arms, the agonizing hours spent in captivity - it was all too fresh, too raw.

My heart raced as I remembered the fear, the uncertainty, the desperation clawing at my chest. I could still feel the cold grip of Greg's hands, the darkness of the office where I was held against my will, the overwhelming sense of help-lessness, and the strangely familiar yet utterly unknown face of the man who came to see me. There was too much happening in my head, too many memo-ries, too much pain, too much fear.

And then, like a cruel twist of fate, those memories triggered something even darker, something buried deep within the recesses of my mind but obvi-ously not deep enough. The face of my stepfather loomed before me, over me. His twisted smile was etched into my memory like a scar, and I knew it always would be.

I shuddered as I recalled the abuse, the torment inflicted upon me by someone who was supposed to protect me. The weight of his crimes against me pressed down on me like a suffocating blanket, gripping hold of my lungs and holding so tightly that I could not draw a complete breath.

Tears mingled with the water streaming down my face as I struggled to shove the memories away, to banish them back into the darkness where they belonged. But no matter how hard I tried, no matter how tightly I closed my eyes, the screaming memories refused to be silenced. Their echoes reverberated through my skull, bouncing viciously against my mind.

At that moment, standing alone in the shower, I felt more vulnerable than I had in years, stripped bare of not only my clothes but of the illusion of safety that I had clung to so desperately for so long. Suddenly, in the chill of the water, I felt a warmth radiate through my body. It took only a moment to pinpoint the source of the comforting warmth. My mate marks heated, and I felt the rush of love and comfort flow through them, from my mates to me. They must have felt my fear, panic, and desperation and were telling me they were there. I smiled genuinely.

Healing would take more than just time. It would take courage, strength, and the willingness to confront these demons head-on. I wasn't sure I was ready to do that alone yet, but as the warmth continued to flow through my body, I knew I didn't have to.

When I exited the bathroom feeling lighter in a few ways, I went to Samara's room to prepare an outfit for the day. She was already up, so I quickly donned some dark leggings and a loose cream-colored sweater.

As I descended the stairs toward the first floor of our safe house, I made a mental list of my questions, and there were many. When I reached the living room, my head was filled to the brim with dozens of daunting problems.

Samara was right. The problems were still here, and I couldn't put off facing them any longer.

Silas and Laz were sitting next to each other on the couch in close enough proximity that they could shift ever so slightly, and their thighs would press against each other. I loved seeing the small ways their new intimacy was manifesting. Samara stood at the kitchen counter cooking something messily, and Orpheus stood with his back to me as his eyes scanned the world beyond the front window. As I approached, they all turned to look at me. They all wore casual clothing, leggings, sweatpants, t-shirts and sweaters. Which wasn't much of a shock for most of them, but seeing Orpheus, my normally suit-clad, perfectly poised mate, in sweats was startling.

"Good morning," I said with a soft and forced smile.

"Good morning, I'm making you some breakfast," Samara offered gently, and I nodded my thanks to her. I suddenly felt the pit of my stomach growl at the prospect of a full meal.

"How did you sleep?" Orpheus asked, his eyes full of concern as he scanned my body, looking for more injuries or signs of pain.

"I slept well, thank you." I crossed the floor and plopped down on an armchair across from the couch Silas and Laz occupied.

We made generic small talk for a few minutes while Samara plated the oatmeal she had made. I ate each bite eagerly and thanked her for preparing it for me. When I was finished, I set the bowl aside and sighed.

"We have a lot to discuss," I stated. Orpheus and Samara moved into the space and sat, Orpheus on the couch next to Laz and Samara on the floor near my feet.

"Are you all ok?" I asked, watching each of them as they met my eyes. Soft smiles and gentle expressions looked back.

"We're alive and stronger, and that's all because of you," Laz replied. "You got us out of there." I shook my head.

"Archer is the one who got us out." My chest tightened at the thought of him. Was he ok? He was downstairs in the basement, right? Had he woken up yet? What was I going to say to him?

"He unlocked the cage, but you're the one who made us strong enough to walk through it," Orpheus said with heat in his eyes. Not the kind that made my core clench but the kind that made my heart swell with pride.

"What do you mean?"

"You know how we each have different abilities?" Orpheus continued.

I thought back to how Samara had healed me, and I had watched Silas shift his form to look like Archer's father back at the warehouse, a shock I hadn't entirely been able to process yet, and Orpheus was able to sense people around him as we exited the warehouse, it seemed overwhelming. But I didn't know much at all beyond that.

"I don't really understand it all that well, but yeah, I know you're all very powerful." I smiled. Pride in my mates was evident in my voice.

"Well, you're right. We were fairly powerful, to begin with, which made it easier for us to hide from Nameless for as long as we did."

I hated hearing about how my mates had been on the run for so long. Never really feeling safe, never settling in one place. It broke my heart. What kind of life was that?

Then another thought occurred to me...was that going to be my life now, too? I couldn't leave grandma, or the store, or Davia. Would they stay with me? Would we ever be safe from the Hunters?

"But you, Athena. Your mate bond, your love..." Orpheus smiled as he said that word. We hadn't said it to each other yet, not out loud, but he said it in every protective measure he took, every comforting moment. He loved me as much as I loved him, and I felt it in his actions every day. He didn't need to say the words for them to be true. "You made us better."

I felt my eyes sting as tears threatened to fall at that admission.

"You gave us some serious upgrades, bookworm," Silas interjected with a laugh. "I haven't even told you all yet," he said, looking around the others and then back to me. "So, you know I can change my form. You saw that."

I nodded.

"Scared me to death, but I didn't have time to panic," I joked, remembering how his hand in mine had suddenly changed, and then looking up to see that haunting face in place of Silas'. "If I had the time to really think about it, I probably would have frozen solid."

"Well, I've never been able to change anyone else's form before," he started, and I heard the others gasp.

"You're serious?" Orpheus exclaimed, and Silas nodded.

"Freaked me the hell out, but yeah, saved our asses."

"What are you talking about?" I asked.

"I changed your form too, bookworm. I hid you from those guards."

It made perfect sense. They had seen me but seemed confused as to who I was. I was so shocked to see Silas looking like the Hunter that I didn't even bother to look at myself. I wondered what I looked like.

"That's a very powerful upgrade," Laz said with a low whistle.

"So, you think bonding with me made your power different?" I asked, running a hand through my damp hair.

"I know it did."

"I could heal without touch," Samara interjected. "That's how I was able to heal you. And I could heal them too." She looked over at her Coven with a sad smile. "Last time, I couldn't reach them. I had to sit there listening to them scream in pain as they endured the abuse Nameless inflicted, knowing that I could help ease their suffering if only I could touch them. That was worse than any physical torture they put me through." My heart constricted.

"I'm so sorry, Samara," I whispered, and she placed a hand on my knee and squeezed gently.

"You helped me save them. You made it so I could protect my family. Thank you," her eyes were shining with unshed tears, and I leaned down to kiss her on the top of her head.

"Do you know anything about what I do?" Laz asked, drawing my attention to them.

"Not really," I admitted.

"I can sense the chemical makeup of different types of liquid. So, your drink that night at the bar..." Their eyes darkened with anger, and someone else in the room growled deeply at the memory of the night we had met.

"You could tell it was drugged," I finished with a sigh.

"Yes, I could." they shook their head, obviously trying to get a hold of their emotions before continuing. "It has come in handy a few times, especially when drinking blood. Knowing if the blood was toxic or had a substance that would hurt us was useful." They folded their hands in their lap and leaned forward, their soft hazel eyes reaching mine. "But now, because of you, I can change it."

They must have seen my confusion because they pushed off the couch and rushed to the kitchen immediately. They returned with a glass of water and put it in my hand.

"Take a drink."

I did, and I loved the way the cool liquid soothed my parched throat. I needed about a gallon and a half, but I didn't want to ruin Laz's demonstration, so I pulled back and held the glass out for them. They placed a hand around mine, gently holding both me and the glass, and closed their eyes. I watched their soft features soften as they focused. I watched the water, but nothing was happening. A few moments passed, and they stepped back, dropping their hand. I looked from the unchanged water back to them.

"Take another drink." They gestured to the glass, and I shrugged and took a sip.

The moment the liquid hit my tongue, my eyes widened. It was an explosion of flavor—strawberry and watermelon flavors washed over my tongue, and I moaned at the taste. Pulling the cup back, I smiled brightly at my mate.

"That was amazing!" I beamed brightly at them. They smiled and sank to their knees before me, reaching for my hands.

"They tried to torture us with holy water. They had it rain from the ceiling, cover every inch of our skin, and it burned horribly," Laz started, and a gasp escaped my throat. "Something shifted in me, and I knew I could change it into plain water to stave off the worst of it."

"For some of us," Silas quipped jokingly. It was then that I realized that my mates had suffered even more than I knew in those dungeons.

"I knew it was bad...but" I started, tears streaming down my cheeks. Laz placed a hand on my cheek and tilted my head to make eye contact with me.

"You made it better," they promised, and I believed them because they made it better for me, too.

"I can feel the emotions of people around me," Orpheus said quietly from his place on the couch, drawing my eyes to him. He stood then, crossing the floor toward the window and looking outside again, avoiding eye contact.

"Ever since I was changed, it's been a constant. No matter who I'm with, where I go, I can feel each person's happiness, lust, guilt, sadness... pain," he whispered the last word, and I clenched my fists in my lap, resisting the urge to rush forward and hold him. "I grew to have a better handle on it, but I could never control it— not really. I just got better at ignoring it. Trying not to pay attention when all the emotions assaulted my senses," he titled his head toward the others, who nodded with a knowing look on their faces. "But it was always there, a direct line from someone's deepest emotions to me."

He took a deep breath, and I mirrored the action. "Some feelings were stronger than others, of course, but when I met you-" he offered a sad smile without looking my way. "I felt you stronger than anyone I've ever known."

"At the diner, you knew I was spiraling," I whispered.

He nodded. "I felt your guilt and knew you didn't deserve it. Not an ounce of it."

I sighed, the fists in my lap relaxing slightly.

"Then I felt your panic," he started, in a voice so low, I had to strain to hear him. "You had that attack at the Lighthouse, and I felt it as if it were my own, from all the way across town." His face was a mixture of amused and pained. "It's never been that strong before. Never in my life, and as you know, it's been a long one." He ran a hand through his hair, messing up the perfectly coiffed image he usually sported. The man before me now was as vulnerable as I was, and a part of me loved that we were in that together.

"When we mated, I felt the power shifting, changing. It got stronger. Like a floodgate had opened, I couldn't shut it down no matter what I tried. I was feeling everyone as strongly as I felt you."

Hot tears streamed down my face again. Mating me had made his power more potent but for the worse. I'd hurt him. I'd made his life harder. I felt so guilty, and then immediately felt even worse knowing he was feeling my guilt at that moment. I felt like shit for forcing him to do all that extra emotional labor. I wouldn't be shocked if he regretted being mated to me.

"I hate that I made things harder for you," I whispered in response. "I never wanted to hurt you."

He turned to face me at that moment, and I could see that his eyes were glistening with tears. However, his face was not twisted in pain or anger. Instead, all I saw in his expression was love.

"Athena, you told me to drown it out when I felt like I was exploding from the inside out. When there was too much feeling, too much pain, too much anger, too much fear. You told me to drown it out."

I nodded, remembering the moment when he had collapsed on the stairs. I recognized the signs of his spiral. I've had my fair share of attacks. I didn't know how literal it was, though.

"You told me to tune it all out, that I was stronger than them, and for the first time in my entire second existence...I was."

My heart began racing as he crossed the room to me and sank to his knees. Laz and Samara had taken a few steps back, giving us this moment. His hands held mine, and his eyes locked on mine.

"For so long, I have wandered through life burdened by the weight of others' emotions, drowning in a sea of feelings that were not my own. Every smile, every tear, every pang of sorrow or burst of joy, I felt them all as if they were my own. But then, you - my perfect, stunning little nymph- reached out to me and offered me something I didn't even know I was allowed to hope for. You granted me the ability to turn it off, to create a sanctuary within myself where I could finally be alone with my own emotions. With your love, you quieted the noise and gave me the space to breathe freely for the first time in far, far too long."

His perfect face blurred behind my tear-filled eyes, and I launched myself forward, throwing my arms around his neck and pulling him in for a kiss. There were no more words to be said.

He drank my kiss as if he were a starved man and I was his only hope at salvation, and I eagerly gave him all of me. When I pulled back, all my mates were smiling at me, and I felt like the luckiest girl in the world despite our current situation.

"I need to call my grandma," I said, watching as their faces fell.

"No," Orpheus replied quickly. I sat back in my chair, pulled my hands from his, and shook my head.

"Yes, this isn't negotiable. I am all she has left, and she's probably terrified. I have to tell her I'm ok." I stood my ground, hoping that my voice seemed as even as I was willing it to be.

"Athena, the Hunters know where you live, where you work... who knows what Archer told them about your grandma before he helped us escape," Orpheus argued, but I put a hand up to stop him.

"That is even more reason why I need to call her."

"Athena, baby, it's too dangerous," Samara chimed in.

"What if they go looking for me and find her instead? What if they find Davia? What if they kill them or take them to get to me?" My heart rate spiked. "I need to warn them."

"You can't tell them anything," Orpheus said through clenched teeth.

"I won't tell them everything, but they deserve to know I'm alive and that they might be in danger."

"If anyone tracks the call..."

"My grandma can barely work her cellphone, let alone track a call." I wasn't going to take no for an answer.

"Athena..."

"No, Orpheus. Listen, I know I can't go back right now." I tried not to think of the possibility that I may never be able to return. That wasn't a reality I was willing to accept. Not yet, anyway. "But I *can* talk to her, and I have to. Please don't fight me on this."

I saw the expression on his face twist with the desire to deny me, but I could see the part of him that understood where I was coming from winning him over.

"Fine, but you cannot say a word about where we are. Time of day, weather, the types of trees outside the window, nothing. Do you understand?"

I nodded, suddenly feeling the weight of what I had to do next settle on me.

He offered me a tight nod before crossing to the security system on the wall and pulling a receiver from the mess of tangled cords.

My fingers danced along the numbers and dialed the only phone number that had mattered to me for so long. Grandma had been my only family for far too long. I had Davia, but she wasn't my blood. Not the way my Grandma was.

I sensed my mates quietly observing me but didn't resent the intrusion. Given the tension of the situation, I understood their apprehension. I was deeply grateful that they recognized why I had to make the call despite our fear.

The phone rang once. Twice. Three times. I took shallow lung fulls of breath into my lungs as each ring added a pound of anxious weight to my chest.

"Hello?"

Her voice was like a balm on a vicious burn. Tears immediately sprung to my eyes.

"Grandma," I whispered.

"Athena?!" Shock filled her voice. "Athena, baby, is that you?"

"It's me," I responded, sniffling.

"Oh, thank the lord, I have been going out of my mind with worry. Are you ok? Where are you?" She rushed out in one breath.

"I'm ok, Grandma. I promise. I'm so sorry that I scared you," I apologized.

"Where have you been? Do you know how long you've been gone? The shop was a mess, and we weren't sure if that man... oh heavens. You're alive. Thank God. What happened?" She continued in a flurry of questions.

I took a deep breath as her questions kept rolling from her tongue.

"I can't tell you that right now. I'm so sorry."

She went quiet for a moment.

"I can't accept that answer," she retorted, the Landry sass seeped through her voice.

"I know it's not fair, but it's what I can give you right now. Just know that I'm ok, I'm alive, and I'm safe...right now." I don't know why I added those last words, but I already felt guilty about lying to her. I didn't want to lie to her about this, too.

"It's those people you met, isn't it? You got way too in over your head with them, and now you're in trouble," she tried to reason, and I shook my head.

"No, no, it's not their fault."

"I should have told you everything," she whispered to herself.

"What do you mean?" I asked, brow furrowing.

"Who is she talking to?" I heard the voice call from behind me. I turned quickly to see Archer standing at the top of the basement stairs. His hair was messy and unkempt, and the circles under his eyes revealed just how little quality sleep he got the night before. But he was standing upright, and that was a positive thing. Maybe. I guess... God, I really needed to sort through my emotions regarding Archer and soon.

"Her grandmother," Orpheus replied, his eyes locked on him, watching him like he didn't trust him. Which was a completely logical reaction, honestly, considering he was the one who kidnapped them in the first place.

"What?" Archer's eyes went wide, and he took a rushing step toward me, but all four of my mates were up, creating a barrier before I could even finish my blink. "Hang up the phone," he commanded with worry in his eyes.

"... I should have kept a closer eye on you, there is just so much going on in this town and with that attack at the shop. I am just so..." My grandma continued on the line. Her anxious pattering filled my ears, and I studied Archer's strange reaction.

"Please, Athena, hang up," Archer begged.

I squinted my eyes at him in confusion, a look that was mirrored on my mate's faces as well.

"Why?" I asked.

"Because there's so much that we still haven't talked about..." my Grandma responded, thinking I was speaking to her, and I tried to focus on both her confusing answer and Archer's pleading request.

Archer gave up trying to move past my mates and locked eyes with me through the window of their blocking bodies. "She knows my father," he uttered quietly. And I think the whole world froze.

"What do you mean?" Samara asked the question I couldn't.

"Why would her grandma know him?" Silas chimed in, taking an intimidating step toward Archer, who, to his credit, didn't cower but just kept his eyes on me.

"Ask her about Jacob Bennett," he urged me, and I let my mind focus on her voice on the phone. Growls erupted from my mates' chests at the name, and all I could see was the desperation on Archer's face. A sinking feeling grew in the pit of my stomach. Jacob. I knew that name, but it couldn't be...

"Grandma," I interjected, slowing her stream of consciousness. "How do you know Jacob Bennett?"

Silence.

My heart sank. How on earth could my Grandma - my sweet, book-loving, disco-centric Grandmother - know the leader of an underground militia of Vampire Hunters? How the hell would those lines ever cross? Unless...

"Athena..." she began, and her tone told me that I wouldn't enjoy whatever was coming next.

"What are you on about, Archer?" Laz asked the Hunter quietly, but he didn't respond, keeping his eyes on mine as my grandmother sighed on the other side of the phone.

"What are you not telling me?" I asked, careful not to let the fear waiver in my voice.

"Where did you hear that name?" She said finally, breaking the silence. Her voice was even, not shocked, but somewhat reserved, like she had been waiting for me to ask this very question for some time.

"Tell me," I urged in a pained whisper as the truth crashed into me. I knew. But I needed her to say it.

She exhaled slowly on the other end, and I braced myself against the wall behind me. "Jacob Bennett is your father, Athena."

The phone slipped like a bullet from my grasp, crashing towards the ground with a thunderous echo. As it fell, the earth seemed to tremble beneath my feet, threatening to swallow me whole. I braced myself against the wall for support, feeling its cold, unyielding surface pressing back against my shaking body. Suddenly, several sets of hands reached out, grasping at my arms and hips, desperately trying to anchor me in reality. Yet, their touch felt distant, insignificant against the overwhelming whirlwind of emotions raging within me.

But despite the haze of confusion, one thing remained crystal clear—his eyes. Across the room, amidst the sea of faces, his gaze locked onto mine with an intensity that sent shivers down my spine. Those soft, hauntingly familiar green eyes were framed by a canvas of freckled pale skin. His dark hair, stained with dye, now failed to conceal the truth that lay beneath as I noticed soft red roots emerging.

In that fleeting moment, the world stood still as the pieces of a fractured puzzle fell into place with a deafening clarity. Archer, the boy with the eyes that mirrored my own, was the brother I never knew existed.

16

SAMARA

Her body went rigid, and we were all to her instantly. I tried to keep shock from showing on my face, but I knew I was failing miserably. The face of our tormentor plagued my vision, and only now I couldn't help but see those subtle similarities between that haunting face and the face of my mate that were unfortunate evidence of the truth behind the words the voice on the phone uttered.

Desperation clawed at my chest as I tried to focus on the present, on helping her through this. Her breathing was shallow, and her eyes darted wildly, searching for reassurance that none of us could genuinely offer. I placed a hand on her shoulder, hoping to anchor her, to pull her back from the edge of panic.

"Stay with us," I murmured, my voice cracking slightly despite my best efforts to stay calm. I pushed warmth through our bond, hoping she felt it. The others closed in, forming a protective circle around her.

Once a source of strength, the bond between us now felt fraught with uncertainty. There was only a brief flash of fear and anger as I tried to separate the man who killed my wife from the woman who stood before me. I wasn't sure how to navigate this new reality. With caution, I suppose. Trust was more critical than ever, yet more fragile, too.

I took a deep breath, trying to steady myself. "We'll get through this," I said, more to convince myself than anyone else. "Together."

She picked up the receiver and held it to her ear with an almost vacant expression gracing her features. "I have to go, Grandma."

"Wait," the muffled voice on the other line called. "Where did you learn his full name?"

"I know his name because he had me kidnapped," she responded with an emotionless tone.

The voice started responding in an anxious tone, but Athena cut her off. "I have to go." Then she hung up. My heart ached for my mate and the pain she was feeling. Her eyes locked on Archer, and I knew she was still processing the explosive revelation, just as we all were.

Laz and Silas stood on Athena's other side and observed her as she took a steady breath.

Athena faced Archer, her posture rigid with tension. Her eyes, usually so full of determination, now held a mix of betrayal and disbelief. I watched as turmoil radiated from her in waves.

"How long?" Athena's voice was barely above a whisper, but it cut through the silence like a knife. "How long have you known, Archer?"

Archer's face was a mask of sorrow and regret. "I only found out recently, Athena. I swear."

Athena's fists clenched at her sides, her knuckles white. "And you didn't think to tell me? You didn't think I deserved to know that the man who had me kidnapped and tortured my mates was my father? That you're my br-" her voice cracked with flooding emotions, and she paused momentarily to compose herself. "Brother?"

Archer took a hesitant step forward, his hands raised placatingly, but Silas bared his teeth, warning him to keep his distance. "I was trying to protect you. Trying to get you out of there. Escape felt like the more pressing thing at the time."

"Protect me?" Athena's laugh was bitter, her eyes flashing with anger. "You think keeping something like this from me is protection? You betrayed me, Archer. How can I ever trust you?"

I felt my barely beating heart ache for Athena. I may not understand the exact pain she was suffering, but I did understand the sense of betrayal that was now tearing at her. I desperately wanted to offer comfort, but Athena had to navigate her reaction to this on her own.

"You're my sister," Archer said softly, his voice trembling. Athena winced at that. "The moment that I found out, I helped you escape. That has to count for something, right? I'm so sorry."

Athena shook her head, her expression hardening. "I don't even know who you are. For all I know, you could be just like him. You kidnapped me!" The mention of Jacob Bennett, their father, hung heavily in the air. He'd taken so much from the individuals in this room. His phantom handprint would forever be scarred onto our souls.

"I'm nothing like him," Archer insisted, his voice desperate with an edge of contempt. "I never wanted to be a part of his world. I never wanted this. I never wanted to hurt you...any of you," he added, tossing glances at the rest of us.

"But you did. And you're still his kid," Athena replied coldly. "And now, so am I."

I watched as Archer's shoulders slumped, the weight of Athena's words hitting him hard. I felt a brief pang of sympathy for him, but my love and loyalty were with Athena. I stepped forward, reassuringly touching Athena's back, a silent promise of my unwavering support.

"He crafted me into a weapon, Athena. He molded my mind, he painted the vampires as the villains, and I believed him," Archer said quietly, his eyes filled with pain. "I am so sorry. But you were right. You have been right all along. My father was framing your Wanderers. He's a monster. As far as I'm concerned, he's the only monster I've ever met." He said those words to us, not Athena, and I hadn't realized how a part of me desperately yearned for that distinction. "I will never forgive myself for believing the lies he crafted, and I just hope you'll forgive me one day. I'll be here when you're ready."

Athena didn't respond. Instead, she turned and walked away up the stairs, her steps steady but heavy with the burden of these newfound truths. Archer watched her retreat with glistening eyes and a furrowed brow.

"Sit," Orpheus ordered the little Hunter, and he nodded solemnly before sitting on the couch. Silas, Laz, and Orpheus were scattered about the room, their expressions a mix of anger, determination, and suspicion. The atmosphere was tense, with each of us eagerly ready to uncover the truth behind Nameless and their long-standing campaign against our kind.

Ever the composed leader, Orpheus leaned forward, his piercing gaze locked onto Archer. "We need answers, Archer."

He nodded.

"I'll answer any question you have if I can."

"Why has Nameless been framing us for so long? What is their endgame?" Orpheus prompted, looking down his nose at Archer.

Archer sighed, running a hand through his hair. "It's not as simple as you think. My father has always believed that vampires are a threat to humanity. He sees you as monsters that need to be eradicated. With or without cause."

"That's nothing new," Silas interjected, his voice laced with frustration.

"But why frame us? Why go to such lengths to vilify us?" Orpheus continued.

"Fear is a powerful tool," Archer explained, his voice heavy with resignation. "By framing you for crimes you didn't commit, my father can rally Nameless support. It justifies their actions and allows them to operate with impunity. They create chaos, and in the aftermath, they step in as the supposed saviors."

Laz crossed their arms with a dark expression. "And you went along with this? You let them continue this charade?"

Archer's eyes flashed with guilt. "As far as I knew, vampires were the villains my father made them out to be." He lifted his wrist and showed us the scar that decorated his skin. "But a person in captivity is bound to react to their circumstances." He admitted softly. His head hanging in shame.

"I never wanted to be a Hunter. Even after this," he indicated to his wrist again. " I hated the idea of hunting another living being. Or sort of living being." He avoided eye contact as he continued. "I didn't know the full extent of it until recently. The Nameless network is huge and well-established. My father is only one person in an army of Hunters who would do anything to erase vampires from existence."

I had been silently observing but finally spoke up. "How do we stop them, Archer?"

Archer met my gaze, his expression earnest. "There is no stopping Nameless. They're too powerful, too connected, too prepared."

"And if I won't accept that answer?" Silas said gruffly.

"There's nothing we can do. We'd have to dismantle their operation from the inside, and I just escaped with any chance of being the inside man. We'd need undeniable proof of your innocence, strategic moves...and death. A lot of death. Maybe they'll stop if you can convince some of them that you aren't the villains. But the ones who don't believe you...They won't go quietly."

Silas nodded thoughtfully. "I'd be happy to deliver them to their deaths."

I rolled my eyes. As much as I shared his bloodlust, we were no match for fully armed Hunters with their current numbers.

"We need a plan. A way to separate the ones who don't believe, weaken their numbers," Laz said quietly.

"I have some information," Archer admitted. "Names of key players, locations of safe houses, and I know the location of the device they used to frame you. But we need to act carefully. One wrong move, and they'll destroy everything, including us."

Orpheus leaned back, considering Archer's words. "We'll need allies. People we can trust to help expose the truth and protect us when the Hunters inevitably retaliate."

"Are other Hunters who, like you, have been lied to? Do you think there are any people who could be made to see the truth?" I asked.

He shook his head. "I have no way of knowing and no idea how to get close enough now to find out."

"Give me the names and locations, Archer. I'll see if I can get some more information." Orpheus grabbed a notebook and tossed it toward him.

Archer nodded and began writing information on the page. He paused, his pen resting just above the notebook's surface, and sighed deeply before meeting our eyes again. "I know I have a lot to prove to you, but I want to help. In any way I can. I'll do anything I can to make it up to Athena."

Silas stood, his expression resolute. "Then let's get to work."

Orpheus nodded to Silas. "Time is against us, but we have the advantage of knowledge now. That's not nothing."

As the group dispersed to strategize, I couldn't help but feel a glimmer of hope. We had a long road ahead, but with Archer's inside knowledge and our combined new abilities and strengths, we finally stood a fighting chance against Nameless and the man who had orchestrated our suffering for so long.

I swore I heard Alora's gleeful chuckle in the back of my mind.

Watch your back, Bennett. The Wanderers are done being hunted.

17

ARCHER

The cool night air was doing little to calm the turmoil within me as I stood on the porch of the safe house. Dark green trees circled the small clearing, acting as a barrier between Nameless and the tenuous safety we've created here. The Wanderers had only sought refuge here because of me, because of my actions. Every creak of the wooden boards beneath my feet seemed to echo the weight of my guilt. I had betrayed Athena, my own sister, and now, the people she cared about were at risk because of me. I wished I could fix it, return to the moment before Doctor Galvin branded me with the mark of the Hunter, and find the courage to step away like I had always wanted, even before I knew about my father's lies. I reached a hand to my shoulder, tracing a finger over the raised white lines of that scar that claimed me as a member of Nameless. Then my eyes caught on the bite mark on my wrist.

Two scars. Two lessons. Two different kinds of monsters. And yet, only one of these scars was given to me by someone who feared for their life. Only one was given out of desperation and fear...and the other out of a desire to control me.

The memories of my confrontation with Athena played repeatedly in my mind. Her eyes, so similar to mine that it was embarrassing to think it took me so long to discover our connection, filled with anger and hurt, will haunt me for as long as I live. She had every right to feel betrayed. I hadn't told her the truth when I learned it, trying to protect her, or so I told myself. But deep down, I knew it was more about protecting myself, avoiding the fallout that the truth would inevitably bring.

543

My father's twisted legacy loomed over me. Jacob Bennett, the man who had raised me to believe in a cause I could no longer stand by, had become the symbol of everything I despised. I had spent years unknowingly perpetuating his lies, and when I finally realized the truth, the damage was already done. Now, I was trying to undo it, but it felt like trying to hold back the tide with my bare hands.

The Wanderers had welcomed me cautiously, a stranger in their midst, but I could feel their skepticism. They had every reason to doubt me, to question my motives. And Athena... I had hurt her in a way I wasn't sure I could ever make right. The bond we could have had as siblings was now fractured, perhaps beyond repair.

Lost in my thoughts, I didn't notice Orpheus approaching until he was beside me. His presence was intimidating and yet grounding, a reminder that I wasn't completely alone, even if I felt like I deserved to be.

"Guilt won't help you now," Orpheus said, his voice calm but firm.

I sighed, running a hand through my hair. "I don't know how to make this right, Orpheus. I've lied, betrayed the people I care about, and endangered everyone. How do I come back from that?"

Orpheus leaned against the porch railing, his gaze thoughtful as he looked out into the wilderness. "Guilt is a heavy burden but can also be a guide. Use it to remind yourself why you're fighting, but don't let it paralyze you. We don't have time for that."

"I can't shake the feeling that I've already done too much damage," I admitted, my voice barely above a whisper. "Athena might never forgive me."

"Maybe not," Orpheus replied honestly. "But you can't focus on what you can't change. What matters now is what you do next. We need your knowledge and your skills. You still have a chance to make a difference."

I nodded slowly, trying to let his words sink in. The guilt was still a constant ache, but Orpheus was right. I had to find a way to move forward, to use that guilt as a catalyst for change rather than a chain holding me back.

"Thanks," I said, meeting Orpheus's gaze. "I needed to hear that."

He nodded, a slight but encouraging smirk on his face. "We all make mistakes, Archer. I've made my fair share. It's how we atone for them that defines us. Now, let's get back inside. I found some information from the names you gave me. We have work to do."

As we reentered the safe house, I took a deep breath, steeling myself for the challenges ahead. As Orpheus and I stepped back across the threshold, the dimly lit interior seemed almost cozy. The others were scattered around the main room, leafing through some files, and I couldn't help but feel almost at ease around them. I struggled to reconcile that only a few days ago, I considered these people before me the biggest threat to my world and safety. It felt foolish now, not that they weren't formidable enemies because I did not doubt that each of them could remove my head from my body and drain my blood in an instant if they felt I deserved it. And the fact that they pulled me out of that warehouse after my father left me bleeding on the ground and healed me, well, that earned them my trust. And respect. I hoped I could earn the same from them in time.

We made our way to a small table in the corner where a map and several files were spread out. I sat across from Orpheus, the flickering light of the ceiling lamp casting shadows on the papers before us.

The file on my father, Jacob Bennett, and Dr. Kline Galvin lay between us.

Orpheus tapped the file thoughtfully. "We've gathered a lot of information about the Hunters you told us about. Samara has been combing through them to see if we can use anything."

I thumbed through my father's file, impressed by just how detailed it was for the short time that they had to find the information.

"His whole life is here," I whispered, flipping through the pages of his past. Even his brief relationship with Athena's mother, Francesca, was detailed along with Athena's birth certificate. Noticeably, the copy did not have my father's name on it, but I wasn't surprised there.

There were several pages about my mother, whom my father married just a few short months after Athena was born. Then, barely a year later, there was me. My mother's death certificate made me pause. I didn't know her, but I felt her absence. There were photos on the pages. My father, with his fiery red hair and bright smile, held me as a child with equally blazing hair while my mother stood by his side and beamed up at us.

It felt intrusive to look through his life as if it were a novel for my enjoyment, each piece of information felt like I was learning about someone entirely removed from the man I grew up knowing. Who was this loving father before me, and why can't I remember him?

"We never knew his first name, not before you told us, and apparently Athena never knew his last," Laz stated, watching me with honeyed eyes. "Now, we know everything there is to know about him."

I nodded, closing the file and sliding it across the table, trying to ignore the sting in my eyes.

"Yes, we've gathered a lot of valuable information so far, but this Doctor Kline Galvin remains an enigma. His records are sparse, almost as if they've been deliberately altered." Orpheus looked down at the file and scrunched his brow in frustration.

I nodded, reaching for the pages and taking a few moments to study the documents. I immediately saw what they were referring to. "It's more than just altered. It's like they've been forged. Everything here feels fabricated."

Orpheus leaned closer, his eyes narrowing as he scanned the documents. "We do know that he's exceptionally skilled at covering his tracks. It's almost as if he never existed before a certain point. No childhood records, family history, or records of ever graduating from any institution with a doctorate program in Occult Studies. Everything starts abruptly about fifteen years ago."

"My dad said that a member of the Galvin line has been leading Nameless for as long as it's been around. We're talking centuries here."

"There's nothing here about any family," Silas said from behind the computer screen.

"If his identity is a complete fabrication, then who is he really? And why go to such lengths to hide his past?" Samara interjected.

Orpheus picked up the single photograph he'd managed to find, an image of a masked Galvin, his posture rigid and composed. Those blue eyes were just as searing as I remembered. "There's got to be a reason. Maybe he's not who he claims to be, or perhaps he has a connection to the vampire community that they're trying to conceal."

I frowned, considering the implications. "If that's true, then exposing his real identity could be our key to unraveling their entire operation. But we need more evidence. Something concrete."

"I have a few contacts who might be able to help us trace forged documents, but I haven't spoken to them since before we were captured the first time. It's risky, but it might be our best shot." Laz interjected.

I glanced around the room, noticing the weary faces of our group. We were all running on fumes, but this lead could be the breakthrough we needed. "If we can find even a shred of his true identity, it could turn the tide in our favor."

Orpheus nodded, determination etched on his face. "Make the call, Laz. In the meantime, we should keep a close eye on the Hunters. They're bound to make a move soon, especially if they are as close to Athena's Grandma as you made it seem."

"Agreed," I said, feeling a renewed sense of purpose. "And Orpheus, thank you. For everything. I know it's not easy to trust me after all that's happened."

Orpheus's expression softened slightly. "Let's focus on bringing Galvin down, clearing our names, and keeping my family safe."

I didn't have the heart to say out loud that clearing their names wouldn't be enough. There were some Hunters who would kill them on mere principle. No, in order to truly save The Wanderers from Nameless, there needed to be no more Nameless.

As Orpheus stood, I returned my attention to the table and the file on

Galvin. The man's cold, calculated gaze stared back at me from behind the mask of the Hunter, a silent challenge. We were on the brink of something big, and our next steps could change everything.

With a deep breath, I began organizing our notes, determined to piece together the puzzle of Doctor Kline Galvin.

18

I sat on the edge of the worn mattress in my tiny room at the safe house, the walls closing in on me with every passing second. The truth felt like a vice around my heart, squeezing tighter with each breath I took. Archer was my brother. The man who had betrayed us, the one I had struggled to trust, was my flesh and blood. And the monster who had orchestrated our suffering, who had tortured my mates, was my father.

Jacob Bennett. The name echoed in my mind like a curse. I felt sick to my stomach, a deep sense of betrayal coursing through my veins. How could this be? How could the man responsible for so much pain be the man who brought me life?

Was I destined to have the world's worst father figures?

I hugged my knees to my chest, rocking slightly as I tried to make sense of it all. My thoughts were a chaotic jumble, each more painful than the last. I had always prided myself on my strength and ability to face any challenge head-on. I had to be strong after losing mom. It was either that or fall apart. But this... this was different. This was a betrayal that cut to the core of who I was.

The memories of our capture flashed through my mind—the fear, the helplessness, the anger. All orchestrated by the man who had given me life. I couldn't reconcile the image of a father with the cold, ruthless man I met in that office. What kind of man could do that to his own daughter? What kind of monster had I come from?

A knock on the door pulled me from my thoughts. It was Orpheus, his presence a comforting anchor in the storm of my emotions. He stepped inside, closing the door quietly behind him. His eyes were filled with concern as he moved to sit beside me on the bed, wrapping an arm around my shoulders.

"I'm here," he said softly, his voice a soothing balm to my frayed nerves.

I leaned into his chest and rested my head on his sturdy shoulder, drawing strength from his warmth. "It's too much, Orpheus. I don't know how to process any of this."

"I know," he murmured, pressing a gentle kiss to my temple.

Tears welled in my eyes, and I let them fall, the weight of the revelations finally breaking through my defenses. "How is this possible?"

He didn't answer but brushed my hair behind one of my ears.

I wiped at my eyes, frustration and sorrow mingling in my heart. "How do I come to terms with the fact that my father is the man who has done all of this?"

"I wish I had the answers for you, little nymph," Orpheus said, his tone careful.

I took a deep breath, trying to steady the turmoil inside me. The truth was excruciating, but I knew I wasn't alone. With Orpheus by my side and the others supporting us, I knew I could face whatever came next. I could survive this. My father might be a monster, but I refused to let his actions define me. We would expose him, stop him, and find a way to heal the wounds he had inflicted.

"What is our plan?" I asked.

He ran a hand idly down my spine. My skin erupted in goosebumps with each pass of his talented fingers.

"We looked into some of the names that Archer gave us or higher-ups in the organization. Information is power right now."

I nodded but felt my chest tighten.

"How are we going to take down an entire organization?" I suddenly was intimately aware of just how...human... I was. My mates were powerful vampires with abilities beyond imagination, made even stronger now by the bond we share. Hell, even the other human in our group now was a trained Hunter who managed to take all four of my mates down alone. I was just...me.

"Are you going to tell me what that face you're making is all about, or am I going to have to turn my power back on?" Orpheus teased, but there was genuine concern in his tone.

I sighed. "I was just thinking about how useless I would be in a fight against Nameless." I looked up at him, and he was gazing lovingly back at me with a soft smile.

"You're not useless, not by a long shot. You made us stronger. That may be all the advantage we need," he assured me with another kiss to my temple. I sat up, turning my torso to face him. The bed creaked under the movement.

The moon was hanging low in the sky, casting eerie shadows through the window of our tentative safety. The weight of my inadequacy felt like iron shackles. My mates, The Wanderers, were skilled and fierce, but even they couldn't always protect us. I hated feeling like a liability, someone who needed saving rather than someone who could fight alongside them.

The thought of becoming a vampire had crossed my mind before, in fleeting moments of desperation, tied in that room alone and separated from my mates. But now, it felt like the only viable option. If I were turned and became one of them, I could fight. I could be the weapon we needed against my father and his Hunters. Honestly, the idea both terrified and exhilarated me, a desperate hope mingled with fear of the unknown. I loved my Wanderers, and the idea of a forever with them was more pleasant than I expected, but then there was the thought of those I'd leave behind. Outlive.

I wrapped my arms around myself, trying to calm the storm inside. Would becoming a vampire really solve anything? Would it make me stronger, or would it simply add another layer of complexity to an already impossible situation? Could I add more stressors to our tenuous stability? The hunger, the immortality, the Hunters, all of it.

I thought about my mates. How would they react to my decision? Would they be happy, or would they try to stop me? And Laz—wise, thoughtful Laz—they had been clear about this choice. About the gravity of such a transformation. Becoming a vampire wasn't a decision to be taken lightly. It was a complete overhaul of one's existence. And for some, it may have been exactly what was needed. But I love my little life as a bookseller in Maine. As much as I tried to escape it, it has become a part of me. Would I be ready to leave it all behind?

I took a deep breath, trying to steady my thoughts. Could I really go through with it? Could I willingly choose to become what my father, my own flesh and blood, hates so deeply? Could I leave my grandma and Davia behind to grow as I remain forever unchanged? The thought of losing more people because of my own helplessness gnawed at me. I had to do something. I couldn't stand by and watch as the people I loved suffered and died.

I sighed. I needed to talk to Orpheus. He was the only one who could help me sort through the chaos in my mind. Laz would try to convince me to think it through. Silas would go through with the change before I even got the sentence out, and Samara would have concerns that kept her from following through. Orpheus, though, would look at this logically. I knew he wouldn't be happy initially, but I had to ask at least. I had to explore every option, no matter how terrifying.

"You should turn me," I whispered as quietly as possible. I wasn't sure if any of the others would be trying to listen in.

Orpheus's heart thumped heavily once.

"No."

His jaw tensed, and his eyes darkened slightly as he firmly responded.

"Orpheus-" I began.

"No," he replied again, standing from the bed. "No, Athena."

"Why not?" I begged in a rushed whisper, jumping to my feet and crossing the room toward him. He quickly brushed past me and crossed to the window.

"Why?" he scoffed as if it were the most ridiculous thing to ask.

A slight pain shot through my chest. Did he not want me to have forever with him? It was petty and childish, but I felt my eyes well with tears, and my stupid heart began to tear.

"Athena, love," he cooed in a pained whisper. When my eyes found him again, he had an expression on his face that I could only place as regret. He pressed a hand to his chest and took a deep breath. "I swear that's not it." He must have unblocked his power because he was staring at me like he could read me so clearly. "I want to spend eternity with you. I've wanted that from the moment my mark appeared on your perfect skin." My fingertips idly traced the raised lines in the shape of a cracked lightning on my throat. I felt my connection with him thrum brightly, and he stifled a moan at the feeling.

"Look where we are right now." He gestured to the window. "We are in a safe house because we are being *hunted* for what we are. Why would you ever think I'd put you through that? I couldn't live with myself if I subjected you to a life of being on the run."

I stepped closer to him, trying to draw his eyes to mine despite how hard he tried to avoid my gaze. "It doesn't matter if I'm a human or a vampire. If you're running, I am, too."

A tear slid down my cheek, and he stepped forward, closing the gap between us to wipe it away. His chest pressed against mine as I looked up into his face. He wore so many emotions in his expression, so vulnerable and open in a way that I knew was hard for him.

"I am so desperately in love with you," he said gently, and the mark on my throat burned warmly.

"So turn me," I answered, admittedly taking slight advantage of this moment of vulnerability.

He sighed, pressing his hand to my cheek.

"It's dangerous," he argued.

"Arguably, being a human right now is dangerous, too," I replied.

"Your grandma and Davia..."

"Would understand if and when I get the chance to tell them."

"Your father..."

"That man is not my father," I interjected.

"This isn't something you can take back, Athena." He brushed some hair behind my ear.

"I know that."

"I don't remember my parents," he whispered quietly, and I gleaned up at him. He made himself busy running his fingers along my hair and shoulder, looking as if he was lost in his own mind. "I assume I had some, once."

My heart tightened.

"The longer you live in this second existence, the more you lose hold of the first," he admitted in a pained whisper.

My heart raced as the realization hit me.

"I didn't notice it until about twenty years in. I'd have blank spots in my memory. Places where things used to be so clear were muddled. After fifty or so years, I couldn't place simple details anymore from my life before I was this," he gestured to himself. "After a century, the names, the places, the feelings, they were all gone. Even if I tried, I couldn't place them." He sighed. "Now? I don't even know if I had family or friends. A life? I can't recall. It's not there anymore. As if I was born the moment I became a vampire, and anything and anyone that came before is gone forever."

My mind immediately drifted to my mom. Her beautiful red hair, her atrocious singing voice, her eccentric dance moves, her love, her heart. I felt a sob break free from my lips.

"It wouldn't be immediate, but over time, she'd be gone, Athena."

Did that change things?

Yes.

No.

Losing her memory meant also losing all memory of *him*. Which arguably would be a benefit.

Dammit.

I withdrew from Orpheus and returned to the bed, climbing onto it and holding my knees to my chest.

"If you want an eternity with us, then we will turn you one day, I promise. When things are safer, and you have thought it through, we will. But, if you want to live a long and healthy human life, that's what we want, too." He settled onto the bed next to me.

"What is that? Fifty, maybe sixty years? Less if I get my mother's disease," I spat. "That's not enough time."

"Eternity isn't enough, Athena." He pressed a kiss to my lip. I tasted the salted liquid of my tears between us. "It never is. But, if I only got one day, I'd still consider myself a lucky man."

I knew we were far from done speaking about this, but his words stirred something so vulnerable in my chest. The part of me that needed his hands, his lips, his love. I leaned forward and let my lips sink into his. His hands cupped my face as he eagerly drank in my kiss. His tongue darted across my bottom lip, and I moaned breathlessly.

Swinging a leg across his lap, I straddled him, not unlike I had that first time on the boardwalk, and I pressed my core against his hardening length.

"Make love to me, Orpheus," I whispered against his lips, and he groaned.

"As you wish," he replied with a devilish smirk. In an instant, his pants were down around his ankles, and he was ripping the leggings and the cream sweater off of me, exposing me deliciously to him.

His eyes scanned my body hungrily, and I relished his attention. My nipples pebbled under the cool air and his gaze, and I felt my pussy tighten in anticipation of what he was about to give me. He lowered his head to my throat and pressed a gentle kiss against his mark. We groaned as the connection thrummed, sending a taunting vibration to my core. His length twitched eagerly, seeking my hot center. I reached between us and lined him up for me before slowly, torturously, savoringly sliding down him inch by inch.

Our breath mingled as I made the slow descent onto him. I felt his heartbeat trying to come to life enough to match mine. When I was fully seated, I remained still, letting our bodies adjust to the onslaught of pleasure. His fingers dug into my hips as he breathed deeply.

"You were perfectly crafted to be mine," he whispered, and I whimpered. Instantly, I felt the burning desire to move, to slam down onto him again, to chase the euphoria I knew he could give me, but I refrained. I was happy to remain frozen in this moment of building anticipation with a man who loves me.

"I'm in love with you too, Orpheus," I admitted in the room's darkness. I watched his face, illuminated by the early evening glow, and was rendered breathless at the smile that spread across his lips.

"Prove it," he challenged teasingly before lifting my hips and slamming me back onto his cock.

I gasped at the delicious intrusion and immediately stopped restraining myself. My hips circled and ground onto him, and his answering moans were exceptionally motivating. I braced myself on his shoulders and rode his cock as if it may be the last time. He pounded into my pussy with punishing but loving thrusts, and I threw my head back, my mouth falling open in a silent scream as he reached the deepest part of me.

His fingers trailed along my sensitive skin sending tremors wracking through my body as he made his way to my clit. Circling the bundle of nerves, he played me like I was a fucking instrument, and he was goddamn Mozart. The sounds I made rivaled the loudest orchestras.

"I need your cum to drip down my cock," he whispered against my skin, and I detonated at the next brush of his thumb. My orgasm erupted violently and quickly. He swallowed my scream with his mouth in a punishing kiss as he pounded through my release. When I returned to planet Earth, he was smiling at me. "That's my perfect girl."

"Was that enough for you, baby?" I teased sensually, and despite the smile on his lips, I saw just how feral that had made him.

"Why don't you check?" He prompted, leaning both hands on the bed behind him and lounging back with a smirk.

I returned the smile and slid off of his cock slowly. We both moaned at the sensation. His eyes tracked me as I lowered onto my knees at the foot of the bed between his legs. "Hmmm," I mused, wrapping my hand around the base of his cock, slick with my arousal. I let my hand rise and fall along his length once, twice. Again and again, slowly, loving how his breath seemed to catch with each pass of my hand. "I think I definitely did what you wanted."

He looked down at me through hooded eyes. "That you did," he agreed breathlessly.

"I wonder what we taste like together," I teased again, and he groaned, throwing an arm over his eyes as he laid back.

"If you don't take me into your mouth in the next few seconds, I'm going to embarrass myself," he promised.

I chuckled lightly before doing precisely that. My lips closed over the tip of his cock, and I sucked him into my mouth. He gasped and gently thrust into my throat. I bobbed my head, loving the power I felt as this powerful creature seemed to crumble beneath my touch.

I licked from base to tip a few times before making a satisfied sound. "We taste amazing," I promised.

"Prove it," he repeated, pulling me up his body and drawing his lips to mine. His tongue sought out mine, and they danced together, our tastes lingering.

He flipped us over until I was pinned on the bed beneath him, and he was above me.

"I need more," he begged, and I knew by the red tint in his eyes that he wasn't asking for more sex. Although by the press of his length against my stomach, I knew he wanted that, too.

"Take everything you need," I said, and he flipped me again until I was face down on the bed. He pressed my legs apart and lifted my hips so that I was kneeling in front of him. I gripped the bed sheets and moaned as he pushed his length against my entrance from this new angle and slid in. I cried out, feeling him deeper than I had before and loving the way every inch of him was claiming every inch of me. He pressed his hips forward, drilling into me over and over at a delicious pace, and I was lost to the sensation of it all. I hadn't even noticed when he gripped my shoulders and pulled me up so that we were both on our knees, with him thrusting inside of me and dusting his lips against my neck. I let one of my hands drift down to my clit, and I pressed against the bundle in tandem with his pounds as he licked my throat.

"Can .. can I?" He asked between thrusts.

"Please," I begged, and in an instant, his fangs sunk into my skin at the base of my throat. I screamed out as another orgasm instantly ripped through me. My body shook, and he had to hold me tightly around my midsection to keep me from falling face-first back to the bed.

His cock pressed into me as his fangs drained blood from my neck, and my fingers kept me feeling like I was floating above my own body.

There was something so intimate about being fed from, and I wasn't sure I'd ever get used to it. It felt like I was opening my soul and letting the other person stake a claim inside of it. My pussy was dripping with my arousal, and I never wanted this feeling to end.

His tongue replaced his fangs on my neck, closing the wound he had made, and I missed the way his bite made me feel instantly, but when he pressed his hand on my spine, directing me to lower my face to the bed again, I forgot what I was thinking about. With a hand on either hip, he began pounding his cock into my drenched cunt, and I couldn't handle the pleasure.

"Fuck," I cried out into a pillow.

He slowed only slightly, and I felt a finger press against my ass. It was tender from last night, but just as quickly as concern bloomed, pleasure replaced it as he spread some of my arousal around the puckered hole.

"I heard you take both of them last night," Orpheus said lustfully. "Did you enjoy it?"

"Yes," I said in a breathy moan. He slid his finger into my pussy, right alongside his cock, and I loved the way it stretched me. When he removed it, he let the arousal circle my ass again.

"I don't get jealous easily, not with them," he continued, adding pressure to his circles until his finger was sliding into me and stretching me. I moaned and pressed my hips back against him. "But, I couldn't stand thinking about how I've never had you here." He ensured I knew exactly where he was referring by sliding a second finger in, and I bit down on the pillow at the delicious stretch. "Can I take you here, little nymph?" He asked gently.

"Please, do it," I begged eagerly. He chuckled darkly and pulled his cock from my pussy. I felt my arousal slide down my thighs, and the moment I began to whimper at the loss of him, I felt his tip press into my ass.

"Relax for me, baby." He ordered, and I did as he asked. Several seconds passed as pain blurred with pleasure. Soon, he was fully seated in my ass, and I was desperately pressing back into him, seeking release. My fingers played with my clit as he began to move.

"You take my cock so perfectly," he praised just as he began to press forward quicker and with more force. Between the pressure of his perfect cock in my ass and my fingers rubbing my clit, I fell apart again. This time, I heard Orpheus follow me with a curse.

Moments later, Orpheus and I had cleaned up and climbed naked into the bed. I laid a head on his chest and hooked a leg over his as we lay together in the blissful afterglow.

"That was beautiful," I whispered into the room's darkness.

He trailed his fingers along my spine.

"Every moment with you is beautiful."

"We could have forever," I whispered. He sighed.

"I know, but I want a forever with you that's not born out of fear," he answered.

"I could help fight."

"I won't change the course of your life because I'm afraid of a little Hunter, Athena." He said it in such a definite tone that I knew he wasn't willing to budge right now. Honestly, I wasn't sure I wanted him to yet. The thought of losing all memory of the woman who raised me was too painful to bear right now.

"Ok, we will put a pin in it... For now," I relented, and I heard him sigh with relief. I buried my head into his shoulder and tightened my hold around his muscular body. God, this man's body should be studied—the perfect ridges of abs, the "v" shape that graced his lower abdomen. Just looking at him had my body wriggling with eager neediness.

I felt so sated, yet a part of me burned for more. I felt like I always would always want more when it came to my mates. Orpheus was right. Eternity would never be enough for us.

"Well, well, well," Orpheus teased. "You still need more?" I felt my face flush with embarrassment.

"Turn that emotion radio off," I said playfully, slapping a hand gently on his chest. He laughed.

A gentle knock on the door sounded, and I didn't bother covering up my naked body because 1. Pretty much everybody in this house had seen me naked already, and 2. If it was one of my other mates, I wanted them to have easy access to offer me the second round I was somehow still in the mood for.

"If that's you, Archer, go away," I called out, a twinge of anger gripping my heart at the thought of the man who was apparently my brother.

"It's me," Samara's voice filtered through the door.

I felt my pussy clench at the thought of her tasting just how aroused I was.

Orpheus laughed again, and I slapped him once more.

"Come in, Samara," Orpheus said, pulling the blanket over to cover himself and leaving me exposed.

She slid through the door, shutting it behind her, and smiled at the sight before her. "Thank you for covering yourself, Orpheus. I would have hated to have to bleach my eyeballs today."

He chuckled, shaking me.

"You're welcome," he said. "What's up?" He asked.

"Well, Archer was asking if he could talk to Athena," she said sheepishly, looking over at me. I felt my fists clench at my side.

"I don't want to talk to him," I replied quickly.

"That's what I told him, but he insisted I ask." She shrugged, and I suddenly felt the flood of love overtake the anger. My mates were always protecting me. I wish they had been there for me all those years ago.

"Athena," Orpheus whispered gently, and I instantly knew what he was going to say.

"I can't," I said.

"Maybe just hear him out?" He prompted, and I scoffed. "Ok, I could kill him for you if you'd rather that?" He offered, and a genuine laugh escaped my lips. He smiled brightly at me.

"That might be a little drastic, but I appreciate having the option."

I looked over at Samara and saw that her eyes were tailing my naked body hungrily, and instantly, all thoughts of anything else were long gone.

"Samara," Orpheus whispered. "I think our mate needs you to taste her." My stomach tightened at the thought of her tongue sliding through my folds, and her eyes glistened with a look that told me she was picturing the same.

"Does she?" She asked, moving toward the bed.

Orpheus manipulated my body around until I was settled between his legs, my back against his chest, and my legs spread wide for my other mate. I gasped at the fast movement, and both my mates chuckled at my shock.

Samara stalked forward like a predator about to feast on her prey, and I couldn't wait for her to devour me. Her tongue darted out to wet her bottom lip, and I felt my legs shake with anticipation. She lowered her face toward my exposed center, and I felt her cool breath on my glistening folds. The chill sent a shock through my body. She pressed a kiss to my right inner thigh, then my left. Slowly. Deliberately. Carefully. Orpheus' fingertips found my nipples and slowly pinched, adding just the right amount of pressure to drive me wild.

I moaned her name, and I felt her hands grip under my thighs and pull my legs even wider for her before she bent down to take the first taste of my pussy. I arched into her mouth and back onto Orpheus' chest at the sensation. She was taking her time, savoring my arousal as she slid her tongue through the folds once more at a torturously slow pace. She hummed happily, vibrating her tongue against my clit, and I gripped her hair in my hands and pressed her face against my center.

She answered my needy plea with another languid draw of her tongue through my pussy. "You are my favorite taste, Athena," she said against my core. After another glacial swipe of her tongue, I groaned.

"Please, Samara."

"What do you need me to do?" She asked, feigning innocence.

"I need you to devour me," I answered with a moan.

"Well, why didn't you say that?" I was about to answer when her fingers slammed into my cunt, and I cried out. Her tongue began assaulting my clit like it was the most delicious thing she had ever had in her mouth. I ground onto her face as she did exactly as I asked. Orpheus worked my nipples in tandem with Samara's now feral laps at my core. Her fingers worked me expertly as she drank my arousal by alternating, licking, and sucking my clit into her perfect mouth.

"Is that what you needed, little nymph?" Orpheus whispered into my ear breathlessly.

"Yes!" I cried out as Samara's tongue replaced her fingers, digging into me. So deep I could almost cry at the euphoria.

I rocked against her mouth like a wild animal, ferociously searching for my release, and she gave me everything I needed. Suddenly, my core tightened, and the orgasm ripped through me, claiming every inch of my body in a blinding inferno of passion.

When my heart rate returned to normal, I saw Samara sitting between my legs, watching me with a beautiful but sinful smile.

"I can't get enough of any of you," I said with a chuckle. "I was so afraid I'd never see you again. Now, I don't want to ever let you go."

Samara grabbed my hand and squeezed. "I know what you mean. If it were up to me, we'd never leave this bedroom."

"Do we have to leave?" I teased.

Orpheus chimed in from behind me. "Eventually, yes."

"But not yet?" I asked hopefully and with an edge of excitement.

"What did you have in mind?" Samara asked, her dark eyes gleaming.

"I need you to fuck me," I answered.

Samara's eyebrows rose with the slightest bit of shock at my forwardness, but it was quickly overshadowed by the heat in her gaze. She shifted on the bed only enough to slip the sundress from her perfect body. Her dark skin was glowing in the moonlight, and I could see the evidence of arousal in between her thighs.

"Touch me, and I rip your hand off," she directed at Orpheus, who held his hands up in mock surrender.

"I'm just here for the show," he replied with a laugh.

Samara maneuvered our bodies so that we were both lying on the bed, my head near the headboard, resting on Orpheus' chest, and her head near the foot of the bed. Our legs were intertwined, and her core was primed to press against mine. When she pressed her pussy against mine, I moaned loudly. My clit was so tender from all the attention it had been getting, but the greedy little fucker jerked to life the moment Samara's arousal slid against mine.

We rode each other like that, slow and sensual, for a few long minutes, just relishing in the feel of our bodies against each other's. Our soft breaths and the sound of our cores meeting were the only sounds in the small room. I felt Orpheus' hardened length behind my back, but he didn't move to interrupt this moment with Samara and me.

There was something so romantic and gentle about the way Samara circled her hips to bring me the most delicious pleasure. I closed my eyes and let myself get lost in the overwhelming feeling of her. Another climax snuck up on me, and I cried out. I heard Orpheus groan behind me as I came down from the mountain of pleasure that Samara sent me to. Her breathing ramped up as she neared her own orgasm, and I dug my fingers into her thigh as she rocked her hips against mine at a punishing pace.

My core tightened as I watched my mate come undone. Her lips fell open on a breathy scream, and I marveled at just how beautiful she was when she let herself go. A few moments later, our breathing returned to normal as we lay there, a mess of limbs and sated bodies.

"That's it. I'm never leaving this room," I joked, and the other two joined me in a fit of laughter.

"Except to go talk to your brother," Orpheus said eventually, and my laughter fizzled out.

"Don't call him that," I whispered.

"But he is," Samara pointed out unhelpfully as she slid her dress back over her body. "He is your brother."

"Why are you two suddenly all Team Archer? He kidnapped you!" I asked, knowing the irony that I was firmly on Team Archer myself before the revelation.

"He also saved you, protected us, and risked his life so we could escape. That sort of loyalty makes up for a lot," Orpheus added.

I scoffed, sliding off the bed and tossing on a pair of leggings and an oversized Led Zeppelin t-shirt from the pile of mismatched clothing I had gathered earlier.

"We're not trying to force you to do anything you're not ready to do," Orpheus said, coming up behind me.

"Jesus put some shorts on at least," Samara exclaimed, accompanied by a gagging sound.

Orpheus pulled his pants back on but kept his eyes trained on me. "I just don't want you to miss out on having more family."

That hit me. Brutal, searing pain caught my heart, and I felt a tear slide down my face. The darkened void that the death of my mother left behind felt even deeper, even more raw, and I could almost feel the empty cavern of pain beckoning for the chance to embrace this new family member. Cruel, backstabbing grief danced in my chest. Suddenly, the resistance melted away, and realization settled. I needed to speak to Archer. He's my family.

"That was a smart tactic," I teased through the tears. Orpheus gripped my chin and turned my tear-filled eyes to meet his.

"It wasn't a tactic." He smirked.

"Fine, well, get out of my way so I can go talk to my long-lost brother," I said with an edge of sarcasm and brushed past my shirtless mate, who chuckled under his breath. Samara gripped my hand and squeezed once tightly before nodding with encouragement.

Exiting the room was easy, going down the stairs was easy, smiling at Laz and Silas when I saw them in the living room hunched over files was easy, but seeing Archer's silhouette through the front door and trying to convince my feet to go to him was impossible. Soft music filtered through the door from the porch and I saw a guitar laying across Archer's lap as he idly strummed.

The melody was gentle, timid, and forlorn. The perfect soundtrack for the moment, honestly. He was talented, that much was obvious. I recalled a conversation we had only a few short weeks ago about our shared love for music and the way a simple song had the ability to tell the most complex stories. He said he played guitar, and I told him I wanted to hear him play one day.

I didn't think it would be like this.

"You don't have to go out there," Silas said from his spot at the kitchen island. I turned my head to him and offered a soft smile.

"I know. I want to," I said, unable to move my feet forward.

"He's helped us a lot," Laz spoke gently, holding up some of the files. "We might actually stand a chance against Nameless because of him." They shrugged as if to say they were just as surprised as I was.

"You all forgave him pretty quickly," I teased, but the humor didn't quite land through my melancholic state.

"Don't get me wrong, I'm ready to rip the fuckers arms off his body if he makes one wrong move," Silas interjected. "But I guess it's easier to forgive people after they save the love of my life."

I offered him a genuine smile, nodded to myself, and took a deep breath before putting one foot in front of the other and heading outside to meet my brother.

19

ARCHER

heard her footsteps before I saw her and knew it was her because of the timidness with which she approached. My heart rate ramped up, and my palms instantly dampened with nerves. However, I didn't slow my strumming as the music poured from the guitar. Music had always been a calming experience for me, creating it, listening to it, feeling it. I needed some of that calm now. Athena settled into the chair next to me on the porch of the safe house. The warm golden glow of the retreating evening sun cast long shadows across the weathered boards, and my fingers danced across the strings. I glanced at her and studied her face as she looked into the distance. How could I not have noticed the similarities earlier? We were not carbon copies of each other by any means, but the strong nose and bright green eyes were identical to my own. I should have noticed it. I should have known she was a part of my family when I met her in her bookstore. I felt so ashamed that I hadn't.

We sat in silence for a few moments as the song continued. The melody was not one I knew but rather just the product of letting my soul lead the way. Eventually, I let the song trail off, the last note hanging in the still evening air.

"You're very good at that," she offered quietly.

"Thank you." I set the guitar up against the side of the house. "I found this in the basement. I haven't played in... a while," I rambled. She nodded.

"You've been busy," she replied with a clipped tone.

I nodded, letting myself feel each ounce of the guilt that stabbed my heart.

"I'm so sorry, Athena," I whispered quietly. She nodded her acknowledg-

565

ment but kept her eyes trained on the forest's edge. I tried and failed a few times to continue, but the words kept getting stuck in my throat. I knew I had to face this and confront the consequences of my actions, but why was it so hard? "I only found out a few minutes before I helped you escape, but I should have told you the minute I saw you."

She looked at me, her eyes softening. "I know, Archer. It's okay. I've thought about it, and I probably wouldn't have been able to focus enough to get out of there if you'd told me then. You made the right choice. It's not your fault."

Relief washed over me, but I could still see the sadness in her eyes. "Thank you for understanding. I just wish I had handled it better. Honestly, I'm not sure I handled it at all."

She nodded, then looked away toward the trees again, her gaze distant. "Can you tell me about him?"

She didn't need to say his name. I knew who she was talking about, the man who connected us. I hesitated, trying to sort through the confusing memories. Some are gentle and kind, some more painful and vivid. There were moments when he was a good dad, teaching me how to hunt, reading bedtime stories, buying me my first guitar, and offering a comforting presence during thunderstorms. But those moments could be so easily overshadowed by his horrible actions. The ruthless decisions, the relentless training, and the way he manipulated and controlled everyone around him to pursue this wicked end goal. Since the moment he confronted me in the gym back at HQ, I've struggled to reconcile the man who cared for me with the monster who caused so much pain and wanted so much death.

"He's not what I would call a good man, Athena. He can be ruthless and manipulative. He believes he's doing the right thing, but his methods are... questionable." I sighed. "He could be a great dad when he wanted to be," I said, my voice tinged with anguish. "But then he'd turn around and do something so cruel, so unforgivable. It's like he was two different people, and I never knew which one I was going to get."

Athena listened, her expression softening with empathy. "I can't imagine what that must have been like, Archer. To catch glimpses of a good father, only for him to prove you wrong. That must have been difficult."

"It was," I admitted, my voice barely above a whisper. That was a truth I wasn't sure I wanted to face. He was my father. He loved me. He wanted what was best for me. That's the truth, isn't it? But only *he* could decide what was best. Only *he* could determine how I lived my life and what I spent it doing.

She listened quietly, her face a mixture of curiosity and sorrow. "I always wanted to know who he was. I thought about him a lot. I was more than content for it to be just Mom and I, but you know there's always that question in the back of your mind. Now, I think I hate that I know."

"I'm sorry you never got to know the best version of him," I said softly.

She took a deep breath, steadying herself. "I'm sorry you had to be raised by a monster."

"It was hard," I admitted, my voice barely above a whisper. "But I think it was all worth it because I met you. You're my sister."

She looked at me, her eyes filled with a mix of pain and resolve. "We have to stop him, no matter what it takes."

"I promise," I said, my resolve firm.

She gave a slight nod, a sign of her willingness to move forward. "My mates mean everything to me. I will do anything to protect them."

"I understand that," I said, relief mixing with the lingering guilt. "I won't let you down again."

As we sat there on the porch, the evening shadows deepening around us, I felt a flicker of hope. It was a long road ahead, fraught with danger and uncertainty, but at least now, we were facing it together. "I want to get to know you," I admitted.

"I'm not that interesting," she replied sheepishly.

"I'd beg to differ," I argued. "You own a small business, and you protected yourself from that asshole, Greg." My chest tightened as the memory returned to me.

Finally, I did it.

I thought to myself as the gas from the canisters spread through the Wanderers' hideout. I waited long enough to ensure the mixture would take hold of the vampires before pulling my truck up the driveway and stepping into the now-destroyed front room. Athena's slumped form was hunched over the unconscious creatures. Shit, I forgot she wouldn't be affected by the gas as a human, stupid oversight. I couldn't risk her catching me here, seeing me, knowing what I'd done. My father wanted me to take her, but I couldn't stand the thought of exposing her to the Nameless nightmare.

She was frantically trying to wake the vampires slumped at her feet when I made my decision. I would get her to safety first, then return the vampires to my father. Maybe he'd be so proud of me, so distracted by the capture of the elusive Wanderers, that he wouldn't notice I didn't grab her, too. But she couldn't see me now; it would ruin everything. Even with this stupid faceless mask on, I couldn't risk her recognizing me. My chest tightened as my heart pounded against my ribcage in anger as the decision was made. I needed to knock her out. Just enough to get her to safety.

I could chloroform her, I thought, prepping a cloth full of the dangerous toxin. But that could keep her out for hours. I only needed her out for ten minutes. Sliding the tainted cloth safely back into my pocket to deal with later, I gripped the weapon at my side. My hand shook violently as I approached the girl I had quickly considered a friend. What a cruel twist of fate this had been. Slamming the blunt end of my stake into her temple, I closed my eyes so I couldn't see the aftermath of her crumpled body on the ground.

Instantly, I felt sick. Guilt and pain bubbled up in my chest, nearly making me lose the contents of my stomach, but I forced it down. I couldn't lose my nerve yet. I couldn't even look at her face as I scooped her off the floor and set her in my truck. Her head slumped gently against the passenger side window. One good thing about it being early in the season was that there weren't many people around when I gently lifted her from my truck and made my way to her store. She would be safe here. Safer than where I was going. I took one last look around the quaint bookstore. Despite the broken front window that was now boarded up, it was a beautiful little sanctuary. I had deeply enjoyed my time there and found myself already missing the afternoons I would spend in the front window with Athena and a cup of coffee. Once I was sure she was safe, I offered her a silent goodbye and slipped out the back door.

I hurried back to the beach house and got to work on dragging the creatures from the wreckage into the bed of my truck. I've never felt so disgusting. With each body piled in the back, I felt the sickly chill of my father's pride, but the guilt was overwhelming in a way that invaded my senses. I didn't feel like myself anymore. How could I? I was just as bad as the creatures in the bed of my truck. I was the monster. I ripped off the mask and tried to drag cool breaths into my constricted lungs as I drove away, intent on leaving this town behind and never looking back when Athena stumbled into the road in front of me. I barely stopped the truck in time to avoid hitting her.

The first look at her had the blood draining from my face. Blood coated her pale skin, and her face was swollen and red. My breath caught in my throat. She wasn't like this when I left her only moments ago. What the fuck happened?

I did this to her. I left her alone. I hurt her.

"Holy shit, Athena. What the hell happened to you?" I asked, sprinting from the car to where she stood, barely remaining upright, on the street before me. Her balance shifted, and I gripped her arms to help her stand. Tears slid down her cheeks. "Athena, talk to me. What happened?" I asked forcefully.

I was seeing red, ready to kill whoever did this to her and then punish myself because I put her in that position.

"Greg," she whispered, and I cursed under my breath. The worst-case scenarios flooded my brain. I left her there unconscious. He could have done anything to her... what if... No. I shook my head and focused back on Athena. I needed to be present to help her. Her legs gave out beneath her, and I slid my arm around her waist and helped her toward my truck.

"Whoa, okay, okay. Here," I whispered, setting her gently against the truck's frame.

"I'm dizzy," she said, gripping the side of the bed and breathing heavily.

"I have some water in my truck. I'll get it." My heart was racing. I couldn't leave her like this. This was my fault. I needed to help her, but how was I supposed to help her with a pile of bodies in the back of my car? I reached into my cab and fumbled for a bottle of water from the bag of vampire-killing weapons I had stashed inside. I couldn't exactly take her to the hospital or the police station with my current... uh...cargo.

"Here, drink this," I said, offering her the bottle. She looked like she had seen a ghost, her eyes focused on something in the back of the truck. "What's wro-" Then I saw it. One of the creature's hands was poking out from beneath the tarp—an unfortunately very distinct hand with recognizable tattoos. I groaned in frustration. How fucking careless could I be? Then guilt flooded my veins. I couldn't imagine what thoughts were running through her mind.

"I can explain, I swear." But I knew I couldn't, and I knew she wouldn't listen. I saw it in her eyes, how her breathing staggered in fear and panic. She was looking at me like I always looked at my father, and I hated how it felt. She opened her mouth to scream, and without thinking, I slid the cloth from my pocket, praying that the toxin was potent enough to work. I clamped my hand across her open mouth and held her body up as she struggled against my hold.

Disgust, anger, fear, hatred.

I had never wanted to disappear more than in that moment.

"I'm sorry," I whispered through sobs that threatened to escape. When her violent struggle slowed and her emerald eyes shut, I helped her into the cab of the truck again, but this time, she wasn't going to her store. She wasn't going home. She couldn't now.

She saw my face. She knew who I was.

She was coming with me.

And there was nothing I could do to stop it.

"I need to apologize, Athena," I started, clearing my throat from the emotions the memory had brought back. "I hurt you."

"I know," she responded with a soft sigh.

"I didn't want to. I wanted to keep you safe, away from all of this." I jumped out of the chair and gestured to the safe house, which was only necessary because of my actions. "I tried to keep you out of it, but then..." I choked up, and tears slid down my cheek. "I swear if I had known Greg would have found you there, I never would... I swear..." I said through body-wracking sobs.

She placed a hand on my shoulder. "Greg wasn't your fault."

"But everything else was." I was broken. There was no other way to describe it. She didn't argue but watched me with glistening eyes. "I spent so long trying to stay on the outskirts of Nameless. Taking only the most meaningless jobs, the least drastic. I didn't want the life dad had planned for me. So, I fought against it for as long as I could. But-" I wiped the tears away and tried to steady my breathing. "I made a mistake, Athena. I let him drag me in and convince me it was the right path, and I feel... I feel like I lost myself along the way."

I felt my knees buckle, and I fell to them on the porch. Athena was quick to join me, kneeling beside my weeping form. She threw her arms around me and pulled me into an embrace that I didn't deserve, but I was selfish enough to accept.

"You made mistakes," she started. "Bad ones." She gripped my chin and turned my head to face her. My gaze met hers, and I saw love there, the kind I remembered seeing in my mother's eyes. "We are not defined by the mistakes we make, Archer. We are defined by what we choose to do next."

I sank into her hold. "I'm so sorry, Athena."

"I forgive you," she replied, and a weight so heavy and violent on my soul seemed to dissipate.

A sudden rustling in the tree line caught my attention. My chest tightened with fear, and I saw the same fear painted on Athena's face as we helped each other stand. "Did you hear that?" She asked, glancing out into the darkness. I nodded, instinctively reaching for my stake, which wasn't there. In an instant, the Wanderers had exited the house and joined us on the porch, their bodies poised for an attack.

"Maybe it's an animal?" Athena said hopefully, but I knew as well as she did that we would not be that lucky.

The silence lasted only a moment before the nightmare confronted us face to face.

The Hunters from Nameless had found us.

At least a dozen Hunters poured into the clearing, armed with violent weapons that I recognized. Before I could react, Silas, Orpheus, Samara, and Laz sprang into action, rushing past us into the open field. Their movements were a blur of speed and precision, honed by years of experience. Silas shouted over his shoulder, "Athena, get inside! It's not safe out here."

Athena's face twisted in frustration. "I want to help!"

"No, Athena. Please. Go inside," Orpheus commanded, his tone leaving no room for argument. Reluctantly, she retreated into the house, her eyes never leaving the chaos unfolding outside.

I turned my attention to the Hunters emerging from the trees. I recognized them immediately, familiar faces twisted with determination. I counted quickly. Fifteen figures spilled into the clearing. Conflict tore through me. Could I really defend myself against the people I grew up with? Could I hurt them if it came down to it?

My hesitation vanished as I watched an arrow pierce Laz's shoulder. They cried out in pain, the impact knocking them off balance. Instinct took over, and I rushed to their side. The arrow was tipped with garlic, its noxious scent filling the air.

"Laz, hold still," I said, my voice steady despite the chaos. I knew how dangerous the arrow was and how to remove it before the poison spread. Carefully, I grasped the shaft and pulled it out, hooking it at just the right angle. The garlic burned my fingers. Laz gritted their teeth, their fangs bared in pain, but I wasn't afraid of them in the slightest. In fact, all I felt was worry for their safety.

"Thanks, Archer," they said through clenched teeth, already healing from the wound.

I didn't have time to respond because the battle around us intensified. Silas and Orpheus fought with a ferocity that left the Hunters little room to maneuver. Samara was a whirlwind of lethal grace, taking down opponents with swift, precise strikes.

I focused on using my knowledge of Nameless's tactics to aid The Wanderers. I shouted warnings, pointing out specialty weapons before they could fall victim to their anti-vampire designs.

One of the Hunters charged at me, a glint of recognition in his eyes. I hesitated for a heartbeat, memories of training together flooding my mind. But the memory of Laz's injury steeled my resolve. I blocked his attack, using the same techniques we had drilled into each other. With a swift motion, I disarmed him, sending his weapon clattering to the ground.

"You're defending these bloodsuckers?" He spat at me with a venomous tone full of disgust.

"They're not the monsters Nameless makes them out to be!" I replied, blocking his next punch.

"Aren't they?" he yelled back, pointing in the direction of Silas, who had his vicious claws hooked into the belly of another Hunter as she cried out. If I'd stopped looking there, it could have convinced me of what my fellow Hunter was saying, but instead, I looked closer. The Hunter, who was being ravaged by Silas' claws, had a dagger buried into his side.

"They're fighting back. You are the ones who attacked us!" I screamed back at him.

"Us? You're one of them now?" His face twisted in contempt.

"Please believe me, Nameless framed them. They want us to kill them all... and they don't deserve it!" I begged him. If I could convince them to listen, there wouldn't need to be any death.

"You're a fool," he replied, swinging his fists again and landing a punch in my gut. I doubled over and saw as he reached for his discarded weapon again.

"Stop, Arthur, please," I begged, but the determination in his eyes was unmistakable. I swiftly disarmed him and buried the blade of his own dagger into his chest. His eyes widened, and he staggered back. Blood spilled from his wound.

"Nisi Nox," he choked out through the blood filling his mouth as he fell to the ground and the life drained from his eyes. I tried not to let my gaze trail across his lifeless form as sickness bubbled in my throat.

I guess in a way, I was still protecting the night from the monsters who threatened to hurt the innocent. It may have looked differently now, but for the first time, I actually found myself proud of the stance I've taken, and the people I've chosen to protect.

I am finally fighting for my safety, and the safety of those that matter to me.

Around me, the battle raged on, a blur of motion and sound. I fought alongside The Wanderers against those who had once been my comrades after failed attempts to get them to see reason.

Orpheus ripped the throat out of a boy who came to my tenth birthday party, while Silas dragged his claws across the throat of a girl I had a crush on during training. The clash of emotions was agonizing to steady myself against. "Please believe me," I begged again before another Hunter ignored my pleas and continued their assault on the Wanderers.

"Samara!" I heard Athena's voice scream out, and I turned to find the female vampire in the battle, each of her arms held behind her. Ropes doused in holy water, searing against her skin as she screamed out. The Hunter held a stake above his head, aimed for the kill.

Then Athena was rushing across the expanse.

"No, Athena, stop!" I called out after her, sprinting in her direction. The other Wanderers heard my call and turned to see the current situation. In their distraction, both Silas and Orpheus were dealt vicious blows by the few remaining Hunters. Silas fell to his knees, and Orpheus doubled over as the wooden stakes were buried deep into their skin. They were lucky that the Hunters barely missed their hearts.

How quickly the tides of this fight have turned.

I sprinted after Athena as she raced past the fallen bodies of Hunters and toward her captured mate. She's quick, too quick for me,

"Athena, don't!" Samara cried out, eyes wide with fear as she approached. The world seemed to slow as the glint of the stake flashed through the air, hurtling toward Samara. My heart pounded in my chest, the scene unfolding with a terrible clarity. In an instant, Athena threw herself in front of Samara, her body moving faster than I could process.

"No!" My screams echoed across the clearing.

The stake pierced Athena's heart with a sickening thud, her eyes widening in shock and pain. My breath caught in my throat, and my feet stilled as Athena sank to the ground, the weapon still lodged deep in her chest, her breathing shallow and labored.

I stood frozen, unable to react. My mind was racing, but my body was paralyzed by fear and grief. The other Wanderers erupted into a fury unlike I've ever seen, their rage transforming them into the monsters of nightmares. Despite their injuries, Silas, Orpheus, and Laz attacked the remaining Hunters with a vengeance, their strikes swift and deadly. The air filled with the sounds of battle—clashing weapons, cries of pain, and the unmistakable scent of blood. Samara took her vengeance out on the Hunters who held her back and the one who had driven the stake into Athena's chest by using the very rope they bound her with to strangle the air from their lungs.

Her primal scream of pain was so palpable I felt it in my very bones.

My feet were rooted to my spot. I was unable to move, breathe, or tear my eyes from the bloodied body of my sister as she struggled to drag in breath. Samara dropped to her knees beside Athena after the last assailant had fallen, her eyes slowly reverting to a more human color and filled with horror and sorrow. "Athena, stay with me. I can heal you," she pleaded, her voice breaking. "Please, don't leave us." She placed her hands on Athena's arms, and I saw a faint white glow emulating from her palms.

I forced myself to move, crossing the chasm of distance. My hands trembled as I knelt beside my sister. "Athena, I... I don't know what to do," I confessed, my voice choked with emotion. The sight of her lying there, so vulnerable and hurt, tore me apart. "Please, Athena," I whispered, my voice trembling. "Stay with us. We need you. I need you."

The other Wanderers joined us, having finally discarded the remaining Hunters.

"Heal her," Silas demanded in an almost inhuman tone. If I could draw my eyes from my sister, I'd see him in his full vampire form.

"She's so weak," Samara cried out, ripping the stake from her chest and pressing her palms onto the wound. Blood pooled beneath her hands and slid past her fingers.

"Athena, baby, you're ok, you're ok," Laz cooed, sliding to the ground by her head and lifting it into their lap.

"It's not working," Samara screamed in frustration and anger. "She's slipping away! This can't be happening, please, not again." Tears poured from her eyes as she screamed.

"Orpheus! Do something!" Silas screamed.

The normally composed vampire looked disheveled and weak, standing bare-chested, covered in blood, and sporting vicious slashes and burns across his skin as he looked down at the scene in shock.

"Orpheus!" Laz echoed, desperation lacing their tone.

"I... I don't.." Orpheus stuttered.

"She's dying!" Samara cried out again, pressing her hands even harder against Athena's skin. Suddenly, all four of them reached up to clutch their chests in pain as if something was stabbing them.

"The bond is severing," Laz cried out through mournful sobs.

"Somebody has to be able to save her," I whispered, reaching for Athena's hand and holding it in mine. Her breathing had slowed so much that I could barely see her broken chest rise and fall anymore. The thought of losing her, just as we've finally found each other, sliced into my heart and sent me spiraling into a devastating landscape of pain and panic. I'd give anything to keep her here. I'd do anything to protect her. She's my family. She's my sister. I can't lose her.

"Turn her," I demanded.

Samara looked up at Orpheus, her eyes pleading.

"She doesn't understand what it means..." he began.

"She'd still be here!" Silas argued in his animalistic voice.

"We'd be condemning her to a life of being a monster," Orpheus said, but his resolve seemed to falter.

"But at least she'd still be here," Samara cried out. "Please, she's almost gone."

I saw the turmoil in his eyes, something maybe the others couldn't recognize, but I could. He knew just how dangerous his existence was and how scary it was to be forced to become something you didn't want to be. Something you don't fully understand.

"Orpheus," I began, getting his attention. He turned his tear-filled eyes to me. "You are not a monster. None of you are. And she won't be either."

He nodded softly, releasing his breath on a shaky exhale before rushing forward and falling to his knees.

"Everyone, drink from her. Just a little. Make it quick," Orpheus ordered, his dominant persona fully restored. I slid back to allow the four of them to surround her. Laz and Silas each grabbed a wrist, and Samara and Orpheus settled their mouths on either side of her neck.

They sank their fangs into her skin and took hurried drinks of her crimson blood before pulling back. "Now," Orpheus commanded again. And I watched as the four of them sank their fangs into their own wrists to let their nearly black blood flow down their arms, and one after another, they placed their bleeding wrists at Athena's mouth, allowing the blood to drip onto her tongue.

"Drink, little nymph, please." I waited to feel disgusted, for the fear of vampires to return, but I only felt desperate hope.

I wanted this to work.

I needed this to work.

Once all four of them had drank from her and pressed their wrists to her lips, they sat back, their chests heaving with ragged breathing.

"Is it working?" Silas asked, his eyes returning slightly to his more human and vulnerable shade.

Samara pressed her hands against Athena's form and closed her eyes as she focused.

"Samara," Laz urged impatiently.

"Hold on," Samara snapped. I could hear my heartbeat in my ears as the moment of silence allowed the weight of the last few minutes to crash over me. Fifteen Nameless soldiers were dead, scattered across the field around me, and now my sister might be following them to whatever afterlife there is.

We huddled around Athena's still form, the air thick with tension and desperation. The Wanderers had done everything they could. Now, we wait.

The night was eerily quiet, and the only sounds were our shallow breaths and the occasional rustling of leaves in the wind. Samara clutched Athena's hand, her eyes never leaving her face. "I can't feel a heartbeat anymore. She's dead."

A sob ripped from my throat, and I cried out—pain unlike any I'd ever experienced pooled in my chest.

"That doesn't mean it didn't work. We're all dead, too. That's how it works." Orpheus insisted hopefully, desperately trying to convince himself of the truth behind his words.

"Come on, Athena," Samara whispered, her voice cracking. "You have to come back to us." Orpheus paced back and forth, his normally calm demeanor shattered.

"What if it doesn't work? What if we've lost her?" Laz spoke. Their voice was raw with worry, each word a dagger to our hearts.

Silas stood and stepped back, his fists clenched, his jaw tight. "She's strong. If anyone can survive this, it's Athena," he said, more to convince himself than anyone else.

I knelt beside her, my heart pounding in my chest. The bite marks on her neck and wrist, the ones we had hoped would save her, looked too small to make a difference now. "Athena," I whispered, my voice trembling. "Please."

Minutes felt like hours as we waited, uncertainty pressing down on us in thick waves. Through every flicker of the moonlight on her skin, every breeze of wind rustling her hair, we watched with bated breath, hoping for a sign of life. Or second life. My mind raced with a thousand thoughts, each more desperate than the last. Had we done enough? Had we acted too late? Would she survive? Would she be upset with us if she did?

The moon cast a cold, pale light over us, a stark contrast to the warmth we so desperately needed—the warmth that Athena so often brought to our lives. I felt like I was trapped in my private hell, fearing the worst but clinging to hope. The silence was deafening, a void filled with our collective anxiety.

Then, a shudder ran through Athena's body. We all froze, our eyes locked on her, waiting for any further movement. Another shudder, and then her eyes fluttered open to reveal bright red pupils. But despite the terrifying sight, relief was the only thing I could feel.

"Oh, thank God," Samara gasped, tears streaming down her face. "Athena, you're ok."

Athena's gaze was unfocused initially, but slowly, recognition dawned in her eyes. She looked at each of us in turn, a weak smile forming on her lips. "I... I'm here," she whispered, her voice faint but unmistakably alive.

We all exhaled. The collective breath we held released with a surge of joy and relief. Silas let out a triumphant shout. Orpheus sank to his knees in gratitude, letting his head fall back as he turned his face to the sky with a relief-filled sigh, and Laz wiped away a tear, their expression softening.

I leaned in close, my eyes wet with emotion. "You scared us," I said, my voice strained. I was worried that whatever transformation there was would take away the parts of Athena that I recognized as my sister, but other than her slightly reddened eyes, she was still just...her.

Athena nodded weakly, her eyes scanning the area. "What happened?"

"We'll explain everything soon," Orpheus pressed a kiss to her bloodied lips. "But we need to get out of here, now, before any more Hunters show up. And you need to feed."

20

ATHENA

 y head was throbbing, and my chest felt like it was on fire. In fact, my whole upper body felt like it was alight with flames, all the way from my sternum, up the column of my throat, and to my eyes. I couldn't make sense of the jumbled mess of memories that led me to this moment. There was an ambush. I remembered that much. Then Silas told me to go inside, and I did despite every fiber of my being telling me not to. Watching from the window, I was forced to stand by and watch my mates and brother taking on skilled and blood-thirsty Hunters. Then I remember Samara's arms being bound, her screams of pain. I felt it through our bond. She needed me. So I ran. Then nothing. I don't recall what happened after that, but looking around, I saw each of their faces. A little battered and bruised for sure, but alive. I sighed in relief.

"What happened?" I asked.

"We'll explain everything soon," Orpheus pressed a kiss to my tender lips, bringing my attention to the strange taste there. "But we need to get out of here, now, before any more Hunters show up. And you need to feed."

"Feed?" I asked, struggling to sit up. Samara helped steady me, and I watched as the others exchanged nervous glances.

"Your injuries were severe," Orpheus started, indicating the stake that was on the ground beside me. I tracked the movement, and my eyes landed on the weapon.

"You jumped in front of a Hunter's stake," Samara whispered. "You saved my life by sacrificing yours," she said adoringly but with an edge of pain.

"Oh, Samara, I'm so sorry," I started, reaching a hand to cup her face. "I hate that I put you in that position again. I didn't think. I just had to save you." Thoughts of Alora flooded my mind, and I felt instantly guilty for my part in this traumatic experience.

Samara pressed a gentle kiss to my lips.

"So you healed me?" I asked after pulling back. Samara glanced up at Orpheus again.

"Stop having silent exchanges and tell me what happened," I said a little more forcefully.

We need to tell her. Samara's voice echoed in my mind the way it had back at Nameless when we were able to create that strange mental link.

"Tell me what?" I asked. Samara's eyes widened.

You heard that? She asked through the channels of her mind again.

Yes, I heard that. I bit back through my mind.

"What's going on," Silas asked.

"She established the mental link again," Samara said.

As she said it, I closed my eyes and focused on the bond I had with my mates. Back at the Nameless headquarters, I had managed to create a link with Laz, and Samara was able to speak to them, but the signal was weak. And no matter how hard I tried, I couldn't do it again. But here, at this moment, I felt each of our bonds so viscerally, like they were tangible threads connecting me to each of them. They felt malleable in my hands. I knew I could pull on them as I needed. I focused on one of them and was pleased to see just how easily the connection formed.

I deserve to know what's going on. I said.

Orpheus' eyes widened.

I can hear you. He replied silently.

I was too confused and afraid to revel in the excitement of the mental connections being stronger and easier to control now.

Good, then tell me what happened. I begged.

"You weren't going to survive. We..." Orpheus responded aloud, his voice choked up. We almost lost you." I tried to stand, but my legs felt too weak beneath me. Samara and Archer both grabbed an arm and helped me to my feet, remaining close enough to keep me steady.

"I'm ok. I'm here," I promise, throwing my arms around his neck.

"I know, but.." he started but paused to breathe. I pulled back and took this time to pull my other mates into an embrace. Silas sank into my arms, finally releasing the tension in his body in the safety of my hug. He pressed a flurry of kisses against my throat, and I smiled at him before moving to grip Laz. They held me gently as if they were afraid I'd drift away at any moment. We shared a brief kiss, and they brushed my hair behind an ear, staring into my eyes with so much adoration I was almost swimming in it. Samara was waiting for my embrace, and she molded her arms around my body perfectly, sinking her hands into my hair and around my waist and pressing me flush against her body.

Then, I turned to face Archer. We had only just settled the distance between us, and I was so afraid that I would lose him before I ever had a chance to get to know him. I tossed my arms around his neck and pulled him close. He hugged me back desperately, just as afraid to lose this bond as I was, it seemed. Suddenly, a pungent aroma filled my nostrils, something almost sweet and sharp. Then I felt it, a sudden, intense hunger. I inhaled deeply, and the scent of his blood filled my senses, rich and intoxicating. And so very mouth-watering.

My vision shifted, a red tint creeping in around the edges. I could feel my front teeth extending, sharp, and aching with a need I had never experienced before. The sharp points bit into the skin of my bottom lip. The warmth of his body and the pulse of his blood became the only thing I could focus on. My throat burned with a desperate thirst, and my mind clouded with a singular, overpowering desire.

Drink.

I tried to pull back, to warn him, but my body refused to obey. The primal urge was too strong, overwhelming any rational thought. Archer's voice became a distant murmur as the sound of his heartbeat pounded in my ears, each thump calling to me, tempting me.

"Athena?" he asked, concern creeping into his voice as he felt me tense. "Are you okay?"

I opened my mouth to speak, but all that came out was a low, guttural growl. Panic flared within me, fighting against the hunger, but it was a losing battle. I could think of nothing else but the need to sink my fangs into his neck, to taste the blood that was so tantalizingly close.

"No," I managed to choke out. My voice was strained and barely human. "Archer, stay back."

He pulled away slightly, his eyes widening in alarm as he saw the transformation overtaking me.

"I... I'm so thirsty," I gasped, my fangs fully extended now, my vision swimming in red. "I can't control it."

The realization of what I had become hit me with brutal clarity.

I was a vampire.

And the hunger was all-consuming.

As I fought to hold on to my last shred of humanity, the scent of Archer's blood was a relentless torment, pushing me to the brink.

I clenched my fists, digging my nails into my palms in a desperate attempt to focus on something other than hunger. "Get away from me," I pleaded, my voice a mixture of desperation and fear. "Please, Archer, go."

Arms encircled my waist and pulled me back against a hard wall of muscle. The loosely coiled serpent at the base of my throat pulsed with energy as Silas held me tight to his frame. His presence instantly calmed me, and the red tint that had colored my world slowly dissipated, but the fangs remained, and my hunger didn't wane.

"You're ok, I've got you, bookworm," Silas whispered into my ear.

"I don't want to hurt him," I replied in a broken whisper. Orpheus approached me with an almost guilty look on his face. The closer he got to me, the more the lightning-shaped mark on my neck pulsed.

"Laz, go get a blood bag from the fridge," he ordered, and my curly-haired mate gave me one last solemn look before rushing off toward the house.

I'm so sorry, Athena. I never wanted to take this choice away from you. Orpheus spoke directly into my mind.

Part of me was thrilled that I was going to be able to spend eternity by their side, but another part of me was terrified of losing the person I've always been to make room for this new version of myself. I sighed, closing my eyes and leaning my head back against Silas' chest.

"The mental link is stronger now," I whispered, trying to avoid thinking about my hunger by focusing on something else. "Is that a vampire thing?"

"Well, yes and no," Samara replied. "I think it's your gift."

I steadied my breathing, trying to force my fangs to retreat so I could focus on this new piece of information.

"My gift?" I asked.

"Your vampire ability," Orpheus chimed in. "Like how I feel emotions, or Samara can heal," he continued. "It was latent as a human. That's why you were able to establish the link a few times, but now that you're one of us, it's been unlocked. I should have guessed that was the case when I first heard about it."

"That's... interesting," I said through gritted teeth as the hunger returned to overtake my senses. I couldn't focus on anything but the burning in my throat and the scent of delicious human blood emanating from my brother.

"Here ya go, darlin'," Laz said as they returned, a bag filled with dark crimson blood in their hand. The moon phases on my upper thigh vibrated as they neared me. They held the bag out for me, and despite the burning thirst in my throat, I hesitated.

"You're going to be ok, Athena. I promise." Samara stepped forward, sending her mark on my wrist, humming with energy, and placing a hand on my arm. My tongue darted out to wet my bottom lip, tasting the sheen of my own blood that my fangs had drawn. The blood tasted good, like a decadent sweet treat, the most delicious of desserts, but the blood within Archer's veins was like sustenance. It called to me with the promise of fulfillment to quench this vicious thirst.

"Drink, Athena. You'll feel better," Orpheus urged, and Laz pressed the bag closer toward me.

Gripping the bag in one hand, I watched as my mates studied me with a mixture of anticipation and guilt. They were so afraid. Afraid for me. Or maybe afraid of me? Were they upset that this was who I was now? Were they feeling forced into an eternity with me that they didn't plan for themselves?

"Stop that," Orpheus commanded softly. I glanced at him, unsure if he felt my emotions or if I unwillingly broadcasted my thoughts to them. "Don't let your mind say those things to you. Don't let your fears make you feel unworthy of this. We love you, we want you, and we are thrilled that you are safe and *alive*." He cleared his throat. 'We're just worried that you'll resent us. That you'll resent me." His eyes turned to the ground, and I felt my suddenly quiet heart ache.

I lifted the bag to my mouth, keeping my eyes trained on my mates in front of me. I let the first wash of the thick crimson liquid cross my lips, and the jolt of thirst was like electricity dancing through my blood. I lost all sense of myself and sank my teeth into the bag, allowing the blood to pour into my mouth.

It was like a blinding light had blurred my senses, warm and vibrant. The first drop of blood touched my tongue, and an explosion of sensation engulfed me. A heady mix of sweetness and iron that seemed to sing through every nerve in my body. The warmth of it spread like wildfire through my chest, igniting a primal satisfaction deep within me.

After every last drop of the delicious nectar was drained from the bag, I licked my lips to savor the final taste, moaning in delight at the feeling of fullness in my chest. I opened my eyes to see four sets of ravenous eyes watching me with lustful hunger, but as my red-tinted eyes settled on the fifth set of eyes, I felt the pointed tips of my fangs retreat, and the color returned to the world as the tint disappeared.

He looked at me like someone might look at a criminal. As if he was disgusted at what I had done and what I had become. The guilt overshadowed the euphoria of feeding. He's only just begun to see vampire-kind as more than the monsters from his nightmares, and here I am, proving those stories right.

"Archer-" I started, my voice finally returning to a tone I recognized as my own. "I am so sorry you had to see that. I swear I wouldn't hurt you," I promised, even though I had no way of knowing if that was the truth. If my mates hadn't stopped me, would I have hurt Archer? Would I have been able to keep myself from draining him? I'd like to think so, but there was so much unknown about my new existence.

"I know," he replied, his face softening. "I'm just-"

"I'm not a monster," I blurted out, a phrase meant for his ears, but it landed on my heart just as hard.

Archer's face contorted in pain as he stepped forward. His hand came to a rest on my shoulder. The proximity only amplified how good his blood smelled, but I found it significantly easier to hold on to the impulses now that I had fed. It helped that I had the presence of my mates at my back, knowing they'd step in if I needed them.

"I know that, Athena." His green eyes met mine, and I saw a light sheen of tears cresting. "God, of course, I know that. You're you. And you're alive. That's all that matters to me."

"I thought vampires weren't alive," I teased gently, an edge of insecurity in my tone. I didn't dare let my hope overshadow the very real possibility that things would never be ok between us.

"You may not be human, but you are alive," he answered firmly.

I threw my arms around him again, all thoughts of sinking my fangs into his throat, a distant memory as the rush of love I had for my brother overtook them all. He held me back, and something shifted in the dark void in my heart. The pain making way for a new connection to take root.

"We need to move. We don't know if they'll send more," Silas spoke up from behind me. Pulling back from my brother, I turned to see the others all agree in anxious eagerness.

"How do you think they found us?" Samara asked.

"My father might have tracked the call you made to your grandma if she told him about it," Archer replied, and I was suddenly reminded about that horrible mess that I needed to process soon.

"So what do we do?" I asked as we began to move through the clearing toward the safe house, averting my eyes and my senses from the dead bodies and spilled blood that littered the expanse. I felt Archer tense as we passed the corpses of his fallen colleagues, maybe even friends, and I gripped his hand tightly in mine. He shot me a thankful glance. "They've proven they will find us, no matter where we hide."

Silas threw an arm around my shoulders and hugged me to his side, pressing a delicate kiss to my head. Laz followed closely behind us, their presence a blanket of comfort as the chilling scene from the clearing threatened to topple my resolve.

Samara and Orpheus stopped on the porch of the house and turned to face us. The five of us stood in a circle, bodies bruised and bloodied. Some of us intimately changed forever. The gravity of the fight that waited for us weighed heavily on us all.

"They will find us again, you're right. But this time, we will be ready. We will never fall to Nameless again," Orpheus declared, his strength and bravery radiating almost intoxicatingly. He promised a future where we were victorious, and at that moment, I felt just confident enough to believe him. His eyes scanned our faces, meeting each of our gazes in turn. Determination burned in those eyes, a fierce strength and power that marked him as a man who would never be a victim again. I understood that determination in a way few others could. His eyes met Archer's, and I saw a look of understanding pass between them, a camaraderie that had my nearly dead heart thumping in my chest.

"Where are we going to go?" I asked in the darkness.

And then, as the moonlight bathed his face, I saw an emotion cross Orpheus' features that I hadn't seen since we were taken. A small smile played on his lips as he said, "Home, Athena. We're going home." Hope. It was hope. And in that moment, I felt it too.

We stood together, a united front against the darkness that had hunted us for so long. Archer and his father's demands for who he should become and who he should hate. The Wanderers and the Hunters that had kept them on the run for their entire second lives, and me and the demons of my past that haunted me in my most vulnerable of moments. We had faced unimaginable horrors alone for too long, but now, with hope lighting our path, I knew we could finally reclaim our lives.

Together.

PART IV

THE UNDYING

PROLOGUE

ORPHEUS

"You're the only one who can keep us from death, Orpheus." The common phrase my mother spoke echoed as I opened my eyes. As they adjusted to the sight around them, I couldn't help but notice that my throat felt raw and pained. The fresh scent of open air assaulted my nostrils. Before me, the Bugeac Plains stretched in every direction, broken by numerous ravines and gullies that sliced through the expanse like veins beneath the skin. Panic consumed me. My heart should have been pounding in my chest from the disorientation, but I noticed with a jolt that it was unnaturally still.

My chest rose and fell as I hyperventilated, feeling the fear grip my unbeating heart as I attempted to piece together the puzzle that led me to this very moment.

I had traveled to Moldova on the trade route with my family's stockpile of grain and livestock to sell at the market. Panicked, I glanced around, looking for any sign of my cart, my animals, or any money received from their sale. When I found nothing, I felt a sinking feeling in the pit of my stomach. Despite the strange fog that hung over the memory of the last several hours, I knew that my family would unlikely survive the coming winter without that money. My mother was counting on me to provide for her and my sister. If I couldn't do that, I was useless.

I was the only thing standing between them and death's doorway.

They'd told me that. They relied on me. And I had failed them.

I stood and began stumbling through the open plains, desperate for a clue of why I was in the middle of nowhere, covered in blood, left with nothing but the clothes on my back. My body felt disjointed, like there was something almost new about it. The morning air's chill caressed my skin, yet I felt no cold. I took tentative steps across the plains, noticing an unfamiliar strength in my limbs. Every sensation was unbelievably heightened. I could feel the texture of each blade of grass beneath my fingers and hear the distant rustle of leaves miles away. My senses had sharpened to an almost painful clarity. The world around me seemed more vibrant and alive, yet I felt detached as if observing it through a veil.

Then, I caught a scent, sweet, warm, and utterly intoxicating. It was unlike anything I had ever smelled, stirring something primal and animalistic within me. I turned, nearly involuntarily, following the scent with instinctual precision. My legs moved with a fluidity and speed that would have shocked me if I had been in the state of mind to analyze it and carried me swiftly across the plain.

In the distance, I saw a traveler, a solitary figure making his way through the wilderness. An almost calm sense of adventure and excitement rippled off of him. I felt a shift within me as I approached, a primal and wicked hunger awakening. My vision seemed to tunnel as I focused solely on the stranger's pulse, faint but steady. My mouth watered, and my fangs, which I hadn't realized I possessed, descended with a sharp ache.

My thoughts returned to the night before, still hazy but slowly coming into focus. I arrived in town late and decided to commemorate the end of my long journey with an ale at the pub. The firelight flickered warmly in the cozy tavern, casting long shadows that danced on the walls as the patrons enjoyed the company of others and the taste of their drinks.

A man, a stranger, commanded the room with his presence and caught my undying attention nearly immediately. He spun animated tales of the unnatural and the demonic. His voice was a deep, velvety baritone that seemed to weave a spell over everyone who listened. He whispered stories of terrible creatures of the night. Of long, sharp fangs. Of blood-thirsty hunters. He argued the validity of his stories with other patrons who were well into their cups. He warned us of the dangers of trusting the monsters of the night.

I recalled how his eyes had lingered on me, an unsettling intensity in his gaze. I remembered the shiver that had run down my spine, a threatening warning I had dismissed as mere theatrics.

As the night wore on, the stranger made his way to my table, seemingly emboldened by how intently I was interested in his tales. He offered to buy me a drink, and I accepted, honestly curious about this enigmatic storyteller and how he became so interested in such tales. We talked long into the night, his stories slowly becoming darker and more vivid. He had produced a flask at one point, insisting I try a sip of what he claimed was a rare wine. The thick, coppery liquid had burned as it went down, and my vision had blurred almost immediately.

Despite my best efforts to recall, that's where most of my memory ends. I had left the pub with him, my steps unsteady, my senses dulled. Whatever liquid he had given me was acidic on my tongue as he led me out of town into the vast openness of the plains, speaking in low, hypnotic tones. There, under the moonlight, he revealed his true nature, his eyes glowing with an unnatural light, his fangs gleaming as he bit into my neck.

The change that had occurred within me was undeniable now. Somehow, I had been transformed into something of nightmares, a creature from the stories I'd only ever dismissed as fiction. The new, animalistic side of my mind begged me to sink my new fangs into the neck of the traveler before me and drain the blood within their veins, yet a part of my human mind desperately clung to the last vestiges of rationality.

The traveler continued on the path, unaware of the predator that had awakened in his midst. As the first rays of sunlight crept over the horizon, I felt the biting sting against my skin. A burning sensation crawled across the pale canvas of my skin. Quickly, I turned away from the traveler and his tempting blood, retreating to the shadows, searching for refuge from the assaulting sun and the world that was forever changed. I'd have to learn to survive in this new version of my existence, and someday, I'd need to embrace the darkness that was now my home.

It took several weeks of traveling only under the safety of the moonlight, but when I arrived at my home, I saw the effects of my failure firsthand. I found them too late. The scene seared itself into my mind, my mother and sister lying lifeless on the cold, hard ground. Their faces were gaunt, their eyes hollow. I had ventured, unwillingly, into the land of the dead, and due to my carelessness, my family had followed swiftly behind.

I fell to my knees before my mother's frail and lifeless body. Her hands folded across her chest as if she had been praying. Praying for me to return, to do what I swore I would, and to protect them. I learned then that even though my heart did not beat, it could still break.

My mother's words whispered to me in a moment of rare tenderness, returned to my mind. "You're the only one who can keep us from death, Orpheus." Those words echoed in my mind, now a cruel reminder of my inability to protect them.

Tears blurred my vision as I reached out to touch my sister's cold hand, the realization hitting me with brutal clarity. I had failed them, but should the occasion arise, I wouldn't fail again.

I clenched my fists, feeling a surge of determination rise within me. This pain, this loss, would not be in vain. I vowed then and there, as I knelt beside the lifeless bodies of the ones I loved most that I would never let this happen again. If I ever let myself care for another person again, I would protect them with a fierceness that knew no bounds.

"I'm sorry, I'm so sorry, I couldn't keep you from death," I whispered, my voice trembling with resolve. "I swear to you, I'll never make this mistake again. If I ever open my heart to another, I will protect them so fiercely that death itself will tremble at my presence. I will not only stand in the way of death's door, but I will burn it down."

The vow took root deep within me, a burning promise that would shape my every action from that moment forward. No one I loved would ever suffer because of my failure again. I would be their shield, their guardian, their protector. And I would ensure that the darkness that had claimed my family would never touch those I loved.

1

ATHENA

My heightened senses were going to take some getting used to. In fact, it all was. Everything about me had shifted in a way that felt so foreign, yet somehow still comfortable. Although, maybe I shouldn't classify the burning in my throat and the overwhelming desire to drain the blood of any living creature near me as 'comfortable.' Familiar, maybe. Which is a wild thought. How could something so unnatural feel familiar? But it did. So, when the first gust of the ocean breeze hit my nostrils, assaulting me with the scent of saltwater, cool air, and comfort, I knew we were almost home. The trip took longer than it should have, but I was forced to travel under cover of night. Orpheus promised that once we eliminated the immediate threat to our lives, we would travel to New Orleans to visit the vampire who gave them the ability to walk in the sunlight. I was already desperate for that day, feeling useless during the daylight hours when the others would be scouting ahead, gathering supplies, or making moves toward accomplishing our goal, all while I hid out in a cave or an abandoned factory, confined to the shadowed corners like a monster.

I felt like humanity was slipping away from me the longer I remained in the dark, but still, I clung to what made me *me*. I'd need that anchor if I were going to survive this.

"What are we going to do about the police? I've been missing for over two weeks. And Greg? What if they ask about Greg?" I asked softly as we slowed our run to a much more comfortable walking pace. Archer slid off Silas' back, grumbling about how 'he wouldn't need to piggyback if we had just rented a car.' Orpheus turned to face me and placed a gentle hand on my cheek. His previously chilled touch felt almost warm against my newly frozen skin.

"We tell them as much of the truth as they need to know, then fill in the blanks. Greg attacked you in your shop, and when you got away, you knew you needed to get out of town in case he tried again. You left with your new partners to get some distance and make sure it was safe for you to return and file a report against him." He caressed my face as he formulated the plan.

"And when they ask why I didn't call them?" I prompt.

His eyebrows furrowed, twisting his stoic face into a more pained look, and he nodded once. "If you feel comfortable, you can cite the lack of assistance this particular station offered during your last report of violence from a male figure."

I sucked in a breath as the memory of the cold dingy room and the detective's even colder judgment returned to me.

"You don't have to say a damn thing if you don't want to," Silas chimed in, his overprotective urges surging to the surface. I ran a finger along the serpents that ran along my clavicle and felt our bond pulse with warmth. He sighed and nodded, a soft smile playing on his lips.

"Am I missing something important?" Archer asked, glancing between us, no doubt sensing my hesitance.

"You've missed a lot, Archer," I replied softly, not with malice but rather with pain. We had missed each other's entire lives because of our father's selfishness. He nodded, content to leave it there for now, but I knew we needed to set aside time to truly get to know each other when things were safer.

Samara came up behind me, laying a hand on my shoulder before addressing the group. "We should head straight to the police department. Then we can go see your grandma," she said softly.

"And Davia," Archer replied. When I turned my eyes questioningly toward him, he shrugged. "She called me while you were at Nameless. She is worried about you." The blush on his face told me there was a little more to the story than that, but I didn't care right now. I needed to get through the next few hours so I could see the people I loved. The conversation I needed to have with my grandma felt like a heavy weight on my chest, but I knew it needed to happen. Maybe I'd see Davia first. I knew that was like prolonging the inevitable, but a furious little piece of my heart that felt betrayed by my grandmother wasn't ready to face her and listen to her explain why she kept so much from me.

We stepped out from behind the canopy of trees and wilderness to see the quaint town of Shockgrove. It was early evening, just an hour after the sun had set. The faint remnants of the day cast a pale orange glow along the water.

Sparkling lights dotted the streets and the pier, sparkling with warmth. I'd spent so much of my life wishing for a way out of this tiny little town and the painful memories that seem so intrinsically tied to it. But in this light, from this angle, knowing all I know now...I can finally see this place for what it is. Home.

My eye caught on the faded lighthouse standing sentinel, overlooking the quiet hamlet. My dead heart ached as I recalled the memories I held there with my mother and how, too soon, they would start to disappear, falling victim to this new existence.

Orpheus, understanding my pain or perhaps feeling it for himself, squeezed his arm around my waist. Laz leaned into me on the other side, kissing gently against my temple. I released a soft sigh, then stepped forward, preparing to face the aftermath of what we had left behind.

Three hours later, after the police had thoroughly and relentlessly investigated my story and extensively questioned each of us, save Archer, who had gone ahead to my house, we were allowed to leave the station. The moon hung in the star-dotted sky, and all remnants of daylight had sufficiently been replaced by the inky darkness of night.

The police, albeit suspicious about some parts of my story, seemed to buy the tale we had weaved completely. I think we were lucky that Detective Barnes was the one who was assigned to lead my case and not her less-than-sensitive partner, Detective Argent. Apparently, there was a security camera on the front of a business just down the pier that caught footage of me, bloodied and battered, scampering down the pier away from The Maine Plotline, followed closely by an angry and feral-looking Gregory. I couldn't shake the involuntary chill that ran down my spine as I watched that footage. The camera, thankfully, did not have the right angle to catch the moment we fought on the pier. So, the police seemed to accept that I got away, found my partners, and got the hell out of town.

The police told us that they had begun to piece together evidence left from the rental house where The Wanderers had been staying. They claimed their running theory was that Greg broke into the house where I was seen after we skipped town, hoping he could find me there.

Detective Barnes assured me she would do everything possible to keep me safe from Greg, and I thanked her. The gratitude felt like ash on my tongue, though. How was it that they believed me now? After everything, all it took was fifteen seconds of blurry footage to prove the truth. But when my shaking, fragile form sat in that room all those years ago, they couldn't be bothered to grant me an ounce of sympathy.

My cold heart ached, and I wanted to cry for the version of me who had to suffer at this department's arrogant and dismissive hands when it truly mattered.

Detective Barnes told me to stay in town. I promised I would unless I felt Greg was going to hurt me again. She urged me to call the station if that were the case instead of running but seemed to recognize the fear in my eyes. A fear I didn't have to fake because while I knew that he went over the railing, I had no way of knowing if he survived the drop and if he was, in fact, lying in wait until his chance came again. Barnes saw that terror reflected in me, and I could tell her leniency was in response to that. A woman understands that fear more than a man ever could.

Now, the five of us stood alone in the Shockgrove Police Station parking lot, a soft moon casting a cool light across our tired faces, but a small weight was lifted. It was just one of many crushing pounds of problems to deal with, but anything that made our load easier to carry was worth it.

"Do you want to go see your grandma? I can go get Archer?" Silas said. I smiled softly. Despite their…shaky introduction, my mate and brother seemed to have formed a bond. Hell, maybe it was the piggyback.

Or it could be the fact that Silas jumped back into the Hunter's den to save Archer from the vicious hands of his father after he risked everything to help us escape.

Probably the piggyback.

"No," I replied quietly. "I'm not ready to hear the answers she has." Silas nodded.

"Do you want to go home?"

Did I? Yes, eventually. But there was someplace I needed to go first.

"I need to see Davia."

Orpheus and Laz agreed to walk me to her house while the others returned to my house to "sunproof it." I tried not to be saddened by the thought of my normally warm and cozy home feeling like a cave when I returned and focused instead on the task ahead of me. Was I going to tell her the truth? Should I? Would that put her at risk in the eyes of Nameless? Would she even believe me? What if she smells too good, and I shift right in front of her? Should I drink before I go in there? Panic was bubbling up in my chest as we walked, and I knew Orpheus could feel it, but he had thankfully not drawn attention to it.

Laz's hand in mine and Orpheus' calming presence at my back was a gentle grounding, reminding me where and who I was. Despite the changes I'd undergone, I was and will always be who I always have been.

"Tell her whatever you need to, Athena. Whatever you'd like to. This secret is yours too now. Yours to share, or yours to keep," Laz offered as they turned toward Davia's home. I didn't even bother asking how they knew exactly where her house was. They had probably been watching out for me during my little staycation while I wrestled with the existence of the supernatural. Something that probably would have freaked me out back then, but now was something I understood all too well now that the mate bond thrummed so loudly in my chest.

"Thank you," I whispered in response as we stopped at the end of her driveway.

"She's going to be glad that you're ok, first and foremost," Laz said softly.

"You should drink a little before you go inside to clear your mind so you're focused only on what you want to focus on," Orpheus said, holding half of a blood bag for me to take. I emptied the contents into my eager mouth, letting the fragrant liquid run down my throat and satisfy the building hunger that never seemed to dissipate entirely.

Thanking him, I handed Orpheus the empty bag and pressed a gentle kiss against his lips. He groaned as the remnants of the blood on my lips graced his tongue, and he deepened the kiss. I barely gathered enough willpower to pull back from his embrace. I took a deep breath and gave Laz a slightly more reserved kiss before making my way up the driveway toward her door. My heart beat once, thumping foreignly against my chest in a way I hadn't felt since my transformation as I lifted my knuckles to tap on her door. It was nearly eleven at night, but I knew she would be up. She was a night owl at the best of times, but she became downright nocturnal when she was stressed. At least we had that in common now.

My knock echoed through her house, and my heightened hearing heard her moving around in her room, making her way toward the door. I glanced over my shoulder to where I had left my mates, but they were nowhere to be seen. I felt them close by, though, in the pulsing of our bond.

You've got this. We're here if you need us. Laz's voice echoed in my mind.

I still hadn't gotten used to that mental link I had created with my mates, but it quickly became my favorite part of this new existence. It eased a part of my anxiety and panic instantly. Something I had never quite had that kind of control over before. It felt empowering in a way I didn't realize I needed.

I love you. I whispered back through the channels of my mind and loved the answering warmth that flooded from Laz's mark on my skin. The phases of the moon just above my hip bone. Transformation. Change. Us.

The door opened, and I inhaled sharply, immediately worried my best friend would recognize that something about me had changed. She knew me

better than I knew myself most times, and I wouldn't put it past her to see
that I was hiding something the moment she laid eyes on me. There she was.
Davia. Her blonde hair caught the light, her blue eyes wide with shock and
relief. For a moment, time seemed to stand still. I had been so nervous for
this reunion, terrified she would see through me, see the monster I had
become. But as her eyes locked onto mine, all I saw was pure, unfiltered
happiness.

"Athena!" she exclaimed, her voice a mixture of disbelief and joy. In an
instant, she crossed the threshold and wrapped her arms around me, pulling
me into a tight embrace. I hesitated, only slightly, as the scent of her blood
invaded my senses. But her warmth and the familiarity of her scent, the real
her, the one beyond the blood, overwhelmed me, and I allowed myself to melt
into her hug.

"Oh my God, Athena, you're okay! I thought... I thought I'd lost you forever,"
she said, her voice cracking with emotion, a bizarre reaction for my normally
stoic and hardheaded friend. She pulled back just enough to look at me, her
hands gripping my shoulders. "Where have you been? What the fuck
happened to you?"

I swallowed hard, forcing a smile. "It's a long story, Davia. But I'm here now.
I'm okay."

She didn't seem to notice the subtle changes in me, the way my eyes no
longer held the same warmth or how my skin was cooler to the touch. She was
too relieved, too overjoyed to question anything. She only saw her friend back
from whatever horrors she had concocted in her mind.

"I was so fucking worried," she continued, tears streaming down her
cheeks. "Get in here," she said, ushering me into her living room. I smiled and
followed behind her, thankful she invited me in without me needing to ask her
to. Allowing relief that she was seemingly untouched by the Hunters to wash
over me. That was yet another horrible possibility that I hadn't let myself think
about, but now that she was here in front of me and safe, I let the fear I'd been
harboring for my best friend drift away.

Davia led me to her couch, setting me down and plopping down right in
front of me, her fingers intertwined with mine.

"Are you ok?" She asked, her eyes scanning my body for injuries. I prayed
she didn't look too closely, or she'd see the raised white lines of my mate bonds,
but I wasn't quite ready to explain that.

"I'm okay, I promise. I'm okay now."

She waited for me to continue, and here I was, finally arriving at the crossroads I knew was coming. I could tell her the story I told the police. All very
rational, and honestly, knowing my history with abuse, she wouldn't question it

for a moment. Or I could tell her the truth. The entire dark, dirty, scary, supernatural truth.

"Athena, what the hell happened?"

I met her eyes, full of worry and confusion. I needed to make a choice. Let
her in on this secret and hope it doesn't paint a target on her back or keep this
massive part of myself from her.

"I'm going to tell you something, and it's going to sound absolutely insane,
and I need you to believe me anyway. Can you do that?" I asked, gripping her
hands in mine. Her skin felt like a blazing inferno compared to mine.

"What are... I don't understand what's going on?" She shook her head.

"Can you promise me that you'll hear what I'm about to say with an open
mind?" I slid forward on the couch until my knee brushed against hers.

"You're starting to scare me, Athena," she said, narrowing her eyes at me.

"I'm pulling the Vagina card," I blurted out, and her mouth dropped open
as her eyes widened in shock. I met her gaze as the gravity of the weird girl-
code contract was enacted. She nodded solemnly, seemingly accepting my
terms.

"Okay," I started, leaning back and taking a long breath. This was going to
be difficult. "I'll start at the beginning."

It came out as a torrent of emotional sobs, and I even started with the easy
part. I told her the truth about what Louis tried that night at the bar, and I
could barely see through my own tears enough to see her cheeks stained with
moisture as well. Her hand clasped mine as she let me continue. I told her how
my Wanderers saved me that night, how they got me home safe. I told her how
Greg confronted me about the brick through the window and then the fight in
the bookstore. I could feel her seething with fury about her old fling and what
he was capable of.

Then, it was time for the hard part.

"This is where I need you to trust me," I prefaced, taking a long, steadying
breath. "The reason I came to stay with you, the reason I needed some space
from them was because..." I paused. "Fuck, this is going to sound crazy."

She leaned forward, bringing her forehead to mine. "I'm here, I'm listening,
I hear you. Just tell me whatever it is. I already believe you."

I squeezed her hand and relished in the moment of intimacy shared with
my best friend. I didn't realize how much I missed her when I was locked away
until now. She meant so much to me, and I was so thankful I had her here in
my arms now.

"I needed space from them because...because I found out they were
vampires." The word slipped from my lips, and I loved how it felt on my
tongue. It was a word that was just a fun thing I liked to read about and

imagine at one point in my life, but now, it was everything to me. It was who I was.

I glanced up at Davia to gauge her reaction, but her face gave nothing away. I took that as an opportunity to continue. "They shifted in front of me and called me their mate. So I promptly freaked the fuck out and ran away." I giggled half-heartedly to lighten the mood. It didn't work. "I didn't want to believe it either, but it's true. They are vampires, and somehow, I am their mate. I belong to them, and they belong to me. We belong together." Whew, okay. I heard it. I was sounding like one of those wackos in the reality shows that people only ever really watched to see that they're relatively normal in comparison to the creeps on the screen.

"I don't understand," she said softly, which was a better reaction than expected.

"They've been on the run from vampire hunters for a while, and one of them actually found us..." this part was going to piss her off. Royally. I saw the way she looked him up and down, the glint in her eye that she only ever got when she liked what she saw. First Greg, then Archer. She was going to seriously freak out when she heard what he did.

"Archer was sent to kidnap them," I stated slowly. "So he did, and because he couldn't leave witnesses apparently, he took me too. That's where I've been for the last two weeks."

She blinked once. Twice.

"You were trapped in a vampire hunter's lair?" She repeated.

"Yes."

"After being kidnapped by a hunter?"

"Yes."

"Because the four people you're sleeping with are your fated vampire mates..."

"Yes."

She leaned back against the arm of the couch and exhaled deeply.

"Vagina card?" she clarified softly, an almost pleading look in her eyes. She wanted me to tell her this was all a joke. She wanted to laugh at my imagination, then kick my ass for scaring her. But I couldn't do that.

I nodded. "Vagina card."

"Well, shit," she whispered with a soft shake of her head. It sent golden tendrils of her hair spilling into her face. "You're kind of living my Twilight fanfic dreams."

The laugh that bubbled out of my throat was two parts shock and one part utter relief. The pit in my stomach seemed to disappear, and I smiled gently at my best friend. I didn't realize how much tension I had been carrying in my body until the moment I could release it. As my muscles uncoiled and my shoulders relaxed, I felt refreshed. But then, the sickening thought occurred to me. She may have been willing to believe me, but would she accept me when she discovered that the monsters weren't just hypothetical anymore, but that I was one of them?

"There's more, isn't there?" She asked, recognizing the pained look on my face. I shrugged, exhaling quickly through my nose.

"You know how the only thing I've ever known about my father was his name?" I prompted, and she nodded. "He's one of the Hunters. He, um, he sent his son to capture us..." I waited for her to put the puzzle together quietly. It took a second. Her forehead creased as her brain sorted the new information into the appropriate categories.

"Holy shit," she said on a breathy exhale. "Archer is your brother?" I nodded. "And he kidnapped you because your father told him to?"

"Yeah."

"Talk about a fucked up family dynamic..." she said, shaking her head with a mixture of disbelief and shock.

"I know this is a lot - " I began.

"No, honey. My breakup last summer was 'a lot', but this is... god, this is on a completely different planet," she interjected.

"There's more." I chuckled darkly.

"Of course there is," she said, reaching forward to take my hand in hers again and squeeze it. "Go ahead, I'm here."

"When we escaped, my father sent Hunters to find us again. We fought, and they almost... They nearly killed.." I stopped, feeling the emotion bubble in my throat and the tears sting my eyes as I recalled the sickening panic that over-took me when I saw that they had Samara vulnerable. Davia's hand gripped mine tighter. "They almost killed Samara, and I couldn't just stand by and watch it. I had just found them, Davia. It sounds fast and unbelievable, but they are my family. They have a piece of my soul that I've been missing, and I couldn't lose that just when I found it. I didn't think about it. I just ran. If I could just get to her, I could do something. I could save her." Tears flowed down my cheeks. "I got to her, I threw myself in the way, and I was hurt."

I glanced up at Davia, trying to memorize the look on her face—concern, love, friendship. Just in case things shifted when she learned of my new development, I could remember this moment.

"I was going to die. Actually, I think I might have literally died there for a second."

Davia sniffled and used the back of her hand to wipe away the tears. "You're about to tell me that you're a vampire... aren't you?"

I scanned her features for any sign of fear or disgust, but all I saw reflected in her eyes was the same love and care with which I looked at her.

"Yeah," I whispered, letting my head fall forward so my eyes were locked on the couch. She touched my chin and raised my head to meet her gaze again.

"Athena Landry, I am your best friend. I noticed something was different with you the moment you walked in here." She held our joined hands up between us. "Your hands are like ice, your skin is annoyingly clear and perfect, and don't get me started on the tattoo-looking things all over you." She chuckled, and I followed suit.

"I may not...really understand what's going on here, and it's hard to believe for sure... but I'm here for you. I believe you, Athena. I love you. And nothing, supernatural or otherwise, could ever change the way I feel about you." Davia wrapped her arms around me and pulled me into a hug, and I melted into her embrace. My heart thumped loudly, bursting to life for a moment with the love I have for my best friend. When we pulled back from the hug, we met each other's eyes and then devolved into laughter.

"If you would have told little high school me about this, I'd probably have an even more dramatic and embarrassing vampire phase than I already did." She laughed, tucking a strand of hair behind her ear. "So, you like.. Drink blood now?"

I cringed. "Yeah, god, that's gross, isn't it?"

She shrugged. "How do I smell? Am I tempting?"

My shoulders shook with laughter. "Honestly, yes. But I just turned, so I think everyone is tempting right now."

"Can I see?" she asked timidly. I quickly bit my bottom lip to try and subdue the pointed fangs that desperately wanted to descend at the promise of blood.

"I'm not completely controlled yet," I replied, ashamed.

"I trust you," she said, offering me her wrist. My eyes were immediately drawn to the blood that ran through her veins like a moth to the flame.

"It's, um, sort of intimate," I challenged, trying my best to force the shift back. I didn't want to terrify her, or worse...kill her.

"Like a sex thing?" She asked, an eyebrow arched in amusement. I hid my head in my hands in embarrassment.

"Not always," I argued exasperatedly.

"Okay then, then take a little sip of La Rosé Davia." Davia took a deep breath and held her wrist to me again, her pulse visibly quickening under her skin. "Show me, please," she said softly, her voice steady despite the tremor I could sense beneath it. I hesitated, fear gnawing at me. What if I lost control? What if I hurt her?

"Are you sure?" I asked, my voice barely above a whisper.

She nodded, her eyes unwavering. "I trust you."

With a shaky breath, I let the shift, which was nearly at the surface, take over. My vision sharpened as my eyes turned red, my ears elongated to points, and my fangs bared themselves. I saw the flicker of surprise in Davia's eyes, but she remained calm outwardly. Her heartbeat, however, betrayed her nervousness, each thud sending a fresh wave of intoxicating scent through the air.

I gently took her wrist, feeling the warmth of her skin against my cool touch. The scent of her blood was overwhelming, far more potent than any of the blood from the bags that I had been surviving on since the transformation. I could feel my instincts clamoring for control, urging me to sink my fangs in deep and drink my fill. But I fought against that monstrous voice, reminding myself why I was doing this.

Slowly, I brought her wrist to my mouth and bit down gently, acutely aware of my new strength and trying not to cause her any harm. The instant her blood hit my tongue, I was flooded with warmth and life. It was unlike anything I had ever experienced. The blood from the bag had been a poor imitation—this was pure, rich, fragrant, and so *alive*. I had to force myself to take only a tiny sip, savoring the taste while battling the overwhelming desire to take more. My willpower was fighting for its life against the creature within me.

After what felt like both an eternity and a mere second, I pulled away, licking the minor puncture wounds on her wrist. To my relief, they closed almost immediately, leaving only a faint mark. I looked up at Davia, bracing myself for her reaction.

Her eyes were wide, filled with shock and incredulity. "I can't believe it," she whispered, her voice filled with awe. "That was incredible. And it didn't even hurt."

I let out a breath I hadn't realized I was holding, feeling a mixture of relief and exhilaration. "I'm glad you're okay," I said, my voice still shaky from the effort of restraint. "I was so scared I might hurt you."

Davia smiled, her eyes sparkling with a strange delight. "You didn't." She reached out, touching my face gently. "You're still you, Athena. Just a lot cooler now."

I laughed.

"Oh my god! We can go to goth night together!" Davia devolved into giddy planning mode, excitedly chatting about the different things we could do together now that I was 'less boring.' I sat back on my heels, listening to her, and felt a warmth spread through my chest.

My best friend believed me.

There was a time when she was one of the only ones who believed me when no one else would. I needed her support then, and I need it now.

I smiled as she droned on and on, and I knew I had made the right choice in divulging this secret to her. I'd let myself bathe in the warmth of this moment for as long as I could because soon, it would be time to speak to my grandmother.

And there'd be no giddy happiness in that discussion, so I'd soak it up now while I still could.

2

SILAS

"We're sunproofing, not preparing for an apocalypse," Samara said, slapping the sheets of wood out of my hands.

"Black-out curtains aren't gonna get the job done, or do you not remember the incident in Tucson?" I challenged, and she shook her head.

"Of course, I remember Tucson. My back was scarred for weeks."

I nodded, the memory of our early morning wake-up call the moment the sun rays spilled through the so-called 'black-out' curtains and burned into our skin.

"Then, this is what we need," I replied, reaching for the sheets of wood again.

"People are going to ask questions if Athena's house suddenly looks like she's prepping for a hurricane," Samara tossed back, pulling the sheets of wood from my grasp, putting them back on the rack, and pushing me out of the lumber aisle.

"Things have developed since the last time we had to sunproof a house," she argued while leading me to the window section of the store.

After an annoyingly extensive question-and-answer process with the employee, who was torn between wanting us to get the fuck out of his store because it was nearly eleven at night and wanting to make one hell of a commission on us, we had purchased three rolls of UV blocking window tint, and two sets of black-out curtains for each window.

After the walk, I stepped up to Athena's little cottage, and instantly, a thought occurred to me.

Hey, bookworm. You better invite me inside.

I felt her amusement through the bond.

Oh gosh, I don't know... I have a lot of valuable things inside... you know. She teased.

Don't make me punish you, baby girl. I taunted hungrily.

What if that's what I want? She answered, and I growled hungrily.

Let me in, baby girl, and I'll fuck you in your bookstore again. I promised. I planned on doing that again, no matter what, but it fits into our game so well.

Of course, you're welcome inside. Mi casa es su casa. Or whatever.

I chuckled, turning the handle and finding myself freely able to step over the threshold.

Do I get my reward soon, sir? She purred.

Fuck, yes. The minute we're alone, you're mine.

Good. She chuckled. *Hey, do I need to invite myself in when I get home?* She asked.

I have no idea. After I turned, I never went back to my old place. *I guess we'll find out soon.*

Stepping into Athena's little cottage was like coming home despite never even setting foot inside before. Archer was sitting awkwardly on the couch, not quite comfortable enough to get comfortable. I stood across the room, my gaze locking onto Archer's. There was a time when that look would have been filled with pure hatred. This was the man who had captured me, nearly destroyed everything I loved for fuck's sake. But now, things were different. Archer saved us and risked everything to do so, so my opinion of the little Hunter shifted.

I took a deep breath, feeling the familiar clench of my jaw before I forced myself to give Archer a slow, deliberate nod. It was a gesture that said everything I wouldn't say aloud, a tentative acceptance of his place in Athena's - and, in turn, my - life.

Archer, standing from the couch, returned the nod with measured calmness. His expression was not smug or triumphant– just quiet understanding.

Samara, Archer, and I got to work quickly, quickly applying the window tint and replacing her cute, sage green curtains with dark, thicker curtains that would keep her alive and safe.

By the time we had finished, it was nearly one in the morning. Archer's mouth opened wide on a yawn, and I crossed the room to him.

"You should go get a room at the motel," I said.

"You kicking me out?" He teased on another yawn.

"Yeah."

His eyes widened in shock at my bluntness.

"Silas," Samara warned.

"Look, it's for your own good," I said, shrugging.

"My own good?" Archer confirmed.

"Yeah, look, this house isn't all that big, and I plan to make your sister scream my name as I pound my cock into her all night, so unless you wanna hear that, I suggest you go get a room," I responded flippantly.

Archer's face twisted in disgust, and he clamped his hands over his ears. "Oh Jesus, don't say shit like that to me." His body visibly shook as a chill ran through his body. Samara smirked and didn't scold me for my brash response. I knew she was just as desperate for our mate as I was. We hadn't spent a single moment alone together since we left the safe house. Not with her stupid brother tagging along the whole time.

"I'm just warning you," I answered. Archer nodded and headed toward the front door.

"I'll be back tomorrow afternoon. I'm going to try and get into contact with some of the Hunters that weren't complete asshats. I think they might listen if we tell them the truth. Tell Athena we can go talk to her grandma tomorrow night after sunset." He stepped across the threshold and disappeared into the darkness of night.

"You didn't have to be so blunt about it," Samara offered, settling onto the couch.

"Tell me you aren't glad he's gone," I challenged, raising a brow as I sunk into the armchair across from her. She shook her head and smiled softly.

"Of course I am. All I have been able to think about since she turned has been her sinking her fangs into my skin and finally marking me as hers."

I groaned, feeling my cock twitch to life at the thought.

Our mate bond is complete, but until she drank from us, we wouldn't bear the mark of her the way she carried ours. A desperate little thrill always filled me every time I saw my coiled serpents decorating her chest, and I couldn't wait to carry a piece of her with me. I needed her to mark me. I wanted her soul tattooed onto mine.

We finally had an eternity together. I wanted to make it count.

"So, you and Laz, huh?" she prompted softly, a little flustered. I met her eyes, searching for any signs of judgment or disgust.

"Only when Athena's involved," I responded, instantly feeling guilty. I wasn't ashamed about my attraction to Laz, and just because our connection was contingent on her involvement didn't make it any less important or intimate. "I mean... We're just, we're together when we are with her," I tried to explain, but I was doing a pretty shit job.

Samara leaned forward, a smile on her lips.

"About damn time."

Now, it was my turn to be flustered.

"What do you mean?" I asked.

"You two have had that intimacy building for as long as I've known you. I never thought it was sexual, just more connected than the rest of us, you know? You've always been the best to comfort each other. When you fight, it's passionate. When we lost Alora, they were the only one who could get through to you," Samara added quietly. I sighed. Every time her name was mentioned, my chest ached.

Losing Alora felt like a piece of my soul had been ripped away and shattered into a million pieces. She was my rock and confidant since childhood, the one person who always understood me, no matter what. We grew up together, facing the world side by side, and now she was gone. I felt lost and angry. So fucking angry. Nothing made sense without her. So I tried to find her in my vices. Danger, drink, drugs, draining... but she was gone.

Days turned into weeks into months, and the pain didn't lessen. It only grew, festering inside me like a fucking disease that was going to claim me. Samara, my partner in pain, seemed to begin to heal from the loss, but I couldn't. And I couldn't understand how she was suddenly okay after losing Alora. Did she even care to begin with? I pushed everyone away, retreating into myself, unable to face the world without Alora. Orpheus and Samara tried to talk to me, but their words felt hollow and meaningless.

Then there was Laz. They didn't try to offer empty platitudes or force me to talk about my feelings or my fucking grief. Instead, they simply sat with me, day after day, night after night, their presence a steady, calming force. At first, I didn't understand why it helped, but slowly, the weight of the loss and the pain began to feel more bearable when they were around.

Laz had a different kind of quiet strength about them, a way of making you feel seen and understood without saying a word. They would sit with me for hours, sometimes in silence, sometimes talking about nothing in particular. They gave me the space to mourn without judgment, and it was exactly what I needed.

One evening, as the sun dipped below the horizon, painting the sky in hues of orange and pink, Laz spoke softly. "Silas, it's okay to feel lost. But remember, you're not alone. We're all here for you whenever you're ready."

Their words broke through the fog of my grief, reaching a part of me I thought had been staked alongside Alora. I looked at Laz, really looked at them, and saw the sincerity in their eyes. They meant every word.

At that moment, something shifted inside me. The pain was still there, but it was no longer suffocating. Laz had given me a lifeline, a way to find my way back from the darkness. Slowly, I began to open up, to let them in. They didn't take Alora's place in my heart— no one ever could— but they carved out their own spot in my soul for them-

selves and helped me remember that life could go on and that I could find a new way to be okay.

"All I'm saying is that you two have a sort of understanding and love for each other that deserves to be explored. I'm happy for you," she finished, and I smiled at my friend.

"Thanks, Samara."

We sat in comfortable silence for a while, enjoying this brief moment of relative peace despite the cloud hanging over our heads, reminding us of the impending storm.

"The Hunters are going to be here any day now," I whispered the truth into the dark. I was so fucking sick and tired of those Hunters playing God. I couldn't wait to get my hands on this Dr. Kline asshole. I had spent a good portion of my time since learning his identity imagining all the ways I'd make him suffer for perpetuating the harm his great, great, great grand-whatever started when he created this fucking organization. I couldn't kill Jacob, as much as I wanted to, because vampire-hunting scum or not, he was Athena's father, and even though I knew she didn't hold any love for him, there's just something about family that changes things.

"I know," she replied.

"Do you think we have a chance?" I asked. She didn't answer right away. Instead, she placed her hand on her chest and smiled.

"With this bond?" She started. "I feel like anything is possible."

"I hope it is," I replied. I didn't want to admit it out loud, but I was terrified. Even more so than last time, Nameless had us in their clutches because this time, I had something even more important to me to lose. If I almost didn't survive losing Alora, I knew that losing Athena would mean the end of me.

No one ever truly wins a war, but I was determined to survive it with everyone I loved still with me.

My ears perked up at the sound of footsteps on the gravel driveway. Three sets. I stood up and waited for the rest of our coven to arrive. The door creaked open, and Athena poked her head in tentatively. Seeing her always seemed to take my breath away. I hoped I never got used to it.

Vampirism looked fucking good on Athena. She's still her. With wild red hair cascading like fire and eyes the same brilliant green that I'd been drawn to since I first saw her in that bar. But there's something different now, a quiet strength that came with her transformation, and it's nothing short of breathtaking.

I watched her from across the room as she entered her home, a new and changed person. I admired the way she carried herself despite the nerves.

I found myself captivated by her. She was beautiful before, a goddess with silky skin, but now she was stunning in a way that defied words. The transformation had brought out a new side of her, one that was both powerful and fucking intoxicating. Maybe it was that, or it also could be the fact that now I got to have her for eternity that made me feral for her.

Yet, beneath all that newness, she was still Athena. The same fire, the same fierce loyalty, the same heart. She glanced over at me as Orpheus and Laz followed behind her, catching my gaze, and smiled. That smile, it hadn't changed. It was the same one that had always made my heart race.

Athena walked over, and as she approached, I couldn't help but notice how the place in my chest where her bond sat burned brighter at her proximity. "What are you staring at?" she asked, a playful smirk on her lips.

"Just you," I replied honestly. "Vampirism looks good on you, bookworm. Really good."

She laughed softly, a sound that was music to my ears and made my cock twitch. "Thanks, Silas." She stood up on her tip toes to press a kiss on my cheek. I groaned at the touch. I was going to absolutely devourer this woman the moment I could. "I think I'm getting the hang of it."

"She drank from Davia and controlled herself beautifully," Laz interjected, pride lacing their tone.

"So you told her everything?" Samara asked.

Athena nodded.

"I had to. She's my best friend."

My heart ached slightly as Alora's face crossed my mind.

"You're stronger than ever, bookworm. And it's... fucking sexy," I teased, letting a hand drift down her waist to settle on her hips.

Her smile widened, and we just stood there for a moment, looking at each other. In her, I saw not just the vampire she had become but the incredible person she had always been.

I couldn't stand another moment of having her in my arms without tasting her lips, so I bent down to seal her mouth in a kiss. She made a short sound of shock but quickly sank into my kiss, and within a few seconds, our ravenous tongues were battling for dominance. Her hands gripped my hair and pulled, the force much greater than what she could have managed as a human, and it only made me harder for her.

"I need to fuck you," I whispered against her lips, and the moan she let out of downright sinful.

"Then do it already," she challenged, and without thinking, I tossed her over my shoulder and headed toward her bedroom. I glanced over my shoulder at the others.

"Are you coming or not?" I teased. I didn't care if Samara and Orpheus joined, I knew they preferred having Athena to themselves, but I needed Laz to come with me. I needed them to watch me make our girl scream, and I wanted to see them squirm as I told Athena how to please them.

I heard three sets of footsteps follow behind us as I stormed into her room and tossed my gorgeous mate down on her bedspread. Samara had the good sense to strip the bed and don fresh sheets while we waited and I was suddenly very thankful. I could not wait to defile them.

She gasped as her ass hit the bed, and I felt the bond in my chest tugging at her, desperate to be consummated by her fangs in my skin.

Soon. But not yet.

Orpheus settled on the chair in the corner of the room, legs spread wide as he sat like a watchful gargoyle. Stoic and rock hard. Samara leaned against the wall by the door with a lustful gaze. Laz, however, knew exactly what I needed from them. They came to a stop near the side of the bed, their hooded eyes bouncing between me and Athena.

"Laz, do you want to make our mate feel good?" I asked, my voice deep and husky.

"Yes, sir," they replied. Athena and I both released an almost feral moan as they submitted to me.

"Undress for us," I said. Us. Not her. This was just as much for me as it was for Athena, and I felt myself getting harder as Laz followed my command, slipping out of their pants and letting their shirt fall open and down their arms. Their cock jutted straight out, and I could see the glistening tip, wet with precum, and I had the surprising urge to dip down and taste it.

So I did.

Leaning over Athena, I brought my tongue to the tip of Laz's length and slowly trailed it along the slit. Laz threw their head back, and Athena whispered profanities as she watched me work. Laz's taste made me even more feral for the two of them than before. I slid their cock into my mouth and took it as far as I could, loving the way my mate beneath me pressed her thighs against my hips.

I pulled off of Laz with a wicked smile and stood up. Both of them were staring at me like I was the only thing in the world that mattered, like they would do anything for me. I wanted to test that.

"Baby girl, I need you to show me your perfect little pussy. Are you dripping for us?" She moved quickly, discarding her pants and underwear and leaving herself bare for me.

"Fuck," I exclaimed, unable to resist sliding my tongue through her perfect lips and drinking her arousal. She was soaking wet, and her hips bucked into my face as I tasted her.

"Laz, have a taste," I demanded, and Laz quickly slid to their knees at the foot of the bed. I stood behind them and watched as they devoured our mate's pussy. She thrashed wildly under their expert tongue, and I soaked up every second of the display as I quickly discarded my own clothes.

"Finger her ass Laz. We're going to take her together again, and I need her ready for me," I commanded, and Laz did as I asked, sliding a finger past the tight rim of muscles at her ass. She groaned their name, her hands tangling with the bedspread.

The sight was almost too sinful to see, and I was seconds away from spilling myself onto both of them. "Lay down on the bed, Laz." Athena whimpered when Laz withdrew their tongue and fingers, but he didn't dare complain.

Laz settled down beside her, their arms pressed against each other. They smiled sweetly at each other as they awaited my next instruction.

"Baby girl, I need you to ride them. Ride them until your cum is dripping down their cock."

Her eyes went wide, but she scrambled to obey. She went to straddle them, but I gripped her shoulders and directed her to face me.

"Eyes on me," I ordered. She nodded, settling in overtop of Laz. She looked back over her shoulder at them and smiled wickedly just before she sank down onto their cock. Watching the way their length stretched her pussy drew curses from the gallery of onlookers behind me. I knew that if I looked at Samara and Orpheus right now, I'd see lust and the darkest intentions painted on their faces, but I couldn't tear my eyes from the stunning creature in front of me.

Her mouth fell open with a gasp as she bounced up and down on Laz's dick. Laz held onto her hips and kept her pace steady and punishing. Just the way I knew she liked it. I leaned forward and took her clit into my mouth, and they both exhaled sharply with a moan as my tongue pleasured both her and them at the same time. It became a delicate dance. My tongue circled her clit, and dipped onto their cock, while Athena slammed her pussy down onto them. She cried out as an orgasm wracked through her body, sending shivers to every limb. I needed to be inside of my mate, and soon. I pulled her off of Laz and turned her so that her chest was pressed against theirs. I had the perfect angle to take Laz's cum soaked cock into my mouth, so I did. Savoring the way the two of them tasted together.

"Oh my god, Silas," Laz cried out.

Just then, I gripped Athena's hips and slid her down onto Laz's cock again. This time, as she rode them, I let my tongue soak the puckered hole that I was going to take to prepare her. When she was writhing in passion on Laz, I pressed the tip of my cock against her tight entrance and pushed my hips forward.

Otherworldly.

That's how it felt. Athena pressed back against me, taking me to the hilt like a fucking champ. Her muscles squeezed me like a vice, and I was seconds from coming and ending the whole thing. I reached around to grip her throat and pulled her up until her back was flush with my front. Laz and I continued to press into her from beneath as I whispered into her ear.

"Time to mark me, baby girl. Make me yours." With one hand holding her throat, I placed the other forearm in front of her mouth. Most of my arms were covered in ink, but there was a spot on my left forearm between two dark, inky patterns that had always been blank. I had always wanted to complete the sleeve, to find something that fit there, but nothing felt right. I should have known I was saving that spot for her. I pressed the patch of unblemished skin against her lips and groaned as her tongue darted out to taste it. Laz slowed their thrusts to allow us this moment, but the pressure of their length up against mine within our mate was deliciously torturous.

Athena's fangs descended and sank into my arm, and I threw my head back on a moan. Euphoria, unlike any I'd ever felt, flooded through my veins. She pulled mouthful after mouthful of my blood past her lips, and I squeezed harder with the hand around her throat. She gasped and pulled her fangs from my arm.

"Now kiss it all better," I demanded, my voice almost unrecognizable in the fog of lust. She stuck her tongue out and waited for me to press my arm against it again. She lapped up the remaining blood and sealed the wound with a little extra sensual flair. When I dropped both hands to her hips, she fell forward onto Laz, gasping for air.

"I think it's time to claim your next mate, baby girl. Claim them while I fuck your ass."

I pounded into her for a few moments, in tandem with Laz's thrust into her pussy. She cried out before pressing a kiss against Laz's throat. I slowed my thrusts, content to simply watch as two people I loved shared their love for one another.

Athena bit down onto Laz's throat, just above the shoulder, and the way she clenched around me should have been illegal. Laz's hands tangled in her hair, and I watched as she made her claim official. Sitting back, she licked the wound closed.

"Baby girl, you deserve a reward for that. Don't you think?" I teased.

She glanced at me over her shoulder, her green eyes shining wickedly. "Yes, sir. I do."

I made eye contact with Laz, a silent exchange, and then we unleashed. Our thrusts into her body were rough and punishing, and she took each slam of our cocks into her like she was made for it. I was so close, and my fingers dug into her hips as she rode us with reckless abandon. She reached her climax first, which only sent me spiraling after her. I came with her name on my lips, and I could feel Laz's thick cock pulse as they spilled into her as well.

I pulled out first, followed by Laz. I helped lay Athena down on the bedspread, and she sprawled out, sated and exhausted. Her perfect body was on display for us. I could see the evidence of our domination spilling from her perfect pussy.

I wanted more. Honestly, I never wanted to stop. But I knew that there were more mates that she needed to claim. I leaned over her and stole a kiss. She melted into it, clearly still riding high from her orgasm.

"It's their turn now, baby girl," I said, tilting my head toward the door and the chair in the corner where her other mates had been watching from. "Put on a good show for me," I demanded with another kiss before sliding off the bed and moving to the wall. Laz joined me, leaning just a few feet from me.

Samara's eyes scanned Athena's naked form, and she exchanged the briefest silent exchange with Orpheus before she rushed forward to join her mate on the bed. I thought I would hate to see the day Samara moved on with someone else. I thought it would hurt to see her happy with someone else. But this was *right*. This was what Alora would have wanted for us. My dead heart felt alive as I watched my friend and my mate fall in love.

Samara wasted no time stripping off her dress and straddling Athena, pressing her dripping core against Athena's. The two of them made positively nasty sounds as they ground their cores against each other. I was so focused on watching the pleasure on my mate's face that I didn't even notice that Laz had slipped a hand around my waist and was leaning their body weight into mine. It felt nice. I held them close and watched Samara bring our mate to another screaming orgasm, and it felt almost... perfect.

I'd do anything to keep this family safe. Anything.

3

ORPHEUS

Athena's fangs sunk into Samara's chest, just above her breast, and I watched with rapt attention as they both came from the sensation. Watching Athena come undone repeatedly proved to be the most challenging test of my willpower, but if I waited, it meant I got her all to myself. As Samara and Athena exchanged whispered admissions of love, I slid my pants off and let them pool on the floor by my feet and let my button-down fall from my form and bunch at my waist. My cock was so hard I was afraid that even the slightest touch would have me erupting.

Samara slid off the bed and smiled at me as she slid her dress back over her head. Athena watched her, thoroughly enjoying the view. "Are you ready for me, little nymph?" I asked, drawing her attention to me.

Her lips were tainted red from the blood she had consumed, and they looked delicious as she drew her bottom lip between her teeth and nodded coyly.

"Come to me," I whispered. My eyes remained glued to her as she slid from the bed and approached me. Her lips were plump, and her hair was wild. She looked freshly fucked, and god, that thought turned me on even more. I never thought I'd share a woman with my coven, but this woman deserves every ounce of pleasure my coven can give her and then some. I couldn't wait to give her all of me.

"Climb up here and sit on my face," I ordered her, leaning my head back on the back of the armchair. She didn't hesitate and climbed up my body to rest her core above my willing mouth. "Sit. Down." I demanded. She pressed her

621

core down against my face, and my tongue dove into her folds, lapping up the collective taste of my coven's arousal. She rocked wildly against my face, and I growled, using my hands to encourage her as she aggressively sought out her orgasm against my tongue. Her hands tangled in my hair as I sucked her clit into my mouth.

"Orpheus!" She cried out, her body tensing as another climax claimed her. I let her ride out the orgasm on my mouth, then helped her slide down my form until she straddled me on the chair. A leg on either side, my erect cock pinned between our bodies.

"I need you to mark me, Athena. I need to wear your imprint on my body."

Her green eyes met mine in a silent exchange, then she nodded, lifting her core until she could sink onto my cock. I groaned as she stretched around me. Her body was perfectly crafted to fit mine, and the moment she sank her teeth into my throat, time seemed to slow to a crawl. Every sensation was heightened, every nerve ending alive with electric energy. Her lips were soft against my skin, her breath warm and teasing before her fangs broke through. The pain was sharp, but it quickly dissolved into something more profound and deeply intimate.

I felt a rush of overwhelming exhilaration as she began to drink. Our connection deepened with each pulse of my blood into her mouth, strengthening the bond that already sat steadfast in my chest. The world around us faded, leaving only the two of us entwined in this intimate and perfect moment.

Her hands gripped my shoulders, grounding me as the euphoria intensified. It was sinfully sensual, the way she moved against me, the way her touch sent shivers down my spine. I could feel her single heartbeat align with mine, our breaths synchronizing as if we were becoming one.

I closed my eyes, surrendering entirely to the sensation of her. The mark she was leaving on me, her mate mark, was more than just a physical imprint– it was a declaration, a promise of forever– an eternity.

As she pulled back, her tongue traced the wound, sealing it with a gentle, almost loving caress. I opened my eyes to find her staring at me, the green orbs glowing with a mix of satisfaction and something deeper, something that mirrored my own devotion.

"You're mine now," she whispered, her voice a soft, intimate murmur that sent a new wave of warmth through me.

"I already was," I whispered back before bucking my hips up into her and bringing both of us back to the edge of a climax. I circled her clit with my finger, and within a few more thrusts, we were falling apart together. A mess of love, limbs, and lust.

As our breathing returned to normal, she chuckled. Sitting there, still wrapped in each other's embrace, I felt a profound sense of belonging. I was marked, I was hers, and nothing had ever felt so right.

Her eyes drifted closed, so I helped her up, and the four of us quickly got her cleaned up and ready for bed. The night of our last mate bond joining had been unfairly cut short, but this time, we would savor this night with her. Each of us now had a brand new mark. Thin raised white lines that decorated our skin, shaped like something so perfectly Athena it could have been nothing else.

A rose.

I smiled at the tiny mark that now permanently decorated my skin and the skin of my coven and recalled how Silas had demanded to get a bouquet for her before the tour that changed everything. She's always been our perfect rose. And now we had the mark to prove it.

The five of us carefully and uncomfortably slid between her bed sheets.

I made a mental note to get us a larger bed if this was going to be the norm. There, holding Athena against my body while her other mates pressed in as well, all of us, healthy, safe, sated... I sincerely hoped it would be.

4

ATHENA

I was curled up on the couch, staring at the covered window. It was midday, but you wouldn't know it from inside here. The sun was a distant memory, and the darkness felt all-consuming, even though it was supposed to be a protective cocoon. I missed the sun's warmth on my skin, the way it used to fill me with energy and light. I missed my bike rides in the wee hours of the morning just as the sun's rays started to peek out over the horizon. Now, I was just grumpy and tired of being confined to the night.

"This sucks," I muttered to myself, drawing my knees up to my chest.

The others thought my grumpiness was cute, but it didn't change the fact that I was miserable. I wanted to go to New Orleans to find the vampire who could give me resistance to the sun. I needed it, and I needed it soon. The thought of spending another day like this, shrouded in darkness, made my sun-sensitive skin crawl.

Laz wandered into the room, their eyes twinkling with amusement as they took in my curled-up form. "You look like a disgruntled kitten," they said, plopping beside me and ruffling my hair.

I huffed, swatting their hand away. "I feel like one, too. I'm tired of being nocturnal. I want to feel the sun again."

Samara joined us, her laughter soft as she settled on my other side. "Patience, love."

"You're so cute when you're grumpy," Silas teased, sliding his hand along my cheek. I pulled my head back and crossed my arms over my chest in a huff, which only drew more laughter from my amused mates.

Orpheus leaned against the doorway, his gaze warm and understanding. "We'll go to New Orleans as soon as we can. Don't let the other's tease you. They were chomping at the bit to feel the sun again, too." He smiled at me, then sighed. "We will prioritize it the moment we are all safe. I understand the loneliness of the dark."

I sighed, the frustration still bubbling under the surface but soothed slightly by their presence and the guilt that I'd only been nocturnal for a few days while Orpheus had spent a century confined to the darkness. "I'm sorry. I know I'm whining, and you all had to do it for much longer than I have. I shouldn't complain."

Silas turned to me, his eyes full of sympathy. "You're still allowed to be upset, bookworm. In the meantime, maybe we can find something to distract you from your grumpiness."

I rolled my eyes, but a small smile tugged at my lips. "Fine, but nothing dirty, ok? My body needs three to five business days to recover from what you all did to me last night."

They all laughed, the sound filling the room with warmth I couldn't get from the sun. For now, that would be enough.

"You know, I wouldn't be surprised if your vampire gifts get an upgrade as well after you marked us," Laz said, smiling.

"Really?" I replied, shocked. My gift was already so powerful I didn't know how it could get any better.

"They're right," Orpheus chimed in. "We each had our latent gifts upgraded, so it would be logical to assume yours would, too."

"What do you think it'll be?" I asked the room.

"Have you felt anything change with your gift today?" Silas urged.

No, it feels the same. I replied via the channels of my mind.

Silas nodded.

"Well, give it time. Mine didn't manifest until I needed it," Laz promised. I nodded quietly, my eyes closed, taking a moment to analyze the strange gift that had settled into my mind since my transformation. It felt like a physical presence, something tangible nestled deep within my consciousness. It wasn't just the mate bond that connected me to Laz, Samara, Orpheus, and Silas– it was something more unique.

This ability to communicate with them wasn't like the telepathic links I'd read about in books or seen in movies. It was different, more intimate. It worked in tandem with the mate bond, wrapping around it like ivy climbing up a tree, using it as a vessel for our thoughts and emotions.

I focused on the sensation, feeling the connecting threads to each of them. The bond with Silas was vibrant and playful, tinged with his unique spark of energy. Samara's bond was deep and soothing, a well of calm and wisdom. Orpheus's connection was passionate and intense, like an eternally simmering fire. And Laz's bond was strong and steadfast, grounding me with their unwavering presence.

I tried to experiment with the gift and sense any additional factions or unique changes. But it all felt the same. Frustrated, I sent out a tentative thought, trying to pull on all four bonds simultaneously.

Can you hear me?

Almost immediately, I felt the responses. Laz's laughter echoed in my mind, followed by a playful, *Loud, and clear darlin'.*

Samara's voice was a gentle caress. *Yes, we're here.*

Orpheus's reply was a warm surge of affection. *Always.*

Silas's presence wrapped around me like a comforting embrace. *We're all with you.*

I took a deep breath, marveling at my mind's intricate web of connections. This ability was a part of me now, an extension of the bonds I shared with my mates. And maybe soon, it might be something more– something that could help us defeat Nameless and begin our lives without fear.

Opening my eyes, I looked around at my mates, scattered throughout the room but connected to me in a way that defied physical distance. I sent out another thought, this one filled with gratitude and love. *Thank you for being here with me and for being a part of me.*

Their responses came in the form of soft smiles.

"I can talk to all four of you at the same time. Maybe that's the upgrade?" I mused out loud.

"Did you try to do that before?" Orpheus inquired.

I thought about it. In the few days since the transformation, I had only ever really tried to speak to one of them at a time. So, I could have done that already, but I just didn't realize it.

"No," I huffed. Laz smiled, patting my head like the disgruntled kitten they assumed me to be.

"Don't worry. If you're going to get something additional, it'll come when you need it most," Orpheus promised.

A knock on the door made us jump to our feet in fear. I hadn't heard any footsteps leading up the driveway, and according to their reaction, my mates hadn't either. I quickly realized in this new life that not many people have the skills to sneak up on a vampire. Unless, of course, they're trained for it.

"Get in the other room, Athena," Silas ordered in a rushed whisper, standing up to face the door, his back tense and rigid.

"I can help!" I whispered. "I'm stronger now."

"Not when the door is open and the sun floods in," Samara reminded me, and I groaned internally before retreating around the corner. My mates prepared themselves and headed toward the door. My heart felt like it wanted to race if it could. Orpheus shifted, letting his vampiric form overtake his human features. His eyes darkened, his ears tapered off to a point, his nails elongated, and his posture became more rigid as his body transformed. I wondered briefly how I looked fully shifted. I was so afraid the first time I saw them like this. So scared of the "monsters" in my bookstore. But now, I didn't see a monster. I saw my protectors and my mates in all their supernatural glory.

Orpheus opened the door, and I slid behind the corner of the wall, instantly feeling a burning warmth from the sun that peaked through the doorway. I tensed, feeling my fingernails dig into the wood on the archway where I was hiding.

"Holy shit!" Archer's surprised voice echoed through my little cottage, and I heard my mates visibly relax. A few moments later, Archer entered, albeit timidly, and the door was shut behind him.

I stepped out from my hiding space and met eyes with my terrified brother.

"You scared the shit out of me," Archer explained, panting and placing a hand on his heart. The elevated heart rate pounded across the room, beckoning me to the running blood within his veins, but I shook my head and forced the impulse away.

"How the hell did you get up to the house so quietly?" Silas sneered, running a hand through his hair.

"I'm used to approaching places silently. Occupational hazard, sorry," he said, holding his hands up.

The five of us took seats in the living room, the tension slipping away but not entirely disappearing. We'd never fully relax until the threat was gone.

"I have some updates," Archer started. I leaned forward, resting my elbows on my knees. "I reached out to a few of the Hunters from my class that I remember, a few that were less... eager to, you know, murder vampires." He winced, and my mates followed suit.

"On a secure line, I'm sure," Orpheus prompted.

Archer rolled his eyes. "Yes, I'm not an amateur."

"So, what did they say?" Silas interjected.

"Kinda ran the gamut, honestly." He shrugged. "A few of them laughed in my face. One person told me that I deserved to be 'staked like those bloodsucking leeches for turning coat.'" He said it so flippantly, but I could see how the words affected him. I reached across the way to place a hand on his. He smiled softly at me.

"Sounds like you made great progress," Silas teased. Samara elbowed him in the ribs, and he grunted.

"Did anyone hear you out?" Samara asked, hopeful.

"Yeah, actually." He nodded.

"How many?" Orpheus urged.

Archer looked down at his hands and played with his fingers idly. "One."

Silas groaned and leaned back, and I felt myself lose any ounce of hope I had allowed myself to feel.

"She won't be able to convince anyone else, but she said she'd feed me intel when she could," Archer announced eagerly.

"That's useful, thank you, Archer," Orpheus asserted.

"She told me that my father hasn't been seen at HQ since yesterday morning," Archer confessed in a whisper. We all knew what that meant. He was on his way, and he'd be here soon.

"Ok, we already knew they'd be on their way. We were ready for that kind of news." Samara tried to sound optimistic, but it fell a little flat.

"She also said that Dr. Galvin was rumored to be coming out of hiding to join him on this hunt." That had all of us holding our breath.

On the journey back to Shockgrove, my mates and brother had let me in on all they had been able to gather about him, which, frustratingly, wasn't much. Galvin was never seen without a mask, a Nameless Hunter staple, but even at Nameless functions, he remained elusive, like a shadow in the night. There was no history about him on the internet past fifteen years ago.

Archer told me everything he knew about him from his time there. Apparently, a member of the Galvin family had been at the head of Nameless since its inception, passed down like some twisted family heirloom. Instead of a watch or a quilt or something, it was a vampire-hunting organization—a legacy of blood and death.

Laz had dug deep on the internet, using every resource, but Dr. Kline Galvin was a ghost. There were whispers and rumors, but nothing concrete. No one knew what he looked like under that mask, and it seemed like he preferred it that way. His true identity was a closely guarded secret even within the Nameless Hunters.

After a mission went south, he had been in hiding for a while. Archer didn't know how long precisely. He hadn't seen him since his graduation day. The day they branded him. I had felt sick to my stomach when he told me about that, marked by the twisted, burning metal and claimed as an agent of death and persecution. I offered to buy him a tattoo to cover it. He seemed interested in that idea.

This mysterious fog surrounding him was infuriating. How could someone so integral to the Nameless Hunters' operations be such an enigma? Knowing that we were up against someone who had managed to remain hidden for so long, someone who operated in the shadows and pulled the strings from behind the scenes, made me uneasy. Information is power, and we had none.

I glanced at my mates, each absorbed in their thoughts. They were just as frustrated as I was. Dr. Kline Galvin may have been a ghost, but he was on his way to haunt us, and we needed to be prepared for anything.

"We will be ready for them," Orpheus assured.

"How can you be so sure?" I stuttered.

Orpheus met my eyes and moved to kneel before me. His fingers caught my chin and tilted my head to kiss my lips. "Because have you ever known me not to have contingency plans?"

I smiled. "I haven't known you that long, actually," I teased.

"Really? See, I think I've known you for my entire life," he whispered softly, letting his lips dust against mine for another gentle kiss.

"I love you," I confided in a breathy moan against his lips.

"Love is only part of what I feel for you," he proclaimed softly before sitting back and addressing the group. "I have a plan to help us should we need it. It's a long shot, but I figured if there were ever a time to take a risky shot, it would be now."

"What did you do?" Silas asked.

"I called for backup," he declared.

I stared at Orpheus, my mind reeling from his words. "You called for backup?" I asked, trying to wrap my head around it.

He nodded, his expression calm. "Yes, we may need reinforcements."

"More vampires?" I probed, my voice barely above a whisper.

"Among others," he replied casually as if it were the most natural thing in the world.

"No," Silas growled.

"Yes," Orpheus replied.

"What's going on?" I asked, looking between the two of them.

"You called Elias?" Silas asked, utter disbelief coloring his tone. I glanced at my mates, who were wearing equally shocked looks.

"He owes us." Orpheus shrugged.

"But then we'll owe him, and do you really want to make that asshole another promise?" Silas bellowed. "I just barely survived the last one!"

"That was entirely different. If my coven is alive and safe, I'll make him any promise he wants."

His words sounded almost muddled as my brain swam with the introduction of this new knowledge. I knew logically there had to be other vampires out there, our kind couldn't be limited to just us, but we had never talked about it. The world of the supernatural had always seemed like a small, contained bubble around my mates and me. Now, with Orpheus' simple statement, that bubble had burst, revealing a vast, intricate web of beings I hadn't even begun to comprehend.

My mind raced. What did he mean by 'among others'? Were there other supernatural creatures out there? Werewolves? Witches? Things I hadn't even imagined? The possibilities seemed endless and overwhelming.

I looked at Orpheus, searching his eyes for answers. "What do you mean, 'others'?" I asked, my voice tinged with curiosity and apprehension.

He gave me a reassuring smile. "Well, if they come, like I hope they will, you'll see soon enough. The supernatural world is much bigger than you think, Athena. Nameless may have dwindled our numbers, but we may not have to be alone in this fight."

I nodded slowly, trying to process this new reality. The shock was starting to give way to a strange sense of anticipation. There was so much more to learn and to understand about this hidden world I was now a part of.

The realization was both daunting and exciting. My life had already changed so dramatically since becoming a vampire, and now it seemed there were even more changes on the horizon. I took a deep breath, steeling myself.

"We need to talk to your grandma to figure out what she knows," Archer insisted, and I felt my stomach twist with pain.

"I'm scared," I confessed.

Samara placed her hand on my back and ran a comforting hand along my spine. My back relaxed slightly under her touch.

"We'll be there to protect you," Laz promised.

"She's at your shop. I walked past earlier today just to check it all out. The sign said she'd be there until close. So, we can probably catch her if we head out as soon as the sun sets," Archer suggested, and my mates all nodded their heads.

The sun would set in a few hours, and I would finally have to face the truth. I hoped I could hold it together.

After the sun finally set, casting long shadows across the ground, we made our way to the pier. I stood at the spot where everything had changed. It was here that I had struggled against Greg, where he had placed his vicious hands on my body and tried to make me submit. It was here where I fought back, and he slipped away into the churning waves below. The memory of that, the fear and desperation, still lingered, but tonight, something else was gnawing at me– was he still out there? I turned away from the railing where Greg was last seen and headed down the quiet pier toward The Maine Plotline. It had been more than two weeks since I had seen it, since that day when Greg had found me there, and everything had spiraled out of control.

The window was fixed now. It felt strange to see the updated visage of the store, so new and pristine when the scars of that night remained etched onto my soul and probably always would. As I approached, I saw Grandma inside, her silhouette moving between the bookshelves. She had been keeping secrets from me, and now, more than ever, I felt the weight of those hidden truths.

The quaint bookstore, once my home away from home, now felt tainted with memories of violence and betrayal. It used to be my refuge, a place where I had found solace among the pages of countless stories. But now, standing outside, for the first time, I didn't want to go inside.

You've got this. Laz promised in my mind.

Taking a deep breath, I pushed open the door and stepped into the suddenly unfamiliar warmth of The Maine Plotline. The scent of books and old wood enveloped me, soothing yet tinged with unease. Grandma looked up from behind the counter, her expression a mix of relief and concern as she saw me. Her eyes flicked to my mates who stood behind me, but she didn't seem afraid or concerned.

"Athena," she said softly, setting aside the book she had been holding. "You're back. You're okay."

I nodded, trying to muster a smile. "Yeah, I'm back." But I certainly wasn't okay.

Her eyes scanned the people at my back. Did she know everything? Did she know who they were? What they were? How much of my connection was shared with her by my father?

Silence hung heavy between us, filled with unspoken words and unanswered questions. I didn't know where to start. My eyes drifted over to the counter. A vase filled with pink roses looked back at me. I felt warmth in my bonds as I saw them.

"I kept them alive for you," she whispered. I took this moment to really study her. The last few weeks had done little to help her health. In fact, she looked worn and tired. Guilt gripped my heart. I hated that I had worried her, that I had forced her to deal with all of this alone, without even knowing if I was alive. Her soft grey hair was pulled back into a braid that traveled down her back. Her floral patterned dress flared out at her feet, and she wore a shawl that gave her an almost Stevie Nicks look. But despite the colorful appearance, her eyes were dull and hollow. Clearly, worry had gotten the best of her.

She came around the counter, her steps hesitant as she approached me. "I'm so sorry, Athena," she said, her voice thick with emotion.

I swallowed hard, the lump in my throat threatening to choke me, before throwing my arms around her neck and pulling her into an embrace. She gasped as she met my icy frame but sunk into the hold. "I know," I whispered. "But now... now I need to know everything."

She nodded, pulling back. Her eyes were filled with a mixture of guilt and determination. "Come," she said, gesturing towards the back of the store where we could talk in private. "Archer, close up the front, will you?" She tossed toward my brother. Did she know who he was to me? Or did she still consider him the friendly stranger I made friends with? "Let's sit down. There's much we need to discuss."

We moved towards the back of The Maine Plotline, my mates following behind, toward where the cozy reading nook I'd spent that evening with Silas awaited us. Soft string lights hung delicately above, casting a warm, amber glow that bathed the area in a comforting light. Ivy vines crawled along the ceiling and draped over the shelves, adding a touch of natural beauty to the cozy space. The plush green velvet couch beckoned invitingly in the corner of the nook, and flashes of all the ways Silas claimed me returned to my mind.

Reminiscing, baby girl? Silas purred into my mind, and I fought off the blush.

Behave. I warned and earned an outward chuckle from him. My other mates glanced his way, but he just shrugged and smiled at me.

Grandma led me to one of the armchairs, its velvet cushions sinking slightly under my weight as I settled in. She sat opposite me on the couch, her expression serious yet tinged with a hint of warmth. Laz and Samara took seats on the open furniture while Silas and Orpheus stood to the side. Archer followed after locking the front door and claimed a seat on the hardwood floor.

As we sat there, the faint scent of old paper and coffee lingered in the air, mingling with the quiet rustle of pages as Grandma reached for my hand. Her touch was reassuring, grounding me in the present moment as she prepared to reveal the truths that had been hidden from me.

She searched my eyes for confirmation that I was prepared for what she was about to divulge. I nodded, my throat tight with emotion. "I'm ready," I replied, my voice steady despite the uncertainty that lay ahead.

"Okay," she began. "I think it's important to start at the beginning and let you know that your father and mother honestly loved each other very much while they were together." My shock must have shown on my face because she quickly added, "I know that's hard to believe considering how little she discussed him, but her opinion of him was colored by how he left, not the love they shared while he was here."

Her eyes filled with a sadness that I only ever saw when she was discussing Mom.

"Jacob Bennett was a good man when I knew him, but he had… unique opinions about the world. Franny tried to see past it," she uttered.

"What kind of opinions," I prompted.

She steadied her breathing. "He believed in the supernatural and in a much more serious capacity than me, believing I can feel your grandfather's spirit sometimes."

I watched her to gauge her reaction. Did she know just how accurate he had been?

"Okay," I said quietly.

"At first, your mother thought it was just a hobby, but it turns out he was part of some organization that was really immersed in that sort of world."

Archer shifted uncomfortably on the floor.

"So, she didn't believe him and kicked him out?" I asked. I needed to know how much she knew.

"No, no. It's a little more complicated than that. He showed her the truth, convinced us that creatures of the night did exist, and they were dangerous."

My mates bristled. I felt the bond in my chest tug as they pulled on it for strength.

"So, you believed in what he was saying?" I asked.

She nodded. "If you'd seen what I had, you would too." I thought back to the office where I was held and the photos Archer had shown me. I wondered if she had seen any of those. Had they been enough to convince her? They might have worked on me had I not already known who my Wanderers were.

"Your father was trying to eradicate the monsters and keep us all safe," she said, and I felt my mates tense at the term. "Franny didn't see it that way."

"What do you mean?"

"You know your mother, she was always a bleeding heart. There wasn't a creature alive she didn't empathize with." She smiled softly as she spoke of her. "She thought your father was just as bad as the creatures he hunted. He thought she was crazy. They fought. When she found out she was pregnant, she gave him an ultimatum. He could renounce his obsession with killing monsters or leave the two of you and never come back."

I felt the hollow pain in my chest intensify. He had chosen his anger and his obsession over being my father. It stung more than I cared to admit. Tears began to pool in my eyes.

"She was broken when he left. I mean, I've never seen her in so much pain. She was pregnant and just had her heart shattered," her voice caught in her throat. I hated the thought of my mother feeling like that. "When you came along, you put the pieces back together."

I felt my mates caressing my bond, comforting me as the new information came in.

"She wanted nothing to do with him. She never wanted you to know him. So, when he wouldn't stop calling to hear about how you were, I saw how it broke her. Each time the phone rang, her smile would drop, and she would retreat into her shell. Eventually, I couldn't take it anymore, so I answered the phone. She didn't know, of course. I was going to tell him off, tell him to leave us alone if he knew what was good for him. But he asked about you, and I could hear it in his voice." She paused, taking a breath. "He was misguided, a downright fool, but he cared about you. I told him you were okay just to get him to stop calling." A mixture of complicated feelings swirled in my stomach at that thought. He cared enough to see how I was, but not to stay? "But then he kept calling me, kept asking about you, and damnit, I couldn't cut him off from you."

We were both crying.

"Now, I think it's your turn to tell me what the hell you meant when you said he had you kidnapped. Because the Jacob Bennett I knew would never do such a thing to his daughter."

I took a deep breath, looking over at Archer, who offered me a soft nod.

"You know the monsters that he hunts?"

Her eyes narrowed in suspicion, but she nodded.

"Well, I am one of those creatures," I admitted into the darkness.

"What?" She stuttered, leaning away from me.

"I am a vampire, Grandma," I declared. She shook her head, studying me as if she was trying to note the differences.

"No, that's not..." her eyes drifted over to Orpheus, then Silas, Samara, and Laz, finally landing on Archer.

"Is this them? The Wanderers?" She asked softly, and I held my gasp in just barely. I felt Orpheus tense, and Silas' knuckles were white from just how tightly he clenched his fists.

"*We* are The Wanderers," I admitted for the first time out loud, although it had been the truth long before the transformation ever occurred.

She sighed, placing her head in her hands.

"Your father told me about them. He told me what to look for and the warning signs that a vampire might be nearby. After that boy from the Craving Crab went missing, I told him I thought they might have been here in Shock-grove...I didn't know..."

"You didn't know that he would kidnap us and try and kill us?" I finished.

She inhaled sharply, her response getting stuck in her throat, but ultimately nodded her agreement.

"Well, he did." I wasn't angry with her. She was operating under the only side of truth she was given, it wasn't her fault, but I couldn't help but feel betrayal seep into my bones.

"Athena," she started. "I'm so sorry. I was just trying to keep you safe."

I knew that. I did. And one day, I'd forgive all of this. I was sure of it. But the sting was so fresh that I couldn't shake it yet.

"Will you introduce me to your friends?" She asked timidly, and my eyes shot up to stare at her.

"You mean it?"

"If they're important to you, they're important to me, too."

"I don't know," I began timidly. "Their stories are theirs to tell." Laz noticed my hesitation and stepped in.

"My name is Laz, ma'am. It's a pleasure to meet you." They really laid on the charm as they tipped their head to my grandma. "I was turned into a vampire after a bunch of bigots in my town decided they'd rather I be dead than queer. Samara saved my life by turning me. Gave me a chance to live long enough to become who I truly was." My grandma listened intently to their words. Tears still flowed from her eyes.

"I was a victim of the LA Times bombing," Silas added. "If Orpheus didn't turn me, I wouldn't have made it."

"My parents used to sell my body to the highest bidder," Samara revealed. My breath caught in my throat. I knew her story wasn't a happy one, but hearing it in such plain terms felt sickening. My grandma felt the same.

"Oh honey..." grandma whispered.

"Orpheus found me one night, and he paid my fee but asked for nothing in return." She smiled over at Orpheus, who looked at her with such love and care that my dead heart nearly burst. "He paid my fee every night for a month. Giving me what I needed to satisfy my parents without forcing me to give away any more pieces of myself."

My grandma placed a hand on her heart as she listened.

"He offered me a way out of that. He gave me my life back."

I love you. I whispered to her via our mental link and felt her tug on the bond in response. Warmth spread through my veins.

"I don't know who turned me," Orpheus interjected. He remained stoic, standing gently against the bookshelf. "I woke up in this new existence completely alone. I struggled, trying to control my thirst and find my place in this world. I was on my own for... a really long time." I heard a slight crack in his voice, which made my heart ache. "Then I found Samara, and then Laz and Silas... and suddenly I had a family again."

He turned his eyes to me.

"And when we found Athena, our whole lives, every ounce of pain, every threat we faced, all the persecution...it was all worth it because finally we had the one thing we had been missing."

"We love your granddaughter, Miss Landry," Laz added.

"We would do anything to protect her, keep her safe, and make her happy," Samara said, smiling warmly at me.

"She's everything to us," Silas pledged like a vow.

My grandma's eyes were full of emotion as she looked around the room at my mates. They landed on Archer. "And you? Are you one of her... partners, too?"

"No!" Both Archer and I shouted simultaneously. Grandma jumped slightly, startled by our adamant denial.

"No, we're not together," I insisted, struggling to keep the disgusting mental image away. "He's Jacob's son."

She gasped, pressing her hand to her mouth. "Oh my word," she started. "You're.."

"Athena's brother," Archer finished.

"You look just alike...I should have seen it," she mused breathily, looking between us. "Are you also a..."

"No, ma'am. I worked with my father until recently. I realized I couldn't stay there when they showed me the truth." He indicated to my mates.

"He helped us escape," I added. She didn't need to know he kidnapped us, to begin with. He felt guilty enough about that without me throwing in his face again.

Grandma nodded softly, tears falling before reaching a wrinkled hand out for Archer. He took it in his and smiled up at her. "Thank you," she said to Archer. "All of you," she directed at my other mates. "Thank you for keeping her safe and for fixing my mistake."

Then she turned to me. "I am so sorry. I love you, no matter what you've become. You are and always will be my Athena."

I devolved into sobs, sinking in her embrace. We cried together for a few moments longer before pulling back from each other, refreshed, changed... altered.

"When did you last speak to Jacob?" Orpheus asked.

Grandma wiped her eyes with the back of her hand and replied, "I called him right after you called me." She nodded to me.

"What did he say?" Silas chimed in.

"I didn't give him much of a chance to say anything. I was confused and scared, and you just told me that he had you kidnapped, so I was trying to get to the bottom of it all. He just asked if you had called the number I was calling him from, and when I said yes, he hung up," she finished.

"He tracked the call somehow," Samara sighed.

"I kept calling back, but he hasn't answered since then."

"Listen, Grandma, he and his organization are on their way here. They're going to try and kill us," I revealed, and she shook her head, fear plastered on her face. "I need you to get out of town for a few days. I can't focus on what I have to do if I'm worried about you."

She shook her head and began to protest, but I held up a hand.

"Please, don't fight me on this. I need this," I repeated, staring directly into her eyes—a copy of mine and my mother's.

"Okay, honey. I can do that for you. Just please be careful. Promise you'll keep her safe," she said to the others.

"We won't let anyone hurt her. You have our word," Orpheus confirmed.

She threw her arms around my neck and sighed. "I'm so sorry."

"I know."

We held each other for another few precious minutes before I urged her to leave. She insisted on going home to pack a bag, but Orpheus, ever the planner, pulled a wad of cash from his suit jacket, which he somehow had the chance to buy since arriving back in town, and handed it to her, telling her to buy whatever she needed when she was out of town.

Grandma seemed to understand the urgency in his voice because she agreed. We walked her to her car, and I didn't take another breath until her tail lights disappeared safely over the horizon.

I leaned my head on Silas' shoulder and gripped Laz's hand on my other side.

"Are you okay?" Silas asked softly.

I nodded without lifting my head from his shoulder. "I'm glad she's safe." The danger was coming for us, and we had to be ready. For now, though, I let myself enjoy the ocean air, savoring the cool breeze and the sound of the waves crashing against the shore under the moonlight.

I took a long breath of the cool night air and sighed. It was moments like this that I missed my mom the most. When I was scared or afraid, she would always be there for me, keeping me safe and protecting me.

I glanced toward the lighthouse, standing quiet and dark in the moonlight. It was where I had shared my last moments with my mother. The memory tugged at my heart. She had known about vampires. She had only the darkest lies about them at her disposal, yet she still chose not to condemn them.

"I want to go to her grave," I said to my mates, my voice steady.

"Are you sure," Silas asked gently, concern in his voice.

"Yeah, I need to feel her," I admitted, and thankfully nobody else interjected. The light of their support overshadowed the darkness of the past, and I found myself capable of focusing on the good memories with my mother rather than the pain of her loss.

"Would you all like to meet my mom?" I asked softly.

"I'd love to," Samara stated first, reaching for my hand. I smiled gently at her before turning to see the others were nodding.

"Archer?" I asked.

"You want me to come too?" He asked, a little incredulously.

"Of course I do," I replied. He nodded, his eyes glistening with the beginning of unshed tears.

The moon was perched high in the sky, casting a silvery glow over the graveyard as I led my mates and Archer through its quiet, winding paths. The night air was warm but not suffocatingly so, typical of early summer, with a gentle breeze carrying the salty scent of the ocean from the cliffs below. As we walked, the rhythmic sound of waves crashing against the rocks provided a melancholy melody that echoed the phantom beats of my heart.

The graveyard was perched on a cliff overlooking the vast, dark ocean, offering a clear view of the ocean, the town, and the lighthouse. I knew this spot was perfect for her when I first came here. Ancient trees stood fiercely on the outskirts of the cemetery, their branches swaying gently in the night air. Weathered and worn by time, the headstones stood in orderly rows, their inscriptions softened by moss and age. There was a serene beauty to the place, a quiet peace that felt less oppressive than the last time I'd visited.

Approaching my mother's grave, a mix of emotions welled up inside me. Grief, of course, for the loss that still ached like an open wound, but also warmth at the thought of introducing my newfound family to her. My heart constricted tighter with each step, memories of her gentle smile and bright personality flooding back.

We reached her grave, the headstone modest but elegant, etched with her name. *Francesca Landry.* Beneath it, a simple epitaph read: *Beloved Daughter and Mother, Forever in Our Hearts.* I knelt, brushing away a stray leaf that had settled against the stone, and placed my hand on the cool surface, feeling the connection that tied us together even in her absence.

"This is her," I whispered, turning to my mates and Archer. My voice was thick with emotion, but I smiled through it, eager to share this moment. "Mom, these are my mates. Laz, Samara, Silas, and Orpheus." I smiled. "I know, I know. Four partners. I can't believe it either. But it's perfect. They're perfect. I love them." I felt tears slide down my cheeks. "I know you would, too. They are really good to me, Mom. They treat me the way you always told me I deserved to be. I'm really happy." A sob lodged in my throat.

"Hello, Miss Landry. It's an honor to meet you," Laz stated first, stepping forward and placing a hand on the gentle surface of the stone.

"She's one hell of a woman. You should be proud of her," Silas joined in, laying his hand next to Laz's.

"We're lucky to know her," Orpheus added, adding his hands to the stone.

"Thank you for keeping her safe and protecting her. We swear to carry on your legacy," Samara finished, placing her hand next to my mother's name.

"She's also dynamite in bed," Silas teased. Laz and Samara both smacked his chest, sending him stumbling back, clutching his pecs and chuckling. I felt the laugh bubble out of my throat and was instantly thankful to him for lightening the mood.

"And Mom, there's one more person you should meet," I glanced at Archer. He was standing behind us, a few feet away. Nerves clearly wracking through his body as he held his fingers in front of him. "Mom. Meet my brother, Archer."

Archer stepped closer, his expression a blend of reverence and sorrow. He knew he was standing at the resting place of the woman who was so removed from him and yet so intrinsically tied all the same.

"Mom," I continued, my gaze shifting between the headstone and my companions. "This is my family now. They've helped me through so much, and I wish you could have met them. I wish you were here to see how far I've come. How much I've survived because you taught me how to."

The ocean breeze picked up, rustling the grass and whispering through the trees as if the world itself was acknowledging our presence. I let the moment wash over me, feeling a sense of peace knowing I had introduced them to her, even if she wasn't physically there to hear it.

"She would have loved you all," I said, feeling the warmth of my mates and brother around me. "Thank you for coming here with me tonight."

As we stood there, the stars shining above us like distant candles, I felt a profound connection not only to my mother but to those who loved me the way she used to.

5

ATHENA

"Bookworm," Silas' whispered words woke me up late the next day. I didn't even know what time it was anymore, my internal clock shifting into this nocturnal creature. I stretched and yawned, turning my head to see Silas, who lay on his side facing me.

"Good morning," I whispered, smiling sleepily at him. "Or evening, whatever it is." He chuckled.

"You slept all day," he noted, nodding to the clock on the bedside table, which read nine o'clock at night. I stretched.

"I'm like a raccoon," I teased, and Silas laughed with me.

"A very sexy raccoon," he smiled darkly at me.

"Stop it," I said pointedly.

"Stop what?" He asked innocently.

"Stop making eyes with me. I just woke up," I joked, and he leaned forward, pressing a kiss to my lips.

"Get up. I'm taking you somewhere," he said before slipping out from the covers and sliding out of the room. I groaned, yawning once more before tossing the covers off of my body and slipping off the mattress. After washing my face and making myself as presentable as possible, I entered the living room.

My other mates were milling about the room, and all stopped to smile when they saw me. I moved to step toward Samara, who was standing by the coffee machine, but Silas' arms circled my waist and kept me in place. I shot him an inquisitive look, and he shrugged.

"You're mine tonight. I already called it," he said so casually. Laz and Orpheus both rolled their eyes while Samara chuckled.

"I don't even get any coffee?" I whined as he dragged me toward the door.

"Trust me, you won't need any help staying awake," he promised quietly into my ear. His sensual vow sent goosebumps erupting across my skin.

"Make good choices!" Laz called out as we stepped across the threshold into the night air. The sky was not entirely black as night, but the sun that had set several minutes ago left the ghost of a painted sky in its wake. A soft orange glow decorated the horizon, and I was in awe as we ventured across town. Silas held my hand in his, and I only minorly noticed where he was leading me.

It wasn't until we hit the pier that I tore my eyes from the previously painted sky and looked at him.

"Where are we going?" I asked as we traversed the boardwalk and passed the quiet storefronts.

"I made you a promise, baby girl, and I always keep my promises." His eyes sparkled with sinful desires, and my core tightened at his words, but they also brought a memory to the forefront of my mind.

"Speaking of promises, you said something about that guy Orpheus asked for help from..." I prompted, and I heard Silas sigh deeply next to me.

"Elias," he confirmed. I nodded.

"What did you mean by you barely survived the last one?"

He ran a hand through his hair, stopping near a bench and gesturing for me to take a seat. I did and looked up at him as he paced near me.

"Elias deals in promises. They're his currency," he started, and I felt the confusion flood me.

"What does that mean?" I asked.

Silas paused, his eyes distant as if recalling a memory long buried. He paced the ground in front of the bench, the dim light casting soft shadows across his face. He looked almost wistful, but his eyes had an edge of caution.

"Fae don't trade in money or jewels," he explained, and I tried to ignore the shock at hearing the word fae used so casually. "They trade in favors, in promises. When Elias makes a deal, it's bound by magic. Once you agree, you're tied to it until it's fulfilled."

I nodded slowly, processing his words. "And you made a promise to him?"

He sighed, running a hand through his hair, the strands catching the light. "I did. Years ago, when The Wanderers were in a tight spot, we had Nameless right on our heels. It was the closest they'd ever gotten, well, until they captured us. We needed a place to lay low, to hide from the Hunters until we could make a plan and escape. Elias agreed to shield us in his Court, but in return, he wanted a promise."

Silas leaned back, his gaze meeting mine. There was a gravity in his expression, a weight that hadn't been there before. "Could have been any of us to make it, but me, being the brave man I am, stepped up to the plate." he smiled wistfully.

"Brave and humble," I teased, he responded by offering me a smirk. "What did he ask for?" I prompted.

"He wanted me to retrieve some weird ass soul crystal from a place called the Shadow Market. It's not a pleasant place. Really fucking dangerous, honestly. It's almost like the supernatural black market, I guess."

I felt my head spinning at all the new information coming into it.

I frowned, trying to imagine such a place. "What happened?"

"It was worse than I'd imagined," he admitted, his voice dropping to a near whisper. "The Market is full of supernaturals who would kill first, then ask questions later. Elias didn't tell me that this soul crystal wasn't for sale... No, the bastard needed me to steal it. But here's the thing about that place. It's got so much dark magic swirling around that the shadows play tricks on your mind, twisting your perception of reality. It was nearly impossible to keep my focus and find the crystal."

My heart clenched at the thought of him in such peril, and I reached out, placing a hand over his. "But you did it. You kept your promise."

Silas nodded, his gaze softening as he looked at me. "I did. Barely. I found the damn crystal and got the hell out of there. Fulfilled my end of the promise."

"What would have happened if you didn't?"

"Fae can enact whatever punishment they see fit for breaking promises to them, so whatever it would have been, I can guarantee it wouldn't have been pretty."

I squeezed his hand, feeling the strength in his grip. "And that's why you don't want us to get help from him?"

He nodded. "If we accept help from that fae bastard, he will ask for something in return," he said, his voice steady but laced with warning. "And I need you to understand that once you agree, there's no turning back."

"He sounds like a monster," I mused quietly, reaching out for him. Silas grabbed my hand and sat beside me on the bench.

"He's not a monster. Not like the monsters we're used to fighting against, at least. But he is bound by the nature of his kind. He will ask for a promise, and I don't want you to be the one who has to make it."

I nodded, understanding the weight of what he was telling me. "I appreciate the warning, Silas. And I promise I'll be careful."

Silas smiled faintly, a hint of relief in his eyes. "I know you will. Now stop saying that word all willy-nilly, ok?"

I leaned against him, taking comfort in his presence.

"Come on, I have a mate to pleasure," he said with a wink before standing up and offering me a hand. I giggled, reaching for his outstretched hand.

He led me to the bookstore, and with each step, I felt my body tighten with anticipation of what was to come. He slipped a key that I didn't know he had out of his pocket and opened the front door. I raised an eyebrow at him, but he brushed me off with a shrug and pressed a hand to the small of my back to lead me inside.

When I stepped inside, I saw dozens of pink rose petals decorating the floor, unlit candles sitting on the counter, tables, and ground, and only the soft, warm glow of string lights illuminated the space, bathing the store in a sensual light. Silas quickly slipped his lighter from his pocket and lit the candles.

"Didn't want to leave them lit while I grabbed you. You know, fire hazard and all that." I chuckled, but it got caught behind the emotions in my throat. This was such a kind gesture. He always made me feel so special.

Once the last candle was lit, he turned to me, his face even more handsome in the flickering candlelight. He stepped forward, his eyes trailing my body, and I felt my skin blaze under his surveillance.

"I feel a little guilty," I confessed, biting my lower lip.

He tilted his head and narrowed his eyes. "About what, baby girl?" I nearly purred at his sensual nickname for me.

"The Hunters are on their way, we have a whole battle to prepare for, and here I am... being selfish," I admitted, hating how the guilt felt like a weight on my heart.

Silas gripped my chin in his fingers and pulled my eyes up to meet his. He glanced at me with a look so full of love that I almost gasped at the enormity of it. "Our lives are in danger," he whispered. "We are going to have one hell of a fight ahead of us. And there's a chance we aren't the same when all is said and done." He didn't want to say it, but I knew what he meant. Some of us might not make it out alive. "That's a real fucking good excuse to be selfish if ever I heard one."

I sighed.

"No, stop that. Listen to me, Athena." He placed his hands on my shoulders and squeezed gently. "You get to be selfish with us, with me. With love," Silas said, his voice gentle but filled with conviction. He reached out and took my hands in mine, feeling the chill of his skin, the slow pulse of life beneath the surface. His eyes met mine, a storm of emotions swirling within them, and I knew he could see into the pain within me.

"You've had so much taken from you," he continued. "The world hasn't been fair to you, and you've faced hardships that would have broken anyone else. But you're still here, Athena. You're still fighting. You've sacrificed so much for everyone else. It's time you allowed yourself to accept love when it's offered."

I felt a tear slide down my cheek, and he wiped it away with his thumb. "You are allowed to be selfish, Athena. You've earned it with every scar on your heart."

I pressed up onto my tiptoes to kiss him. He slid his arms around my waist and held me there as his mouth devoured mine in a soft, sensual kiss. His lips parted only slightly, giving me just enough room to sweep my tongue inside and brush against his. He moaned and sank into my embrace. When he drew back, I almost protested, but then I saw the devilish look in his eyes, and a shiver of anticipation traveled down my spine.

"Time to make a choice, baby girl," he instructed softly. "I can either make sweet, sensual love to you, make you feel just how special and cherished you are in each kiss, each brush of my skin, or thrust of my cock. I can be gentle and loving."

I choked on air.

"Or I can fuck you like the eager-to-please naughty girl that you are," he admonished in a commanding tone that had me quivering in his hold.

I moaned aloud.

"So, which one will it be?" He asked, pressing a kiss on my collarbone where his serpents rest. I let my head fall back as the bond between us thrummed with eager ecstasy.

"Fuck me," I whispered, leaning forward for a kiss.

"Ah ah ah.." he said, pushing my shoulders back and keeping me from pressing my lips to his. I groaned in frustration. "Use your manners, baby girl."

"Fuck me..." I said again, looking up at him through the curtain of my lashes. "Please, sir," I finished. He groaned deliciously at my words, our own special little phrase. Our own special wicked game. I couldn't wait to play. I loved being with him without any pretense or games, but there was something so appealing about pleasing him this way. It was a game I only ever wanted to play with him.

"You're going to be such a good girl for me, aren't you?" He asked, gripping the back of my neck and forcing my lips to his. I sank into his punishing kiss like butter. My whole body felt heated and warm despite the chilled touch.

"Yes, sir, I am," I swore eagerly. Loving the way I could completely disappear into this place of submission and yet still feel so confident and powerful with him.

"You're going to go to our couch, remove your clothes, and sit there with your legs spread nice and wide for me, and you're going to do it now," he demanded, his eyes alight with lust. I nodded and rushed down the aisles of the bookstores toward the velvet couches. My core was fluttering with eagerness, and I felt my nipples pebble against my shirt. I ripped my shirt over my head and slid my jeans off as fast as possible. I had no idea how close he would be behind me, and I wanted to be ready like he told me to be when he arrived. I was so eager to please him. I felt the urge to be perfect for him in every move I made.

When I was stripped naked, I slid onto the couch and pulled my legs wide. The soft blowing wind from the air conditioner felt nearly sensual against my exposed and eager center. I could feel just how wet I was, but I didn't dare touch myself or relieve the ache because I was a good girl.

I sat there, spread wide and waiting for a few silent minutes. It was torturous as I strained to hear his breathing or any movement from the store. Finally, I heard his footsteps, and my chest heaved as he approached.

"Should we read together again?" He asked from somewhere in the stacks of books. I felt alight all over.

"Yes, sir," I replied.

"Good answer," he breathed quietly, and I licked my bottom lip, trying to distract myself from the ache between my legs. "I'm going to read you a passage, baby girl. And you're not going to move a single inch."

I gasped.

"You're going to be so turned on you can't see straight. Your pussy is going to be soaking wet and begging for relief, but you won't touch yourself. You will not move, do you understand?"

I nodded.

"Words, baby girl. I can't see you, so I need to hear your dirty words," he demanded.

"Yes, sir. I understand." I choked out in my raspy, breathy voice. My arms hooked under my knees and held my legs wide, and I braced myself against the back of the couch, ready for the beautiful torture he was getting ready to inflict.

"'I never wanted anything more in my life than to dip my tongue down and taste her soaking wet pussy.'" He began, and I instantly knew this would be a challenge. "'Her cunt was wet and ready for me to claim as my own, so perfect and tight. Made entirely for me. So, I slid my tongue through her folds, lapping up her arousal like it belonged to me, which it did. She did. She always would.'" I felt my pussy tighten at the dirty words and the images it sent toppling into my mind.

"'Her taste was something so sinful, I knew I'd never be able to forget how it felt on my lips. When I pressed my fingers into her cunt, and her walls tightened around my fingers, I knew she would give me everything I asked her to, and I planned on asking for everything.'"

I was breathing heavily, and my eyes darted around the space, looking for a glimpse of my sinful mate and his watchful eyes.

"'She came on my fingers, her body spasming beneath me as she rode my tongue and fingers to the edge of euphoria. I couldn't wait a moment longer. I needed to be inside of her. I needed her core to squeeze my cock. I slammed into her, her pussy still fluttering with the aftershocks of her orgasm, and then I fucked her.'"

My head fell back against the couch, my eyes falling closed, and I fought against the urge to press my fingers against my more-than-ready pussy.

"'My cock slammed into her over and over and over again. Her breasts bounced against the force, so I had to take the pebbled peak into my mouth. She arched into my mouth, and I couldn't help but circle the clit at the apex of her thighs. That tight bundle of nerves was so eager, so read for my touch that she nearly exploded after just one touch.'" My clit throbbed in almost painful anticipation. I felt my hands wander closer to my core, leaving fiery paths along my thighs on their descent to my pussy.

I just needed a little relief.

I pressed my fingers against my clit, but just as soon as the touch was there, it was snatched away. I opened my eyes to see Silas, now shirtless, standing over me. My offending wrist in one hand and the open book in the other. He glared down at me, disappointment in his gaze.

"You broke the rules, baby girl," he chided. I pouted, hating how defeated I felt.

"I'm sorry, sir, I had to," I replied, trying to sit up, but he kept his hold on me tightly and kept his body positioned between my spread legs so I couldn't close them if I wanted to.

"What should your punishment be?" He mused, his eyes alight with sinful desires.

"I'll do anything," I pleaded.

He thought for a moment, then smirked. He turned the book to me, and I took it in my free hand. He let my wrist go, and I instantly gripped the book to avoid breaking the rules again and reaching for his deliciously exposed body.

"You're going to read for me now, baby girl." I nodded, my eyes drifting to the page and preparing to read, but then he moved and drew my attention back to him. His fingers made quick work of his jeans button, sliding them down his legs and releasing his hard cock from the confinement of his pants. My jaw dropped as I took in the sight of him– the perfect specimen.

"Read, baby girl. And accept your punishment."

I had no idea how this was a punishment, but I barely tore my eyes from his cock and began reading.

"'Her body writhed beneath my punishing thrusts. She slammed down onto my cock as I pressed my body into hers. Her nails tore down my back, and I couldn't contain my hips from pistoning, fucking her like she deserved.'"

I heard his soft moan, and my attention diverted back to him to find him softly stroking his cock, just inches from my soaking wet center. I groaned in near pain. One of my hands reached for him instinctively, but he gripped it with his free hand and returned it to the book.

"Bad girls don't get to touch me," he promised, stroking his length sensually.

"Silas," I whined.

"Read, baby girl. Accept your punishment, and then if you're good, I'll fuck you," he vowed, and the promise was almost too exciting a proposition. So I pulled my gaze from his stiff and eager length and continued reading.

"'She was going to come, and I was going to feel every inch of her fall apart beneath me. The way she fell into an orgasm was so sexy. Her core tightened around my cock, squeezing me until I could feel my balls tighten and my climax rise. Her back arched, and her mouth fell open as she screamed my name. I pounded into her as her orgasm beckoned my own.'" I heard him moan, and the sinful sounds of his hand sliding along his cock was almost enough to draw my eyes away again, but I didn't dare. I wanted my reward. "'I emptied myself into her, her core taking all of me the way she was designed to. Her body was mine, and I was hers.'" I finished in a breathy whisper.

I closed the book and looked up at Silas, who had slowed his strokes and was staring down at me sinfully.

"That's my good girl," he praised, and I preened under the adoration. "You need me, don't you?" He asked, his eyes looking down at my glistening pussy.

"Yes, sir," I begged.

"Say it," he said, leaning forward slightly, bringing the tip of his cock to just about an inch away from making contact with my swollen clit. I threw my head back and fought against the urge to push my hips up to meet him.

"I need your cock, sir. Please," I cried out.

The first press of his head against my clit was like a bomb detonating. I cried out his name but kept my body still. He slid the tip along my pussy lips gently, teasingly. Never quite pushing in. The sensation was almost too much.

"Oh my god, baby girl. You are so wet," he said, dropping the facade of my dominant sir just slightly. "I could just slide in if I wanted to."

"Only for you," I promised, earning me a hum of approval. I felt my body tingle with pride.

"I am going to fuck this pussy like you've never been fucked before," he swore, his eyes turning feral. The red tint shone through.

"I dare you," I challenged.

His eyes flashed darkly, and he smirked, pressing the tip of his cock against my clit again, and I arched into it. "Oh, is that so?" He asked, sliding his cock down my pussy toward the entrance and pressing in just enough for me to feel the slight stretch but not enough to satisfy my wanton need. "You dare me?" He asked teasingly.

"Please, Silas," I begged, but he pulled back, leaving me pussy empty and eager.

"Let's get one thing straight, baby girl," he said just as he pressed his cock against my entrance again, pressing forward a little more than last time, but still not nearly enough before pulling back again. I sighed frustratingly. "You do not get to challenge me when we play our little games," he said, sliding his cock up and down my pussy lips coating it in my arousal. My lips fell open on a gasp. "Tell me you understand."

"I understand," I replied with a moan.

He slid his cock down until it pressed against my ass ever so slightly before sliding back up my soaked folds.

"You are mine to play with, mine to command, mine to fuck," he said, the look in his eyes so feral and ferocious I almost growled in response. The nearly animalistic side of me fighting for dominance.

"I need you, Silas. Please, sir. Fuck me like you own me," I begged.

Then he slammed his hips forward and sheathed his cock so deep into my aching pussy that I let out a guttural scream. The sound was almost inhuman as pleasure erupted through my body. I was so tightly wound that the first orgasm ripped through me unexpectedly and wracked through my body.

"Yes, that's it, baby girl, grip my cock as you come," Silas demanded as he slammed into me over and over again. His words were broken and strained as he fought against his building climax.

He slammed into me, making good on his promise to fuck me like an eager-to-please naughty girl. I so rarely let myself let go the way I did when we played this game. It was so freeing and so dirty.

His cocked slammed into me, and I was falling apart all over again as he claimed my body as his. His mouth closed over one of my nipples, and I arched into his hold. My body felt worshipped, every nerve ending wholly wound up and tingling under his expert touch.

"I'm in love with you," I called out, an exclamation in the heat of the moment. His eyes softened, the dominant 'sir' slipping away to reveal my Silas.

"Fuck, I'm in love with you too, bookworm," he swore gently before slamming his hips against mine again and stealing my breath. His fingers found my clit and pressed deliciously sinful circles against it until my stomach muscles were clenching, and I was climaxing all over again. He leaned over me, bracing himself on the back of the couch as he came too, his body jerking violently as his orgasm wracked through him. We sat in silence for a few moments, his cock remaining idly inside of me as our breathing slowed and our bodies stopped trembling.

"I don't want you to leave," I whined, locking my ankles around his back and holding him to my body. He smiled down at me.

"I'm not going anywhere, baby." He picked me up, keeping me pressed against him so that his cock would remain pressed inside of me. He was sitting down on the couch, leaning back so that he was horizontal, and I was straddling his body. I leaned forward, pressing my cheek against his chest, and counted his heartbeats for a long while.

"I love playing that game with you," I whispered sheepishly, suddenly more self-conscious about my submissive state.

"So do I," he promised, tracing lines down my spine with his fingertips.

"I never thought I'd ever be able to be vulnerable like that with someone ever again," I admitted quietly, avoiding eye contact.

"After.." he started, and I nodded.

"Yeah," I finished for him. "I used to wake up in the middle of the night and feel his hands on my body. Like imprints." I shuddered. "I never felt so weak, so submissive. All I could do was lay there and let it happen. I couldn't fight back." His arms closed around my body, holding me tightly to his chest.

"I hate that I didn't find you early enough to save you from him," Silas said, seething beneath me.

"You are saving me, all of you, every single day," I sat up a little, just enough to look into his eyes. "With everything you say and do, you're all saving me from the pain of those memories. Orpheus makes me feel like I have agency again and can ask for what I need. Samara makes me feel like I can be sensitive again and let people in. Laz shows me that my scars can be stories and that I'm stronger because of them. And you... You give me the freedom to let go, to trust someone again, the way I haven't been able to since he took what he did from me."

Silas ran a hand along my face, tucking a lock of hair behind my ear.

"You saved my life, Silas," I swore and kissed his lips. He drank my kiss delicately, sensually, savoring every moment of it. I felt his cock twitch to life within my core.

"I'm going to make love to you now, Athena," he promised against my lips.

"I dare you," I challenged with a wink, rolling my hips tauntingly.

When Silas and I had had our delicious fill of each other and arrived back at the house, I was sated and happy. Silas kept an arm around my shoulders and led me to the kitchen island, where my other mates gathered around a Shock-grove map. We sat hunched around the kitchen island, the air thick with tension as we discussed our plans. The room was dimly lit, the soft glow of the overhead lights casting warm shadows on the walls. Despite the relatively calm atmosphere, I could feel the undercurrent of urgency in our conversations as we strategized our defenses against whatever might come next. Every day we sat here strategizing was another day closer to the Hunter's inevitable attack. I could feel that, and so could everyone else.

Laz was leaning against the counter, and their brow furrowed as they jotted down notes on a pad, their gaze flicking up to meet mine with a reassuring smile. Samara sat beside me, her fingers tapping rhythmically on the counter-top, deep in thought. Silas and Orpheus were across from us, engaged in a quiet discussion, their voices low and focused.

"We need to make sure we're ready for anything," Orpheus said, his voice steady but determined.

Silas joined in. "They won't stop coming, and we can't afford to be caught off guard."

Samara nodded, her eyes reflecting the same determination. "We could call the covens in Maine to set up defensive wards, maybe?"

"If you think they'd use their magic to protect vampires, you will be sorely disappointed," Silas chuffed.

"Covens? Like witches?" I gasped.

"It's a big world, bookworm," Silas added, tossing me a sly smirk. My head felt like it was spinning.

"We can't ask them, but we do have other potential reinforcements coming," Orpheus promised.

Just as Silas was about to respond, the kitchen door swung open, and Archer rushed in. I flinched instantly, a reflex now due to my painful reaction to the sun's rays, but luckily, no sun spilled through the doorway. It was well into the evening, nearly midnight. Time had gotten away from me. We were all startled, not having heard his approach, a testament to the stealth he'd honed through years of Hunter training. I relaxed the moment he locked eyes with me, but he didn't. His presence was charged with a panicked intensity. His eyes were wide with anger and panic, and his usually calm demeanor rattled. I heard his heart rate racing, pumping his blood through his veins.

"We need to go to the lighthouse," he said, his voice urgent. "Right now."

The suddenness of his entrance and the tension in his words shocked us. Silas and Orpheus exchanged a quick glance, their expressions shifting from curiosity to concern.

"What's going on?" Orpheus asked, his voice calm but wary as he approached my brother.

"They left a message," Archer replied, the words heavy.

A chill ran through me at his tone, a sense of foreboding settling in my gut. I met Archer's gaze, seeing the worry etched in his features. Whatever message had been left, it was enough to shake him.

Without hesitation, we moved as one, gathering what we needed and following Archer out the door. The night air was cool against my skin as we hurried to the lighthouse, a sense of urgency propelling us forward.

The walk was silent, each of our heads on a swivel, the gravity of the situation pressing down on us. As we approached the lighthouse, its silhouette stark against the night sky, I felt a mix of dread and determination.

As we reached the entrance, Archer paused, his eyes scanning the surroundings before he turned to us. "Be ready," he said, his voice low but persistent. "We don't know what we're walking into."

We paused at the base of the base of the lighthouse, and I breathed in deeply, letting the scent of salt and seaweed fill my lungs. This place, which meant so much to me and carried so much love and so much pain, was once a place I called our spot but had been tainted. I could almost hear my mother's laughter in the wind and feel her presence beside me. The nights I spent here with her flooded my mind. I remembered how we came here and sat at the peak, talking for hours as the waves crashed around us. She always made me feel safe, even when the world seemed to be falling apart. Her smile, gentle touch, how she would brush a stray lock of hair behind my ear or tell me everything would be okay. All those little things that made her my mother. Standing here now, I felt her spirit wrapping around me like a comforting embrace, preparing me for what was next.

Silas' voice broke through my thoughts. "Shit."

"What is it?" Laz asked.

"See for yourself," he said, pointing to the side of the old beacon. We shifted to his position to see what he was referring to. My heart sank as I took in the ominous symbol. Two offset triangles and a stake. Two words painted in bright red paint dripped like crimson blood down the side of the lighthouse.

Nisi Nox.

It was only my whispered words that cut through the emptiness of the chilly night air.

"They're here."

6

SAMARA

I felt their presence the moment they arrived. Turning over my shoulder away from the Nameless mark, I saw them approach. Nameless was here. Fear gripped me, a cold, unyielding terror that had the potential to paralyze me. But I couldn't afford to be scared. We needed to fight for Athena, for our survival...for Alora. My gaze darted around, taking in the faces of my mates and Archer, all of whom wore determined expressions despite the fear flickering in their eyes.

I scanned the Hunter's ranks, counting quickly. At least sixty. Shit. Then I saw her. Athena's best friend, Davia, was held tightly in a wicked embrace by one of the Hunters, her face pale with fear as she cried out and fought against their hold. A surge of anger and protectiveness shot through me, but it was Athena's reaction that nearly broke me. Her eyes blazed with fury, and she stepped forward, ready to charge and rescue Davia.

"Athena, no!" I grabbed her arm, pulling her back. "That's what they want."

She stopped, her chest heaving with rage and desperation, her eyes red and fangs viciously bared, but she knew I was right. Charging in blindly would only get us all killed. We needed a plan, and we needed it now. I sent my power out toward Davia, shocked to find that it was not only powerful enough to reach her at this distance but enough to heal the pain in her arms from where the Hunters had roughly grabbed her.

Finally, my eyes landed on Jacob Bennett. His eyes were wild, and his face was twisted in almost wicked determination. Alora's face flashed in my mind. There was a time when I wanted his death more than I wanted anything. But now I had Athena, and for some cruel reason, he was her father. I'd kill him for her, but I'd also spare him for her if she asked me to.

"Up the steps," Archer hissed, already moving toward the lighthouse.

We retreated up the winding staircase, the narrow space offering a temporary reprieve from the overwhelming numbers below. Each step echoed with the sound of our hurried ascent, the weight of the situation pressing heavily on us.

At the top, we paused, trying to catch our breath and form a strategy. I could feel the panic rising again, but I forced it down. This was no time to lose control.

"Athena," I whispered, turning to her. "We need to think. We can't save Davia if we're dead.

She nodded, though her eyes remained fixed on the direction of her best friend below as the Hunters continued to surround the lighthouse. Her hands clenched into fists, the frustration palpable. "We need a distraction," she said, her voice tight. "Something to draw them away from Davia."

Orpheus nodded. "I'll go. I'm fast enough to lead them on a chase."

"No," Laz interjected. "We stay together. We can use the lighthouse to our advantage. Force them to come to us one by one." I glanced around, seeing the agreement in everyone's eyes. It was risky, but it was our best shot. We couldn't afford to let fear dictate our actions.

The moment the Hunters started up the lighthouse stairs, the atmosphere shifted. I felt it. We all did. The clanging of their boots echoed up the spiral staircase, each step sending a jolt of tension through my body. I steeled myself, knowing my role in this battle was to heal and keep us all alive.

Orpheus and Silas were the first line of defense.

As the first wave of Hunters breached the top of the stairs, the two of them dispatched them quickly and precisely. They fought side by side, a perfect blend of brute strength and lethal grace. Orpheus's sharpened nails flashed in the dim light while Silas's raw power sent them flying back down the stairs, knocking down approaching Hunters behind them.

A sudden clatter caught my attention, and I turned to see Laz on the deck, a bucket of rainwater in their hands. Their eyes glinted with determination as they stared at the liquid within the vessel. They offered me a hopeful shrug, then pushed past Silas and Orpheus to pour the bucket's contents down the stairs. The liquid splashed onto the Hunters below. Screams filled the air as the acid burned their faces and hands, rendering some lifeless and sending the others stumbling back in agony.

Despite the chaos, I kept my focus on healing. Whenever one of them took a hit, I was there, my hands burning with healing energy. Cuts closed, bruises faded, and the pain in their eyes dimmed as I focused my energy on them.

Eventually, the Hunters regained composure and continued their assault. Silas and Orpheus held the line as best they could, but a few slipped past, rushing toward Laz, Athena, and me.

Athena was initially distracted by the sight of Davia below, but as the Hunters flooded the area, she finally joined the fray. This was her first time fully utilizing her vampiric abilities in a fight, and she took to it with a natural adeptness that was both awe-inspiring and terrifying. My dead heart thumped viciously with fear and worry for her. She seemed to be holding her own quite well, evading their attacks. If I weren't so afraid of losing her, I'd be proud.

"Athena, behind you!" I shouted, seeing a Hunter sneaking up on her. She spun around, catching his arm mid-swing and twisting it with a sickening crunch. With a swift kick, she sent him tumbling down the stairs, adding to the growing pile of bodies below.

Orpheus and Silas kept the line, their coordinated attacks keeping the Hunters at bay. Laz, having emptied the bucket, joined the fight with elongated fangs desperate to sink into the Hunters' flesh.

Despite the overwhelming odds, we fought with everything we had and held our own against the constant onslaught Nameless.

But the battle was far from over. More Hunters kept coming, their determination and anger unwavering and relentless. I moved between my coven, healing wounds as they happened, and they kept happening. We were outnumbered.

"There's too many of them!" Laz cried out as several more Hunters spilled out from the staircase and began attacking. Silas screamed as a poisoned blade sliced across his torso. Athena's eyes snapped toward the sound, and distracted, she took an arrow to the chest. She writhed in pain. I sent my magic out toward both of them, desperate to keep them safe, when a flying fist knocked me back.

I hit the ground and groaned at the pain that was radiating through me at that moment. The Hunter who had managed to hit me stood above me, a wooden stake poised to slam into my chest. I threw my legs up, slamming my feet against his chest, and sent him flying back, toppling into another Hunter, which gave Orpheus the advantage he needed to rip their throats out.

"Athena, Archer," a familiar, eerie voice called from the base of the lighthouse. The Hunters stilled at the command of their leader.

I shook with fury. How dare he say her name. How dare he speak to her.

"Come down here and join us. We don't want to harm humans," Jacob bellowed from the ground below. The Hunters at the staircase ceased, paused in a tense standoff with Silas and Orpheus as they awaited the result of his offer.

Athena and Archer shared a brief look at each other, their faces and clothing covered with the blood of their father's Hunters, before walking toward the ledge of the deck. They leaned against the railing and looked down at the man below.

I took this brief respite to soothe my coven's injuries. The wound on Athena's chest where the arrow had pierced was deep, and there was a toxin there that seemed to come from the arrow before she had removed it. I focused all my energy on that wound, banishing the toxin from her blood and healing her. She visibly relaxed when I finished.

Silas' chest was the worst of our injuries. It bled profusely because of the anticoagulant that the blade was laced with. I had to focus intensely on that one to ensure he was healed. It would take more than I could give now, but he was at least upright and breathing.

The others had minor cuts and bruises that I worked on as Athena, and Archer glanced down at their father. This fight was far from over, but if I had anything to say about it, we'd all make it out of here alive. Bennett would never take another person I loved from me.

7

ARCHER

"You are fighting for the wrong side," my father called out to us from his place on the ground. My teeth ground against each other, and my jaw tightened as my eyes saw that his arm was now barred across Davia's throat. She looked so scared, so afraid, and all I wanted to do was protect her. Get her as far away from all this as possible. She didn't deserve to suffer at the hands of my father.

"Let her go!" Athena seethed.

"I will, when you both come down here, where you belong," he claimed. I rolled my eyes.

"I don't belong anywhere with you, asshole," she replied, pure pain in her voice.

"Archer, you know better than this. You cannot seriously want to fight for those monsters... to die for them?" He spat, nothing but vitriolic hate in his tone.

"I'd rather die for them than believe another second of your lies," I growled back.

"You won't win this fight, don't be on the losing side," he pleaded, and to his credit, behind the hateful rhetoric, he did sound like a concerned father.

"Why won't you consider that you're wrong?" I begged, desperate for the man I once called my father to replace this vicious villain before me.

"Because those creatures are evil, and they deserve to rot in hell like the abominations they are!" His arm tightened around Davia's throat, and she cried out.

663

"Let her go right now, or I will make you," I threatened, my hands gripping the railing so tightly that I was nervous that I may actually break it.

"My mother was right about you," Athena blurted, even-toned and angry. My father's face paled.

"Your mother doesn't understand," he argued.

"Are you willing to kill your son to prove this point to yourself? Are you?" I howled. He shook his head but didn't vocalize a response.

"What about me, dad?" Athena cried, and everyone took a collective inhale as the word spilled from her tongue. "What about me? Would you kill me? Would you kill me after leaving us to feed your stupid obsession?" She screamed, and his face dropped.

"Athena.. I.." He stuttered.

"Answer me!" She sobbed.

"You don't understand," he pleaded wild anger in his eyes. I eyed the point of contact where his arm pressed against Davia. I wouldn't let him hurt her. I'd jump off this damn tower to stop it if I had to.

His face twisted into an almost unrecognizable mask of fury. I had always feared him and sought his approval, but now I saw him for what he truly was, a man consumed by his own darkness.

"Dad, let her go! And just leave. We are no threat to you." I shouted, my voice echoing against the cliffs. The ocean roared below, a fitting backdrop to the chaos unfolding around us.

He shook his head, tightening his grip on Davia. "You don't understand, Archer. This is for your own good. For all of us. I'm protecting humankind."

Anger and sorrow twisted inside me, but I couldn't let it consume me. I had to stay focused. "This isn't the way. Let her go, and we can talk."

He sneered. "Talk? If you two won't join me, then there's nothing left to say."

Before I could react, the Hunters surged forward, attacking with renewed ferocity at my father's twisted command. Their numbers seemed endless, and despite our best efforts, we were overpowered. I fought alongside my sister and her mates as Hunter after Hunter arrived up the staircase at a rate even we couldn't keep up with. Blood and sweat mingled, and the weight of each strike grew heavier.

A Hunter that I remembered from headquarters broke through our defenses, slashing at Silas with a serrated blade. He grunted in pain, stumbling back into Orpheus. While they were distracted, another Hunter struck out against them with a garlic-laced whip. It struck Orpheus across the face, leaving a blistering red line. He winced. Athena called out for her mates, which only made her more of a target. The Hunter to her left reached out and got their hands around her neck, squeezing as she fought against them. Laz and I jumped to assist her, but another Hunter pulled me back. He landed a blow across my face, and the sickening crunch echoed through the night air as my nose broke. Samara was healing us as fast as she could, but the injuries were coming too quickly.

We were losing. The realization hit me like a punch to the gut, much more painful than the one I had just sustained to my face. We couldn't hold out much longer.

We were going to lose.

A bright flash of light erupted from the broken light beside us. Bright, gold, shimmering light spilled into the space, cutting through the night sky like a blade. Fighting ceased as Wanderer and Hunter alike shielded their eyes from the assaulting light.

When the golden pool of light began to dissipate, my eyes adjusted to the scene around me. Similar, and yet somehow completely different. There was another figure on the deck of the lighthouse now, tall and slender with shaggy black hair flowing like a river of midnight, wearing almost regal attire and a circlet of ivy. His eyes glowed with an ethereal golden light as he gracefully moved through the remaining Hunters in the tower. With a flick of his wrist, he sent daggers of what looked like shimmering light speeding toward them, their weapons clattering uselessly to the ground.

On the ground below, a second figure, buff and imposing with dark skin and shaggy hair pulled back at the nap of his neck- charged into the fray. He swung a massive sword with effortless strength, holding back the Hunters, who remained on the ground with ease.

A third figure, a red-headed warrior with fierce determination in his glowing eyes, appeared beside my father and Davia. With a quick, precise motion, he disarmed my father, pulling Davia away from his grasp. My father's eyes widened in shock as the red-headed stranger slammed a shimmering fist against his temple, knocking him flat out.

The regal one near us flourished his hand, and an icy chill emanated from his magic. The air around him shimmered with energy, a palpable force that made the hair on the back of my neck stand on end. A surge of energy erupted from him, spreading out in a wave that washed over the battlefield. The Hunters froze in place, their weapons mid-swing, their expressions locked in various states of shock and anger. I blinked, trying to comprehend what had just happened. The Hunters were suspended in mid-motion as if time itself had stopped for them.

I glanced over the railing to find he had also affected the Hunters on the ground.

"Elias," Orpheus panted, offering a hand for the stranger. "I see you got my message."

The tall man, Elias, took Orpheus' arm and held it. "Just in time, it would seem." Orpheus shrugged, pain coloring his expression.

Uninterested in the welcome party, I sprinted down the steps, desperate to see if Davia was safe. Weaving carefully through the frozen Hunters that littered the steps, I heard the others follow behind me, but I didn't turn to look. I had to get to her. I had to see her.

Spilling out of the lighthouse onto the clearing, I immediately saw the two additional strangers, each gripping one of my father's arms as he hung limp and knocked out in their hold. They eyed me curiously as I sprinted toward Davia.

I stopped just short of pulling her into my arms, looking her over for any injuries. "Davia, are you okay?" I gasped.

Her eyes met mine. I could see that she had been crying. Her blue eyes were bright and mesmerizing. She was just as captivating as she had been the first time I saw her. She opened her mouth, and I thought she was going to say something to me, but instead, her palm struck against my cheek, sending me reeling back from her slap. The sting in my cheek was vicious. I cupped my cheek with a hand and glanced back at her.

"That's for kidnapping Athena," she said, and I didn't have any time to react before her knee came up into my solar plexus and sent me toppling to the ground on all fours with a grunt. She leaned down so that her lips were by my ear. "And that's for lying to me about it."

"Davia!" Athena's voice called from behind me. Davia stood and rushed forward to embrace her friend. I felt the warm caress of Samara's healing against my stinging cheek and aching stomach. I sent her a thankful nod, and she smiled softly at me.

I stood and turned to watch Davia and Athena cry into each other's arms. I smiled, appreciating for a moment how fiercely these two protected each other. It was the kind of relationship I had never really had with anyone, but I was definitely starting to feel for my sister, and her mates, too, I guess, which was a wild turn of events.

"Thank you for your help..." Athena directed to the strangers who had arrived in the light. I took this moment of relative peace to really study the newcomers who had saved the day. The regal-looking one that Orpheus had called Elias was pale. His sharp cheekbones and attire reminded me of portraits of royalty I might find in a history textbook. The redhead who held one of my father's arms had cropped hair just above his ears and wore much more modern attire than the others. Sporting dark wash jeans and a Henley.

The buff one, who looked like a gladiator, wore what could only be described as a suit of armor you'd see at a Renaissance faire.

They were a mess of genre that frankly had me even more confused now that I got a closer look.

"Elias," he offered. "And this is Ronan," he indicated to the red-head. "And Jasper." The tank of a man grunted his acknowledgment. "Two of the most trusted members of my Court."

"Court?" I asked, eyeing them.

"You don't know who we are?" Ronan chimed in, his voice like molten lava with how much disdain was laced in the tone.

"He's not a vamp, Ronan," Samara replied. "And she's a fresh-turn."

Ronan nodded, and Elias stepped forward to Davia, gripping her hand and pressing a kiss against her knuckles, making my blood boil. "And you? What is your relationship to the supernatural?"

She stood her ground against him, seemingly unaffected by his imposing nature, as she ripped her hand back. "I'm a human, and you are in my space, so I kindly ask you to back the fuck up."

I heard Orpheus and Silas inhale sharply at that, bracing themselves for retaliation. I prepared myself to jump in if it seemed like she needed it. But instead, a smile spread across his lips, and he laughed darkly.

"We appreciate your help, Elias," Laz chimed in, trying to pull his attention away.

"Well, you're not quite out of the woods yet." He indicated to the frozen Hunters who were poised to attack. I wondered how long he could hold them in their place. "We are always willing to make a deal. Orpheus knows that," Elias answered, smiling coyly at him before glancing back at Davia.

"Alright then, get on with it. What do you want?" Silas challenged.

Elias tore his eyes from Davia and smiled at Silas. The almost diplomatic way he surveyed him sent chills down my spine.

"Tsk tsk tsk, is that any way to thank your backup?" Elias asked tauntingly. "I don't have to assist. Would you prefer to handle them on your own?"

"You have our gratitude, and you will have your promise, whatever it is. Name it," Orpheus declared, sending a look of warning to Silas, who huffed but nodded. I sensed a story there, but now wasn't the time to dive into it.

Elias shared a look with Ronan and Jasper, a silent exchange. Jasper nodded to Elias rather quickly, without much fuss. He seemed the quiet type. Ronan, however, looked pissed, anger burning in his eyes, but eventually he nodded too. Now having whatever confirmation he needed, Elias turned back to the group.

"Well, in exchange for helping you with your little Hunter problem, as you are aware from the last time you asked me for my assistance, the price remains a single promise."

"Oh yeah, we remember," Silas quipped under his breath.

"Name it," Orpheus said, ignoring Silas, and something about the way Elias smiled had my stomach dropping.

"I want this one to promise to spend an entire year with me at my Court," he said, pointing at Davia.

"Not a chance," I said at the same time as Athena called out, "No way!" Davia's eyes widened, and she took a step back. I moved a step closer, trying to put myself between her and the royal asshat.

"I said you'd have a promise from me," Orpheus argued, trying to calm the chaos for the moment.

"No, you said I'd have my promise. Whatever I want. I believe you said. Name it," he taunted darkly. I felt my fists clench at my side as fury built up in my chest.

Orpheus cursed under his breath.

"You should know to be careful with your words by now, my dear friend," Elias said.

"She's not going anywhere with you," I demanded.

"See, that's not how this works, love. If you want us to do as you ask, I need my payment." Elias titled his head, offering me a condescending look.

"Fuck you," Athena spat. His eyes lit up with glee at the challenge in her tone. He stepped forward, tenting his fingers in front of him.

"I understand. If you don't want to make the promise, we can always leave..." He lifted his hands, wiggling his finger. I saw the Hunters begin to twitch, their movement returning to them in tiny increments.

"Elias...please," Samara begged, eyeing the pack of Hunters around us. She knew as I did that we weren't guaranteed a win if left to our own devices.

"The promise is all it will take," Elias confirmed.

"There has to be something else you want," Orpheus urged eagerly.

"Afraid not. My terms have been set," he replied flippantly. My heart rate sped, fury boiling just beneath the surface.

"That's not fair!" Athena cried out.

"It seems we are unable to come to an agreement on this. We shall take our leave now," Elias said smugly, lifting his hand as the Hunters' reanimation sped up. Any second now, they would be back to attacking, and we would be outnumbered. I braced myself for the second round.

"Wait," Davia called out. All our heads turned to face her. "I'll do it."

"What?" I exclaimed.

"Davia, no…" Athena challenged. Davia placed a hand on Athena's cheek and nodded fiercely.

"I can't lose you again, Athena," she blurted before taking a deep breath and closing her eyes. "I was so scared. You're my best friend, my sister, and I thought you were…" she cried softly, tears stained her cheeks. "I brought Louis and Greg into your life. I did that. I'm the reason they hurt you."

Athena started to protest, but Davia shook her head. "No, don't try to take this guilt away. If doing this saves your life, then it is the easiest decision I will ever make."

Athena was crying, her shoulders wracking with sobs.

"Besides, you know I've always wanted to take a year off to travel," Davia added with a chuckle. They embraced, and I saw Athena nod softly.

"Are you sure?" Athena whispered. My chest tightened… No, she wasn't going to actually do it, was she?

"Let me do this for you," Davia pleaded.

"Thank you, Davia," Athena confessed, and I stepped forward involuntarily.

"No, not a chance. You are not going with these strangers, Davia. We know nothing about them. What if they hurt you?" I was fuming.

Davia turned to glare at me. "Not all strangers are like you, Archer."

It stung, but I deserved it.

"You can't go…"

"It's not your choice to make," she retorted.

"Then I'm going with you," I blurted out, and shock colored her expression.

"What?" Davia asked just as Athena stepped forward and gripped my arm.

"Archer…" Athena started.

"Just to keep an eye on you, make sure you're safe," I justified. I still was not even sure what I was saying, I only knew that I needed to do this.

"I don't need your help," Davia argued, but I saw it. The slight twinge of relief in her features eclipsed the fear behind her mask of strength and indifference for the briefest moments. She was afraid and needed me, even if she wouldn't admit it.

"I know, but I'm offering it anyway. Please, let me go to be there for you if you need me." I met her eyes, and a silent understanding passed between us before she nodded.

"So, do we have a promise?" Elias prompted. I turned to see the look on his face, and he seemed almost hopeful.

Davia gripped Athena's hand and smiled, turning her icy glare to the figure before her. "Archer and I will join you in your Court for one year." She didn't meet my gaze, but my heart lept at the trust she placed in me.

"Say it," Elias commanded darkly, holding his hand out for Davia. She placed her palm in his. He then turned to me and held his other hand out for me to take. I held his eyes as I did.

"I promise." We both said in unison.

A small crack of thunder erupted from where our hands were joined, and a bright golden light danced around our arms. I shielded my eyes until the light began to dissipate. In its place was a faint golden vine of ivy climbing up her forearm, and when I looked, I wore a matching mark on my skin. Elias smiled down at his arms, which also bore the mark of our promise.

I felt changed. Different. I knew that what we promised would change everything, and there was no going back from it now. At least she wasn't in it alone.

"Great," Elias said, giddy happiness on his features. "Shall we finish off your Hunter problem then?" He directed to Orpheus, who looked lost.

"Yes," he answered, shaking his head.

Elias nodded to the others, Jasper and Ronan, who set my father's body down on the ground and moved to stand before the Hunters, who were still frozen.

"Are you going to kill them like that?" Laz asked.

"Where's the fun in that?" Ronan answered with a wicked smile just as Elias dropped the magic holding the Hunters. The battlefield once again erupted into chaos, but this time, we had the advantage.

Elias stood at the center of the fray, his hands glowing with mysterious energy. With a flick of his wrist, he sent magic bolts crashing into the Hunters, knocking them back and creating barriers to protect us from the Hunter's onslaught.

Jasper, the towering figure of strength, easily tore through the Hunters in front of him. His shaggy brown hair whipped around as he swung a massive sword, cleaving through enemies like they were nothing more than paper. I suddenly found myself incredibly grateful he was on our side. Ronan, the red-headed warrior, moved with a supernatural stealth. He slipped through the shadows, striking with deadly precision. One moment, he was there. The next, he was gone, leaving a trail of incapacitated Hunters in his wake.

Silas and Orpheus joined the fray with a savage fury. Their fangs bared as they let the pain and anger of all the years that Nameless hunted them fuel their strikes. They moved like predators, their vampire instincts making them formidable, but their fury making them unstoppable.

My eye caught on Laz as they ran toward the cliff's edge, pursued by several Hunters. Panic gripped me as they approached the ledge, but just as they reached it, they spun on their heel to face their assailants. Their features were more vampire than human as they focused on the mist from the crashing waves that spilled around them. The water from the wave rained down on the Hunters who had chased Laz, and the moment the liquid hit their skin, they screamed and clutched their burning faces. The smell of burning flesh filled the air, and I tried not to look at their melting skin and instead focus on the Hunters ahead.

Samara stood back, trying to keep each of us healed and in the fight while Athena moved with deadly precision, her movements a blur as she took on a Hunter. With a swift, clean motion, she knocked him out, her eyes cold and determined. She had fully embraced her new vampiric strengths, and it showed in the way she fought. I thought maybe I'd be afraid to see her like this. But she was powerful, and I felt the kind of pride that could only ever be reserved for her—my sister.

And then there was me. My sole focus was protecting Davia. She clung to my side, accepting my help without hesitation. Utilizing my training, I managed to fight off any Hunter who came too close. Her trust in me gave me the strength to keep going.

As the last of the Hunters fell, a heavy silence settled over the bloodstained battlefield. We stood together, breathing heavily but victorious. The immediate threat was gone, and we had a moment to catch our breath for the first time in what felt like forever.

Elias lowered his hands, the glow fading as he looked around at the aftermath. Jasper and Ronan stood tall, their expressions a mix of relief and exhaustion, while Silas and Orpheus wiped the blood from their fangs, their eyes searching for Athena. Laz stepped away from the cliff and stood near Samara, who healed their skin from the burns they sustained from their acidic waves. Athena, her fingers still dripping with blood, smiled softly at her mates.

I turned to Davia, who looked at me with wide eyes. "Are you okay?" I asked, my voice rough with worry.

"Yeah, I'm fine," she answered, and I almost believed her. She rushed over and hugged Athena, and the two of them devolved into exhausted laughter.

"Thank you, Elias," Orpheus said, stepping toward him. Elias bowed his head in acknowledgment before turning to face Davia.

"Take your time. Get your affairs in order," he spoke calmly as if he hadn't just been in the heat of a wicked battle. He pulled a card from his pocket and held it out for her. She took it, and the shake in her hands was almost imperceptible. But I saw it. "Meet us here when you're ready."

She nodded her silent agreement.

"What are we supposed to do about them," Athena whispered, her eyes wide as she took in the bloody mess surrounding us. There were bodies littered across the grass and spilling into the lighthouse. Bright red blood darkened the grass at our feet. It was a horrific sight.

"I'm not sure," Orpheus admitted, and I could tell that he hated not having the answers. Anal retentive bastard.

Elias waved his hand before him, sending a rippling wave of magic out across the field. The bodies dotting the space slowly disappeared behind the shimmering veil of his magic. The blood spilled along the ground sank into the earth, leaving no trace of the battle that had occurred here or the death that remained.

"Consider that one a freebie." Elias winked as he looked over his shoulder at Ronan and Jasper, who stepped forward to flank him. "Until next time." The bright light that heralded their arrival erupted again, and I once again found myself shielding my eyes. What the hell was it with those assholes and bright lights?

Athena was wrapped in the embrace of her mates, sharing an intimate moment of relief, so I averted my eyes to give them their privacy and walked over to my unconscious father, crouching down to see him clearly. He was sprawled on the grass. His face looked almost peaceful, which felt like such an oxymoron. He was a vicious man, a violent creature who wanted death and destruction.

He was also my father.

"You didn't have to do that," Davia whispered as she approached. I kept my eyes trained on my father's face but shook my head.

"Yes, I did," I admitted.

"This doesn't make up for what you did," she said. I stood but didn't turn to face her.

"I know."

We stood silently, avoiding each other's eyes for a few prolonged moments until Athena joined us.

"What are we going to do about him?" She asked softly. I shrugged.

"I don't know," I replied. We could kill him and ensure that he would never hurt any of us again, but I honestly didn't know if I was capable of doing that.

"We can secure him for now and decide when we get a chance to talk to him," Orpheus interjected, moving forward to pick my father's form off the ground.

"Good idea,' I said, trying to hide the lump in my throat and the indecision in my soul.

"Let's go home," Athena said, reaching for her mate's hands.

I followed behind them, their giddy cheeriness palpable, but I couldn't help but feel the weight of those words.

Home.

I didn't have a home, not anymore. Shockgrove could have been, maybe, if I had enough time. My sister was here, and her family was. I could have been happy here. This place could have become home to me someday, but that thought was thwarted by the climbing vine of ivy on my forearm and the promise I had made.

I wouldn't take it back, even if I could, but a selfish, lonely part of me wondered if I'd ever find a place to call 'home.'

8

ATHENA

There was only one word to describe how I felt now that the battle with the Hunters was done.

Relief.

I wasn't naive enough to assume we were entirely out of danger. Dr. Kline Galvin's absence from the lighthouse battle was notable. I'm sure he'd be here, with reinforcements of his own, and we would tackle that when it happened, but I also knew the importance of celebrating the little wins. And right now, this was a little win.

I didn't want to think about the promise Davia had to make to secure us the victory, but if Orpheus trusted this Elias guy enough to ask him to help us, then I trusted him to take care of her while she fulfilled her promise to them. Archer looking out for her definitely lifted a weight off my chest.

She was going to be ok. They both were. And because of their promise, we had won the battle even if the war was far from over.

We walked Davia home. I offered for her to stay with me, but she waved me off. "As if I want to hear you getting railed by your sexy vampires? No, thank you, I'm perfectly fine here," she added. I hugged her again, whispering my thanks. She deflected them all, telling me that she would do anything in the world for me. I told her the same.

"Promise me you'll come see me before you go," I demanded into her hair as I embraced her.

"I recently learned to be wary of that word, but I will. I swear." She winked and disappeared into her home. I looked over at Archer, who watched after her with yearning alight in his eyes. I wasn't going to press him on it, but I was glad to know she would be there with someone who seemed to care for her as I did.

Orpheus carried the limp body of my father to The Maine Plotline, careful to avoid the cameras that the police divulged were on the pier. I didn't comment aloud on the irony of tying him up in my office as I had once been tied up in his, but it didn't escape me.

"He'll be out for a while. Ronan packs one hell of a punch," Silas mused, almost admiring the red-headed fae's handiwork.

"I'll guard him tonight," Archer said.

"I'll stay with you," Silas chimed in. The two shared a look of camaraderie, and my heart warmed at the sight.

"Call us if you need anything," Orpheus commanded, indicating the phone on the desk. Silas nodded before coming over to me.

"Get some rest, bookworm. Don't let those rabid animals keep you up with their mouths on your pussy all night," he teased with a sinful look in his eyes.

Archer gagged, smacking Silas' arm. "What did I say about saying those things in front of me? Fucking hell, Silas..." He stalked off toward the front desk, shaking his head as if trying to dispel the mental image, and I watched him leave, chuckling.

"You did that on purpose," I scolded playfully. He acted offended, pressing a hand against his chest.

"Who me? Never." he smiled, sweeping me up into a spinning embrace. His lips met mine as he slowly lowered me to the ground. His tongue dipped into my mouth, and he moaned as our tastes mingled. His hands tangled in my hair, and my breasts pressed against his hard chest.

"I love you so much, Silas," I vowed against his lips. He glanced down at me, his arms caging me against his body, and smiled so warmly that I felt the icy chill of my skin slip away under his gaze.

"Hmm, say it again," he commanded softly.

I pressed a kiss to his lips. "I." Kiss. "Love." Kiss. "You." Kiss. He smiled into my kiss and drank me up.

"Go, we will watch him tonight. This can all wait for tomorrow," he promised, and I traced a finger along the slight stubble on his jawline, trailing down his chest and then his arms. My fingers trailed along the inky swirls of his tattoos and stopped just above the raised white lines of my mate mark. A blooming rose. I traced it, loving how my bond with him seemed to alight within my chest as I did. He leaned down, pressing his lips to his mark on my chest, and we both groaned as the bond pulsed deliciously.

"We're definitely going to be experimenting with that later," he teased, flicking his tongue along my collarbone where his serpents were. The moan that escaped me was entirely involuntary.

"We will see you tomorrow, Silas. One of us will come to relieve you," Orpheus said, patting him on the back and throwing an arm around my shoulders.

"Take good care of our girl," he called out as we stepped away.

"Always," Orpheus replied, pulling me closer to his side.

Laz and Samara trailed behind us as we returned to my cottage. I glanced only briefly over at the lighthouse. Standing sentinel and abandoned as if it hadn't just been the sight of a massive battle with countless casualties.

If I thought about it long enough, I'd find myself feeling queasy and sick at the thought of all those lives lost, but they made their choice. They chose hate. They would rather follow a cause mindlessly than consider that they might be wrong. My father was wrong. About me, about The Wanderers, about the supernatural. His Hunters were fighting for the wrong side, and I wished it could have been different. I wished it didn't have to come to that.

That lighthouse had seen far too much death.

One death that broke my heart and the others that set me free.

When we arrived back at my little house, I eagerly rushed in and disrobed. The scent of blood was thick in the air, and I couldn't bear to be covered in it a moment longer.

"Clothes off," I ordered to my mates.

"Silas told us to behave," Laz jested, but they made quick work of the button of their pants.

"I don't want you three trailing blood over my house," I retorted, turning to face them. All three of them had gone still, their eyes glued to my naked form.

I rolled my eyes, playfully annoyed at their distractibility.

"Clothes, now," I repeated before turning on a heel to head for the shower. "I have room for one more in the shower with me for whoever listens the fastest."

I didn't bother turning to see if they had heeded my offer, but I heard the tell-tale rustling of clothes and a few choice curses as elbows were thrown. I chuckled as I turned the shower faucet and let the water heat to an appropriate temperature, which I was learning in my new vampire form wasn't quite as scalding as I used to prefer but was now a more comforting lukewarm.

I slipped inside the shower to stand beneath the running water, averting my eyes from the blood running down my body and circling the drain. I just focused on the feel of the water as it danced on my skin. I heard someone approach and slide in the shower behind me, but I didn't turn to see who it was. I didn't have to. As their hands slid around my waist, I felt my bond with Laz flicker to life within my chest at their nearness.

"You won the race," I mused, leaning my head back onto their chest. Their hands circled my body and held me tight against them.

"Orpheus is fuming," they boasted, and I laughed.

The water poured over our bodies, rinsing us clean from the horrific events of the last few hours. The steam rose around us, wrapping us in a warm, hazy embrace that starkly contrasted the chaos we had just survived. I closed my eyes, letting the water cascade over my face, and tried to let the tension melt away. But my mind was a whirlpool of memories and emotions, each one clamoring for attention. The past few days have been challenging, to say the least.

"You wanna tell me what's on your mind?" Laz whispered into my ear, and I sighed softly.

"It's been a rough few days," I admitted. The confession only scratches the surface of the emotional turmoil swirling inside me.

"You could say that again," they agreed. Their fingers trailed delicate lines along my hips.

"I'm okay, though," I promised.

"You don't have to mince words with me, Athena. It's okay if you're not okay." They rested their chin on my shoulder and hugged me tight to their body. I gripped their arms, which were wrapped around me and held tightly. Their support felt so comfortable that the small wall I'd built around my emotions began to crumble, and tears fell freely from my eyes, mingling with the water pouring over our heads.

"He didn't want me," I wept, admitting the words out loud felt even harsher than when they were nagging at my heart.

Laz's arms tightened around me, spinning me in their arms to face them. I buried my head into their chest and cried, the sobs wracking my body with a force I couldn't control. Laz's hand stroked my hair, their touch gentle and soothing.

"It's okay to cry," they whispered. "But just know that he doesn't deserve your tears."

I clung to them, the warmth of their body grounding me in the moment. "It just hurts so much," I choked out. "He chose his stupid obsession over me. Over both of us." There it was, the heart of it. He hadn't just left me. He left my mother. The kindest soul I'd ever known. He chose hate and violence over a life with us, and it crushed her.

Laz's arms wrapped tighter around me, their embrace a fortress against the pain. "He's a damn fool," they said softly. "It is his loss that he will never know the amazing woman you have become. The woman your mother raised you to be."

Their words broke something open inside me, and the tears came even harder. I let myself cry and mourn the loss of the father I never knew. Laz held me through it all, their presence unwavering.

"I don't know if I can kill him if it comes to that," I admitted, my voice muffled against their chest. "But what if he won't see reason? What if he still wants to hurt us? What do I do then?"

Laz pulled back slightly, tilting my chin up so that I had to meet their gaze. Their eyes were filled with an intensity that took my breath away. "You don't have to make that choice alone, Athena. We're in this together. Every step of the way."

I nodded, trying to believe them. "I feel like I'm drowning."

"Then let us be your lifeline," Laz said firmly. "Lean on us. Lean on me. We won't let you drown."

Their gentle caress gave me a glimmer of hope. I took a shaky breath, trying to steady myself. "I need you," I whispered against their skin.

"You have me," Laz said, their voice fierce with conviction. "Always."

I clung to that promise, letting it anchor me. The water continued to pour over us, but the storm inside me began to calm.

"Thank you," I whispered, my voice still trembling but filled with gratitude.

Laz kissed my forehead, their lips warm and reassuring.

As the water washed away the remnants of the battle, I felt a spark of hope reignite within me.

"Kiss me," I pleaded, and they gave me the slightest nod before pressing their lips to mine. Their kiss has always been more calm, more simmering. I relished in the slow build of passion as their hands slid around my waist and pulled me taut against their torso. I felt their length harden against my stomach, and a small whimper of excitement escaped my lips.

"Laz," I moaned against their lips as the inferno of their slow and steady kiss was getting torturous.

"Yes, darlin'?" They asked teasingly.

"I need you," I repeated, but this time with a much darker and sinful connotation. They smirked.

"I'm yours," they confessed, leaning down to lift me and hitch my legs around their hips. I yelped as the ground disappeared below me, and I was pressed up against the wall of the shower. My limbs wound tightly around their frame. "You know, I love sharing you with Silas," they began, sliding a hand between us toward the apex of my thighs. "I love watching him slam into you and having him tell me exactly what to do to make you scream." Their finger brushed ever-so-slightly over my clit, and I bucked against their hold, but they didn't give me any more than that. Just a delicate touch that was so gentle I almost cried out. "But you and I, like this…" they whispered, sliding their finger through my folds and eliciting a dirty moan from my lips. "These quiet moments where there's nothing else but the two of us, our bodies, our souls." They slid a finger into my heat, and my head fell back to rest against the tiles behind me. They teased me for a few moments, drawing their finger out of me at a deliciously sinful pace before pressing in again. My body was so tightly wound I was nearly about to explode. They withdrew and reached down to grip their length and notched it at the entrance of my pussy.

"This is my happy place," they said as they thrust inside of me. I groaned and cried out their name. My nails dug into their shoulder blades as I circled my hips and pressed down against them.

We made love there against the shower wall, with no sense of rush or reckless abandon, just slow, sensual, and purposeful thrusts. Their body joined to mine in a way so intimate it almost brought a tear to my eye. I let my tongue run along the mark at their throat, my rose, and they shivered at the sensation.

"Please, do that again," they demanded softly. So I did. I let my lips and tongue worship the piece of their skin that now belonged to me, and their breathless moans told me that they loved every second of it. They shifted so that their fingers could dance along my hip where the phases of the moon were forever embedded on my body, and the moment our marks were both being worshiped at the same time, the bond pulsed within us, sending a shock of ecstasy through my body and sent me toppling into a climax. Laz's thrust sped up, and they grunted their release with my name on their lips.

When our breathing returned to normal, I felt it—the single beat of our hearts, synchronized and strong. My smile stretched across my face. They slowly lowered me so that my feet hit the shower floor but kept their hold on me until I was steady enough to stand on my own.

We washed each other off then, taking turns exploring each other's bodies while rinsing away the grime and memories of the day.

When the water began to turn cold, I begrudgingly suggested that we leave so the others could shower as well. Instantly feeling guilty, I asked them to strip out of their clothes and then left them without a shower for over a half hour.

I'm so sorry. We're almost done. I projected to Samara and Orpheus.

Don't be sorry. That's my favorite sound in the world. Orpheus replied smugly.

We are more than content to wait, love. Take the time you need in there. I could tell that she didn't just mean time to shower. She must have recognized the pain I was in and the aggravation I needed to work out.

Laz hopped out of the shower and brought me a towel, wrapping me tightly before doing the same. We exited into the bedroom, and I smiled, seeing Orpheus and Samara standing facing the opposite direction, entirely naked, not sitting so they didn't get my furniture messy.

"Oh my god, I'm so sorry," I chuckled. "The bathroom is all yours."

Samara smiled thankfully. "I'll be quick," she promised, jogging past me into the room. Laz excused themself, averting their eyes from the other two, and disappeared into the living room, leaving me alone with Orpheus. I turned my attention to him. His eyes trailed the water droplets that traveled across my skin, running down the valley of my breasts. His gaze was so heated that I almost felt the water itself burn me under his supervision. I took this moment to appreciate his naked form. I never really took the appropriate amount of time to just stare at my mates. Something I planned to rectify immediately. They were all beautiful. Like stunningly so. His shoulders were broad and toned, while the planes of his stomach were hard and rigid. He, like Laz, bore scars from a time before I knew him. And judging by the age he had only ever really alluded to, it was a time long before. His hair was tousled from the fight, but he looked as if he had rinsed off the blood that had splattered his face and exposed skin off in the sink.

I stepped forward, standing before his bare form, with only a towel between us.

"I have something for you," he professed softly. I smiled up at him.

"I don't need anything," I whispered, the truth in my statement ringing out in the air between us.

"You do, and I want to be the one to give it to you." He reached over to my bedside table where a blue cloth-bound journal sat. My eyebrows furrowed as I looked at it. He held it out in between us.

"A journal?" I asked, gripping the gift in my hands. He nodded gently, a look of guilt crossing his features.

"I told you briefly about the...unfortunate side effects of our nature," he started, and my breath caught in my throat. "I have lived a very long time. And I do not regret this new existence of mine. It brought me to my family. It brought me to you." He reached up to grip my arms, tears cresting in his eyes. "But what I do regret is that I never wrote it down—the life I had before. I have no recollection of my family or who I was before I was this. I don't know if I had any siblings, if I played with them if I got along with them... I don't know if I had a father who taught me how to be a man. I don't know if I had a mother who loved me." The tear slid down his cheek, and I felt the familiar sting in my eyes as I let his words sink in. One day, I would forget my mother, too. "I have no recollection of being turned. Did I ask for it? Was it my choice? It's all gone because I never took the time to remember it while I still could." Regret was painted so clearly on his face.

He reached for the cover of the journal in my hands and drew it open to the first page.

'Remembering Francesca Landry'

The words scrawled in small letters tore me apart at the seams. Tears poured down my face. I pulled the journal close to my chest, already feeling an emotional connection.

"Write it all down, Athena. Tell her story in these pages so she will live forever alongside you," he vowed, and all I could do was nod. This gift was something so sweet and yet so perfectly sentimental.

"I can't express how much this means to me. Thank you," I replied, my voice hoarse and full of emotion.

He leaned forward to bring his lips to mine. I leaned into the gentle and comforting kiss. The journal was pressed against my heart and pinned between the two of us—a perfect place for it.

Samara slipped out of the shower, a towel wrapped around her glistening body, and smiled at me.

"You gave it to her?" she indicated to the journal between us.

Orpheus nodded.

"Good. I look forward to learning more about the woman who made you who you are." My heart constricted with love. There was something so incredibly beautiful about the people I loved, wanting to know about the person who loved me before they could.

"Thank you, " I repeated. Orpheus kissed my forehead before side-stepping me and entering the bathroom.

Samara squeezed my hand before slipping out of the room, leaving me alone with the empty journal.

I discarded the towel and quickly donned an oversized t-shirt before sliding onto my bed and opening the journal to the second page. My pen hovered over the page hesitantly. There was so much I never wanted to forget about my mother, so many moments and joyful memories that I desperately wanted to cling to. Where would I even start?

I guess the best place to start is with the most important.

Athena,

If you're reading this, it means you're starting to forget your mother. The way her smile lit up a room, the way her eyes crinkled when she laughed, the warmth in her embraces, and the love she felt for you, so let me remind you.

These pages will one day be filled with specific memories, moments in time that you shared together that impacted who you became. There will be stories about your inside jokes and the joy of sharing your family business. The strength she had to protect you and to stand up for you even when it meant her own heart was shattered. We will get to all that, the good, the bad, and the ugly, because remembering it all is important. To know that she was always there through every wonderful and painful memory.

But there is one thing that, even if you forget all those stories and all those memories, you should know. Something you should always be aware of no matter how far removed you get from your human life.

Your mom loved you.

She loved you with a love so fierce and so powerful that you felt empowered to take on the world as long as she was by your side. She loved you so completely that you never felt the absence of your father as void. She loved you in a way that made you strong.

The memories are important. The stories matter. But if you only remember one thing, let it be that you were loved.

My tears slid down my cheeks, staining the pages of the journal as I wrote. My mates allowed me these quiet moments alone with my journal and the memory of my mother. A few hours later, my hand was cramped, and a dozen or so pages were filled with some of my favorite memories of growing up with my mom.

The creaking floorboard had my head snapping up to see who was there. Orpheus leaned against the doorframe, wearing a tight white tee and loose-fitting flannel pajama pants. I smiled at the relaxed nature of it.

"How long was I writing for?" I asked, looking over at the clock on the bedside table.

"Couple hours, it's nearly morning," he admitted. I smiled, sliding my new favorite journal into the bedside drawer, then sliding under the covers. I glanced over at him.

"You joining me?" I asked, holding open the comforter. He smirked and sauntered over to slide in beside me. Nestling beneath the comforters, I curled up next to his muscular frame, resting my head on his chest. We lay in silence for a few moments, and I took a moment to count his heartbeats. Silas had once described his heart rate as 'racing' around me. Which, for a vampire, it was. I lay on his chest, breathing as he breathed, letting his infrequent heartbeat comfort me.

"Thank you for giving me a way to remember her," I said, breaking the silence. His fingers traced idle lines along my back as he replied.

"I wish someone had been there to tell me to do the same," he mused.

"Do the others keep journals?" I asked.

He shook his head. "Samara doesn't have an enjoyable history. She never deemed it worth remembering. In fact, I think she often wishes for time to speed up so that she will wake up one day and finally forget what her parents did to her."

Those people were monsters. How could they have done that to my perfect Samara? My heart broke for my mate and her pain.

"You know Laz's story, they would rather forget the pain and betrayal, and I honestly get it. Their scars, though, those act as an unwritten journal. A vicious map of those memories. I'm afraid they'll never truly forget what they did to them. No matter how desperately they may wish to."

My hold tightened on my mate, sending a pulse of love down the bond I shared with Laz. They answered back by tugging on the bond, bringing a smile to my face.

"Silas brought the only person he cared for from his previous life with him, so he didn't need to remember anything else."

I instantly felt guilt and pain surfacing. How was it that I had so much worth remembering and my mates didn't? It wasn't fair.

"Hey, hey, whatever you're thinking...cut it out," he said, reaching for my chin and lifting my eyes to meet his.

"You have your powers turned on?" I asked.

"Not right now, I just know you, little nymph."

I snuggled into his side. His fingers danced along my hip, brushing slightly along the exposed skin where my t-shirt had bunched up.

"You really do," I mused. "I feel like I've known you all for my whole life. Is that a mate thing?" I asked.

"That's a love thing," he confessed.

"Kiss me," I begged, and he obliged, leaning his head to meet my lips with his. It was soft, lazy, and exploratory. We didn't rush but instead took a moment to really feel each other's kiss and commit the feeling to memory. My core tightened, and I felt myself growing wetter the more his mouth devoured mine.

After a long while of just exploring each other, he pulled back. "You should get some rest." I may have pouted because he chuckled softly, shifting me around so that my back was pressed against his front. He pulled me tight against him, his arms circling my waist and holding me in place.

"No fair," I whined.

"You told us you needed three to five business days," he teased. "And Laz already broke the rule."

"It was supposed to be a joke," I grumbled beneath my breath, and his body shook behind me with laughter.

"You're insatiable," he commented coyly.

"Well then, I guess it's a good thing I have four of you to satiate me," I tossed back with feigned aggression. He laughed again, the sound melodic and intoxicating.

"Go to sleep, little nymph," he ordered softly.

"I'm actually thinking I might go find Samara," I taunted, shifting to get up, but his arms closed around me tighter.

"You wouldn't dare," he whispered playfully against my ear.

"Watch me," I teased, wiggling my backside against his growing erection. He released a deep growl.

"You want my cock inside of you? Is that it?" He asked, all playfulness replaced by pure, intense lust.

"Yes, please," I replied with a giggle, like a damn sex-starved woman. His hands danced along the bare skin of my thigh, nearing my apex with each tortuous pass. After a few passes without any relief, I swirmed, pressing my ass into him again. "Touch me," I begged.

"Patience will be rewarded, little nymph," he promised, smirking against my throat.

He continued his vicious exploration of my body, trailing his fingers so near to where I desperately needed him but never quite bridging the gap. It may have been minutes or hours, but by the time he let his fingers brush against the lips of my pussy for the first time, I was a dripping mess, completely lost to my lust.

"You are always so ready for me, aren't you?" he whispered darkly.

I nodded my answer, unable to find my voice amidst the cloud of passion.

"And when I touch you, will I find you soaking wet for me?" He asked, dancing his fingers against the lips but not quite dipping into my heat. I spread my legs, bending my left leg over his hip to give him all the access he needed.

"Yes, I'm so wet for you, Orpheus," I vowed in a whispered cry.

"Guess I'll have to see for myself," he said before sliding his fingers through my wetness to find my clit. I bucked into his touch, every nerve ending so sensitive that I was nearly climaxing already. "Fuck," he whispered in awe. "You are perfect, Athena."

I wanted to reply, I might have, but he stole my words by sliding two fingers directly into my pussy. Stretching me so deliciously that words were a long-forgotten memory to me. He took his time, slowly exploring every inch of me with skillful fingers. I was a wanton blubbering mess by the time he pulled his fingers out and inserted them again, slowly and deliberately.

"More," I begged incoherently.

"Patience," he replied, but his voice was strained, as if he, too, was having a hard time controlling his urges and was reminding not only me but himself. He slid his fingers in and out of me at an achingly deliberate pace. I felt so tightly wound, so impossibly turned on, that the second his thumb pressed against the bundle of nerves at the apex of my thighs, I exploded. My orgasm rippled through my body, and Orpheus held me tightly through it, pumping his fingers in and out to prolong the ecstasy.

"So perfect," he mused as he watched me come undone under his touch.

When I came down from the climax, he didn't remove his fingers but instead continued his relentless pace. I groaned, feeling the tightness in my lower belly return with each punishing stroke of his skilled fingers.

"I love feeling you fall apart in my arms," he confessed sweetly.

"I need you," I begged my voice nothing but a breathless whisper.

He slowly removed his fingers, relishing in each inch. And lined his cock up from behind me. He shifted his hips slightly, giving him perfect access to enter me from his position behind me. But he didn't. He sat there with his tip notched at my entrance and held my hips still so I couldn't squirm down to take him inside of me.

"Orpheus," I cried. "Please."

He pressed his hips forward so achingly slow that each new inch inserted brought with it a shiver of lust and anticipation. When he was finally seated entirely inside of me, my walls stretched around him. He paused, unmoving.

"This is where I belong," he admitted into my hair, his breathing rapid and strained. He circled his hips but didn't move to thrust. I loved how full I felt of him. I felt him in every inch of my body, knowing that was his intention. "I'd look back for you," he whispered, and I turned my head to meet his gaze.

"What?" I said, breathlessly.

"The story of Orpheus and Eurydice," he confirmed. It had been a while since I'd read the story, but I recalled the gist of it. "Hades told them that they could leave the underworld and be together as long as Orpheus never looked back to see if Eurydice was still following him." He circled his hips again, and I moaned at the sensation. "He was so overcome with love, so afraid to lose her, so terrified that she had been left behind, hurt, or lost, that he turned back. He gave up a potential future with her just to ensure her safety in that moment." His lips pressed a kiss against my throat where his mate bond sat. The bond vibrated enticingly, which had me tightening my muscles around him. He moaned. "To love someone is to look back. And I'd look back for you, little nymph," he vowed just before he withdrew his cock and slammed it back into my dripping cunt.

I cried out his name as he finally gave me everything I needed. His cock hit each delicious part of me, which because of his torturous build-up, had been rearing and ready for him. My muscles tightened as I felt the climax build at his now aggressive pace. He held my hips in pace and pressed into me, over and over and over, each thrust filled with more love and promise than the last. He dipped a finger down the front of my stomach and pressed against my clit as he continued to slam into me from his spooning position.

My vision blurred as the climax swept me away. I felt warmth spread down my legs as my release coated his cock. I didn't even have a moment to feel embarrassed because he pulsed into me with reckless abandon, his breathing becoming shallower as he neared his own release.

His hips jerked as he fell apart, and I rode him through it all. A few moments passed before he slowly withdrew from me and helped me up from the now-soiled sheets.

"I'm going to need to buy more sheets if we're going to keep ruining them," I whispered. I glanced over at Orpheus, and we devolved into laughter.

"There are several sets on their way already, along with your new bed and a waterproof mattress topper," Samara said, slipping in through the bedroom door with a fresh set of sheets in her hands and I shook my head, trying to piece together what she had just said. Laz was close on their heels, their heated gaze washing over my body before helping Samara strip the mattress.

"I'm sorry, what?" I asked.

"You didn't think the five of us were going to fit on your queen mattress comfortably forever, did you?" Orpheus replied nonchalantly, reaching forward to tuck one corner of the new sheet under the mattress.

"I.. well, I.." I stuttered.

"An Alaskan King should be arriving tomorrow afternoon," Laz excitedly said. "Don't worry. I measured it, and it'll fit."

My gaze bounced back and forth between the three of them. "You bought us a new bed?" I asked.

"Yes," Orpheus replied, smiling. Seemingly amused by my shock.

"And more than enough sheet sets for us to ruin at least two a day," he answered, smirking sinfully.

My eyes stung with tears of pride and joy as I watched three of my mates make my bed. It was such a mundane yet beautiful action.

"You bought us a bed," I repeated, a love-filled sob lodged in my throat. They glanced over at me, mirroring my emotions in their expressions.

"This is forever, Athena," Samara promised, stepping forward to grab my hands in hers. Her soft skin against mine sent a buzz of happiness rushing through me. "We are all in, and this place... this place is your home as long as you want it to be. So, yes, my love, we bought us a bed. One big enough to hold every ounce of our love for you."

I knew we couldn't stay forever, but I hoped it'd be longer than a few days.

I threw my arms around her neck, dragging her into my embrace. Her skin felt silky and smoothed against mine, and I cherished how her perfect curves fit delicately against mine.

I pulled back, meeting her warm brown eyes.

"Thank you," I spoke to her softly. "All of you, thank you so much."

When are you going to realize that we would do absolutely anything for you? Samara whispered into my mind. The corners of my lips lifted into a smile.

I guess I'm just trying to believe that I deserve it. I admitted. She tilted her head, her eyes softening.

You deserve all of it and more. She let her hands dance over my arms, and I felt the warmth of her healing powers seep into my body, mending the bruises that still dotted my skin.

Thank you for kissing it better. I said again, the words I knew I'd be speaking to her for the rest of our eternity.

"We should get some rest," she answered aloud. "Sleep with me tonight?" Samara asked hopefully. I beamed back at her.

"You heard the lady," I said, raising my voice for the others to hear but keeping my eyes from hers. "She's got dibs tonight."

Laz and Orpheus feigned disappointment, but I saw the look on their faces when they saw how Samara was looking at me. The way she held me. The way she loved me. They were once afraid she'd never feel that way again. They were happy for her.

Once the others vacated the room to make their beds on the various couches in my living room, I gripped my mate's hand and led her to the freshly made bed.

We settled in, comfortably entangled beneath the sheets, our limbs and bodies eager to keep the other as close as possible.

"What are you thinking about?" I asked, studying the contemplative look on her face. She smiled down at me.

"I'm thinking about how Alora," she replied in a melancholic whisper.

I sighed, tightening my hold on her. "I think about her a lot," I admitted, tracing my finger along her chest where she now bore my mark. The small white lines of the rose stood out so stunningly against the canvas of her unblemished ebony skin. Our bond hummed in my chest.

"You do?" Samara breathed shock in her tone.

I nodded. "All the time." I felt my chest tighten. "I constantly find myself wondering if she was my mate, too. Did I lose her before I ever got to have her? I have no way of knowing, but it hurts to think we may have had what you and I share. That I may have had another person to love if my father gave her the chance."

Samara pulled me closer to her chest.

"I think about that, too," she admitted quietly, stroking my back.

"Tell me about her?" I prompted. I felt her chest rise and fall with a long, painful breath. Her heart beat once beneath my cheek.

"What do you want to know?" She asked, pressing her lips against my hair. Her almost floral scent filled my nostrils, and I inhaled deeply.

"Everything."

And so she did. I listened intently as Samara shared with me the memories of her chosen. Her wife. I laughed with her. I cried with her. I held her hand when it shook and wiped her tears when they blurred her vision.

My heart ached alongside hers for the woman whom my mate loved.

We held each other as she recounted their stories and told me how brave and strong she was. I knew the sun had risen for the day, not by any filtering light. The tint and curtains concealed those, but I could hear the birds sing their song, once a sound that had welcomed me to a new day was now beckoning me to sleep.

"I would have loved her," I whispered, exhaustion overtaking me.

"She would have loved you right back," Samara replied softly as I drifted back to sleep.

9

ARCHER

The sun was starting to rise, casting a soft glow through the edges of the heavy curtains in the office of The Maine Plotline. I stood there, staring at my father tied to a chair, waiting for him to regain consciousness. The sight of him bound and helpless brought a storm of mixed feelings, each one crashing against the other.

I leaned tensely against the desk, my fingers drumming absently on its surface. The familiar smell of books and aged wood was comforting, yet the tension in the room was palpable. The quiet was interrupted only by the ticking of the old clock on the wall and the soft rustle of pages as a breeze slipped through a crack in the window. Athena and I created our bond in this store. It was where we became friends. Where we got to know each other, and now it was the place that held the father who betrayed both of us. I hoped his presence wouldn't forever taint my memory of this place. This is where the love for my sister blossomed, and I didn't want him to take that away from me, too.

Looking at my father, I couldn't help but feel a pang of regret. This was the man who had raised me and taught me how to survive in a world that aimed to hurt us. But he was also the man who had been so lost in his crusade that he'd rather hurt those he 'loved' than admit his mistakes.

The ropes around his wrists and ankles looked tight, cutting into his skin, which was pink and raw from them. I wondered if they hurt. I wondered if he cared. He had always been so strong, so unyielding. Seeing him like this felt wrong like I was looking at a ghost of the man I once knew.

I took a deep breath, trying to steady my thoughts. When he woke up, what would I say to him? How could I face him, knowing what he had done? The anger I felt was real, but so was the sorrow. I wanted answers, but I wasn't sure I could handle it if he didn't submit. If he didn't listen.

The clock ticked on, each second stretching into an eternity. I rubbed my temples, feeling the weight of the night's events bearing down on me. This wasn't just about me anymore. It was about Athena, about her newfound family, and all the supernatural lives that had been torn apart by his choices.

His eyelids fluttered, and I straightened, my heart pounding in my chest. This was it. The moment I had dreaded and anticipated in equal measure. He groaned softly, his head lolling to the side before he slowly opened his eyes.

Our gazes locked, and for a moment, neither of us said anything. The silence was deafening. The man before me was a stranger, yet he was my father.

"Dad," I said, my voice barely more than a whisper.

He blinked, recognition dawning in his eyes, followed by a flicker of something I couldn't quite read. Regret? Resignation? Or just the cold, calculating look of a man who had lost control?

"Archer," he replied, his voice hoarse. "What have you done?"

The question hung in the air, heavy and loaded with meaning. What had *I* done? What had *he* done? The lines were so blurred I didn't know where to begin.

"We had to stop you," I said finally, my voice stronger.

He didn't respond immediately. He just studied me with those piercing eyes that had once commanded my respect and fear.

"Where is Dr. Galvin?" I asked. I had a million questions to ask him, but the most pressing threat was, without a doubt, the impending arrival of Nameless's elusive and mysterious leader.

My father scowled, his bruised face twisting wickedly. "You know better than to say his name aloud. If he's coming for you, then you won't stand a chance. You'll never see him coming," he spat. "You've chosen the wrong side, kid."

"Don't fucking call me a kid," I warned. His eyes widened in shock.

"I was always hoping you'd finally grow up. Just never thought you'd be so foolish when you did," he said quietly.

"Tell me about the weapon in your drawer. The blade that emulates a vampire bite." If he was surprised I knew about it he didn't show it. "And don't try to deny it. I've seen it."

"What do you want to know?" He said, meeting my gaze.

"Did you kill all those people, the ones in the files? Did you frame The Wanderers?" Tears stung my eyes.

"Fuck no, I'm not a monster, they are!" He retorted.

"Then why do you have that weapon?" I shouted back.

"When Galvin tells you to keep something safe, you do it," he spat. I ran my hands through my hair anxiously.

"You never asked what it was? Why he had it? What it did?" I probed.

His lips were pressed into a hard line. "It wasn't my place," he answered.

"You're kidding me," I spat. "You had proof that he was framing vampires in your damn drawer, and you think it wasn't your 'place' to ask why!?"

"You don't understand.."

"Who is Galvin? Who is he?" I interjected.

"What the fuck are you on about? He's the leader of Nameless, and you know that as well as I do."

"No, Dad, I mean, who the fuck is he? There's nothing about him anywhere. Past fifteen years ago, he was nothing but a ghost. Have you ever even seen him without his mask? Do you even know anything about him?" I was screaming, but I couldn't stop myself if I wanted to.

He started to respond but quickly snapped his mouth shut. His turmoil was reflected in his eyes.

"Silas, I need your help," I called out, knowing the tatted Wanderer was listening. The door to the office creaked open, and the long-haired vamp slipped inside. My father winced, pushing back against his chair in an attempt to put as much space between him and Silas as possible.

"Get him out of here," my father hissed.

"He's not going to hurt you," I promised, tossing an apologetic look at Silas, who was undoubtedly itching to do just that.

"You've aligned yourself with monsters, Archer."

"This *monster,* as you call him, climbed back into the window of Nameless, risking being caught, imprisoned, and tortured for the third time just to carry my beaten and bloodied body out of there after *you* had me nearly beat to death. Tell me, would you rather I be dead?"

Something that resembled guilt flashed in his eyes.

"I'm going to try and prove to you that you're the one who's been fighting for the wrong side," I said, lifting the sleeve of my shirt to expose my wrist. The scar I bore from Evangeline stared up at me.

"Why bother?" He asked.

"Because if you can see reason if you finally see the truth, then maybe I won't have to decide if you need to die."

His breath caught in his throat, and his mouth fell open. He shook his head, tears brimming in his eyes.

"Please, just try to have an open mind," I whispered before holding my arm out for Silas. I hadn't told him my plan, so I hoped he wouldn't be upset with me, but I couldn't think of another way to show my father the proof. I know Athena had mentioned that it was a rather intimate experience, but I had come to trust Silas. This little display had worked on me, after all. But I wasn't quite as far gone as he seemed to be.

Silas gripped my wrist in his hands, offering me a tight nod before letting his fangs descend and his features shift. My father squirmed in his chair, kicking his feet out to push himself back, but he was stuck. He couldn't move. He had to watch this.

The moment Silas' fangs pierced my skin, I winced, but it wasn't as painful as I remembered it. Maybe my fear had something to do with it. My skin didn't tear or rip as it had when I was wrestling it away from Evangeline's desperate bite. In fact, after the initial sting, if I sat completely still and allowed Silas to drink...it didn't feel painful at all. It felt almost good. Like that tingle, you get when someone plays with your hair. I watched him drink a few thick mouthfuls of my blood before he retracted his fangs and swept his tongue along the wound once before dropping my wrist from his hands.

I held my blood-covered wrist out for my father to see. His eyes were latched onto the two deep puncture wounds and surrounding smaller teeth marks to either side. Together, we watched as the wound closed, shrinking so slowly that it seemed as if nothing were happening at all. Within a few moments, the fresh wound was completely gone, leaving only a tiny blood stain and the scar that had once felt so volatile but now represented something much bigger.

My father looked up at me, glancing between the two of us.

"Impossible," he whispered.

"And yet..." I urged.

"We drink human blood," Silas interjected, his features still more vampire than human. "But we don't take life carelessly. We don't kill aimlessly and without cause. Not all of us, at least. Everybody is capable of evil. You are a case in point. But would you have me eradicate all humans because of the actions of one evil man?" As Silas spoke, his eyes returned to their everyday honeyed shade, and his features softened to reveal the humanity beneath the creature. But I was starting to recognize that humanity existed in both versions of him. It just looked a little different.

"This isn't right.." My father replied, nearly to himself.

"I know that it's hard to look at a belief you've held for your entire life with a critical lens because that means admitting that you've been wrong. But please, for my sake... For Athena's sake. Can you consider even just for a moment that you may be wrong?" I begged, tears slipping from my eyes, repeating the words that Athena had once said to me.

"She's amazing, dad. She's strong, she's powerful. She has the kind of heart you and I could only ever dream of having." Tears spilled from his eyes. "She turned out amazingly, considering all the shit she had to go through after you left them. After you chose hate over a life with her."

He shook his head, not in defiance, but to stave off the onslaught of emotions.

"One of your Hunters killed her," I whispered, and his eyes snapped up to meet mine, his chest rising and falling quickly.

"She's.. She's dead?" I watched the panic in his eyes, hoping that this moment of fear would be enough to convince him to listen to reason.

"She was," Silas answered through his teeth. Anger poured off of him in waves. I knew he was thankful that she had turned, but he hated the circumstances surrounding it. It wanted it to happen on her own timeline.

"Was? No... You don't mean," he stuttered, his eyes frantically bouncing back and forth between the two of us.

"They saved her," I confessed. My father's face twisted in pain and disgust.

"You turned her?! How could you! You condemned her to a life of misery," he spat, thrashing against his bindings.

"Only if you don't stop this fucking crusade!" I answered crudely. "The only threat to her life now is you, Dad! You!" I shouted, my voice trembling with a mixture of anger and desperation.

He paused at that, his eyebrows pinching together as tears continued to flow from his pained eyes. His shoulders slumped, and for the first time, he seemed smaller, less imposing. The lines on his face deepened as he let my words sink in. For the first time in my life, I felt like maybe he had actually heard what I said.

His lips parted, and he took a shuddering breath. "Archer, I... I never wanted it to come to this," he said, his voice barely a whisper. The raw vulnerability in his tone was something I had never heard before, and it caught me off guard.

I shook my head, trying to process his words.

He took a deep breath, the weight of guilt pressing down on him. Finally, he looked up at me, his eyes full of regret and sorrow.

"I don't know how to look past this," he admitted, his voice barely more than a whisper. "But I don't want to lose you. Either of you."

There was a long pause, the silence filled with our unspoken pain. And then, he said something I had waited my whole life to hear.

“I'm sorry, son.”
“That’s not enough,” I confessed, feeling my chest tighten. “But it’s a start.”

10

ATHENA

I stirred awake to the gentle sensation of lips brushing against my neck, a warm and familiar touch that immediately brought a smile to my face. I didn't open my eyes just yet, savoring the moment. Samara's kisses were soft and lingering, each one sending a delightful shiver down my spine.

"Good morning," I murmured, my voice still husky with sleep.

Samara's lips curved into a smile against my skin. "Morning," she whispered back, her breath warm and sweet.

I finally opened my eyes, slightly turning to meet her gaze. Her deep, enchanting eyes were filled with affection, and I felt my heart swell with happiness. There was a softness in her expression that made me feel cherished and adored.

"You're up early," I said, running my fingers through her dark, silky hair. "Or late, I guess," I amended, glancing at the clock that read eight p.m. I was going to need to get used to this whole nocturnal thing because we weren't going to make it to New Orleans anytime soon with all the shit still going on here.

She shrugged, her kisses trailing up to my jawline. "Couldn't resist waking you up this way."

I chuckled softly, the sound vibrating against her lips. "It's pretty good as wake-up calls go."

Samara leaned back slightly, her hand resting on my chest, fingers tracing lazy patterns on my skin. "How are you feeling?"

I took a moment to assess myself. The past few days' events had been intense, to say the least, but right now, lying here with Samara after last night with my mates, I felt a rare sense of tranquility. "Better now," I replied honestly, reaching up to cup her cheek.

She leaned into my touch, her eyes closing briefly. "Good," she said, opening her eyes again to look at me. "You deserve to feel good."

I smiled, pulling her closer for a kiss. Her lips were warm and inviting, and I lost myself in her sweet, familiar taste. When we finally broke apart, I rested my forehead against hers, feeling an overwhelming sense of gratitude for this moment.

"You deserve to feel good too, you know," I offered coyly, smiling innocently at her.

"Is that so?" She replied playfully.

"Hmm, mmm," I said, sliding beneath the blankets and settling between her legs. Her thighs fell open, revealing her center to me, and I moaned in appreciation when I saw that she was bare and ready for me.

I decorated her thighs with simple little kisses, gentle and prolonged. She sighed breathlessly with each one. My mouth neared her core, and I felt her arch her back.

My tongue darted out to wet my bottom lip, eager to feast on my mate. God, she was perfect. The first swipe of my tongue through her slick arousal had us both groaning. She tasted sweet, a perfect blend of flavor, and I drank her eagerly. Alternating between dipping my tongue into her pussy and sucking her clit. Her hands tangled in my hair as she held me tight to her core. As if I'd ever want to leave. I felt so powerful at that moment to have my mate writhing beneath me, her body shaking as I pleasured her. I was so wet I couldn't stop myself from reaching down and pressing my free hand against my aching clit. The action had me groaning, which only sent more sinful vibrations through her.

My fingers slid into her wetness as my tongue circled her clit, and she cried out, her orgasm tearing through her. I drank every last drop of her eagerly.

She tore the comforter from above me, bathing me in the soft, warm light from the bedside lamp. The look in her eyes could only be described as feral. She gripped my shoulders and directed me to lie on my back with a gentle but forceful push. I gasped at the movement. My head hung just barely off the foot of the bed. My legs spread for her as she pulled the hem of my shirt up. I lifted my shoulders from the bed, expecting her to tear the shirt completely off, but instead, she stopped just above my eyes, sending my sight tumbling into darkness and pinning my arms to the side of my head as she tightened the shirt.

My mouth fell open on a moan.

"You trust me, right?" She asked, kissing my clavicle once she was satisfied with her makeshift blindfold.

"Always," I vowed breathlessly, writhing as Samara's mouth hovered over my heated icy skin. All of my other senses were heightened even beyond their new capabilities. I could hear the shifts in her breath, the way her skin moved against the bedspread, the way her fingers dug into the sheets beside me. My nipples pebbled as her breath dusted over them. Her tongue darted out and took one peak into her mouth, and I arched into it. She suckled softly, applying just enough teeth to drive me wild. My hands balled into fists, desperate to reach for her.

She repeated the attention on the other side, careful not to let any other part of her body touch mine.

"You get your new bed today. I figured we could say goodbye to this one together," she whispered against my stomach as her breath trailed lower and lower.

"Yes. God, yes, please," I rambled.

I heard her shift on the bed, pulling her mouth away from where I needed her, and I groaned. She shifted something around in my bedside drawer, and I felt my body shiver in anticipation. It was such a terrifyingly beautiful thing to be completely at the mercy of my mate. To give myself so completely to her and not feel an ounce of reservation. To have one of my senses dulled, the way it had been *that* night, and still feel like I have all the power.

My mates had given me my life back. They'd erased his vicious touch from my memory and replaced his imprint on my soul with theirs.

I felt a tear of love and gratitude slip from the corner of an eye, and just when I prepared to say something to thank her for what she was doing for me, her tongue slipped between the lips of my pussy, and I bucked against her.

"Fuck," I whispered.

"I intend to," she replied wickedly against my core. Then something phallic shaped and warm pressed against my opening.

"What are.." I asked, wondering briefly if one of my other mates had joined us. But then Samara pressed a button, and the vibrator roared to life against my clit, and I cried out at the feel of it.

"Oh my God," I cried out. Samara pressed kisses against my inner thighs as she held the toy against me. She pushed it there, circling it slightly until my whole body shook. Just when I thought I was going to disappear into oblivion, she pressed the head of the vibrator into me. The moan that slipped through my lips was downright pornographic.

She fucked me with the vibrator, alternating between slow and sensual thrusts and hard and punishing ones. The vibrations echoed through my bones, and I couldn't control my violent shaking as my orgasm built and built within me. Her mouth came down onto my clit, somewhere between worship and punishment, and that was all it took to send me toppling into the climax to end all climaxes.

"Holy shit, Samara," I exclaimed loudly as my release soaked the toy and my mate's face. She kept the toy pressed inside of me but turned off the vicious vibrations to give my body a moment of reprieve.

"Athena," she whispered, her voice soft and admiring. "I wish you could see how perfect you are when you scream my name."

I squirmed under her hold, unable to form coherent thoughts in my post-climax blissed-out state. She gently slid the toy from me, making sure I felt every inch of the removal before I was once again writhing.

I felt the bed shift as she positioned herself over me, her legs entangling with mine. I felt the heat from her exposed core hovering above mine, but she didn't press down to meet me. With a hand, she reached up, slowly removing the blindfold from my eyes and gifting me with the sight of my stunning, naked mate looking down at me from her position of power over me. When my vision was cleared, she still didn't move to close the distance between our bodies. Instead, she just held herself there, tantalizingly close but still too far. Her mocha eyes held mine, and too much passion to explain adequately flowed through us. This was love. Passion. Lust. Healing. Safety. She was all of this for me, and by the depths of the look she was giving me, I knew that I was all this for her, too.

"Make love to me, Samara," I whispered. She brought her lips down onto mine and locked my mouth into a passionate exploration before slowly lowering her core to press against mine. We moaned into each other's mouths at the first brush of friction. She maneuvered her hips expertly, chasing her passion and bringing me to the brink of mine. Our breath mingled, coming out in pants. Her breasts pressed against mine, and I let my hands explore them, delicately playing with each peak as her pussy slid against mine.

"Oh fuck," I cried out as my stomach tightened and the orgasm crested.

"That's it, baby. Come for me," she begged, thrusting her hips faster. I threw my head back, arching against the foot of the bed, my hands clasping around her neck and holding her into place as I circled my hips to grind against hers.

"Oh my god," I think I said, but it may have been incoherent as the cascade of euphoria claimed me, toppling me into a body-shaking orgasm. Samara rode me through my climax, her body tense as she chased her own release. She met me at the cliff, and together, we dove off into the ravine of pleasure below. I'm not sure we could have held each other tighter if we tried. When our breathing returned to normal and the delicious tension in our bodies melted away,

Samara slid onto the bed beside me, smiling up at me with an exhausted, sated smile.

"Good morning," I whispered, chuckling. She laughed, burying her head in the crook of my neck.

"Good morning," she replied softly.

We lay there for what felt like hours, and simultaneously not long enough.

"I need to see my father," I admitted quietly to the room's darkness. Samara's gentle touch slid against my arm in comfort.

"I know," she said.

We slid off the bed, and I already missed the warm haven of safety while I prepared myself both emotionally and physically for the long evening ahead of me.

I slid into one of my comfortable sweat sets, soft heather grey pants that hugged my curves while still remaining loose and comforting, and a matching cropped hooded sweatshirt. I sat down and allowed myself the simple joy of applying a full face of makeup for the first time since before I was captured. I hadn't realized how much I missed the creative outlet makeup had become for me until I no longer had it. As I painted my eyelids and contoured my cheeks, I thought about how this makeup felt almost like a shield, something to help me brave my next task.

I tamed the wild red strands of my hair into a low ponytail, and finally, I was ready to face my father.

Stepping into the living room, I found Laz and Samara sitting at the island. They each had a mug in front of them, and I could scent the blood all the way from where I stood. Samara slid another mug over to me. I gripped the cup in my hands and marveled at how normal this felt despite the contents as I drank down the delicious liquid. I wasn't used to drinking human blood yet, but the coppery taste still shocked me when it hit my lips. While vampire blood from my mates had all the flavor of human blood, maybe even more so, it did little to quench the hunger in the pit of my stomach. Like eating all the mouthwatering and decadent sweets in the world, it clearly had a superior taste but was not sustainable. Blood from the bag was, of course, not the same as from the vein - thanks to Davia, I knew that now - but it was enough to keep the stabbing hunger that always lay beneath the surface at bay.

"Where's Orpheus?" I asked. Samara and Laz shared a tense look. "What's going on?" Panic rose in my chest as I reached down the bond of him. The fear settled slightly as I felt him there on the other end.

"He's searching for Greg," Laz replied. My breath caught.

"What?" I stuttered.

"He's a potential threat, and in case you haven't noticed, Orpheus is a little bit obsessed about protecting you," Samara added.

"Has he found anything?" I asked.

"Not sure, we haven't had a chance to get new phones yet," Laz shrugged. I instantly sent out a thought to my mate.

Are you ok? Why are you doing that alone? Have you found anything? My nervous stream of consciousness spilled through my mind.

Good morning, Athena. Orpheus replied teasingly. *Yes, I'm perfectly well. I'm just gathering some intel and following trails, and I'm perfectly capable of doing that alone. And not yet, but I won't give up.*

I sighed, feeling the tension in my shoulders relax.

Please be careful. I pleaded.

You don't need to worry about me, little nymph.

I will anyway. I promised.

I know. He replied, and I felt him tugging on the bond, sending a wave of love and warmth down the bond to my heart.

I nodded, releasing a long breath, and leaned against the island before me.

"Are you ready?" Laz asked, coming behind me and caging me against the island with their strong arms.

"As ready as I can be."

They slid my ponytail to one side and pressed a kiss against the back of my neck. I turned to face them and pressed a soft kiss on their willing lips.

"Alright, let's do this," I said, gathering as much bravado as possible.

Together, we strolled through the evening streets of Shockgrove, my footsteps echoing off the familiar buildings. It was early summer, and already tourists were trickling into town, their presence a reminder that these peaceful streets would soon be filled with noise and activity. The thought made my chest tighten. I needed the tension with the Hunters to be resolved soon. The idea of innocent people being caught in the crossfire of my war was too much to bear.

My heart pounded in my chest as I approached the pier and my bookstore. I was nervous beyond anything I'd ever experienced. It's not every day that you need to confront the father that kidnapped you. Facing him was inevitable, and I couldn't keep putting it off. I took a deep breath, trying to steady my nerves, and reminded myself that I wasn't the vulnerable little baby that he left behind. I was stronger now, and I had my mates and my brother. I had a whole life filled with love and earned strength that he didn't get to be a part of.

As I walked, I noticed the early signs of summer everywhere, the vibrant green leaves on the trees, the colorful flowers blooming in the gardens, the warm, bright stars dotting the infinite landscape of the sky, and the gentle breeze that carried the scent of the ocean. Normally, these sights and smells would comfort me, but today, they only reminded me of a home that was tarnished by my father's hate.

A few people passed us on the pier as they closed up shop and headed in for the night, and I envied them for a brief moment. They had already lived their day in the sun and light and were retreating to darkness to sleep, and yet my day was only just beginning.

As I reached the front door to The Maine Plotline, I hesitated for just a moment before pushing open the door. I was shocked to see the 'Open' sign flipped and a few figures inside with arms full of books. My shock doubled when I saw Silas behind the cafe counter, my baby blue half-apron tied around his waist. He got the last croissant from the display case and handed it to the middle-aged woman while Archer ran the cash register. The two worked in perfect synchronicity, smiling and laughing with the customers while sending them on their way. They hadn't noticed us yet, and the smile that was plastered on my face was impossibly large.

I held the door for the two customers as they exited with their goodies, smiles on their faces.

"Thank you, dear," the woman said, smiling at me, which made the soft wrinkles at the corner of her eyes even more prominent. She was gorgeous, a beautiful example of aging gracefully. The gentleman, her husband, I presumed, nodded his thanks to me and then slung his arms over her shoulder, and the two of them walked down the pier, stumbling playfully as they laughed and joked with each other. My heart warmed. I was lucky, I got to spend a different kind of forever with my mates, but there was a certain beauty to growing old with the people you love that felt so enchanting. I'd never see the way grey hair would look on Orpheus, the way Samara's skin would soften, the wrinkles that might decorate Laz's face, or how Silas' tattoos would fade beautifully into his skin.

I wouldn't trade my version of eternity for anything, but I appreciated the reminder that every eternity is different, and none is more beautiful than the other.

The welcome bell echoed through the shop as we slipped inside. I smiled at the two behind the counter, my heart full of warmth.

"You opened the shop today?" I stated, my voice cracking with emotion. Silas came around the counter, sliding off the apron and wrapping me in a hug.

"Of course we did," he whispered against my hair.

"We know this place is important to you, and well, you showed me how to work most of it when I spent time here with you, so it was a no-brainer." Archer reminded me. The images of the lazy afternoons spent in this very shop getting to know the man I had no idea was my little brother returned to me. Less tainted as they had once been. Maybe one day I'd look at those memories fondly without the dark cloud of the Hunters marring it.

"Thank you both," I said, sliding out of Silas' hug to embrace Archer. He held me tightly, sighing with relief, like he felt that I might finally decide I'd had enough at any second and choose to hold his mistakes against him.

"Bold of you to open for business with a hostage in the back office," Laz jested as they flipped the sign to 'Closed' and locked the door, but I could see the actual nerves beneath the humor-filled words.

"We had a little chat with him this morning. He knew to keep quiet if he wanted a chance to speak to you," Archer started nodding to me. I glanced between the two of them.

"And?" I prompted.

"And," Silas began. "Your little ex-hunter here thought it'd be a fun little trick to make me drink from him right in front of dear old dad."

A shocked gasp escaped my lips.

"Well, that's one way to rip the band-aid off," Samara acknowledged under her breath.

"What did he do?" I asked.

"He's got a lifetime of ingrained beliefs to sort through. It's not a switch that can just be flipped. I didn't even buy into the whole 'vampires are evil' idea all that much, and it still took me some time to sort it all out," Archer stated. I nodded. "But he was certainly shaken."

Shaken was good. Shaken meant that the foundation he built his lies on was unsteady and could be rebuilt with the right truths.

I didn't want him as a father. I didn't need him. I already had a mother who meant the world to me, and I was not looking to replace her. But I didn't want to kill him. I wanted his beliefs to change for Archer's sake. I wanted to spare my brother the pain of needing to decide his fate or losing him.

"We can work with that," I expressed before taking a few steps toward the closed office door.

"Want backup, bookworm?" Silas asked as I brushed past him.

I shook my head. "No, thank you. I need to face this alone," I admitted before letting my hand settle on the doorknob.

The door creaked open, and I was met with my father's familiar yet weary, face. His eyes widened in surprise at the sight of me, and for a brief moment, we just stared at each other. Then, taking another deep breath, I stepped inside and closed the door behind me.

My father sat tied up in the chair, his face a twisted mask of anger and desperation. He looked up as I entered, his eyes scanning me with a mixture of confusion, disappointment, and something else I couldn't quite place.

"What a difference just a few days will make," he mused. "It appears we have switched places."

"The only difference is that you deserve to be tied to that chair," I chided back but took a slow breath, trying to compose myself. I needed to remain calm for this if I was going to accomplish what I'd come here for. To change his mind about us.

"You're one of them now," he whispered, and my fists clenched at my side. He said it in a tone so accusatory that I could almost taste the judgment.

"Because your Hunters killed me," I retorted calmly. I couldn't look at him, so I quickly turned and glanced at the books that lay on the desk beside me, letting their worn covers ground me.

"It was never my intention for that to happen," he whispered, and the genuine regret in his tone had caught me off guard. "I only ever wanted what was best for you, Athena. Even before you were born."

I shook my head. "You believed leaving us behind to commit murder was what was best for me?" I bit cooly.

"I believed that leaving you both to protect you from monsters who could harm you was," he replied.

I sighed. Disappointment for the man before me coursed through my veins. "Well, you were right about one thing," I started. "I was better off without you, your hateful rhetoric, and frankly cowardice views. Leaving me to be raised alone by my mother was the greatest thing you could have done for me. So perhaps, for that, I should thank you."

"Does she know that you're one of them? One of those inhumane creatures?" He asked, and I felt a jolt of pain in my heart. Grandma had told me that he didn't know about her death, and for the briefest moment, I felt a sting of pity for my father.

I crossed my arms, leaning against the doorframe, trying to steady my breath and mask the storm of emotions swirling inside me. "I can't believe you can't see the humanity in me," I replied, my voice colder and sharper than I intended, like a shard of ice.

He struggled against his bonds, his frustration etched deeply into the lines of his face. "How can I when you're part of the very thing I've spent my life fighting against?"

I shook my head, stepping closer, feeling the cold seeping from the wooden floorboards into my veins. "I can't see any humanity in you either."

His eyes narrowed, his anger flaring like wildfire. "Does she know?"

I shook my head, trying to fight the sting of tears.

"Because you're ashamed to tell her because you know it's wrong!" He spat.

"No," I whispered, but he continued.

"She may have a soft spot for the creatures, but she wouldn't want her own daughter subjected to a half-life!"

At that, something inside me snapped like a brittle twig. "She's dead!" I blurted out, the words ripping from my throat before I could stop them.

The room fell into a heavy, suffocating silence. My father froze, his eyes widening in shock, the anger in his expression melting into a look of raw, unfiltered pain. "What...?" he whispered, the fire in his voice replaced by a tremor of disbelief.

"She's dead," I repeated, my voice softer now but no less pained, each word like a dagger twisting in my heart. "Cancer. Few years ago now."

The news hit him like a sledgehammer, and I could see the impact of my words in the way his face crumpled, the lines of his features sagging under the weight of the revelation. He cared about her. That much was clear. But he had cared about his crusade against vampires more. And for that, I wasn't sure I could ever forgive him.

He looked up at me, his eyes filled with a sorrow that mirrored my own, a silent reflection of the pain and loss we both carried. "I'm sorry," he said, the words I had unknowingly waited my whole life to hear. "I'm so sorry, Athena."

We just sat there for a moment, the weight of our shared grief hanging heavy in the air like a thick fog.

"I know I couldn't be the father you needed, not when your mother and I disagreed on something so fundamental," he continued, his voice cracking. "You deserved so much better than me. I admit I was glad when your grandma told me that Franny had moved on. That you finally had someone to fill the role I couldn't. I was a little jealous." My chest tightened in response to the prickling fear at the mention of him.

Suddenly, the floodgates opened. I felt the tears I had held back for so long spill down my cheeks. My defenses crumbled, and I let out a shuddering sob. My mates had done such a great job of keeping the vicious memories of him at bay, but here they were, slipping back into my mind like an unwelcome visitor.

Whiskey. White teeth. Selfish hands. My step-father and what he took that did not belong to him. The snapshots of the worst night of my life flashed in rapid succession. His haunting face reminded me of just how helpless I felt, and despite the new power flowing in my veins, I felt like that powerless little girl all over again.

The memories felt so violently real and vibrant after all this time. I don't know why, but my vision flashed with a golden light, and I couldn't stop it. I felt the memory almost project from within me, finding purchase in my father's mind. It was like a rush of emotions, and the images poured out. The dark room, the harsh words, the physical and emotional torment I had endured. I was sharing my pain, my trauma. He saw it and felt everything, just as I had.

The vulnerability of sharing those memories hit me hard. It was as if I was exposed, and every painful moment laid bare not just for my father but for the world. My breath hitched, and for a brief moment, I felt like I was spiraling, losing myself in the trauma all over again.

But then, like a lifeline, I felt the presence of my mates. Their love, strength, and unwavering support wrapped around me, pulling me back to reality. Laz's calm reassurance, Samara's gentle encouragement, Orpheus's protective nature, and Silas's steady strength were all there, reminding me of who I was now. It was because of them that this power of mine had grown. Their love made me stronger.

I took a deep breath, grounding myself in their love. What I suffered through no longer felt like a weakness but a testament to my strength. Of what I had been able to endure in spite of him.

My father's expression shifted, the realization of what I had shown him sinking in. His eyes widened, and for the first time, I saw a flicker of understanding, maybe even regret.

With a final deep breath, I let the memories fade from his mind, pulling my newly expanded gift back into myself. I let my mind trace along the gift's edges, knowing there was more to it. I'd have time to explore it later.

I finally registered my mate's voices in my head, frantically checking in on me. They had felt my panic through the bond.

I'm okay. Thank you. I replied to my mates when I had regained my composure.

"What... what did you just do? I could see. I thought I saw..." Jacob asked, his eyes wide with concern. It was a strange look to see on his face. I didn't share this part of my history easily, not when I knew firsthand how some people reacted to it. And it was not a weapon I wanted to wield to hurt my father. My pain didn't need to be his, but all of a sudden, I wanted to share it. Not out of maliciousness but because it has made me who I am. Scars and all. It was the hardest thing I've ever had to survive, and I did it.

"That man abused me," I whispered.

He looked up at me, guilt and concern etched into his features. "Athena... He.. didn't.."

"He raped me," I admitted, the words like venom on my tongue.

My father's face twisted in agony, and I saw his body tremble. "No," he breathed, shaking his head. "No, I didn't know. I never knew. If I had..."

"He was a monster," I said, my voice breaking. "He took what didn't belong to him without regard for me or my mother. He hurt us both in ways neither of us have ever, or will ever truly heal from. He is the demon that haunts my nightmares. He is the violent creature I wish you could have protected me from."

He bowed his head, his shoulders shaking with silent sobs.

"I'm so sorry," he whispered over and over again, his voice melting with his cries into a soft cacophony of pain and regret. I stepped forward, kneeling before my father and gripping his chin to bring his eyes to mine.

"I don't need your guilt or your apologies," I said, not with venom but with strength and resolve. "I need you to hear me."

His tear-filled eyes met mine, and he nodded, the most broken I had ever seen him. In this light, he almost looked like me.

"When I was lost when I was broken... when that human piece of filth almost destroyed me..." He winced. "It was The Wanderers who taught me to love again. It was those gentle, beautiful, protective creatures out there who saved my life. They grabbed each broken shard of my heart and pieced me back together until I finally felt whole again. They are not monsters. They are my lifeline."

Tears slid down his face, the picture of a broken man whose very resolve was shaken to its core. I stood, suddenly feeling unable to face him like this.

I turned on a heel and sped from the room, rushing past the faces of my waiting mates and brother.

I could see from my mate's faces that they had heard the conversation with their exceptional hearing, but Archer looked at me with a hopeful expression.

"I need to get some air," I responded, feeling the twinge of panic return.

"What happened in there?" Archer asked eagerly.

"Just give me a second," I replied.

"Are you okay?" Laz asked, taking a tentative step forward. I nodded and took a deep breath.

"Yes, I just need to clear my head for a moment." I smiled shyly at them. I stepped toward the counter, plucking one of the pink roses from the vase. The aroma was so sweet and strong to my new senses that I instantly felt calmed. "I promise I'm okay. I just need a second. I'll be right back," I promised, taking the rose and heading toward the back door through the stacks of shelves. It would be safer to break down back there where no one could see me.

I stepped out the back door of the bookstore, the soft creak of the old wood blending with the sound of the ocean waves crashing against the pier below. The salty evening breeze greeted me. I twisted the stem of the delicate pink rose in my hand, letting the sting of the thorns pressing against my skin keep my mind from wandering too far into my memories.

The conversation with my father replayed in my mind like a storm of emotions swirling within me. I felt like I had finally broken through to him, made him see the pain and the truth. But the cost of dredging up those old memories was a weight I hadn't been prepared to carry again, and I needed a moment to process it all. Strange how that worked. Trauma. I could feel the safest and most secure I ever had, and still, those memories could sweep in and undo weeks, months, even of work.

I walked to the pier's edge, the wooden planks slightly damp beneath my feet. Staring out at the vast expanse of the dark ocean, I let myself feel the weight of everything. Tears blurred my vision as I looked down at the rose, the symbol of my new life, my new family. It was beautiful, but like the thorns, it also reminded me of the pain I had endured to get here.

My power was shifting and growing. I could feel it like a living thing inside my mind, expanding and evolving with each passing moment. I had shared my memories with someone else, letting them peek into my past. It was both exhilarating and terrifying. I took a deep breath, focusing on calming myself. But even still, it felt like there was more left to be discovered.

And then, out of nowhere, a sharp pain exploded at the back of my head. The world spun, and the rose slipped from my fingers, falling into the dark waters below. I barely had time to register what was happening before everything went black.

Darkness enveloped me, pulling me away from the pier, the ocean, the rose, and the memories of my father. My last conscious thought was a desperate hope that my mates would find me, that I wouldn't be lost to the darkness forever.

11

ORPHEUS

How do you find someone who might be dead? Start at the scene of their supposed death, of course.

That's why I found myself stripped down to my undergarments and wading through the chilled water under the pier in the early morning. I'd left Athena in Samara's capable arms last night and instantly knew what I needed to do. I needed to find the bastard who attacked her. I needed to relieve the stress of this unknown variable from her life and from ours.

There was no sign of a body in these waters, but any signs of an escape may have washed away in the several weeks since it occurred. One thing was clear to me, though, if he had died, his body would have washed up on shore. This spot was too close to the beach, too public. No, he was alive. He was out there. Biding his time, I was sure of it. I knew predators. I spent most of my second life hunting them.

I made my way to the beach rental that he and Louis had secured and found old police lines. Of course, they'd searched the place and came up with nothing. I slipped in past the police tape and looked around. Both Greg and Louis had left their things behind, and there was no sign that he had returned for anything at all.

From there, I moved on to the motels in town, each one turning up nothing but dead ends and false leads.

As the evening wore on, and the moonlight bathed me in its glow, I felt my anxiety tightening around me like a vice. My thoughts kept drifting back to Athena, the image of her face, her eyes, and the fear that something terrible was happening to her, gnawing at my insides. I felt her panic a few minutes ago, powerful and raw. I wanted to alleviate the burden of some of her struggles even more. I had to find Greg before he chose to act.

Finally, I remembered my powers. I had been so focused on the physical search that I had neglected the tool that could, in theory, lead me straight to him. I silently cursed myself for getting so comfortable with the emotional silence Athena's mate bond had gifted me that I forgot to utilize one of the best weapons in my arsenal. Taking a deep breath, I closed my eyes, let my senses expand, and the switch flipped on. It was like trying to find the right radio station amid a sea of static. The emotions of the town's inhabitants swirled around me, now more overwhelming because of the start of the tourist season, a chaotic blend of everything from fear to excitement to sorrow and joy.

I tuned out the noise, focusing on a single thread, searching for the particular brand of malice that Greg exuded. It was difficult, almost overwhelming, but then I felt it, a sharp, vindictive emotion cutting through the background hum, hatred, nearly palpable in intensity, laced with a sickening sense of anticipation.

I locked onto it, following the thread through the maze of feelings around me. Greg's emotions were intense, burning with a dark satisfaction that chilled me to my core. I couldn't quite place his location. Too many other emotions were pricking at the edges of my consciousness to get that specific. He was planning something, and it was coming to fruition. A surge of fear and determination rushed through me, nearly knocking me off balance.

Without wasting another moment, I sprinted toward The Maine Plotline, toward Athena. She was there, and if he was going to act, it would be there. Panic and urgency drove me forward, my thoughts singularly focused on finding Athena before Greg could get to her. The sense of dread in my gut intensified with each step, but I couldn't let it slow me down.

As I ran, the faces, memories, and moments flashed before my eyes, Athena's laughter, strength, vulnerability. I had to find her, protect her. My heart pounded in my chest, and with every beat, the need to save her grew stronger.

I just hoped I wouldn't be too late.

Athena! I called out in my mind. But when no response came, I felt the pit of my stomach deepen. *Athena! Are you there?*

I tugged on the bond. Still there, still strong. But she didn't tug back.

I reached the front door and pounded on the glass, drawing the attention of the figures littered inside. I counted quickly. Athena wasn't there.

Laz barely had time to unlatch the door before I rushed inside.

"Where's Athena?" I asked, fury incarnate.

"Whoa, what's going on, Orpheus?" Samara asked, but I brushed past, looking around the stacks of books for my mate.

"Where is she?" I repeated, tossing open the office door, revealing Jacob Bennett. His eyes were red-rimmed from tears, and his shoulder and head slumped in defeat, but there was no sign of Athena.

"She stepped outside for a second," Silas responded, and I turned to glare at him, not bothering to shut the door to the office.

"And you let her go alone? With all the threats out there?" He looked like he wanted to fight back, but he saw the fear in my face, and his features softened.

"What happened?" He asked.

"I'll check the back," Archer said, bursting into action, heading toward the back of the shop.

"What's going on?" Jacob asked from inside the office, but I couldn't even focus enough to respond to him.

"Orpheus, breathe for a second," Samara said, touching my shoulders. I felt my breathing slow, but the panic didn't subside. "What is going on?"

"I felt Greg, I felt him. He's going to try something," I explained.

"Okay, okay," Samara replied, nodding as fear crossed her features.

I hear Archer's footsteps returning quickly, and the sinking feeling deepened. "She's gone," he croaked out.

The Wanderers devolved into a panic of epic proportions while I fell to my knees. Trying to focus on Greg's emotions again.

"Where the fuck are you?" I whispered.

I couldn't pinpoint it, not with how strongly my coven was feeling things. Their panic and anger overpowered the channels of my mind. I tried to push past their overwhelming reactions, but too much was happening, and too many feelings filled this small space for me to look beyond it. Then I felt a wave of guilt, so strong and so unlike any I'd felt before. My head snapped up to meet eyes with Jacob Bennett.

"Who the fuck took my daughter?" He asked fury in his words.

"A human," Archer spat back, running a hand through his hair.

Jacob damn near growled his response, his face etched with a desperation I hadn't known him to be capable of. His eyes, red-rimmed and hollow, pleaded with us. "I want to help find Athena," he said, his voice trembling with fear and anger. "Please, let me help."

'Absolutely fucking not," Silas exclaimed.

"Not a chance." Laz contributed while Samara scoffed her discontent.

"You're not going anywhere," Archer exclaimed.

Archer and my coven stood their ground, distrust, and anger radiating from them. Samara's eyes narrowed, and Silas's fists clenched at his sides. They weren't going to let him do a damn thing, not after everything he had done. But for some reason, I felt drawn to his emotions. I watched him, I felt the shift, something genuine and raw breaking through the surface.

I reached out with my power, feeling his emotions as if they were my own. Regret, guilt, and a newfound determination coursed through him. It was like a dam had broken, and he was finally seeing the consequences of his actions. Something Athena had said had gotten through to him, and he was seeing the other side of things for the first time. For the first time, he felt guilt.

"He's sincere," I said, rising from my knees and stepping forward. "She got through to him." I spoke with an edge of pride, and it felt almost euphoric, but the reminder of our current predicament quickly dispelled that feeling.

Jacob turned to me, tears welling in his eyes. "I know I've done terrible things to you. To all of you. And I am sorry for that." The room fell silent, the tension thick. I looked into his eyes, searching for any hint of deception. But all I saw and felt was a broken man, desperate to make amends. I searched his emotions for any sign of insincerity, but it wasn't there.

"She told me what you all did for her. How you saved her when she was drowning." His face twisted in anger again, and I felt the fury-filled hatred aimed at her stepfather. Jacob Bennett and I finally had something in common. "If you only let me do one last thing before you kill me, let me help bring her back."

For a moment, no one moved. Then, slowly, I nodded. "Alright," I said, feeling the weight of my decision. "You can help. But there won't be a second chance if you even consider betraying us."

Jacob nodded, a flicker of hope in his eyes, and his hope licked at the edges of my senses. "I understand. Thank you."

I stepped forward, intent to release his bindings, but Archer sidestepped into my path.

"Are you sure, Orpheus?" He asked. I studied the man before me. He looked so much like Athena and so much like the man bound to the chair just behind him, but he was also so incredibly individual. The pain in his eyes was unique to him.

His emotions were tumultuous. Anger and disappointment were at the forefront, but a tendril of wild hope danced around. He so desperately wished for his father to have changed, for him to finally see the right side of things.

"I can't say with any ounce of certainty that he won't hate vampires for the rest of his life," I said, glancing over Archer's shoulders at the broken man. "But he loves Athena, you can't fake that. He will help us find her."

"We don't need his help," Silas argued. "We can take down a puny human. Hell, she can take him down herself now, too."

I felt Laz and Samara's silent agreement in their emotions.

"What if we run into Galvin? We may need his expertise. He may be the only edge we have." I nodded to Jacob.

"I hope you're right," Archer whispered, stepping to the side and out of my path. I moved forward, ready to release the man who had tortured us. The man who had killed Alora. The man who had been the source of our turmoil for years.

The man who had given life to my mate.

"I hope I am, too," I replied and sliced through the ropes at his wrists.

12

ATHENA

I woke up slowly, instantly feeling a table's cold, hard surface beneath me. My arms and legs were bound, but as I looked around, I quickly assessed the situation. I felt tired but not weak. I did have a massive headache stemming from where I was hit, and the throbbing pain was enough to keep me from establishing the mental link with my mates, but I could feel my supernatural healing already starting to take effect. I'd keep trying to reach them until I could get through. The bindings were simple ropes, nothing that could hold me if I decided to break free. My captor had no idea what I was and just how little these bindings could hold me and that mistake would cost him.

The dim light filtering through a small window high on the wall cast eerie shadows across the space. An old fishing warehouse, I determined by the smell of rotten fish and the sound of the waves so nearby. My senses sharpened as I took in the musty scent of old wood and metal, the faint sound of wood creaking somewhere nearby. There was no one in sight, but I knew better than to assume I was alone.

As I tugged experimentally at the ropes, I confirmed what I had suspected, there was nothing here made to hinder my vampiric abilities. No Hunter tricks, no special restraints. This wasn't the work of the Nameless Hunters or Doctor Kline Galvin. This was Greg.

A cold fury settled in my chest. He thought he had me right where he wanted, but he had no idea just how wrong he was. I could easily rip through these bindings and disappear into the night, but he'd still be out there, still planning something to hurt me. I allowed myself to relax on the table, deciding to wait. Let him think he had the upper hand. Let him come to me.

The seconds ticked by, each one feeling like an eternity. My thoughts drifted to my mates, my friends, and my brother. I knew they would be searching for me, but I was on my own for now. And that was just fine. I could handle Greg. I smiled at just how true that statement felt.

I turned and saw a phone sitting atop a tripod facing me. There was no indication that it was on, but I made a mental note to be careful about overtly using my abilities in front of it.

I listened intently, focusing on the faintest of sounds. The creak of a door opening somewhere in the building. The soft shuffle of footsteps. He was coming. My muscles tensed, ready to spring into action. The waiting was almost over, and soon, Greg would learn just how big a mistake he had made.

Greg burst into the room, his face twisted in a mask of anger and frustration. The moonlight gleamed off his sweaty forehead. His eyes were wild, darting between the phone and me with a volatile mix of rage and desperation.

"Athena Landry," he spoke, his voice nearly unrecognizable, maybe on purpose to avoid his voice being identifiable on the camera.

"Gregory Holden," I replied, letting a soft smile play on my lips. His lips turned up in a snarl.

"Don't say my name, you fucking bitch," he snapped.

"Why not, Gregory Holden?" I taunted. He growled, nearly stepping into the camera's frame, but paused and took a breath.

"You're trying to piss me off, so you can justify killing me like you did with Louis," he claimed.

I narrowed my eyes at him.

"Not that I want a reason for anything like that, but you did kidnap me...so.."

"Shut the fuck up!" he interjected.

I shrugged, trying to show just how indifferent I was. I had been in positions like this far too many times in my life, but for the first time, I felt like I had all the power. It was intoxicating. This man had once terrified me, but now I pitied him.

"Why won't you just admit it?" He roared, his voice echoing off the metal walls of the warehouse. "Why won't you confess to what you and your fucking harem did to Louis? I know you're involved. I know you all are!"

I remained still, my gaze steady and defiant. The ropes binding me were a mere inconvenience, a temporary hold that I had no intention of letting him know I could easily escape from. Instead, I leaned my head back against the table, feigning nonchalance. My heart was calm, even as his rage intensified.

"I told you before, Gregory Holden. Your 'friend' tried to rape me, and my partners pulled him off of me and sent him on his way." On his way to hell, but he didn't need to know that part.

"No, he didn't, you fucking slut!" I felt the bubble of anger slip through my calm exterior. I had been called my fair share of names, such as that, when the town first heard about what my stepfather did to me. They affected me greatly at the time, but now they stung me differently.

"Don't call me that," I warned. "Louis was a rapist and an asshole who drugged me because he couldn't get what he wanted from me. My mates sent him on his way... and if he never returns to Shockgrove, it would be a better place."

Greg's face flushed a deep, angry red. He stormed over to the phone and slapped it, making it jolt. "Don't play games with me, Athena! This is your last chance to come clean. I know you killed him, and you're going to confess."

I could see the steam practically pouring out of his ears. It was clear he was expecting me to crack, to break under the pressure of his accusations. Of the bindings that he secured around me. But I refused to give him the satisfaction. I met his gaze with an unyielding calmness, a smirk tugging at the corner of my lips.

"I'm not afraid of you."

I was surprised by just how much truth was in that statement.

Greg's fury seemed to reach a boiling point. He kicked the tripod, sending the phone toppling to the ground. I had no idea if it was still recording, but the lens was faced down. His eyes narrowed, and he marched over to me, grabbing a fistful of my shirt and shaking me violently. The ropes tightened painfully around my wrists, but I remained silent, not giving him the reaction he was so desperate for.

"You're not afraid because you're arrogant," Greg spat, his breath hot and furious. "But you will be. You'll confess, or I'll make you wish you had."

Despite his threats, I stayed calm, forcing myself to breathe steadily, even though his hands burned into my skin. My mind was already working on the escape plan. Greg's temper was his greatest weapon, and it was also his greatest weakness. The more he raged, the more control I had. I wasn't playing the victim, and I wasn't submitting. And that, more than anything, seemed to enrage him further.

"You're a fucking whore. You can't say Louis tried to rape you and then spread your legs for four fucking people at the same time," he growled in my face. His hand slipped into the waistband of his jeans, and for a brief moment, I feared that he might try to replicate Louis' attempt, but there was no lust in his gaze. It was only fury. His hand returned with a knife this time, and on instinct, my body tensed with fear. He must have seen it because he smiled wickedly, stepping closer.

"I told you you'd be afraid, slut," he whispered into my ear, pressing the knife against my throat.

I'd reached my breaking point. Ripping through the bindings at my wrists, I felt myself cry out in anger, in fury, in contempt for all the times people underestimated me, every time they tried to break me down or chip away pieces of me until there was nothing left. I moved too quickly for Greg to even comprehend. The knife bit into my skin only slightly, but once my hands were free, I twisted it from his grasp. My arms barred around his throat from behind, and I pressed the knife against his neck this time. "And I told you not to call me that," I growled into his ear.

"What the..." he stuttered, shock in his tone.

"I'll give you one chance. Get the fuck out of this town. Take your fucking vendetta with you and leave me alone," I asserted, feeling every ounce of strength in my soul.

My headache began to subside just in time to hear my mate's worried and frantic calls. Just as I prepared to respond, to ensure them I was safe, I felt their presence as they busted into the space. Their eyes searching frantically for me, their forms nearly shifted, but just human enough not to alert Greg to their nature.

Trailing behind them was Archer, who looked terrified. And then, surprising me entirely, was my father. His form took up the rear of the group, he stood tall and menacingly, prepared for a fight, but my mates weren't registering him as a threat to them. What did that mean?

"Athena!" Orpheus' voice was a mix of relief and surprise as my Wanderers rushed forward. Relief was evident on their faces.

I turned to them, my heart pounding. "You came."

Greg's face twisted in confusion and anger. "What the hell is this?"

Jacob, my father, stepped forward, his face a mask of fury. Before Greg could react, his fist connected with his jaw, sending him reeling. "That's for hurting my daughter, you piece of scum," he spat.

Archer moved swiftly, taking over and securing Greg, his eyes flashing with barely restrained rage. I turned from Greg, finally feeling able to let my guard down, and fell into the embrace of my mates. Their arms wrapped around me, grounding me, and for a moment, I felt safe amidst the chaos.

"Thank you," I whispered, my voice breaking. "Thank you for coming."

Orpheus gripped my face in his palms, his eyes searching mine. "Are you okay?"

I nodded. "I had it under control," I admitted, loving how that truth made me feel.

"Of course you did," Samara added proudly. Archer handed off a dazed Greg to Silas and embraced me. My gaze shifted to our father. He stood a little apart from the group, watching me interact with my mates with an intensity that made my breath catch. I moved towards him, Archer's hand secured in mine, my voice low so Greg couldn't hear from where he stood, thrashing in Silas' hold. "You came to save me? With them?"

Jacob's eyes softened, and he nodded. "Saving you was the only thing that mattered to me, Athena. You are both more important to me than anything. I'm sorry it took me this long to see it. I've fucked up. A lot. And I'd like to make up for it if you let me."

I glanced over at Archer. Jacob had abandoned me, but he had let someone hurt Archer, ordered it, in fact. How could you come back from something like that?

"Fucked up is putting it lightly," Archer hissed.

"I know," Jacob replied, hanging his head.

"But for Athena's sake," Archer said as he glanced at me. "I'll give you the chance to earn my forgiveness."

I felt a slight moment of hope blossom between the three of us. We'd never have a relationship like the one I used to dream about, but maybe we'd have something different. Something more... us.

"Thank you, both of you."

Just as he finished speaking, he suddenly recoiled, his face contorting in pain. I couldn't move. I couldn't even breathe. He stumbled forward, doubling over at the waist. That's when I saw it, the arrow lodged deeply in his back, piercing his heart. "No!" I cried out, the sound ripping from my throat as I rushed forward to him, catching him before he fell. Archer joined me, our father collapsing into our arms. We settled him onto the ground, my eyes unable to look away from the arrow.

My heart was in my mouth, terror and pain overwhelming me as I held my father. "No, no, no," I whispered, tears streaming down my face.

The others were already reacting, their eyes scanning the area for the threat. But all I could focus on was my father, his blood staining my hands as I tried to keep him upright. "Dad, stay with me," Archer pleaded, his voice trembling.

"Where the fuck did that come from?" Silas growled, holding tightly to a thrashing Greg.

"Keep your eyes peeled," Orpheus commanded angrily.

"Samara, please!" I cried out, my throat raw as I screamed. The blood on my hands was thick and warm, and I didn't even notice the hunger over the fear. She rushed over, but before she could place her hands on my father, another arrow emerged from the darkness and slammed into Greg's throat. Silas jolted, his face wide as he saw just how close it had come to hitting him. Greg's steps faltered, and he pressed a hand against his throat. Dark blood spilled from the wound as he fell to his knees.

"Don't even think about it," a sinister voice whispered from the darkness. The sound sent an eerie chill down my spine. And that's when I heard it, a loud, high-pitched ringing. I pressed my hands against my ears, trying to drown out the offending noise, but it persisted. I felt the power within me slip away as if it was retreating from the noise. My mates spun, putting their backs to each other, each straining painfully from the noise.

"What's going on?" Archer asked frantically, watching me shake my head in pain.

Samara focused her gaze on my father, a frustrated grunt coming from her. "He's blocking our gifts. I can't heal him."

"No, no, no," Archer spat. "Please, stay with me."

"I'm.. so sorry. Both of you," he sputtered, and I felt my dead heart crack. "I love..."

The light drifted from his eyes, and I knew that without Samara's healing abilities, he would be gone soon.

The air felt charged. This was it. I could feel it. The moment that either vampires or Hunters emerge victorious. There would be no draw. Two were walking in, and only one could walk out. I squeezed my father's hand, knowing that the only way to save him would be to win, and stood.

My father's blood dripped from my coated hands down my arms as I let the shift take over. My vision reddened, and my claws and fangs elongated. I lifted one arm and tracked my tongue from elbow to wrist, letting the jolt of fresh-from-the-vein human blood spur my strength. I felt my mates prepare, joining me in a formation. We were about to take on *the* Hunter himself. And if I had anything to say about it, we were going to fucking win.

ORPHEUS

Why the fuck did I turn it off? I scolded myself. The moment I found my mate, I had to flip it all off because the relief and the anger were all too much, and all I wanted to feel was her and her alone. So I turned it off. I let the emotional radar quiet in my mind, and because of that, I missed the Hunter-sized threat heading directly for us.

I let my guard down, and we were ambushed.

And if we lost anyone here tonight, it would be my fault.

I tried to switch it on now as the eerie voice bounced through the warehouse, but whatever device he had was dulling our senses... leveling the playing field. Hunters had been fighting against vampires for centuries, finding ways to use our advantages against us. I shouldn't be surprised that Galvin brought a little toy like this.

Amidst the panic and anger of my own emotions, I felt the tingle of familiarity claw at my mind. The voice echoing through the chamber gnawed at me. I don't recall running into him at the headquarters during either of our ventures there, but for some reason, his voice sent a wave of recognition over me. But I couldn't place it.

The scent of blood was thick in the room as both Greg and Jacob Bennett bled out on the floor at our feet. Archer was pressing his hands onto Jacob's form, trying to staunch the worst of the bleeding. Greg was dead. I heard the last pump of his heart only moments ago, and now he was gone. I couldn't say I was distraught that the man who injured, stalked, threatened, and kidnapped my mate was dead, but I didn't want the Hunters to be the ones who rid the world of him.

"Hello, Kline," I said to the void of darkness. My senses were dulled by the device emitting the high-pitched screech, so I couldn't tell where exactly he was. It almost felt like he was everywhere.

"Orpheus," the voice whispered in a hiss. "I wish I could say it's nice seeing you again."

I tried to hide my confusion from my face. "Sorry, I don't recall us ever meeting. Perhaps you didn't make much of an impression," I replied tauntingly. Silas was at my back, and Laz and Samara were standing to my side with their shoulders pressed together. Athena stood near Jacob Bennett, and my eyes kept glancing at her to ensure she was okay. Her form had fully shifted. She was stunning. Her vampiric features were hauntingly terrifying, with a beauty only she could possess. Still, I didn't enjoy the reason for her shift.

The voice chuckled in response, sending an eerie chill down my spine. Why the hell was he able to affect me like this? I shook my head, trying not to let the nagging feeling get to me.

"You have grown a spine since last we met." Then, finally, stepping out of the shadows was Doctor Kline Galvin. The doctor stood before us, his figure cloaked in the Nameless Hunters' familiar yet unnerving white mask. His body was strong and built, every muscle seemingly coiled and ready to strike. His stance was firm, exuding an aura of confidence that made the air feel heavier. He was not a man to be underestimated, and his presence alone was enough to send a shiver to my extremities.

From behind the mask, his eyes were cold and calculating, scanning the room with a predator's gaze. There was something about him that tugged at my subconscious. The sensation was like an itch I couldn't scratch, growing more insistent with every second that ticked by.

But for the life of me, I couldn't place him. His identity remained just out of reach, hidden behind the mask.

As he stalked forward, I glanced around, sure that he wouldn't come alone to fight us. He must have backup here somewhere, and I wouldn't let him distract us from that threat.

"We need to be vigilant. There has to be others," I whispered under my breath so the Doctor couldn't hear me. My coven was on edge, ready to spring into action at a moment's notice, but we remained still, poised for the attack we knew was coming.

He lifted his crossbow and took aim at none other than Jacob Bennett. "Bennett, Bennett, Bennett," he mused disappointedly. "You know what we must do to traitors, don't you?" Archer stood, placing himself between the arrow and his father. "Ah, Archer, right? I knew I saw weakness in your eyes that day. I'd hoped I was wrong. But it seems you got your backbone from your father." With Samara's ability hindered, if Archer took a hit, we might lose him too. I couldn't watch Athena lose both of them tonight. I took a menacing step forward, and Galvin aimed at me.

"I'm done following your lead, Galvin. What you're doing isn't right," Jacob seethed through gritted teeth.

"Is that so?" He tilted his masked head, and I almost felt the wicked smirk.

"I won't let you hurt my family," Jacob sputtered, blood spilling from his mouth. Archer's pain was so evident on his face I didn't need my gift to feel it. He knew, as we all did, that Jacob wouldn't survive without healing.

"I forgot the part where I said I cared what you thought," Galvin mused before aiming his crossbow again. He moved so fast that even I couldn't see it until the arrow flew through the air. I tried to move and call for Archer, but the arrow found its target, lodging in Jacob's neck. A violent sob ripped from Archer and Athena's throats. It was a cry of pain, of anger. Of loss.

The briefest image of Alora with a stake in her heart flashed in my mind.

"Dad! Please! No!" Archer cried, but it was too late. Jacob was gone.

Athena readied herself to rush toward Galvin, but Silas placed a hand on her shoulder, keeping her back.

"Why don't we make this interesting?" Galvin said as he gripped a remote from his pocket. Pressing the button, he sent out another wave of that ear-splitting screech. The moment the sound intensified, it felt like a knife slicing through my senses. My head throbbed, and my vision wavered as I tried desperately to focus on the threat before us. I felt my strength falter and my hearing deafen. He had the upper hand, and that fucking pissed me off. He stood there, a crossbow in hand, arrows at the ready, the pointed tips glistening in the soft light of the warehouse.

Then he attacked.

Every arrow he loosed flew with impossible speed and precision, soaring toward its mark with deadly accuracy. The first struck Archer in the leg, and he fell to his knees with a cry of pain. Athena quickly rushed to move him behind a stack of crates, the only cover we could find in the chaos of the warehouse. He cried out and clawed out for his father, but Athena pried him away and got him to a fraction of safety despite his protests.

The high-pitched device was crippling us. Our enhanced senses, strength, and speed were all dulled, and we were barely more than human. Once her brother was safely tucked behind the cover, Athena's eyes darted around, trying to pinpoint the source of the sound. Silas and Laz were already strategizing, their minds racing even through the pain.

"We need to find that device and shut it down," Silas hissed, his voice strained. "We won't stand a chance against him otherwise."

I nodded, pushing through the agony. "I'll draw his fire. Laz, can you track the source?"

Laz, despite the grimace on their face, gave a determined nod. "I'll do my best."

With a deep breath, I dashed out from behind the crates, making myself a moving target. Galvin's eyes followed me, another arrow already knocked and ready. I dodged, trying to make it difficult for him to get a clear shot, but my speed was hindered. An arrow whizzed past my ear, so close I could feel the air shift.

"Come on, you bastard," I muttered under my breath. "Keep your eyes on me."

Laz was moving, too, their eyes scanning the rafters and corners of the warehouse. Another arrow flew, grazing my arm, but I kept moving, the pain secondary to the mission at hand.

"There!" Laz shouted, pointing to a small device mounted on the upper level of this warehouse. How long had he been planning this? Did we walk directly into his trap? How did he know Greg planned to pick this location? "It's up there!"

Athena's eyes met mine, a silent understanding passing between us. She was still weakened by the sound as we all were, but she gathered her strength, her determination glistening in her red eyes. "Silas, give me a boost."

Silas positioned himself under the catwalk of the upper level and cupped his hands together. Athena stepped into them, and he launched her upward with all the strength he could muster despite the stinging pain. She caught the catwalk's railing, her fingers gripping tightly as she swung herself up.

Galvin's attention snapped to her, but before he could react by sending an arrow, I hurled a heavy crate in his direction, forcing him to dodge. It bought Athena the precious seconds she needed.

She reached the device, her fingers working quickly. The sound intensified momentarily, a final burst of agony, and then– silence. Blessed silence. The relief was immediate as our senses sharpened, strength returned, and the fog lifted from our minds.

Athena dropped back down, landing lightly beside me. "That's much better." She stretched her neck, shaking off the last remnants of pain.

Galvin's eyes narrowed, realizing his advantage was gone. "You think this changes anything?" he snarled.

But it did change everything. With our full powers restored, we were ready. He let a few more arrows fly in quick succession, but we were able to easily dodge them as we made our way to his side of the warehouse, where he had remained in relative safety until now.

"Holy shit," Laz exclaimed next to me, and I turned to see their face just as an arrow pierced my shoulder. I hissed, quickly pushing Laz behind the crates and evading another lethal blow.

"What is it?" I asked through gritted teeth. The pain was sharp, and I felt the toxic tip slowly seep into my blood system. I reached up, ripping the arrow from my skin, gritting my teeth at the pain as it pulled through my tender skin, but instantly felt the toxin stop its maddening disolvement.

"I can feel his blood," Laz said, their eyes glassy and wide.

"What do you feel?" I asked as Silas tossed another crate at Galvin, which crashed against the wall. I looked over and saw Samara was focused on healing Archer's wounds. Archer was pale empty, his eyes unfocused and glistening with tears.

"He's not human, Orpheus," Laz said finally, and my head snapped to face them. Shocked.

"What do you mean, he's not human?" I asked in a hushed whisper as another round of arrows lodged in the crates behind which we were hidden.

"I can feel the venom in his blood. He's a vampire, Orpheus. He's one of us." Laz whispered it, but if what they said was true, it was loud enough for Galvin to hear. The barrage of arrows slowed, and I heard the man sigh.

"A vampire," I said quietly, knowing he heard me. If he was, in fact, one of us, it meant he could hear everything the same as I could. "You're a vampire who hunts vampires..." I was still trying to wrap my mind around it when I stood from behind the crates to look him in his fucking traitorous eyes.

He tilted his head slightly as if considering whether to answer. Then, with a chilling calmness, he spoke. "You really don't remember me, do you? Perhaps I can help jog your memory."

With deliberate slowness, he reached up and removed the mask, revealing a face that sent a jolt of recognition through me, ripping through the recesses of my lost memories and tearing a piece of them free. The features were exactly the same as they had been all those years ago but held a more menacing glow, and there was no mistaking the man who had haunted my nightmares until his visage disappeared into the lost memories of my human life.

The one who had turned me.

Realization crashed over me like a tidal wave, leaving me reeling. "You," I whispered, the word laced with a mixture of shock and anger.

"Me," he replied, a cruel smile curling at the edges of his lips. "It's been a long time, hasn't it? And now, it seems, our paths have crossed once more."

The tension in the room ratcheted up a notch, and I could feel my mate's concern through our bond. The Wanderers were coiled like snakes, ready to strike at the right moment. They were prepared to fight, ready to protect, but they also sensed the personal nature of this encounter and gave me this moment to confront the phantom of my history alone.

"Who is he, Orpheus?" Samara asked.

"My sire," I whispered, my eyes locked on his figure as the blurry memory of his face clarified in my mind.

"You're a hypocrite," Athena hissed, and Galvin sighed.

"I'm a Hunter," he replied.

"How can you hate what you are?" Silas demanded. "Why kill your own kind?"

"I simply admitted to myself what our kind has shied away from for centuries... we are monsters, and this Earth would be better off without us tainting its soils with our unnatural existence."

I'd heard that kind of radicalized speech before from Hunters or humans with unfortunate knowledge of our supernatural existence. Still, I'd never heard that kind of violent diatribe from a member of our own community.

"One day, I woke up from my blood-hazed stupor of murder, bloodlust, and violence and saw what I had become. I was disgusted when I saw who I was and what I had done. I knew then that my purpose in life was to eradicate every last one of us from this plane of existence... and when my task is finished, I will follow to the fiery pits of hell where we belong." His eyes darkened into the signature red as he spoke.

"Why turn me? Why make more vampires if you're trying to eradicate us?" I spat at him. Disgust and anger colored my tone.

He sighed. "Because I was no match against some of the more powerful of our kind. Not when they'd been gifted their unique and unnatural abilities." He spat the word unnatural like a slur. "Myself? I wasn't gifted any abilities in my new existence. At least, I didn't think I was. But when I created my first heir, I realized that when he matured and developed his gift. I was able to siphon it for myself."

"You made me an heir?" I whispered, putting the pieces together. Heirs were different than turned vampires, they required a more detailed turning ritual, and the benefit was a blood tie that lasted as long as they lived. I glared at the man in front of me. Disgust blooming in my chest. How could I be tied to a monster like him?

"Don't feel so surprised, Orpheus," he taunted, hinting at his ability to feel my emotions. I growled, my chest vibrating. "I made vampires, so I could finally build an arsenal of powers to use against the very vampires I created."

"How many," Samara asked, her voice quivering.

"How many heirs have I created? Or how many have I killed?" He clarified with a wicked smirk.

"You bastard," Silas tossed out.

We weren't acting or rushing forward because my coven had likely put together the same thing I had. If this man was the vampire who turned me, he was ancient. His strength was undoubtedly unmatched by any of us. And if he was telling the truth about his ability, he may have powers unlike any we've ever seen running through his veins.

Somehow, he'd managed to outnumber us all on his own.

"So," he began. "My sired..." he whispered softly, sending a wicked shiver down my spine. "It's time for you to be sent to where you belong. I will win, and you will die. You can fight if you'd like. But this ends today. The Wanderers will die tonight."

I glanced at my coven. Their eyes met mine with the same burning intensity I felt reflected in my own heart. We had so much to fight for and live for, and we were not going to go down without a fight.

I clenched my fists and let the shift take over completely.

"You're going to regret the day you created me," I promised before rushing forward into a losing battle.

14

PLAZ

Galvin moved with inhuman speed. His every step was a blur as we squared against him. I still hadn't shaken off the shock that hit me when I felt his blood and noticed the vampiric venom that danced within. We rushed forward, but my chest tightened because I knew we were going up against someone with an arsenal of abilities we'd stand no chance against. But we were going to try.

Our bodies clashed in a flurry of blows and claws, but Galvin managed to stave off the worst of our attacks with ease. Our speed was entirely unmatched by his. Galvin chuckled darkly, offering me a vicious smirk.

One moment, we were standing on solid ground, and in the next, everything shifted. The warehouse walls twisted and stretched, the floor beneath us undulating like the surface of a stormy sea. It was disorienting and terrifying. The image was so believable that I had to focus hard to keep my balance. The air seemed to hum with his power, and I could see my friends struggling to adjust to the new reality he had painted for us in our minds.

"It's not real!" I screamed out.

Galvin laughed, his form flickering as if he himself were made of shadows.

"Maybe not, but this is," he taunted as he waved a hand, and the floor beneath us turned into quicksand. My feet sank immediately, the thick, heavy sand pulling me down. Silas and Orpheus were similarly trapped. Their movements slowed as they tried to free themselves. Samara and Athena, light on their feet managed to dodge the space barely.

Panic surged through me. We would be at his mercy if we didn't counter this quickly. I closed my eyes, reaching out with my power. I focused on the nearly liquified ground beneath us, willing it to solidify. The sand resisted, considering it wasn't my common medium, but I pushed harder, my control over the contents of the mixture at my feet, fighting for dominance over Galvin's control of our minds.

Slowly, agonizingly, the quicksand began to solidify. I could feel the resistance of Galvin's power, a dark, malevolent force pushing back against me. But I persisted. I wouldn't let him win. With a final, concentrated effort, the ground beneath us hardened, turning back into solid earth, allowing us just enough time to distance ourselves from the depths of Galvin's abilities.

"Move!" I yelled, urging my friends to take advantage of the brief respite.

Silas charged forward, his strength and anger renewed. Orpheus followed, his eyes glowing with predatory fury. I couldn't imagine being told that I was sired by an evil man like this, let alone his heir. Athena moved with deadly grace, her blood-covered claws gleaming as she struck at Galvin. I focused on the air around us, trying to make sense of the lingering effects of his reality warping. What was real, and what wasn't?

With a flick of his wrist, Galvin summoned a torrent of water from seemingly nowhere. The liquid swirled and formed razor-sharp blades that sliced through the air. Samara barely managed to deflect one of the blades, her healing powers working overtime to mend the shallow cuts it left behind on her skin.

Orpheus lunged at Galvin, his fangs bared, but Galvin was ready. He conjured a wall of flame that forced Orpheus to retreat, the heat searing his skin. He screamed out, clutching at his arm. Athena tried to take advantage of the distraction, her claws aimed at Galvin's heart, but he vanished in a puff of smoke, reappearing behind her with a mocking smile.

"Is this the best you can do?" he taunted, his voice echoing around us.

The frustration and fear in my coven was palpable. We were outmatched, and Galvin knew it. He was toying with us, using his numerous gifts to keep us on the defensive.

Silas lunged forward, managing to land a blow across Galvin's chest. He grunted in pain and recoiled, but Galvin whispered something unintelligible before Silas could manage another hit. Silas's whole body froze, his muscles bulging from the effort.

"Silas!" I heard Athena cry out.

Slowly, my friend turned to face us, his body rigid and tense. His eyes were red and feral as they scanned over us as if he were looking at us for the first time.

"Silas?" I asked, not recognizing the look in his eyes or the way he tracked us like prey.

"Well, what are you waiting for?" Galvin said, and before I could react, Silas lunged again. This time at me. His claws dug into my shoulder, and I screamed out as pain radiated down my arm.

"Silas, what the hell?" I grunted, pressing my hand against the wound.

He didn't reply, but I don't think he could have even if he wanted to. There was an almost wicked haze over his eyes as he glared at me. Galvin had done something to him. He was controlling him somehow. Silas growled at me, drawing my attention back to him. His eyes were vacant, his expression blank and glazed. I knew it wasn't him, it was Galvin's twisted control that had taken over, but it hurt more than I cared to admit to see him looking at me like that. When he lunged, it was with all the power and ferocity I had come to love about him, but now it was turned against us.

"Silas, please!" Athena cried out, desperation tinging her voice as Silas lashed out again. I tried to fend him off without causing him harm, but he was too strong, too relentless.

Orpheus and Samara moved in tandem to get to me. Their efforts were a coordinated dance to subdue our friend without hurting him. But his blows were powerful, and one struck my lower abdomen, sending a searing pain through me. I staggered back, clutching the wound, blood trickling between my fingers.

"Silas!" Athena pleaded, tears in her eyes as she sprinted toward the trashing Silas. She tried to reach him, to break through the fog of Galvin's control, but it was like shouting into the wind. He was deaf to our cries. Orpheus and I gripped each arm while Samara tossed her arms around his neck and held him barred.

We struggled to hold him, our muscles straining under his violent strength. "We need to do something," Orpheus grunted, barely managing to keep Silas's arm from breaking free.

Athena stepped forward, determination etched on her face. "Hold him still," she commanded. I tightened our grip on Silas, my heart heavy with the knowledge that we might have to hurt him to save him.

She reached up and placed her hands on Silas's face, her fingers trembling. He tried to pull back, grunting, but she did not relent. "Silas, come back to us," she whispered, her voice filled with raw emotion.

For a moment, nothing happened. Then, Athena's eyes flashed gold, a brilliant, otherworldly light. My breath caught in my throat. I'd never seen anything like that before. It was beautiful. Perhaps even more shocking then was that as Silas' eyes met Athena's, they mirrored that same golden flash.

There was a tense silence as the glow enveloped them both, and I could feel the power dance in the air.

Slowly, Silas's body began to relax. His struggles ceased, and his eyes cleared, the golden light fading. He blinked, confusion giving way to recognition. "Athena..." he murmured, his voice hoarse.

We released him, and he stumbled into Athena's arms, clutching her like a lifeline. "I'm so sorry," he whispered, flicking his eyes to me, his voice breaking. Athena held him tightly, her tears mingling with his.

"It's okay," she soothed, her fingers brushing through his hair. I nodded my agreement. "You're back with us now. That's all that matters."

"How touching," Galvin teased. "Have you realized that I cannot and will not be beaten yet?" As he raised his hand again, the air around us seemed to thicken, turning into a suffocating fog that choked the breath from our lungs.

The fog seeped through my nose, burning my lungs as it enveloped my senses. I doubled over, coughing out the offending fog, but the more I tried to dissolve the toxin in the mist, the more it poured in.

I fell to my knees, my body tired, my power weak in the face of Galvin and his overwhelming abilities. No wonder Nameless had survived for this long. This vampire was damn near invincible.

I felt the bond in my chest vibrate with panic. Athena's fear gripped and pulled at the thread of our connection. She was desperate to reach us.

He's too strong. She cried into our minds, her physical voice far too injured by the fog to say anything out loud.

We can't give up. Samara.

We need something big. Silas.

"Vampires are the devil's mistake, and I will not stop until every last one of us is rotting in hell," Galvin seethed, his voice thick with rage and fury.

Just as I expected the fog to drown me, a deafening crunch permeated the space, and the fog immediately dissipated. I jumped to my feet quickly, ready to fight whatever Galvin had planned for us next. He was cradling his head, his venomous blood pouring from his ear, where a hatchet was buried into his temple. I glanced around in shock, and that's when I saw them.

Bursting through the warehouse door, pouring in through the open windows, and slipping in from the shadows were dozens of vampires. Some faces I'd recognized from our brief meetings in passing, some I'd never seen before. But they all had one thing in common. Their faces, bodies, and souls each carried scars dealt to them by the one man now standing alone in the middle of us all.

These vampires, these survivors, once scattered and afraid, were now united with a single purpose. To reclaim their lives and their freedom and take down Nameless once and for all.

A familiar older woman led the survivors, her long black locs swinging as she moved with a grace that commanded respect. Her skin was deep ebony, and her eyes burned with fierce determination. She raised her hand, and the vampires behind her surged forward, a wave of vengeance and hope. I recognized her gentle features from when we met her in New Orleans when she gifted us the ability to walk in the sunlight.

"We meet again," she said in her comforting, thick cajun accent, nodding toward Orpheus.

"Zula, you got my message," Orpheus said, relief flooding his voice.

"We all did," she nodded to the menacing crowd of furious vampires around.

"He's a vampire," Orpheus warned. Zula nodded.

"Of course he is," she hissed.

"You think backup is enough to stop me?" Galvin seethed, pulling the hatchet from his head and letting the blood pour from the wound. "You only saved me the trouble of tracking every last one of you *monsters* down!" He cried out, his features shifting feral. "I look forward to delivering you all to your deaths." He said before he struck out again. But this time, the vampires descended on him.

The air was thick with the scent of blood and the metallic tang of fear as we fought against Galvin. They were a sight to behold. Vampires who had been in hiding for years and hunted relentlessly by the Nameless Hunters. Their eyes gleamed with determination and a fierce desire for vengeance.

I could see the desperation in Galvin's feral eyes. He summoned shadows to obscure his movements and conjured fire to burn us, but we were relentless. He had to fight off blow after blow as dozens of vampires swarmed him. We fought with a ferocity born of years of anger and fear. We wanted their freedom, and we were willing to die for it.

Despite our new numbers, Galvin's ancient and overwhelming powers still gave him the upper hand. He moved quickly, striking out with deadly precision, sending several of our reinforcements scattering across the floor, blood pouring from them.

But he was also growing nervous. The constant barrage from all sides was wearing him down. He couldn't keep this up forever. We just needed to survive long enough to weaken him.

Just then, an idea so big and impossible formed in my mind. It was crazy and wild enough that it might actually work.

"Orpheus," I called out, rushing over to him. He glanced over at me, and I saw his face. Blood smeared across his features, and already violent bruises bloomed on his cheeks. "I have an idea," I rushed hurriedly.

"What is it?" He asked. I turned my gaze to Galvin, who fought off the barrage of attacks, but only barely, and let my power wash over him.

His blood pumped violently in his body as a result of his exertion. I let my power dance through the veins under his skin, feeling the venom pulsing within it. The venom that created this monster. The venom that made him one of us. The venom that gave him immortality.

The venom that I was going to remove.

"We will never defeat him like this," I admitted, and Orpheus's angry face only confirmed the truth I already knew. "But what if he was mortal..." I whispered and saw the recognition flash on his face.

"You think you could?" He asked, incredulously but hopefully.

I let the power take hold of the venom, analyzing it until I felt every ounce of it within his bloodstream. It was so thoroughly intertwined with the human blood that remained in his body that it took me a while to find the edges of it all. To identify the pieces of him that were mortal versus what was this supernatural amalgamation before us. My head began to ache as I pressed against the very edge of my power. I closed my eyes and strained.

What's going on? Athena's voice in my mind called out.

Laz has an idea. Orpheus responded for me.

I was thankful because I couldn't do anything other than focus on the edges of the venom, tracing out each ounce of it.

What idea? Athena prodded.

They're going to make him mortal. Orpheus said his confidence was supportive but perhaps too premature. I felt blood trickle from my nose as my head throbbed.

They're in pain. I can feel their injuries. Samara cried out.

They're going to push too far. Silas responded as well.

You are strong enough to do this, you always have been. Athena's encouraging words landed in my heart, and I felt our bond pulsing with life and energy. She sent me a bolt of strength, almost implanting an image of my success in my mind. And that was all I needed to grasp hold of the venom.

And then I willed it to change.

Galvin screamed, an unearthly screech of pain as I evaporated the very essence of the vampire within him from the inside out. His scream echoed off the walls, sending the other vampires into an almost standstill as they covered their ears and watched as the corrupted heart and soul of the Nameless Hunters writhed in pain.

I felt something I could only describe as relief when the venom was gone, and his blood ran clear. My whole body felt weak, but the satisfied smile on my lips wouldn't fall away.

The screams subsided, and instead, he curled in on himself, panting. The vampires waited with bated breath. I felt Athena come up to me, tossing her arms around my throat, and instantly, the pain in my head dulled as Samara pressed a hand against my temple. Silas stopped near us, towing a pale and ashen Archer behind him and holding Jacob Bennett's body in his arms. I met their eyes gently, smirking.

Then I whispered words that changed everything. "He's mortal."

"No, no, no, no!" Galvin cried out.

An incredulous chuckle bubbled from my lips, and my coven followed suit, devolving into a disbelieving laugh. At the same time, the other vampires turned their malicious and hungry gazes back to the weak figure before them. They were more than prepared to take their lives back, to exact revenge for the years of torment and fear. They stalked toward him as he cowered.

But all I wanted was to leave this place and this chapter of our lives behind us. "Now's our chance," I said, glancing at my coven. Athena, Orpheus, Silas, Samara, and Archer nodded in agreement, their tired faces filled with relief, not a hunger for vengeance. We didn't need to finish him ourselves. We had done enough. This was their moment, their victory to claim.

"Let's go," I whispered.

We turned and made our way to the exit, our arms wrapped around each other. As we stepped out of the warehouse, I could hear the sounds of Galvin's desperate struggle behind us. The other vampires closed in on him, finally gifted their revenge. His screams were quickly swallowed by the sound of tearing flesh and snarling creatures.

We didn't look back. The night air was cool against our skin as we pushed through the doors, leaving Galvin to his fate. He had terrorized us for too long, but now he had faced the consequences of his hatred. The other vampires had seen to that.

For the first time in this second existence, I felt a sense of freedom. We had survived. We had won. And now, we could start to rebuild our lives, free from beneath the thumb of Nameless.

15

ATHENA

The three days following Doctor Kline Galvin's death were a whirlwind of emotions, tensions, and pain.

On the first day, we buried my father.

The sky wept as if mourning what could have been, the drops falling in a steady, mournful rhythm on our umbrellas. I stood at the grave's edge, the damp earth clinging to my boots, feeling a profound emptiness. I wasn't sad about losing him, I hadn't known him as a father, only as a distant, conflicted figure. What weighed heavily on my heart was the loss of what he could have been, the potential for redemption that would never be realized.

Archer stood beside me, his face a mask of grief and confusion. He was torn up, struggling with the complexity of his emotions. The man we were laying to rest had caused us so much pain, but he was still Archer's father. I felt his anguish like a physical weight, and my heart ached for my brother. He believed there could have been good in our father, even when all evidence pointed otherwise, and I think I was starting to believe it, too. I reached for his hand and held it in mine.

We had to bury him at night, as the sun was still my enemy, although I did have plans to rectify that very shortly. The moonlight was obscured by thick clouds, making the cemetery feel like an ethereal, almost otherworldly place. The rain soaked through our clothes, but none of us seemed to care. The Wanderers stood with me despite my insistence that they didn't have to. I knew my father had hurt them in ways more vicious than he ever harmed me. Yet here they were, a testament to the bond we shared and their unwavering support for me.

Orpheus, Silas, Laz, and Samara formed a protective circle around Archer and me. Their presence was a comforting reminder that we still had each other, even in the face of a loss this painful. Laz's hand found mine, their touch grounding me in the moment. Silas' stoic presence was a pillar of strength, while Samara's gentle caress on my back offered solace. Orpheus, ever watchful, scanned our surroundings, unable to shake the centuries of looking over his shoulder in only one day. I feared he'd be breaking his hard-learned habits and healing from his fear responses for a very long time.

The rain mingled with the tears on Archer's face, his grief pouring out silently. I wished I could take his pain away, but all I could do was stand by him, share the weight of his sorrow, and hope that time would eventually ease his heart. I let my mind send Archer a memory, the only good memory I have of our father. The moment he asked our forgiveness and when we granted him the chance to earn it.

My vision flashed gold as I sent the memory to Archer, and he squeezed back, choking on tears as he relived the moment with me.

A heavy silence fell over us as the final shovelful of earth was placed over the grave. I turned my head, seeing the distant silhouette of my mother's headstone. I couldn't bear to bury him beside her, but I think she'd want him to be near enough for me to visit if I ever wanted to. She was just selfless enough for that.

Archer knelt, placing a single pink rose on the freshly turned soil, his fingers lingering on the petals as if hoping to find some connection, some resolution. His shoulders shook with sobs. I knelt beside him, wrapping my arms around his trembling form. The ground was cold and wet beneath us, but that discomfort was far from my mind. All I could focus on was my brother's grief and the overwhelming need to comfort him. "I'm here, Archer," I whispered, my voice barely audible over the rain.

He nodded, his breath hitching as he tried to compose himself. "He could have been better," he choked out, his voice breaking. "He could have been so much more."

I hugged him tighter, the cold rain soaking us both. "I know," I said softly.

Together, we said goodbye to the father Archer mourned and the father I never had the chance to.

On the second day, Davia and Archer left to fulfill their promise.

The evening was heavy with the weight of goodbyes as I stood with Davia at the pier's edge, the salty breeze mingling with our whispered words. The waves lapped gently against the wooden posts below us, and I tried not to think of how many times it would crash between now and when Davia and Archer could return in one year's time. Davia's eyes glistened, her lips pressed into a determined line as she held back her emotions.

"What did you tell your parents?" I asked, eyeing the set of baby blue luggage at her side.

"Marketing Bootcamp," she replied flippantly. "They've been pushing me to leave the theme park for a while and branch out into bigger things." Her voice held an edge of regret. "Honestly, I found an online course I'm going to take while I'm there, so I'm not even lying."

"I hate that you have to do this," I whined, holding her hands in mine.

"Listen, as far as I'm concerned, it's a free vacation. And honestly, I would have promised even more years if it meant keeping you safe and alive." She squeezed my hands. Tears stung my eyes.

"I love you so much, Davia. You are my best friend," I vowed.

"Damn straight." She smiled. "I hope you realize that this better solidify my maid of honor spot in whatever weird quad blood-ritual wedding you're going to have. Okay?" She teased.

I chuckled. "You secured that spot the moment you told me you'd rock my world if you were into vagina," I smiled up at her. She pulled me into her, her arms tightening around me.

"Be careful, ok?" I whispered into her hair.

"Listen, I may have promised I'd be there for a year, but I didn't say shit about anything else. I'd like to see them try anything. Give me an excuse to use this new pepper spray I bought." She seemed confident, as always, but I noticed the slight twitch of fear cross her face. She was being brave for me. I hated it.

I nodded, my throat tight with emotion. "You're braver than anyone I know, Davia. But you don't have to be brave for me."

She sighed softly. Her smile dropped slightly as she gripped my face in her palms.

"I'm brave *because* of you, babe. You're kind of a badass survivor. You know that, right?" She pressed her forehead against mine, and together, we breathed, the rise and fall of our chests syncing. "You make me feel like I can be too."

She hugged me tightly, her warmth a brief solace against the chill of impending separation. "I'll be back before you know it. A year is like a second to you now," she pointed out before pulling back. "Besides, I have your back-stabbing brother to keep me company."

I noted the look in her eyes. Outwardly, there was hatred, but I saw something else glimmering beneath the surface. I smirked. "Don't be too hard on him. I already forgave him."

"Yeah, yeah, well, I haven't made him suffer enough yet," she tossed before dragging me into one last hug. We held each other for a moment longer, and then she pulled away, her steps hesitant as she walked toward Archer, who was waiting nearby.

Archer's expression mirrored my own turmoil. His usually steadfast eyes were shadowed with grief. As Davia joined him, he took her bags and tossed them into the trunk of his rental car.

I walked over to my brother, my heart aching at the sight of him. We had been through so much together, and now we were being torn apart again.

"Archer," I began, my voice trembling. "I don't want you to go. I just found you. How am I supposed to say goodbye now?"

He looked at me, his gaze softening. "Athena, this isn't goodbye. You're the only family I have left. You're never getting rid of me." He chuckled and grunted as I threw my body at his.

I hugged him fiercely, feeling the familiar strength of his embrace. "Stay safe, Archer. Keep Davia safe. And come back to me."

He pulled back slightly, pressing a kiss to my hair. "You stay safe, too, Athena."

I nodded, blinking back tears. "I will."

"I love you, little brother," I admitted, and his answering tears were filled with relief and adoration.

"I love you too, sis," he confessed, playfully punching my arm.

"Don't go kidnapping anybody," I teased, and he rolled his eyes.

"I'm not making any more promises," he said, the double meaning obvious.

With one last lingering look, he released me and turned to enter the car. A hollow ache settled in my chest as I watched them disappear into the distance. The pier felt emptier, the world a little colder.

But I knew this promise had to be kept, a sacrifice they made to ensure our future. And though the goodbye was painful, at least they had each other.

Arriving at my little cottage, I tried to ignore how Archer and Davia's absence already had a pit growing in my stomach, but the void they left was too obvious.

I felt one of my mates press a kiss on the back of my neck and slip their arms around my waist from behind.

"They'll be ok, little nymph," Orpheus promised into my ear. "Elias is a bit of a jackass sometimes, but he's fair and honest. He won't harm them."

I nodded half-heartedly but bit my bottom lip.

"You don't believe me?"

"Silas' last promise begs to differ," I pointed out.

He gripped my arms, pinning them to my sides.

"Would I ever lie to you?" He asked, running his nose along the column of my throat. A shiver descended down my spine as I took in the hungry gazes of my other mates as they watched.

"No," I replied, breathily. My core tightened at his touch.

"Do you need a reminder of how devoted we are to you? Do you need us to show you why we'd never lie to you?" He asked tauntingly, letting his breath dust over my neck. I gasped sharply at the sensation.

The real answer. No, of course I didn't. These four showed me they loved me in every action. In every breath, in every movement. They remind me every day how lucky I am to have found them.

The answer I gave? "Yes, please."

I was such a liar.

A dirty, horny liar.

But I knew it would be worth it when Orpheus turned me in his arms to face him and devoured my lips in a punishing kiss. I sank into it, my arms, now free from his clutches, hung around his neck and pulled him to me. My hips pressed against his, desperately seeking friction.

His teeth bit my bottom lip, his fangs nipping at the skin there and flooding our mouths with the taste of my tangy blood. He moaned.

"Your taste haunts me, Athena," he licked my lip, drawing more of the blood into his mouth and sending a jolt of pleasure directly to my pussy. "It's all I can think about, all I can focus on."

He kissed me hard again, and this time, I dug my fingernails into his back. Groaning, he tangled his hands in my hair, holding me to him, unable to break free if I wanted to. I didn't want to.

"I need to taste more," he growled, and that was all the warning I got before he turned me around again and forced my torso forward, bending me at the waist so my face was pressed against the arm of the couch. I gasped as pleasure and shock mixed. My eyes caught Laz's, who was sitting on the sofa near my head, their hand gently stroking their length.

Orpheus hooked his fingers in my pants and pulled, taking my underwear with it and leaving me deliciously exposed to him. My ass was up, my face smushed into the material of the armrest, in such an undignified position I should have been self-conscious. But I couldn't think of anything but his tongue spearing into my cunt.

I cried out as he lapped up my arousal with eager swipes of his skilled tongue.

"Oh fuck," I cried out, gripping the back of the couch and bracing myself against his assault. Laz smiled at me with hooded, lust-filled eyes but made no move to touch me. Neither did Samara, who had come around to the back of the couch and looked down at me from her position, and Silas, who had kneeled next to the couch, a wicked smirk plastered on his face as much as I desperately sought their touches, I knew, like they seemed to know, that this was Orpheus' turn.

And boy, was he making the most of it.

His fingers dug into my thighs as he continued his relentless attack on my clit. My legs trembled, but he held me still. The pressure built in my core, a sensation I'd only experienced once before. His tongue worshipped my clit, and suddenly my arousal was squirting from me. Soaking his face. I cried out, weakly sinking my head and shoulders into the armrest as the aftershocks of my explosive orgasm wracked through me.

Orpheus hummed appreciatively, licking up every drop of my climax from his lips and my quivering pussy.

"That was the hottest thing I've ever seen, baby girl," Silas said, devilishly biting his lower lip.

I was too lost in the bliss of my orgasm to notice that Orpheus had stood and removed his pants. "Hold on to the couch," Orpheus commanded as he slammed his cock into me in one powerful stroke. I screamed out his name as he slammed into me over. Pistoning his hips like a starving man who could only find salvation within me.

My walls tightened around him, squeezing him, and he moaned. His breath was shaky and ragged as he neared his climax. He reached around, pressing his fingers against my clit as he fucked me.

I was a wanton little thing, crying out for more of his touch even as he pleasured me. He sped his hips and, therefore, his fingers, bringing himself to the edge of sanity and reason. He came with a roar, his cock pulsing inside of me and had me circling my hips, chasing after him to my own release.

We caught our breath, remaining still, just enjoying how our bodies were so in tune with each other. When he pulled back, removing himself from me, I opened my eyes and saw the feral looks in my other mates' gazes as they watched me.

"Our turn now," Silas said, pushing away Orpheus, who stepped back with a chuckle. I began to stand, but I felt Silas press a hand against the small of my back, keeping me bent over.

"I quite like this position," Silas mused, running his hands over my ass cheeks and down my legs, purposefully ignoring my soaked slit. "Let's put you to work, though, shall we?" He teased before gripping my hips and sliding up two feet to the left. The quick movement had me reaching out in front to brace myself. My hands braced against Laz's chest as we came to a stop with my head hovering just above their hard, aching cock.

I smirked up at them as they gently cupped my face. "What Silas is trying to say, in his caveman ways..." Laz kissed my lips softly. "Will you pleasure me with that perfect mouth of yours?" I moaned and nodded, my mouth falling open. Laz lifted their hips to relieve themselves of their pants, their cock sprung free, and I wasted no time circling the head with my tongue and sliding the whole thing into my mouth. Laz's head fell back, and they tangled their hands in my hair.

"That's my fucking good girl," Silas praised, and my whole body preened at the compliment.

"I'm going to fuck you now, baby girl." I shivered in anticipation. "Your job is to make our Laz cum before I do. Can you do that?" He asked, his fingers brushing against my swollen pussy lips. I sighed around Laz's dick and nodded.

A sharp slap came down on my ass cheek, and I jolted forward, my lips popping off Laz's cock in surprise.

"Use your words," Silas demanded darkly. I turned over my shoulder so I could meet his gaze. He was staring down at me like a man possessed. His eyes were hooded and eager, his breath coming in ragged spurts.

'Yes...sir," I replied, and then he was slamming into me. I fell forward, resting my head on Laz's chest as Silas fucked me hard.

"You're losing the race," Silas pointed out, and I suddenly remembered where I was. Stupid Silas and his mesmerizing dick. I dropped my mouth to Laz again and got to work. The sounds of their pleasure mixed together into a sinful cacophony, and I wanted nothing more than to keep eliciting those sounds for the rest of my life.

I took Laz as far down my throat as I could and then let my tongue dance along the tip as Silas pumped into me, hitting a part so deep that it had my body shaking with each punishing thrust.

Laz pumped their hips up, pressing their cock into my mouth, their abs tightening as they neared their climax. Silas, too, sped up, his thrusts becoming jerky and unstable as he prepared to fall over the edge of oblivion with me.

The three of us exploded into passion, one right after the other. I didn't know where my orgasm ended, and theirs began, but for several seconds, there was nothing but blinding passion.

Silas withdrew from my core just as I lifted my mouth from Laz's cock, licking my lips and smiling up at them.

Silas let go of his hold on my hips, and Laz helped me sink into the couch by their side. I hummed, satiated, and happy, loving the feel of their skin on my cheek. Silas knelt down, pressing their lips against Laz's, and I watched with rapt attention and a heart full of love as they found pleasure in each other. I felt delicate brushes of fingertips along my thighs and looked over my shoulder to see Samara. Her eyes were locked on mine and my skin felt heated under her chilled touch. She slid her fingers across the canvas of my skin delicately, not rushing, not expecting. Just relishing in the feel of my skin, and I leaned into her.

"I want you to touch me," I whispered to her, feeling as if we were the only two in the room but still feeling spurred forward by our audience.

She smirked, brushing her fingers across my pussy. She groaned at the wetness she found there. "You know we love you, right?" She asked, sliding her fingers along the slit again. I let my head fall against the couch as my legs fell open to give her more room.

I nodded in an almost lustful haze.

She circled my clit with one of her fingers gently, and my stomach tightened as the pleasure soaked through my limbs.

"You are everything we've always been looking for," she continued, pressing one finger into my heat. "I wanted love that didn't come at a price."

Laz smoothed their hand over my hair. "I wanted someone to see me for who I am, scars and all, and accept me anyway."

Silas sat near the edge of the couch on the ground, his eyes bearing into mine. "I wanted someone who would miss me if I left."

"And I.." Orpheus added from the armchair he'd taken residence on. "I wanted this. All of you. A family."

I felt tears sting my eyes, but the pleasure that Samara was gifting me chased the tears away.

I breathed deeply, loving the way Samara's fingers felt as they slid inside my slick channel. And then I let my mind drift to the first time I saw them. The way their bodies called to me, the way my heart instantly felt like it had been captured by the sinful strangers who saved me. I replayed the moment in my head and shared it. My vision blurred gold as I sent the memory to them as well. Their eyes flashed golden as they each joined me in that moment. The moment when it all began. The moment I fell for The Wanderers.

When the memory drifted away, and the golden hue dissipated, I felt the collective sigh of happiness and contentment. But it didn't last long before Samara's hands turned eager, and she slammed her fingers into me, bringing me to the brink once again.

She slammed her lips onto mine and kissed me like I was everything she needed. And I kissed her like I would never get enough.

When I came, soaking her fingers, she hummed happily before taking her fingers into her mouth and licking up my arousal.

I couldn't move, so instead of getting dressed, I simply pulled a blanket off the back of the couch and draped it over me. Laz and Samara cuddled into my side while Silas slid in next to my feet. Orpheus smiled at us from his spot across the room.

I felt their energies shift. An almost anxious cloud of worry blanketed the room. Orpheus and Laz shared a look.

"What's wrong?" I asked, pulling the blanket up to my chin. They didn't respond, but again, they shared a look. This time, Silas diverted his gaze and stared at the ground. I sat up, pulling the blanket tight against my chest.

"What's going on? What are you telling me?"

Laz cleared their throat. "We, um, well, we were talking about something, and we wanted to offer you something," they said timidly.

"Okay, what?" I asked, anxiety spiking.

"You know how we defeated Galvin?" They prompted.

"Yes..."

"We did something we never thought would ever be possible. We gave someone their human life back," Laz continued, looking down at their hands.

It all came into brutal clarity then.

They were offering me my humanity back.

My memories of my mother. My days in the sun. My small town for the rest of my days.

"Oh," I said, sorting through the mess of emotions that flooded through me.

"Is that something you want, bookworm?" Silas asked nervously.

Was it?

Did I want my old life back? I let the reality of what they were offering settle in my mind momentarily and tried to analyze my reaction to it.

"You're conflicted," Orpheus said.

My eyes flicked up to meet his. "I'm not," I answered.

"We won't be upset, Athena, if this is what you want," Samara added, squeezing my thigh.

"I don't."

They stared at me.

"I don't want to change this. This is my life. This existence, with you for the rest of eternity. This is who I was meant to be, and you are who I was meant to be with. This is my life, and I wouldn't change it for anything."

I heard their collective sighs of relief.

"Thank you for offering, but that version of me wasn't who I wanted to be. This is who I wanted to be. Thank you for giving me the chance to become her."

I met their smiles with my own.

"Ever since mom died, this place hadn't felt like home anymore," I whispered. "But right now, it does." I sighed. "I'll miss it."

"Why would you miss it?" Orpheus asked.

"Because we're going to be leaving?" I theorized. They were The Wanderers, after all. The very name implied nomadic tendencies.

"Athena, baby," Samara said, caressing my face. "This is your home, and for as long as it can be... It'll be ours, too."

"What?" I said, sitting straighter. "But you're The Wanderers, you wander," I emphasized.

"Darlin', we've been on the run pretty much from the moment we turned," Laz looked over at their coven. "I think I speak for everyone here that planting roots sounds perfect right about now."

I glanced around, finding the others nodding emphatically.

"We're going to stay here?"

"For as long as we can, Shockgrove is home," Orpheus confirmed, and I squealed in delight. I hadn't admitted aloud how much I would miss this place when we left. I knew that we couldn't stay forever. The neighbors would grow old one day, and we wouldn't, but that was long enough away that I didn't have to think about it now. All I cared about was that *this* was home, and *they* were home.

On the third day, I finally felt the sunshine again.

Zula, the New Orleans vampire with the gift of sun resistance, offered to perform her ritual on any other vampires who had assisted in the death of Galvin and Nameless. Fourteen vampires, including myself, met with her under cover of night at The Maine Plotline, and she gave us a chance at a sense of normalcy.

"Athena, is it?" she asked, her Cajun accent thick and warm.

"Yes, thank you, Zula, for coming to help us. Your numbers won this battle for us," I replied, gently clutching her hand.

"Not the battle, Ami." She patted my cheek, warmth radiating from her in waves despite the chill to her touch. "We just won the war."

I swallowed the lump in my throat and nodded, trying to fight back the tears that threatened to fall. Nameless had kidnapped me, tortured my mates, and killed Alora, but what they'd done to me and my mates was only a small portion of the hate and violence that they'd caused at the orders of Galvin. Nameless had been a black cloud of death and fear for vampires for centuries, and those vampires who survived them long enough have suffered greatly from their bigotry.

"How old are you?" I asked but quickly bit my tongue. "I'm sorry, you don't have to answer that! I was just wondering how long you've... yeah, sorry, never mind," I rambled.

She replied with a soft chuckle. "I have no way of knowing, for sure, but I'm pretty positive I am the oldest living vampire. So old that I remember a time before our King and Nameless."

I gasped.

"I've lived a long time, seen many things, and survived even more." She sighed. "I used to hide away in my compound. Afraid to step outside. But what kind of life is that? When your Orpheus sent us a message, I knew it was time for me to step out of the shadows. No matter how afraid I was. Or how much pain I harbored." She took a deep breath. "They took my mate," she said softly, eyes downturned. "Now, he rests peacefully for the first time."

I nodded my acknowledgment, knowing my emotions would betray me if I tried to speak.

"I met your Wanderers once before, a persistent bunch of fools," she teased. "They begged me to help them, to give them an advantage over Nameless. It wasn't till I saw the pain in their eyes and felt the sorrow in their souls that I knew they'd been hurt, as I have, by the Hunters."

She closed her eyes.

"They'd taken someone from them, too," she finished. "I recognized the broken pieces of their hearts because they looked like mine."

She turned her head toward the front of the store. Other vampires who had been freshly gifted the ability to walk in the sunlight were excitedly chatting with my mates, who seemed to enjoy the camaraderie of a community. Something else the Hunters had kept from them.

"They were barely living a half-life when I met them. Their wounds were fresh and raw. I think I gave in and performed the ritual just to give them something to live for. Our kind's numbers had dwindled too much to lose any more to broken hearts."

I let her words wash over me as I studied my mates' faces. How much pain have they suffered, and how long have they carried the weight of their trauma?

"Those vampires there," she indicated toward them, a slight smirk on her lips. "Those are vampires who have been made whole again. And I can see that they have you to thank for that."

I smiled. Watching my mates smile and laugh was like a balm against the burn of the scars on my heart.

"You've been around a while," I started. "Is it common to have multiple mates?"

"Well, no..and also maybe?" She must have seen the confusion on my face because she cleared her throat and continued. "There have not been many in our history. But it was not completely unheard of in incredibly powerful covens or with descendants of the royal family," she clarified. "But there's no way for us to know if it would have been more common had our kind not suffered a genocide of devastating proportions at the hands of Nameless." I nodded. "What is your vampire gift?" She asked.

"I can talk to my mates in my mind, from great distances too, it seems. And I think I can make people see what I want them to see, share memories," I added tentatively. "I haven't had much time to explore it, but I projected my memories into someone else's mind." I tried to ignore the sting of thinking about my father.

"Mental projection," she mused, nodding as if it made sense.

"You've heard of it?" I asked eagerly.

"I have," she replied cautiously. "The projectors I've met have something slightly different, but it sounds familiar. They have been able to establish an almost lethal grip on other's minds. Able to bend them and shape them as they desire. I bet if you needed to, you could too."

I shook my head.

"I hope I never need to," I replied, not enjoying the feeling in the pit of my stomach.

"We agree on that." She rubbed her chin. "The projectors I've met each had suffered something unimaginable. Something that made them feel so alone that their souls called out to the fates for someone to connect to. Someone to understand. Someone who can see and feel what they do." She nodded when she saw the recognition on my face.

"If I had to guess," she started, smiling at me. "I'd say it's not your gift that ties you together, but the experiences that gave you your gift in the first place."

"You're telling me that because I suffered, because I went through unimaginable pain, the fates or whatever wanted to reward me with multiple mates so I wasn't lonely?"

"I'm telling you that what you survived yesterday is what gives you your strength today." she clarified, gripping my hand in hers. "Trying to understand fate is like trying to bottle a feeling. Useless. And a waste of the moment."

I nodded. Enjoying the way that thought made me feel.

"Are you ready to walk in the sunlight again, Athena?" Zula asked, her smile warm and comforting. I nodded.

"Yes, yes, I am."

The ritual was quick, but the pain was vicious. She helped me lay down on the couch at the back of the Maine Plotline and whispered words over my body while her hands dusted touches along my skin. It started as a low hum of energy in my bones, a vibration almost like I was sitting in a massage chair. It wasn't painful at first, but it was slowly growing more aggressive. The pinpricks of pain grew into stabbing shooting jolts as the power seeped into my blood. It was agony. The fire seemed to course through my veins, igniting every nerve ending. I clenched my fists, nails digging into my palms, trying to anchor myself through the pain. My muscles began to tremble uncontrollably, the spasms wracking my body. It felt like I was being torn apart and remade, every cell of my body rebelling against the intrusion.

My vision blurred with tears, and I could barely make out Zula's form through the haze of pain. She placed her hands on my shoulders, and I could feel her power surging into me, a force both ancient and overwhelming. The heat intensified, morphing into a searing sting that felt as if molten lava were being poured into my veins. My skin felt too tight, as if it would split open at any moment.

I couldn't contain it any longer. A guttural scream tore from my throat, the sound raw and primal. The fire inside me roared, consuming everything in its path. Every nerve was alight with excruciating pain, each breath a struggle against the searing heat.

"It's almost over," Zula murmured, her voice cutting through the torment.

I forced my mind to drift to Laz, Samara, Silas, and Orpheus. Their faces, their love, their unwavering support. It gave me something to hold onto, a lifeline in the sea of agony. The burning began to ease, replaced by a deep, pulsing ache that resonated through my entire body.

I opened my eyes, and the world came back into focus. The pain was still there, but it was a dull throb compared to the searing agony of before. I felt...different. A new energy coursed through me, a resilience that hadn't been there before.

Zula helped me to my feet, her grip firm and steady. I saw my mates had come to surround me, their faces a mixture of pain and sadness. They did not want to see me in pain.

"I told you that you didn't have to be here for this," I whispered, my throat still feeling raw from the cries.

Silas hugged me first, but Laz and Samara quickly joined in. I chuckled, feeling the pressure of their bodies on all sides.

"Get in here," Silas grunted toward Orpheus.

"I thought I told you I don't share," he joked, a teasing heat in his eyes. Silas reached his hand out, gripped the front of Orpheus' button down, and pulled him into the embrace. We devolved into a fit of relieved laughter. I caught Zula's eyes as she nodded, smiling before turning and leaving us.

I held tightly to them. My mates. My heart. My happy ending.

I could live forever and still never get enough of them. I guess it's a good thing I had an eternity.

ACKNOWLEDGMENTS

I cannot thank you all enough for joining me in this world and falling in love with Athena and her Wanderers the same way I have. There are countless people who deserve to be thanked for their support in making this series a reality.

First, to my husband for being my first Beta reader and biggest cheerleader. Thank you for always being there to hype me up.

Then, my mother. You not only taught me how to tell a good story, but your support is the reason I get to do this. So thank you.

If you are in my family, thank you so much for picking up this book and supporting me. Truly, it means so much to me. Now, please put this book down and don't read it. I mean it. Please. This isn't for you. This novel will not make good conversation over the Thanksgiving dinner table. I'm not above begging. Please. Thank you.

And finally, to all of you who grew up loving sexy vampires. I hope you are ready for the supernatural ride of a lifetime.